The Isles

Moon Isle

Vinderla
Territory

Broken
Harbor

The Gates

Sun Isle

Singing
Mountains

Agora

Hive

Sky Isle

Abbey

Bay of
Teeth

The Last
Tower

The
Craters

Star Isle

Lightlark

ALEX ASTER

THE LIGHTLARK SAGA

BOOK 3

AMULET BOOKS • NEW YORK

For anyone who has ever looked for strength in others and found it in themselves.

Cataloging-in-Publication Data has been applied for and may be obtained from the Library of Congress.

ISBN 978-1-4197-7378-5
eISBN 979-8-88707-518-1

Book design by Chelsea Hunter

Printed and bound in the U.S.A.
10 9 8 7 6

ABRAMS The Art of Books
195 Broadway, New York, NY 10007
abramsbooks.com

HOME

Isla Crown watched the man she loved disappear as the world fell away.

The other man she loved gripped her arm with the desperate hope of holding onto a dream before waking. Her stomach dropped; her ears rang—

Clashing swords and howling dreks turned to silence.

"You're home," Grim said, his voice breaking in relief; and then she was ensnared in the familiar place against his chest, her cheek below his heart. It was instinct to breathe him in, to hold him close.

Home. Something in her marrow unfurled.

Another part recoiled.

She tore herself away. Looked down. Her armor and hands were covered in blood. Her lips tasted of salt—sweat and tears from the battle.

She considered everything she had done . . . everything she was . . .

She wanted to run. She wanted to tear down these hallways the same way she had the first day they met, she wanted to portal back to Lightlark, back into Oro's arms—

But she was here for a reason. Isla would kill either Oro or Grim, according to the oracle. It was fated. Now, knowing what she had done in the past, all the people she had killed . . . she didn't trust herself not to hurt the Sunling king.

Grim approached her slowly, tentatively. His voice was gentle. "Heart." He offered his hand again, his knuckles raw and caked in what had to be both his and Oro's blood.

Heart. Hers was split in half. One part wanted him more than anything—*remembered.* Another wanted to stab him through the chest again.

She took his hand.

Grim's wide shoulders melted in relief until she said, "Take me there."

He knew what she meant. As much as she wanted to hate him, as much as she wished her hatred of him would stick, take root in her bones and overgrow like a neglected garden, he knew her. *He really knew her.* "Isla—"

"Take. Me. There." Her voice was a guttural rasp. She could have portaled herself with her device or with his power, but the idea of using any scrap of ability after seeing what she had done with it made her want to retch. Grim studied her for a moment longer before curling his fingers around hers, and then the room disappeared. Her stomach flipped again.

Ash stuck to every surface of the landscape, a layer of poisoned snow. Houses lay in charred piles like pyre wood. Nothing stood tall anymore. The village had been brought to its knees.

Her cry cut through the silence like a scythe. Bodies big and small curled against the ground and hardened into rubble. Some were indefinable shapes against the stone.

You did this, a voice in her mind said. *Monster.*

No. She hadn't meant to, she—

Memories flitted beneath her eyelashes. She saw herself visiting this site, mourning the same action in the past. It hurt. It hurt so much; she was a wound that refused to scab. She wanted to bleed. She *deserved* to bleed. Still, her pain meant nothing—these people were dead because of her.

Because of her power.

She turned to Grim, eyes burning. "You should imprison me. I—I'm a criminal. I'm worse than any thief or murderer, I—" Grim caught her as she began to collapse.

"This was not intentional," he said, steadying her shoulders.

She choked on her breath. "Does intention matter when hundreds of people are dead?"

His eyes were sad. "It does."

She tore herself away from him. "You would say that. Of course, you would say that."

Tears caught in the back of her throat as she thought back to the battle on Lightlark, blood everywhere, dreks shredding the sky with their talons. *Ciel dying, Avel cradling her twin's body.* "They didn't have to die." A sob scraped against her ribs. "*Why,* Grim? Why did you have to attack?"

"You know why." His words were quiet. He stepped closer, but she walked back, refusing to bridge the gap between them.

She did know. She could almost see it now, the action that had caused all of this death—the uncontrollable power she had unleashed to save Grim, killing her in the process.

He had brought her back, by binding his life to hers, but it was just a temporary solution. Only Lightlark's portal to another world with infinite power offered a permanent one.

"You could have told me. We could have talked about it. We could have told Oro—"

"Oro will die if we use the portal. He wouldn't have agreed to it." He was quiet for a moment. Then, "*You* wouldn't have agreed to it."

Of course, she wouldn't have. Lightlark's portal was built into the island's foundation. Using it would mean the death of Lightlark and Oro, who was bound to it as king.

She shook her head, wincing at the death around her. "You really would have let Lightlark fall? You would have doomed the rest of the realms while leading yours into a world we know nothing about? For one woman?" It didn't make sense.

Grim frowned. "Not for one woman," he spat, like the words insulted him. He stepped toward her. "For my wife."

Wife. The word unlocked a thousand memories of them, a year before the Centennial. Fighting. Falling in love. Marrying. All moments she hadn't remembered, up until recently. She squeezed her eyes shut in frustration. "You know what I mean. *One life* to risk thousands. That is *criminal.* Selfish. Monstrous."

Isla could feel Grim getting closer. When she opened her eyes, he was right in front of her. "Heart," he said steadily. The spikes on his shoulders made him look like a demon. His blood-slicked armor glimmered in the moonlight. "If waging a war for one woman is a crime, then please do consider me a criminal." Closer. "If killing thousands to keep you alive is wrong, then consider me a villain." She now had to tilt her head to see him clearly. He leaned down. His breath was hot against her mouth. "If loving you this much is my downfall . . . then consider me already on my knees."

Her voice shook. "That's disgusting. You—you're a monster." She said the words and knew it made her a hypocrite. The ground they stood on now, the hundreds of deaths around them . . . she had done it *for him.* To save him.

We are monsters, Hearteater, Grim had said to her, back during the Centennial. He had been right.

But that didn't mean she couldn't change.

Grim had promised to end the battle, if she returned with him. Too many lives had already been lost. Lightlark had been *losing.* "Call back all your warriors and dreks. Immediately."

"It's already done." In his hand, the sword that controlled the winged beasts appeared. "It's over."

It was the same sword they had searched for, in the past. The one she herself had unlocked for him to use.

This was all her fault.

The dreks had killed so many. She had led her friends into bloodshed. Her own husband's forces had cut them down.

The survivors must think her a traitor. They must think she had been lying to them this entire time. That fact *killed* her, but her feelings didn't matter if going with Grim guaranteed their safety. "Command all the dreks to remain underground and put the sword back in the thief's lair. Swear you will never use it again."

She expected Grim to put up more of a fight, but the words fell easily from his mouth: "I swear it."

She pushed her luck. "Swear you won't try to use the portal again."

This time, he said nothing.

"*Swear it.*"

"If I do, you will die here," Grim said. "We all will."

Grim's life was tied to all of his subjects'. Now, all their fates were tied to hers. She looked around, at the bodies. The lives she had already taken. "You shouldn't have bound yourself to me." She closed her eyes again and tears swept down her face.

Grim's thumb traced her jawline, smearing the tears away. "I would do it again," he said, his voice a deep rasp against her ear. "I would do it a thousand times over, heart; you should know that. I will choose you over the world every single time."

Which meant it was up to her to save it.

THRONE

Isla could have locked herself in her room for months, she could have drowned in regret and grief. She had in the past, the first time she discovered what she had done.

But her tears wouldn't keep Grim from using the portal on Lightlark. They wouldn't help her understand the oracle's deadly prophecy. They wouldn't ensure her death didn't doom thousands. Only action would.

So she buried her feelings down as deep as they would go and decided the only way to ensure Grim didn't plan behind her back again was to be part of every meeting. Every event. Play the part of his wife, because it would gain her access.

Starting with the burial ceremony, the next morning. Grim had given her his room—*their* room—and she woke at dawn. Lynx had nearly torn apart Grim's stables in the moments they had been parted, and now he watched her from the corner of the room—his green eyes simmering with worry—as she braided her hair into a crown, in the Nightshade style.

She chose her dress carefully. Here, surrounded by enemies, her image would matter.

That was why, when she was ready, she reached for her golden rose necklace with shaking fingers. It was the only thing she had left of Oro, other than her memories. Tears slipping down her face, she unclipped it and slid it into her pocket.

In the mirror, she hardly recognized herself. The Wildling green and red were almost gone—replaced by a black dress with the faintest of roses beaded into the bodice. She looked like a Nightshade's devoted wife.

It was a lie, she thought, as she portaled into Grim's store of weaponry. That was where she found their stock of the healing elixir, the one that the Wildlings had been making for battle. Much of it had already been used, but she took the majority of what was left, drew her puddle of stars, and sent them through to Lightlark's infirmary.

It was a risk, but hundreds of injured warriors would die without the healing properties. It was the least she could do to help, after bringing them into battle. Nightshade had endless fields of nightbane, the flower the elixir was made from. They wouldn't miss it.

She closed the portal and was back in her room just before Grim knocked.

"You don't have to go," he said, studying her swollen eyes. He lifted a hand as if to wipe a tear from her jaw; but then, seeing the expression on her face, seemed to think better of it.

Her voice was cold. "I know. I'm going anyway."

On Nightshade, bodies were buried. Warriors were put to rest on a sacred stretch of land overlooking the coast, beneath mounds of ash.

The air smelled of flesh and salt. It blew her hair back, revealing the black pins she'd added. They were tipped in black diamonds to complement her cape. The necklace Grim had given her, with the large glimmering black diamond, was now purposefully visible against her throat.

Some gasped at it. She heard whispers about the stone around her neck. It was a symbol of their marriage. Perhaps they hadn't believed their union was real until they saw the necklace.

It didn't seem to make a difference to the Nightshade families who eyed her with hatred as she walked through the rows of the graveyard, toward the newest mounds. She couldn't blame them.

"Traitor. You don't belong here," she heard someone mutter. They were right. She belonged on Lightlark, mourning the deaths of the

people who fought alongside her. Now, she pretended to honor the same warriors that had cut them down. She felt disgust, and hatred, and anger alongside families that cried out in grief.

Also, guilt.

Flashes of ash and bone had filled her dreams. Lynx had woken her that morning with a nudge of his head. The sheets had been on the floor. There were scratches down her arms, as if she had clawed herself. Her ribs still hurt from her racking sobs.

Now she buried those emotions. This was not the time to feel anything. Not when that same ruinous power prickled just beneath her skin, waiting to be unleashed.

As Grim spoke in remembrance of the dead, she clung to every word, searching for indication of a veiled plan or threat against Lightlark. All he offered were condolences. A line of warriors stood behind them, their heads bowed, and swords dug firmly into the dirt. When Grim's speech was over he waved his hand, and some of the ash that coated the graves rose toward the sky.

"My court will meet in the throne room tonight to discuss our plans," Grim told her, after meeting with every family.

She kept a vise around her emotions, lest he wonder why he'd piqued her interest. "Is there a place for me?" She studied his face, scanning for any irritation at her request.

She found none. "There is always a place for you," he said. "I made your throne myself."

He had: She remembered it now. Grim had crafted it with his own shadows.

Hours later, she walked toward that throne like a ghost. Memories blurred, past and present bleeding together until they were one.

She remembered the outrage when Grim had announced her as his wife to his court—as his equal—right before they left for the Centennial. Grim had made it clear that anyone who didn't respect her didn't

have a home on Nightshade, and so the dissent was not erased, not pulled out by the root and banished, but permitted to grow like a weed in secret.

This room . . . these thrones . . . She recognized these faces that stared her down, the space filled to the brim with high-ranking soldiers and nobles.

They bowed for her because Grim would have gutted them if they didn't. Only he remained standing. He watched her walk toward him with an admiration typically reserved for the gods. But there were no gods here.

"Your ruler has returned."

No one dared protest.

A woman watched from the corner of the room, one palm resting at the intersection of the curved swords that formed an "X" on her chest. Isla felt a vestige of recognition from her past. It was Grim's general, Astria. Her long black hair was tied back into a single braid. Her high, pale cheekbones made her face seem even more severe.

Her dark eyes slid back to Isla's, after sweeping across the room for any threats against Grim; and they narrowed, as if spotting the greatest threat of all. From the first moment they had been acquainted, Isla had known that Grim's general didn't dislike her . . . she just didn't trust her.

Astria would be a problem. Being here, in her enemy's land, would mean lying to Grim. Isla would need to hide her true purpose as she sought to identify her options. Grim's sense of reason was clouded by his feelings for her, but his general would see things clearly.

Isla reached the end of the aisle, and Grim took her hand. He helped her onto her throne.

Shadows moved curiously beneath her skin like extensions of Grim himself, but she didn't dare flinch as the crowd rose to their feet.

Isla had the sudden urge to unleash her power. She was surrounded by enemies. Some of these faces she recognized not from the past, but from the battlefield.

For Oro, she would sit among them. She would learn their plans. And, if they put him and Lightlark at risk, she would stop them.

"What now?" A voice dared break the silence. Isla knew of only one soldier foolish enough to speak so boldly. She found the source immediately, a hulking man who was difficult to miss. He wore armor shaped for his great stature. His hair was a single long patch down the center of his head. No one dared stand too close to him, even with his hands covered. It seemed no one wanted to be caught touching him. He was a powerful Nightshade who could control a person by touching them, an ability in their realm that had become rare over the centuries. Grim didn't acknowledge the man, who continued talking as though he had a death wish.

"We were winning. Don't think we don't know why we retreated." He stared pointedly at her, gaze fixating on the stone resting between her collarbones. "That necklace. It is an abomination for—"

"Tynan." Grim's voice was as cold and cutting as the shadows that stilled beneath her. No one dared move a muscle. "My father was known for taking the tongues of his soldiers, you'll remember. Following orders doesn't require speaking, isn't that what he used to say?" He frowned. "It's a wonder he let you keep yours. Perhaps that needs to be rectified."

To his credit, Tynan stood tall, though his metal-encased fingers clashed together in anger. He was dangerous. But not to Grim. Grim's power was as undeniable as the tide. The force of him was felt in the room. He could kill every one of them without leaving his throne, and they all knew it.

"Hundreds were lost," Tynan continued, his voice shaking in fury. "Over a woman, over—"

Grim raised his hand, and Tynan froze. The Nightshade made a gurgling sound. "That *woman* is my wife," Grim said clearly. "And your ruler. You serve her." He released his hold, and Tynan staggered forward. "Now bow."

"Ruler, I—"

"I said bow."

Isla watched the man, his eyes flashing with hatred, as he sank to his knees.

"Lower."

The man placed his hands on the floor, gauntlet clashing against the stone.

"Lower."

Tynan's shoulders shook with undeniable rage as he pressed his forehead to the floor.

"Now," Grim said, leaning back in his chair. His voice turned almost casual. "We might have retreated . . . but we did not lose Lightlark."

Isla stilled.

She turned her head very slowly to face Grim. He didn't even look at her. Panic spilled like poison through her chest. "Quite the contrary," he continued. "We have reclaimed our greatest chance at overtaking the island. Three rulers founded Lightlark, including my ancestor." Only then did he turn to her. "And hers."

Isla wasn't breathing.

"The king of Lightlark is in love with her," Grim said, as if it were a joke. As if she had been a spy sent in to make Oro, King of Lightlark, fall in love with her to gain access to his power. The court laughed. The soldiers began to murmur. Her rage turned into a wildfire. Isla's hands gripped the side of the throne, the shadows' sharp edges digging into her palms, nearly drawing blood. She wanted to silence them all. She wanted to drown them with the power that

surged like a rogue wave within her. She wanted to strangle Grim. Especially as he said, smirking, "Now we have everything we need to take Lightlark."

Isla watched every soldier and member of Grim's court file out of the room, her blood boiling to such a degree, it was a wonder she didn't catch fire. Finally, the doors closed behind the last of them.

Her blade was at his throat in an instant. She pinned him to his throne. Her words shook with anger and betrayal. "You manipulative, villainous—"

"As much as I would love to hear the end of that sentence," Grim said, seeming unconcerned by the blade beneath his chin, "do save your barbs for a different time, when you actually have reason to hate me."

She bared her teeth. Everything he had just said—

"I'm not planning on invading Lightlark, heart."

She blinked, incredulous. "You *just said*—"

"I know what I said. I told them what they wanted to hear, to buy some time." He searched her eyes. "The portal would have saved you . . . and it would have also saved my people."

She lowered her blade the slightest bit. That, she hadn't expected. "Saved them from what?" The dreks were their biggest threat in the past, but they were gone. Grim had banished them below, and hidden the sword again, just as she had asked.

"Storms," he said simply. "The deadliest you can imagine."

It was the first she was hearing of this. And she had explored Nightshade for a year before the Centennial.

He must have sensed her confusion, because he said, "They used to happen every few centuries, on and off, then decades, then every few years. They are unpredictable, and every one has gotten worse. Hundreds die during the storm season."

Hundreds? She frowned, and he nodded.

"It's not just the weather. They bring sickness. Creatures. Entire villages have been razed by beasts in the night. The tempests are deadlier than the curses, even. The dreks appeared during one of them, and never left."

"How do you know there will be a storm season?"

"There are signs," he said. "The tides change. Certain animals burrow themselves. It lasts about three months. The whole winter this time, if I had to guess."

Isla swallowed. Hundreds of Nightshades were in danger, then.

Perhaps they were already doomed. Her own lifespan was uncertain . . . if she killed Grim to fulfill the prophecy, all of them would perish . . .

No. She refused to accept that fate. The oracle had made it seem like her future was etched in stone, but if there was a way around it, she would find it.

"I'll help you. I'll help you stop the storms."

He raised a brow at her. "You don't think I've tried?"

"You've never tried with me." They had worked together before. The memories of it blinded her for a moment. Her breath became unsteady. "Work with me. Buy us more time, enough for us to find another solution that isn't the portal."

Buy *her* enough time to change her fate.

He hesitated. Then, nodded.

She sighed, leaning back, only to realize she was still pinning him with her legs.

Grim's gaze slowly slid down her body, catching on the hem of her dress, riding high up her thigh. Her skin prickled with cold.

For a moment, she imagined his hand curling around her hip, dragging her forward against every inch of him. She imagined arching her back, pulling her dress over her head and—

It wasn't her imagination, she realized. It was a memory of something they had done, and her cheeks burned. Grim watched her with darkened eyes, his hands firmly glued to the sides of his throne.

He was her enemy. She was disgusted by her thoughts.

Forget burying her feelings. She needed to smother them. Burn them.

She stood, straightening her dress. "Tomorrow, then." She gave her sweetest smile. "If I find out your threat of Lightlark is real, I'll find a use for all those pretty blades you left for me in my room." There were rows of them, all perfectly angled to fit the many slim pockets in the pants that hung in her wardrobe. "Just because we're married, don't think I won't gut you."

Only when she reached the door did she hear him say, "I would expect nothing less, wife."

FORGE

Before she worked with Grim to stop the storms, she needed to do something for herself.

Burying her feelings hadn't worked, not really. She couldn't trust herself to keep them in check, and she now knew the ruin they could cause when mixed with her abilities.

She needed to ensure she would never kill another innocent again. She needed to keep her powers contained.

Only one person knew how to create such an enchantment, and the last time she'd seen him, she'd stabbed a knife through his eye.

"Here to take the other one?" the blacksmith said. He was sitting in his forge, back turned to her as he polished something on his worktable. Even seated, he was more than a head taller than her.

She remembered how that towering man had hunted her through his forest like prey, sensing her blood. He had craved its ability, to hammer into his weapons. Back then, she had thought herself powerless. She hadn't understood why he had been so desperate for her blood, but she did now.

It was risky traveling here without telling Grim. The blacksmith had more than a few reasons to want to hurt her.

"If you're wondering if I'm going to drain you of your enchanting blood, do allow me to put that fear to rest," he said, without turning. "You happen to be the last person in this world that I would kill."

She frowned, partially insulted. "Why?"

"You're better use to me alive."

That made her pause. "And just what do you plan to use me for?"

He didn't answer. He just continued his polishing.

She ran her tongue across her teeth. Best to jump right into it.

"I need a way to restrain my power. Keep it under control. Can you make something like that?"

Once, she had dreamed of having ability. Now that she had access to more power than anyone in all the realms, she would do anything to have it taken away. It had made her into a weapon that no one—including herself—could control.

Her mind flashed the images. Ash. Shadows of bodies. *Death*—

His chair creaked wildly beneath his weight. "I could with the proper metal. It is rare, however. Coveted. I'll have to melt other creations down to make it." He studied her for a moment. Two. His gaze slipped to her necklace, and his eyes gleamed with interest. She wondered if it was his own making. "My help comes at a cost."

She was happy to pay. Anything to smother the power like fire in her veins, anything to ease the fear that any turn of emotion would lead to more death. "Fine. How much?"

"Not coin. I want something only you can give me."

Isla remembered what he had said, about how she was only valuable to him alive. Was it because he needed fresh blood? Her hand inched toward the dagger sheathed against her leg. He was the tallest man she had ever seen. She had the thought that he could crush her skull in his hands without much effort. She wondered if now was a good time to run. "What do you want?"

The blacksmith stared her down, single eye filled with fire. "I want you to kill me."

Isla blinked at him. "I—I'm not sure I understand."

"You understand perfectly."

His request didn't make sense. "Why me?" He could have found death numerous ways over the centuries, if that was what he wanted.

That was when she remembered what the blacksmith had told her right after she had put her dagger through his eye. "*You weren't supposed to be able to do that.*"

"A ruler far before Grimshaw cursed me to never be able to die, so that they would never be rid of my abilities." He motioned at his forge. "No one else in this world can create what I can. They knew that."

"My flair circumvents that."

"Your *father's* flair," he corrected. It was rare for non-rulers to be born with flairs, but her father had been powerful, and immune to curses.

He would have known her father. She had a sharp need to drain him for details, to ask for any crumbs of her father he might give her, but the blacksmith didn't seem intent on indulging her for long, and she had more pressing matters. Like the blacksmith asking her to end his life.

Isla didn't want anyone else to die by her hand. That was the entire point of using the metal in the first place.

He seemed to sense her indecision. "Allow me the mercy of rest," he said. Isla wondered at the idea of living forever. Never having the peace of death.

"You're sure?"

He nodded.

"Fine. I'll give you until the end of winter to change your mind. If you still want this . . . I'll do it."

The blacksmith's mountainous form seemed to shrink a bit in relief. Then, he turned toward his forge.

She watched him take down two daggers from his wall of creations. They looked ancient, their hilts covered in symbols she didn't understand. And their blades . . . they shined brightly, more than they should have in their condition. Next to the fire, in the bright

light . . . the metal almost glimmered. He didn't waste a moment before melting them down. Flames erupted from a device, filling the forge with heat.

Watching the blacksmith cast was mesmerizing. He worked expertly, diligently. Under his process, the strange metal changed color, before melting completely. It glittered brightly in its new form, like a bowl of stars. He didn't use a mold. Somehow, he was able to pour the liquid metal into his hands, without burning them. Somehow, he was able to shape it himself. This was his power.

She suddenly regretted making a deal to kill him in a few months.

The metal began to harden beneath his fingers. Before it was set, he motioned for her to outstretch her hands. She did, wondering if she would be burned by the blistering material, but under his control, they did not touch her skin as he closed them around her wrists. With a sweeping of his fingers, the metal cooled completely.

Then, it was done.

"What is this metal?" she asked. It glimmered brightly under the light, like a thousand diamonds were trapped within.

"It's *shademade*," he said. "Made from ancient power."

"They won't break?"

He shook his head. "It is designed so that only the person who puts them on can release them. And me. My enchantments always have safeguards."

Good. She wouldn't be asking him to release them anytime soon, however. The moment the bracelets had closed around her wrists, her shoulders sagged with relief. Her eyes stung with unshed tears.

It was so . . . quiet. She had almost forgotten what her mind had been like, without having to constantly block out the endless connections waiting to be formed around her. It had worked.

Her power was gone.

***

Grim insisted on having dinner with her before they began working together. She rushed into the room several minutes late, only to find him sitting perfectly still at the end of the table, looking content to wait forever, if needed.

As soon as she entered, he stood, his eyes widening slightly, as if she was something to marvel at. He took in her dress—long and embedded with thousands of black beads. It had been waiting in her wardrobe. It seemed he had made good on his promise to hire a tailor for her, after he had ripped so many of her dresses apart. She wore it because it was expected. The last thing she needed was Grim's court questioning her motives even more than they already did.

Grim didn't look suspicious at all. He smiled.

Then his eyes caught on her bracelets.

"Hearteater," he said carefully, his deep voice making her chest feel tight. "If you remember, there's a closet of jewelry for you just off your quarters." There was. It was filled with centuries' worth of ancient gems, mostly featuring black diamonds. Not that any of those stones rivaled the one against her throat.

She ignored him and the ridiculous sparks spreading through her at something as simple as his voice as she walked to her seat opposite his own at the long table. They were both seated at the heads. It made for an impractical dinner. Now, as he continued to study her bracelets, she was grateful for the space between them.

Until Grim appeared at her side and gently took her wrist in his palm. He hissed, touching the metal. "What did you do, heart?"

"What I had to," she said, turning her attention to the goblet of wine in front of her. It smelled slightly floral. She took a sip.

"You don't have to hide yourself," Grim said. "Not with me. Not here. Not ever."

She wanted to tell him that she needed to hide *most* here, because despite hating him, she loved him, and that love had made her do horrible things.

She wanted to tell him that she remembered everything in vivid detail. Like the time they had forgone dinner entirely, and Grim had wrapped the room in shadows and laid her on this very table and—

Grim must have felt the shift in her emotions, because his eyes darkened. As though he too was remembering.

He eyed the side of the table, as if he could see the memory. As if he could taste it.

Isla swallowed, and his gaze shifted to her throat. Her necklace suddenly felt very heavy against it, though it had rarely bothered her before. Her skin prickled on instinct, and—

"You visited the blacksmith." His words interrupted her thoughts.

She didn't deny it. Grim only frowned, then returned to his seat across the table.

They ate in silence. The meal was perfect; he had purposefully ensured her favorite foods were made—charred vegetables, spiced grains, buttered potatoes. Still, she didn't say a word, and it was up to Grim to break the tension.

"Your leopard bit the gardener," he said. At night, Lynx slept with Isla; but that day, she had let him roam free.

Isla frowned. "What did the gardener do? Lynx doesn't bite unprovoked."

Grim narrowed his eyes. "That beast tried to bite *me*. And I haven't done anything but house and feed him."

"You provoke him with your very presence." She took another sip of wine.

Grim sat back. He picked up his own wine. Casually turned it in its glass. "So, is this it, then? You're going to pretend to hate me?"

She was out of her chair and on her feet in a moment. "I'm not pretending," she spat, glaring.

He stood too. "Really? I can feel your emotions, heart. If you're going to lie, you should get better at it."

Her hands shook at her sides with anger. "I'm not lying," she said, raising her voice. "You're only lying to *yourself* if you thought waging a war would get me back here to be your loving, naïve, idiotic wife!"

Any amusement left Grim's expression. "I didn't wage a war to get you back here. I did it to try to save you."

"And how did that work out?" she demanded, her voice echoing through the room.

Grim was silent. His eyes weren't gleaming anymore. Any light in them had shuttered away. She had hurt him. Good.

They stared at each other from each end of the table, chests heaving, her heart hammering.

She wanted to hurt him more.

She wanted to rush into his arms.

She was two people—Isla from before the Centennial, who married the Nightshade ruler; and Isla from afterward, who had battled against him.

"I—I can't do this," she said, meaning it. She couldn't sit here having dinner, pretending Grim hadn't been her enemy just days before. She couldn't pretend he wasn't *still* her enemy.

She couldn't pretend there wasn't a prophecy that said she was just as likely to kill Oro as she was him.

She darted for the door. Grim appeared in front of it right as she reached for the handle.

"Please," he said, his eyes wide. Desperate. "Please don't go. I'm sorry. Hate me," he pleaded. "Hate me all you want. Hate me forever. Just—just don't leave." He took a step toward her. "I love you, Isla. I need you."

She didn't need Grim's ability to read emotions in order to understand the depths of devastation in his eyes. To know she really was his heart, the center of his life, and she had been ripped away from him. She had left him. She had chosen Oro, and it had clearly left its mark.

But he had done it to himself.

Her voice was shaking as she said, “You had me. And you lost me all on your own.”

She didn’t think his devastation could deepen, but it did. And this time, when she shoved past him, he didn’t stop her.

WRAITH

Isla stared at the necklace against her pulse and wished she could rip it away.

She really couldn't do this. Sitting across from Grim, sleeping in the room they once shared—it was too easy to slip into the past. Too easy to forget that half of her heart belonged to someone else—someone she had fought the urge to run back to every moment since they'd parted.

Oro. Her eyes burned as she thought of him. As she remembered the look of pure devastation on his face when she took Grim's hand. Even when they were nearly gone, he had reached for her.

He had reached for her.

It had been only two days, but it felt like a lifetime away from him. Her hands curled in fists, her marred palms biting in pain. This wasn't how the battle was supposed to go.

By now, she was supposed to be on a stretch of golden sand, just him and her, Oro's favorite everything in his favorite place. She closed her eyes and could almost see and feel it—her cheek pressed against his warm chest, his hand making lazy strokes down her bare back, the unrelenting sun blazing against every inch of her skin.

She opened her eyes.

Instead, she was in this cold castle. Staring at herself in a mirror. Wishing she had never agreed to put on this damn necklace.

Nothing would break it, she had tried. Only in her death would it be released.

Soon, then.

Her jaw tightened; her teeth ground together. *Enough.* She was done speculating about how much time she had left, or the prophecy's meaning, or whether her fate could be changed at all. She needed answers.

Unfortunately for her, the only person who could give them to her—the oracle who had given the prophecy in the first place—was dead.

She sighed, moving toward the wardrobe, then stilled.

The oracle was dead . . . but she'd had sisters. Other oracles who hadn't awoken in thousands of years. Cleo had captured them.

Something dangerous—something like hope—began to bloom in her chest.

If she found Cleo's fleet, if she found the oracles . . . they could tell her more about the prophecy. About the time she had left. Maybe even how to change her fate.

It was a risk. Cleo was her enemy now more than ever. Isla didn't have powers; she would be easy to kill, if she could even locate the Moonling's fleet. Cleo's ships could be anywhere. They would likely be on their way back to the Moonling newland by now.

No, she realized. Not the Cleo she had come to know. Cleo wanted to go through the portal more than anything; it was the only way to be reunited with her child. She wouldn't simply retreat to her isle—she would have a plan. Grim's portaling power was essential to getting to the otherworld. Cleo would attempt to convince Grim to reconsider his decision.

The Moonling would be heading to Nightshade.

Isla's steps were quiet as she paced the room. Even if she was right, the sea was vast. The journey from Lightlark to Nightshade was long.

If only she could fly. If only she hadn't given up her powers.

She could portal back to the blacksmith right now. He could take the bracelets off. It would be so easy. She could even have him put them back afterward . . .

Isla pulled that thought out by the root. That was how it would start. Excuse after excuse, reason after reason, until the bracelets were off more than they were on.

Until something terrible happened again.

The ash. The ruin. The bodies—

No. She didn't need power. She hadn't needed it for most of her life.

She would find Cleo's fleet without it.

A bouquet of flowers lay outside her door. Dark red roses. She wanted to burn them.

A note was attached. It was scrawled in his sharp script, the same handwriting as the invitation to his demonstration during the Centennial.

I'm sorry, it said. *Please have dinner with me. Again.*

She wasn't going to go. She had left the flowers untouched. But as she took a ride on Lynx's back, mentally considering ways to find Cleo's fleet, she remembered another creature.

A tiny bundle of scales.

She had spent the rest of the day looking for him in the castle, without any luck. He wasn't in the stables either. By late afternoon, her chest twisted with worry.

Where was he?

Grim looked entirely too pleased to see her that evening. He stood immediately when she entered, then portaled to her chair to pull it out for her.

For the first few minutes, they ate their food in silence: him looking up every few moments, studying her, as if cataloging what she did and didn't enjoy; her trying her best not to care that he had meticulously planned each course to coincide with things she liked. Again. Strips of seasoned meat cooked all the way through, fluffy grains, root vegetables spiraled into ribbons. There was a chocolate dessert course. Of course there was.

Being this close to him made memories expand, like they were a sea trying to drown her. Some, featuring the tiny creature.

"Where—where is he?" she demanded, heart sinking behind her ribs. What if the little dragon was dead? She hadn't spoken his name in ages. "Wraith." Her voice broke on the word.

Grim's grin put her at ease. He hadn't necessarily liked the creature, but even he wasn't sinister enough to smile at its demise.

"I was wondering when you would ask."

"I looked for him, in the castle."

Grim made an amused sound. "He doesn't sleep inside anymore."

She remembered Grim glowering whenever the tiny dragon would take his spot in the bed. She glared at him. "Why not?"

"I'll show you." Isla followed him out the doors of the dining room, onto a wide, curling balcony. Salt burned her nostrils, her hair whipped back wildly. She squinted. All she could see was endless ocean. "Wait here," Grim said before she could ask questions, and then he was gone.

Isla tapped her fingers against the stone impatiently as she waited. She hoped Grim had treated Wraith well in her absence. He was just a tiny creature in need of help.

She remembered the day she found him struggling to walk, his little leg injured. She had slowly healed it with the Wildling elixir. He would cry when she rubbed the nightbane in, and she would hold him tightly until he slept. He was small enough to fit directly over her chest, and that was where he preferred to be, despite Grim's grumbling that the dragon had stolen his wife.

That moment, that life, had felt like home once. Now, she remembered and felt hollow.

She was leaning over the balcony, wondering why Grim had told her to wait here and why he was taking so long, when a gust of air sent her flying backward.

Stone dug sharply into her back as she landed.

Midnight-carved wings wholly blocked the moon, casting clawed shadows across the balcony. Her hair whipped behind her as they flapped. With a horrible scraping, talons almost as large as her body gripped the ledge, causing pieces of stone to crumble into the ocean. The talons were familiar. One was slightly crooked.

Wraith.

The tiny bundle of scales was now a full-grown dragon. And Grim was riding him.

Still sprawled on the floor, not daring move an inch, she watched as the dragon dipped his head down to study her. Her hand trembled as she slowly moved to touch his face. His scales were cold. He sniffed her.

Then the dragon leaned back and cried into the sky. She was off her feet in a moment as Wraith threw her into the air with his nose. He caught her using his neck, and she slid down his rough scales, narrowly avoiding falling when Grim caught her by the back of her dress, sending beads flying. He hauled her in front of him while Wraith screeched happily toward the stars.

Grim's eyes seemed to glimmer under the night sky. "I've never seen him so excited."

Isla gaped at him. "How—it's only been a few *months*. He—"

"Grew."

It was an understatement.

"Do you want to ride him?" he asked.

Before she could respond—and the answer was *no,* for this was just another form of flying, which she decidedly hated—Wraith took to the air, and Grim caught her around the waist to keep her from being cut to ribbons against the cliff.

Her scream was swallowed by the wind as Wraith shot into the clouds. "Hold on," Grim whispered into her ear, and that meant holding onto *him*.

She sat facing him, pressed firmly against his torso, her head tucked into his chest. Her legs wrapped around his waist. Straddling him.

It was an unfortunate position, but she didn't dare loosen her grip around his neck, not when the alternative meant hurtling to the ground below. Her ankles locked behind him, and she felt Grim go still beneath her.

This was familiar. Even as fear dropped through her stomach, so did an ember of heat. He overtook all her senses. He smelled of soap and storms and something distinctively him, and she fought the impulse to run her lips across his neck, his jaw. He seemed to be dealing with a similar level of restraint.

No. He was her enemy. She despised him.

"Wraith," Grim finally said, his voice a dark whisper against her ear, skittering down her spine as he instructed the dragon to land. When he did—and not gently—Isla ground against Grim with the impact, and she made a sound like a whimper. Grim made a sound like a growl.

Then, Wraith turned over, and Isla slid into an undignified heap on the ground. She couldn't be too upset at the creature; he was still young. Wraith grinned at her with his massive teeth, in what would have been a horrifying smile if she didn't see within it a glimmer of the little dragon he had once been. He bent down to rub his head against hers, which knocked her back onto her backside.

Grim tried and failed to hide his laugh as he watched her from across the clearing. "He's still getting used to his size."

Wraith huffed, as if he could understand Grim's words. Then the dragon proceeded to do the last thing Isla expected, which was lazily roll onto his back.

Grim sighed in a long-suffering way. "Insolent creature," he said. Then, *Grim* did the last thing she expected and began rubbing the dragon's stomach.

Wraith's foot moved wildly in delight, and Isla watched with her mouth dropped open.

Grim shrugged a shoulder. "It was easier when he was the size of a shield."

"And how exactly did he become the size of a hill?"

Grim continued while he turned to face her. "It was difficult returning without you," he said quietly. His voice told her *difficult* was a mild way to put it. "We missed you." He looked at Wraith.

"You bonded," she said, in awe, thinking of her own connection with Lynx.

He nodded. "It was what he needed to grow. It happened rapidly."

A spike of happiness shot through her at the thought of them both finding such a bond. Leaning on each other.

It quickly withered when she remembered why, exactly, he had returned without her. He had taken away her memories. He had left her out of his plans. He had made decision after decision without her.

He seemed to sense her shift in emotions, because his tone turned serious. He walked over to her and did yet another unexpected thing. Slowly, gaze never leaving hers, he went on his knees and bowed his head before her. He was so tall, his eyes were level with her chest. "I'm sorry," he said. "When I returned, I regretted taking your memories away every day. It was my fault this all happened. I—all I ever tried to do was protect you."

"By lying to me?" she said, her voice sharp as the blade on her thigh. "By turning me into some pawn? Some clueless puppet?"

"I didn't—"

"You *did*," she said. "You did over and over again, and I trusted you, like an idiot." He lurched back, as if her words had burned him.

Isla closed her eyes. She wanted to leave him here, on his knees. She wanted to tell him she hated him.

But his regret, she realized, she could use to her advantage.

"If you're truly sorry, then swear you will never work behind my back again. Swear you will never enact a plan without telling me. Swear it on our marriage." She gripped the stone around her neck.

Grim rose to his full height. He pressed his hand over hers, on the black diamond that now always remained visible. "I swear it, heart."

Words meant little, she knew that, but she could see the regret on Grim's face. She knew how much their marriage meant to him.

She hoped it would be enough to keep him from razing the world, simply to keep her.

They were supposed to be working together. "You said the storms brought deadly creatures. Like what? Where?"

"I can take you to a place that was hit particularly badly tomorrow, if you wish."

She nodded. She wanted to see it. She wanted to understand the storms and the devastation that was coming for them.

She wanted him to be distracted from her own plans. For, as they flew back to the castle, Isla watched Grim's movements carefully. The placement of his hands. The scales he touched, in a wordless communication with Wraith. How he bent low against the wind.

She watched, because she had just discovered her way of finding Cleo.

Grim could have portaled them to the village in half a second. Instead, she asked if they could take Wraith.

"Do you—do you think you could teach me to ride him?" Her tone was casual. Curious, even.

Isla expected him to see through her, to realize she must have an ulterior motive if she actually wanted to learn to *fly* the creature that had made her nearly retch just the day before. Instead, he only smiled. Something about that made it feel like a blade was scraping against her insides.

"Of course, heart," he said.

There it was, that blade again.

Wraith slept in a specially made stable, on the other side of the castle, away from the rest of the animals. Apparently, there had been some sort of incident that had required his relocation. Something about trying to play with the other creatures with his teeth . . .

The dragon's wings lifted happily when he saw her. He leaned his head down, so it was level with hers. Smiled.

He breathed out, and the force from his nostrils nearly swept her off her feet.

Grim caught her with a firm hand against her spine. She tried not to focus on the way he lightly ran his fingers down her back before he dropped it.

Wraith's head lowered to the ground as Grim approached, not in deference, but in clear command. He wanted his head rubbed, and Grim complied, stroking the spot between his eyes. Wraith made a deep sound of satisfaction.

He looked over his shoulder at her. "You can portal onto his back—with your device, of course. Or mount him like this." She watched Grim effortlessly climb up Wraith's scales.

It looked easy enough. She approached Wraith. Rubbed her hand exactly where Grim had, which made the dragon smile. His teeth were nearly as big as her entire body.

Wincing, she gripped one of his scales. It was rough beneath her palm, and firm. When he was smaller, his scales had been smooth, almost soft, but now they were strong as armor. With a little maneuvering, she gained purchase, climbing first to his shoulder, then onto his back. She sat in front of Grim, leaving some distance between their bodies.

"May I?" he asked.

She looked down to see his hands hovering just inches from her waist. She nodded; then his fingers were curling around her hips, and

he was effortlessly sliding her toward him, until she reached a place where her legs were almost perfectly molded to Wraith's spine.

"Better?"

She nodded, not trusting her voice to sound even remotely casual, not when he was still touching her.

"Finding places to hold on is obviously important," he said, his voice right in her ear. One of his hands lightly covered her own. "Here." He guided her hand to a ridge. "And here." He gripped his fingers around hers, showing her the right spot. "His hearing is impeccable. He can hear instruction even in the sharpest winds."

She hoped neither him nor Grim could hear the ridiculous beating of her heart as she leaned back, finding herself settled right between his legs.

"Do you have to sit so close?" she said sharply, her voice far too hoarse.

Grim said nothing as he shifted away from her. Good. She tilted back and forth, testing her position. She dried her sweaty hands on her pants, then gripped the places Grim had indicated.

"Go on, Wraith," she said, chin high, when she was sure she was ready.

Isla was expecting a slow ascent. A few more moments to mentally prepare.

Instead, Wraith took just one step before shooting into the clouds.

Her stomach lurched; she lost her grip completely. She flew back, soaring breathlessly for half a second until she crashed into Grim's chest, and he curled one arm around her, pinning her against him. Somehow he kept his grip, even though he was only holding on with one hand. A curl of darkness had her realizing he was using his shadows to keep himself steady.

"That's cheating," she told him, voice breathless with panic. Those same shadows inched toward her. They twined around her hips gently, reverently, extensions of Grim's own arms.

Grim made an amused sound. "What an interesting way to say thank you." He leaned down to say right against her temple, "You're the one who decided to part with your powers, Hearteater. You can't blame me for using mine."

Wind stung her cheeks. Wraith dipped, and she used the momentum to lurch forward, away from Grim and back to her hand placements. She wouldn't have his shadows keeping her secure when she rode Wraith alone. She would need to learn how to do it the hard way.

Her fingers were slick with sweat. Her thighs burned with effort as she fought to stay still. Her eyes watered from Wraith's speed. Wraith tilted slightly, and she gritted her teeth against a rush of nausea as she peered at the ground far below.

She wondered, for a moment, about the first time Grim rode Wraith. He wasn't particularly known for his patience. Part of her wished she could see it, the way they had bonded.

When she was relatively sure she wasn't about to slide off, she risked a look at Wraith's wings.

They were glorious—slightly translucent and massive, light filtering through like a shade. He soared through the sky in a smooth arc.

Most of the time, anyway. When they caught a trail of wind, Wraith turned sharply, riding the current. He was clearly still a child playing with a newfound ability, tilting side to side, then up and down. Her arms shook with the effort of holding on. Her stomach lurched.

"Wraith," Grim said smoothly. "Isla is going to vomit, it's going to land on me, and I'm going to be far less inclined to rub your stomach."

Wraith straightened immediately. The ride was smooth for several minutes, until he began lowering.

"You'll remember, his landing needs some work," Grim whispered behind her, shadows circling her waist once more.

"What—"

Her voice was swallowed by the wind as they suddenly dropped what felt like a mile in one fell swoop. Her body lifted from Wraith's back, hovering, until the shadows tightened, pulling her back in place. Her breath caught in her chest as the ground came into view. Closer. Closer.

Wraith's wings spread for just a moment before they landed, and then they were sliding through the dirt, his talons ripping up a slice of farmland, dirt exploding everywhere, before finally stopping at the edge of a village.

The dragon looked over his shoulder at them, grinning.

Grim sighed in a long-suffering way, then portaled them off his back.

The village was comprised of quaint houses constructed from either river stone or wood. She could see the edge of a modest square, with wagons selling produce. There were the beginnings of a fence built around it all, stopping just shy of complete, as if someone had given up just before finishing. A few people were visible beyond it, but they weren't moving. No, they were stopped. Staring.

The man closest to them dropped the harvest he was carrying, his mouth falling open as Wraith flipped onto his back, shaking the ground itself, hoping to have his stomach scratched. Grim ignored him.

Silence, then screaming. Mostly coming from children, who yelled excitedly as they flooded through holes in the not-completed wall, followed by mothers who screamed with far less excitement.

When they saw Grim, even the children paused. Bowed. There were whispers—*ruler*.

Then, their attention turned to Isla. More whispers. They bowed again. Some eyed her with suspicion. Some mothers looked at her with more fear than the dragon behind her.

She was used to it.

Whereas the others seemed frozen in shock, an old woman stepped freely beyond the small crowd that had formed. She used what looked like a fire poker to support her gait. Her hair was silver, her eyes were sharp, and her smile was kind.

"What brings you to our village?" she asked, her booming voice completely at odds with her age.

Grim turned to look at Isla. He was going to follow her lead, apparently.

She straightened. There was so much blood on her hands, but stopping the storms could mean saving hundreds of people. She needed to know what she was up against. "We—we had some questions regarding the storms a few years ago, and the beast it brought. Do you remember it?" Grim had filled her in before they left the castle. This village had been attacked by a creature no one had ever seen before, or since.

"Remember?" the old woman said. "I'm still finding blood stains in my floorboards."

Isla swallowed.

"Follow me." Isla and Grim exchanged a glance; then Isla nodded. The woman led them down the long dusty road, the villagers' eyes following them all the while, until they arrived in front of her house. She pointed at places on the floor of her modest kitchen that were undeniably stained crimson.

"Snuck through the window. Attacked my husband. He survived, somehow, though not with all his limbs. He's gone now."

"I'm sorry about that." Isla hesitated. "What did it look like? The creature?"

The woman pursed her lips. Wrinkles sprouted from them like roots across her pale face. "Teeth. That's what I remember. Lots of teeth. Oddly shaped too . . . crowding the mouth. It looked like a shadow, almost, slithering across the floor."

The creature was eventually killed, Grim explained. Its teeth had been sold over time. There was nothing left now for them to look at.

The old woman shook her head. She sank into her seat with a groan. "I always said those damn storms were getting worse. They're harbingers of the end, I tell you."

The other villagers told them similar stories. Some died by running out of their homes into the night, thanks to the curse. Others were mauled by the great teeth that were described slightly differently, depending on who was speaking.

Most were far less welcoming than the old woman, at least, to Isla. She didn't miss the way they studied her when they thought she wasn't looking, like she was yet another creature, come to ruin them.

She also noticed how they looked at Grim—not with fear, which she expected, but with reverence. Some used the opportunity to air grievances, and Grim took notes. He promised solutions. He made plans to have people in his court follow up on every concern. She didn't know why this shocked her, but it did.

All of the villagers seemed terrified of the start of another storm season. Some got to work packing their most valuable belongings and leaving them by their doors. There were tunnels built below Nightshade during the curses, to allow for nighttime travel. They had been used as shelters before, but the tempests were unpredictable, coming down without warning. Killing before anyone had a chance to run.

As they left, Isla turned the old woman's words in her head. She had called the storms harbingers of the end. She couldn't stop thinking about it.

Especially, when, just days later, the storm season started early.

STORM

Wind rattled the windows. Rain hit the glass with the force of throwing stars. Some of it had been frozen solid.

She stood, watching. Listening. Even through the thick stone exterior, she could hear it now, howling. The sky had gone a strange shade. Whorls of green and purple peaked between clouds, illuminated by flashes of light. The stone rumbled with thunder.

The old woman's words might usually have been enough warning to keep her inside . . . but the storm was the perfect cover for her own plans.

Before she could think better of it, she was in her training clothing and portaling to Wraith's specially made stable. His head had been down in boredom, but he rose as she stepped toward him. He flashed his great teeth at her.

Guards typically patrolled outside. Tonight, they protected the castle's exterior, the sides that weren't facing the cliff, against any creatures. She had watched them from the windows, forming a perimeter, decked in thick armor. Grim had told her to stay inside—the palace was built well. It was secure.

She needed to hurry. Wraith's dark scales shimmered as he stepped out beneath the moonlight. Rain slipped down them.

The weather might be good for staying hidden, but it would make it far harder to stay on.

Maybe this was a mistake. Maybe it wasn't worth the risk . . .

A memory of Oro flashed in her mind. Sitting among the wildflowers. Her golden rose necklace still around her neck.

According to the prophecy, she might put a blade straight through his heart.

She thought of the village. The ash. The ruin.

As it stood, her death would be the end of everyone on this island. Including Grim.

If anyone knew how to change her fate or extend her life, it was the oracles.

She took a step forward. Wraith did too, as if to meet her. "Would you let me ride you? Alone? In the storm?"

In response, Wraith bent down, offering his neck for her to climb. She only made it three scales up, before slipping, barely catching herself. Her heart was in her throat. She didn't dare breathe until she hauled herself onto his back. Her grip was tentative, at best. She swallowed. She didn't even have to say a word. The moment her seat was secure, Wraith stepped one foot forward. Another. And then shot up into the clouds.

The sky raged like a battlefield. Thunder and lightning dueled, one striking and the other responding. Night seemed to shatter all around her, and the rain was thicker than it should be, striking like throwing stars. Isla ducked low, holding on to Wraith for dear life, fear settling in her stomach.

It wasn't just the height. Something about this storm was wrong. She shouldn't be up here. Not alone. Not when her life was now tied to all of Nightshade's.

"Watch out!" she shouted, as a full-sized tree was launched toward them. Wraith moved at the last minute, careening left, and she fought to stay on, her teeth sliding painfully together as she smothered a scream. An entire forest had been ripped away by the storm, and it circled them, flying past, riding endless winds.

Wraith moved to dodge each tree, and her stomach dropped as he turned sharply upward, to fly farther into the clouds.

Up here, the sky changed shade. It was what she had seen shards of, from the castle window. The purple-tinged clouds, the greenish tint. She tasted power on her tongue, smelled it, like copper, like blood. Power from what? They climbed higher and higher, until they were drenched in it. The air felt heavier, alight, full.

Lightning struck, not far. It gleamed like a branch on fire.

Wraith's wings flapped faster, shooting like an arrow through the sky, dodging projectiles. She held on tightly as he swerved. It was a wonder she hadn't slipped off. Only fear had kept her steady. Her head was bent low. Rocks of ice pounded against her arms, sure to leave bruises. Still, she held on.

The purple deepened the farther they went. The green seemed to glitter.

Out of nowhere, her chest began to ache.

Her heart. It began to burn, as if the seams of her scar were breaking. She risked a look down, half expecting to see her shirt soaked in blood, but there was nothing but rain.

Her hands wrapped tightly against Wraith's ridges, she folded over as the pain became stabbing, like a blade was carving her heart out little by little, trying to wrench it through her ribs. She screamed.

Wraith turned to face her. She could barely see the land below; it was a blur beneath them. Her grip tightened.

Then, a flash of light. A monstrous strike of lightning flared through the sky.

It blinded them. Wraith didn't see the tree until it was too late. It crashed against them with such a force, Isla was knocked clean off his back.

And then, she was falling.

She screamed until her voice went hoarse, and her limbs flailed helplessly. The force of the air was too strong; she couldn't move her arm, couldn't pull the necklace. Couldn't reach for the starstick she had tucked down her spine. Couldn't do anything as the wind howled around her, and she fell alongside the rain.

Her body broke through the storm, hurtling toward the ground. It rushed up to meet her.

With a breath-stealing thud, she was knocked back against a set of scales. Wraith had caught her on his spine, just feet before the dirt. He reared up, and her body flew off again with the force, but her hands held on. He lowered again, and she molded herself to him.

Go back. Go back. It was the voice of survival in her head, knowing she wouldn't get lucky the next time she fell. This was reckless. Foolish.

But she needed to find the oracles tonight. Grim couldn't know she was seeking them out; he couldn't know about the prophecy. Especially since she might very well kill him to fulfill it.

Unless she could change fate. The oracles' information could save them all. That was what kept her going.

Below, the ocean raged, peppered in whitecaps, like the sea had grown teeth. The waters between Lightlark and Nightshade were vast. Part of her knew the impossibility of finding anything out here, especially in the darkness, but Cleo had an entire armada. They would be together, like a legion.

She hoped she would get lucky. She hoped she was right.

The storm weakened away from Nightshade, but it did not disappear completely. Would Cleo's fleet be sailing away from it? Or would they be harnessing the power of the upturned waves to get to Nightshade even faster?

For hours, she watched the endless dark beneath her, waiting for any sign of the Moonling, her grip never loosening.

Nothing but waves.

She nearly gave up. Almost told Wraith to head back.

Then she saw it. White sails like ribbons in the storm, whipping wildly. Hundreds of them. It was a wonder the tempest didn't swallow them completely.

There.

Cleo's ship was the largest. It had extra sails that rippled like silk. "Keep circling, but higher," she told Wraith.

Then she slipped off his side, holding her starstick.

For a moment, she was falling again, hurtling through the storm.

Then, she was on a deck.

Her knees buckled under her; her legs weakened from fighting to stay on Wraith's back. She slumped against a pillar, hiding behind it, rain plastering her hair over her face. The wood below was white oak, crafted from the pale forest she had seen on Moon Isle.

Yells swirled around her, Moonlings struggling to tame the sea and keep the ship steady. She needed to move. Quickly, she looked around, squinting through the storm. A light. There was a light on, in what looked to be the captain's quarters. *Cleo.*

The oracles would likely be below. Another touch of her starstick, and that was where she went.

It was quieter down here. She took a shaking breath, shivering, not realizing how cold the rain had been until she was out of it.

Her legs shook as she got to her feet, leaning against a barrel. She slid the lid off with a grunt. Food. Almost every barrel was filled with it. Still . . . the Moonlings wouldn't last forever on water and fish without resupplying.

What was their plan? Would Grim allow them to get food from Nightshade?

It didn't matter now. All she cared about was finding the oracles.

The last time she had seen them, they had been frozen in ice. She wondered if Cleo thawed them or kept them entrapped.

Only one way to find out. She opened every single barrel, every crate, until her arms were sore.

No sign of them.

She searched every inch of the hull. She considered that they might be on another ship, but no . . . Cleo wouldn't let anyone as important as the oracles out of her vicinity.

They were above, then. If they were freed from their ice, they might be locked in a room. She touched her starstick. Winced, wondering if she was about to be surrounded by Moonlings.

The room she had appeared into was, mercifully, empty. Waves pelted the windows. The wooden ship groaned.

The space was large. Luxurious, even. She looked around, searching for any sign that the oracles might be staying here.

The more she looked, the more she realized every part of the cabin had been meticulously crafted. Moonstone floor. Expertly carved paneling.

It was a room fit for a ruler.

A floorboard groaned behind her.

Before she could take a single step, the sea crashed through the window, knocked her off her feet, and slammed her against the wall.

Isla's body shook as she tore against the icy restraints. She was trapped, splayed, just like she had been during the Centennial.

Cleo tilted her head at her, watching with pursed lips. "You must enjoy getting captured. You're so very good at it."

Isla spat at Cleo's feet, and the ice hardened further, nearly choking her.

Then, all at once, the ice turned to water, and she fell on the floor, gasping for air. She gripped her dagger immediately. Held it in front of her as she got to her feet, ready to strike.

Cleo looked bored. "What do you want, little Wildling?"

There was no use in hiding it. Cleo could have killed her, and she hadn't. There must be a reason.

Her teeth were chattering. "The oracles. Where are they?"

Cleo's answer was immediate. Emotionless. "Dead."

Something within Isla wilted. "You're lying."

"You aren't worth lying to," Cleo said flatly.

Isla had her dagger to Cleo's heart in a flash.

The Moonling barely spared it a glance.

"Why?" Isla demanded. Her hand was shaking.

Cleo only blinked. "Isn't it obvious? I took their prophecies and killed them so that I would be the only one to know the future."

Fury battled within Isla. She wished for her powers, so she could tear the ship to pieces, so she could shatter the sky and sea like a storm. It was this dangerous anger, this serpent within her always ready to strike, that was why she needed to keep the bracelets on. She knew that, yet still yearned for that power so she could paint the sky the shade of her endless rage.

"What did they say?" Isla roared, knowing she was foolish for even asking. But she had to try.

Cleo's smile was serpentine. "So much about *you*. None of which I will share, of course." In a flash, the Moonling hit her square in the chest, sending her back with a whip of water. Her dagger hit the ground. A half dozen ice blades were positioned at Isla's throat, like a death necklace. Cleo stood above her, still amused. "Fear not. Your end will come in time, but not from my hands."

In time.

Isla would have given anything to know when. To know how. To know how to stop it. To know any sort of explanation, or guidance, or hope that the oracle was wrong, and her fate could indeed be changed.

She felt so alone. The only two people she wanted to confide in were the ones she was in danger of killing.

"I'll give you anything," Isla said, meaning it. The anger had been put out and replaced by pure desperation. She was trembling, back against the corner of the room. She had never felt more powerless, and it had nothing to do with her lack of abilities. What was the point in having any power at all, when she couldn't even control her own destiny?

She had never imagined willingly being at the Moonling's mercy, but for this, she would beg. "Please. You must want something. Tell me what the oracles said, and I'll help you get it."

"All I want is my child back."

The only way to do that was to go to the otherworld, where souls could rise again. Getting there would require the death of all Lightlark. Thousands, including Oro. It wasn't an option.

Cleo seemed to see it on her face, because her expression completely hardened. "Leave now. Don't make me tempt fate."

Isla gripped her portaling device and obeyed.

It had taken hours to get Wraith home. Portaling them both while flying with her starstick hadn't worked. She'd had to wait until they reached land, where she could draw her puddle. By the time they went through and reached the stable, the storm had nearly crested. Wraith rolled onto his side and fell asleep immediately. Isla shivered as she portaled back into her room, barely meeting Lynx's gaze as he snarled at her, displeased. She closed the doors to her bathroom and winced as she lowered herself into the steaming tub, the one she had once shared with Grim.

Now it was just her, knees against her chest, tears slowly falling down her cheeks.

The oracles were all dead. There was no one left to ask about her fate. No one left to help navigate the prophecy.

There was no easy option. Each would break her in different ways.

Oro was the obvious choice. Her life wasn't bound to his.

She refused. She loved him—and, even if she didn't, she couldn't doom all his people and the island.

Grim's death would also kill thousands, including her.

Then, of course, there was the fact that she might not have long to live at all anyway. How much time did binding Grim's life to hers give her? The oracles might have known.

As she tightly gripped the edges of the tub, pinching her lips against a frustrated scream that would wake half the castle, part of her wished for her life before the Centennial. A fool locked in a glass room, thinking the only thing she would ever want was freedom. She remained in the tub until the water went cold.

First thing in the morning, a knock sounded on her door. She expected to find Grim there, to visit the other villages affected by the storms.

Instead, she found an attendant. He stood on the opposite side of the corridor, as if afraid to get close to her.

"Yes?"

"You have visitors," he said. "They're waiting in the throne room."

She frowned. "I do? Who?"

"Your guardians."

NIGHTBANE

"The last time I saw you, you tried to kill me," Isla said.

Terra only huffed in twisted amusement as she regarded her. "The last time I saw you, you were bleeding yourself out for power." She cocked her head. "How did that work for you?"

Isla might have lunged at her before. Now, after last night, she didn't bother summoning the anger. She was drained.

And Terra was right. Bleeding herself out to amplify her abilities had been reckless.

Still, the longer she stared at her old teacher, just standing there as if she hadn't lied to her for her entire life, the more a fury built in her bones. Hating her was easy. Terra had held her limbs to flames, had abandoned her in the middle of a storm, had knocked her unconscious with the hilt of her sword countless times during training.

Poppy, on the other hand . . . Isla watched her guardian nervously raking her nails against her thick skirts and wanted to sink to the floor. Poppy had held her hand while she received treatment for the injuries she received while training. Poppy had hummed while making tea filled with honeycomb. If Terra had been the blade, Poppy had been the balm. "Little bird—"

"Don't call me that," Isla snapped.

"Isla," Poppy corrected, her eyes darting to Terra nervously. "We can return another time, if—"

"I banished you," Isla said, her voice raising. "You killed my parents. You killed the last ruler of Wildling. You—"

Terra sighed impatiently, and the anger Isla had tried to bury came creeping back up. "I did hope surviving the Centennial would make you less of a fool."

The air around her changed, sharpened. The color drained from Poppy's face as she stared somewhere behind Isla.

"You'll watch how you speak to my wife in our home." Grim's voice was as piercing as the blade at his side. It would have made her blood go cold, if she weren't the wife in question.

Terra didn't seem concerned that Grim could turn her to ash without so much as a glare, as she barked a laugh. "And a coward too? Needing your demon husband to defend you?"

She stepped forward, drawing her blade from its sheath. In half a moment, it was aimed at Terra's throat.

"Speak to either of us that way again, and you'll find you won't be able to speak at all," she said steadily. Poppy paled even further. "I might have saved your life during the Centennial, but I am not beyond ripping your tongue out of your skull." The violence of her words shocked her, but she did not backtrack. She did not shrink into herself.

If Terra didn't like it, then she could only blame herself. This was who her guardian had trained her to be.

Terra almost looked impressed for a moment. Then, she frowned. She looked tired. Her voice barely contained any acid as she said, "Hate us for a thousand different reasons, but I'm putting an end to one of them once and for all. We did not kill your parents."

Isla didn't know what she had expected Terra to say, but it wasn't this. She bared her teeth. How dare she lie to her so blatantly? Did she think she wouldn't do as she promised and kill her on the spot?

"You *admitted* it," she said.

Terra did not deny that. She said nothing at all.

Why accept the blame? It didn't make any sense. "Liar."

"Yes. A thousand times," Terra said. "But not now. Not about this."

She could know for certain. She could reach for Oro's flair. She had used Grim's before, she could—

With the bracelets, she couldn't. And she wasn't going to take them off. Not for anything.

She forced her face back to indifference. It didn't matter now. She had far bigger issues. "I assume you didn't come here just to clear your names."

"No," Terra confirmed. "We came to tell you about the nightbane."

She frowned. "What about it?"

"It's dead."

Dead? "How much?"

There was a pause. Then, "All of it."

Once, the dark violet flowers had made up fields of star-shaped petals. Isla had stood here with Grim, marveling at their existence. They were miracles, every single one, capable of both life and death—healing and killing.

Now, they had all shriveled up and died. Isla picked one from the ground and watched it turn to ash between her fingers.

"We salvaged what we could," Wren said beside her. It had been a relief to see the Wildling leader safe.

Isla knew she needed to address her people. It had been days since she had returned.

Wren's leadership in her absence was a gift. The Wildling told her about the castle Grim had relocated them to, an abandoned estate with fields fit for farming and more than enough room for all of them.

Grim appeared minutes later, and Isla did not miss how Wren watched him warily. She turned her attention back to the wilted flowers.

"Secure any of our remaining elixirs," she told Wren. "We have seeds from the newland, right?" The plant was notoriously slow to grow. For the time being, the healing elixirs would be limited.

Wren nodded, bowed her head, and turned to give orders.

Isla studied the ground. *The storm.* She remembered how Grim said it had ruined lands before.

Grim was silent by her side. She could feel his tension. His worry. It echoed her own.

The destruction of nightbane was a massive blow. The scarcity of the drug it was used to create would only intensify unrest. Many people of Nightshade relied on it daily.

And, without the healing elixir it made, people would die from injuries that could previously be mended. They had just lost one of their greatest assets.

This had just been one storm of a season. It was just the beginning.

"We need to know about the origin of the storms, if we're going to stop them." They needed more information.

She needed more information.

The question was asked from desperation. She tried to keep the urgency out of her tone as she said, "You don't have oracles here, right?"

She didn't dare hope. She didn't dare breathe.

"No," he said, and she closed her eyes. Fought against the rush of sadness. Then, "The closest thing we ever had was a prophet, but he died a long time ago." *A prophet?* "His order survived, but they only speak to those who make the climb."

"The climb?"

"Up to their base. It's at the top of a mountain."

She blinked at him. "You never tried?"

"Of course I did. When I reached the top, they refused to let me in."

She frowned. Grim was their ruler, and he seemed well-liked by his people. "Why?"

"My father killed the prophet." Oh. Perhaps sensing she was going to ask why in the realms Grim's father would do that, he added, "He refused to share his prophecies with him."

Her desperation was so sharp, she knew he could feel it. "Maybe they'll speak to me. I'll make the climb." She said the words casually, but her heartbeat was anything but.

Grim just looked at her. "It isn't a simple mountain. There are tunnels within, and they shift unnaturally. There are beasts inside. The climb is a test, created when the prophet still lived. Only those who survived it were deemed worthy of his knowledge."

She gave him a withering look. "And you think me incapable?"

He glared back at her. "Of course not. But all power is nullified in the mountain, it's a sacred place of unusual ability, and—"

It didn't matter. The bracelets did that anyway. "You think just because I can't use my powers, I'm powerless?"

Grim blinked at her. "*No*," he said, looking as though he was trying to choose his words carefully. "But without them you are vulnerable." *Vulnerable.* She hated that word, even though he was right. "I'll go with you."

"I don't need your help."

"Perhaps not. I'm coming anyway."

"I—"

"Every single person who has tried to make the climb in the last century, other than me, has died. Your death means the death of my people. Any information they can provide about the storms is critical to us all."

That, she could not argue with.

She shifted on her feet, considering, and Grim just watched her, leaning against Wraith. She had so many secrets. She wished he would just leave her alone.

But if the prophet-followers wouldn't allow him in . . . he wouldn't hear her questions. If he could help her make it to the top, so be it.

"Fine. Where is this mountain?"

THE CLIMB

According to Grim, the ascent would take a full day. Two, possibly, depending on what they encountered.

She wanted to back out. Not just because of the danger, but because she wasn't thrilled about having to be trapped with him for hours on end, in close quarters.

As much as she denied it, Grim was right. Her feelings told a different story than her mind. Logically, she knew she should hate him. She knew he was the enemy.

Her emotions were still tied to memories.

She pushed the feelings down. Buried them as far as they would go. They didn't matter. They were only a distraction from her purpose.

They each carried supplies. The packs were small, to allow for easy movement. Water, food, and thin blankets were strapped to their backs. Swords and daggers were at their fronts. She wore her training clothes.

"Any warnings?" she asked, as they lingered at the entrance. It was a simple arch, leading into a single tunnel.

Grim looked at the dark passageway warily. He shook his head. "None that would do any good."

And then they were plunged into darkness.

"We should have brought an orb," she said, feeling around. They were less than ten steps up the path, and she couldn't see in front of her anymore.

"I did during my climb," Grim said. "It burnt out immediately. It was considered power, I suppose." Great.

She felt around in the dark, looking for a ledge, only to drag her hand completely down Grim's stomach. It was hard as marble, rippling with muscle. She snatched her hand back before she went any lower. "Sorry," she said quietly.

Grim's voice was deep and rattling, and too close for comfort. "Don't apologize," he said. "You can touch me wherever you like, wife."

She rolled her eyes even though he couldn't see it and blindly took a step forward, desperate to be as far away from him as possible. "Good to know, but irrelevant, as I don't plan on it."

"If you say so."

"I *do* say so," she hissed. She took another step that wasn't actually there and lurched forward. Only Grim's hands on her waist kept her from knocking her teeth in.

She stood very still, his breath right against her ear. "Careful. There are over a thousand steps to go. I can carry you, if you'd like." His tone was almost mocking.

With one of her senses muted, she focused on the others. Grim's voice, echoing through the tunnel, deep and scraping against some aching part of her. His cold, muscled body behind her back. His large hands still on her waist, fingers gripping her hips.

Isla placed her hands on Grim's and felt him stiffen.

Then, she shoved away from him.

She took it slow. The steps were uneven, so she felt each one with the tip of her foot before advancing. It was a long process. By the time a pocket of light appeared in front of them, they had been climbing for hours.

In the ceiling, bits of crystal glowed, creating a trail through the tunnels. Still, her eyes strained with effort in the limited light. Her calves began to burn.

Isla put down her pack and sank to the floor. "How far are we?"

"Not even a fifth of the way up."

She groaned. The prophet-order better be worth it. He handed her water, and she took a long sip. The tunnels were full of dust that dried her lips and tongue.

"We're lucky we haven't come across any creatures. I'd had at least two encounters by this point when I last was here."

A clicking noise echoed somewhere far away. It could have been anything. Vermin. Shifting rocks.

Then, it got louder.

Grim began to pack his bag once more. "Spoke too soon." He looked up at her. "Have enough water?"

She nodded. He took the pouch from her. "Good. Now run."

Clicking filled the tunnels. Their steps scraped against the stone floor as they ran, side by side, dust kicking up around them. They hurtled around each corner, her hand dragging along the rough wall as she turned. At the last one, she dared look over her shoulder.

That was when she saw them.

Curved-over creatures with talons that clicked as they crawled through the caves, their horns like crowns of daggers. They were almost as wide as the tunnels themselves. If the beasts caught up to them, Isla and Grim would be torn to shreds.

Faster. They needed to go faster.

Her legs ached as she pushed forward, but it wasn't quickly enough. The creatures were advancing. She had to slow down for fear of crashing into another wall.

The tunnels diverged again, and instead of choosing the one with the path of lights overhead, she dragged Grim in the other direction.

He followed her lead without slowing. "Is there a strategy I should be aware of?"

She motioned at the tunnel. A light smattering of crystals barely lit their path. The clicking was getting louder. They were right behind them. "Look. The walls are getting smaller."

Ever so slightly. It was a gamble, to see if it would continue to narrow. They ran and ran, and Isla wondered if perhaps she had led them down the wrong path. If there was only one right one, and they had lost it. Doubt nearly choked her.

Then there was a terrible high-pitched noise as the creatures' horns began to scrape against the walls.

Hope made her run faster. Just a little farther. They just needed to get a little—

She fell, skidding on her knees. One of the horns had torn a gash down her leg. Her scream echoed through the tunnel, and she turned around, arms in front of her, ready to be shredded—

But the creature was stuck. It snapped its wild teeth at her, just inches away, but did not reach her. Its horns were caught.

Before she could sigh in relief, the other creatures slammed behind it, sending the beast lurching forward. A moment before its jaw locked around her leg, Grim pulled her to her feet. He examined her wound. "The cut isn't deep. Can you walk?"

She nodded, but at the first step, her knee nearly buckled with the pain. It didn't matter. They had to keep going, lest the creatures break their horns and fit through.

They raced down the tunnel, slower than before, around a different corner, before she collapsed to the ground. Grim began to diligently wrap her leg with supplies from his pack. He was right: It wasn't deep, but it stung.

It would be difficult climbing the rest of the way with an injured leg, but they didn't even have the option of turning around. Not with the horned creatures completely blocking their path. The only way through was up.

"Ready?"

She wasn't. The pain burned. The tunnel was growing darker again. She didn't know how much she would crave light and greenery

until she was completely without it. Still, she stood and took the hand Grim offered.

He hadn't taken this path on his previous journey—neither knew what they would face. For an hour, they walked in silence. The tunnel kept getting smaller, and smaller, until Grim's head nearly brushed the ceiling. The floor slightly tilted downward, instead of up. They could be going the wrong direction. It didn't matter now. They didn't have another choice anyway.

The silence bred endless thoughts, especially this close to Grim. All the questions she had wanted to ask him, the ones she had kept buried for months after the Centennial.

"You thought working with Aurora would save my life, didn't you?" she asked.

She shouldn't care. It was in the past.

But she did. She cared a lot.

His eyes hardened. She could tell he didn't like thinking about it.

"Her plan promised us all Lightlark's power. I thought it might be enough to sustain your life for centuries, until we found another solution. I was going to move my people from Nightshade, away from the storms."

Aurora had tricked Grim into believing the prophecy to break the curses involved a Sunling king having to fall in love with a Wildling ruler—*the history that had to be repeated.*

She had used him, just like she had used Isla.

"You didn't think to tell me? You didn't think to include me?"

He stopped dead in his tracks. She did too. They faced each other. "All I thought about was your survival. I regret it. I told you that."

Regret wasn't enough.

"I fell in *love*, Grim," she said, her voice rising, echoing through the tunnels. "I fell in love with someone else, while I was married.

And I had no idea." He winced. Her words hurt him. *Good,* she thought. She wanted him to hurt. She wanted him to *understand.*

"Do you have any idea what it feels like to betray someone you love? Without even trying to?"

"Yes," he said through his teeth. He meant her.

She stepped forward. "You don't know what love is."

"I don't?" he said, bridging the space between them. "I waged a war for you. I bound my life to you."

"I didn't ask you to!" she screamed. She shook her head. It ached. Her eyes stung.

So much death. So much loss. She knew she should be grateful that he had brought her back to life, but part of her wished he had just let her die. The world would have been better for it. So many people wouldn't be in such imminent danger. When she said it aloud, Grim growled with anger.

"Don't ever say that. Don't ever *think* that. You have saved far more people than you have killed. You have power that threatens the gods." He frowned down at her bracelets. "Even if you insist on keeping it contained, you have it. I might have saved you because I love you, but you are meant to live. You are meant to use this power."

She didn't know how he could speak so reverently about power that had caused so much destruction. She wished she'd never had it at all. She wished she hadn't ever explored the world with her portaling device.

"I wish you'd never loved me." It was true. It would have made everything so much easier. It would have saved so many lives. She pressed the heels of her hands to her eyes in frustration. Anger built behind her ribs. She dropped her hands and looked him right in the eye. Her voice was sharp. Barely recognizable. "I wish I hadn't given myself to you, like a fool. I wish I hadn't let you betray me, and lie to me, and manipulate me, and I *hate you.*" Her chest was heaving. "*I hate you, I hate you,* and I would throw this damned necklace into the sea if I could!"

Grim reared back, as if she had slapped him. His eyes glistened with hurt. She had never seen him look so wounded, even when he'd had a dozen arrows through his chest.

She instantly regretted her words. But why? She had meant them, hadn't she?

He took a step away from her. She took a step away from him, in turn—and nearly slipped.

Water. Just a puddle of it, spreading slowly. Eating away the rock beneath it, creating a mirror. She blinked at her own reflection, hazy in the faint crystal light.

Then, it came rushing like a river.

She looked up at him. Their gazes locked.

"Run," she said, and they did. The water was gushing now. Rising to her ankles, then her calves. It kept growing until it knocked her off her feet, and then she was paddling, gasping for air. Soon it would fill the tunnel. They would drown.

Her limbs ached as she swam as fast as she could, fighting to stay above the water. She managed a gulp of air before being pulled under by the force of the current. When she surfaced again, there were only a few inches remaining between the top of her head and the rocks above.

The tunnel was endless. It was no use fighting it.

She stopped swimming. Grim did too. She lifted her head as high as it would go, greedily swallowing air.

Grim faced her.

In his eyes, she saw unfiltered fear. The same fear she had seen moments before she had died.

They found each other's hands through the water.

"I—I'm sorry, I—"

"I know, Hearteater," he said. He pulled her close, and their foreheads touched. This couldn't be it. This wasn't her fate.

She thought of all the people who would die because she was reckless enough to insist on going on the climb. The children. The innocents. The same as before, when—

The floor. It had curved downward. It had confused her, but now she realized it might be their salvation.

The tunnel had split throughout their journey, left and right. What if it also split top to bottom? They had been fighting against the current, trying to remain above the water, when perhaps they should have been letting it take them. With the last gulp of air, she said, "The tunnel is going down, the water pressure is increasing. Sink to the bottom. Follow the floor. Stop fighting it."

Grim met her eyes; his were filled with trust she didn't deserve. He nodded.

It was a risk, but the water was at the ceiling now anyway. Isla stopped swimming. Stopped struggling. So did Grim. She blew out the air in her lungs in one long stream and sank to the bottom. The current was even stronger down there.

In a rush, it raked her across the bottom of the tunnel, her shirt the only thing keeping her skin from being ripped apart. Faster. *Faster.* The water took them down, then farther, and she felt stone above her, as she moved through a different tunnel, a tighter one. Hope engulfed her. Maybe she had been right.

Just as quickly, panic closed in as closely as the rock that surrounded her. The space had become as narrow as a tomb. What if it narrowed further and she got stuck? She would drown in seconds. She was drowning *now.*

The pressure in her chest built. Roaring filled her ears. Spots clouded her vision. She came to a stop.

Then one great surge pushed against her feet, and she was careening forward, downward, faster than before. She was thrown in every direction, rock scraping her bare skin, her throat constricting, her head throbbing, lungs burning. Just when she thought she couldn't take it

any longer, she flew forward out of the tunnel, where she landed in a pool of water. She let out a choking sob as oxygen flooded her lungs.

Grim.

He broke through the water next to her a second later. His eyes were wild, and their intensity didn't dim as he found hers. She was coughing, gasping, feeling like she was going to retch but seeing him safe, knowing they had survived the tunnel—

Their arms were around each other in an instant. She didn't realize she was shaking or crying until he smoothed his large hands down her spine. "You're okay," he said, as if he was saying it to himself as well. "Because of you . . . we're okay."

They had nearly drowned. Her lungs still burned. She buried her face in his neck as he carried them through the pool, toward its edge. He whispered soothing sounds against the top of her head. His hands continued their gentle strokes up and down her back as she trembled against him. She was freezing. He was naturally cold; but compared to the water he was warm, so she clung to his chest. *Safe.* She felt safe in his arms. She knew it was wrong; but when he hauled her out of the water, she found herself grieving the loss of his skin against hers. She braced for more chill, but the rock was surprisingly warm beneath her hands.

After retrieving her pack that had gotten lost in the spring, he hauled himself out of the pool and straightened to his full height, towering over her. His clothes were molded to his body and dripping, their runoff forming a puddle at his feet. She swallowed, heart still hammering.

Then he began removing his clothing.

Logically, she knew it was because they were wet. They needed to dry off before they advanced. They would freeze in their drenched clothing, especially in the cold tunnels.

But there was nothing logical about the way she watched him. About the way she couldn't bring herself to look away from his chest,

muscled to perfection and marred by a single unhealed scar. Or his legs. He was built like a statue. Like a warrior. She swallowed.

"You're leering at me."

She immediately found somewhere else to look. "I am not."

"Leer away, wife. I don't mind."

Isla scowled and pulled herself to her feet with a groan. Her leg still ached. Her breaths remained labored. Meeting his gaze, she began to take her clothing off too, slowly, piece by piece. She watched his throat work. For all his smugness, he turned away a moment later, seeming very preoccupied with laying his clothing perfectly across the rock, alongside their soaked blankets.

Just like him, she kept her undergarments on. She laid her clothes out flat. Then, she rested against the rock. It was warm—comfortable, even—a balm against the spiking chill of the pool. The groan that escaped her as the stone pressed against her skin was mortifying. She pressed her lips together as her skin flushed.

Any hope that he hadn't heard her died when she turned to find him staring. No. He was *leering*. Just as she had.

She wasn't sure he was breathing.

They wouldn't survive the rest of the journey if they both died of hypothermia. She tried to appear unaffected as she motioned toward the space next to her. "Are you going to warm yourself, or just stand there with your mouth hanging open?"

Grim didn't even try for a retort. His eyes didn't leave hers as he slowly lowered himself to the ground next to her, careful not to touch her skin.

Sleep. They needed to sleep. Their bodies were spent from the journey. Now, the inside of the mountain was quiet, but who knew what they would soon face?

She turned away from him, pressing her eyes shut.

Cold air hissed through the tunnels of the cave, making her skin prickle everywhere. She shivered. Sleeping on her side wouldn't

work. Not like this, anyway. Any part not touching the warm rock was numb. She shifted slightly closer to Grim and found that it helped.

"You're freezing, aren't you?"

She didn't deign to respond. She wasn't used to the cold. The Wildling newland was always warm. Terra had tried to train her in as many different environments as she could, but even the worst of trials hadn't been close to this.

"You hate the cold."

She did. He knew her. *Bastard.*

He shifted slightly closer to her. She stiffened. "Who likes the cold?" she asked, tone biting.

"I do." She knew that too.

Still, she laughed without humor. "You must be thrilled about our current circumstances, then."

"No, not particularly. I'm watching my injured wife shiver like a leaf in a storm in front of me."

She glared at him over her shoulder. "Stop calling me that."

"A leaf in a storm?"

Her eyes narrowed further.

"Wife?"

"Yes," she hissed.

"No."

She flipped to completely face him. "What do you mean, *no*?"

"No," he repeated. "You are my wife." His gaze dropped to her necklace. She didn't so much as move as he dragged a finger down her throat, then across her collarbones, tracing a slow circle around the massive stone. He leaned in. His breath was hot against her pulse as he said, "I'm your husband. I'm *yours*." His voice was nearly a growl as he said, "And you . . . *wife* . . . are *mine*."

A warmth dropped through her. She tried to ignore it. "I don't see *you* wearing anything around your neck."

He didn't so much as falter. "That can be arranged."

She gave him a withering look that didn't hold any real bite. Not when his finger was slowly tracing the path from her collarbone to her chest, stopping just short of the thin fabric she wore.

"Cold, Hearteater?"

"No," she said, with all the conviction in the world, only to follow his gaze and see that her chest was very clearly peaked and visible through her undergarments.

She stiffened, and Grim dropped his hand. She shivered involuntarily at the loss of contact, the loss of the tiny bit of heat.

All she wanted was to be closer, but she forced herself to turn around again. She wrapped her arms around herself, covering her chest, and tried to forget who was behind her.

Minutes later, she was still freezing. She couldn't take it any longer. The prophet-followers were her only hope of obtaining more information about the prophecy. If she didn't at least rest a few hours, she wouldn't have the strength to press forward.

That was what she told herself, anyway, as she scooted back and said, "Do you—do you mind?"

"No. Come here." His arm circled her waist. He gently dragged her back, cradling her against his chest.

And then, she was enveloped by him.

She was finding it hard to breathe normally. The fabric of her underthings didn't create any kind of barrier. It was just skin and muscle, and his hard edges against the softest parts of her, and heat flowing through her as soon as the cold was banished.

Being this close to him was like being in a storm, wrapped in everything *him*.

This was wrong. How did they end up here, on the ground, in nothing but bits of fabric, folded around each other?

He was her enemy. She was in love with someone else.

She knew she should get up, but she didn't want to. She was tired, hurt, and cold, and all she wanted was to lay here, for just a little while, and be relieved that they had survived.

Comfort—that was what she needed, and what he offered her as he wrapped his body fully around hers, shielding her from the cold. She leaned into his touch just a little too much. She felt herself sigh when his nose ran down the length of her neck. She shifted back, pressing against him, some part of her finally relaxing, as if it had waited a long time to be back in his arms.

Only for a little while, she reminded herself.

She thought it even as her eyelids drooped, and she was smothered by sleep.

She awoke wrapped in Grim's arms. At first, for a few strange moments, she didn't know where she was—only that it felt familiar to be surrounded by the smell of storms and spice and something distinctly masculine. To be held in these arms. She let out a peaceful sound and wriggled back, against him. Against something hard.

She stilled. Her eyes flew open.

The cave greeted her. She didn't dare breathe. Want flared within her like a wildfire, but she buried it down, instead forcing herself to scuttle forward, away from him. He was awake. Of course he was. He probably hadn't slept a moment, lest they be caught unawares by some creature in the cave.

She turned, and they stared at each other. For just one second, the air between them felt taut, like a single move could break the illusion between them. Like one movement forward, one word, or one rasped breath could lead to them tangled together on the floor.

She rose to her feet. Grim did the same, and she didn't dare stare at him, not again. She turned and began dressing. Her clothes were dry now. Not just dry, but warm.

Without glancing at him, she made her way to the tunnels. There were a few paths to choose from. Each had different colored crystals embedded in the ceiling.

She had led them through the last tunnel, and it had nearly gotten them killed. It was his turn. "Choose," she said. He moved ahead of her, and they walked through the mouth of his chosen tunnel in silence.

At first, it seemed as though Grim had picked a good path. For miles and miles, the worst thing about it was the climb. They had gone down, and now they were forced back up, to a degree that seemed impossibly high. Her calves burned, and she feared falling backward, rolling all the way back down. Likely breaking her neck in the process. She leaned forward, angled over her knees, steadying herself. Her breathing became labored.

Her leg had bled through its bandages again. She could feel the blood dripping down her ankle. Filling her shoe. Crusting between her toes. It was impossible to stop here, in the narrow space, the floor curved and treacherous.

Times like these made her grateful for her training. It was hours until the path became level. She nearly sank to her knees in relief but worried she wouldn't be able to stand again if she did. The muscles in her legs were all stiff. The nerves were either numb or burning with exertion.

They had to be close. She didn't think she could last much longer.

The crystals in the ceiling became more plentiful, until they led to a wide cave. A clearing. Beyond it, another tunnel entrance awaited.

But it was blocked.

"What," she asked, not daring speak beyond a whisper. "Is that?"

A dark shadow concealed the entrance—a monstrous figure with long, thin limbs. It reminded her of a grasshopper, if grasshoppers grew to be twenty feet tall.

Its skin was iridescent. Every time it breathed, every inch of it rippled.

It turned sharply toward her. It had no face.

Isla backed away, placing her hand on the blade at her hip. She waited for it to advance. But it did not. It simply stood at its post in front of the tunnel, facing them.

"We're going to have to get past it," she said.

Grim sighed. "Any ideas?"

Without a face, did the creature have all its senses? As a test, she reached down, grabbed a rock, and threw it to the other side of the clearing.

It hammered wildly against a wall. The sound echoed.

The creature didn't move an inch. Interesting.

It had sensed her, somehow, though . . . if not from her speaking, then from what? She took a step forward and nearly slipped in a dark, wet streak by her heel. That was when she realized it.

"Blood. It senses blood."

Grim looked from her leg to the creature. "I think you're right."

Isla knelt to the ground.

"What are you doing?" he demanded.

"What do you think?"

She began to undo her wrapping. He stopped her, with a hand over hers. "Keep it on. I'll cut my arm."

She shook his touch away. "You said it yourself. This is a test to see if they'll let me in at all. It has to be me." Grim didn't seem happy about it, but she didn't really care. She hadn't been nearly shredded, or drowned, or trapped in this dusty tunnel system only to stop short of speaking to the order of prophet-followers.

No. They were getting past this creature. She was going to get answers about her fate.

"Get ready to run." She stepped into the clearing.

Before she could throw the wrapping to the other side as she'd planned to, the creature lunged. It knocked her off her feet in a flash.

One of its thin legs pinned her down, pushing into the center of her chest with surprising strength. It was a wonder it didn't crack through her ribs. Her head spun. She could smell more blood—likely from her head this time—and the creature began chittering.

It lifted its foot. Only then did she see that there was a mouth at its bottom, rimmed in teeth. It inched toward her head, as if to swallow it. As if to rip her face off and eat everything beneath it.

Before it could get any closer, she cut its leg off with her sword.

The creature seized above her, emitting a high-pitched sound. She rolled out of the way just as another mouth-tipped foot shot down, right where her head had been.

"Go," she screamed, rubbing a hand along the back of her head, and finding it wet. Yes. Blood. She rubbed it on the walls, then stumbled at the force of the creature slamming against it. It was right behind her. Right behind—

She ran through the tunnel.

It was still right behind her.

It was a split-second decision. She gripped her sword tightly, then dragged it down her calf, tearing her wound open again, coating it in blood. Then, she stopped running. She turned and planted herself in the center of the tunnel. Outstretched her arm just in time—

And watched the creature skewer itself on her blade.

She was panting. Her leg was a fire of pain.

Grim cursed, moving quickly to wrap her opened wound as she twisted her sword, until she was sure the creature was dead. "Climbing is going to be difficult," he said.

"Good thing we won't be." She could see the end of the tunnel from over her shoulder. The crystals above their heads flashed, as if in welcome.

Below them sat a door.

The moment Grim was done wrapping her leg again, she began limping toward it. The pain had faded away. All she felt was the cold rush of relief. She had made it.

The door had no handle. That was fine.

She stepped forward and knocked, slamming her fist against the stone. Her skin broke. Blood coated it.

For moments, nothing happened, and she banged harder. Harder.

It finally opened just a sliver, rattling the cave. Enough room for a single robed individual to step through.

A hood hid their face. The figure turned to her, then Grim, then back. A bony finger peeked from the robe and pointed right at her.

It was clear. Only she would be allowed through. They had expected this. She turned to look at Grim, and he nodded. She could almost sense the words in his intense gaze—he was right outside. He might not have powers here, but he would rip the doors off their hinges and get to her if she needed him.

A few days ago, she would have glared at him, but now . . . after what they had faced . . . she nodded back.

The doors closed behind her with a thud she felt in her bones. Inside, hooded figures faced her, in perfect lines. They bowed, their white robes gleaming through the darkness. It was almost as if they had known she would be coming.

It was almost like they had been waiting for her.

Every wall was shimmering black rock. A scattering of the same crystals from before were embedded in the ceiling above.

The hooded figure led her down corridor after corridor, until they turned into a small door, cut into the rock-face room. It promptly closed behind her.

She turned and startled.

A woman appeared from the darkness itself, seated on a slab of rock that hadn't been there before. Another seat appeared before her. Then, a table between them.

There was power, at least, here in their base, it seemed.

The woman before her lowered her hood. A large scar cut across her face, slicing through her lips, her brow, and one eye. Her smile was wide and warm, completely at odds with her height and muscular figure. This woman used to be a warrior. She could see it in the small scars along her fingers. She'd had the same ones, once, before Poppy had healed them away with their elixir, thinking them ugly.

She took the seat she offered.

"I'm Eta. Welcome to our peak, Isla, ruler of Wildling." A book appeared on the table. Its pages were thick and yellowed. Eta trailed a leathered, scar-crossed hand along its spine. "Our dear prophet," she said reverently. "The book is bound in his skin. The words are written in his blood."

She fought the urge to vomit. She had clawed her way to this very seat. Part of her wanted to come out and ask about her prophecy, but no. She had to start off small. Judge whether she could give her any useful information at all.

"I'm here to find out how to stop the storms on Nightshade. Did your . . ." she motioned toward the book with a wave of malaise, "*prophet* have anything to say about them?"

Eta gently traced the edges of the book, though she didn't look down at it. No, her gaze was fixed on her. She was studying her closely. She looked almost amused.

Isla shifted uncomfortably under her gaze but was relieved when she nodded.

"To stop them, you must close their source."

"Which is?"

"The portal. The door left open."

She blinked. No, she couldn't have heard her right. "The one on Lightlark?"

Eta shook her head. "No, no, that is a bridge. The one here is simply a door, left ajar."

She leaned forward. She wasn't sure she was breathing. "You're saying there's a portal on Nightshade?"

"Of a sort."

Grim couldn't have known about it. If he had, he would have used it. He wouldn't have attacked Lightlark.

"How do you know?"

"It's how our prophet got here. He came from another world entirely. It's how he knew everything that would occur. It had been written."

The prophet had come from the otherworld?

She didn't mask her interest. No, she couldn't do anything but demand, "Where is it?"

"No one knows. The prophet's records of it were stolen." Eta reverently flipped through the book's well-worn pages; and upon closer study, Isla saw a large portion of its beginning was missing. Pages had been ripped away.

"If someone found the portal . . . could it be used?" It could be the solution to all her problems.

Eta shook her head. "It is simply a rip between worlds, a torn seam. Anyone from this world would die making the journey—the power required doesn't exist here. Portaling between worlds has a price, just like power has a price."

Power has a price. She knew that better than anyone.

"The portal on Lightlark. If it had been used, it would have killed us too?"

She shook her head again. "Not necessarily. That portal is a bridge, built to fuse two specific worlds, so the connection is stronger. It does most of the job itself, you might say." She pursed her lips. "Still, many would have died. Only the strongest would have made it through. Many *did* die, in the creation of Lightlark. Their bodies were used as the foundation of the island. It gave it power. Did you know?"

She didn't. Her voice was a frustrated growl. "Why is there a portal on Nightshade at all, if it can't be used?"

"That, I do not know. What I do know is that it is like a hole in a dam. And it is growing. Things are being let *in*. Storms and creatures that don't belong here."

"Can it be closed?"

Eta nodded. "The prophet knew how. He simply wasn't able to, before he died."

To stop the storms, they needed to find the portal and close it. She had gotten the answers they needed.

Now was the time to ask about her own fate.

"Did the prophet speak about my prophecy?" Part of her wanted to rip the book from her hands.

Eta seemed to sense that, because it suddenly vanished. "Yes, it's all been written. You've been told all you need to know. Goodbye, Isla World-maker."

No. She had so many more questions. Her hand flung out, forming an iron-clad vise around her wrist before she could leave. She looked up at her, eyes wide. In fear? No. In curiosity. "How long do I have to live?"

She shook her head. "That, I do not know. Only the augur might be able to tell you that."

"The augur?"

Eta nodded. "He was one of us, once. Now, he lives deep in the woods, behind a curtain of water. He studies blood. He might be able to read yours and tell you how much time you have left."

Studies blood. That made her more than a little uneasy, but she was desperate for information.

"What is his price?" She knew well enough now that just like power and portaling, information also came at a cost.

"Blood, naturally. I believe hearts are preferable." She watched her, amused, but didn't say anything about her people's former curse.

Isla's teeth dragged together. Her entire goal was to not kill another innocent, but she would find a way around that.

Eta's wrist still in her unrelenting grip, she said, "My prophecy. Does it—does the book have anything about *who* I kill?"

The oracle had said that the choice was still in flux. She was just as likely to kill either ruler.

"No. Only that you will plunge a blade into another powerful heart, and it will mark the start of a new age."

"Can it be changed? Is it possible that the prophecy is . . . wrong?"

Eta looked almost sad for a moment. She smiled weakly. "Every single thing that has been written in this book has come to pass."

Her eyes burned. Her throat tightened. She released the prophet-follower's wrist.

No. There—there had to be a way . . . she had to be *wrong*—

Her look was nearly pitiful. "A warning for you, Isla Harbinger. There is a traitor in your midst that would like to see you dead. One of your own."

It was the last thing she was expecting to hear. "A Wildling?"

She nodded. "It is written. One of your own betrays you. One of your own has *already* struck against you."

Betrayed her how? "What do you mean?"

"The nightbane, of course."

The fields of dead flowers. Poisoned by a blight. "That was the storm."

She shook her head. "The storm was used as a cover. A Wildling poisoned the flowers."

A Wildling. That didn't make sense. The nightbane benefitted everyone. Her people spent months cultivating it. Why would one of them destroy it?

"Find the traitor. Stop them, or they will be your ruin."

"How do I find them?" she demanded.

"Follow the snakes."

The snakes? "What—"

Before the word left her mouth, Eta was gone.

Grim straightened as she stepped back outside the doors. He looked relieved, until his gaze dropped to her leg. It had bled through again. She hadn't even felt it. No, she had been too busy turning Eta's words in her head.

Every single thing that has been written in this book has come to pass.

The book had to be wrong.

Grim ducked to replace her bandages. From the floor, he looked up at her, and it made her heart stutter. "Well?"

She considered not telling Grim about the portal. She knew he would hope, just as she had, that it was a solution to their problems.

But she had to tell him something—and she would need his help finding it.

She told him everything about the portal. She sensed his excitement at the idea of another way to the otherworld, then watched it wither when she told him it couldn't be used, not without killing them in the process.

"Do you have any idea where a portal might be?"

He shook his head with certainty. "No. With my flair, I would have sensed it."

She had figured as much. So, where was it? Where could it be hidden, where the ruler of the land wouldn't have encountered it?

The storms were connected to it. Perhaps they could be the key to finding its location. There was one person who knew more about tempests than any of them. "I'm going to visit Azul."

Grim looked surprised, but he didn't try to change her mind. She was trying to help his realm, after all.

But that was not the only reason she wanted to seek out the Skyling.

The walk down nearly broke her. Grim offered to carry her several times, and she was close to letting him, but somehow, they left the darkness of the mountain. Before she saw even a shard of sunlight, Grim was portaling them back to the palace.

Her leg was soaked in blood—the wound was worse, deeper now from the strain of her movements. Her head was spinning. They had run out of bandages. Grim was gone in an instant.

When he returned, he held a coveted vial of healing elixir. Before she could say a single word, he was pouring the liquid directly onto her wound. She gritted her teeth as her skin slowly sewed back together.

Only minutes later, when the pain had dimmed, did Grim say, "Hearteater. Why is there only one vial of healing elixir left in our weaponry store?"

There was no use in hiding it. "I sent the rest to Lightlark."

She watched his shoulders stiffen.

Isla knew what it looked like. Nightbane was one of Nightshade's greatest resources, and now it was gone. Every remaining vial mattered.

She had sent almost all their store to the enemy.

It was a betrayal, treasonous.

But she wasn't even sure who the enemy was anymore. All she knew was that the elixir belonged to *her people,* and she chose what she was going to do with it.

Grim was silent. She readied herself to see anger or frustration in his expression . . . but all she saw was pain.

He stood. Handed the near-empty vial back to her.

He didn't say anything, which was almost worse.

"You can't expect me not to care," she said, out of nowhere. "I was preparing it for them, that was my home, I was—I was—"

She couldn't get the words out. Her eyes stung, thinking of Oro. Of everything they had built together, over months. Trust. Love.

And she had shattered all of it.

"I understand," he said, and he looked like he did. Or, at least, like he was trying to. Most of all, he looked full of regret. He closed his eyes for a moment. Opened them. "Can you ever forgive me?"

She knew what he was asking. From the moment she had arrived, she had made it clear she resented him for everything. He was asking if they could ever go back to how things were before. If she could ever truly love him.

No, she wanted to say.

Instead, she said, "I'm not sure." It was the truth.

He nodded. She was surprised when he said, "You're right. I don't know what love is. I don't know how to love. If you ever gave me another chance to love you, I would learn. I would learn the right way to love you."

Then, he left.

STORMSTONE

"I hear congratulations are in order." Azul's booming voice overtook the room. She hadn't seen him since before the fight between Lightlark and Nightshade, when the Skylings had voted for their ruler not to participate.

So, he had heard about her marriage. "Who told you?"

"Who do you think?"

"Zed." The Skyling was fast as lightning. He hadn't ever truly trusted her. Now, she knew he never would.

Azul nodded. "I heard the king is . . . inconsolable." He studied her, as if waiting for her reaction. She showed none. If she thought too hard about Oro, and their life together, and the betrayal he must feel right now, she would start crying, and she didn't know if she would ever stop.

Instead, she raised her head. Azul stared pointedly at her necklace. "What would you have had me do?"

"Well, to start, you could have not married him."

Isla ground her teeth. "When I met him, I was a naïve puppet that had only ever known the confines of her room. Then . . . after the battle . . . it was the only thing to stop the killing. To stop the death. To stop everything."

He shook his head. "No, you knew what he was when you married him. You knew how many people he had killed. You know *now.* Why stay? To stop a war? You are not a fool, Isla, so stop playing one. Do not think for a moment that Grim won't invade again. Nothing in the world can come between him and his sights set, not even you."

She hoped he was wrong.

"I stay because I'm a monster too, Azul."

He gave her a look. "You are many things, Isla Crown, but you are not a monster."

"You're wrong. That is why I came here."

"To tell me I'm wrong?"

"No. To tell you the prophecy."

Isla hadn't told anyone. But someone needed to know. Someone needed to keep her accountable.

She needed to be careful with who she trusted; she knew that. But Azul was the most trustworthy person she had ever met. And, perhaps more than anyone, she trusted *herself* the least.

She told him every single word. Azul listened, frowning. "It is certain?"

"According to the oracle, yes. One or the other."

For a moment, it looked like he pitied her. Then, "So which one is it?"

She shook her head. "I don't know. I really don't. But either way, as it stands . . . either death would mean the end of thousands."

Nexus bound all people to their rulers. It was a curse.

"Why are you telling me this?"

She looked at the ground. Part of her felt shame. "I don't trust myself. I've made every decision with my heart . . . and it has ended in ruin. I wanted you to know the prophecy, in case I ever lost myself. In case you saw me about to make the wrong choice."

He nodded.

"How are the Starlings?" She thought of Maren, who had told her about nexus in the first place. Cinder, her cousin, who was the most gifted Starling she had ever seen.

"Taken care of. Our newland has more than enough space for them." She supposed it helped that the realm was small,

unfortunately, due to their previous curse. "They're conducting a vote soon, I hear."

Right. Isla had promised to make Starling a democracy and to yield her rule should they vote for another leader. It seemed obvious they would choose one of their own.

She'd thought of Nightshade's storms as a localized problem, but she now realized the portal could affect all the realms. Especially if the torn seam between worlds was growing.

"What do you know about storms?" she asked him.

Azul looked slightly amused. He studied her carefully. "What do you know about flowers?"

Fair. "How do you stop them?"

He seemed to consider this. "Storms are filled with energy. Powerful Skylings can shape them, manipulate parts of them. *Stopping* them is more difficult. It would mean cutting them off at their source."

There was no time for secrecy, not with Azul. "What if their source was a portal?"

Azul frowned. It was an unfamiliar expression on his face. "I've never heard of anything like that."

"There's a portal on Nightshade." His eyes widened ever so slightly. "Not one that can be used. It's a torn seam between worlds. Creatures are being let in. Storms. I need to find it and close it."

There was a fold between Azul's brows. His thumb was thrumming down the side of his chair. Silence.

"What is it?"

He hesitated for just a moment. Then, he said, "We read omens in the clouds."

"And?"

His head lowered. His voice was nearly a whisper. "They warn of a storm to end all storms. A reckoning."

She thought of the woman in the village, calling them a harbinger of the end. "When?"

He shook his head. "I'm not sure . . . But a storm is coming, Isla, I can feel it." He dipped his chin as he said. "One unlike any we've ever seen before."

Chills swept up her arms.

"Wait here," Azul said. He flew out of the room in a flash. When he returned, minutes later, he was holding a cage, with a bird inside. It was sky blue with a grey beak. Small enough to fit in her palm.

"This is a stormfinch. It can sense a storm before even Skylings can." She had never heard of such a creature. "Before the next storm . . . It will start singing the most beautiful song you have ever heard."

This would save countless lives, she thought. It would give Nightshades time to get underground before the tempests struck.

She gingerly took the cage. It was ornate, with swirling designs across its side.

"When she sings, I want you to get as high as you can. Then, I want you to hold this." He slipped one of his largest rings off his fingers and handed it to her. It had a large light blue stone, like a bird's egg.

At her questioning look, he said, "It has a shred of storm trapped inside." *A shred of storm?* She squinted, holding the stone up to her eye. Faintly, she could see something spinning within its depths. She gasped and stared at him.

He cracked a smile. "You didn't think I wore all of these just for decorative purposes, did you?" She studied all the stones he wore, on his fingers, around his neck, on the buttons of his cape. "They are all imbued with storms. They amplify my powers significantly. Precious stones can trap power." He nodded at the ring in her hand. "Trap part of the storm in it, and the stone should lead you to its source." *To the portal.*

"How?"

"Break the stone with power. The storm will be released and called to its origin. Follow it."

Her grip on the bird's cage tightened. "Thank you," she told Azul.

Isla went to turn on her heel, but he called her name, and she just barely caught something he had thrown her.

Another ring. *Her* diamond ring. The one she had given to Azul before the battle for safekeeping. She looked inside. Something flurried.

"I added something to it. A shred of power for you to shape how you wish." It seemed to hum against her hand, just like the other stone. She swallowed. She didn't deserve this. If he had seen what she had done with power—

"Everyone can be redeemed. You are not a monster, Isla."

She wished she believed him.

"You are *not*," he repeated. "I know one when I see one. I knew something was wrong with Aurora from the very beginning."

Aurora.

Some empty corner of her mind ached. She had been her best friend. She had been a stranger.

As she portaled away, she remembered the one thing she had left of her friend turned enemy. The only thing she had kept.

She had meant to go to Grim, to show him the stormstone, to hang the bird's cage in the castle, but instead, she went to the Wildling newland. She went to the room she had been locked in, almost like the stormfinch.

A charred mark marred the center of her former room. The door had been ripped off its hinges. She had done that, in a fit of anger, proof that her bracelets were necessary. Now, even as she called for her power, it didn't even whisper back.

Her wall of swords reflected her face in garish angles as she searched for the one object she had kept from the Starling newland.

Aurora's feather.

She found it in a drawer. Upon closer inspection, it was just a simple white feather. Its weight didn't signal any importance. A single flame would kill it, a single gust of wind would spirit it into the forest. She had found feathers just like it during her training.

So why had Aurora kept it in an orb?

Why had she kept it a secret?

Isla strummed a finger down its spine, and the barbs shivered in waves, like a pond disturbed by a stone, a breeze humming through treetops.

Strange.

She thought of Azul's words, how stones could be imbued with power. Could feathers?

Her finger continued its path until its point, and she flinched, nearly dropping the feather in surprise. Its tip was as sharp as her dagger's. A drop of blood dripped down her finger like a tear. The feather's white point now gleamed red.

If it was this sharp . . . perhaps it was meant for writing, she thought, before finding a pot of ink and a ream of parchment in another drawer.

She wrote a single word. *Isla*.

Nothing happened.

What did she expect would happen? She nearly snapped the feather in annoyance. She should burn it. She should throw it into the forest. It was useless, just like her former friendship.

Aurora had betrayed her, but she was dead.

If the prophet-follower was to be believed, she had another traitor to deal with.

TRAITOR

A Wildling had destroyed the nightbane. One of her own was working against her. It still didn't make sense. Why would a Wildling kill one of their greatest assets? According to Wren, her people were thriving on Nightshade.

It was time for her to see it for herself.

Lynx snarled as Wraith landed behind them, so closely, she was nearly knocked off his back. Grim had insisted on accompanying her here, though he didn't know about the traitor. When it came to anyone harming her, he seemed to operate by a kill first, ask questions later philosophy. No, she would find the Wildling traitor herself. She ran her hand down Lynx's neck as she dismounted, and he took off, immediately followed by an eager Wraith, as if they were in some sort of race.

A castle sat on the edge of a cove, surrounded by farmland. Its bricks were shining black, almost silver, and its towers were spiked, as if covered in crowns. A ring of water around it glimmered beneath the sun. Its door was a bridge, laying across the moat, perfectly aligned with a pathway of cobblestone and patches of grass. A small village sat nearby, abandoned for decades.

That was where Grim had taken the Wildlings. "They chose this place," he said, from just behind her.

A castle with a town next to it. Something about it tugged at her bones.

"It was your father's. It's yours."

Her father.

He had been Grim's general, a powerful Nightshade, from a prominent family. That was all she really knew about him, besides his flair.

A question snagged in her mind. She couldn't believe she had never asked it before. Perhaps she had been too afraid of knowing the answer. "Do I—do I have any surviving family?" The castle had been abandoned, but it was possible they lived somewhere else.

Grim nodded, and she nearly drowned in hope.

Her eyes burned. "I do?"

Her entire life, she had been taught her family was dead. The idea of that not being true, of her having someone out there . . .

He could sense her excitement, she knew that, but still, he had a strange expression on his face. A tentative one. "A cousin."

A cousin.

Family.

She wanted to meet them. How could Grim have hidden them from her? She scoured her memories but came up short. She had never met a relative, not even in the past.

"Who is it?" she demanded.

He looked suddenly nervous. "Roles in my court go blood deep. Certain lines have served the same positions for centuries. Millenia, even."

Isla's smile dropped. She knew what he was saying. Who her mysterious cousin was.

Grim's current general, Astria. The woman that looked at her as if she was a snake curled around Grim's neck, slowly tightening.

Astria must have known they were related. She must have known and still didn't trust her at all.

"Oh," Isla said.

Grim portaled her to the castle's entrance and was gone.

The inside of the palace was surprisingly welcoming, coated in a layer of black marble. Her people looked happy to see her. She might

have suggested they convene all together, but no. If she was going to find the Wildling traitor working against her, she was going to have to speak to each one of them separately.

One woman approached her immediately. Her name was Calla. She had short hair and freckles across the bridge of her nose. Her eyes were wide as she told Isla about what had happened a few days prior, during the storm.

"I was out in the field, when the ground began to shift. I could feel it . . . pulsing, almost. Then snakes crawled from the dirt. Dozens of them. As if called by the winds. I've never seen anything like it."

Follow the snakes. That was what Eta had said.

Perhaps it had been Calla. Maybe she was trying to blame the storm for the nightbane loss. How else would she know about the serpents?

Isla's suspicions withered after a few hours, when she spoke to the rest of the Wildlings. A few had been with Calla the entire time. Several had seen the snakes. They were described as being half green, half black.

According to them, all Wildlings had been around the keep during the storm. The nightbane fields were across Nightshade. Without portaling, getting there would take several hours.

Unless they were all lying—unless they were all working against her—she couldn't put the blame on anyone yet.

For hours, she sought each of her people out. The result was twofold—getting to hear their grievances and experiences thus far on Nightshade while also considering if they might have destroyed the nightbane.

Most seemed happy here. It should have pleased her, but, as time went on, it unnerved her. The prophet-follower had been clear. There *was* an enemy among her people.

Was her judgment so faulty, that she couldn't spot them? Were they truly that good at hiding from her?

She had been betrayed, time and again, by people she had trusted. Perhaps *she* was the problem. Perhaps she should trust no one.

Everyone was a suspect. Everyone could be lying to her.

Again, she briefly considered going to the blacksmith and having him take off her bracelets. She could use Oro's flair to see who was telling the truth . . .

No. It wasn't worth the risk or useful, unless she planned to ask each of her people point-blank if they were the ones that destroyed the nightbane. Perhaps it would come to that, but not yet. She didn't want her people to panic.

By the end of the day, she wasn't any closer to identifying the traitor. It was dusk when she found Wren in the castle stables. She was tending to a tree with strange branches that curved and moved wildly.

No, not branches. When Isla got closer, she realized they were snakes.

Snakes. Isla stilled, remembering Eta's words.

Wren simply smiled. She brushed the tree, and a serpent slid right down her knuckles, wrapping itself around her arm. It was light green, with shining black eyes. Its scales were hard and reflective, like armor. She recognized the faint patterns on its scales. It was poisonous.

Wren smoothed a finger down the snake on her arm. "I brought them here from the newland. Their venom cures sickness, when mixed with the right flowers." She glanced at Isla and smiled. "Don't be afraid. I trained them myself. They don't bite Wildlings."

Was Wren the traitor Eta warned about?

Isla shook the thought away. Besides these snakes not looking like the ones that had been spotted, Wren had never given her a reason not to trust her. If there was anyone close to her that she didn't trust, it was her guardians. They had lied to her time and time again.

They had been her first suspects, until she learned Terra and Poppy had taken charge of maintaining the fields of nightbane. They

had been healing Wildlings with it, and even Nightshades who came to them for help.

Why would they then kill the creation they had painstakingly worked on for months? It didn't make sense. Unless there was something she was missing. A bigger purpose.

Isla lived in Grim's castle. She needed to stay focused on finding the portal and changing her fate. Any chance at finding the traitor hinged on trusting someone who lived here, alongside her people. Someone who could keep an eye on things, in case there was another event like the nightbane.

The snakes seemed to watch her, wrapped around their branches, as she took a step forward. "I believe a Wildling destroyed the nightbane. Not the storm."

Wren frowned. "Why would any of us do that?" Her shock seemed genuine.

"I'm not sure yet. But if anything else happens . . . if you see anything suspicious . . . tell me," Isla said.

Wren nodded.

Isla slowly extended her arm toward the tree. A single snake slithered from the pack, down a branch toward her. She tensed, waiting for it to sink its fangs into her skin, but all it did was trail down her wrist. It coiled itself around and around like a bracelet.

"Take her for a while," Wren said.

She did.

By the time she returned to the castle, Wraith was in his stable. Her starstick was in her room, so Lynx followed her through the halls, eyes narrowed at the snake slithering up and down her arm. She thought about the traitor. She wondered if they were operating right in front of her nose.

That was when she felt it—Grim's power, radiating off him. It made the air feel thicker, heavier. She told Lynx to wait for her and

followed the power toward the throne room. The door was open just a sliver. Hushed voices sounded just beyond it.

She stood there, listening. At first, she heard just words. *Risk. Attack. Future.*

Was Grim having a meeting without her? She thought about Azul's warning, that nothing and no one, including her, would stop him from invading Lightlark.

Was he already doing it against her back, despite his promises not to?

She neared the opening, bowed her head, and listened.

A scraping voice. She vaguely recognized it as belonging to a bald officer who had sneered at her more than once.

"We are your council. If we cannot speak plainly, who can?"

There were some murmurs of approval. A few voices she couldn't make out.

Then, the officer's again: "There is a snake in our midst, ruler, and you are blind to it."

Grim's voice was as cold as the stone she was leaning against. With predatorial calm, he said, "A snake? *Speak plainly,* then. Tell me exactly what you mean."

There was a frustrated sound. "The temptress in your bed is a serpent waiting for the right moment to strike. She is a traitor. Can't you see—"

He was cut off by a gurgling choking sound, followed by the thud she knew as a person dropping to the floor.

Quiet.

Then, "Does anyone else have any doubts about my wife?"

Not one word.

She took a step back. Another. A small council had intervened to warn Grim about her. *A snake,* they called her. A traitor.

Isla couldn't even be mad.

Because, depending on how the prophecy was fulfilled, it could very much be true.

Grim didn't believe them. He trusted in *her*. It made her chest twist uncomfortably. They were right. She was working behind his back, lying to him about her true intentions. She had come here, knowing the prophecy, knowing there was a good chance she would kill him. As suspicion rose, her questions seemed more pressing than ever. How long did she have to make the decision? How long did she have to live?

According to the prophet-follower, there was only one way to find out.

THE AUGUR

If the augur wanted blood, she would gladly give it to him.

Lynx glowered at her as she crept past him to the wardrobe in the middle of the night.

Clad in her dagger-filled pants; boots; a long-sleeved, thick fabric wrapped around her hands and forearms; a hood over her head; and a scarf draped over the bottom of her face, she portaled away with her starstick.

It took a few tries to find a larger town, complete with a market, roads that twisted and converged in no decipherable pattern, and plenty of shadowy rooftops from which she could watch.

She could likely kill anyone, but she wouldn't harm innocents. No; if she was going to kill someone, they would deserve it.

Though the curses were gone and Nightshades could go out after dusk, it seemed centuries of habit weren't broken in mere months. Or perhaps they were worried about being caught in a storm. The streets were quiet. She leapt across rooftop after rooftop, listening. Studying.

It took a few hours before she discovered its underbelly—a shard of city that had thinner alleys, establishments with basement levels carved into the ground, and bars that didn't ever seem to close. This would be the spot. She watched, fascinated, for a few nights, discovering people's routines. A large, bowlegged man went to the same brothel every other night, like clockwork. Just beforehand, he would visit the bar next door for courage. Every morning, just before dawn, he emptied the contents of this stomach in the streets before wobbling home.

Another man—slender and tall with spikes on the back of his boots—lingered by the door of the brothel for hours without ever stepping foot inside. At first, Isla figured he was shy, but when a woman stormed out to demand he leave, she learned he had been banned.

The man didn't leave after that night. He just got better at lurking in the shadows. Isla had her sights on him, but—though making the women of the brothel uncomfortable was certainly deplorable—he hadn't yet done anything worth his life. He would, though. She was sure of it. She just needed to wait.

It happened two days later. Isla was sprawled across a rooftop that had a view all the way to the harbor, when a scream split through the night.

The sound made her think of the hundreds of innocents—of the ruin she'd inflicted. How they must have screamed, hoping someone would save them. How *she* had been responsible . . .

She was on her feet in moments, leaping across rooftops, bolting toward the sound. It was coming from an alley that ended in a point: three buildings that had sagged together over time, fighting each other for foundation.

There was the slender man—choking a woman who looked no older than she was.

She landed behind him in a crouch. She took her thinnest knife from its place against her thigh and slid it right into his back.

The man cursed and dropped the woman immediately. She fell to the floor, gasping, clutching her throat with shaking fingers. The man made to turn around—presumably to hit her—but his efforts simply pushed him more firmly onto her blade.

Isla had never stabbed someone through the ribs . . . *through their back*. There wasn't anything honorable in it. But, then again, a man choking a woman in an alleyway didn't deserve an honorable death.

He whirled and grabbed her other wrist, perhaps meaning to break it, but the snake she wore there as a bracelet over her metal ones struck out, piercing his vein with its jaws. Without power, she needed to take precautions.

Isla sighed. "Now *that's* going to be painful," she told him. "Right into the bloodstream." She shook her head ruefully. "Stabbing your heart would be merciful."

She drew her blade sharply from his back and kicked him to the ground, far from the woman he had nearly killed. He vomited as he flipped over. His face was turning a peculiar shade of blue. He began spasming. The poison was already working.

She hardly recognized her own voice. "I've grown tired of being merciful."

The woman flinched when Isla reached out to her.

"It's okay," Isla said, her voice gentler now. "I've been where you are." She met the woman's eyes, thinking back to all the times she had faced near certain death.

"Thank you." The woman accepted her hand, allowing Isla to help her to her feet and escort her back to the town's main street, leaving the man to choke on his own bile.

By the time she returned, he was dead. The alley was quiet. There was no one to witness how she carved his heart right out of his chest. It was bloody work, cutting through the ribcage; his organs were still warm.

The augur wanted a fresh heart? He was going to get it.

Just like Eta had said, the augur lived deep in the forest behind a thin waterfall, guarding the mouth of a cave like a door. It didn't take long to find it, on Lynx's back. Without so much as a word, she threw the sack with the heart in it through the curtain of water and waited.

Minutes later, her own sack was thrown back through—empty—nearly hitting her face. If the action wasn't already clear, the voice from behind the curtain certainly was. It said—

"More."

Greedy creature.

Isla returned three times—with three different wicked hearts—and was told the same thing.

More.

How much blood could one being need? What was it even being used for?

There hadn't been another storm in days, but she could feel the energy in the air, as if the sky was holding its breath. It had slowly shifted into an ominous, darker blue. Grim was busy preparing the tunnels and developing a system of bells that would warn each town of an incoming tempest as soon as the stormfinch began singing.

Now that they knew there was a portal, he had searched for it himself, on Wraith's back, unsuccessfully. She knew, because he gave her updates in his scrawled writing on letters he left outside her door, along with flowers, every morning.

She had let them pile up. She didn't roam the halls anymore, in fear of running into him.

He had defended her. He had *believed* in her. She told herself she avoided him because he was a distraction from her work to get answers from the augur, but the truth was, she couldn't face him.

At night, she portaled to the different villages, much to Lynx's irritation. She heard things, from the rooftops. Whispers. Loud jeers. It wasn't long before she heard about *herself.*

The snake queen, they called her. *The Wildling snake.* Just like the council that had tried to warn Grim.

A traitor in our midst. A lover of the king of Lightlark, come here to spy. To destroy. The words filled her with rage—and also with hurt, because what if they were right?

She didn't want to be a traitor. She didn't want to pretend. She didn't want to be all the things they thought she was.

The next time she showed up at the augur's door, she speared her sword into the soft dirt just in front of the waterfall. He wanted more?

Eight dripping hearts were skewered on her blade. It had taken days of searching for her victims, and only one night to end them all.

Her voice was a low growl. "If you want these, you'll have to come out and get them."

Silence. There were only her ragged breath and heartbeat and the waterfall beating against the pool to mark seconds in the night.

Then the curtain of water parted, and the augur stepped through.

Isla stilled. The augur had smooth skin, as pale as the curve of the moon, covered in dark markings as thin and delicate as the weaves of a spiderweb. They glimmered mysteriously, like the ink had been melted straight from a starless night. His eyes were dark crimson voids. He didn't have a nose—just a hole where it should be, a skull clear of its cartilage. He was tall and wore the same robes as the prophet-followers, without the hood.

"What do you do with the blood?" It wasn't her most important question, but the words spilled out of her as she watched him pluck her sword from the ground. He eyed the hearts appraisingly. Hungrily.

"I'll show you." He motioned with his chin toward the waterfall.

She had worked days to get to this point, but now she looked at the entrance to the cave and wondered if she was making a grave mistake—if Eta had tricked her. She had no powers; only daggers and her snake. She had never encountered a being with bloodred eyes before.

As if sensing her hesitance, the augur said, "You're scared. Good. You should be afraid, Isla Snake-queen. You should be terrified of everything that makes up this wretched land."

He stepped over the pool separating her from the cave and passed through the waterfall.

She followed him.

Water hit her for a moment, soaking the crown of her head, and then—darkness. The cave was carved from smooth black rock. She walked blindly forward, following the white flash of the augur's robes and the high-pitched scrape of her heart-laced sword he dragged behind him.

Soon, there was a light, the faint twinkling of sparkling rocks embedded in the ceiling like a cluster of stars. Beneath it sat a shimmering pool.

A pool of blood.

Isla stopped short. Her hand crept toward her throat. One pull of her necklace and Grim would be there; she knew that. But then he would know she had sought the augur. He might start to listen to those rumors about his traitorous bride.

The augur looked amused. "I do not fear the ruler," he said, as if knowing the significance of the necklace. "He should fear me, as I know the properties of blood. Blood tells such secrets, doesn't it?"

His gaze never leaving hers, he slowly removed the first heart from her blade, held it in his hand above the pool—and squeezed.

There was a ring on his thumb adorned with a blade curved like a talon on its underside, and he used it to cut through the tissue. He pressed harder. *Harder.*

She watched him drain the heart of every drop of blood, the red liquid sputtering from between his fingers until he threw the spent organ behind him, to a corner of the cave. Creatures chittered there, fighting over the pieces. She swallowed the bile building in her throat.

The augur looked over at her as he did the same thing to the second heart. Then the third. He looked amused.

"Your people have done far worse to hearts," he said, his fist tightening for the fourth time.

"They did it because of a curse," she responded, forcing herself to watch. "They did not relish it." She wouldn't shy from her actions anymore. If this was the price required for the information she needed, so be it. "You still haven't answered my question."

"Right. What I do with the blood." He threw the last of the hearts to the corner, where a mound of insects with a tangle of legs had gathered.

He handed back her bloody sword. She took its hilt with tentative fingers. Then he made his way toward what looked like stone steps leading into the pool. At the top of the first one, he turned toward her. Extended his hand.

The augur raised a brow when she didn't immediately take it. "You want answers . . . yes?"

Yes.

But she needed to know he could give her the answer she needed. "Can you tell me how long I have to live?"

He nodded.

She swallowed down her disgust and bent to release the snake onto the rock. It slithered and curled, head raised, as if pleading with Isla to reconsider. Still, she stepped forward. Took the augur's hand. It was spindly; his bones protruded through his skin. His grasp was cold as the cave itself. Together, they walked down the steps.

Blood. She had seen it before, had felt it on her skin, but not like this. It was thicker than water, noticeably so, and rippled only slightly as she moved through it. First, it was at her knees, then her hips, and then her ribs, and she fought the urge to retch. The scent of metal prickled her nose; there was something else in the air.

"You feel it, don't you?" The augur said, watching her far too closely. "Power . . . it's in the blood, you see."

Blood is power. The past whispered the words, and the memory of her and Oro sank its teeth into her before she could shake it away.

She ripped her hand from the augur's in the middle of the pool. "How does this help me get answers?"

Quick as a serpent, he struck. Metal glinted in front of her, then disappeared. Her cheek burned in pain. He had cut it with the talon on his thumb. She gasped, nearly tripping back in the pool. Her hand rose to her face, her fingers slick against a small trail of blood.

The augur brought the talon to his lips and slowly licked the blood off it. His eyes seemed to grow even redder as he said, "Interesting." He began to laugh. "You are the greatest thing that has ever stepped foot into my cave, Isla Thorn-tide."

Then she was dragged down through the blood.

An invisible grip clutched her ankle, forcing her to the bottom of the pool. She kicked, but her foot didn't hit anything solid. Her mouth opened with a silent scream, filling with blood.

I shouldn't have come. She reached toward her necklace—but before she could touch the stone, spectral ties seized both of her wrists too.

She was drowning not just in blood but also in power. It was everywhere, flaying her skin, calling to something deep inside her chest, an incessant knock on a locked door.

Flashes of something, obscuring her vision, intruding on her mind. Memories. But they weren't hers. Voices filled her head, *so many voices*. There were laughs and sighs, but then there was *screaming*. Everyone was *screaming*, all she felt was pain, and anguish and—

One moment she was fighting for her life at the bottom of the pool of blood. The next, she was gasping for air, her fingers clawing at her throat. The snake crawled across her chest, as if trying to wake her. She opened her eyes to find herself on the smooth stone beside the

pool. Blood muddled her vision. It filled her ears, cloaked her lips. She turned to the side and retched once. Twice.

When she looked up, blinking away the blood, she saw the augur pacing just a few feet away.

A moment later, she was on her feet. Her blade pressed against the tattooed skin of his neck. "You tried to kill me."

He looked amused. "I would love to kill you. But, sadly, I cannot."

"Why?"

"I know what was written, and I am but a servant of the book. Your fate is on one of the very last pages. I'm curious to see where your future goes from there." He smiled, revealing teeth that had been shaved into spikes. They were still tipped in her blood. "You felt it, didn't you? The power of your blood, calling to the rest? The strength of it all?"

He spoke of it with such relish, it nearly made her sick. His robe, previously white, was now stained crimson.

"Your blood spoke to me in many tongues. You wear your fate like a crown of blades. Doesn't it hurt?"

Her snake hissed, slithering farther up her forearm. Isla frowned. Part of her screamed to slit the auger's throat, to be done with it. All he was doing was speaking riddles and nonsense. "What?"

"Your blood . . . all that power, stirring beneath your skin. Doesn't it *burn*?"

It had. But not anymore. "My bracelets keep it contained."

At that, he laughed. It pealed through the cave. He shook his head, skin slicing slightly against her dagger. He didn't seem to care. "You can defang a snake, but the poison remains."

Perhaps he was right. Perhaps she was lying to herself if she thought the bracelets changed who she was. What she had done. Or her fate.

Enough. She had come for answers and, so far, had gotten nothing. "How long do I have?" she demanded, digging the blade, made

sticky with blood, into the top layer of his pale flesh. More blood joined it.

He sighed. "Yes, your lifespan. You died. Life was given to you, leeched from another."

She nodded. She knew that. "And?"

The augur frowned. "In your current state . . . you won't last past the storm season."

She stumbled back. Her hand trembled as she sheathed her dagger. Grim said it would likely last the entire winter. They were already weeks into it. "You're certain?"

He nodded.

Thousands dead. All because of her.

No. "I need more time. How do I get it?"

A slow smile formed across the augur's face. It stretched his pale skin too taut. His pointed teeth glimmered. "You asked several times what I do with all the blood. It helps me with readings. Amplifies my power . . . but also gives me time." He motioned toward himself. "You can see the price paid. Every method to extend life has one."

She glanced at the pool of blood. Shuddered. "What are the other methods?"

He pointed toward the markings on his head and neck. "Skyres. The ancient markings." She hadn't ever heard of skyres, though she had seen something like the augur's markings once before on someone. But that person was dead.

"Teach me."

He shook his head. "I cannot. I do not know myself. The prophet made these skyres, you see . . . he did so in secret. He never allowed anyone to witness the art."

She studied them carefully. They looked complicated.

The augur sighed. "Find the portal, Isla Stormheart. It has power. Take it. *Use it to live.* Its fate is tied to yours. Find the portal . . . find your fate."

"Do you know where it is?" She didn't want to wait for another storm to find it.

He shook his marking-covered head. "No. The prophet knew its location. He wrote it in pages bound by his blood . . . but they've been lost." She remembered the torn-out parchment from the book. "Centuries before the curses, a follower of the prophet's word stole them and set off toward Lightlark."

Lightlark? The mention of the island made her pause with both curiosity and longing. It was an effort to shift back to the reason she was here.

"Do you know how to close the portal when I find it?"

He shook his head again. "Only the pages know." That wasn't useful, if they were as good as lost.

She needed to wait for the next storm, trap it in the ring, and follow it to the portal. If the augur was to be believed, its power could give her life, *time*. She would take it, then find a way to close it.

The augur licked his thin lips with relish. His tongue dragged along his pointed teeth. "Such blood . . . Use it wisely, Isla Cursecure. Your parents gave you such gifts." *Her parents.* He eyed her bracelets. "Such blood . . . such blood, wasted."

"How can I make sure it isn't wasted?" she asked. Her life . . . she wanted it to be worth something. She wanted to have done more good than bad.

"*Use* it." The augur smiled. His sharpened teeth glimmered in the limited light. "Learn the truth of who you are . . . and your path will become clear."

He motioned toward the wall. There, carved into the rock, she saw a drawing. It was a woman with snakes wrapped around and around her arms, her neck, her chest. She looked—

She looked like *her*.

"What is that?" Isla breathed, reaching out to trace the lines in the stone that looked ancient. Weathered.

"The future," he said, reverently.

"Is it—is it supposed to be me?" The woman looked fearsome. Wicked.

The augur looked at her curiously, crimson eyes swirling. "Do you want it to be?"

She backed out of the cave, throat tightening.

"Not to worry. You will be back, Isla Heartblade," he said, his voice echoing through the cave as she tore out of it. "It has been written."

SNAKE

She and all of Nightshade wouldn't survive the storm season, unless she could find the portal. Unless she could extend her life long enough to change her fate.

Part of her felt rage. Her life had barely been her own. Since she was a child, she had trained for the Centennial. Then, she found herself the ruler of two realms. Now, she was practically a walking corpse, her life tied to another, on borrowed time.

Freedom was what she had craved since she was a little girl, but fate was the ultimate restraint. It was the glass in her room, caging her; it was the bracelets, keeping the worst of her at bay.

The stormfinch sat watching her from inside its cage. She watched it back, willing it to sing. Willing a storm to break, so she could find the portal. Its beak remained closed.

It always stood in the same place. No matter how many days she left the door open, the bird never tried to fly out.

"You're smarter than I am," she said. For years, all she had wanted was to leave her room in the Wildling realm. She dreamed of adventure, of freedom.

Look where that had gotten her.

She was lonelier than ever, out of necessity. It wasn't like Grim hadn't tried to seek her out. Along with her favorite flowers, her favorite foods had been brought by attendants. He knew them all, and she didn't think too hard about that fact.

The plates were all empty now, and she craved a bit of comfort. Something warm and sweet that would make her forget, for just a few moments, that there were only a couple of months left of winter.

It was long past midnight. She left her room, stepping carefully over the built-up pile of flowers, intending to find the kitchens. The halls were empty.

She walked through them, taking the long way to avoid the room Grim had been staying in, since he had given her his quarters. Part of her wanted to go there, to seek comfort in *him,* but no . . . her heart was too confused already. What she longed for was a friend.

What she longed for was a home.

There was an emptiness in her that had always existed. A place where perhaps a mother or father or friend would have gone. Celeste had filled it for a time, but she hadn't been real.

So much hadn't been real.

She remembered the carving on the augur's wall. Her, looking the part of the vengeful snake-queen the people here believed her to be. She could almost see the serpents now, slithering around her arms. Hissing. She could almost feel them, cold scales slipping against her skin, even though she had returned the serpent she often wore to Wren an hour ago. It felt almost familiar. Almost *right.*

She turned the corner and hit something solid. Before she knew it, she was pressed against a cold wall. Her hand reached toward her blade on instinct but was pinned by her side before her fingers could curl around the hilt.

Grim rippled into visibility before her. His grip on her wrist was loose. She could easily escape it, but she didn't. She remained very still, even as his thumb gently brushed across her pulse. It was getting faster. He could feel it. He tilted his head, looking down at her with a preternatural focus.

She was grateful she had scrubbed the blood from her skin, from her hair, from her clothes; but under his unrelenting gaze, she wondered if he knew where she had been. If he knew that while it

seemed she worked for his realm's benefit, she was also making plans without him.

She lifted her chin. "Following me?"

A slow smile spread across his face. "Always."

He leaned down, and she didn't move a muscle, even as his lips inched closer. Closer. She swore her traitorous pulse must be hammering beneath his thumb, because his mouth curled in wicked amusement. Part of her wanted him to bridge the gap between them. Part of her wanted any comfort he could offer her, especially now, especially with everything falling apart. Instead, his lips swept past hers, dragging across her cheek all the way to her ear to say, his voice like a finger down her spine, "You've been avoiding me."

She swallowed. He traced the movement of her throat with his gaze. "I've been trying to get information. About . . . about the portal." It wasn't completely a lie. She kept her emotions steady.

His lips were still inches from her ear. He leaned in, as if he could smell her feelings, as if he could taste them. Lower. His mouth pressed ever so gently against her pulse. She didn't think she was breathing.

Then, he abruptly pulled back. Stared down at her, with eyes filled with something like fury. Something like worry.

"What happened?"

Of course he could sense her sadness.

She said nothing. She wondered what he would read into that—if it would make him suspicious of her comings and goings—but, if anything, he only looked more concerned.

He couldn't have known she had been looking for the kitchens, but that was where he brought her, before she could blink.

Without saying a word, he began preparing something, moving around the room in a familiar, practiced way.

The words stumbled out of her. "You cook?"

He pretended to look offended by her surprise. "Is that really so hard to believe?"

“Yes,” she said, leaning against a counter. The dark stone was cold against her spine.

His gaze slipped down her body for just a moment, and she became aware that she had left her room in one of the nighttime outfits from her wardrobe, two small pieces of silk that left swaths of skin uncovered. His eyes darkened.

Then, he turned back to what he was doing. She watched as his hands worked quickly. Diligently. He was chopping something up and putting it in a pot. She couldn’t see exactly what it was. What she could see were his broad shoulders. His muscled back.

He faced her again, and she quickly shifted her gaze. “I learned during training. I often found myself alone. If I wanted to eat . . . I needed to cook.”

She knew little about his upbringing, other than a few mentions of it in the past. She knew he had undergone extreme training to be a warrior. It was difficult to imagine him without the comforts of his castle.

Now, though, as she watched him stir something in a pot, she could picture it. Grim, hair curled around his ears the way it was now, messy from a clear lack of sleep. His wide shoulders draped not in a ruler’s cape but in a black fabric that didn’t look soft at all, not soft enough to sleep in. She wondered if he had any comfortable clothes. All she remembered was him in his training clothes, or armor, or formal attire, or out of it.

The thought made her cheeks burn. She heard a scrape of movement—Grim, finding a mug. Pouring something into it.

That was when she smelled it.

She met his eyes. She must have looked far too excited, because he smiled again, like he treasured her excitement, like he would do anything to make her make that exact expression again.

He carried it over to her; and in her happiness, in her anticipation, she slipped her fingers over his around the mug. Together, they held it. Together, they brought it to her lips.

She groaned, tasting the chocolate. It was velvety, rich. Hot compared to the cold of the stone still against her back. Her eyes fell closed, savoring it.

When she opened them again, she found him studying her. He looked transfixed. Before she could make another move, he gently took the mug from her hands, set it on the counter beside her hip, and brought a thumb to her lips, which she imagined were covered in chocolate. He brushed against them, and she shivered.

She didn't know what came over her—perhaps the reminder that her life was fleeting—but when he moved to drop his hand, her own came down over it.

Grim went still. His eyes bore into hers, waiting. Waiting for her to tear away from him the way she had so many times before. She didn't; and slowly, so slowly, his calloused fingers curled around her jaw. Threaded through her hair. Her fingers molded over his.

They just stared at each other, until his gaze dropped to her lips. The corner of his mouth lifted. "Missed some chocolate." His voice sounded strained.

Her own was breathless. "Then get it."

He made to move his thumb again, but she kept her hand firmly over his. He frowned. Then, his eyes seemed to go wholly black as he understood her meaning.

With a gentleness that had her heart racing, he slowly, so slowly, dipped his head.

He was the ruler of darkness. He was a brutal warrior who had killed a member of his court in cold blood simply for speaking ill of her. Now, he was almost trembling as his lips hovered inches from hers.

Slowly, reverently, his tongue traced her mouth, licking away the chocolate, and she was burning, she was aching. She wasn't sure she was breathing when he took her entire bottom lip into his mouth—and slowly dragged it through his teeth, tasting her completely.

That was it. In this moment, she didn't care what had happened or about the prophecy; she wanted him. She wanted him so badly, her skin felt raw, needy, ready. Her lips were swollen as he stared down at her, his chest heaving just as much as hers.

She wanted him to lift her onto the counter behind them by the backs of her thighs. Wanted him to settle between her legs, drag his tongue over the rest of her heated skin, taste her everywhere.

He could feel that want. Feel that aching need. She could feel his own, against her stomach. It nearly made her ask for everything she wanted.

Instead, she said, "Thank you for the chocolate."

And went back to bed alone.

The scrape of a boot against the floor awoke her.

Before she could move a muscle, every single one in her body tensed as if turned to stone.

A hand was curled around her wrist.

A gravelly voice said, "The whispers are true. You don't sleep with the ruler."

Tynan. She fought against his iron grasp on her bones, but she couldn't even summon a groan in response.

"No, no . . . you can't move at all, can you?" She heard him tap his foot. Her eyes were wide and glued to the ceiling. Tears streamed down her face after just seconds of not being able to close them. "The ruler seems to believe you are special in some way." He spat at her. "But you are just a distraction. An enemy."

She knew the sound of a sword scraping its scabbard. He forced her head back with his power, controlling her every muscle, stretching the skin of her neck taut. Her body trembled with the strain of trying to overpower him.

"The ruler has gone weak. *You*, Snake, have made him so. With you gone, we're going to invade Lightlark. We're going to finish what

we started." He leaned down until his putrid breath was right against her mouth. "You don't even know how priceless this necklace is, do you? Only in death is it released . . . so I'll just have to kill you."

No. He didn't know her and Grim's lives were tied together. He didn't know killing her would secure his own demise.

Tynan gripped her wrist so tightly it was a wonder the bone didn't break. She would have cried out if she could.

The sword came into her view as he lifted it high over his head. She watched the flickering of her hearth's flames reflect upon it.

A low growl sounded in front of her.

Tynan might have been right about Grim not sleeping in her chambers . . . but whoever had told him that information clearly didn't know about the leopard that did. The one who was barely visible when he slept in the corner of her room, sinking into the shadows.

A roar, and then her wrist was released. Her limbs were freed of the invisible vise.

She doubled over and gasped for air. Sweat streamed down her back and the middle of her chest.

Tynan was thrashing on the floor, holding a hand against the gash Lynx had made in his neck.

Lynx's teeth gleamed with his blood as he awaited her instruction.

Grim landed in the room with a crack. His wide eyes went straight to her, quickly assessing her state, then to the bleeding man on the floor.

His hands were shaking. His voice was not the predatory calm she had come to expect.

No, his words were laced in pure fury as he bent down, grabbed Tynan by his bloody neck, and said, "My wife? You dare threaten *my wife*?"

Tynan made what must have been a gurgled plea that didn't translate into words.

Grim bared his teeth at him, his mouth turning into a twisted smile. "You have no idea how much I'm going to enjoy killing you."

Shadows spilled across the floor, poisonous and ruinous, nothing in the world could stop them—except for the hand Isla placed on Grim's shoulder.

At her touch, he stilled immediately. He looked up at her.

"Let me," she said, in a voice she didn't completely recognize. His shadows instantly retreated. Tynan's eyes wildly searched the room, as if looking for a final chance at escape. But there would be no escape. He was injured, unable to wield his ability. She wasn't frozen in her bedsheets any longer.

She took the dagger at her thigh and plunged it through his heart. Blood spurted through his ribs, down her hand, but she only twisted the blade deeper. Deeper, until the tip dug into the floor.

Something within her seemed to sing.

As she watched the life leech from his eyes, Isla realized with horror and fascination that taking it felt good.

Tynan wouldn't have been the only one in the Nightshade court who wanted her gone. She needed to send a message.

Grim's people didn't need another reason to hate her. But she would gladly give it to them.

Air was stolen in sharp gasps throughout the room as Isla strutted through it. They had all gathered before Grim, who watched her from his throne. His posture might have been casual, but there was nothing mild about the lingering fury in his expression.

Snake queen? She would be the villain they already believed her to be.

Her black dress had thin straps and a plunging neckline. The fabric clung to her skin like a sheet of water, its loosely curled ribbons streaming gently onto the floor. Thin, poisonous snakes curled around her waist, sliding up and across her chest, keeping her decent, slithering.

Two more wrapped around each of her arms. They hissed at the closest nobles as she passed them by, making one stumble onto the floor. The thinnest snake of all curled around her neck like another necklace.

Their looks of horror weren't about the snakes, however—though each was poisonous. No; they stared at what she gripped loosely in her hand, emitting a line of dripping blood next to her.

Tynan's head, held by the hair.

She reached Grim's throne and threw it at his feet.

"Eat," she said, and the snakes slithered down her body and raced to the floor, sending the closest people screaming. Their poison worked instantly, melting flesh from bone. The creatures devoured his eyes and tongue in front of the crowd. They swallowed the remaining flesh, and his eyes, all in front of the crowd. Wren had trained them well.

Someone loudly vomited. Another fainted.

Grim forced them to watch. Isla stayed until Tynan's head was no more than a skull.

"Well," she said, her voice echoing in the silence. "If anyone else wants me dead, you know where to find me." Then, she turned on her heel and left the throne room, her snakes not far behind.

"That was quite the display."

Isla stopped brushing Lynx's fur to find Astria standing behind her, posture straight as ever, donning those curved crossed swords on her chest.

"Thank you," Isla said. "I was sick afterward, but it's the show that counts, right?"

Astria made a huffing sound that almost resembled a laugh. Then she frowned. "Tynan had it coming. For someone ordered to wear gauntlets all the time, he found plenty of excuses to go without them." Isla felt a rush of joy at having been the one to end them. It didn't seem

like the first time he had ventured into a room at midnight and made a person a prisoner in their own skin.

Grim's general reached a hand toward Lynx, and Isla opened her mouth, ready to warn Astria that Lynx had developed a reputation for biting Nightshades.

But, to her surprise, her bonded allowed Astria to touch him. He only started to growl when she got too close to his ears.

"So," Isla said, looking the woman up and down, trying to find some similarity. "How long have you known?"

Astria's hands absentmindedly drummed her swords' hilts. "That you're my blood? Grim told me right before you were married." She frowned. "Right after I suggested you might be a spy and he should consider putting your head on a pike."

"Nice," Isla said, knowing how lucky Astria was to have escaped that conversation with her life. She began brushing Lynx's fur again. "And the fact that we're related changed your mind?"

"No," she said, considering her. "It isn't ever too late for Grim to take my advice."

Isla looked over her shoulder at her. "And it isn't too late for Grim to get a new general. I hear the position runs in the family."

Astria smiled. Then laughed a little.

Isla smiled too.

She bent down to clean between Lynx's pads. He made a peeved sound and tugged his foot back. She glared up at him. "Do you really want another rock incident?" she asked him. There had been a stone lodged in there for a week, and it had gotten infected. For as tough and ancient as Lynx was, he had been awfully dramatic during the days of resting his foot.

He begrudgingly lifted his leg, and Isla spotted a pine needle lodged right between two of his pads. She shook her head, and tried to pull it out, but it was stuck. Lynx growled.

"Here," Astria said, bending down low. She pulled it out quickly, and the leopard roared. Then he glared at Astria, who took a few steps back. She watched Isla work until she was done, and then said, "I looked for him, you know."

Him. By the intensity of her tone, Isla knew exactly who she was talking about. Isla slowly rose to face her cousin.

She remembered what the augur had said: *When you learn the truth of who you are . . . your path will become clear.*

She was desperate for any detail about her parents. She wanted to know them, even through the eyes of others.

"I searched the newlands with the ruler, just in case there was a chance he was alive. Then . . . when too much time had passed . . . I grieved him." Her nostrils flared. "He was like a brother to me, and I don't understand his choice. I don't know why he chose *her.*"

Her mother.

Lynx growled low.

"He wasn't . . . an *emotional* person," she continued, eyes studying her bonded. "I can count on a hand the number of times I ever even saw him smile. He wasn't cruel, no . . . but serious. About his duty. About serving his realm." She frowned. "Now that I know he didn't die, that he *left* . . . I can't respect his decision. I can't respect what he did."

Isla understood. Even though she was talking about her father, and not in the greatest light, Isla appreciated that Astria was even talking to her at all, let alone telling her something so personal.

Isla knew what it was like to choose her heart over duty. If that was what her father had done, she couldn't judge him. But things were more complicated than that.

Her father and Grim had searched for the sword that controlled the dreks together. Her father had found it.

"He stole the sword, to keep it away from Grim. He must have believed Nightshade was better off without it."

He must have believed Grim would use it to overtake Lightlark. He must have been trying to save the island, the same way she was now.

Astria shook her head. "Even if that's true, that wasn't his call to make. We serve our rulers. Their word is law. We are their sword. He knew that."

Isla didn't know what to think. She just wished that she had known her parents. How different her life would have been, if they had survived . . .

It made her think about what Terra and Poppy had said. If they really didn't kill her parents—which she wasn't quick to believe—then who did?

It also made her think about the Wildling traitor. They hadn't struck again, to her knowledge, but dissent was dangerous. What was their end goal? What did they want?

"You have his frown," Astria said, knocking her out of her thoughts.

"Excuse me?"

"It's exactly the same. Almost uncanny. Everything else, I suppose you got from . . . her." Astria studied her closely, as if trying to imagine what her mother would have looked like.

Part of her wanted to forget their connection at all. Why develop a relationship with someone now, when they all didn't have much time left? Another part, the little girl who had sat in her room and dreamt of having a place to belong, refused to let this opportunity slip by. "I don't have any other family," Isla admitted, and immediately felt exposed, like she had shown far too much of herself.

Astria studied her. She raised her head. "I don't either."

Isla didn't know why that was a comfort, when she should have been sad that they had both lost everyone related to them. "I suppose we have each other," Isla offered.

Astria's suspicious gaze did not falter in the slightest. But, after awkward moments passed, she said, "Yes, well. I suppose having you is better than having nothing."

Isla's smile spread across her face. "And here, I was thinking you incapable of giving me a compliment."

Another day passed without a storm. She was restless, impatient, knowing it was what she needed to find the portal. With her starstick, she brought Lynx to the Wildling newland, if only to feel a whisper of home. They tore through the familiar woods, his legs stretching happily as he leapt into trees. He had missed it, she realized. Both of them had.

Part of her wished she could feel the forest, its heartbeat, but the bracelets made everything quiet. Dead.

By the time they approached her old room, it was dark out. She left Lynx outside and portaled her way in, with the goal of retrieving some of her old knives. The ones Grim had provided were nicer than any she had ever had, but she missed their familiar feel in her fingers. Their simplicity.

She walked toward her vanity and began opening drawers. There were a few simple blades inside that she hadn't used in years. She grabbed one of them, a simple dagger, without any markings.

And dropped it.

Its tip nearly went through her foot. She didn't even look to see where it had landed.

Her eyes were caught on the piece of parchment before her, and the white feather atop it. It had been weeks since she had written her name on the page.

Now, there was a new line below it.

Hello Isla, it read.

The words themselves weren't what made her stomach drop—it was the handwriting, which she knew almost as well as her own.

Aurora's.

FEATHER

She had seen Aurora's writing hundreds of times before. She still had scraps of it, from when they used to share books and write notes to each other in the margins, back when Aurora was disguised as Celeste.

She rushed to her secret hiding spot, and there it was, one of the last volumes they had ever read together. She flipped through the pages, looking for the curls of ink and finding them. Her spine turned to ice. It was undeniable as she compared the letters.

Her hand trembled as she took the feather, half expecting it to twist out of her grip. She wrote beneath it.

How is this possible?

She dropped the feather and waited. Silence. She could hear her own heart beating as the seconds ticked by. Just when she was about to begin wondering if she was losing her mind, the feather stood upright by itself. She watched it slide across the paper and carefully write a sentence that made her blood run cold.

All that is buried eventually rises.

The feather dropped dead on her parchment.

Isla nearly tripped as she stumbled backward. This was impossible. She had killed Aurora. She had plunged her dagger into her heart, had watched her fall into a chasm.

It had to be a trick. A faulty enchantment.

Only one person would know for certain.

***

"Have you ever created something that allows one to speak from the dead?"

The blacksmith was busy hammering away at some creation. He had been working with the same material since the last time she saw him, the *shademade* metal. It glimmered beneath the flames of the forge. He carefully put his tools down.

Instead of answering her question, the blacksmith only outstretched his hand. He grumbled with impatience. "I'm assuming you've brought the object. Best to just let me see it." She hesitated, wondering if she could trust him not to share this discovery with Grim.

But no. The blacksmith only cared about his death, and she was the only one who could give it to him.

She produced the feather from her pocket and placed it in his awaiting palm. He held it with remarkable care, eye gleaming as he studied it. "It writes words from the dead? You're sure?"

"One dead."

"On its own?"

She nodded. "I watched it write a sentence as if a specter's hand held it."

The blacksmith hummed. "Interesting." He squinted and studied its every inch, seeming to find traits she couldn't see. "I smell your blood on it," he said. "Your power woke it."

She frowned. "Even with the bracelets on?"

He glanced at her. "Your blood is power, Isla. The bracelets don't change that." She thought about the augur tasting it and shuddered. He turned his attention back to the feather. "Not my creation, but I recognize its charms. A shred of a soul has been stored within it."

A shred of a soul. So, it wasn't Aurora's words from the dead . . . but a small piece of her she had left behind.

He tilted the feather at her. "Look at its tip."

She squinted. There, she noticed a tiny layer of metal. It glimmered like a thousand diamonds trapped inside.

Shademade.

"This is very old enchantment. It predates this land itself."

"What does that mean?"

"It is not of this world."

Not of this world.

Isla frowned. "You—you don't mean . . ."

"It's from the otherworld."

How did the blacksmith even know about the otherworld? Isla was under the impression very few people did. "How do you know?"

"Because that's where I'm from too."

Isla blinked. She had only ever met one other person who seemed to be from the otherworld, the ancient being that had taught her to wield her Nightshade abilities. Remlar. "That—that would mean you're—"

Thousands of years old.

He just looked at her.

"Tell me about it. What is it like?" The words slipped out of her mouth before she could stop herself.

He lifted a shoulder. "Even if I wanted to, I can't. The more time spent here, the more the otherworld is forgotten. It was by design, you see. To keep us from wanting to return. I don't even remember its name."

How did Aurora get her hands on an object from the otherworld in the first place? "Are objects from the otherworld common here?"

"No. Most were destroyed over the millennia, or stripped of their enchantment by me, following orders." He took the blade from his belt, then positioned it beneath an orb of light. She watched as the metal glimmered, as if a thousand stars were trapped within it. "Here. This is how you can always tell what is shademade. What is otherworldly."

She took the feather back. She knew she should have put it back in the drawer. Forgotten about it. Burn it, maybe.

She didn't.

Isla stared at the writing for days. She kept the scrap of it in her pocket, alongside the golden rose necklace.

Hello Isla.

Words, from her former best friend. The one she had killed.

Part of her wanted to reply, and longed to speak to her friend the way she had for years, confiding in her every time she had felt alone.

"Celeste doesn't exist," she told herself, as she rode across Nightshade on Lynx's back. "You need to remember that."

Lynx made a sound beneath her, as if he could sense her inner turmoil. She stroked the top of his head. In flashes, she was seeing his perspective, the land rippling before him. Then, there were pieces of something else. His own lost friend.

Her mother.

She saw her in his memories. Laughing, in a forest. Turning around in a circle, making flowers bloom in a torrent around her. As Lynx tore across the island beneath her, she watched, and she couldn't get enough.

Isla saw her own room. It looked slightly different than it did now. There were no swords against the wall. There was no paint across the glass of the greenhouse. No, her mother hadn't had a reason to hide. She had been born powerful. From what she could see, she was a skilled wielder.

Did she have a flair? She watched, waiting to see something out of the ordinary, but all she saw was nature.

Then, she caught a glimpse of her father. Dark hair. Pale skin. She watched him look at Lynx, but from his view, it was almost like he was looking at *her*. She felt a tear slide down her cheek.

He showed her something else. A flash of golden hair. Amber eyes.

Her grip on his furs tightened.

Lynx had always liked Oro. She had worked to bury any memory of him down; but just as Aurora had written, *all that is buried eventually rises*.

Isla should have moved her hand—should have told Lynx to stop—but she didn't. She watched greedily, remembering Oro's smile, the way it made tiny crinkles form next to his eyes. The way those eyes would glimmer when he was happy, like sun sparkling atop water.

She watched their first kiss, when he had pinned her against the tree. She heard Lynx's low growl, stopping them as Oro's hands ran up her sides. She heard them both laugh. For a single moment she felt that happiness, as if she was there. As if she had been portaled into the past.

The images stopped as quickly as they had started.

They had reached the stables, and Lynx made a huff of annoyance.

Wraith. He was outside his stable with Grim, who looked to be at the end of washing his scales.

Face still flushed from the memories, she cleared her throat. Worked to bury her feelings again. "I'm surprised you don't give someone else the pleasure of bathing a full-grown dragon."

Grim sighed as he put the giant sponge he had been using back in a bucket. Wraith was covered in soap and bubbles. Isla didn't think the tubs of water used for the other animals would be even remotely helpful.

"He only allows me to do it. Temperamental creature," he muttered. Wraith only grinned down at Isla and Lynx.

Isla watched her bonded consider the dragon, unimpressed. He didn't care for him, not really. She smoothed the space between his ears with her hand, sending images to him. Wraith as the tiny bundle

of scales she had discovered limping near the cave. Wraith in her arms, his wings tucked tightly against his body.

Lynx's muscles relaxed a bit beneath her. Isla slid off his back and watched Lynx and Wraith regard each other for a few moments longer, Wraith far more excited. Then, Lynx turned away with a huff, in the direction of the dried meats the stableman had begun offering him, to try to curry his favor.

Isla watched as the soap on Wraith began to fizzle. "How do you plan on washing him off?"

Grim glanced over at her. "Care to see for yourself?"

No. She still had nightmares about slipping off his back in the storm. Nearly hitting the ground. But Wraith looked so heartbreakingly excited that she sighed and allowed Grim to portal them both onto his spine. It was slippery with all the soap, but Grim pinned her in place with his shadows, called Wraith's name, and they were off.

The flight was short, and the dragon began to tilt toward the ground as soon as the fields turned to forest. She knew what to expect by now and steadied herself for their landing. He curved, then plunged in the direction of a spring. Wind blew her hair back, roared in her ears, made her eyes water. Her muscles tightened as she braced herself.

Wraith's wings flared out before they crashed right through a pond.

Isla gasped, and her lungs would have filled with water, if Grim's translucent shadows weren't still enveloping her. Only when he met her eyes, when he was sure she wasn't still in shock, did he let them drop, and she was encased in water.

Wraith fell slowly, like a rock sinking down to the bottom. He rested there for just a moment, before kicking off, and surfacing.

Isla desperately sucked in air as they crashed through, water sputtering, and she turned to Grim, glare already in place.

His dark hair was stuck to his forehead. He didn't seem to mind that he was soaked through, his cape a wet shadow across his shoulders.

Isla shoved him off Wraith's back and had the pleasure of watching him crash into the water. Wraith turned his head to face Isla, and she could have sworn he was smiling.

She was smiling too, until a rope of shadows pulled her right in after him.

She would have sunk to the bottom, weighed down by all her daggers and sword, if it wasn't for the arm that curled around her waist. Slowly, like he had all the time in the world, she felt Grim reach into the slits of her pants, long fingers expertly pulling out dagger after dagger, throwing star after throwing star, and tossing them all to the edge of the bank.

"How many blades does one person need?" he asked, incredulous, as his rough hands gently traced down her legs, fingers curling around her thighs, looking for more. Isla felt like she might be close to drowning again, for very different reasons.

"Several, when she's married to a demon."

He only grinned. She threw her sword to the bank herself, then shoved away from Grim, able to swim on her own.

"What is this place?" she asked. There was a thick waterfall falling into the deep body of water, reminding her, with a chill, of the augur's home. Wraith was currently beneath it, clearly happy as the water hit his back, scrubbing off the soap.

"A pocket of beauty on Nightshade. A rare one."

It had been a while since she had swum for leisure—and not when she thought she was dying. She liked it, the feeling of the water through the roots of her hair, the way it seemed to soothe her aching muscles as she pushed through it. The water was cold, but she didn't really mind. By the time she pulled herself out of it, and onto the bank, she felt like she could roll over and fall asleep.

The grass was soft beneath her. The sun wasn't strong, but it gradually warmed her skin. She was so relaxed she didn't even try to move when Grim lay right beside her.

Her eyes were closed as he carefully and slowly slid every one of her knives back in place, fitting them against the curves of her body, in the pockets that were specially made for her, by him. She shivered, feeling his fingers brush up her thighs as he pushed them each in. He left her sword in her open palm. "In case you need to use it," he said, dark voice skittering down her bones. She would have rolled her eyes if they were open.

She had just managed to drift to sleep, when a thousand droplets of water pelted her every inch.

"Wraith," Grim growled, and she opened her eyes to find the dragon staring happily down at them, after having flapped his wet wings.

Wraith didn't do anything but sink down into the grass. He rolled over, but Grim glared at him, refusing to rub his stomach.

The dragon turned to her.

"Traitorous creature," Grim muttered.

Isla had to fight to hide her grin as she stood, and obliged Wraith, running her fingers down his scales as his talons happily scratched at the sky.

Wraith made joyful sounds, and she found herself smiling. Laughing. She hadn't really realized it, until she turned, only to find Grim staring at her.

Her smile withered away, replaced by guilt. She didn't deserve to be happy. She didn't deserve to have this time to enjoy when so many lives were at risk.

"The storm is taking too long. There hasn't been another storm in days," she said. "There has to be another way to find the portal."

Grim's expression turned serious. "I've tried. I've visited any surviving elders. I've gone through all the ancient records; none speak of

a portal. I've flown across nearly every mile of Nightshade and haven't felt even a whisper of my portaling power."

She had tried too. The augur had been helpful in other ways, but their best bet was still Azul's ring.

Isla sighed. Grim continued to watch her. There was a fold between his brows. He opened his mouth, then closed it. He looked . . . almost nervous.

"What is it?" she demanded.

"Would you marry me?"

Her look was withering. With the hand that wasn't still scratching Wraith's stomach, she lifted the stone at her neck, and let it thud between her collarbones. "Didn't we already do that?"

"My people believe you're a traitor. Your display with Tynan didn't exactly disprove that point."

Her eyes flashed with anger. Her stomach swirled with panic, remembering everything she had overheard. "He tried to assassinate me."

His gaze mirrored hers in intensity. "I know," he said, standing. His height was surprising, even now. "And he deserved to be eaten by those snakes while he was still drawing breath. But discontent and suspicion continue to spread to the people. It grows and grows, like a weed. An uprising would only hurt us all." He sighed.

Grim, she had to admit, was right. "Fine. What do you propose?"

"A wedding."

She remembered their first. It had been small—only Astria there as a witness. Isla had worn an embroidered dress that told their story—nature meeting shadow. Life melting into darkness. She'd had flowers in her hair.

"How in the world would that help? Your court hates me."

"They doubt your commitment to me. To us. Some are convinced you're a spy from Lightlark." She watched him, wondering if he ever had that fear. If he ever doubted her motivations. "A ceremony would show a unified front. The people of Nightshade are removed from the ongoings of the palace. They only hear rumor, and they are suffering. Everyone still feels the effects of the storm. A distraction—even for a few hours—would benefit everyone."

"Fine," she said, even as her stomach twisted. Marrying him once was one thing. *Twice?* If news of another wedding reached Oro, what would he think? He would hate her.

Good, she thought, with a bite of sadness. She didn't deserve him. Loving him would ruin him, if she let it. He needed to forget her.

"We'll have a wedding."

HEARTRIPPER

Isla dreamed of snakes slithering across her skin. She dreamed of drowning in them. She dreamed of them wrapping around her throat—

She awoke panting. Lynx's green eyes glowed through the darkness, watching her warily. Her head was pulsing, feverish.

Follow the snakes . . .

It was still dark outside. She hadn't planned on visiting the town, but she grabbed her daggers and slipped on her clothes.

Waiting for the storm had made her restless. The augur had said she would be back to his cave—that it had been *written*.

She didn't yet know the right questions to ask, but she figured it wouldn't hurt to pay in advance for his services. That was what she told herself, anyway, as she prowled the streets night after night. It was easier than admitting that she got a twisted sort of satisfaction in seeing the life leave the eyes of those she had seen hurt others. That with every kill . . . something inside of her was growing. And there was never a shortage of people to hunt down. Even as she killed the worst in society, over and over, more seemed to take their place, like relentless weeds.

She had a favorite perch, a rooftop where she could get a wide view of the city. That night, she found something waiting for her. A piece of fruit, and a pastry. It was warm in her hands. Buttery in her fingers. Still, she didn't eat it. It could be poisoned.

The next night was the same. Another offering.

The following evening, she arrived early, and waited on a different rooftop. She watched a woman climb up the stairs inside the

building and leave the gifts. She recognized her clothes. She was the woman Isla had saved.

Tonight, the gift was some sort of pie. It smelled of potatoes and meat and herbs, and even as her stomach growled in hunger, she didn't eat it. The woman had seemed kind . . . but she couldn't trust anyone.

She watched the streets for hours. It was quiet, so she made her way down to walk, sticking to the shadows. She made five right turns in a row, in a useless circle.

That was how she knew someone was following her. She could hear their footsteps splashing the puddles between misaligned stones in the road, just a few yards behind. Whoever it was, they weren't skilled at stalking. They were clumsy, and careless.

Satisfaction rooted deep within her. She figured one of these days a friend of one of those men she had killed would come after her. Her skin buzzed with excitement as she climbed up the gutter of a building and waited. Once they turned into the alley, she pounced, jumping from the rooftop.

She nearly had her blade against her stalker's throat, when she realized she knew them.

The woman who had been leaving her gifts. She had pale skin, freckles, and curly dark red hair that she wore up in pins.

She grinned, not looking too upset that a dagger had just been pointed at her. "This close, you look far less menacing than I thought you would," she said, seeming stunned as she looked Isla up and down. Even though half her face was covered with her scarf, Isla didn't like how closely she studied her.

"Stop following me," Isla said, trying to make her voice as firm as possible. "Stop leaving me things."

The woman just tilted her head. "I meant no offense. Just gratitude. I don't know how to repay you."

"You don't need to," Isla said. "Just please keep yourself safe."

With one final nod, she turned on her heel.

"Help me, then."

Isla turned around again. "What?"

The woman raised a shoulder. "Teach me."

Isla just stared at her.

"It's not the first time something like that has happened. Teach me to defend myself, in case you're not there to save me next time." Isla almost laughed. She shouldn't be teaching anyone anything. But the woman just looked at her. She blinked.

Isla sighed. "If I teach you this, will you leave me alone?"

The woman nodded, grin widening.

"Fine."

Isla looked behind her. Paused. When she was confident she wasn't about to be ambushed, she took out one of her daggers—one with its own sheath—and handed it to the woman.

She beamed. "My name's Sairsha, by the way."

Isla ignored her. "The blade is sharp. Make sure not to stab yourself while trying to wield it." She took another dagger between her fingers, and demonstrated the right way to hold it. "Like this."

Sairsha tried a few times before getting it right.

She nodded. "Keep it sheathed. If you're being attacked, the best thing to do in your case is run. If that's impossible, then first try to go for their nose. Or their groin. If none of that works, use the dagger. Get in a strong stance." Isla demonstrated a simple one. "And go for anywhere you can. The stomach is a good option. The ribs are hard to get through. The neck . . . is messy." She closed her mouth, wondering if she was doing more harm than good. "If you aren't skilled, the dagger is more likely to be used against you. It's a last resort."

Sairsha nodded. She carefully sheathed the weapon, pocketing it like a treasure. Her voice was reverent. "Thank you."

Isla didn't say anything in response before she turned and left.

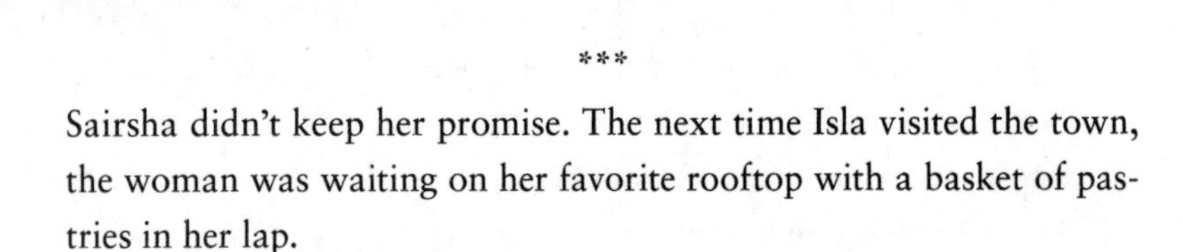

***

Sairsha didn't keep her promise. The next time Isla visited the town, the woman was waiting on her favorite rooftop with a basket of pastries in her lap.

She smiled and waved, and Isla turned on her heel and left. The next night was the same. She was close to visiting another town entirely, when she finally found her spot empty.

Good. The woman had given up.

Not an hour into her watching, Sairsha noisily opened the door opening to the roof. "Oh you're here already! I had—"

Isla had her hand over her mouth in less than a moment. "What do you think you're doing?" she demanded.

"Helping you," she whispered from behind Isla's fingers. She held up something in her hand, as if to show her.

It was the dagger Isla had gifted her.

She dropped her hand. "If I tell you to leave, will you listen?"

The woman shook her head. Isla sighed.

They ended up on the rooftop, side by side. Sairsha chewed the pastries loudly, crumbs falling all over her lap.

At least she was being quiet, Isla thought, until Sairsha was done with her food and said, "You've saved many of my friends, you know."

Isla didn't look at her. She just stared ahead and wondered when this woman would leave her alone.

"We feel safer nowadays. Fewer incidents happening. It seems people are afraid of the consequences. You've earned a reputation."

That wasn't great. She would need to start going to other villages.

A door opened below. Laughter spilled onto the streets. It closed, muting them. "Have you been there before?"

It was a bar. She had watched its entrance plenty of times but had never been inside. She shook her head, grateful the scarf over most of her face had kept still.

"I could use a drink. Let's go."

Isla ignored her.

"The beer's terrible, but the food is good."

Isla offered her a noncommittal nod.

"The company's not bad either, except—"

Isla turned to face her. "If I go, will you *actually* leave me alone?"

Sairsha nodded. Isla sighed, then found herself scaling down the building, while Sairsha took the stairs. This was foolish. She should just go into an alley and use her device to portal away. She should find a completely different town. She should wait at her window until another storm finally broke.

But, she realized, she had come to crave the routine of this town. It had given her some semblance of control over her life. She liked this rooftop and the bars around it, the alley that was especially convenient for killing.

So she stepped inside the bar.

Someone near her turned lazily in her direction, then froze. He whispered something to the person next to them—a short woman—and she startled. It continued, person after person whispering, then staring, until the room went quiet.

Isla went still. Her hand inched toward her dagger and starstick, as she wondered which one she would use first.

She shouldn't have come. It was a risk, even with a scarf disguising most of her face. The people of Nightshade hated her. If they knew she was Grim's wife—the *snake-queen*—she might not be able to portal before they attacked.

Sairsha just laughed. "Don't mind them. They're just in awe of your presence." *They knew.* She took a step backward.

"It really is you," a voice said, as Isla turned to run. "The heartripper."

Her hand paused just inches from the door handle.

Heartripper? She needed to start adding more variety to her killings. Clearly, she had made it her signature.

She breathed again.

"Told you I knew her." The woman linked arms with Isla's, and she had to physically stop herself from wrenching away.

A man with a weathered face and bald head nodded at her as she passed. "Thank you for all you've done," he told her, before continuing his conversation.

Slowly the attention shifted away from her.

"Get you anything to drink?" Sairsha said, as she led Isla to a pair of empty stools that looked very close to collapsing and were covered in a film of substance, likely dried drink.

"No," Isla said, keeping her voice as hushed as possible. They didn't seem to know who she was beyond heartripper—yet—but she didn't need to make it easy for them to figure out her identity.

Every time someone in front looked over their shoulder at her with curiosity, she tensed. She reminded herself that it would take hardly any time to portal away. Or to touch her necklace, summoning Grim in an instant. But then, he would probably end up killing every single person in this room. And wondering why his wife was in this bar to begin with.

Sairsha returned a few moments later, slamming a large mug in front of her. "In case you change your mind," she said. "Our little saint must be parched."

Saint. It was laughable how ridiculous that word was, when applied to her.

Isla nodded in thanks, not planning to take a sip.

The woman seemed to sense the reason for her hesitation. She raised an eyebrow, found an empty mug on a table, poured half of the offered drink in it, raised it in cheers, and took a hearty sip.

"Decidedly not poison," she said with a wink. Then, she turned around again and joined the others.

Curiosity got the better of Isla a few minutes later. When no one was facing her, she quickly pulled down her scarf, took a tentative

sip, and fought to keep herself from gagging. Yes. Decidedly not poison.

Still, decidedly disgusting.

Again, Sairsha did not keep her word.

They formed a routine. After Isla was done roaming the streets, she would visit the bar for a few minutes. It was filled with the same people every time.

"Why do you come here every night?" Isla asked her one day.

Sairsha shrugged. "I was looking for a sort of family." She smiled as she looked over at the others. "We all know each other. We have meetings, sometimes, to try to make our town better. Our future better. We're joined by purpose. And that, I've found, can be stronger than blood."

Purpose.

Each night, they would share a drink; and every time, Isla would pretend to like the warm beer that tasted like it had long gone sour. But Sairsha seemed to love it and would throw her head back and laugh as she told Isla stories about her family and growing up in a small mountain village. It was nice.

"What do you think of the ruler?" Isla asked one day, curious.

Sairsha thought long and hard. "He's fair. Much fairer than his father, or any before, I've heard. Whenever there is some sort of problem, he is always the first one there. He doesn't just send others. During the curses, he himself built the tunnels with his great power. He spent years creating them. Making sure we were all safe and had enough provisions. He would hand-deliver them."

She didn't know why this shocked her, but it did.

Isla remembered him struggling against the dreks. Taking the brunt of the attack himself. Appearing in her room, ravaged by wounds and shadows.

He didn't just hide behind a palace. He was there, in the thick of it, every time. He put the needs of his people above his own.

Except when it came to her.

She had just crept into bed that night when Lynx nudged her.

"Let me sleep," she said, turning toward the other side. She barely got a handful of hours of rest a day, thanks to her insistence on playing vigilante every night.

Lynx made a growling sound and pushed her off onto the floor.

She landed in a heap of blankets and glared at him through the darkness. "What is it?"

His green eyes glowed just inches in front of her. He motioned toward the glass. The window.

There was a faint knocking sound, clearly not the wind. The stormfinch was asleep in its cage.

Knocking?

Lynx looked insistent.

She reached toward her necklace, and Lynx growled.

Isla dropped her hand. "Fine. If I die, it's your fault," she said to her leopard, and grabbed her blade instead.

She ripped the curtain back.

Her dagger dropped to the floor.

There was a figure, right outside her window, filling it like a god.

Oro.

STORMFINCH

Panic gripped her chest. This had to be a dream—an illusion.

But Oro's amber eyes were clear, he was *right there*. Even without her powers, she could feel the link between them, fainter than before, thanks to the bracelets.

For a moment, she felt joy, warmth, relief, like being plunged into the sunlight after weeks in darkness.

Fear replaced it.

If Grim found him here, if anyone did, he—

She opened the window and pulled him through it.

Oro nearly collapsed onto the floor. He was cold, shivering. He had dark crescents beneath his eyes.

He had flown here, across the world. It must have taken days.

"What are you doing here?" she demanded, searching wildly for his pulse. It was still strong. It was a wonder he wasn't nearly dead.

Oro only looked at her. He seemed lost for words for a moment. Lynx brought over a blanket with his teeth and draped it over him.

Treacherous creature.

Oro reached back and pet Lynx on the leg. He curled up behind him and purred.

"What are you doing here?" she repeated. Her voice was hushed. Any sign of panic, and Grim would be here in an instant. It was his room, after all. *Their room.*

This was bad. Very bad.

"Our bond weakened. I was worried something had happened to you."

She lifted her wrists, to show her bracelets. "They block my power."

Oro frowned. His gaze trailed up her arms, to her chest, to her face. He searched her quickly, as if looking for any sign that she had been hurt. Then, his gaze roamed across the room, as if half expecting to see that she had been locked in a prison.

"You flew across the world to make sure I was okay?"

"Of course I did," he said sharply. His breathing was labored.

"You could have sent someone else. The *risk,* it—"

"I didn't trust anyone else." He looked at her, and she understood his meaning. He didn't trust anyone else not to kill her on sight. She was the traitor.

Yet—he was here.

Tears gathered in her eyes. She couldn't believe it. So many nights, she had clutched the golden rose necklace to her chest and thought of him before burying the emotions down.

Isla knew she should send him away. She knew she was a risk to him. But she couldn't stop herself from slowly reaching a hand to touch his face. His eyes closed as her palm pressed against his cheek. As her fingers grazed his lips. She made to move, and his hand curled around her wrist, keeping her there.

"Oro," she said, her voice a rasp.

"*Isla.*" And the way he said her name . . . it was nearly her undoing. She nearly threw her arms around him, nearly kissed him, nearly did a thousand stupid things that would only end in more confusion and heartbreak.

But then a sound cut through the darkness. A pitch like a talon scraping the night itself, nearly painful, wholly beautiful.

Her hand still against his face, they both slowly turned toward the intricate cage in her room, and the small blue bird sitting within it. Dread and hope dropped through Isla's stomach.

The stormfinch was singing.

She turned to look at Oro, eyes so wide they watered. They had just seconds. Grim would hear the bird. He would portal here, so they could go into the storm.

She had to get to Grim first. Keep him away from her room. If he found Oro here . . .

Flashes of their battle echoed in her mind. Blood, everywhere. Her, screaming at the sky, watching them nearly kill each other.

Her voice tumbled out of her. "I have to go." She stood, immediately missing the faint heat that had started radiating out of him. "Stay here. Stay hidden."

The stormfinch continued its singing. It was getting louder. Grim would be on his way.

Oro's brows came together. He looked half ready to demand to come with her, but before he could say a word, she grabbed her clothes in a fist, then the starstick, and portaled into Grim's room.

He was standing in its center, looking half a moment from going to her.

"Hearteater," he said, mouth barely moving, as if on instinct. His eyes filled with surprise and happiness for less than a second, before they narrowed in confusion. He was staring at her night clothes. Likely wondering why she hadn't changed in her own room.

Her heart was hammering so loudly, she wondered if he could hear it. Her emotions were unbridled. Grim was feeling a canvas of relief and devastation and fear—

"I—I need help," she said quickly.

The stormfinch was still singing. She could hear it faintly, even from down the hall. Would Grim want to go to it?

She turned around in a flash, offering her back to him. "The buttons. I can't reach them."

It was a lie. She was grateful he wasn't Oro, because he would have seen through her in a moment, with his flair. There were only five

buttons. She could easily twist and get them, but she made a frustrated sound and pulled her hair over her shoulder, to allow him access.

For a moment, he didn't move an inch. He must have already alerted a guard, because somewhere far away a bell started ringing, warning the nearby villages of an incoming storm. The warning would spread across Nightshade.

They didn't have much time. They needed to get up into the skies quickly and follow Azul's instructions.

Yet time seemed to stand still as Grim's cold fingers brushed against her spine. Her shoulders hiked.

"Sorry," he said, somewhere close to her ear. "You're . . . very warm."

She swallowed, pulse racing, thinking about the Sunling skin she had just touched. The warmth that had filled her like a gulp of summer air.

Panic spiked, knowing he was still in her room. Just a few walls away.

She turned to look at Grim right in the eyes, attempting to distract him from wondering about anything. "It's fine. Don't stop."

His gaze didn't leave hers as he undid the next button. Then the next. Then the next. Until all of them were done, and her straps were hanging off her shoulders, back completely exposed. Body turned away from him, but eyes on his, she let the night dress drop to the floor. Watched his throat work.

Then, she turned toward the wall. She shrugged on her long-sleeved shirt and pants. She didn't know if he was watching, but by the time she had everything in place, he was facing the wall.

"Ready?" she said.

He nodded.

And he portaled them both to Wraith.

***

The night was starless. The darkness seemed to simmer, full of something she couldn't see but they both could feel.

Wraith moved silently through the sky, farther and farther up until Nightshade was lost below.

"Worried, Hearteater?" Grim said, leaning in so she could hear him through the wind.

She swallowed. Of course she was worried. Oro was in her room—in *Grim's* room—at the very center of the land of his enemies. He had flown across the world. He could be discovered in an instant. How long would he wait?

"The storm," she said with all the confidence she could muster. "It's our best chance at finding the portal."

It was true. They had waited weeks for this moment. Her thumb fidgeted with Azul's ring. An energy coursed through it, the storm inside gently swirling.

Grim was silent long enough for her to peer over her shoulder at him. He was staring at her.

She knew him, so she could see the slight disappointment in his expression, the hint of sadness. "What?"

He tilted his head at her, ever so slightly. "I'm just wishing you didn't feel the need to keep so many secrets from me."

Her limbs went boneless. Feelings spilled through her, unchecked—surprise, and guilt, and fear. She knew he could feel them. Knew it was useless to say, in a voice like it was dragged out of her, "What secrets?"

Did Grim somehow know about the king in her room? Or the prophecy?

She felt the sudden need to run, though she didn't know how. She had forgotten her starstick back in Grim's room.

Just when she nearly lost her grip on Wraith's ridges, palms slick with sweat, he said, "You went to see the augur."

Relief filled her—and was almost immediately replaced with wariness. "How do you know that?"

His eyes narrowed at her. "You're dying. You don't think I've been trying to find every way possible to save you?"

Right.

She should have known—should have expected that the same man who had waged a war to save her wouldn't simply accept her fate.

She should have been relieved that he was pursuing an avenue to save her and Nightshade that didn't end in Lightlark's destruction. Instead, all she felt was worry. How much had the augur told him?

"And?"

Grim dropped her gaze, then. He was looking below at the dark clouds that had begun to gather. His jaw tightened. "As I suspected, the only chance at permanently saving you is the otherworld."

She knew her death was imminent . . . but it didn't make it burn less to hear it said. Only a few months of winter remained. Every day was colder. Would she ever feel the heat of summer again?

"Reconsider," Grim said, meeting her eyes again. His voice was firm. Desperate, even.

"What?"

"Using the portal on Lightlark." He leaned toward her. He let go of Wraith with one hand and reached toward her cheek. His fingers were trembling and cold against her skin, so at odds with Oro's heat. "Reconsider. Let us go through it. Let—let me save you." His voice broke on the words. It seemed supremely difficult for him to hold back on simply taking her to Lightlark right now and carrying her through the portal himself.

But he was listening to her. He was respecting her wishes. He was *trying.*

Her eyes stung as she shook her head. No matter how much she wanted to live—truly *live,* with freedom her position would never

allow—she wouldn't doom thousands to death, just to save herself. "I can't. I—"

Her skin prickled. The wind shifted into a different pitch, a sharp sound that made her wince. Something in her body seemed to sing, pulled toward a force she couldn't see. Her scalp felt sensitive, the metal of her bracelets trembled against her pulse. Grim lurched forward, as if to shield her, just before the skies around them shattered.

Her breath was knocked out of her lungs as she was thrown against Grim's chest. He caught her with a hand around her waist as Wraith was flung back by a gust of wind that seemed intent on shooting them down.

The sky had gone that strange shade again—green and purple whorls formed around them. Her ears rang. She fought to breathe.

Something hit her in the arm. Her blood was hot against her frozen skin.

"Something's wrong. We're leaving," Grim said.

Her words came out raw. "No! It's our only—" She cut off sharply as her leg was sliced, down to her ankle, right through her clothes. Impossible. Her pants were made of fabric that was supposed to be nearly impenetrable.

"Enough of this." Grim extended his hand, to portal them away.

Nothing happened.

He froze behind her. Tried again. She could hear his frustration like a growl. Then, he was lunging forward, to block another object soaring through the air, right at her face. He caught it in his fist.

He flinched like it had burned him, before dropping it. It looked like a piece of metal, but charred, aflame.

It looked like her bracelets.

"My power isn't working," he said over the roaring of the wind. This storm . . . it was so much worse than the previous one. There hadn't been metal in that one, not that she had seen. Wraith was moving quicker than ever. In seconds, she could barely keep her eyes open

against the force of the tempest. The dragon whipped sideways suddenly, nearly sending her off his back.

The shademade metal fell like hail. The pieces were getting larger. She ducked, barely dodging a clump the size of her fist.

"We should turn back," Grim said, his grip on her tightening. Wraith dropped to avoid something she couldn't see, and her stomach lurched.

"Not yet. Tell him to go higher."

"Heart—"

"*Tell him*," she said, looking down at the ring upon her longest finger. Nothing was happening, not yet. They must not be in the heart of the storm.

He cursed, then shouted orders to Wraith. At first, she feared he had ignored her wishes and told the dragon to turn back to the castle. Instead, they began to rise through the skies.

It was worse up here.

The energy was almost speaking to her, a whisper, a thinly forged dagger flaying her skin. The metal pieces were smaller but more abundant, thick as rain, nicking her every inch.

"We're not going any higher," Grim said.

"But—"

The sky chose that moment to rumble and shatter around them. Lightning struck, thunder answered.

"Fine," she said through her teeth. She made sure her grip was tight. Grim didn't have his shadows to keep her in place. If she fell, it would be to her death.

With a steadying exhale, she lifted one arm into the air, offering the ring on her finger to the tempest.

One second. Two. Three.

Something scratched against her finger. It was the metal, shifting, turning slowly around her skin, by itself. It was almost as if the shred of storm inside the ring was trying to escape. It was pulsing, like a

heartbeat. She looked up to see it faintly glowing. It seemed the power inside was calling out.

With a flash that nearly blinded her, the storm answered.

Lightning. Barreling right toward her. Stopping just short of the ring, blinding her completely for seconds.

She tasted power on her tongue, like metal in her mouth, like *blood*. The stone felt hot against her finger, absorbing a piece of it.

Another strike, this one far too close, and Wraith was propelled away by the force of it, wings flapping wildly to regain balance. Grim gripped her hip with one of his hands to keep her steady.

She lowered her arm and stared down at the ring. Inside, green and purple wove together with the shred, in thin, braid-like strands. They formed a new, sparkling color.

This was the key to finding the portal. The key to saving Nightshade.

According to the augur, the key to giving herself more time to live.

A searing pain erupted in the back of her head, from something that had cut across it. *The metal*. It was getting bigger now, even up here.

"Duck!" Grim yelled through the roar, and she did, but it hardly helped. The storm had thickened. She was pelted by metal in all directions, like an army of throwing stars, until Grim covered her entire body with his.

She remembered him shielding her from the arrows in the cave. Remembered him taking every single one. He did the same thing now, getting stabbed a thousand times by increasingly large pieces.

His powers still weren't working. If they were, he would have wrapped them in shadows. He would have portaled them away.

They were stuck in this storm.

Grim shouted orders for Wraith to descend. They lost air quickly as Wraith dropped—so quickly, that Isla's hand slipped.

And with it, her grip on the ring.

She watched in agonizing slowness as the ring fell through the air, down toward Nightshade, disappearing through a thick layer of clouds.

Her only chance at finding the portal. Gone.

On instinct, she went after it. She had no plan, no powers, no starstick—before she jumped over the edge, Grim was hauling her back.

"What the hell do you think you're doing?" he demanded as he pinned her in place, shielding her with his body as they continued their descent. Blood dripped from every exposed inch of him, he had been cut in a thousand places, but he didn't seem to be focused on anything but her as his eyes filled with rage.

"We need to land!" she screamed. "That was our only chance!" She didn't recognize her own voice, her own insistence, her own recklessness.

Her life was tied to thousands, but in that moment all that mattered was that shred of storm.

She didn't have any other rings on. Could she use another stone to trap the storm? *Her necklace.* She reached for the stone around her neck.

But before she could wrap her fingers around it, a roar cut through the storm like a blade carving it in half.

"What in the realms is that?" she whispered, Grim's breath hot against the top of her head, Wraith's scales wet and cold beneath her cheek. She slowly turned her neck, to look up.

The sky had gone red.

And from those blood-brushed clouds emerged a creature emitting spirals of flame.

No. Not flames.

Lightning.

She turned to Grim. "Can Wraith—"

"No," Grim said and he—he sounded afraid. Afraid like when she was dying in his arms. In a desperate push, he pressed them both

down against Wraith's cold, rain-slicked scales. He shouted against the roar of the storm, and Wraith began to tilt down, to retreat.

It was too late.

Streaks of lightning darted toward them, illuminating everything, splitting into shards. Roots on fire.

One hit Wraith right in his neck, and he seized. His wings went still. He tilted to the side.

And then, they were falling.

BROKEN

Her chest burned.

It was like her scarred skin, right where the heart of Lightlark had marked her, was aflame. That sensation was what woke her as she fell through the sky, wind whipping her wildly through the air.

Grim. Wraith.

She tried to look around, but she couldn't see anything past the blinding mist.

Wind whipped wildly, tossing her through the air as she plummeted, her skin raw and bleeding. This was it. Her powers were gone. The metal would have muted them anyway. Her limbs flailed as she fought against the inevitable.

A sob scraped against her throat as the clouds cleared, and she managed a look at the ground that was rushing up to meet her.

It was replaced by a wing.

She crashed against the leathery skin, and then against someone—Grim. Wraith had caught them both, and folded into himself, shielding them from the metal that had already marked them everywhere. Cocooning them in his wings that didn't work any longer, as they fell. Fell.

They crashed like a shooting star, and then, there was only darkness.

She gasped, coughing up water. Her throat burned with salt. Her eyes stung as she fought to open them, as she gripped anything she could—

Only to find herself on land.

Grim was in front of her, holding her hair back as she retched seawater. "What—"

"My power returned just before we hit the ground. I portaled us to the sea for the impact, and then back here." She turned to see they were on an unfamiliar cliffside. It was freezing, a cold she felt in her bones. A layer of snow frosted everything.

Her chest was still burning.

Wraith.

Her knees nearly buckled as she tried to stand, stumbling away from Grim's help, looking around frantically, only to find Wraith on his side, a few feet away. She rushed toward him, dragging herself forward, everything sore.

She pressed a palm against him, tears already blurring her vision.

"He's injured, but alive," Grim murmured. His voice was pained.

His wings. They were torn up and bloody, shredded from the scraps of metal flying through the sky, some still imbedded into his leathery skin. There was a starlike mark on his neck, where the lightning had struck.

It must have hurt immensely. Still, he had shielded them. Wrapped his wings around them, even as he was falling toward the ground. He had sacrificed himself to save them, without any hesitation.

Tears swept down her cheeks. This was her fault. It was her fault they were even in the storm in the first place. She should have listened to Grim—should have let him turn them around.

It was all for nothing. The ring was lost. They could search for it, but they'd been so high up . . . it could be anywhere.

She looked to the sky. The storm had moved on. She could barely see it now, though she narrowed her eyes, searching for another pair of wings. "The creature—"

"Is gone. The storm cleared . . . and with it . . . everything."

Isla's knees finally buckled, and the snow was cold against her legs as she buried down into it.

She blinked, and they were back in the stables. Wraith was groaning, breathing in a way that sounded like it hurt.

"Where's the remaining healing elixir?" she demanded. The vials in the castle were gone, but there had to be more.

"If there's anything left, it's with the Wildlings."

"Get it. Heal him," she said, knowing he would. They had bonded. She could see the worry clear on his face.

She wanted to stay with the dragon, take each piece of metal out of Wraith's wings herself—but there was something she needed to do first.

Grim eyed the dozens of tears in her previously impenetrable clothing. The blood that stained it. "Let me help you first," he said, stepping toward her.

He was going to portal her to her room. Help wrap her injuries. Help her into new clothes.

The room that Oro was currently standing in.

"No," she said, so loudly, he stilled. "Please—please go with Wraith. I—I feel so guilty." It was true. He would be able to feel that guilt now, mixed with undeniable panic. "Portal me to your room, please. I'll get the starstick, fix myself up and meet you at the Wildling keep."

She wasn't breathing as she watched him watch her—studying her closer than she cared for at that moment.

He could ignore her wishes and help her anyway, portal them both right now. It wasn't like he hadn't done that before.

Slowly, he reached his hand toward her.

His fingers curled around hers.

The stables faded, replaced by his room. She grabbed her starstick, and portaled to her own.

She was immediately engulfed in warmth. She seized, whipping around to see if Grim was there too, if he had changed his mind—but there was only Oro, arms wrapped around her, his heat almost biting against the cold of her skin.

"You're freezing," he said into her temple.

Past him, she saw the stormfinch sitting quietly in her cage. Lynx towered behind Oro, eyes wide in worry. Teeth barred in fury.

"What happened?" Oro asked, looking just as concerned as Grim had a few minutes prior. She was covered in cuts and blood; her hair and clothes were still wet.

There wasn't time to explain. She had to get Oro out of here. She needed to get back to Grim quickly, lest he come and check on her.

"Come back with me. For good."

Oro's words were firm. Pleading.

She closed her eyes. They still burned from tears and salt water. "I can't. You know I can't."

His warm hand pressed gently against her cheek, and her shoulders hiked. She opened her eyes to find his staring her down, lit like they held flames.

"I know you think you being here is the only way to save Lightlark, I know you did it for us, but *you* cannot be the cost of this. I won't let you be. There has to be another way, another—"

"There *isn't*." He didn't understand. "If you kill Grim, I'll die, and so will all of Nightshade."

"Killing him isn't the only way to stop him. You could help us. We could imprison him. No one would have to die."

"*I'm* going to die," she said. "Soon." And before that, according to the prophecy, she would plunge a blade into either Grim's or Oro's heart.

"We'll find another way." He didn't look defeated . . . he looked determined.

Oro wasn't going to stop fighting for her; she knew that, even though he should. She remembered Enya's words. Him loving her was dangerous. It made him weak.

Even without the prophecy, she was bad for him. She made him forget his duty. Made him do reckless things like risk his and all his peoples' lives by traveling across the world to the land of his enemies. The king she had met at the Centennial would never have done that.

She was poisoning him.

She didn't deserve him, and she was ruining him.

Break him, a voice in her mind said. *Make sure he never looks for you again. Make him hate you.*

Her heart was burning again, breaking, but for entirely different reasons. Tears fell down her face. She missed him so much. She missed his touch, but also so much more. She missed their conversations before bed. The way he would warm her socks because she always had cold feet. The way she would catch him studying her, as if he always knew this was temporary, that it would end, and he wanted to commit her to memory.

She didn't breathe as his thumb slowly swept down her jaw, to her lips. As his calloused skin scraped across her mouth. It continued down her neck, until he reached her necklace.

He dropped his hand as if he had been burned.

His eyes darted to a corner of her room. It seemed in her absence he had noticed the pile of daggers she had taken from her pants. They were still bloodied. She hadn't cleaned them yet.

For him to be safe, he needed to forget her.

For him to stop looking for her, he needed to hate her.

"I use those to kill people," she said steadily. He met her eyes. They narrowed, because he knew she was telling the truth. She didn't drop his gaze. "I put the knife through their hearts . . . and I enjoy it. I roam the streets at night, looking for people to kill. I smile as the life leaves their eyes."

He shook his head. Even as his own power was telling him she wasn't lying, it seemed like he didn't believe it. "No. You don't."

"*I do*," she said, stepping into him, getting as close to his face as she dared. "There is so much blood on my hands, they'll never be clean. I'm the enemy, Oro. Stop looking for me. You won't like what you find."

He took a shaking breath. "I don't recognize you, love."

"You're not supposed to."

She grabbed her starstick, then him, and it was done.

They were back in his room.

Their room. They had shared it for months. Part of her ached, truly ached, to just crawl back into that bed. Let Oro help her get warm again, let that warmth be a bonfire that lived permanently in her bones, making her feel safe and loved. Go to the beach with him, the one he had promised to take her to.

She wanted it so badly, it nearly brought her to her knees.

Oro must have seen it on her face. He lit the great hearth in his room, to warm her, then caught her wrist in his hand.

"You don't have to go back." He was looking at her neck. At the necklace that marked her as Grim's wife. "We can find a way around it. You have a choice."

She had two necklaces. One, permanently on her neck. Another, she kept in the pocket of the pants she most often wore. The one with the golden rose he had made her.

It nearly killed her, but she reached her hand inside. Gripped the gold.

It pained her to say the next few words. "I know," she said. "And I made it."

Isla handed the golden rose necklace back.

In his eyes, she saw unfiltered pain. Gone was the cold, heartless king of Lightlark. No, this one had a heart.

And she had broken it.

She was about to portal away, when the balcony door to his room burst open. Zed walked through. "You're back, you—"

He spotted her immediately, and he didn't hesitate. He was fast, faster than them both. In half a second, he had his bow ready, and before her hand reached her starstick, he had three arrows careening toward her.

One pointed at the center of her head. One at the center of her heart. Another at the center of her stomach.

Oro threw his power out, a Starling shield that blocked the arrows.

But not all of them. Not in time.

She looked down and saw one sticking through her stomach.

Oro's heat filled the room. He roared. "What did you do?" he demanded, and Zed was suddenly chained to the floor by glittering sheets of Starling sparks.

There was no regret in Zed's face as she fell to her knees. As pain flooded her chest like a wildfire.

"What you wouldn't," Zed said.

Oro reached toward her, calling water from the balcony to heal her. He took the arrow out, and she screamed. He worked to close the wound. She couldn't stay here. She had to go. As soon as it was mostly stitched, she reached for her starstick and said, her words just a gurgled rasp, "I'm marrying him again." Oro didn't know the circumstances, but he didn't need to. All he needed was to hear that she was telling the truth. "I made my choice. It isn't changing. Don't seek me out again."

And then she was gone.

Zed had nearly killed her.

She portaled to the Wildling keep, took one step, then collapsed to the ground. Grim was there in an instant, cradling her in his arms. Yelling orders.

Grim's shadows were everywhere. "Who did this to you?" he demanded, but she didn't say a word.

His power raged around them, growing more ruinous as he began to understand her silence. His voice was raw as he said, "Don't tell me. If it's anyone you care about, Isla, don't say a word. Because nothing will stop me from wiping every ember of their existence from this world."

She knew it was a promise. He had done it before.

Oro would certainly hate her if Grim killed all his closest friends . . . but she couldn't do that to him. They were the only people he had, especially now that she had left for good. So she remained silent.

She heard Wren's voice, but her eyes wouldn't open. The world felt too heavy, like she was being dragged underwater.

"This is the only full vial left," she heard Wren say.

Grim didn't hesitate. "Use it."

"Wraith—" she gasped. The elixir was meant for the dragon. "*Please.*"

Grim hesitated for a moment before he said, "I'll restitch her wound myself. Use the vial for my dragon."

Good. *Good.*

Commotion. Then, something cold against her skin. Pricking it. *Breaking it.* Redoing the stitches that were already there, the ones that had broken because she had left before he could finish. Grim had to know who had made them.

He had to know, and it had to be killing him.

She thrashed in Grim's arms as he sewed her skin back together. She gasped for air. His snow-cold hands ran down her back. "I know, heart," he said gently. "I know."

Zed had wounded her.

She shouldn't be shocked. She was a traitor. Everyone knew securing Lightlark's safety meant ending Nightshade.

It was still a surprise, though. The betrayal felt raw, more painful than the wound itself.

She had been too careless. Of course it was a danger going to Lightlark at all, especially without her powers.

She grieved Oro. They could never be together. Not when she saw what she had turned him into. Not when his friends hated her enough to try to kill her. There was no going back from that. She hoped he forgot her. She hoped she never saw him again.

AFTERMATH

The storm cleared, and with it, her chance at finding the portal.

Entire villages had been torn apart by winds that were described as hands dropping from the sky, scraping away everything in their path. Wicked, twisted creatures had been spotted again, attacking villagers in the most rural areas of Nightshade, too far from the tunnels to use them for shelter. Their bodies were never found. The only remnants of them were the puddles of blood staining their floorboards.

Without the healing elixir, the injured died.

This was just the beginning; she could feel it. Azul was right. A storm was coming, unlike any this world had ever seen. They needed to find the portal, and close it, before the next one.

If only she hadn't lost the ring.

Wraith was still recovering. She visited him once she could leave her bed. He purred weakly. Lynx sat with him in the stables, watching over him.

If the dragon wasn't injured, she could retrace their flight path, try to find the stone . . . but she knew it was little use trying. It could be anywhere.

Grim was busy helping the people of the villages that had been destroyed, though she couldn't help feeling like he was avoiding her.

He had to suspect she had been with Oro. Would he think she had been going back and forth this entire time?

Would he think her a traitor, just as his court had warned?

At night, she didn't sleep. Stress made her toss and turn in her bed. She needed an outlet for it.

She portaled back to the rooftop.

Sairsha was already there, waiting. She looked up at her. "Wondered if you were coming tonight," she said. She had an entire bottle of wine with her.

Isla sat beside it. She didn't say a word for several minutes, lost in her own thoughts, until Sairsha tipped her head back, taking a long swing of the drink.

"Something wrong?" Isla asked, her eyes trained on the street. At first the woman's presence had been annoying. Now, it was a comfort.

Sairsha drank deeply. "The storm destroyed my house."

Isla whipped to face her. "Really?" She shouldn't have been shocked. Dozens of homes had been decimated.

She nodded. "Not the one I live in currently. The one I grew up in." She shrugged. "Haven't been there in a while, just strange to see it all gone." There was a faint clinking as she put the bottle down. "Family's all dead. Some were taken by the curses. Others by the storms, over the years. Others just by time. The house is all that was left, and now that's gone too." She shrugged. "The place I live now is fine. The bar is fine. It just makes me wonder if the only home I'll ever have is lost."

Isla knew what it was like to feel like home had been ripped away. "I'm sorry," she said. "I hope you find another home. A better one."

At that, Sairsha smiled. "I hope so too." Soon after, she left her alone.

The next night, she returned. She met Sairsha at the bar. A group of women were chatting excitedly about the upcoming wedding. They were talking about the dresses they had sewn specially for the occasion.

"I heard the marriage is fake," someone said. "I heard they can't even tolerate each other."

Another person grunted. "I suppose we'll see soon."

Isla was grateful for the scarf as she grimaced, trying not to think about the fact that Grim hadn't so much as spoken to her in the last few days.

She had assumed the ceremony would be cancelled due to the storm, but now it seemed more important than ever. Morale was low, but talk of the tempest had been replaced by excitement for the wedding.

Days passed without storms, and Isla spent the mornings looking for the ring and the evenings on her rooftop.

That night, she was tracking a man who had killed his wife and was now on the run. She had been watching him for days, waiting for the perfect moment, for he was rumored to be a powerful wielder. She couldn't use her abilities, so she would need to surprise him.

She was waiting in the alley he had stashed his belongings in, when he entered it. Before he could summon his shadows, she was there, taking advantage of his surprise. The Nightshade was against the wall before he could blink, her blade was through his windpipe before he could summon a scream. Blood ran hot down her hand, seeping into the black fabrics she would throw away by the end of the night.

With his last remaining energy, his hand produced a shadow sharp as a sword, and she sighed. He was still too strong, even with a knife sticking out of his throat. She had been changing up her killing techniques, not wanting her reputation as heartripper to spread, but now she didn't have much choice. *Heart it was.*

She forced her blade out of his neck and through his chest.

The man lurched against the wall, and she frowned. Still not dead. She pushed the blade deeper. He was stronger than she was used to.

"A little harder, heart," a voice said close to her ear. "Need to get through the ribs."

Isla startled, and the man she had pinned beneath her blade lunged, but a strong hand curled over hers, keeping her steady. With

his added strength, she went right through his heart. The man slumped down the wall.

Isla turned slowly to face Grim, who was looming over her. She swallowed. Excuses filled her mind. She opened her mouth to voice one of them, but Grim tilted his head at her, daring her to try to explain her way out of it.

He seemed amused by the shock on her face. "You didn't really think I didn't know what you were up to, did you?" She froze. How much did he know? He raised a brow. "Beautiful woman wearing snakes and killing wretched men with blades through their hearts? The *heartripper.*" He stepped toward her. "That could only be my wife."

She just blinked at him. "You—you don't . . . care?" He wasn't upset. He wasn't disgusted. There was something about him seeing the worst of her—and not flinching.

He shrugged a shoulder. "Kill anyone you want, heart, especially these bastards. Kill me, if it will make you feel better."

A stone sunk in her stomach, knowing the prophecy.

A moment later, she had him against the wall, dagger to his throat.

Grim didn't so much as look at the blade. He only looked at her. Eyes never leaving hers, he reached up and slowly dragged her dagger down his chest, cutting through fabric and skin, until it reached his heart. Then, he patted her hand and said, "Go ahead. It's yours anyway."

Her chest was heaving. Her every nerve was aflame. For one gleaming moment, it was just them, the way it had been before. They were just inches apart, only her blade between them, but she wanted—*needed*—to be closer. She went on her toes just as he leaned forward. Their lips just nearly touched, and she gasped.

The dagger slipped from her fingers, made slick from all the blood, but he caught it on its way down, and gently—ever so gently—slid it back into the pocket against her thigh, the metal curving slightly around it. He didn't drop his hand. His bloody fingertips slowly trailed

up her leg, and she was suddenly burning. He gripped her hips, and she ached for him.

Then, in a flash, he swung her around, so she was the one with her back pressed against the wall. He raked his fingers up the sides of her stomach, pulling her shirt up in the process, until his thumbs curled around the bottom of her chest.

They were both covered in blood, but she didn't care. She couldn't think straight.

His lips slipped down her jaw, her neck. He dragged his teeth across her pulse and made a deep sound of approval. His voice rumbled against her throat as he said, "I love it when I make your heart race."

Her sensitive chest tightened. She was desperate for more.

This was wrong, it was so wrong, but she also didn't want him to stop.

"Hearteater. As far as I'm concerned, you killed me the day you met me. I've never been the same." His lips trailed back up, across the corner of her mouth, all the way to her ear before he whispered, "I'll see you at the alter tomorrow."

Then he disappeared, leaving her pressed against the wall.

CLASP

Isla had hoped for storms. Not only for another chance at finding the portal, but also because they might have wiped away the tents that had been built outside the castle, for the wedding festivities.

None had arrived. Excitement for a distraction had only grown among the people.

A Nightshade ruler had never taken a wife before.

That morning, there was a knock on her door, and a group of women filed inside. They painted her nails and her features, and brushed her hair, and put jewels on her wrists, all without saying a word to her. She wasn't sure if they were ordered not to speak to her, or if they simply didn't want to, but she sat in silence, waiting—*hoping*—for the stormfinch to sing. It just stared at her.

When they were done, she had red smeared on her lips, just like the first time she had ever seen Grim. She had kohl on her eyes. She had pink on her cheeks. It all accentuated her natural features, but Isla hadn't worn so much makeup in a long while. Her hair was left down, but the front pieces were pinned back by clips coated in black diamonds.

The dress left on her bed wasn't the one she had been married in. No, that one was in the wardrobe. She had seen it and blocked it with her other dresses, because every time she saw the fabric, all she could think about was how Grim had *removed* it, and there was no room for any of those thoughts, especially after what had happened the night prior.

A mistake.

Agreeing to this wedding was a mistake. It was getting far too easy to *forget,* and that had always been her problem, hadn't it?

The dress was black, the requisite color for a Nightshade bride. It was strapless, perfect for putting her necklace on full display. The bodice was tight, and then there was tulle beneath her skirts, making it wider. There were long black gloves that slipped easily over her bracelets. They reached far past her elbows. They reminded her of Celeste's gloves. They reminded her of the gloves she had worn at the Centennial, the one she had wrapped around her eyes, when she had struck the crown—

Off Oro's head.

No. She needed to forget him. She was marrying his enemy.

Again.

There was a knock. It was time.

She opened the door and was relieved to see a familiar face. *Astria.* She threw her arms around her, before she could think better of it. They barely knew each other. Still . . . she was the closest person she had.

Astria let out a shocked laugh. "You'll cut your dress," she said, but Isla was careful with the swords. She sighed and stepped back.

"How do I look?" she asked her cousin.

Astria lifted a shoulder. "Painfully beautiful."

Isla raised a brow. "No insult?"

She shrugged. "I'm sure I'll think of something before the night is over." She took Isla's arm in hers and walked her down the corridor.

"He sent you, didn't he?"

Astria nodded. "He thought you might want . . . family."

"Are there a lot of people there?"

"Anyone who could make the trip, did," she said. "The ones who can't see the ceremony will be at the festivities afterward. They'll go on for more than a day."

"What are Nightshade weddings usually like?" Astria had been at her original one, but it had been quick and nontraditional. They hadn't had an audience. Grim had made it special.

"There's a ceremony," she said. "Some sort of hand ritual. Then, necklaces are presented, as is custom." She nodded toward Isla. "You already have yours, of course."

Isla froze. Was she supposed to have one for Grim?

Astria dragged her along, not missing a beat. "This is where I become useful," she said, pulling a simple chain from her pocket. It reminded her of the one Grim had worn during the curses, with the charm that made him impervious to them. She handed it to Isla. "A family heirloom."

Isla took it. It was cold and smooth against her fingers. She gripped it like an anchor through her confusing emotions as Astria continued to lead her through the castle. She wasn't sure where they were going, until they reached the end of the wing.

Then, she remembered.

The Nightshade castle had always made her feel like she was drowning in ink. Every surface was black. Most windows had been built over during the curses, and the floors were gleaming sheets of dark marble. It felt like being underground, trapped, without any sunlight or nature.

But, on its edge sat an orb of life.

Grim had built it for her.

It was a greenhouse. The walls were glass, and every shade and shape of flower bloomed before her. A fountain sat at its center, with a statue of a smiling woman holding her tiny dragon, flowers in her hair and between her fingers.

Standing in front of it was Grim.

There were hundreds of people in the room. Watching. Judging. Even more were outside, observing from beyond the glass.

But it might as well just have been them.

He was wearing armor without spikes and his shining black cape. Her own dress had a sheer cape with roses knitted into the fabric, a nod to her Wildling realm.

Grim had chosen this place. He must have known it would feel like home. He must have known it would mean a lot to her that he had included the Wildlings, who had their own section right behind him.

She remembered Grim presenting the greenhouse to her. It was her wedding present. She had always bemoaned the lack of color and life here, so he had built her this. A spot of life in Nightshade, just for her, his Wildling wife.

She stepped forward.

The crowd watched her. Some looked curious. Others regarded her like an abomination.

Grim looked at her the same way he had at their first ceremony. Like she was the beginning and end of his world. Like he would be content to live in this very moment forever.

He broke into a smile. People whispered. They seemed unnerved by it. She wondered if his people had ever seen him smile.

He reached out his hand.

She took it.

When she turned, she finally noticed the woman behind Grim, the one who would be handling the ceremony.

Eta. The leader of the prophet-followers. She frowned. Why was she here? She hadn't even considered that she left the mountain.

Had Grim made the climb again to ask? Had they let him in this time?

She didn't seem to be the only one surprised by Eta's presence. Members of Grim's court—and many of the guests—whispered, watching.

"Today, it is my honor to join the ruler of Nightshade with the ruler of Wildling. A powerful union that has not existed in millennia."

She paused and looked around meaningfully at the guests. "A union that was fated. A partnership that was *written*."

Silence, then whispers. She guessed many on Nightshade held the prophet's opinion in high regard, because many in the crowd gasped at this revelation.

Grim's idea to have the wedding to gain support for their union was working.

She was told to face Grim. To raise her hand. He was told to meet it. His hand was huge, engulfing hers. His fingers gently slid against her own, callouses scraping. Sparks whispered down her arm at his touch.

"The clasp," Eta said, and Isla assumed she meant the necklace, the one she had for Grim. She dropped it in the prophet-follower's grip with her other hand.

Eta tied the necklace between their fingers, joining them, the chain wrapping around and around. She supposed if it wasn't already around her neck, her own would be part of the ceremony too.

"And now, they are bound, until their last breath," Eta said. She nodded at her, and Isla undid the necklace's clasp.

Grim bowed before her. There were a few whispers, murmurs, indignation that the great ruler would bow to her, but she ignored them.

He lowered his head. For a moment, she hesitated.

Once the necklace was clasped, it wouldn't ever be released, not until his death. She remembered the prophecy.

Would it be at her hand?

Part of her wanted to drop the necklace. Run out of the room.

But she was Grim's bride. It was a decision she had made, in the past, and now, again, in the present. As much as she hated it, as much as she wished things were different . . . she cared about him. She really did.

Isla clasped the necklace.

It was done.

Grim stood, towering over her. His eyes were glistening. He took her hand. Music began to play. People began to form around them, circling them. "Now, we dance. It marks the start of the festivities."

She nodded. She could do this. She could stand here and pretend like emotions weren't thrashing within her, battling. Like she wasn't both radiantly happy and horribly disappointed in herself. Like her heart wasn't currently breaking and mending at the same time. Like it wasn't split to begin with.

His other hand went to her waist.

"I didn't know you were capable of dancing," she told him, as he moved through the steps with surprising precision. It was easy, he was leading her in a circle, but he did it perfectly.

Grim tilted his head at her. "I'm capable of anything, with the right motivation."

"And the motivation right now?"

"Not stepping on my wife's toes."

She swallowed. Looking at him was too painful. No, not painful. Too familiar. Too *pleasurable*. She wanted to hate this. Her gaze returned to the glass, to all the flowers around them.

"Did I make the right choice?"

She nodded. That, she could admit. "It's my favorite part of the castle." She smiled. "I was so touched that I cried when I saw it," she said, the memory fresh in her mind. She turned to face him again. "You thought I didn't like it and were prepared to fire all of your gardeners."

The ghost of a grin played on his lips. "I was prepared to *kill* all of the gardeners, heart," he gently corrected, and she wasn't even sure if he was joking.

Afterward, she had demonstrated to him just how much she had liked it, right here, against the greenhouse glass. She blushed. That time right after their marriage had been a frenzy, a race to who could know each other most intimately.

Grim's hand flexed against her lower back, as he felt her shift in emotions.

Isla was quick to change the subject. She didn't remember ever giving him a marriage gift. She hadn't known it was custom. She frowned. "Did—did I ever give you anything?"

Grim looked at her, and this time he did smile. "Heart," he said, eyes glistening again. "You gave me everything."

She looked at him. Really looked at him. For a moment, she allowed the iciness to thaw. She allowed herself to feel the emotions guilt had buried away.

She loved him.

It wasn't something she could change.

Grim's leg pressed slightly against hers as he twirled her, and she watched him frown. Slowly, one of his hands dipped, knuckles trailing down her thigh—and the dagger she had strapped to it.

"Is this for me?" he asked, voice faintly amused.

Their faces were just inches apart as she said, "Maybe."

He held her closer, lips brushing down her temple, and said, "Wait until the end of the song, at least."

For a moment, she allowed herself to melt into him. To pretend that this wedding was done purely out of love and celebration, and not as an elaborate distraction. She let herself fall fully into his gaze, their eyes locked like a vow, speaking to each other without words, the way only people who knew each other could. The way only people who had fought distant dangers and sacrificed their lives for each other could.

Grim made an amused sound as he brushed against her waist, and the hidden pockets there. She had tucked throwing stars inside.

He clicked his tongue, then leaned down to say into her ear, "Only my wife would come to her own wedding armed to the teeth."

Isla's hands slowly dropped down his chest, smoothing across the rough material he always wore. "Only my husband would know the places I keep my blades in the first place."

The corner of his lip twitched upward. "You forget I know you, wife." He leaned in closer, so his words were pressed right against her ear. "I know you have a blade here." He touched the curve of her arm. "And here." He gently stroked the pins in her hair that yes, she had sharpened into weapons, should she need them. "And here." His fingers ran up her thigh past the other blade—dangerously high, almost to her hip—to where she kept yet another dagger. He brushed against it, leaving blooming heat behind, and she swallowed. He straightened again.

"That's all you know about me? Where I keep my weapons?"

He shook his head. "No."

"Tell me."

His face turned serious. He leaned in, so only she could hear him. "I know you prefer the other wedding dress but didn't wear it, because you want it to stay ours. I know you hate that we're dancing in front of a crowd right now. I know you're hoping a storm will interrupt the ceremony, so it can all be over." He leaned in even farther. "I know you have nightmares every night, and it kills me—*kills* me—that I'm not there to hold you through them, the way I was before. So, instead I send whatever I can. Your favorite foods. Your favorite flowers. I know you've killed dozens of people who should have rotted in our prisons long ago, and I know why you do it. To keep the beast within at bay. To funnel your anger and skills into something that maybe looks sort of like *good*."

Her breath hiked. How could he know that? He must have felt her jolt of surprise, because he pressed his forehead to hers.

"I know that, because you and me, we are the same shade, Hearteater. I knew it the day you stabbed me through the chest while our lips were still locked. I knew it when you looked at me with such hatred, such fury, but never *fear* . . . not even knowing who I was, and what I had done." His lips brushed across her cheek. She wasn't sure she was breathing. "I knew it when you gave up your life for mine, because for you . . . only for you . . . I would do the same."

Grim gently pulled away. His eyes burned into hers, as he gently tucked a loose lock of hair behind her ear. "You are the only person who has ever seen any good past all the blood on my hands, Hearteater."

And he was the only one who hadn't made her feel shame for who and what she was.

"You see, I used to have nightmares too, heart." He did? She must have looked surprised, because he said, "You wouldn't know. They all stopped when I met you."

The nightmares stopped.

Something sank through her chest, something she had buried deep inside, bottled for fear of what it would to do to her.

Something like trust.

They were still dancing. For the last few minutes, she had almost forgotten she was in the center of her own wedding, but when Grim spun her around, she spotted a smirking solider. Someone she recognized. She had faced him on the battlefield.

That trust wilted.

These people . . . they had been killing her friends just weeks before. They had been attacking *her.* Now they just stood to the side, drinking from black goblets and murmuring.

If anyone on Lightlark saw her, right now, twirling around with the ruler of Nightshade, as his *bride,* they would be disgusted.

She was a traitor. She was a villain. She was everything they said she was.

Grim was right. They were the same. No one could understand her mistakes the way he could.

She wasn't sure if that was a good thing.

He tenderly moved her head so their gazes met again. "I know you're still angry. I know you don't yet forgive me. Tell me what to do, and I'll do it. Tell me how to fix this."

Her eyes burned. For all of their good memories, there were bad ones, things she didn't know if she could ever forgive. "I—I don't know."

Grim nodded. For several moments they danced in silence, looking away from each other. In the absence of words, she thought about the betrayals. The heartbreak. He seemed to sense her anger and sadness, because he said, "Don't worry. It'll be over soon."

She laughed without humor. "And then what? They'll all watch as you take me to bed?" The way they were watching them now, as if expecting their every movement, looking for lies, it wouldn't shock her.

His eyes darkened for just a moment at the mention of it. Then, he frowned. "Of course not."

The music was slowing. The song was nearly over. "Good," she said, getting close to him. To the crowd, it must have looked like she was leaning close to her husband, to whisper something loving into his ear. "Don't even think about visiting my chambers tonight."

Then, the song was over. And he should feel lucky, she thought, that she didn't reach for her blade.

Drink was served by the barrel. She sipped from a glass and frowned. It would take a while to get used to the thick, strong Nightshade wine. The ones Grim chose for dinner were lighter, more floral.

He did know her. Every single thing she touched or consumed in this castle had been carefully hand-selected by him.

Her people, at least, seemed to be enjoying themselves. She counted all of them. Every single one of her people was invited, but two. Terra and Poppy.

Some small part of her felt guilty not having them there. They, out of anyone, had been with her the most in her life. They had raised her.

She buried the feeling down. Just like Grim, they had betrayed her. They had betrayed her *mother.* And, more than that, it wasn't as

if this wedding meant anything. The true one had happened many months prior. This was just a show.

Everyone was dancing. The party had moved outside, beyond the greenhouse. Music was played in wild plucks, people swayed in the grass, there was laughter, and smiles, and *celebration*. Grim had been right. The ceremony would raise spirits. It would foster hope.

He was on the other side of the lawn, speaking to members of his court. She took a long sip of her drink and wondered if she was supposed to be staying by his side. If everyone would believe it was odd that she wasn't. Somehow, he seemed to sense her gaze, because his eyes met hers. He raised his drink toward her, in a silent cheer. She gave her best attempt at a smile, still angry from the end of their previous conversation.

It must have looked more like a grimace, because a moment later, a voice behind her said, "Very convincing. You look more inclined to murder me in my bed than to lie with me in it."

She turned to the side, where Grim had portaled, and gave him her sweetest smile. "Really? And I was trying so hard to mask my true feelings."

He barked a laugh, and the people around looked genuinely concerned. She wondered if they had ever seen their ruler even chuckle. "You're scaring the guests," she murmured against the rim of her glass.

Grim looked faintly amused. He opened his mouth to say something, but, just then, a guard frantically rushed over. He whispered something to Grim. He only nodded, not letting a hint of trouble show on his face.

She knew better. "What is it?"

He motioned for her to follow.

She wasn't the only one who had seen the guard, who had sensed his panic. The celebration seemed to wane. People were watching them, stopping their conversations. Some began to whisper. She didn't

know what the guard had told Grim, but it couldn't be good. And this was meant to be a distraction.

So, she grabbed Grim by the shoulders, pressed him against the nearest tree, and kissed him.

At first, he looked alarmed, eyes opened wide.

Then, he seemed to forget all his people were watching, or he just didn't care, because he threaded his fingers through her hair, cradled the back of her neck, and kissed her ravenously.

His tongue swept into her mouth and his taste—she had almost forgotten. Had almost forgotten how one brush of his tongue inside her mouth melted down all of her emotions and forged them into a single gleaming, unrelenting want. She groaned before stifling the sound, but it only made the act more convincing. His thumbs grazed her throat as he held her, calluses scraping, making her shiver, until he reached her necklace. With a sharp movement, he pulled the diamond and growled into her ear, as if the word had escaped, "Mine."

In response, she pulled the chain around his neck, forcing his lips back to hers, and said against them, in a voice she hardly recognized, "*Mine.*"

That seemed to be his undoing. He turned her around in a flash, her spine hitting the bark, and dragged his lips down her neck, toward her chest. Her breathing hitched, ending in a high-pitched sound only he could hear. He rumbled his approval against her collarbone.

There were cheers, somewhere. The music became louder.

This was likely enough of a distraction, but the drink made her bold enough to chase exactly what she wanted, so she moved his hands down her body, slowly, exactly where she had imagined them for weeks, and he made a low sound of pure need. One hand gripped her hip bone, thumb making broad strokes across the thin fabric, inching toward the center of her need. His other swept down her spine, her nerves raw and full of want, before stopping just short of her backside,

as if he had finally realized that everyone was watching. No. She didn't want him to stop. She rose on her toes, so that his hand slid, and he laughed darkly against her lips.

Her own fingers trailed down his chest, exploring, remembering, pressing against muscle like stone. She didn't want any fabric between them, she wanted to feel him, feel the heat that was currently pressing against her stomach dragging through every aching part of her. She broke the kiss to whisper, "Carry me," into his ear, and then she was off her feet. He turned—

And they weren't at their wedding anymore.

No. They were on a cliffside. He was still carrying her. They were both breathing far too quickly.

"That was convincing," he said. His voice was casual, but his eyes were like two pools of ink, darkened with want. He looked like he was on the edge of his sanity. Like one word from her could snap his control completely.

Part of her was relieved he had known it was an act. The other part wondered what would have happened if Grim had portaled them into their room instead.

"What did the guard tell you?" she asked.

At that, his gaze returned to normal. He set her down. "He told me that."

She turned, and any heat she had felt before withered away. They were at the burial site they had visited just weeks before.

And the graves had been destroyed. Dirt was everywhere. Ash had been scattered.

Anger flashed in Grim's eyes. It was enormously disrespectful to the dead. She knew that, but it wasn't what made dread sink through her chest.

This wasn't a simple job. Hundreds of graves had been desecrated. It had been done quickly, for guards typically monitored these sites. It was only empty because of their wedding.

There was something else. A single serpent, waiting in the center of one of the dug-up mounds. It rattled its tail, then sank back into the dirt. *Follow the snakes.*

This was the work of a Wildling.

She reached behind her, down the back of her wedding dress. Her starstick was warm in her palm.

"Where are you going?" Grim asked.

She didn't answer. She left her husband on the cliff. In her dress, the bottom now muddied, she swept into her family's stronghold.

Isla found them in the dining room of the castle. Poppy was sniffling, eyes red and bloodshot like she had been crying. Terra sat next to her, eating dinner in silence.

Poppy jumped up when she saw her. "Litt—Isla," she said. "You came to see us." She saw the expression on her face and frowned.

Isla couldn't find it in her heart to feel badly. No, not when she felt such anger. Such conviction. Her smile was pure hostility as she walked toward them. She hardly recognized her own voice as she said, "Everyone was at my wedding . . . everyone except the two of you."

Terra looked up at her, bored. "We're aware. Poppy's been crying about it for hours."

"That's how I know."

Poppy frowned. "What do you mean?"

"How I know it was *you*. You killed the nightbane. You destroyed the gravesite. *You* are the traitors I was warned about, you want me dead!" Her head pulsed. Something stirred painfully in her veins, like her power was rising, fighting against the bracelets' hold. "My parents weren't enough for you, were they? You needed to kill me too?"

Poppy looked at Terra. She looked . . . almost afraid. "Isla . . . are you all right?"

Terra got to her feet. "Enough, you sputtering fool," she said. This was it, wasn't it? Isla reached for the blade on her thigh.

Poppy gasped at the sight of it.

Terra's frown only deepened. "We didn't kill the nightbane. We didn't destroy any gravesite. And, for the last time, we did not kill your parents."

Lies. Liars.

"Stop lying to me!" she said, and she felt her power flare in her chest, felt it be stopped by the metal. Her heart was hammering. Her eyes burned.

They had never loved her. They had never cared for her. All they had done was *lie to her, and betray her, and use her.*

She clutched her necklace, before she could stop herself. Grim was there in half a moment.

"I want them imprisoned."

Poppy cried out.

Grim looked unsure. "Heart, are you—"

"I said I want them imprisoned," she said. She could feel something in her chest unfurling. Rage and vengeance spreading. "Or does my word mean nothing here? Am I ruler simply by name? Is my throne a prop? Does this marriage mean anything to you?"

He swallowed. "If this is what you wish."

It was what she wished.

She strode out of the castle, away from Poppy's cries and Terra's curses.

WRITTEN

Her guardians were the traitors. She shouldn't be surprised. They had betrayed her before. So why did it hurt so badly? Why did it make her question everything?

"You're making a mistake," Wren told her.

No. She was finally finding the strength to rid her realm of those who would rise against her.

Did they not understand that the future of all their realms hung in the balance? Did they not see that a *storm worse than any before* was coming?

Did they think she *wanted* to imprison some of the only people she had ever loved? Did they think it made her feel *good?*

Of course not. They didn't know she was on borrowed time, that she had just *weeks* left to make these hard decisions, to change her fate and save them all, even if it broke her heart. Even if it broke *her.*

There had to be another way to find the ring—at whatever cost.

The blacksmith didn't look particularly happy to see her. He didn't even turn to face her; instead he continued to work diligently as he said, "It isn't time."

"I'm aware." She had been counting down the time he had left almost as closely as she tracked her own. The end of winter—the end of the storm season—marked both of their deaths, even if he didn't know it. "Do you have a device that can track something?"

"Be more specific."

Her voice had an edge. "I lost a ring. I need to find it."

He paused his work. Gently put down one of the large metal tools he had been holding. “No. I used to, many millennia ago, made from the blood of a ruler with a tracking flair. But it was lost, and his ability with it.”

Lost.

“And that’s it? There isn’t any other way?”

He shook his head.

That might have been the end of it . . . but he had paused slightly. For a fraction of a second.

“There is, isn’t there?”

He sighed and turned to face her, looking tired. “Not one that is practical.”

“But possible?”

The blacksmith shook his head. “I suppose. But—”

“Tell me.”

He studied her. “The person I’m speaking of . . . the ruler with the tracking flair. He bound his power to a marking.”

She frowned. She didn’t know that could be done. “What does that mean?”

He leaned his massive arm against the side of his worktable. “It is part of an ancient, dangerous art. When crafted correctly, markings have power. They can call upon ability long lost.”

Isla took a step forward. “You’re talking about skyres, aren’t you?”

The blacksmith stilled. His forge seemed to still with him. “What did you just say?”

“Skyres.”

He blinked, as though clearing cobwebs from his mind. “How do you know about that?”

She wasn’t about to tell him about her visit to the augur, though the blacksmith almost certainly knew he existed. They were both obsessed with powerful blood, for very different reasons. She held his gaze, unblinking. Shrugged a shoulder.

"You will get yourself killed."

"I'm dying anyway," she spat back.

He frowned. Shook his head. "It's unnatural. I've seen even the most honorable people transformed into demons over time. Like all power, using skyres has a cost. Often, it's your soul."

Chills rippled down her arms, as if his very words contained power. As if he was giving her an omen.

She had been warned against power before. From Oro. From Grim, even.

But there was only a month and a half of winter left. Now she was getting desperate. If extending her life, if saving all those bound to it, had a cost . . . it only made sense that it would be her.

"Tell me."

He shook his head. "I cannot. I don't know much about them; it was a lost art even in the otherworld. Even if I had the completed skyre from the tracker, I wouldn't know how to help you use it. Doing it wrong has disastrous results. It's best you don't even try."

She stared at him for one second. Two. "What do you mean, the *completed* skyre?"

The blacksmith heaved a heavy sigh and turned to face his wall of weapons. He looked through rows of daggers before he found the one he was looking for.

"This is half of the marking: his personal flair. All I know is the rest should be made up of one of the original skyres."

She asked for a piece of parchment and a quill. Slowly, she traced over the marking, until the lines were perfectly imprinted on her page.

"It won't work for your purpose," he warned. "A tracking skyre needs to be bound with—or onto—a portion of what you're looking for. The marking helps each piece call to the others. It forms a connection."

And she didn't have a piece of the ring. Or the storm within it . . .

Azul hadn't enchanted it; it didn't contain his blood. There wasn't an easy way to find it, even if she could figure out the skyre.

She was back at the beginning of her search, but something about the markings made her curious. Perhaps there were others that could help her now.

"Thank you," she said to the blacksmith. He might not know the art of skyres. The augur might not either.

But she knew someone who had.

They were dead now.

Though . . . perhaps that didn't mean the information was lost.

Back in her room, the feather's tip glimmered slightly in the light. She picked it up carefully, ready to drop it at any second.

Isla had to know whether the small markings she had seen on the Starling's pale skin—during a rare time she had allowed her long gloves to slip down her arms—were the symbols she was searching for.

Do you know how to draw skyres? Isla wrote.

She watched the feather rise with bated breath, as the feather wrote:

Yes.

Isla couldn't trust Aurora. She knew that better than anyone. She herself had plunged a blade through her former best friend's heart.

Aurora would betray her just like she had before. It would be foolish to follow anything the dead Starling said.

Still, before she had shoved the feather back in the drawer, she had asked,

Would you teach me?

The answer was immediate. *Yes.*

Why would you help me?

There was a minute of nothing. Two. Then, the feather rose and wrote, *Redemption.*

It was a word Isla identified with, though she still didn't trust her. There had to be another way to find the portal. Something she was missing.

That night, she funneled her rage and pain into visiting three different towns. Hunting down those who had wronged others.

By the time she reached her rooftop, she was starving. Thirsty. Sairsha and her usual basket of goods awaited her. They hadn't seen each other in days.

"The little savior is tired," Sairsha said, stretching her legs long across the roofing. There was the aftermath of a pastry in her lap, crumbs everywhere.

"Don't call me that," Isla said weakly, sinking to the place next to her.

Sairsha only smirked. "Is heartripper preferable?"

Isla winced at the name. It wasn't the worst she had been called. The truth was carved out of her. "No. I don't like names, or titles. They come with expectations. And I so often fall short of them."

A ruler of Wildling who didn't live among her people. A ruler of Starling, who had given her position up, since she wasn't the best choice. A wife of a Nightshade she would likely betray, because it made sense to kill Grim to fulfill the prophecy, if they were all going to die anyway. It was a thought she had kept suppressed, but the weeks of winter were dwindling down without progress.

They were all going to die. Because Grim gave her life.

She shut her eyes against the images. The ash. The bodies. She was responsible for so much death, and there was so much more to come.

Isla felt something smooth against her hand. Sairsha had placed a bottle of wine in it. She was shaking her head at her. "Don't do that. Don't underestimate yourself, when you're trying. So many people never bother. They decide they can't make a difference, so they don't even try. And trying . . . that's the hardest part. Not succeeding, but all the trying it takes to get there."

Isla raised a brow at Sairsha. "You sound like an expert."

Sairsha laughed. "No. But I had a sister once, and she told me the same thing. I'm just repeating her words. She—now *she* was truly a

savior. Half our village was in the path of a landslide. Every storm, it would get worse. She was determined to stop it, even though everyone told her it was impossible. Inevitable."

"Did she stop it?"

Sairsha's smile was sad. "No. She was buried under the rubble while trying."

Isla's throat worked. She wondered if the prophecy, and her fate, was her own form of a landslide.

Inevitable.

After a few moments of silence, Sairsha turned to her and said, "Why do you do this? Why do you care about us?"

Isla fiddled with the cap at the top of the wine bottle Sairsha had handed her. How much to say? Lies were easier to tell when wrapped with truth. "I want to make amends. Get redemption . . . for the things I've done." She noticed how easily she echoed the feather. Echoed *Aurora*.

Sairsha nodded sagely. Her eyes went to the knives and sword on Isla's waist, and she wondered if the woman was thinking about how much blood had crusted on those blades. Isla drank some of the wine and winced at its sour bite.

"I joined a group out of a need for redemption too," Sairsha admitted. "I was a thief on the streets when I happened upon them. They gave me hope that my skills could be used for something good. Something important."

Isla wondered what group Sairsha was talking about; but when she opened her mouth to ask, she found she couldn't form words. Her face had gone still. Her vision began to swim in front of her. Sairsha's concerned face became a blur.

She needed to go. Something was wrong. Isla's hands gripped the rooftop to lift off of it; but her limbs were useless, buckling beneath her. She fell over onto the roof with a thud.

Sairsha's distorted face peered at her from overhead.

Isla had consumed dozens of gifts during her conversations with Sairsha.

Only one had been poisoned.

Isla awoke coated in sweat. Her hair clung to the side of her face, and there was a rushing sound, a roaring. Still, even over it, she could hear her heart. It was pounding desperately, as if in warning, saying *get up. Get up. Get up!*

Her eyes flew open, and that was when she saw the roaring sound was a river. There was a tiny island in the middle of it, a massive stone that the water churned around. She had awoken in its center.

Around her stood a group of people she recognized from the bar.

They had changed. Instead of their worn clothes, they now wore flowing robes, with hoods that cast shadows across their faces. Each was belted with a scabbard and sword.

"What—what are you doing?"

The bald man she knew as Ragan stared at her, eyes gleaming with something like excitement. Something like hope.

Two men stood next to him; she'd exchanged polite nods with them once or twice before.

Then, standing the farthest away, was Sairsha. She had the nerve to smile at her.

Isla wasn't bound. They hadn't even taken her weapons. Fools. "So. You know who I am."

Sairsha's smile widened. "Yes," she said, far too enthusiastically. "We know exactly who you are." What were they going to do, sell her for ransom? Imprison her?

Had Sairsha planned this trap the entire time?

Isla slowly rose and realized with a shot of horror that while they hadn't taken her weapons, they *had* taken her starstick. "What do you

want?" She motioned at her daggers. "If you wanted to kill me, you really should have taken these." They wouldn't know their lives were bound to hers. She wondered how much she should say.

Sairsha laughed. It was a pleasant sound, completely contrary to the circumstances. "Kill you? Quite the opposite." She stepped forward. All the others did too, pulsing like a living body. With them surrounding her, there was no backing away, only backing toward one of them. Sairsha's smile brightened, her eyes wide and reverent. "Isla Crown, we have waited hundreds of years for you."

She couldn't have heard her correctly. This . . . this had to be a dream. Her head was still pulsing with pain, from the poison. "What are you—"

"This is your destiny. It is written."

"No." Her voice barely made a sound.

They were prophet-followers.

"What's going on?" Isla's eyes were wild. She turned in all directions. She was surrounded.

Metal sliced through the night as they each pulled swords from their scabbards in one fluid motion. They dug the blades into the rock and did something Isla never expected. They went to a knee before her.

"Please," Sairsha said, her voice thick with emotion. "Accept our gifts."

They rose at once.

Gifts? Did they think she was raising an army? Isla didn't understand.

"You . . . you're confused," Isla said, turning quickly, afraid to give any of them her back.

"No," Ragan said, his voice booming. "The prophet never made mistakes. Everything that was written has come to pass."

Sairsha's eyes gleamed with fervor. She was buzzing with energy, and so were the others. As if something big was about to happen. Isla

felt the same dread, the same prickling on the back of her neck, that had come just before the breaking of the storm. "I wish you could read his teachings. His book is full of wonders. And you . . . he spoke so much about you."

"What did he say?" she demanded. Eta had hinted at her destiny.

Sairsha smiled. "He said that at the end of the world, a girl will be born from life and death. The girl will either destroy the world . . . or save it. She would be either a curse . . . or remedy." Sairsha's grin grew even wider. She was shaking with excitement as she said, "Don't you see? You are the girl. The one that was promised."

Isla shook her head. Tried to back away. These were fanatics.

Sairsha still smiled as tears streamed down her face. She was so, so happy. And Isla didn't understand at all. Her smile never faltered as she said, "We were chosen to help you. We have waited so long for you to be revealed to us."

Chosen? By who? For what?

"We offer ourselves to you," Ragan said, volunteering his sword for her to take. "And hope we are worthy."

She tentatively took the sword by the hilt, not knowing what was going on, but certain that she would rather it be in her grip than his.

Ragan smiled wide. He closed his eyes.

And ran himself through with the blade.

Isla screamed, the sound filling the world. Her ears began ringing. She dropped the sword, and his body along with it. Blood pooled at her feet. She hadn't wanted to kill him . . . but he was dead.

What had he done?

What had *she* done?

Something in her chest flickered, almost in satisfaction. That didn't make sense. She didn't *want* to kill. She didn't *want* to feel as though she had gained something from it.

Grim's words from their wedding were in her head: *I know you've killed dozens of people who should have rotted in our prisons long ago, and I know why you do it. To keep the beast within at bay.*

There was a beast inside of her, she had known that for a while. It enjoyed taking life.

But that wasn't who she was.

Isla slowly looked up from the body, only to see the rest of them smiling at her, offering her their own swords. She backed away as much as she could. "What are you doing? What is wrong with you?"

Sairsha shook her head. "Don't be concerned, Promised," she said, smile still bright on her face. "You will take us somewhere else. Somewhere better."

What was she talking about? She couldn't promise them anything.

"Please," Isla said steadily. "Just give me my portaling device. Let me go. I don't want any part of this."

"But it's the part you must play," Sairsha said. "It has been written."

They pushed forward in unison, and Isla was forced to put her own blade up.

"I won't kill you," she said, backing away, shooting a look at the wild waters behind her. If she could make it in the river, the current would help her get away.

But she needed her starstick. In the wrong hands, it could be ruinous.

She could clutch her necklace. Summon Grim. But that would likely lead to everyone here dead, and that was exactly what she was trying to avoid.

"Oh, but you must," Sairsha said. She put her arms to the side, baring herself for a blow.

No. She refused. This was madness.

Sairsha's face fell. "We hoped you would understand. But you still have much to discover." She looked to the others. "We insist."

"I said *no*," Isla repeated. "Leave me alone. I'm not the person you're looking for. I am not the girl. I have not been *promised*."

Sairsha smiled again. "You are *everything* he said you would be."

Then, she struck.

Isla folded over with the blow. She hadn't been expecting the hilt to the face. Blood ran down her temple. The act of having killed Ragan swirled in her chest, burning, unleashing feelings she didn't want to harbor.

Hunger. Part of her wanted this fight.

When Sairsha went back for another hit, Isla kicked her square in the chest. Sairsha flew across the rock, landing on her back. Good. She didn't have to kill them. She just needed to subdue them, get her starstick, and leave.

It seemed they were intent on forcing her hand, though.

The men she had never spoken to shot forward, and, suddenly, she found herself fighting against two swords. Their blades sliced the night sky to pieces, and she grunted as she worked, still tired from whatever poison they had given her. She managed to hit one man in the face with her hilt, but he was relentless, returning just moments later, blood spurting from his nose.

Sairsha was on her feet again. "It doesn't have to be difficult. This death is not permanent."

Isla twisted away from a blow and just barely managed to avoid what would have been a nasty scar on her arm. "How many times do I have to tell you?" she yelled. She slipped her fingers into the pockets woven into her pants and pulled out two throwing stars. They gleamed as they flew, hitting one of the men right in the shins. He collapsed to the ground, and she hoped he stayed there. She whirled to meet the other's blade. "I am not going to kill you."

The other man came to her from behind, and she shoved him back with a hilt to the forehead. He fell back, and there was a horrible crack as his head hit the rock.

He stared back at her with empty eyes, dead.

No.

The other swung at her, and she fought back to meet his blade. This time, though, he let his sword drop. He didn't deflect her blow.

Instead of meeting metal, her blade went straight through his heart.

Ringing sounded in her ears. She backed away. No. *No.*

She looked up, and the woman's red hair had fallen from its braided crown. She was staring at her, tears glistening on her cheeks. And still, despite the blood at her feet, smiling.

"Go, Sairsha," Isla said, her voice barely a whisper. "*Please.* I won't fight you."

"But you will." Sairsha closed her eyes. She took a breath—

And her shadow began to move on its own. It peeled from the ground and rose, in Sairsha's exact shape. The shadow had a sword.

It leapt forward, wicked, baring its teeth and tearing into Isla's flesh with a bloodthirsty ruthlessness. She screamed out as the shadow's teeth sank into her shoulder, as solid as the ground beneath her feet. It was an impossible ability, a fine-tuning of Nightshade power. She hadn't even seen Grim do anything remotely like it.

Groaning, she managed to shove the shadow away, but it did not tire. If anything, it was invigorated. It leapt at her; sword raised high— and Isla ran hers right through its center. The shadow instantly dropped to the ground and melted right off the stone, ink swirling into the river.

"Thank you." Isla looked up to see Sairsha's robe soaked in blood, right in the middle. Right in the same spot she had stabbed the shadow. She collapsed.

Isla's knees buckled.

She knelt next to Sairsha, pressed her hands against the wound, ripped off part of the robe to try to stop the bleeding. It was no use. Blood puddled in her hands, and Sairsha just smiled. "Thank you for this honor."

And then she went still.

Her starstick was in Sairsha's scabbard. Isla took it in a shaking hand and stood, stepping over the bodies around her. Blood coated their robes and streamed down the rock in rivulets, before being swallowed by the river.

Isla lifted her head to the sky and screamed.

SECRETS

She arrived in her room covered in blood. Lynx growled, and Grim was there in a moment. She didn't even look at him as she passed him by. She didn't even tell him to leave as she stripped off her clothing in a pile and turned on the bath.

"Who?" he finally asked, the word as sharp as a shard of ice.

Her head rested against the side of the tub. She stared at the opposite wall and felt nothing. "Doesn't matter. They're all dead now." Her words were emotionless. He didn't have to know about their supposed prophecy, or the *promised,* or the other words that had driven them to madness. A madness they had been willing to die for.

Grim portaled the crimson-soaked clothes away. She didn't protest when he took the soap and gently helped her wash the blood from her temple, and back, and shoulders. She didn't bristle when he began slowly washing it out of her hair.

She closed her eyes and wondered why death always seemed to follow her.

"Change your mind yet?" Isla asked. Her voice was hard. Unfeeling.

The blacksmith didn't falter. "Not for a moment." He turned. "But I see that you did."

Isla didn't say a word as she held her wrists out in front of her. "I'm done pretending to be powerless," she said. If she'd had her abilities, she would have been able to get away from the sect. She could have saved them.

"My dear," he said, his gravelly voice like scraping rocks. "You've never been powerless a day in your life."

With his touch, the bracelets fell onto the table.

"I'll see you in a month," he said. Then, he got back to work.

Isla thought to herself that he seemed remarkably busy for someone who was readying himself to die.

"Light reading?" She was thumbing through a tome that was as thick as her head and could be used as a solid shield, should she ever need it.

A tracking skyre wouldn't help her find the ring, but perhaps another type would. She had hoped to find some trace of them in the library, so she wouldn't have to trust Aurora. She had gotten nowhere. The blacksmith and augur were right. It was a lost art.

Astria was standing in front of her, wearing her typical armor. She never took it off, and Isla wondered aloud if she slept in it too.

The general asked in an even tone, "What do you mean, sleep?"

Isla blinked, immediately taking herself out of the imaginary consideration for applying to be Grim's general, when Astria leaned back, and said, "A joke." She pulled what looked like a handful of nuts from her pocket and began eating them. "And the answer is: Yes, sometimes, when I'm too tired to change out of it." Her eyes slid from the nuts in her palm to Isla's book, curious.

Isla slammed it closed, emitting a formidable cloud of dust that immediately provoked the biggest sneeze of her life.

To her horror, when she opened her eyes she found a small pile of peonies in front of her, as if her hold on her abilities had momentarily slipped.

Astria stopped mid-chew, staring, her mouth agape. "Did you just . . . did you just sneeze *flowers*?"

Isla felt a flush of red creeping across her cheeks. "No."

"I *saw you*."

The petals hadn't come from her nose; that was ridiculous. Still, she knew what it looked like. Isla ran her tongue along the front of her teeth. "If you tell anyone, I'll kill you," she informed the general. "I'll go right for the gaps in your armor."

Astria folded at the waist, laughing. She laughed and laughed, voice echoing up the tower, until a small man marched out from the stacks, hand in the air—already halfway to chastising—before seeing *who* he would be speaking to. Then he abruptly turned on his heel and left. Astria continued to laugh until she reached up and dabbed at her eyes with a piece of cloth she kept in a pant pocket.

"Are you . . . *crying*?" Isla asked, incredulous.

Astria turned to her, and, with the same steady tone said, "If you tell anyone, I'll kill you."

Isla made a gesture signaling a truce.

Her cousin finally composed herself enough for Isla to break in. "So. Did he send you here to find me?" She hadn't seen Grim in a couple of days. The skies were swirling with color again, and he was preparing his people for another potential storm.

Astria gave her a sharp look. "I'm his general, not his clerk. Your wedding was a special circumstance."

"Then why are you here?" The rest of the library was relatively empty.

Astria narrowed her eyes at her. "I'm sorry, do I look like I don't read?"

Isla raised a shoulder. "Do you?"

"I do, thank you."

Isla stared at her expectantly. When Astria continued loudly chewing on her nuts, Isla asked, "What do you read?"

A nut cracked between her teeth, and she picked away a curl of skin. "A little of everything, I suppose. Some history, here and there, though those are usually horribly overwritten. Some mysteries. Romances too."

“Romance?” Isla asked, her interest piqued. She and Aurora used to trade books, but their selection had been limited. “There’s romance in this library?”

“Oh, yeah,” Astria said. “There’s a Starling writer from the last century whose works were smuggled in a few decades ago. Guess by who?” She smiled mischievously. “There are a few books by Nightshade writers as well, but many of them . . . well, many . . .” She made a face like she was vomiting.

“Many what?”

She snorted. “Many are about the ruler. Not by name, of course. But you can tell. The main characters are all tall, dark-haired, broody, powerful. It’s ridiculous how many women are in love with him.” She laughed, then stopped short, seeming to remember she was speaking to Grim’s wife. She cleared her throat. “Sorry.”

Isla didn’t care, though she would love to see the look on Grim’s face when he found out his library housed fantasies about him. She would likely wake up the next morning to the library aflame. She smiled at the thought of it.

Then her joy wilted. Lately, happiness seemed like flowers that withered before she could pluck them for herself.

She wished the book in front of her were a mystery or romance. Instead, she had been flipping through a multi-century look at how the curses had impacted society on Nightshade, hoping to find any mention of skyres. In summary: negatively.

Isla looked up at Astria, who had gone back to eating her nuts, and realized one of her greatest resources might have been right in front of her all along.

She wouldn’t ask her about the skyres; no, she couldn’t, not when her cousin was loyal to Grim. He couldn’t find out she was looking for something that would eat at her soul . . . but the augur had mentioned figuring out her history. *When you learn the truth of who you are, your path will become clear.*

Perhaps the answers she was looking for were somehow related to her parents.

"My father."

Astria slowed her chewing. "What about him?"

What about him? She started with the little she knew. He was one of the few non-rulers in history born with a flair. "How did he discover he was immune to curses?"

Astria rolled the shell of a nut between her fingers. A smile tugged at the side of her mouth, before melting back into a frown. "It was an accident. He fell asleep outside or something, and woke up to the stars. Realized the night didn't kill him."

"Was he interested in curses? Given he was immune to them?"

Astria nodded. "He would talk about the other realms' curses for hours. He pitied the Starlings. And, of course, the Wildlings." She looked pensive. "He envied Grim's flair, though. Always wanted to travel. Always wondered what was beyond our borders."

"Do you have a flair?"

She shook her head. "No. Just good at killing." She grinned, then continued to chew her snack. "You know . . ." she said after a while, then trailed off, her voice cautious, as if she hadn't yet decided whether to finish her sentence. Whatever interest she found in Isla's face seemed to convince her, because she continued, "Your father. He liked maps."

"Maps?"

She nodded. "You won't find many here, in this library. Exploration was nearly impossible during the curses. Couldn't really keep an entire crew below deck in the middle of the sea all night, right? But your father . . . he searched them out. From before the curses. Collected them. Started making his own."

"Why?"

Astria lifted a shoulder. "Who knows why he did anything he did? He always wanted to leave. He was great in his role, but he hated it. Even I saw it, and I was far younger." She was looking beyond Isla

now, as if ensnared by a memory. "When your father was eight, he built a boat out of driftwood and tried to set sail at the castle cove." She huffed. "The idiot didn't realize how big the waves were; he really thought that he could make it. No one could come rescue him, because he did it in the middle of the night, thinking it was best chance of getting away. My poor aunt sobbed at the window, watching him holding on to the boat for dear life, nearly drowning. The waves eventually washed him ashore. He was sent to training not long after."

Isla swallowed, finding her throat dry. Her father had been desperate to see outside the world he had been born into. Just like her.

"Do you have any of them?" she asked quietly, trying to keep the emotion out of her voice.

"The maps?"

Isla nodded.

"They should all still be in his room. It's untouched. He lived in the castle once he became Grim's general, but he only ever kept his most personal items in his own home."

Isla nodded, lazily paging through the useless tome in front of her, waiting for Astria to leave. After a few more minutes of conversation, she did, and Isla wasted no time falling through her puddle of stars, into her family's castle.

According to the Wildlings at the entrance, the main bedroom was on the top floor of the keep. Isla made her way up the stairs, speaking to a few of her people. They seemed more somber than usual; Terra and Poppy's imprisonment hadn't gone over well.

A few more women passed her on her way, and then she was alone, facing the last door in the hall, the only room on this side of the floor. Isla quickly realized why it had been left untouched.

The door didn't have a handle.

It didn't even have a keyhole. Isla frowned. How was she meant to get in? From the outside? She supposed she could break a window. Or simply break down this door with a weapon. Or portal in with her starstick.

She placed a hand against it to test its strength—and with the slightest touch of her fingers to the wood, the door creaked open.

Isla jumped back, almost expecting to find someone there.

But the room was empty. She hesitated on the threshold and the door opened wider, like a hand beckoning her inside.

Isla didn't know if the room was enchanted or if it recognized her as her father's blood, but it didn't matter.

At first glance, the room was nothing special. It was empty save for a mirror, bed, and wardrobe. But as she stepped forward, shadows fell from the walls like brushed away cobwebs, revealing stacks of books. Letters. And, most of all, rows and rows of maps.

Astria had been right. Her father had been born with the heart of an explorer. An entire wall was made up of layers of parchment overlapping at the edges like a quilt and painted over with meticulously drawn coastlines. She recognized Nightshade, Lightlark, and the newlands.

There were a few other shapes she hadn't seen on any other map. Unexplored areas, by the look of it.

The largest of these was far beyond Nightshade, to the west. It was a large piece of land, separated from the rest of the map by a row of tiny islands, sitting like guards. Strange. How could something that large not have been developed in all the years since the curses? It seemed special. In fact, it was the only uncharted body of land with a name, etched in with precision. Her breath caught as she read it.

No. That couldn't be right.

Its name was *Isla*.

MIRROR

Her heart thundered in her chest. This didn't make any sense. Why did her father have an island with her name on it, when he had lived here before he had ever even met her mother?

Isla.

It had to be a coincidence. Her name meant island. Perhaps it didn't mean anything at all.

But what if it did?

Isla removed that sheet of map from the wall, rolled it up, and placed it in the pocket of her cape. She moved around the room, to see if there was anything that could help her now, anything that might indicate the portal, but all she saw were letters between him and family members, detailed maps of Nightshade, and books upon books about the other realms. She flipped through one about Wildlings, read the first sentence of the middle chapter, and nearly snorted.

Wildling women have fangs that curve out of their mouths like pythons, they have claws like panthers—they drink blood in buckets.

Is that what her father had thought of the Wildlings before meeting her mother? She wondered for a moment about their story. How they met, and where, and how they had fallen in love.

Part of it she could guess, given the details she already knew. Her father had escaped with the sword, using the portaling device he had stolen from Grim. Somehow, he must have ended up on the Wildling newland. Her mother must have happened upon him, and, for some reason, they had chosen not to kill each other.

Isla swallowed, realizing how closely it matched her own story. She had somehow ended up on Nightshade, using the starstick. Grim had happened upon her. And—though she had stabbed a blade through his chest during that first meeting—they had decided not to kill each other.

Yet.

Life and darkness. Opposites in so many ways. One power created, the other destroyed. It seemed like a pairing that could never work, not really. Perhaps they were too different. Perhaps her own parents' joining had been wrong.

She remembered what the prophet-followers had said, before their death. *A girl will be born. She will either destroy the world . . . or save it.*

She wouldn't be the cause of more destruction. She would find a way to close the portal and buy herself more time. She would use that time to change her fate.

This map . . . it had to mean something.

There was only one way to find out.

Map in one hand and starstick in the other, she imagined the island in her mind's eye, felt around for it, tried to visualize it, tried to pin down its place in the world. She fell through her puddle of stars.

Then she was drowning, pulled down by a relentless current. Only her last-second instinct to reach her arm high over her head kept the map from disintegrating in the water. She had landed in the middle of the sea—a wave crested, about to pull her under again. She closed her eyes tightly and used her starstick to whisk her away. Anywhere. *Anywhere.*

She landed roughly. Her cheek was scratched from the shell-laden beach, her landing had dragged her across it. The sand was dark, volcanic ash. She peeled herself up from the ground, coughing up water, folding over, her mouth and eyes full of salt. Her fingers felt around for her map and found it damp—but whole. She carefully opened it up, tying the corners down with rocks so it could dry. She didn't have

fresh water, but once her tears cleared her vision enough to see properly, she carefully folded the map into her pocket.

Four tries later, she found herself on a wider coastline.

The rest of the islands had been barren, lifeless, but this—

This might as well have been the Wildling newland. She could see the forests from the beach, rising high. She could hear squawks and growls and the chitter of insects. She could feel endless gleaming threads, reaching toward her like fingers. This place . . . was alive. She half-expected a group of people to approach, but no one came.

She needed a better vantage point.

In the days since she'd had the bracelets removed, she had been hesitant to use her power. It had been buried so long, she feared it would rush up in an uncontrollable wave.

That was part of why she was here. According to this map, the island was far from any other inhabited land she knew of. If it was empty; it could be the perfect place for her to explore her abilities again, without fearing ruin.

She just needed to ensure it was the right location.

Breathe. It was almost as if she could hear Oro in her head. She slowly filled her lungs, wincing, her airways still dry with salt. She carefully focused her mind, like an arrow. Then, without daring open her eyes, she shot into the sky.

It was a risk. She could fall, she could propel herself too high; but for a moment, she let go of her fear, and of gravity, and her stomach dropped—

Then, there was just peace. Silence. Weightlessness.

She opened her eyes and nearly vomited. The land was so far from her feet. She gasped and fell, screaming, hands pinwheeling, before stopping herself.

Breathe, she commanded.

Hurriedly, she studied the coast, the islands nearby. She had memorized the map by now. This was it.

This was Isla.

With the rush of relief, she lost her grip on the sky, and fell—the ground rushed up to meet her.

She shot her arm out, and a burst of energy helped cushion her fall. Still, she landed roughly against the sand.

Every bone and muscle ached, but she forced herself up, because she had found it—the island only her father seemed to know about.

From the sky, she had seen just how large the island was, but tonight, she would start with this forest. As soon as she took a step inside, it seemed to quiet.

Isla went still. She couldn't believe what she was seeing.

Fruit, everywhere. Hanging plump from trees, the forest was heavy with it. The ground smelled sweet from the fruit that had fallen and broken open. She reached up and grabbed one, smelling it, recognizing it. This was a variety Poppy had fed her as a child once, and never again. Isla had asked, and Terra had said the tree had died.

Because of her.

Because of her powerlessness.

Now, she knew that had been a lie. So many lies.

Isla bit into the fruit and groaned. Its yellow juice dripped down her face as she ate ravenously. It was the sweetest variety she had ever eaten, and there were dozens of them—*hundreds*—hanging right there.

It was impossible. Nightshade didn't have many varieties of fresh fruit. In the aftermath of the storms, it was barely getting by, yet there was this land with endless food. Endless resources.

How did Grim not know about it?

She quickly used her abilities to weave a basket with vines. She filled it to the brim with fruit, portaled into a Nightshade village, left it on a doorstep, and did it again. Again. Again. Until her arms were sore, and that tiny patch of island was bare.

A small difference, but a difference all the same. *Trying,* she thought, with a bite of bitterness in her chest.

She spent the rest of the night eating her way through the woods, trying everything. Eventually, the native creatures seemed to get used to her presence, because the snakes began to slither. The birds began to call to each other. A boar with wild, twisted horns darted in front of her and was gone.

By the time Isla found a pool where she could scrub the salt and sand from her skin, she wondered if her father's biggest secret wasn't his own death, his wife, his child—

—But the island.

She hadn't traveled here only to see a piece of her parent. No, this island would serve a purpose.

Still in the center of the water, Isla reached into the deepest crevices of her power. Into all the places she had buried her ability, and emotions, and sanity.

And let it all come rushing out.

The water around her exploded upward before turning into steam. Waves of petals and trees broke through the land around her. The air itself seemed to shatter, wind howling. Shadows coated her arms, wrapped in sparks.

The beast within her—the one that made her powers deadly—uncurled. She gave into it, only here. Only in a land where she couldn't hurt anyone.

As her power unleashed across the island, the monster within felt relief.

Isla awoke in the middle of the night, shivering from another nightmare, only to find a serpent curled at the foot of her bed.

She hadn't gotten another from Wren in a while. Where had it come from? Cautiously, she reached out to grab it, but the serpent slithered onto the floor.

Lynx was still asleep, curled in the corner. Isla stepped out of the bed, and lunged toward the snake to catch it—

But it was too fast. It slithered beneath the door frame. She crept into the hall, following it around the corner, only to watch it be joined by more snakes. They were all the same dark green color with black specks, moving as one, as if each were pieces of the same whole.

Follow the snakes.

She did, even though the traitors had been captured. The serpents were relentless; it was as if they were trying to lead her somewhere, tell her something. She followed them until she turned a corner and nearly crashed into a wall adorned with an intricate mirror.

Her reflection stared back at her.

She was covered in snakes. They were wrapped around her arms, her stomach, her throat, squeezing—

She gasped, and they were gone. They weren't on the floor either. They had vanished, as if they had never been there to start with.

Slowly, she inched back down the hall, her heart hammering, only to crash into something solid. She seized, then whipped around, and Grim gently grabbed her wrists before she could reach for her hidden dagger.

"Hearteater," he breathed. "What are you doing?" His voice sounded faraway.

She blinked, and it was as if she was plunged back into this moment, into the hall. She heard a faint screeching.

"Did—did you see them?" she asked, squinting against the darkness, searching for any sign of them.

Grim frowned. "See what?"

"All the snakes," she said, as if it was obvious.

"Heart," he said, knuckles running across her forehead. "Are you all right?"

"I'm fine," she told him, stepping away from his touch. She drew her brows together, studying him. "You look like a demon."

"Thank you," he said.

"That wasn't a compliment." She shook her head. "Why are you in armor?"

"The stormfinch," he said. "It's singing."

That was the screeching.

Hope flared within her. *Finally,* another chance. She still had the other ring Azul had returned to her . . . he had trapped a shred of storm inside. Perhaps it would work.

Quickly, she got dressed and slipped the second ring on her finger. Without Wraith they couldn't fly, so Grim portaled them to a location just outside one of the rural villages. Some of his people lived far from the tunnel system, so he would bring them to safety himself.

Rain had just started to fall; it was cold on the crown of her head. A flash of lightning soon joined it.

The clouds above began circling ominously.

Villagers rushed out of their houses at the sight of their ruler. He portaled them all to the castle. Isla took more, using her starstick. After everyone was evacuated, they went to another town.

Bells were still ringing faintly from other villages. Warnings of what was about to come. Villagers began pouring out of their houses again, possessions pressed to their chests. But, before Isla and Grim were past the wall surrounding the cluster of houses, the first tornado touched down.

Then another.

Another.

Grim's power shot out. He portaled a few screaming people away, as the tornado barreled right toward them. Then his own abilities faltered.

Just like the last one, this tempest was full of tiny pieces of shade-made metal, swirling everywhere, stabbing into surrounding trees and grazing her skin, nullifying power.

"Hearteater, get down," Grim said, before pulling her behind the stone wall. The storm roared behind them, sending trees and bricks flying. She reached for her power, but it had dimmed. Gone, as though she were wearing her bracelets.

There were screams.

There was nothing she could do.

This—this was why they needed to close the portal. She held the ring tightly, waiting for it to tremble in her hand, to heat—but nothing. She was too far away.

Isla made to stand, and Grim pulled her back down. "You'll get yourself killed," he said over the roaring; but he meant all of them.

He was right. She closed her eyes tightly, wind bellowing around them, the ground peeling away in coils, dirt smattering against her every inch, metal cutting through her clothes, and knew that getting close enough again would be almost impossible.

It seemed like hours before everything went still again. Grim stood first, then helped her up.

She choked back a sob.

Destruction. Death. Bodies . . .

It was just the beginning.

For a week, there was a new storm every day. The season had started in earnest. Each time, Isla attempted to capture part of it; but she never got close to a tornado again. Most of the tempests raged far above—and with Wraith still injured, she couldn't go that high. Her Skyling ability wouldn't work, thanks to the metal.

Every death—every quiet morning after, watching the aftermath, seeing the ruin—made her remember.

Ashes. Bodies. Destruction.

There was less than a month left of winter when she finally took the feather between her fingers again.

And wrote, *Teach me.*

SKYRES

Skyres draw power from blood.

That was what Aurora said.

They can only be formed with shademade metal.

She had been practicing the symbol for days, on parchment. Aurora knew one, she said. One to funnel power. To control it.

It was exactly what she needed. A replacement for the bracelets. A safeguard in case her visits to the island to unleash her power weren't enough.

Now, she was ready to try it on her skin.

Shademade. She could have gone to the blacksmith and asked for another dagger, but its tip would have been too broad for her purposes. No, the feather was perfect.

She followed Aurora's instructions. Skyres were most effective when bonded with objects of great power, to use as ink. She unearthed a ruby that had been passed down through generations of her line. One that was said to have been made by the power of her ancestor. Slowly, she pressed against it with the feather's tip. Not expecting much to happen.

She watched, transfixed, as the glimmering metal went right through the gem. The stone's center became almost liquid, coating the end of the quill in sparkling crimson ink.

If the feather did that to a stone, she wondered what it would do to her skin.

Act immediately, while the source is fresh, Aurora had said, so she didn't wonder for long. Pinching her lips in anticipation of a scream, she dug the tip of the feather against her arm.

Fire erupted through her veins, as if her blood had been set aflame. She screamed, grateful she had portaled to the Wildling newland, where no one would hear her. Sweat poured down her forehead, mixing with tears. She had never experienced such pain in her life, not when she had purposefully lit her arm on fire for the Centennial, not when she had been struck in the heart by an arrow.

It was almost enough for her to stop. Still, her fingers trembled as she mimicked the symbol she had practiced hundreds of times already. The delicate curve, the swirling lines, the tiny details.

Every single line has to be right, or your skin will flay from your bones. The skyre becomes a curse that will consume you.

She gritted her teeth, trying to keep her hand steady. When she finished the final sweep of ink, she dropped the feather and collapsed onto the floor.

Her arm was bloodied, the skin broken. It looked wrong. It looked like she had been bitten by a strangely fanged beast.

But slowly, the ink began to glisten. Shine. Until the skin around it tightened, painfully, melting into the marking.

It was done.

Her blood was roaring in her ears, searing through her body like lightning. She lifted her trembling hand, testing the skyre.

It was supposed to funnel her powers. Control them.

Energy spiraled out of her palm in a green-tinged crest. She jolted in surprise, watching as it hit the wall with precision, searing through one of the swords against the stone.

Slowly, she approached the singed metal. Studied the hole that had gone right through the wall.

Perfectly circular. Perfectly controlled.

She stared down at the gleaming ink upon her skin, thin as the weaving of a web. With it . . . her abilities felt like they had been forged into a weapon in her hand—a sword, or dagger, or throwing star, that she could throw with precision.

It was a shortcut. It came at a cost. She heard the warnings in her mind, but they didn't matter . . . not when so many other lives were on the line.

Aurora was still her enemy . . . but she had helped her. The skyre had *worked.*

Do you know any other markings? She scribbled desperately.

The response came quickly. It made Isla's heart sink. *No.*

Isla nearly grabbed the pen, before it started moving again. *But I know where you can find out.*

She found Grim in the greenhouse. In his black outfit, he looked like a demon at the center of an oasis, shadows staining the ground around his feet. They puddled as he turned around to face her.

"What are you doing here?" she asked, joining him at his side. There was a balcony up a spiral staircase, overlooking all the nature. He was leaned against its ledge.

He blinked as if he had been lost in his mind. "I come here, sometimes. To think." His gaze shifted to her. "To remember."

Remember.

"Things . . . things were different back then," she said, eyes glued on the fountain in the center. The one with a statue of her, smiling, holding a baby Wraith in her arms.

She could see him nod in her peripheral vision.

"*We* were different."

He had fallen in love with a person who had barely left her room. Who had never known an intimate touch. Who had never known power.

She had fallen in love with a ruthless warrior who had planned to kill her, at one point.

"Sometimes I think our love was cursed from the beginning. That it started with so much hatred . . . so much blood . . . it could never lead to anything good."

He was silent. She turned to face him, only to find him frowning. "From the first moment I saw you, I didn't stop thinking about you, and I hated it. I thought you were a curse. Hatred was a lot easier to admit to myself than love. It was a lot more familiar." He shook his head. "I . . . I'm sorry for ever hating you."

"I'm sorry too." She had stabbed him in the chest during their first meeting. She had kept countless secrets from him. She had chosen someone else over him. Right at this very moment, she kept a prophecy from him that could lead to his death, by her own hand.

"I've never loved anyone," Grim said, and she turned sharply to face him. "Not until you."

His face was clear. His eyes were earnest. It made her sad. "That can't be true."

"It is. I started to believe I was incapable of it . . . of any of the feelings I sensed from others . . . of loving someone so much, I would die for them, without question." He leaned against the ledge again. "I would watch, sometimes, in the villages, a family walking down the streets, smiling. A husband and wife with their arms linked. I thought it impossible to be that happy. I thought love was the greatest lie. The most outrageous fantasy." His eyes narrowed. "I hadn't . . . I hadn't ever imagined myself happy. I didn't think I would ever deserve it. Not after everything I had done." His body tensed, as if he had been snagged by a memory. "When I was young, we were trained to be ruthless, to have heart trained out of us."

Isla's voice was barely a whisper as she settled beside him, staring out at the greenery. "How do you have the heart trained out of you?" She wondered if she should even ask.

Grim raised a shoulder. "You ensure a child is never loved." His throat bobbed as he swallowed. "There was one guardian I grew attached to. Against orders, she would tell me stories from her village before bed. She brought me one of her own child's balls to play with. She . . . cared for me, and I cried saying goodbye to her. My father

found out and had her executed. He made me watch." Tears burned her eyes, fury at his father for being a monster, anger for the childhood that had been ripped away from Grim.

He glanced at her. "'Love is a disease,' my father used to say. 'Love kills kingdoms.' So, he tried to rid me of it."

In their world, love did kill kingdoms. When power could be shared, it could be taken. As Isla thought about the oracle's prophecy, and the sacrifice he had already made for her, she couldn't help but think—

His father had been right.

"I come from a long line of heartless men, modeled after Cronan." Her jaw set at the mention of Grim's ancestor, who had founded Lightlark with Horus Rey and Lark Crown. "His cruelty was seen as strength. According to my father, he was the model we all fought to emulate. Even the most barbaric of practices."

"Like what?" Again, she wondered if she should even ask, but she wanted to know him, know the childhood that had made him into someone he considered a monster.

His eyes blazed with fury. "Cronan had children. Many, many children, as much as he could." He swallowed. "He buried them beneath the land, their power fed it."

She stilled against the ledge. "He killed his children?"

"All except the strongest. And that was how the line continued."

Isla gaped at him. No. She couldn't be hearing him right. Her eyes stung. "You—you can't mean . . ."

Grim nodded. "Every Nightshade ruler before me has had dozens and dozens of children. Has raised them until they were of age. And has forced them to compete to the death."

No.

She had heard of Grim's brutal training. Never once had she considered that there were others. His siblings, who he must have been raised to think of as his rivals.

"So, you—you . . ." she couldn't say the words.

Grim, mercifully, shook his head. "I was spared by my flair. The moment my father found out about it, he slaughtered the rest of his children himself."

Isla was crying. Grim had always been alone . . . but he hadn't needed to be. He'd had *family*. And they were all dead. No wonder he hated his father. No wonder he had fought against love and connection.

"But you . . . you don't have children," she said, confirming. He had told her as much in the past, when she had inquired about the line of women she had once joined.

"No. From the moment my father died, I knew I couldn't do it. I knew I would never be able to . . ."

Isla grabbed his hand. She felt sorry for all the innocent children, brought into this world to die. She felt rage for the rulers who had killed them, all for power.

"I'm sorry," she said, meaning it. She knew what it was like to grow up alone.

Isla understood now, more than ever, why Grim had been ready to go through the portal for her.

She was all he had.

Slowly, her fingers settled between his, and a chill swept up her arm at the contact. He looked at her like he had so much to say, but not enough words and not enough time. His thumb brushed across her knuckles, scraping them just slightly, and she shivered. He reached her wrist and swept the inside, across her pulse. Frowned. His gaze slid down to her bare wrists. He raised his brow slightly in question.

She hadn't seen him since she had gone to the blacksmith. "I decided to stop hiding."

"Good," he said. "I married all of you, Isla. Not just the good parts. Not just the good days. Don't hide from me."

It was in that moment that she realized she had been hiding from herself. She wanted so much, and it shamed her.

Half of her loved Oro—always would.

The other half loved Grim. Unconditionally. The same way he loved her. Theirs was not a gentle love, it was a bleeding love. And she was done pretending she didn't want it.

If she was going to save Nightshade, and change her fate, she needed to work with Grim—not against him.

Tears swept down her face again.

His eyes widened. He looked like he wished he could kill anything that had made her upset. "What is it, heart?"

She shook her head. "I trusted them. The people I killed the other day, when I was covered in blood. I—I thought they had become my *friends*." It sounded so stupid, saying it aloud. She sounded so pathetic. But Grim only listened. He did not judge her. "And . . . my guardians. They—they—"

He held her as she cried. This was what she deserved, she knew. She had betrayed countless people as well.

"I want to go somewhere," she said, her chest rattling with sobs. "Just with you. Like before."

They didn't have much time. They were well into winter now. The augur had been clear—her fate and lifespan were somehow tied to the portal. They needed to find it. All of their lives depended on it.

She watched Grim hesitate.

"There's another palace," he said, his large hand sweeping down her spine, gathering her closer to her chest. "We can go there, for a few days. I think—I think you'll like it."

She nodded against him. Perfect.

It was exactly what she had been hoping he would say. Exactly the place Aurora had described. The skyre on her arm, made invisible by Nightshade shadows, seemed to pulse.

It was an excuse, but it was also the truth. With so short a time left, she wanted to enjoy part of it for just a few days. Give in to the desires she could no longer ignore.

She and Grim . . . as much as she had tried to fight it, as much as part of her hated herself for it, they were more alike than they were different. They understood each other.

She was done pretending she didn't love him. She was done burying her feelings down, hoping they would die.

It might have made her a villain. It might have been wrong.

But she wanted him.

Isla found her original wedding dress in the wardrobe. It was pristine. Perfect. Hung in a way that made it look like art on a wall, a piece Grim might have often looked at.

Her fingers swept down the silk, across the ties of the bodice, and she remembered standing while the dress was created around her. She remembered the look on Grim's face when he first saw her. She remembered when he went to his knees and pressed his forehead against her legs and whispered something into the fabric like a prayer.

She slowly took it off its hanger.

The buttons down the back were difficult to hook herself, but she bent her arms, and with every latch there was another memory, another moment. He had imprinted himself upon her life, and she wasn't sure if there was any way around it.

Before she could think better of it, she was in front of his door. She didn't need to knock.

The door swung open, and Grim's eyes widened, just slightly. She hadn't often surprised him, but when she did, she cherished it.

The dress had long sheer sleeves made up of intricate embroidery. The design told their story, whirling shadows meeting blooming flowers. The bodice was low and covered in petals, the design of vines and stems curling out of them, against her skin. The fabric was tight against her waist and stomach, and the silk below was smooth, all the way to the floor.

"Heart," he said, blinking more than usual, as if trying to discern a dream from reality. "What—"

"I'm ready," she said. She took a step forward. "I'm ready to try again. To be your wife. Truly."

The look he gave her was so earnest, so disbelieving, she couldn't imagine she had ever thought him heartless.

Slowly, his gaze never leaving hers, Grim went to his knees before her. He took her hands as gently as if they were made of glass and bowed his head. Tears swept down the sharp panes of his face. She had only seen him cry once before, and it was when her heart had stopped. It made her own eyes burn. "I won't pretend I'll ever be a good man," he said. "But I'll be good to you." His words were a promise she could feel in the center of her chest, the bridge between them dark and gleaming. He smoothed his lips across her knuckles. "I will make us happy, heart. I swear it."

She wanted that. With every part of her, she wanted this to be real. She wanted to pretend she could change her fate: that she could save them all, have a happy ending.

Grim rose to his full height, eyes still never leaving hers. She carefully wiped his tears with her thumb, and he shivered. "Our wedding night," she said, slightly breathless. "You remember it?"

His eyes darkened, then. "Only every night."

"Good," she said. She stepped into him. His body was hard and cold against her. "Do it all again."

Grim didn't hesitate. One moment she was firmly on the ground, and the next, he had reached down and swept her off her feet.

He turned around and portaled them so smoothly that she didn't even realize they were in their room until they were facing the bed.

She had anticipated he would want to do this here. Lynx was gone. Isla had already brought him to the stables. She'd had to leave him several pieces of dried meat and blankets to make up for it.

Ever so carefully, Grim set her down in front of the bed. She slowly slipped out of her shoes, shrinking slightly before him.

"May I?" he asked, motioning toward her dress, the words so soft she barely heard them.

She nodded and turned around. He gently moved her hair over her shoulder, and his featherlight touch made her shiver. Just like their wedding night, every sense seemed to be heightened, her skin as sensitive as if she had never been touched before. Her toes curled at his breath on her neck and his rough fingertips against her spine as he began to slowly undo the buttons. Every scrape of him against her skin had her burning. Restless.

There were too many damn buttons.

He laughed darkly. "Patience, Hearteater," he said, and a thrill went through her as he used her old name. "We have all night." She felt his breath against the shell of her ear, and it made her shoulders hike. "And I plan to enjoy every moment of it."

She twisted to face him. "If I recall correctly, we didn't leave this bed for days."

Grim laughed again. "Greedy for more, when we haven't even started, Hearteater?"

"Always," she said, and felt the last button open. Her entire back was bare to him. Just as she got used to the cold air upon her skin, he swept his rough knuckles down her spine, and she arched, aching. The fabric fell off her shoulder, and he pressed his lips against it, making his way up her neck, across her jaw. She shivered at his touch, her want surprising her, rising just as forcefully as she had tried to bury it down.

The dress fell to the floor, and Grim made a noise that almost sounded pained. She had found the pieces of lace in her dresser too, the ones that barely covered anything.

"My memory is useless, when it comes to you," he murmured. "You're always so much more beautiful than I remember."

"And you're still fully dressed." She was impatient, needy. She pressed her hands against his shirt and watched it turn to ash, revealing a chest so broad and muscled, he would have looked like a flawless statue, save for the scar next to his heart. The one she had given him. He had kept it, a vestige of her.

"Getting back at me for all the dresses?" he said, his voice dark and amused. The ones he had ruined, by ripping them off her.

"Exactly."

His pants were next. Now, they were on equal footing. Before she could touch him again, he bent down and picked her up by the back of her thighs, lifting her onto the bed. Then, eyes never leaving hers, he knelt before her again.

She gasped as he hooked his fingers beneath her knees and dragged her to the edge of the sheets, right below him. His breath was hot against the center of her, and she groaned.

"You have no idea how many times I've imagined this," he said. Her lace was gone with a single movement, and he didn't waste a moment with teasing or games. No, he seemed to be as starved as she was. Her head fell back with the first press of him against her, toes curling, eyes squeezing closed.

Then, she arched off the bed. His hands gently pinned her hips down against the sheets, thumbs stroking her sensitive skin. He was slow, and gentle—until he wasn't. She dug her heels against his back until she was moaning into her own shoulder and fisting the sheets. Then she was being dragged beneath an endless sea of pleasure, until her muscles tensed and she was shattering against him.

She sat up, dazed, limp, her skin feeling raw and covered in sparks.

He slowly rose from the floor, and she watched him with wide eyes, beyond words. She watched as he slowly climbed up the bed, leaning over her. Then he tucked his arm beneath her and dragged them both to the head of the bed.

He slowly kissed his way up her body—her stomach, then her sensitive chest, peaked with need. He took his time there, and she gasped as he scraped his teeth, then his tongue across her. She was molten, squirming below him, desperate for more.

"Please," she said. She locked her legs behind his back, reaching for him. In response, he slowly, very slowly, took one of her arms and placed it above her head, her knuckles pressed against the silk sheets. Then he did the same with her other arm.

He reached between them, and she gasped as she finally felt him push against her. He slowly inched forward. His thumb swept across her palm, and he moved carefully, gently, his body shaking with restraint. He went in and in and in, until she couldn't think around the pressure, couldn't breathe around it; and then he sighed against the crown of her head, and she groaned as he reached a place that made her spine feel like a bolt of lightning.

Then he started to move, and nothing in the world had ever felt so good, so right, so saturated. She was breathless, breaking, mending, and it was better than she remembered, this feeling, this fullness.

He held her by the wrists as he drove into her, and she moaned into his mouth, panting, lost for words, lost for sanity. She knew he could feel her emotions, every crest of pleasure, every inch of need and want.

He growled as he hauled her up against him, as if he couldn't feel enough of her; and she groaned at the contact, her sensitive chest scraping against his cold skin with his every movement. She hooked her arms around his neck and bit down against his shoulder to keep from making even more noise.

In a flash he sat back on his feet, lifting her upper body to face him. At this angle, she could feel everything, every inch of contact between them. He moved, and her head fell back as she took everything he gave her, his body finding every aching spot in hers and filling it.

Grim grabbed her by the side of her face and kissed her deeply, his tongue stroking the roof of her mouth as she shuddered against him,

all of her going taut, then loose. He pulled her back onto his chest, and kept going, faster, and she kept kissing him, as if she could show him with her lips and tongue how good this all felt, because words would never be sufficient.

She bit his bottom lip as he found a spot that felt like the place between stars, and he kept going, never tiring, muscles hard as stone beneath her. She met him stroke for stroke, grinding her hips, chasing her pleasure; and when she found it and cried out against his mouth, he flipped them over and drove into her again, pulling her close. He gasped as he pushed into her one final time, his shadows flaring around him, shuddering through the room.

On their wedding night, he had broken all the windows. Tonight, it seemed he had remembered and taken precautions against it.

"Again," she said, panting, not a moment later. "Do that again."

He laughed darkly in the space between her neck and shoulder. He kissed the length of her neck. "So impatient," he said against her skin. But then he flipped her over, and he did.

WINTER

The winter palace was made of harsh arches that mimicked the mountains around it. A thin layer of snow clung against the stone and glass exterior as if it was wearing a sheer blanket, and the windows were as dark as lifeless eyes, like the entire castle was sleeping.

Howls of wind blew her hair back and clawed at her cheeks. The cold was voracious, striking in a thousand swift bites. Grim didn't seem to mind it as he took a few steps forward. "It wasn't always empty," he said. "I remember it full."

"What happened to everyone?" she dared ask.

"They died. Every single one."

She felt a bite of pain, remembering what he had told her. Everyone Grim had ever truly known was gone. Everyone except for her.

"Did you spend a lot of time here as a child?"

He nodded. "From the time I was born, until I started my training. This area is called the Algid, the northernmost part of Nightshade. Here, it snows all the time."

The forever winter here was a reminder of her fate. Of the limited time she had left to change it.

"Has it been abandoned for long?"

"Not completely. The grounds are maintained, and the main chambers are attended to, in case of a visit."

She turned to him. "I don't remember coming here. Why didn't you take me?"

He frowned. "It's cold. You hate the cold."

The moment Grim stepped foot inside the castle, flecks of silver lit up within the stone of the interior, a million lights around them, like stars buried in the night sky. Isla gaped at them.

"It's a special stone," Grim said, glancing at her. "Lights up when it senses Nightshade power."

It reminded her of Starling. She told Grim, and he nodded. "The realms aren't as different as we make them out to be."

Grim showed her down hall after hall, room after room. She saw a few attendants who bowed, then went on their way.

By the end of his tour, Grim seemed lighter. He ran his hand along the back of a chair carved in an intricate style she had never seen before.

"You look . . . happy," Isla said, watching Grim take all of it in.

He nodded. "As a child, I was happiest here."

"Why?"

"Because my father lived in the other castle," was what he said.

"We can be happy here," she said, putting her hand on his. Remembering the words he had told her before he had taken her to bed.

And, even as she hid her true purpose for being here, she meant it.

Grim had portaled in a wardrobe full of soft fabrics. Sweaters, pants casual enough to sleep in, thick tights to wear beneath her dresses. There were capes with hoods lined in furs, and gloves that would reach her elbows. It wasn't all black, either.

"I thought you would appreciate color," he said. The color in question was a mix of white, greys, and the occasional Starling silver, but she was grateful.

"This was thoughtful," she said.

He looked almost sheepish. "All I ever think of is you."

Isla stepped close to him. She went on her toes and didn't even come near his height. "Remember when we first met?"

"Of course, I remember." He pulled his shirt up, revealing the silver slash on his chest. "You made it difficult to forget."

She rolled her eyes at him as he smoothed the fabric back down. "The Grim I first met would have been disgusted by the words that just came out of your mouth."

Grim scowled. "Does this end in a point?"

She flicked his nose, and it seemed like he was trying very hard to glare at her. He ended up pulling her close to him. "My point is . . . people can change."

His face softened. "If they have a reason to," he said, reaching down to run his rough fingertips across the side of her face. Even that simple touch felt like sparks trailing down her skin.

"I want to see you relaxed," she said.

"I am relaxed."

He was wearing three different types of swords, a cape, and wraps around both of his arms. His spine was soldier-straight.

"Right." She frowned. "I don't think I've ever seen you in anything . . . casual." She walked over to his own wardrobe and tore it open. Cape. Cape. Cape. Cape.

She turned around, exasperated. "You wear it when you're alone too?"

He just looked at her.

"No." She shook her head and grabbed his hand.

"Where are we going?"

"Take us to the closest village," she said. Her plans could wait. If they had a couple of days together to celebrate their union, she wanted to enjoy them. "This time, disguise us as something fun."

In the valley of mountains that resembled carnivorous teeth sat a village draped in snow. The houses were quaint, roofs like folded pieces of parchment, glistening with frost. Smoke rose from stout chimneys like steam from tea. She had never seen a place so beautiful.

Isla gaped at Grim. "I can't believe you weren't ever going to take me here."

Grim gave her a look. "Who said I wasn't?"

She stared at him. "We were married for *months,* and I can't seem to find this particular place in my memories."

He grabbed her hand. "We're *still* married," he said. "And you hate the cold. I thought we established that."

She nodded down at her cape, which was lined in fur and the softest fabric she had ever known. Her dress was made of thick wool. Beneath it she wore soft tights and boots that went up to her knees. "Not so much when I'm dressed for it."

No one paid them much attention as they walked through the village, and Isla knew Grim had disguised them with his power. Children played in the snow, their cheeks pink, their words coming out in clouds. Shops featured pastries and licorice in their windows.

"I used to steal those, when I was a child," Grim said, nodding at the candy.

She glanced at him. "Villainous from your first breath."

"Precisely." He looked thoughtfully at the shop. "My father didn't allow candy, or games, or anything he thought would make me weak. My guardians were good at enforcing his wishes." He shrugged. "But I discovered my flair at a young age. When they thought I was sleeping, I was here, stealing candy, and watching the other kids play."

She tried to imagine a child Grim. Messy black hair, pale face. Alone.

It was exactly what she had done with her starstick, once she had discovered its ability. Grim's power—even though he hadn't known it at the time—had provided them both with an escape.

"When I was old enough to be trusted with money, I walked into the store, dropped a pile of coin on the counter, and walked out."

"Enough to pay for all the licorice?" she asked, looking up at him.

"Enough to pay for the shop, if I wanted."

She pulled his hand. "Let's go, then." He started to refuse, but then he gave up, and let her lead him inside.

"One of each," Isla said at the counter, and Grim chuckled behind her, remembering when he had said the exact same words at the Centennial. When they were brought a pile of different flavored strands, he sighed and stared at her over the table.

"This was much more charming with chocolate," he said.

"Yes," she agreed, nodding her head solemnly. "It wasn't at all alarming that the villainous Nightshade was feeding me chocolates."

A smile played on his lips. "You liked it."

"Of course, I liked it," she said, grabbing one of the licorice strings. "It's chocolate." She motioned at him. "Now, should we get started?"

Isla watched Grim take a bite, and his eyes closed as he slowly chewed. A smile almost crept across his face. "It tastes exactly the same," he said, disbelieving. "Centuries later, and it hasn't changed."

She chewed on a piece, and it was fine—it wasn't chocolate. But seeing the joy it brought Grim made her love it.

They took the rest wrapped in paper for later. Then the real fun started. She found a shop that sold clothes and pushed Grim into a changing room. "What are you doing?" he demanded.

"I'll get options," she said. "You can try them on."

He looked at her as if she had lost her mind. "I'm not changing in a store," he said, as if the idea was ridiculous.

"Fine," Isla said, throwing her hands up. "You'll just have to buy options without knowing how they look. You might not end up getting anything you like."

Grim looked exasperated. He turned to the shop-owner, handed her a mountainous stack of coin, and said, "One of each."

"You're leering at me again," Grim said.

She really was.

He was wearing a soft, long-sleeved black shirt and casual pants. No cape. No boots. No spiked armor.

Just him.

Something about that was doing strange things to her composition.

For her part, she felt like she had made an outfit from a cloud. She wore one of Grim's new sweaters, like butter against her skin and deliciously oversized, and a thicker version of the tights he had brought her.

Most of her life, she had either worn dresses with bodices that cut off her air supply, or armor that weighed her down like an extra layer of gravity. Only recently had she known the comfort of thick, smooth fabrics against a cold night.

She walked over to him as he cautiously eyed her. "Isn't this comfortable?"

He frowned down at his outfit. "It's fine."

She made a sound of indignation. Her hands smoothed down his chest, the fabric softer than silk beneath her fingers. She groaned. "Tell me you can *feel this,*" she said, looking up at him. His eyes had darkened.

"Suddenly," he said, "I'm liking it more."

She beamed at him.

There was a small fireplace in their room, and they sat in front of it, watching the snow and trading stories from their childhoods. Isla told him about how she would sneak sticks and leaves in her pockets during training to build dolls out of them. One was named Stick-man.

"Creative from your first breath," Grim said, and she flicked his nose again.

Grim told her how he had first discovered his flair. He was seven years old, in this very castle, and had just been locked inside of his room, as a punishment for allowing himself to be struck during training. He had banged on the cold glass windows and had wanted to be somewhere warmer. Somewhere different.

When he opened his eyes, he was on the beach below the Nightshade castle to the south. He had almost driven himself mad trying to get back to his room, in time for his guardians to check on him. He had managed to portal back just before dinner.

No one had noticed the sand in his shoes.

He had kept it a secret for as long as he could, knowing that once he shared the news with his father, his movements would be more closely monitored. It wasn't until the portaling became a strategic fighting advantage that he shared his flair. By then he had mastered it, having traveled across Nightshade and beyond.

It was the same flair Cronan had been born with thousands of years before. She knew now how the comparison must have weighed on him. How it would have put even more pressure on him to become as monstrous as his ancestor.

"Are flairs usually passed down through family lines?"

Grim shook his head. "Besides rulers, only very few familial lines have flairs. It isn't guaranteed and is rare." Grim must have seen her confusion, because he added, "It is strange you have the same flair as your father. But anomalies happen."

Speaking of family. "I talked to Astria."

"Did you?" he sounded wary. Perhaps a bit amused.

"Yes. She told me she strongly advised you to stick my head on a pike."

Grim's shadows surged, but his smile was playful. "She's very loyal to her family," he deadpanned.

"Yes, I gathered that."

"So. What did you say in response?"

The edges of her mouth twitched. "I told her that I heard the position of general runs in our family, and that I would be happy to replace her."

Grim's chest shook as he laughed. "You want to be my general, Hearteater?"

She shook her head. "No. That would require listening to you. And I think far too highly of my own ideas to be able to do that."

He laughed again. Fighting a smile, she thought it was the perfect time to tell him what Astria had told her about the romance books in the library. The ones about him.

His amusement withered away. He scowled. "Astria's idea of a joke."

Isla grinned. "No. Not a joke."

He narrowed his eyes at her. "And you know that how?"

Her smile brightened. "Because I read one."

Grim shook his head at her. "That library's days are numbered."

"I thought you would say that. So, I wanted to let you know I really like the library. And I would be very sad to see it reduced to a pile of ash."

"Too bad," he said, without any bite.

It seemed like a perfectly normal time to ask, "Does . . . *this* castle have a library?"

He nodded. "It does." Hope gleamed within her. He sensed that hope and frowned down at her. "If you're looking for any more of those books, I can assure you this collection isn't the romance variety." She swallowed. She had almost forgotten how careful she had to be with her emotions around him, especially when she was hiding something.

She raised a brow at him. "Why not?"

"It's our most ancient texts. Every piece was curated by my ancestors."

Good.

MAZE

Gardens stretched behind the palace, overgrown but still beautiful, coated in a layer of ice and snow. Isla watched them from the wall of windows as she sipped from the mug of hot chocolate that Grim had handed her when she had awoken.

He shamelessly stole the mug and took a sip from it. She narrowed her eyes at him, and he lazily smiled before pressing his warmed lips against hers and handing the drink back.

"What's that?" she asked, spotting the border of a tall hedge. It seemed to turn a sharp corner.

"The maze."

She frowned. "Maze?"

He nodded. "It's ancient, older than the castle itself. Do you want to see it?"

Of course, she wanted to see it.

They got dressed in their winter clothes, Isla putting on layer upon layer, like some sort of ornate pastry. Grim led them outside, past the sprawling gardens, around the castle.

They walked until they reached the mouth of the labyrinth. It was enormous, with frost-caked hedges reaching more than triple her height. The tunnel was like a hallway that split ominously.

There was an energy to it like a shield. Power, pulsing, in a mysterious way she had and hadn't encountered before.

They stepped inside.

“This was my favorite place, as a child,” Grim said. He made a turn, and she followed him. “My guardians were replaced every year, to keep me from forming an attachment to them. They never stayed long enough to learn the maze.” He trailed his hand along the thick shrubs. “I used to hide here. I used to hope they would never find me.” He frowned. “My father learned, and I awoke one day to see the maze on fire. I thought it was gone forever, but the maze is stubborn. It took centuries to grow back, but it did. And its power never wavered.”

Another turn.

“Power?”

He nodded. “The maze is dangerous. No power can be used within it, not even Nightshade. Which is why my father had to use a match to try and destroy it.” She thought about her bracelets. Was there a deposit of the same ancient metal beneath? It reminded her of the Place of Mirrors, but even Wildling ability could be used there.

“So, a ruler could die here,” she said. She had assumed if they got lost, she could use her abilities to cut through the hedges or fly out herself. But now, when she reached for her power, she found only its embers. Grim nodded. “The maze has killed countless of my extended family members, if lore is to be believed.”

Isla swallowed. She wondered at how casually he walked through it, brushing its hedges like an old friend.

“You aren’t . . . afraid?”

He shook his head. “No. Because I know the way.”

Isla studied his every turn, memorizing it, just in case. Starving to death in a maze was not how she wanted to spend the last moments of her life.

The maze was enormous. Her feet seemed frozen solid when they finally reached the middle of it.

At the center sat a coffin.

“Cronan,” he said, before she could ask.

The Nightshade ruler was buried there. The maze had been built around his grave.

She studied the coffin, knowing now why power was drained here. It was completely made of sparkling black metal. *Shademade.*

She didn't know where Lark Crown was buried, and Oro had never mentioned anything about Horus Rey's body. Perhaps the knowledge had been lost with time.

Since they couldn't portal out of the maze, they had to walk out of it. The ground was damp, and their footprints had been frozen solid by the time they exited. It became a trail out of the labyrinth, leading their way out. By the time they were in the gardens again, Isla was shaking.

"The library has a fireplace," he said, and she nodded, anticipation building in her chest.

In moments, the fire was raging. The hearth was so large, even Grim would be able to walk into it. The flames were unnaturally high, nearly brushing against its ceiling.

Frost melted down her skirts immediately, forming a small puddle around her shoes. Without thinking about it, she slipped out of them and undid her cape. It fell to the floor. She looked up to see Grim watching her.

Now that she had given up on burying her feelings for him, they surged forward at every opportunity. She didn't fight them as her eyes traced his body, his damp shirt pressed firmly against every muscle in his chest and stomach. She didn't look away from a gaze so hungry, so intense, that her skin prickled beneath it. His chest was rising and falling just as he looked at her, like it was an effort to keep still in her presence, to battle against the growing want that she could see right in front of her.

It was a frenzy.

Her lips crashed into his, and then her freezing fingers were weaving through his hair, still damp from the cold. His tongue was hot against hers and she moaned. "I need you," she said against his lips.

He seemed to need her too. With a burst of power, the texts and papers on the table behind them were swept to the floor, and then he was bending her over it. He pulled her stockings down, and then she was filled with pulsing heat. She clawed at the table, sending cracks forming along the thick wood.

They were ravenous, starved; nothing was enough. Soon she was kicking her tights off completely, and he was hauling her against the wall.

No—not a wall. She discovered it was a bookshelf when books began crashing down around them, falling from their shelves.

"Don't stop," she said, her ankles locking behind him. She formed a Starling shield around them, the books flying wildly.

"I never intended on it," he said, as the wood groaned behind her.

She woke up draped in a half dozen blankets. Grim must have portaled them here to make her comfortable. The fire crackled just a few feet away. Somehow, they had ended up on the floor, right beside it. She remembered now, how Grim had groaned as she had climbed atop him, how he had pulled her down against his chest afterward. Their clothing was strewn across the floor, along with dozens of books. There were gaps in the shelves he had pressed her against.

"We made a mess," she said. Grim waved the thought away.

"I'll put them back," he said. His power began to work, but she shook her head.

"I—I want to look through them," she said. "I've never had a library to myself—not like this. Not without restrictions."

"Now you have several."

She told the truth. "Maybe there will be something to help find the portal."

He brought her some fresh clothes, and she slipped them on, before moving to the table. She began stacking books with her power. Grim watched her.

She turned to face him. "You're distracting."

“Am I?”

Isla looked from the cracks in the table, to him, laying in the fabrics with nothing on, shadows from the flames playing across his pale skin. He was already ready again, and part of her wanted to go back to him, but—

Grim laughed. He walked over to her, kissed the top of her head, and said, “Enjoy your library.”

Then, he was gone.

The room suddenly felt too empty. But she had a job to do. She found her discarded dress and pulled something from the interior pocket.

The feather.

She struck its point against her palm, watched the blood burble, and wrote on a fresh piece of parchment.

What am I looking for?

A book cursed closed, the feather wrote. Isla wasn’t sure she understood. How could a book be cursed?

She didn’t suppose it would simply be sitting on a shelf, and she hoped it wasn’t one of the ones that had fallen to the floor.

Most of the books didn’t even have titles, or covers; they were simply leather-bound. She had to flip them open and read a few paragraphs before moving on. After doing so for hours, she realized it would be weeks before she got through the entire collection. And she had only a few hours before Grim would summon her for dinner.

If the book was important, it would be hidden. She studied the walls, looking for levers or special panels. She remembered searching the libraries on Lightlark, and looked in the hearth too.

Nothing.

It was only when she was stacking the books she and Grim had knocked down that she realized one book had remained in the middle of the center row, when all others around it had fallen.

Strange.

She shook the shelf, waiting for it to fall loose. But it didn't move an inch. As if it was stuck.

Or enchanted.

Isla grabbed one of the sliding ladders and climbed to the shelf. She studied the book carefully without touching it, not wanting to force it out with her abilities and potentially harm it.

It looked just like the others. Thick black leather cover, creased by time. Spine engraved in a swirling pattern. There was just one thing that set it apart. Strange stains against its pages.

Isla expected it would take all her might to pull the book free. But the moment her hand curled around it, the book released its hold, and slid against her fingers.

Strange. She climbed down and set it on the table. It had a force around it, power she could feel clicking against her bones.

It was only when she went to turn the page that she realized the stains upon it were blood.

Isla stumbled back just as the book flew open. *Cursed.* It was supposed to be *cursed closed,* according to Aurora. She expected an attack, a storm to rise from its pages, blades to careen through the air . . . but there was nothing.

Only parchment and faded ink.

Her flair had saved her.

Her father was the only person she knew of who'd had her flair. If the book was cursed, then perhaps it hadn't been read in millennia. Even though, judging by the blood, many had tried.

She sank into a chair and rushed to flip through the pages, reading as quickly as she could.

If she had been expecting page after page of skyres . . . she was wrong. Every page was blank.

She grew more frustrated as she flipped through them. "Help me find the portal," she begged in a whisper. She needed to close it, stop

the storms, stop the death. She needed to use it to extend the time she had. She needed to hope it would be enough to change her fate.

The pages remained empty until the very end.

Undeterred and without any other options, she flipped from the beginning and tried again, to see if she had missed something.

This time, ink began to form. It was as if the book changed every time it was read. A few sentences were revealed, far away from each other. Most didn't make sense out of context.

Then, on the last page, there was a skyre. An ornate marking that looked almost like a rose, encased in an orb.

It had no description. Part of her itched to simply paint it upon her skin, to test it out . . . but it would be a risk. It could do anything. She remembered the blacksmith's warning.

She flipped back to the first page and started again.

Grim surprised her by taking her to the village for dinner. He must have noticed how much she had loved it.

The restaurant was full, and Grim frowned at all the noise and chaos, but Isla couldn't hear enough, couldn't see enough. It was lively, the villagers dragging chairs to other tables, having conversations over groups of people, laughing, and smiling, as if they weren't in the middle of the storm season. As if they lived each day to the fullest, anyway.

When she looked at Grim, he was already staring at her.

"What?"

"You . . . would be happy here," he said slowly, studying her face for her reaction.

She hadn't really thought about it. But . . . even as much as she hated the cold, this village was alive in a way she hadn't seen before. The community had survived centuries of curses. It was clear that the same families had known each other through generations. It was beautiful.

Grim ordered charred meat with whipped potatoes and got something completely different delivered by the boisterous owner. Isla smiled behind her hand at the look on his face. Still, he ate it, and she ate off his plate when she decided his was far better than hers.

"Just take it," he said gruffly, pushing his plate to her, and reaching over to take hers.

"It's so much worse," she said, watching his face as he took a bite. "It was a horrible trade."

"It is," Grim confirmed. Isla smiled, pushing his food back, but he stopped the plate with his hand. "I told you I would give you anything, remember? That includes my clearly superior mystery dish."

He dutifully ate everything on his plate, and then the rest of hers when she was done. Afterward, he dragged her into an alley, and she moved first, pinning him against the wall and kissing him until he sighed into her mouth.

"As much as I enjoyed that, I had more innocent motives for bringing you here," he said, sucking his bottom lip, as if to savor the taste of her. He motioned toward light peeking around the corner. "Chocolate," he said. "It's a chocolate shop that—"

She pulled him to her. "That is so incredibly thoughtful," she said. "And I love chocolate in a way that is probably concerning. But I want something else right now." She looked at him. "Do you understand?"

By the way he portaled them back to the castle—and what he did afterward—she knew he'd understood perfectly.

UNLEASHED

The winter palace seemed oddly removed from the rest of the world. Outside, nothing was heard but the faint calling of birds; and at night, nothing was seen but an endless sheet of stars.

As she stared out the wall of glass windows, she wondered how this place had survived centuries of storm seasons. She had seen the force of the tempests—and all they had destroyed—in just the last few months. She kept waiting for another one, but the sky here was still blue.

Grim said he wanted to show her something outside, and he motioned toward a set of clothes he had pulled from her wardrobe. She squinted at the pants that would disintegrate in the snow, socks that were meant for inside, and undergarments that weren't at all suited for any type of exercise.

"What?" he asked as a smile played on her mouth.

"Nothing," she said, pulling pants made of thick leather, a tight band and shirt to keep her chest warm and in place, and a long-sleeved shirt. "You know remarkably little about how women dress, for someone who's been alive for half a millennium," she said. He had likely asked an attendant to help him create her wardrobe.

Grim gave her a look. "Might I remind you, I was never meant to marry. I was never meant to have a woman in my quarters for more than a few hours."

She smiled at him. It was true. She remembered the challenges of having the original ceremony. The surprise and outrage of the court.

Isla realized this room—the one that must have been his father's centuries before—would never have had a woman living in it. Now her things were everywhere.

When she was dressed, Grim studied her, as if committing the pieces to memory, annoyed at having gotten it wrong before. She smiled as he led her out into the gardens.

They could have portaled anywhere, but they walked for miles, talking about everything from what was going on at the castle to how Lynx and Wraith were getting along.

"Your leopard is oddly protective of a creature that is several times his size," he said.

"His name is Lynx," she corrected, for the dozenth time.

"But he isn't one," Grim said, for also the dozenth time, exasperated. "You're calling him by a different type of animal."

"He likes it," she said, glaring at him.

"Fine," he said. "*Lynx*," he frowned at the word as if it had insulted him, "is oddly protective of the aptly named Wraith."

She rolled her eyes at him. "Wraith might be huge, but he's still a child. Lynx is older." She sighed. "I'm just relieved Lynx hasn't held Wraith's bonded against him."

Isla didn't see the ball of snow until it was crashing into the side of her face.

She whirled around, fingers pressed to her temple. Grim was already holding another one.

"Don't," she said.

He threw it, and she only barely ducked in time.

"You said you're ready to stop hiding." He motioned at the fields around him, and the mountains at their back. "There's no one for miles. Except for me." She looked at him pointedly. "You can't hurt me," Grim said.

"Overconfident?"

"Try," he said.

"No."

"Try."

"*No.*"

The ball of snow hit her right in the center of her chest. She gave him a look. "Fine. Remind yourself you begged me to put you flat on your ass when it hurts."

If they were going to duel, she wasn't going to use balls of snow.

He didn't know about her skyre. He had kissed every inch of her skin last night, but it had remained hidden by Nightshade power. His *own* power, that she had used.

Which meant he didn't know about her newfound control.

She flexed her hand toward the ground, and a sword of ice formed down her arm, the sharp point sliding against the snow. It didn't feel like she was using Oro's powers. No . . . this felt like her. If Grim was surprised by seeing her using Moonling ability, he didn't show it. He just summoned a sword made of shadows that twisted and calcified.

Then, he struck.

Isla turned away at the last moment, then hooked her leg around his. With all the force she could muster, she knocked his legs from beneath him, but he was ready for her. Before he hit the ground, he was on the other side of the clearing. "Portaling isn't fair," she grumbled.

Grim chuckled. "Might I remind you, wife, that you have access to the same power."

She did.

She portaled into the mountains, and he was right behind her. Their swords clashed, and then she was gone. Higher. They portaled their way up the cliffside, swords battling.

When he appeared right behind her, she swept her arms wide, and sent a wave of snow over him. She grinned, watching it glide down the mountain, but then she turned, and there he was. He sent her back

with the force of his shadows, but she was already propelling herself into the air with a burst of Starling energy.

She landed with a crouch on the mountain top and waited for him. Waited.

A snowball hit her right in the ear.

She bared her teeth and turned around, finding Grim standing there, looking very pleased with himself.

Isla slowly stood and, eyes never leaving his, summoned her Starling shield, feeling it form from her toes, up her legs, her stomach, her chest, down her arms, over her neck. It was a glimmering second-skin, a fighting suit of stars.

Grim's eyes trailed her body. "Impressive. What a striking star you make."

Isla launched forward and, with the force of a meteor, crashed into him. Grim fell back with a whoosh, and she was pleased to have knocked the breath from him. They rolled across the clearing, just nearly falling off the side.

He landed above her, caging her in with his arms on either side of her face. His body was pressed against every angle of her.

Grim's eyes swept down her form again. "I've never taken a woman on a mountain before."

Just when he made to kiss her, she disappeared, leaving him in the snow.

Behind him, she said, "And you never will."

Grim laughed darkly. He was behind her in an instant. "Will you be mad at me when I launch you off this peak?" he whispered in her ear.

Cocky demon. His shadows swarmed her, but she was too fast, she froze his shadows solid, and they fell into the snow. She shot herself back with a burst of energy, then began throwing ice dagger after ice dagger, aimed at his heart, his head, his neck. Each turned to ash

just an inch before landing true. In response, he sent an army of snowballs in her direction, which bounced off her Starling shield. They didn't touch her, but the force against her shield hurt.

It was too thin. She needed thicker. And she needed to wipe that self-satisfied grin off his face.

Isla shielded herself completely in energy, arms crossed in front of her. She called every inch of her force around her. Then, when Grim was close enough, she exploded.

Grim was launched off the mountain so quickly, he was just a streak of shadow.

And Isla was left smiling.

He was waiting for her at the bottom of the mountain, leaning against it, looking awfully whole for someone who had just been hurled off a peak. "Unleashed suits you, Hearteater," he said.

She couldn't agree more.

Grim woke her up early, with his lips against her head. "Wraith is getting restless. I'm going to take him flying. I'll be back soon."

She should take Lynx for a run too. But she needed to spend more time going through the book. So far, she had only collected a handful of skyres, without knowing how to use them. He couldn't know about her research.

He left, and she returned to the library. The pages flipped over and over, revealing just a little bit more each time.

Most were pieces of skyres. A select few were whole. None had descriptions; not yet.

She was slouched in the chair, her cheek resting against her palm, as she flipped through and a sentence caught her eye. She'd hardly finished reading it before it settled, disappearing.

Slowly, she sat up.

It wasn't a skyre . . . but it was something important. Something she would need, once she discovered the right marking.

It read, *Bones hold more power than blood. The most powerful skyres must be formed with them.*

If she was going to close the portal—if she was going to extend her life—she would need infinitely powerful bones.

She knew where to get them.

Snow fell weightlessly around her as she stopped at the mouth of the maze, still clutching the book in her hands, in case she needed a different skyre.

Uncertain, she took a breath. She had memorized the turns Grim had taken, as a precaution. Still, Isla wondered if she was making a grave mistake as she stepped inside the labyrinth.

Power hummed somewhere inside the hedges, smothering her own. She could feel it biting against her cheeks, her fingertips.

It was quiet. Too quiet, almost, as if all life had been stolen within its walls. She imagined what it would be like to be trapped forever, to go crazed inside, searching for the way out.

The book seemed to hum in her hands. She opened it as she walked, flipping through the pages, seeing what might be revealed to her.

Nothing.

Just blank parchment. Not even a single marking. She frowned. Closed the book again.

By the time she heard the growl, it was too late.

The creature was on her, its teeth sinking into her calf as she screamed. The smell of her blood filled the air, and she kicked as hard as she could, foot finding hard skin. It was enough to get the beast off her and give her a chance to run.

That was when she saw what it was—a snarling four-legged creature with a squished, angry face, and tusks coming out of its front. Something about it was twisted. Wrong.

A creature from the storm. From the otherworld.

But there hadn't been a storm in weeks . . . unless there had been one far away. Unless the beast had been hiding all this time.

Its skin was plated in patches of scales like armor, and it roared, head to the sky, as if communicating with something. It sniffed wildly in the air, and Isla realized with a start that it didn't have eyes.

Smell. It went off smell, and hearing, similar to the creature in the mountain.

Her ankle was bleeding badly. She would need to return to the coffin later. She took off toward the maze's entrance, limping as fast as she could, shaking hand keeping a firm grip on the book, and froze.

Three more beasts awaited her.

They smelled her immediately, the one she had kicked in the face catching up. And all Isla could do was run. Into the maze she went, ankle screaming in pain as she ran as fast as she could, weighed down by her heavy fabrics. She tucked the book into the front of her dress to keep from losing it and soaked her cloak in her own blood. When a turn came up, she threw it in the other direction, over a hedge, and watched all four creatures lunge the opposite way.

She tore back down the path, but she had turned too many times in their pursuit. The directions she had memorized were now useless.

She was lost.

Ripping sounds reached her as the cloak was turned to shreds. Then, roaring. They were hungry. They had gotten a taste of her blood and wanted more.

Isla pressed against one of the hedge walls, panting, trying to keep quiet. They would smell her here. It was little use.

The growling was right behind her now.

If she was lost, she needed to get up, atop the hedges. She felt around her person. She had two daggers. Nearly useless against the scaled beasts . . . but she could use them to climb.

She stuck her blade into the thick hedge and heard the creatures erupt in growls. They had sensed her.

Her other blade reached high above, and she cried out as she hauled herself up, her ankle bleeding down the plants. Just three more stabs of the hedge should do it, she told herself. Then, she would be safe. The hedge was tall; she didn't think they could climb it.

She reached back to strike again—

And was dragged off the wall by a set of teeth.

Isla's breath left her as her back hit the ground. All she could do was watch as four sets of teeth hovered, snarling, ready to pounce.

The book against her chest was the only thing shielding her body from being ripped open, and it didn't stand a chance against those teeth.

The book.

Just as they leapt to finish their meal, Isla pulled the book out of her dress, hoped Aurora was right about it being cursed, and flung it open.

At first, nothing happened.

Then, an otherworldly scream cleaved through the air like a clap of thunder. Isla watched as nothing short of a demon crawled through the pages. It was winged, and sinewy, and didn't have a face, other than a mouth with more teeth than she had ever seen in any type of beast, rows of them, sharp as stacked blades. It hit the ground in front of her, resting on the talons of its wings and even the four-legged creatures backed away.

They didn't stand a chance. The demon lunged forward and ripped them to ribbons. Blood spattered as the creatures fought, covering Isla in it, but she wasn't safe. Not yet. When the demon was done with the beasts, it could turn for her . . . and she was still lost in the maze.

She tucked the book back against her chest and began to climb.

At any moment she could be torn to shreds. She could be pulled back off the wall. She knew that, and she kept climbing and climbing,

dragging her bloody ankle behind her, until she reached the top and hauled herself over it.

The castle gleamed in front of her, just beyond the gardens.

She was right. The hedges were compacted, strong. Covered in a layer of ice.

Solid enough for her to run atop them.

She should go back to the palace, before she bled out . . . but she turned toward the coffin, glimmering in the center of the maze.

This could be her only chance to visit it without Grim. As soon as he saw her injury, he would be suspicious. She might never get this opportunity again. "You're going to regret this," she said to herself, before taking off toward the glittering metal.

She ran down row after row, until there was a gap. She needed to jump. She did, over and over, using skills honed from prowling the towns, jumping from rooftop to rooftop. On her last leap, her ankle twisted below her, and she hit the side of the opposite hedge with a thud that stole her breath, before sliding to the ground. Her head spun. Her body was sore everywhere. But she was close. She had seen it. Ignoring the pain, she got to her feet, turned the corner, and was nearly blinded by sparkling metal.

Her breathing labored, she inched toward the coffin. Curled her hands around the side. Pushed.

Nothing happened.

She tried again. Heaved against it with all her might. But it didn't budge. Almost like it was enchanted.

Or cursed.

She remembered what the blacksmith said. Her blood was power. She didn't spare a moment before smearing the blood from her ankle across its opening.

Immediately, the blood began to spread, melting across the coffin. This time, she pushed—and it opened.

She looked inside, expecting to see a corpse. Waiting to steal a bone to use for her skyres.

But the coffin was empty.

Impossible. Had the body been moved? Stolen?

A screech like a talon across the sky shattered the silence, and the maze seemed to tremble around her, in anticipation.

The creature. It had finished with the others, and now, it would find her. She tucked the book to her side, scrambled to the closest hedge, and climbed for her life.

She ran, dragging her ankle behind her, along with a trail of blood. She had lost so much already.

After the next jump, she collapsed against the top of the hedge, her vision blurring. Her head spinning. She dragged herself back up, letting the pain pulsing through her ankle anchor her consciousness, but she stumbled, dropping the book. She didn't even see where it landed.

Already, she could barely feel her hands and fingers. This was bad.

Then it got worse.

There was rustling behind her, and she turned to find the demon from the book crawling up to the top of the hedges.

She whipped around and ran faster. Faster. So fast, she barely saw in front of her; all she knew is she needed to *move*. The castle was right there. So close. But her head was spinning now.

And there was one more jump left to the outer ring. She didn't think she could make it, not when her entire leg now had gone numb from the loss of blood. It was freezing. She sunk to her hands and knees and felt the ice, slippery beneath her palms. The cold seemed to stick to her, crawling into her lungs, stinging against her wound, slowing her breathing. Her eyes fluttered closed.

Somewhere behind her, the demon from the book screamed again, and she folded over, covering her ears.

There was an answering roar.

She recognized it immediately.

Grim.

With renewed hope, she flung herself through the air, just barely making it across the way. She hung off the side of the hedge and groaned as she pulled herself atop again with her last remaining effort. Just a little farther.

Stars spotted her vision. She saw the mouth of the labyrinth and forced herself forward. There. Just there.

She crawled to the edge, and her fingers were cut to ribbons as she reached within the thorned hedge for purchase. She tried to climb down the wall without her daggers, but she had lost too much blood. Her vision went black, and her hands went wholly numb. She fell halfway down—

Into Grim's arms.

Snow melted against the window; the glass heated by the roaring fire beside it. It was the first thing she saw when she awoke.

She was still in the winter palace, then. Flashes of the maze came in spurts. The four-legged creatures. Her ankle, torn open by their teeth. The demon from the book. Her running atop the maze.

She looked down at her ankle and found it wrapped around and around, in bandages already soaked with blood—but not as much as there should be. Grim was in the process of changing them.

When he saw her awake, he knelt beside her in an instant.

She strained to get up from the chaise he had dragged next to the fire.

"Creatures—"

"I saw them," he said. "Or what was left of them." He looked at her in question. She was good with her daggers, but even she could not shred a creature of that size the way that demon had.

"Something saved me," she admitted.

That was when Grim held up the book. He must have found it within the maze. Isla's reflexes made to fling it across the room, to warn Grim not to touch it.

Then, he held up the head of the faceless demon that had crept out of it.

Oh.

"It saved me," she said, a little sad to see it dead, even though it had hunted her.

He raised a brow at her. "It tried to tear me to pieces."

Fair.

Isla had seen the demon at work. Sometimes she forgot how powerful Grim was.

Then came questions she wasn't prepared for. "What were you doing in the maze, Isla? What is this book?" The pages had remained blank for him, then.

She stilled, wondering how much to say. She remembered how his advisors had warned him . . . had called her a traitor. A snake. Even now, though, Grim didn't look upset . . . no. If anything, he looked confused. Hurt.

She told part of the truth. "I thought it might help me find the portal."

He blinked. "Did it?"

She nodded. "It did."

It had all come together on her way out of the maze.

He looked at her expectantly.

"The portal is the coffin."

Grim's eyes narrowed, considering.

"It's empty. His flair was portaling." *Bones hold more power than blood.* "I think . . . I think his bones created it, *became* the portal."

Grim bit the inside of his cheek in concentration. "The maze . . . it hid its power."

She nodded.

Isla expected to feel melting relief—they had found the portal. But it didn't even look open. She had no idea how to permanently close it, or if that was even possible, when she couldn't use power around it.

She sighed, leaning back, and caught a glimpse of glimmering ink. The swirl on her arm that she had previously kept hidden. Her sleeves had been torn by the beasts and thorned maze. It was fully visible between the tatters.

The shadows she had kept over them would have been released in the labyrinth. She had passed out before being able to put them back.

Grim had clearly seen it, while he had healed her. Slowly, she looked up at him. He didn't drop her gaze as he said, "What, Heart-eater, is that?"

BONES

Isla told Grim everything about the skyres. About the augur's words. About her dwindling timeline. About the feather she spoke through. At first, the words came out slowly, but then, in a relieved rush. She was grateful to be burning at least some of the secrets between them.

The entire time, Grim just sat there, almost unnaturally still, as if forcing himself to be silent to let her finish.

Then, he said, simply, "No."

"No?"

He shook his head. "No. Your soul will not be the price to pay."

"Then what will?" she demanded. "Who will?"

He was silent.

"I'm going to keep using them," she said firmly. "This—this guilt. This blood on my hands. It will never be erased. But any sacrifice I have to make to do more good than bad . . . to make sure everyone doesn't die with me . . . I'm going to do it. It's my choice."

His eyes blazed into hers. They stared each other down.

Grim didn't agree with her . . . but she knew he wouldn't dare take away her choice. Not again. Begrudgingly, he nodded.

Grim looked away. For a few moments, there was silence, as he leaned over his knees, his hands pressed against them. He looked pensive, deep in thought. Then, he said, "I said I would choose you over the world, every single time." He glanced over at her again, and she nodded. "It's true. I would burn the world for you, in a moment. Without question." His throat worked. "But that doesn't mean I want

us to live in its ashes." He sighed, and it seemed to move through his entire body. "I don't want the world to die, heart. I've been trying to search for solutions. I thought . . . I thought maybe we could have a child."

She stilled. An heir would resolve his life being tied to his realm.

"The augur's read of your lifespan clearly makes that impossible," he said. He was right.

But the idea of having a child with him . . .

"It made me happy," he said, quietly. "It made me wish for another life. Another universe, where it was just us, just our family. One where we were free from all the responsibilities that bind us."

"I want that too," she said, the words a whisper. Her eyes burned, thinking about it. "A life with nothing binding me. It's what I've always wanted."

He almost smiled. He brushed away a tear that had slipped down her cheek. "We aren't supposed to want anything," he said gently. It was true. She had learned that from the time she could learn at all. Rulers were born simply to serve their people. Her life was not her own.

She leaned into him, and he gathered her to his chest. She buried her face in his shirt, her ear pressed against his heart. She relished in its beating. "Somewhere, out there, nearby, or in another world completely, there someone who got everything they wanted. It will never be us." She looked up at him. "But for them . . . for them, I'm happy. I hope they know how lucky they are."

"I'm not happy for them," he said. "I envy them."

She smiled. "I envy them too."

His arms tightened around her. He whispered, right against the crown of her head, "I'm holding everything I've ever wanted."

Isla turned and looked up at him, only to find him studying her.

His eyes were almost glimmering with intensity. "You said before, I don't know what love is . . . but I do. I know it means us being infinite. It means our fates being tied together regardless of where we are,

or whether we live or die." He trailed his knuckles down her cheek. "I'm not sure of much in this world, Isla, but I am sure of this. My love for you doesn't know reason. It doesn't know limit. It doesn't know death. In every universe, every timeline, I am yours . . . and you are mine."

She kissed him as snow began to fall outside the glass window. She held him and thought to herself that this moment was perfect.

It was almost easy to pretend that there weren't a million problems waiting beyond, like distant arrows aimed at this glass house, ready to shatter it.

The augur eyed her as she stalked toward him, having stepped through his waterfall without an invitation. He was standing at the ready, as if he had been expecting her.

"I wondered when you would show up," he said. "Where are my hearts?"

Her grin was poisonous. "I'll feed you the one in your chest, if you'd like."

Slowly, he smiled, stretching his sickly skin taut, his pointed teeth glittering. "Oh, the prophet would have liked you . . ."

"Speaking of him," she said. "I'm assuming you have his blood."

He didn't make a single move that signaled surprise.

"You have more than that . . . don't you?"

The augur lifted a bony shoulder. "I have his skull. And, of course, blood."

She imagined stealing their dear prophet's body might have been what had gotten the augur ousted from the mountain.

They knew where the portal was—but not what to do next. There was a path to find out she hadn't yet explored, mostly because she had believed it impossible. Now, she was desperate. "The lost pages of the prophet's book. They speak about how to open and close portals. Right?"

He nodded. "They detail exactly how the prophet got here."

"They were written in his blood?" She needed to confirm.

He nodded again.

"If I put a tracking skyre on his bone . . . would it lead me to it?"

He seemed surprised. "You learned how to form it?"

No. She hadn't. But the book from the winter castle had given her several original markings. It was dangerous—and painful—but she would try each one, until she got it right. "Not yet. But I will."

The augur regarded her curiously. For a moment, it looked like he was going to say something. Then, he seemed to think better of it and scurried deeper into the cave.

He returned holding an object far smaller than a skull. It gleamed in the limited light. He motioned for her to outstretch her hand, and she did, watching as he dropped it in the center of her palm.

A tooth.

"Write the skyre on this, with your blood. Follow it closely."

She nodded.

"Oh, and Isla?"

"Yes?"

He reached out, just as something dripped from her face. Crimson stained his finger, and he licked it away.

Her own hand rushed to her lips . . . only to find them coated in blood. She was bleeding from her nose. From the corner of her mouth.

The augur tutted. "The price of the skyres," he said. "I can already taste them in your blood . . . souring it." He frowned. "It will get worse, the more you make." He eyed the tooth in her palm. She curled her fingers around it.

"Such guilt you wear," he said, licking his lips. "I taste it so sharply. You want so badly to be the hero in this destiny."

She remembered what the prophet-followers had said. That she was destined to either save the world . . . or destroy it.

The augur seemed to know it too.

"You are made from both light and dark, and so much more. You don't even know it. But you will. Soon." He sighed. "The traitor. She's been uncovered. She's rising."

"*Traitors,*" Isla said, confused by his words. "My guardians."

He looked surprised. His crusted lips nearly cracked and bled from how wide he smiled. "No . . . you don't know. The traitor . . . she's closer than you realize."

"What do you mean?" she demanded, her fist tightening around the tooth.

But the auger only laughed. He turned and walked deeper into the cave, the blood in his pool rippling as he passed it by. His laugh echoed, until it, like him, disappeared.

Grim found her on Lynx's back, halfway to the castle. Wraith had recovered enough to fly. He landed, his wings shuddering slightly with the impact, but when he saw Isla, he smiled.

She rushed to him, and he bent his head low to brush it against hers, sending her flying back, against Lynx, who grumbled.

He too, however, looked pleased to see Wraith flying again.

She turned to Grim, and her smile slowly shrank. "What is it?"

"Another gravesite has been ransacked. Worse than before."

The augur's words were fresh on her mind as she said, "Take us there."

He did. They landed in front of a gravesite.

Isla's mouth went dry. She didn't dare say a word.

The graves hadn't just been desecrated . . . they had been *raided.*

"The bones are gone," Astria said. She had been waiting in the clearing.

The holes were empty. Barren.

She could almost hear the augur's pealing laughter echoing through her skull. "Terra and Poppy. Are they still imprisoned?" she asked Grim.

He nodded.

"Take me to them."

The prison was on an island off the coast of Nightshade. Large waves crashed against its exterior. One side had windows, the other did not. Guilt stabbed her through the stomach, knowing this is where she had sent her guardians.

They were led in front of her, still restrained. The prison itself had been built thousands of years before, from glimmering shademade metal. No power could be used inside, so they had been brought outside, to her.

Poppy looked afraid. Terra looked murderous.

Isla had sworn to herself she wouldn't use Oro's power, but she had to know. She had to be sure. She closed her eyes. Reached for the connection.

Part of her wondered if it wouldn't be there. Part of her *hoped* it wouldn't.

But, clear as a beam of sunlight, she felt it in her bones.

She grabbed onto it.

"Tell me again," she said slowly. "Tell me again all that you did not do."

Terra looked ready to gut her, but she said, "We did not destroy the nightbane. We did not desecrate any graves. And," her voice was clear as day, "we did not kill your parents."

Poppy repeated the words.

Isla waited to feel the bitter taste of a lie on her tongue. She readied to feel it like poison in her veins.

It did not come.

They were telling the truth.

***

Isla didn't know what to believe—what to feel. Her sanity was unwinding within her. Everything she had believed to be true was a lie. She had locked up her guardians, and they had been innocent. She no longer trusted her own judgment.

It was the middle of the night when she turned slowly in the sheets, next to Grim. His wide chest was bare, illuminated by a sliver of moonlight peeking through the curtain they had rushed to close when Grim had grabbed her on her way out of the bath.

She carefully moved his arm from her waist and left the bed. Her steps were quiet, careful, but Grim awoke anyway. "Hearteater?" he asked quietly, his voice thick with sleep.

"I'll be right back," she told him, and headed into the bathroom. She waited until his breaths slowed again.

Then, she portaled to her island.

Grim knew she was using skyres . . . but he didn't need to see the pain it took to create them.

The tooth glimmered in the moonlight.

She spread out the pages before her—four full skyres she had managed to get from the book, and the half of the tracking skyre. They were supposed to fit together somehow.

Her tests would be run on another object—a piece of bark she had peeled from a nearby tree.

Her eyes closed. She breathed deeply. Then, she dipped the feather's tip into her vein, until it gathered her blood like ink. She winced against the slight burn, but that wasn't the hard part, no.

The moment she began to create the shape upon the bark, the edges of the skyre forming, her veins began to heat.

Please be right, she thought, remembering what the blacksmith had said about making markings incorrectly. There was a price.

As her shape closed, she paid it.

Her body seized. She began thrashing on the ground, she barely missed biting her tongue. Instead of feeling fire through her veins, she

felt as if each one was being plucked out of her body, torn through her skin. Her scream scraped roughly against her throat; it seemed to swallow the world.

The pain—it was too much.

Her powers rose up to the surface, that beast within her lashing out.

Plumes of black smoke barreled through the woods and down the beach, ending in flames that hissed into ice when they met the sea. The forest floor lifted like a carpet and became a field of thorns.

She screamed and screamed, the pain and power it called blinding her, eating all her senses, until it all became too much, and the world fell into darkness.

The noon sun peeked right through the treetops. She squinted against it, then rose, only to find herself covered in dirt.

Pain surged through her, a reminder of last night.

She had messed up the skyre, and it had nearly killed her. The peel of bark sat buried beneath a layer of soot, glimmering with her blood.

She didn't know if she could do this again, until she got it right. She didn't know if she would survive it.

Her body was sore. Her power was spent, scraped clean. She nearly fell over as she made to stand. Her head throbbed. She had dreamed of the village again—the screaming, the darkness, the chaos.

How long had she been asleep?

Isla portaled back to her room and found it empty. She cursed. It was already past noon. Grim would be well into his day already and wondering where she had disappeared to. He would be getting worried. As she changed out of her clothes, she noticed the commotion outside. Soldier boots. Orders. Panic.

Grim portaled in a moment later, his hardened expression shifting to relief when he saw her.

Then, his gaze dropped to her bare feet, which were covered in dirt. "Where were you?"

"The Wildling newland," she said, the lie escaping her with surprising ease. Isla wanted to tell him about the island. But there was something about it belonging to her father—something about him having kept it a secret—that made her hold back. She turned toward the bathroom. "I was experimenting with the skyres. What's the panic?"

"There's been an attack. Many people are dead."

Isla stopped in her tracks. She whipped around. "Another storm?"

He shook his head. "No. An attack."

"What? Where?"

"A town to the northwest," he said, studying her. "It's one of our military bases. But civilians died too."

That didn't make any sense. Who would attack now? Oro certainly wouldn't. He didn't want war and wouldn't kill Nightshade innocents. The rest of the realms didn't have the motive or resources.

Poppy and Terra might have done something out of vengeance, she thought. But no—she had already wrongly accused them of murder before.

"Why would anyone attack Nightshade? How would they even get access?" Almost the entire island was surrounded by reefs, making it nearly impossible to reach by boat. Cleo's fleet could only anchor to the north. She supposed the perpetrators could have flown, but it was a long journey, and the Skylings were peaceful people. There was no need to start a war between realms, not now.

"We're not sure. We just have initial reports, we're working to get more witness accounts."

Isla nodded. Good. "Are we going to the town?"

He looked at her. "Do you want to?"

"Of course I want to."

She turned to the dresser and began putting on a new set of pants, boots, and a long-sleeved shirt. A bath would have to wait.

As she made to put her hair up, however, Grim said, "You should stay. Get cleaned up; I will take care of it."

Isla froze, fingers still against her roots. "You want me to stay?"

"You didn't sleep last night." He brushed his lips against her forehead. "Rest, heart. I'll be back soon."

Then, before she could protest again, he was gone.

Isla's eyes narrowed at the door. There was something he wasn't telling her.

She slipped into the hall. Keeping to the shadows, she followed him all the way to the throne room, where his legion waited. Just before he entered, Astria stopped him at the doors.

Isla pressed against a wall around the corner, far enough not to be sensed but close enough to listen.

"Yes?" Grim said, even more gruff than usual.

"More witnesses," her cousin said. "They're all saying the same thing, ruler."

"They're confused. They don't know what they saw."

Astria was silent for a few moments before she spoke again. Her voice was resolute. "Is that what you're going to tell them to say?"

Grim made a sound like a growl.

"They're reliable witnesses. Previous soldiers. They are certain in their accounts."

"And what, exactly, are they claiming they saw?" Grim demanded.

"A Wildling, coming up from the ground. Leveling the town with power they have never seen before. Pulling bodies straight into the dirt. Suffocating them."

Isla wasn't breathing. A Wildling attacked a town on Nightshade. A Wildling with power they had never seen before. None of her people had power like that, at least that she knew of. She supposed they could be hiding it, but to what end? They were happy here.

It was the traitor. She was still out there.

"They saw *her*, ruler," Astria continued. "Their description matches her exactly. One of the witnesses has seen her in person, at the court. He confirmed it."

Her.

She meant Isla.

Her blood went cold, then boiled. How could Astria accuse her of such a thing? Did the fact that they were family mean nothing to her?

Grim's voice was a growl as he said, right in Astria's face, "Are you accusing my wife of destroying a town?"

Astria did not back down as she said, "She's done it before."

BLOODLESS

Isla didn't stick around to see Grim's rage, but she felt it, the castle trembling around her. She raced to their room.

A town was destroyed. And they thought she was responsible.

That was why Grim hadn't wanted her to come, why his eyes had lingered at the dirt on her body.

Did he think she did it too?

Did he suspect that if she showed up at the town, they would point to her and scream? Like she was a villain who had returned to finish them off?

No. It wasn't her.

Just as she denied it, a sliver of doubt spiraled through the back of her mind like a blade. She had dreamed of destroying the village. She had woken up later than usual, covered in more dirt than expected. The skyre had been made incorrectly. She thought of the auger and blacksmith's warnings, the price of using the markings.

Had she attacked the village unknowingly?

Had the monster that had been growing within her taken over while she slept?

No. Tears swept down her face.

No.

She shouldn't have taken the bracelets off. She shouldn't have trusted herself, even with the skyre. *Especially* with the skyre.

Isla needed to see the ruins. Maybe she would remember. Maybe it would be clear that she'd had nothing to do with it.

She knew the general direction of the village, but it took one of her father's maps and five tries to get it right with her starstick. By the time she landed, encased in shadows, Grim was already there with his soldiers, searching through the rubble.

Her knees nearly buckled. It looked so much like the village she had destroyed.

A baby wailed. A woman cried out for a daughter she still couldn't find. Her hands were bloody from desperately digging through rubble.

Instead of ash, there was dirt. Everywhere. It was as if the ground had swallowed the town, had dragged the bodies beneath. A few lifeless hands were sticking up through the ground, in a final call for help.

Someone grabbed her hand and she gasped, realizing she had lost hold on her shadows. "Hearteater," a voice said. Grim.

He wrapped them in his own shadows, shielding them from the world.

"I didn't do this," Isla said. She couldn't have. That was what she told herself. She shook her head. Tears rolled down her cheeks. "I swear it."

"I believe you," he said instantly, before pulling her into his arms. Her cheek against his chest, his hand cupped the back of her head.

Grim trusted her. Immediately.

As he held her, hand smoothing down her spine, she couldn't help thinking that he shouldn't.

She's done it before.

Astria's words had gutted her with more efficiency than any blade could. She couldn't even be mad at her cousin, because she was right. Isla had unintentionally killed hundreds in the past.

Who was to say this wasn't her either?

She knew the facts. Nightshades had *seen* her. Who was she to question their testimony?

She barely slept, afraid that if she did, her body might act on its own, relive its nightmares again and again. Grim's arm around her now felt more like a precaution.

"If I leave in the middle of the night . . . follow me," she told him before bed one night, and he just nodded. That was the furthest she could go in acknowledging that the attack might have been her. Grim's eyes were clear of any judgment.

Kill anyone you want, heart, he had said before. *I will never judge you.*

His words had once been a balm, a sigh of relief that someone could see the worst in her without flinching.

Now, she wondered if it had been permission for the worst part of her to roam free.

Follow the snakes. The words echoed through her head as she attempted to draw the skyres, paying the price with every try until she finally got it. She didn't feel any rush of triumph when the skyre gleamed upon the tooth.

Follow the snakes.

She remembered the augur's laugh when he realized she hadn't figured it out, she didn't know who the traitor was.

When you learn the truth of yourself, your path will be clear, he had said. She thought of the sculpture on his wall. Her, wrapped in serpents.

She thought of her dreams, of drowning in scales.

She thought of seeing the snakes in her mind, crawling through the halls, leading her to a mirror. To her reflection.

Skyred tooth in pocket, she visited Wren and watched as every snake on the tree turned toward her. She stilled as they inched up her legs to wrap around her chest and arms, as if summoned.

Follow the snakes. She had.

And they had all led to her.

***

Grim was sitting on his throne when she entered the room. He looked exhausted. Still, the shadows at his feet puddled when he saw her.

He was in front of her in an instant. "What is it, Hearteater?"

He studied the snakes still curled around her body, hissing.

"What if it was me?"

"It wasn't." He seemed certain.

She shook her head. "What if I'm what everyone says I am? What if I'm a traitor? What if I'm a monster? What if I end up being your downfall?"

Grim's look was fierce and fearsome as he caught her chin in his palm. He tilted her face toward his. "Then I will defend you until my last breath."

Her voice trembled. "You can't mean that."

"I do."

"You shouldn't," she said. "It's madness. It's . . ." The floor began to tremble.

She frowned. "What—"

Isla was flung back as the castle's foundation lurched. Only Grim's shadows kept her from crashing against the wall.

There was a moment of stillness, of silence.

Then the castle began to shake in earnest, as if it was being slowly pushed off its cliff. Another storm—a big one.

The doors slammed open as Astria rushed inside, her two blades in her hands. It was the first time Isla had seen her since she had accused her of destroying the village.

"There's an army at our steps," she said, out of breath, her eyes narrowing at Isla. "They—they look like ours."

"What do you mean they look like ours?" Grim bellowed.

"They *are* ours," she said.

That didn't make sense. Was this a coup? But Grim's entire army wouldn't dare rise against him. His death would mean death to them all.

No. This was something else.

Windows began shattering from above, in the highest corners of the chamber, one by one, glass raining down, fracturing against the marble.

Branches and rocks like blades skewered from every direction. Guards up on the balcony were sucked out of the room.

Grim reached for Isla, seeming to anticipate something she couldn't; but just before his fingers met hers, the ground below her feet split open like a broken stitch.

And she was swallowed up.

Isla was dragged through the ground, a tunnel forming below her feet. If it wasn't for the Starling shield that she made around herself and her snakes, they would have all been shredded along the rock. She fought against the invisible hold, clawed at the walls with her power, but whatever this was, it was stronger.

Just when she managed to overpower it, she was deposited into a room. She was deep underground. It was dark save for fireflies, stuck against the cavernous ceiling.

In front of her stood a woman. She had long dark hair, large eyes, and tan skin. There were vines wrapped around her arms and legs. Her clothes were nothing more than a tapestry of woven branches, flowers, grass, and leaves.

"You're Wildling," Isla said, thinking back to the vines and branches that had crashed through the castle. "You're the Wildling that attacked the village." Her resemblance to Isla was uncanny. She now understood why, from a distance, the witnesses had believed it to be her.

But Astria had spoken about a Nightshade army. That was impossible. Were the Wildling people planning a coup behind her back, with this woman at the helm?

"You don't recognize me, do you?" the woman asked. She was speaking softly, but her voice seemed to echo, resonant in a way Isla had never heard.

She didn't. And though Isla had barely been a ruler to her people, she knew them all. "No. Should I?"

The woman looked sad. "No. I suppose you shouldn't."

Isla felt around for her powers. They were right there, just like her blades, waiting for her to take them.

But this woman had attacked a village. She had ambushed Grim's castle. She apparently had an army. She had captured Isla for a reason. Before she escaped, Isla needed answers.

"What do you want?" Isla demanded.

The woman smiled. "To make this world anew."

Whatever she'd been expecting to come out of the woman's mouth wasn't this. "What do you mean? What do you want with the Nightshades?"

"Simple," she replied. "I want to kill every last one of them."

Isla's vision narrowed to a tunnel. Whoever this was, she was done listening to her. Fast as lightning, Isla's fingers curled around a blade at her thigh, and she threw it right into the woman's chest before she could blink. Isla watched the metal pierce her heart.

The Wildling looked down. She didn't collapse, didn't bleed, didn't die. All she did was frown, and Isla watched in terror as her knife slowly inched out of the woman's chest and dropped to the floor, clean.

Impossible. Isla gathered all her power—energy, fire, ice, vines, shadows—and unleashed it onto the woman. The Wildling was punctured in a hundred different places at once. One arm was sliced clean off.

Isla was panting, waiting for the woman to drop dead. Waiting to feel the curl in her bones at yet another kill.

But it never came.

Isla watched in horror as all the gaps in her body filled again, without a single drop of blood. As her arm was remade, before her eyes, the arteries and skin growing like bark and vines.

"You didn't let me finish," the Wildling said, sounding annoyed, as she stood again to her full height. She took a step forward, and Isla backed away, until her spine hit the wall. "I want to kill every last one of them . . . and use them to build something better. A new world."

"What makes you think you can create a *world*?" she asked.

She smiled. "Because I've done it before."

The snakes around her began to hiss. They started to uncurl. Isla watched as every serpent slowly slithered down her body, one by one . . .

And went to her.

They wrapped around the woman's arms and chest, just like the etching in the cave. *The future* the augur had promised.

That was when Isla realized the woman looked like her, more than just from a distance. They shared features. They had the same lips. The same cheekbones. The same exact shade of green eyes.

The Wildling's smile was wicked. "Now you're getting it. It's nice to meet you, Isla. I'm Lark Crown."

LARK

Lark Crown. Her ancestor. One of the three founders of Lightlark.

"But you're—"

"Dead?" She motioned down at herself. The snakes continued to wrap around and around, tightening. "As you've seen, I'm hard to kill."

Icy fear spread through her chest . . . but part of Isla was relieved. All those times she had felt so alone—she wasn't. She had Wildling family. She had someone who knew what it was like, having these uncontrollable powers. "Where were you?"

"Buried. By someone I trusted."

Isla didn't understand. Lark must have known that, because her gaze softened. She looked so much like her. So much like her mother—at least the glimpses Lynx had given her.

"Worlds are built on bones, you see. So many needed to die to feed the lands when we made Lightlark. So much power had to be given. Including our own."

"For the heart of Lightlark," she said, her voice just a whisper.

Lark nodded. "The heart had more than that. It was stolen from the world from which we came. A seed of endless ability." She could feel a whisper of that power in her heart, where it had marked her. "Nightshade didn't have that. Cronan used his children for power, burying them, but one line could give only so much." She curled her lip in disgust. "He was supposed to die, to give the ground what it wanted: some of the original power born of the otherworld. Instead, he used me to anchor it." Vines exploded out of Lark's hands, coating

the ground, brambles with thorns everywhere. "He buried me in metal that leeched my power, so I could not use it to escape. My strength fed the land for millennia until I was set free." By who?

Then, Lark's words sank in. "Cronan . . . is alive?"

His coffin was empty, but no . . . it was impossible.

Though Lark standing here, in front of her—that was impossible too.

Lark nodded, and a chill crested along her arms, remembering everything Grim had said about him.

"Where is he?"

"Back in the world from which we came."

"He used the portal here," Isla breathed.

"He *created* the portal," Lark said. "He drained me of as much power as he could, over and over, until he had enough to use his flair and rip a hole in this world, to the next."

"But it should have killed him . . . the journey." She remembered what the prophet-follower had said about the portal.

"He is more powerful than you can imagine," she said. "He could have made it himself, but the power he stole from me ensured he would stay alive." That fact seemed to haunt her.

"How do you know he wasn't killed?"

Lark tilted her head at her. "His curses have survived. They were each bound to his blood. They would have died with him."

His curses.

She had so many questions, but few of them mattered now, when Lark was here before her, threatening to destroy their world. "Why do you want to create a new world? Why do you want to kill everyone?"

"It's what I should have done in the first place. I should have killed Cronan and Horus and built a world from their bones. I won't make that mistake again."

Lark meant to kill Oro and Grim and build a new world with their power.

Anger formed a flame in her heart as her power surged forward. But her ancestor was impossible to kill. The best thing she could do now is get as much information as possible, anything she could possibly use to defeat her.

"And me?" Isla dared ask.

She understood the prophet-followers' warning now. Lark was the Wildling traitor that wanted her dead. Not Terra. Not Poppy. Not Wren. Not any of her subjects.

Lark was the one who killed the nightbane. She was the one who turned up the graves. She was the one who killed those people.

She was the true snake-queen.

Her voice was emotionless. "I planned to kill you too, but you might be more useful to me alive. You have access to all the realms' power." She looked at her as if she could see through her. "The heart of Lightlark has marked you. I can feel its energy. I need its power to create a new world. You will help me find it."

How could she believe Isla would give up on her world so easily? "I'll never help you. I don't care if you're my blood."

Lark tilted her head. "Is that true? You're so lonely. I can see it all over your face. You're alone in this world, Isla. No one understands you. You're a traitor everywhere."

How could she know that?

"I know you better than you think," Lark said, smiling. "You are so much like me. You have no idea."

Isla bared her teeth. "I would never kill innocents for power."

"Oh? But haven't you?"

She felt like she couldn't breathe. Suddenly, the darkness, the muskiness of the rock, the narrowness of the underground . . . it felt like the world was closing around her.

"I can give you life, Isla," Lark said, and time seemed to still.

The word was barely a whisper. "What?"

"I can save you. You have seen what I can do."

She had seen.

She wanted to live, she wanted to save Nightshade. But not at the cost of this world.

Isla needed to warn Grim. *Oro.* They had no idea what had been awoken. They had no idea what was coming.

"Think about it," Lark said, seeming to know what was going to happen next.

Isla reached above and formed a tunnel in the ground, her skyre directing her Wildling abilities, sharpening them. She crashed through the rock until she surfaced, sunlight spilling all around her. She was panting, her heartbeat like a merciless drum in her chest. She coughed up dirt.

This couldn't be real. This couldn't be happening.

Isla turned. The Nightshade castle glimmered in the distance.

It was surrounded by an army. *Grim's* army, just as Astria had said. They wore the black shining armor.

She took a deep breath, then shot into the air toward the keep, using her Skyling power. She landed roughly on the steps in front of the door, guarding it from the coup. Searching for Astria or Grim.

She barely got her arms up before a weapon was upon her. She felt the force of the blow through the crown of her head as her blade rushed up to meet a sword longer than her leg. She wasn't prepared—she wasn't in armor.

The warrior went to skewer her through the stomach, but she whirled to the side and cut off his hand with a blade-like slice of Starling energy. It fell to the floor, and she stole his sword.

She expected blood. Screaming. Cursing.

Instead, the warrior's hand fell, and he didn't even look like he noticed. He kept advancing.

This was not Grim's army.

This was something worse. Something buried that had risen.

She thought about all the graves that had been ransacked. She thought about how Lark had been able to regenerate herself.

Before she had time to even consider the possibility, the warrior pulled another blade from his belt and attempted to stab her in the throat. She ducked and struck her stolen sword through the gaps in his armor, right in the stomach. It stuck all the way through him, but he didn't so much as falter.

Dozens of soldiers were closing in. She was surrounded. Grim's true army was approaching now, portaled in spurts by their ruler, but it was impossible to see who was who, when they wore the same metal.

Confusion, clashing swords, chaos, as the warriors discovered what they were up against. Then, death. Soon, she could tell which were Grim's soldiers by all the blood. By the bellows of pain, as they fought an enemy that felt none.

They were losing.

She shot into the sky, flying high above. She could wipe the army clean with a burst of her ability, especially with her skyre. But the soldiers were all interspersed, battling one another. What if she injured Grim's army as well?

Did she care? She remembered their brutality as she had fought against them on the other side . . .

Yes. She did care. To have any chance against Lark, they would need Grim's forces.

She closed her eyes, focusing on the seed of power in her chest. The world dimmed. Her panic quieted. Her abilities were a horizonless sea and her skyre was a gleaming sieve, filtering it through, shaping it into a scythe. Her marking burned as she summoned its control, trading it for a shred of her essence. She breathed in. Out.

And unleashed.

Her arms flung out, and from her fingers, silver sparks exploded, smothering the world, rippling, targeting only the bloodless soldiers. They fell into shards, breaking until they were nothing but indistinguishable pieces.

Grim's army stopped. Looked up at her.

And they started to run, fleeing as if she was the enemy about to strike them down. She found herself smiling. That was what they expected. They hated her. She found herself wondering if she should do it. Wondering if she should give into that rage, that revenge. Especially the cowards who ran, when there was a battle right in front of them.

In the end, she let them flee. Let them fear her.

Some remained. They stood firm in their places. She nodded down to them.

Then she threw her arm out, and shadows formed a tidal wave, washing over the entire army, swallowing only the ones who didn't bleed.

When the darkness cleared and Grim's remaining forces found themselves whole, they advanced toward the next wave of bloodless soldiers.

Again and again she struck, clearing the way for the Nightshade warriors. Still, Lark's soldiers were relentless, attacking from all sides; and some of Grim's army were cut down, no match for an enemy that felt no pain. That didn't bleed. That kept going, even while missing limbs.

She raged until all the bloodless army was vanquished. She breathed heavily, nearly spent—and that was when she heard them. Distant screams coming from the direction of the closest village.

They needed her.

As she raced through the sky, she saw mile after mile of warriors marching as one.

Thousands of them.

Bigger than Grim's current army. Millennia worth of dead, risen.

Her throat went dry. There were too many. And they were headed toward all the villages, as if to recruit new soldiers.

One had already been infiltrated, the wall around the town turned to rubble. The bloodless warriors were clogging the streets, advancing, marching over dead bodies that were being pulled into the soil. Dead *innocents.*

Villagers screamed as they ran away, only going quiet as the soldiers cut down everyone in their path.

Ash. Bodies. Shapes—

She wouldn't let these people die.

With the force of a meteor, Isla landed in the streets, right between the bloodless soldiers and the villagers in their path.

She gathered the remaining power in the center of her chest—and set it free.

Oro's flames—fire tinged in blue—exploded out of her, filling the tunnel of the town. It raged, eating the bloodless soldiers, burning them, until their bodies came apart before her. When it all ran out, she could barely breathe, and only singed armor remained. She folded over, chest heaving.

A crash sounded behind her, and she whirled around, hands up, ready to strike—only to find Wraith standing in the middle of the town.

Grim was on his back.

She was in his arms in a moment.

He looked her over frantically. "We searched everywhere. Lynx was tracking your scent—"

She didn't realize she was crying until Grim frowned and wiped her ears away, cupping her face. "Heart," he said steadily. "Who took you?"

She told him everything. Who the traitor was. What she looked like. What happened when Isla delivered what should have been a dozen deaths upon her.

Grim had been right. The recent deaths . . . *it hadn't been her.*

It had been something far worse. "This army . . . it falls only to rise again. Even with limbs missing. Even with their *heads* missing."

"I know. Hundreds of people are dead."

"Then her army will only grow."

She looked around at the injured villagers. The blood painting the streets. The screams and cries surrounding them.

Her power was spent; she felt ready to collapse, but they couldn't leave the other villages defenseless. "We need to go," she said. Grim nodded.

They raced to get on Wraith's back, and then they were off.

Nightshade had been overtaken. Every single village was being swarmed by soldiers. They were everywhere, like an endless plague, worse than the storms.

"Call back your forces," she told Grim. "Portal any of your people in our path away. So we don't end up killing them all."

Grim did.

She watched them retreat, building up her strength. Calling upon her skyre, using it to leech her of more power, to fill her with all that was left.

Then, from Wraith's back, they both raged. Fire met shadow and killed everything in its path.

She knew Grim was one of the most powerful rulers. She had seen him fight. Still, she hadn't been prepared to watch his shadows swallow the world. They rippled across the entirety of his land, devouring everything for miles. Even the trees were cut down, the ground wiped clean.

He could skin the world clean of life. She could see that. It might have scared her before, but now she almost smiled, watching the soldiers become nothing. Watching *everything* become nothing.

Her shadows joined his, filling in every gap, until they formed a united wall, an endless surge that made the ground itself tremble in

fear. She threw all of herself into it, every bit of pain and fury and pulse of the skyre. Isla screamed as the power was scraped out of her, as every bit seemed to be eaten up.

"You're going to hurt yourself," Grim said, but she kept going. Children were dying. Innocents. She heard their screams, and they mixed with the ones she'd heard in her head constantly for months.

They landed in another village, and she started to fight with a shimmering starblade, formed from energy. Everything in her path died. Over and over and over she fought, blinded by purpose and rage. She used every ability in her arsenal, and when one was snuffed out—sapped to the dregs—she reached for another. And another. She fought, and depleted her power, until it was just a whisper, and then she used her swords.

She didn't stop until Wraith was behind her again and Grim's hand was on her hip. She whipped around to find him covered in dirt and blood.

She realized with horror it was his; the soldiers couldn't bleed. She raced to find a major wound, but it was mainly cuts.

"They're gone, heart," he said.

"What?"

"They just . . . left. Like they had been called off. Their bodies went straight through the ground."

Lark must be replenishing her forces.

She remembered what Lark had said . . . what she had offered. *Life.*

But this wasn't life. Not truly. Her forces had been drained of their souls. They were just bodies.

Grim looked spent. More exhausted than she had ever seen him. "She has an endless army. One that can never die. Never be stopped."

There would be no winning against a force like this.

Screams still rang around them. The cries of the injured and dying. Grim portaled them all to the Wildling keep. They didn't have

any healing elixirs left, but they had basic remedies. It wouldn't be enough. People would die . . .

This was what Lark had wanted, she knew, rage boiling through her veins. She had killed the nightbane so more people would die when she attacked. So that more people would join her army.

This entire time, Lark had been planning against them.

Grim portaled her to her room so she could get her starstick. She needed to help get more people to the Wildling keep. But just as she went to grab it, it glowed. Then pulsed, as if trying to tell her something. Tentatively, she grabbed it.

When she fell through her puddle of stars, it wasn't to her family's home.

The blacksmith was pacing his forge. For once, he looked happy to see her. It was hot inside, as if he had just finished making something.

He handed her a dagger by the blade.

She frowned down at it. "It's not time yet. Not for a couple of weeks."

"I've called in my favor early." He looked restless, a single eye glued to the entrance, as if he was waiting for something. "I trust you've seen her?"

Lark. Of course. Isla nodded. Understanding washed over her. "Has she visited you?"

"Not yet," he said. "But she will." His tone was ominous.

Isla realized then that the blacksmith must have been the one to put Lark in containment. She asked him, and he confirmed.

"If she's this powerful, how did he do it?" Isla asked. "How did Cronan trap her? How did he wound her?"

He smiled ruefully. "He didn't. Lark loved him. She cannot be incapacitated, but she sleeps, just like the rest of us."

"He took her while she was sleeping?"

He nodded.

For a moment, she almost felt bad for the Wildling. She couldn't imagine such a betrayal. Cronan was truly ruthless.

"We don't have much time," the blacksmith said. "That's why I summoned you."

She frowned. "How did you do that, with my portaling device?"

He tilted his head at her, single eye narrowing. "Who, Wildling, do you think made it?"

Of course. She owed him so much, for creating the one thing that had made her childhood tolerable.

"And I've made you something else." He unveiled what he had been working on for months—a suit of armor. A breastplate fitted exactly to her measurements, by the look of it, and crafted from the thinnest metal imaginable. Sleeves of tightly woven chainmail and boots of leather and metal. Pants of the same material. The metal was a sparkling silver with roses painted onto the wrist plates. It glimmered beneath the light. *Shademade.*

This was what had been keeping him busy.

"Why?" she asked, in awe at the beauty of his craft.

"You will need it."

"To fight Lark?"

He nodded. "For that . . . and so much more."

But he had begun working on this before Lark had attacked. "How—"

"I'm sure by now the prophet's followers have found you."

Pain lanced through her as she remembered Sairsha and the others, dead by her hand. She nodded.

"I never believed in their prophecies . . . not until I met you. And then I understood. Who your parents were . . . your flair . . . it all began making sense."

"What did?"

"That you were born to either destroy the world or save it."

She paled at his words, the ones she had heard before. Isla shook her head. "I don't want this armor. I don't want this role."

"Yet they're yours anyway." He presented her with a set of knives, which fit into thin pockets in her armor. Every little piece had been considered, crafted for her. Her eyes burned, looking at it. "Remember, Isla. Weapons are nothing without those who wield them."

He looked past her, as if seeing something she couldn't. He frowned.

"She's coming."

Isla imagined he'd made enchanted devices to warn if anyone was nearby. Or maybe he could sense the Wildling's blood. He was suddenly rushing, looking around his forge as if making sure he didn't miss anything.

"I can't be killed, but I can be compelled," he said. "My skills have been twisted by people like her for millennia. She will use me to destroy this world, just as she did to make it. She needs me. Do not allow her to have me."

Isla shook her head. "But I might need you," she said, tears sweeping down her cheeks. "I—I might need you to help me save it."

The blacksmith paused then. Smiled. "You have always had everything you needed." He handed her one of the daggers from her armor. It was sharp and efficient. Perfect for just this task. "Now, make it quick, Wildling." She gripped the hilt. Hesitated.

"Your name," she said. "What is your name?" She had never asked before.

He squinted. His eyes glazed over, as if seeing past her, to another life. Another world. "I—I don't remember," he said softly. His gaze focused again, as he looked to the door. "She's almost here. Now, Wildling."

Isla struck.

Just before the metal touched his skin, his hand curled around the blade. "I remember now," he said quickly. "Ferrar. My name is Ferrar." He let her go.

Ferrar gasped as the blade went through his heart. Tears traced Isla's cheeks, one after the other, as he slumped over. She fought with all her strength to keep him upright, but he was too heavy, so she sank to the ground alongside him.

Brambles began filling the forge. She could feel Lark's power overtaking it.

She wiped her cheek against her shoulder and tried to grab the suit of armor, but it fell apart into several pieces, too many for her to carry. The ground shook with Lark's power, and Isla refused to leave without Ferrar's gift, not when it was the last thing he had ever made. She didn't have time to put it on. With her Starling power, she forced her armor into the air, its pieces hovering around her. She quickly shaped them like a puzzle, into something like a shield she could carry on her back. She pulled her new blade free from the blacksmith's body.

By the time Lark stepped into the forge, she was gone.

When Isla finally appeared in front of the Wildling stronghold, she felt knee-wobbling relief to see that it had been left alone, for now. She wondered if Lark would spare her own people.

She sank to the ground as Lynx came running toward her, green eyes bright with worry. He buried his head against hers. She gripped his fur and cried. He showed her images—flashes of waves of warriors, cutting everything down in their path. Him, looking for her on the ground, while Wraith and Grim searched from the skies.

"I'm okay," she told him, feeling his panic as if it was her own.

She couldn't say the same for hundreds of Nightshades.

When the last of the injured were carried inside, she went to Wren. Terra and Poppy were nearby, helping the wounded. She explained everything to them.

Lark was their ruler . . . not Isla. Lark was infinitely more powerful. She was the original creator of their world.

And Isla? Beyond breaking the curses, she hadn't given her people much reason to be loyal to her. She just hoped they wouldn't stand against her.

There was one thing she could offer: an escape. Though something in her grieved, she carefully handed her starstick over to Wren. "Use this to portal our people away, should you need to. Go back to the Wildling newland. Bring Lynx, if he's not with me."

Wren nodded. Isla taught her to use it.

Grim portaled them back to the castle steps. There, Astria was waiting. She was covered in dirt. Her arm had been badly cut and was now wrapped.

"Burn the dead," Grim ordered. "Dig up any other grave sites and burn the bones."

Astria looked wary. Isla understood. The outcry when the graves had been desecrated had been sharp. Warrior cemeteries were places of honor.

Still, she didn't question Grim.

The general took off to follow his orders.

Isla watched him carefully. As the rush of the battle slowly faded away, realization settled in her bones.

When she had told him who had taken her . . . he hadn't looked as surprised as she should have. Lark Crown was one of the three founders of Lightlark, and she was *alive, here, on Nightshade.*

It was at that moment that she remembered something Oro had said, back at the Centennial. He had said that Grim was the only thing standing between them and a greater darkness.

"You knew," she said. Her chest felt hollow. "You knew Lark was alive. You knew she was buried below."

He stood, expressionless. He didn't deny it.

She took a step. "You *both* knew. You and Oro."

They hated each other. Why would Grim share information like that with his enemy, and not her?

Grim nodded, confirming her fears.

"You . . . you both kept it from me. Why?" Something deep within her cracked. It was another betrayal. Grim looked almost afraid, as if seeing the shift inside her. It had taken so long for any trust to be rebuilt between them.

She wanted to be angry, she wanted to feel betrayed, but she also knew it would make her a hypocrite. She had kept so much from him, even now, even after letting him in.

"I told Oro at the Centennial, before the trials started, so he wouldn't try to kill you. He knew your death wouldn't fulfill the Centennial prophecy; it wouldn't end your familial line. It was also a way to prevent him from trying to kill me. My line's power trapped her. Only my power can release her. Upon my death, she would have been freed."

Grim tried to take her hands, but she wrested them away.

He frowned. "Many of our histories have been buried, but Oro knew that Lark had been just as ruthless as Cronan. She killed *thousands* to form the land; she made it from their bones. Freeing her would mean the end of the world, and we both knew it." He studied her. "That is why you couldn't know. She's your family. She's part of your realm. We thought you might one day be compelled to visit her. Free her. She can only be released with my line's power, and—"

She had access to it.

Lark had been freed anyway, somehow. If not by either of them, then by who?

Everything he said made sense. But she still burned with betrayal. Not just from Grim . . . but Oro.

He knew she'd had family. He knew her ancestor had been imprisoned deep below Nightshade, forced to power the land. Lark might be a monster, but her imprisonment was torturous. Twisted.

Power in bloodlines were shared. It meant Isla's ability, as vast as it was now, was limited by Lark's existence.

She wasn't the only one.

"Cronan is alive," she said. Lark had told her as much.

Grim stilled. "That's impossible."

"All of this is impossible."

They stared at each other. Their ancient ancestors still lived. The fact that they were both this strong meant their lines were infinitely powerful.

It also meant her death wouldn't be the end of all Nightshades. Grim's wouldn't be either.

She could kill him to fulfill the prophecy . . . and his people wouldn't die. Not if Cronan still truly lived.

But she would.

The choice remained impossible. She loved both Oro and Grim. And though the prophecy had taken over her life since the oracle had made it, Lark was now their greatest threat.

They didn't have a chance against her. They both knew it. "Lark can't be killed. Her army is endless."

"So what do we do?" Grim asked. The great Nightshade warrior was asking her for her plan. And she had one.

"Nothing in this world can stop her," Isla said. "So we need to send her to another one."

Grim's eyes narrowed as the meaning of her words became clear. "The portal."

She nodded. "We need to open the portal on Nightshade and send her through. Then close it behind her."

Grim shook his head. "We don't know how to do that."

He was right. But she knew where she could find that information. "The prophet's book had pages missing, containing information on how to open and close portals. If it still exists . . . it's on Lightlark."

Grim stiffened at the mention of the island.

"I'm going to go find it." She took the tooth from her pocket, skyre gleaming in the sun.

“I’ll go with you.”

“No. Lark could be back any moment. You need to protect your people. You need to ensure there are people left to save.”

In the past, he would have stopped her. He would have insisted on coming anyway. He would have made the decision for her.

Now, he only gathered her in his arms, pressed his lips to the crown of her head, and said, “Come back to me, wife.” His voice broke on the word. “Please.”

She looked up at him. Nodded. She didn’t have her starstick anymore . . . but she had access to Grim’s powers. She had used his flair before, when she had saved his life. It had taken every ounce of emotion and ability she hadn’t known she possessed.

Even now it was difficult, reaching for that bridge between them, finding that elusive portaling power. Gripping it. She gritted her teeth against the effort to hold it firmly. A bead of sweat trickled down her forehead. Her skyre glowed.

Finally, she clasped the power.

And portaled to Lightlark.

GATES

If Isla had been expecting the tooth would lead her straight to the prophet's missing pages, she was wrong.

She landed at the edge of a forest. The trees had golden leaves and plump fruit like miniature suns.

She was on Sun Isle.

Focus, she thought to herself, feeling the rush of emotion swelling within her. Nightshade was in danger. Thousands of innocents were in danger. *Grim* was in danger.

The world was in danger.

She had only been on the isle once. It felt like forever ago now. She had never been past the palace.

The tooth stirred in her pocket, warm against her thigh, pulsing with power.

The missing pages had to be nearby, even if she couldn't see them. She walked through the forest until she saw a flash of something tall and glimmering through the treetops. The tooth heated, leading her toward it.

She stepped out of the woods and swallowed.

Massive gates stood before her, wrought in twisted ornate gold. They had to be over a hundred feet tall.

She took a step forward, and the tooth in her pocket nearly seared into her flesh, through the fabric. Its message was clear—the prophet's blood-inked pages were on the other side.

Her hand reached to touch the burning metal. She pushed.

Nothing happened.

She pushed harder. It didn't so much as tremble beneath her hands.

Her power was nearly spent from the battle. Her body was aching. Neither mattered when Lark threatened the world. With a steadying breath, she bent her knees, then took off into the air, the delicate weaving of the metal right in front of her face, until she was above it. She moved to fly over it—

And was met with resistance, like an invisible shield rippled out in all directions, where the gates couldn't reach. It was as solid as the metal itself.

Lark's forces could be rising at that very moment. She didn't have time. She reached for Grim's power, straining with effort, meaning to portal to the other side.

It didn't work.

Her landing rattled her bones. She frowned as she lifted her hand, energy spiraling out of it, enough to turn the gates into a mangled mess.

Nothing happened. The gates were impenetrable. Shielded.

Not for long. She fell back into the forest. Closed her eyes. Breathed in and out, felt the woods whispering around her.

Threads, reaching out.

She pulled all of them.

Trees were ripped from their roots, scraped until they were sharp, until they were tied together to form a massive battering ram. Her hand shook as she kept it levitating, moving the ram toward the entrance. She sent her shoulder back, intending to slam it through the gates.

And was knocked off her feet.

Her back collided with a tree behind her. She lost her grip on the ram, and the forest shook as it fell to the ground.

There was a blade at her throat.

And amber eyes pinning her in place.

Oro wasn't breathing. Isla was breathing far too much, panting in his face. His golden hair was disheveled, his clothes were darker than usual, and he was staring her down like she couldn't possibly be real.

His eyes slipped down her body, slowly, and she felt his gaze like rough knuckles dragging down her neck, her chest, her ribs, her hips, her legs. Then, his eyes were meeting hers again, and it was undeniable, this force between them, an energy quivering like a strike of lightning.

It was almost enough to forget his dagger against her pulse.

He looked down at it, as if remembering. Still, he did not lower it. No, if anything, his grip tightened. The metal dug sharper against her skin. He leaned forward, and she didn't know if he meant for his hips to pin hers against the tree; but that was the result, and she swallowed against the blade.

"I should kill you," he murmured, his lips so close to hers. "I should really kill you." She couldn't help but think this was the same position they'd been in when he had first kissed her. She could almost taste him, the summer and heat and fire—part of her wanted him to do it now.

No. She shook away that thought. She loved Grim. She had just been with him—

But her heart was split in half. And one piece belonged to the king in front of her, holding his blade against her pulse.

Until he straightened, leaving her sprawled against the tree, heart thundering for conflicting reasons.

"What are you doing here, Isla?" he asked. There was no friendliness in his tone. No *love,* though she could feel it, a shining bridge between them. "Are you here to kill me too?"

Her blood went cold, remembering the prophecy. But he didn't know about that . . . not unless Azul told him, which she didn't believe.

His words sunk in. "What do you mean kill you *too*?"

His gaze was sharp as his knife. "Do you really think I don't know?"

"Know what?"

His voice shook with anger. "You murdered the entire coastal guard. Twenty warriors."

She frowned. "No, I didn't."

Isla knew how unbelievable that was. She had killed innocents before. He had watched her lose control. She had *told him* about how many people she had killed, to get him to hate her.

But she didn't need to convince him.

Oro blinked as he realized she was telling the truth. "They . . . they saw you. Witnesses saw you."

Dread curled in her stomach. No. Lark couldn't be here that quickly. It was impossible. She had seen her, just hours before, across the world.

She told him about Lark and her attack.

His expression turned to stone, melting into his familiar seriousness, but he was not wholly shocked. Of course he wasn't.

Her voice trembled. "You always said you didn't lie to me, but omitting the truth, what is that? Isn't that a lie?" She could feel power radiating out of her, Starling energy gathering in her fists, along with her anger. "You knew about Lark. You *knew* I had family. You knew, and you didn't tell me."

Oro's gaze softened, just barely, a flame dimming. "Isla—"

"You were afraid I would seek her out, weren't you? Wake her?" Maybe she would have. She didn't know. The promise of family might have made her foolish. Still, he had kept it from her, and it hurt. She shook her head. It didn't matter now. She was awake, and somehow had already gotten to Lightlark.

She had less time than she thought.

"There's a deadly portal on Nightshade. I'm going to banish her through it; but to do that, I need to get past those gates."

Oro studied her for moments, in silence. Weighing her words. Sensing the truth in them. Finally, he eyed her discarded battering ram. "That wouldn't have worked."

"Why?"

He walked toward the gates. "Because only my bloodline can open the gates."

She wondered if that extended to her because he loved her. The augur would know. Seeming to sense her thoughts, he looked away and nodded. "Yes. Should you have done it correctly, they would have opened."

"What is the right way?"

He ignored her question. Instead, he said, "If I let you through, I'm going with you." She had figured as much. She didn't pretend he trusted her for a second. His throat worked. "Lark is all our problem now. Especially if she's here."

She didn't want him to go with her. Any time near him was torture. Any feelings she had tried to bury were now rising in full force.

But they were on his isle. Perhaps he could help her get the pages she needed.

"Fine."

"You should know, there's a reason only my bloodline is allowed inside."

"Why?"

"Apart from holding our greatest enchantments . . . it has some of our harshest temperatures. Even Sunlings could die in the heat."

"And . . . power can't be used on the other side?"

He looked over at her as he approached the gates. "It can. But the elements can be stronger than our abilities. They can weaken us. Drain us."

"So why have it at all?"

“Heat brings us strength, if you know how to use it. My ancestors used to come here to gorge on power. When I came of age, and mastered my Sunling abilities, I was locked here for a week, to prove that I was worthy of our line.”

“Has anyone . . . has anyone in your line *not* survived it?”

He nodded.

He and Grim had more in common than they ever would have admitted.

She swallowed, considering the gates. The place beyond seemed deadly—an endless expanse of twisted rocks and sand. Though, if that was where the tooth was leading her, she didn’t have a choice.

“Open it,” she said.

He ran his hand down the metal. There was a gold thorn there that she hadn’t noticed. It sliced down his hand, drawing blood. It dripped.

Then, with a magnificent groan, the gates creaked open.

For nearly an hour they walked in silence through a canyon of twisted rock, painted in hypnotic, orange, wave-like stripes. The path through was narrow and strangely formed, but at least it offered shade.

She had dreamed about this, about being able to talk to him again, but now . . . now she couldn’t find the words. She didn’t know if she should apologize or let him continue hating her.

Oro still loved her. She could feel the bond between them, as strong as ever. Killing him wouldn’t destroy Lightlark, not while she still lived.

He was walking slightly ahead, bending beneath the twisted stone. She could do it. She could take the dagger in her pocket and plunge it through his heart before he even sensed her movement.

It would fulfill the prophecy. Grim would be safe.

She knew it; and still, her hands remained firmly by her sides. As it stood, her life was almost over, unless she could find the portal and

take some of its power before closing it. Being bound to Lightlark would only put more innocents in danger.

They continued walking as the ground turned to orange dirt. The air became heavier. She considered discarding layers of clothing; but the sun was beating so heavily, she was afraid her skin would burn. She conjured a starshield above her for a few hours, before her focus began to wane. Oro was right. The heat was like a current, dragging her energy away.

"Conserve your strength as much as possible," Oro said gruffly beside her. "It's only going to get hotter."

It did.

The heat intensified, thickening until it felt like she was treading through water. She lifted her shirt to wipe her brow. Sand stuck to her sweat-covered skin as they traveled through it. Her legs began to strain against the friction, her feet sliding. Even Oro began to look tired.

"Isn't the heat supposed to energize you?" she asked pointedly, her voice dry and raspy.

His look was piercing. "It feeds my Sunling abilities, which I have no intention of using." Good. She didn't know if she could take even another degree of heat.

Hours later, it felt like she was steaming in her clothes. She started peeling layers off, starting with her shirt. Oro didn't look at her as she took it off, tying it around her shoulders to protect them from the burn. Next was her tank top, which had stuck to her body like a second skin. Soon, she was only in her pants and the fabric she wore around her chest. Her daggers were heavy against her legs, weighing her down.

She treasured each of them. But one by one, she began discarding them, until only one dagger remained.

The tooth pulsed against her leg, leading her forward. Her pace became slower, until her feet were barely moving. It was then that she

realized she might not make it to the missing pages at all. She had never felt this shade of heat before, a warmth that seemed capable of drowning her.

She swallowed and found her throat raw and aching. *Water.* She needed water, but there was none around. Just endless sand.

Her steps began to slow to a glacial pace. Her head developed an aching pulse. Eventually she stopped, hands on her knees. Breathing unsteadily.

Oro stopped with her. "There's an oasis. It isn't close, but it exists."

An oasis.

The promise of water was enough for her to start walking again. A faint breeze brushed against her cheeks. She closed her eyes tightly against the sand and spread her arms wide to get as much of the cool air as possible.

Oro cursed beside her.

She opened her eyes the slightest bit, and it looked like . . . it looked like the desert was *rippling.*

She squinted, wondering if the heat was making her see things, but no. She couldn't just see it; she could *feel* it. The ground trembling, as something like a rogue wave rushed toward them.

It overtook everything in its path, smearing away the sun itself. Distant mountains disappeared. It was swallowing the horizon whole. It kept going. Right toward them.

"What—"

"Sandstorm. We need to get inside *now.*"

Her voice was crazed. "Inside where?"

Oro didn't answer, he just took her arm and started running. He had been here before; he had survived this. Her knees nearly buckled as she tried to match his pace.

She was slow, slower than she ever had been, and certainly slower than the storm. Oro didn't look over his shoulder. He didn't falter. He dragged her to the right, parallel to the sand whisking around them.

They should be heading away, she thought; but she followed him regardless, not sure if she would be able to move without him helping her. If he let go, she would just sink into the sand. She would die.

She thought of Grim. Nightshade. They were counting on her to survive this.

But the storm had reached them.

The sand hit her like a battering ram, and she would have fallen to the ground if Oro hadn't kept her steady.

"Keep going," he yelled over the roar of the wind; and, through sand that nearly blinded her, she saw it. A cluster of dark orange rocks. A hole in one side. Shelter.

Sand grated her skin raw. It was already burned from the sun, and now it stung as if she was being flayed. She gritted her teeth and kept going.

She had survived many storms before. She would survive this one too.

That was when she remembered the stormstone, the second one Azul had given her, the one she wore now.

She didn't need to track a storm anymore, but Azul had said gales were engorged with power. Ability that could be captured. It could be useful against Lark.

She began to slip the ring off her finger.

"Faster," Oro said right in front of her, but she couldn't see him. No, all she could see was golden sand, scraping like teeth against her skin. She could barely breath. It was getting in her throat. "We're here." Oro had reached the opening.

She dropped his hand before entering.

He lunged for her, but she planted herself against the wall of sand and faced the storm. It roared like a beast, increasing in power, winds raging, nearly knocking her back, but she stayed firm. She did not fall. She did not falter. She closed her eyes and raised the stone above her head, the same way she had before.

The diamond trembled in her palm. It shook as she captured the storm in her fist, feeling its strength in her bones.

Warm fingers curled around her arm and dragged her into the cave.

She collapsed on the ground, gasping for air, coughing up sand. It had torn up her throat. It had filled her mouth. When she could breathe again, she tried to open her eyes, but they stung too much. Sand was caked on her eyelashes and on every inch of her skin.

"What the hell was that?" Oro demanded.

She said nothing as she slipped the ring back onto her finger, as she scrubbed against her eyelids again. After several minutes, tears washed them clean, and she wondered how she had any liquid left in her body.

The space was small. Sand blasted outside, in a torrent, stronger than before. Without shelter, they would have suffocated in it. She leaned against the stone at her back and flinched. It was hot as coals.

The entire cave was hot, without so much as a breeze from the outside. Heat had been trapped within. They might have been spared the storm, but she could die of dehydration in here.

"How long will the storm last?" she asked, eyes darting to the entry, at the flashing wall of gold.

"Hours, sometimes."

Hours?

She wouldn't survive hours in here. Not with all the heat. Not when she was already boiling.

No use in waiting. Wincing against the feeling of the fabric shifting against her raw skin, she slowly peeled the rest of her clothing off, until she was naked. She crossed her legs and pulled them to her chest, in an attempt to cover anything she could.

Isla wasn't sure Oro was breathing. He was just watching her, looking like he might be close to losing his mind. Sweat slipped down

her neck, between her breasts, and he traced its path with his eyes. Swallowed.

For several minutes, Oro sat very still. He didn't move a muscle. Then, as the heat intensified, made warmer by their body heat, he took off his shirt. His pants were next.

She knew she shouldn't, but she watched his own sweat slide down his chest, down muscle as hard as the rock behind her. For a moment, she imagined tracing it with her finger. Feeling his golden skin against—

Isla turned away.

It was too hot. It was messing with her head. She couldn't think straight.

She reached for the link between them, to use Moonling ability to freeze the water dripping down her chest, hoping to offer some sort of relief, but her energy was nearly depleted. Only a single bead of sweat turned to ice, before her power flickered away.

"Here," Oro said. He reached a hand toward her. "May I?"

At first, she tensed, and he dropped his hand. She was *naked*. But then, she understood his meaning. She understood what he was offering.

Cold. *Relief*. She should say no. He was her enemy. He'd had his blade against her throat just hours ago. She was married to someone else.

Still . . . she found herself saying yes.

Oro gently, very gently, ran his hand down her arm, and her every nerve awakened. She was coated in sweat, but he didn't seem to mind. Under his touch, the water cooled, and she groaned as his icy hand smoothed across her heated skin.

She pressed her lips together against the sound, for it was far more sensual than she had meant it to be. Oro's throat worked as he moved to the other arm. Everywhere he touched was soothed, calmed. She

was greedy for it. Desperate. She took his hand in hers, making him tense, and placed it on her forehead. She closed her eyes and sighed. It dulled the ache. *He* dulled the ache.

After a few moments, she opened her eyes to find him staring down at her. *Amber eyes.* She had missed that color. The heat was doing wild things to her head. She remembered a time just like this, during the Centennial, when he'd had his hands on her, to heal her. She had only been in her underthings. She remembered, and it made her forget herself. Forget the other half of her heart. She couldn't help but move his fingers down her face, her jaw, her throat.

"Isla," he said, his voice dark and rasped, and it made her remember even more. She dragged his hand down her chest, to her heart. His fingers were long against her bare aching skin, and she sighed again.

"It feels so good," she said, barely knowing what was coming out of her mouth. "It feels so good when you touch me."

His eyes darkened. His other hand was splayed next to her head, stiff with restraint, veins taut. He didn't dare move, not unless she guided him.

And she did. She slipped their hands down her chest. Down her stomach.

An ache began to build. An ache for him, an ache from the past. *A memory.* She started to remember the day before the battle, and everything they had done.

"I'm sorry," he said.

She stilled their hands.

Sorry? Why would he be sorry?

His thumb gently swept across her stomach, over a scar that hadn't yet completely healed. The place Zed had put an arrow through her.

"He's imprisoned. It doesn't erase what he did—he, he shouldn't have—"

"You put him in a cell?" she asked, part of her sanity returning. He nodded. Zed was one of his oldest friends. *But he had tried to kill her.*

Her thoughts seemed to slither free from the grip of her mind. Everything was slippery. Everything was magnified, especially this ache within her.

She guided his hand lower again. Lower, until his knuckles traced a path between her hip bones, leaving her skin prickling.

"Isla, I think you inhaled too much sand in the storm." Oro was saying, somewhere far away. "It has power. It can . . . heighten senses. Emotions."

Yes, that was what she felt. *Heightened.* Every nerve was on fire.

He began to move his hand away, but she said, "Please. Please don't stop touching me. Never stop touching me."

But he did. He looked pained, but he gently removed his hand. "Sleep, Isla, if you can."

Sleep. She didn't want to. She was suddenly burning, more than she ever had in the desert. But, as she rested against the warm floor, sleep reached her quickly.

And she dreamed of the night before the battle.

GOLDEN

Isla had surprised Oro in his chambers. The following day, everything could change.

She wanted a piece of happiness, a slice of summer, something to hold on to during the bloodshed. So she had put on a red dress that molded against her every inch. And now, she waited.

Isla felt his heat before she saw him, a radiance that nearly brought her to her knees, and then he was filling the door, and staring at her, and she wasn't sure he was breathing. He had gone still, fingers still curled around the door's handle.

She smiled, pleased. "I take it you like it." Her voice was a rasp she almost didn't recognize.

His own was strained. "If by like, you mean I want to tear it to shreds with my teeth, then yes. I like it very much."

His words were like embers catching fire, a heat dropping right through her. She wanted him now. She wanted everything.

He closed the door behind him and stalked toward her, eyes intently studying her dress the way she had watched him study maps and battle plans. He looked at her like he was trying to navigate the easiest way under it.

A moment later, he had her against the wall, and she inhaled sharply. He ducked toward her mouth, but she stopped him with a hand against his chest.

"Can we pretend?" she asked.

"Pretend?"

"Pretend for just a moment that you're not the king, and I'm not your enemy." If only. If *only*.

He frowned. She didn't like to upset him, but she secretly loved it when he frowned; it reminded her of the Centennial, back before she had admitted to herself that she could tolerate the Sunling king. "Isla," he said against her forehead. "You could never be my enemy."

Her voice trembled. "I'm Nightshade. I opened the portal without realizing. I helped him find the sword. I made it possible for Grim to destroy everything."

Anger flared in his expression. "You didn't know. Most of this happened in the past."

"Can we pretend there's no past, then? That it's been you and me from the beginning?" She wanted that so badly. More than anything.

For a moment, she wondered if he would send her away.

But then he said, right against her lips. "Tonight . . . we can pretend anything you want, love."

Need prickled her skin. They had all night. All night to pretend like they might not all die the next day. "I want you to do something for me. I want you to make my dress gold."

He seemed confused. "I'll call for Leto after all this is over."

A smile tugged at her mouth. "No." She looked down at her dress and was met with the sight of her chest, straining against the low, tight bodice. She heard him swallow, also watching her. "The one I'm wearing. Turn it gold."

She knew what gilding meant to him, the trauma behind it. She wanted to take that trauma and turn it into trust.

He hesitated, so she went on her toes, and said against his mouth, "I trust you. You won't hurt me." It was true. He was the only person in the world who had earned all her trust. Then she whispered, "Turn it gold. *Please*."

The hand he had pressed against the wall next to her head flexed.

Slowly, slowly, his fingers lightly gripped the side of her waist, thumb rubbing down, and they both watched as the red fabric of her dress gave way to the thinnest gold foil, down her stomach, to the floor. It was an impractical choice. The gold foil was so thin, even the slightest movement would rip it.

He made a primal sound, watching, seeing her in his realm's color. Just when he was about to reach for her lips again, she said, "Now melt it off me."

His brows came together. "I'll hurt you."

"You won't."

Before he could protest again, a Starling shield raced across her skin.

His eyes widened in surprise, then intensified, taking in the gold and glittering silver. She felt powerful. In control.

"Now," she repeated. "Melt it off me."

It didn't seem like she would have to ask him again. He ran his knuckles down the center of her chest, to her stomach, and watched the dress melt down her body like a candle, revealing every inch of her little by little. The gold slipped into a puddle that hardened in a circle around her feet, and she was completely bare in front of him. Her Starling shield fell away.

The way he was looking at her . . . it made her remember when he said, *I wish you could see yourself the way I do. You would never doubt yourself again.* "You're looking at me like I'm something to worship," she said, nerves swirling in her stomach.

He made a low sound of need as he stepped forward, leaning into her. His voice was just a rasp as he said, "Do you want me on my knees for you, love?"

Her answer was immediate. "Yes."

"Are you sure?"

She nodded, ready. She felt raw, needy, desperate to feel him. "I think I might die if you don't touch me."

Slowly, eyes never leaving hers, he sank to his knees before her . . . and that heat turned to a pulsing, relentless ache. "We wouldn't want that," he said.

Then, he gripped behind her knee and hooked her leg over his shoulder.

She gasped. At the first press of his mouth, she bucked against him, making a sound that mixed with a whimper, and he pinned her against the wall with a hand against her lower stomach. She writhed below him, pleading, making the types of promises that made him growl against her.

Her pleasure was a wildfire, razing the world, setting it aflame, flaring with every stroke, every nip. Their eyes were locked when it all crested. She gasped. Her hand hit the wall, and energy spiraled out of it, cracking the stone in several directions. For a moment, they just stared at each other, eyes ablaze. Chests heaving. No one had ever made her feel this way: cherished, like the full force of the sun was upon her, shining, melting all her troubles away. She trusted him fully, and that trust deepened every moment they shared. Every connection.

Oro gently set her on the ground again, and she shook her head, spent and still aching for more. "How are we ever going to leave this room?" she asked. She meant it.

"If it was up to me, we never would." Then, he reached down, swept her into his arms, and carried her to the bed.

As soon as her body pressed against the silken sheets, she reached for him. Her hand pressed against his chest, and they watched as his shirt burned away, the flames licking his skin. She was using his power.

He looked at her like he was seeing her for the first time, like she was something wondrous and rare, and she couldn't take it anymore. She wanted everything with him. She wanted it while they still could. Who knew what the next day would bring?

With a burst of energy, she pulled him under her and climbed atop him, straddling him. Slowly, she ground her hips against his, and they both groaned at the contact. Her head fell back, and she balanced her hands behind her as she moved against him, pace quickening.

"I want you," she said, panting. "I want all of you."

He sat up, gripped her backside, and shifted them both until his back hit the headboard. Her hands fell to his shoulders, and he reached his own hand between them.

She gave him a look that said that wasn't exactly what she meant—that she wanted *all* of him—but when he touched her, she groaned, and her eyes fell closed again. "More," she said, reaching down to direct him where she wanted him, deeper. When he did, she gasped and leaned down to press her forehead against his. They were both breathing too quickly, sharing breath, and she looked him right in the eyes as she said, "I love you. I could never not love you."

I love you.

He pressed his thumb where she liked it, and she curled her nails into his shoulders.

She moved on him with abandon, arching her back, wanting it to last, wishing this fire she felt when he touched her would rage forever. He stared up at her, transfixed, his other hand curved around her hip, tightening when she cried out.

"*Oro*," she said, eyes blazing into his as her body tightened and he sat up quickly, as if he couldn't help himself. His hand at her hip curled around the back of her neck, and he pulled her lips to his, tongue stroking her through her pleasure. It was a savage kiss, hard and desperate, like they might not see another night, like he could memorize the taste of her.

"I love you too," he finally said when she stilled, melting against him. "No world exists in which I do not love you."

At that, she pressed her lips against his neck, and went lower. Lower. Suddenly, she was off him and removing the rest of his clothing.

"Isla—" he said.

"*Oro*," she responded near his hips, looking up at him, before continuing her exploring.

The first press of her lips against him, he fisted the sheets in his hands, and they burned away beneath his fingertips.

The rumble of her laugh against him seemed to undo him, because he groaned.

She groaned too, the sound melting into a gasp. Her body twisted.

Only to scrape against hard rock. A dream. It had been a dream of a memory, and—

At once, she remembered herself. Where she was.

Who she was with.

Oro sat on the other side of the cave, watching her. His eyes had darkened to a shade she had just seen, in her mind. He looked like he hadn't slept at all.

She opened her mouth. Closed it. "I—did I say anything. . . . in my sleep?"

"My name. Constantly."

Right. Her cheeks burned. "I—"

"Nothing I haven't heard before," Oro said, before standing.

Her eyes slid to the entrance, and she saw that the storm had cleared. "Why didn't you wake me?" she demanded.

"You looked like you were enjoying yourself."

Anger replaced any remaining shred of want. Then, shame. *Enjoying herself.*

The longer it took her to figure out how to close the portal, the more people would suffer. How could she be this guided by feeling?

What would Grim think, with her gone so long? Would he panic? Was he okay?

If something happened to him because she was taking too long, she would never forgive herself. She shook the sand from her clothes quickly, dressed, and met Oro outside.

The sun was gone, and part of the heat had lifted. The tooth in her pocket trembled. Still, even though it was supposed to lead their path, Oro stepped in front of her.

She frowned. "How—"

"There's only one structure out here, past the gates. Unless your pages are buried in the sand, I know where we're going."

Oh.

In the relative coolness of night and after a bit of rest, she moved across the desert quicker than ever.

It was hours before her head began to throb again from dehydration. Her tongue felt heavy and rough in her mouth. It hurt to swallow.

Her eyes stung with every blink. Her sunburnt skin was painful to the touch. Everything felt dry, and she was desperate for the oasis Oro had promised.

By the time dawn broke, the tooth was practically shaking out of her pocket. They were getting close. Still, as the heat of the day intensified, her eyes began to close. She muscles went slack. She would have fallen right into the sand if it hadn't been for a strong arm curled around her waist.

"Hey," he said, somewhere above her. "The oasis is up ahead. You can make it."

It was easy for him to say. He was Sunling. He was used to this unrelenting heat. It invigorated him, in some ways. She tried to reach for his power, seeing if it might give her a surge of energy, but she was too weak now. None of it held. It felt like she was falling again, and he jerked forward to catch her.

Then, she was off her feet and in his arms.

Her eyes opened the slightest bit, crusted in sand that they had kicked up on their journey, only to see Oro above her, looking forward.

He didn't slow in the slightest, even though he was now carrying her. If anything, his pace quickened.

She should insist he put her down. Instead, she almost melted into his touch. Being Grim's wife made him her enemy, yet she trusted him more than almost anyone.

That trust made her body stop fighting. She went in and out of consciousness. Her senses were snuffed out, one by one. Sun seared her skin, burning it, until suddenly, she was plunged into water.

Isla gasped and gripped Oro in shock. Her arms curled around his neck; her chest went flush against his.

The oasis. The water was hot, but with Oro's ability it cooled, and she almost whimpered in relief, clinging to him, afraid she would lose consciousness again and drown.

"May I?" Oro asked, a hand outstretched.

She nodded, and his fingers carefully slipped across her skin. She flinched, raw, burned red; but under his touch, her pain eased. Carefully, he healed her burns, using his limited strength on her.

Her eyes closed, and she tried to focus on anything else but the careful, practiced way he touched her, like he had done it a hundred times before, because he had. He knew her body . . . and she knew his.

He was just healing her, she told herself. Helping her. It was innocent.

But there was nothing innocent about her pulse quickening. Or the heat that dripped down her spine.

"Thank you," she whispered, far too close to his face, when he finished.

Then she fell backward, and he released her into the water.

Isla let herself sink. She relished the smoothness, the cold, the way the roots of her hair were massaged, how the sand separated from her

body and clothes. She pooled water in her hands and drank greedily, quickly.

"Slowly," Oro said. "You'll make yourself sick."

She wanted to drink the entire damn oasis, but she listened.

When she was satiated, she swam to the edge of the pool and turned away from Oro, then began stripping off her clothing. She rinsed each item and set them out on a cluster of smooth rocks to dry. It was only when she had sunk back into the water that she realized they were both naked inside of it.

Before—in the cave—that had been different. She hadn't been herself. She had been fighting to survive in the heat. She'd been asleep.

Now she had most of her sanity back. She looked down. Her chest was nearly exposed, and she sank deeper. Covered herself with her arms.

Oro's brows rose. She could practically read his mind. It wasn't anything he hadn't seen before, hadn't touched before, hadn't tasted before. But things were different now.

At least, they were supposed to be.

Traitor. The word echoed through her mind. In this very moment, she wasn't quite sure who she was betraying. Maybe everyone, including herself.

His fiery eyes pierced right through her. "Are you happy?" he asked, out of nowhere.

Her answer came too quickly. "Yes."

He looked unconvinced, and Isla almost asked him if it had been a lie. She *was* happy. She loved Grim.

But she loved Oro too.

The pool was shallow. She watched as he slowly approached her, water rippling around him, as if rushing to move out of his way.

Under the sun, in this place, he looked like a god. Golden hair turned darker by the water, wild strands clinging to his forehead. Sun-kissed skin over rippling muscle.

He got closer, and closer, until he was towering over her.

"Why did you get married again?" he asked.

She remembered why she had told him about it in the first place. To make him hate her. To make him forget her.

She still hoped he would.

Oro had warned her before about using blood for power, and that was what she was doing now, to an even greater degree. Her skyre was still hidden by the thinnest snip of shadow, but if he learned about it, he would be upset. He wouldn't understand.

She was dangerous. Reckless. Even without the prophecy, he deserved better. One day, she could hurt him without even meaning to.

"I married him again because I wanted to," she said, hoping the statement held enough truth. Oro looked unconvinced.

He leaned closer, until his breath was against her forehead. "So that's it? You're my enemy now?"

She swallowed at his proximity and nodded.

He tilted his head at her. "That's what you want?"

Yes. "I do. I—I hate you."

He only dropped his gaze to her lips, then her collarbones, then her chest, still almost completely visible in the clear water. Then, he leaned down, breath skittering across her bare skin, so he could say, right against the shell of her ear, "Say that to me when you aren't moaning my name in your sleep, and I might believe you."

Then, he lifted himself out of the pool and got dressed.

After that, they walked in silence. She tried her best to stay as far away from him as possible, to bury this building attraction, and he seemed content to do the same.

They kept going, walking all through the night until the horizon shaped into a mountain range, and she spotted a structure in the distance.

Relief nearly made her knees buckle.

A palace had been carved into the entire side of a golden cliff. It looked like a castle trapped in stone. Its façade was made up of thousands of sunlike symbols and countless doors. There were statues, stairs, and endless columns.

"What is this place?"

"A tomb," Oro said, stepping past her. He stopped at the front. She made to walk through the door, but he caught her wrist. "We can't enter yet."

"Why?" They didn't have time. Nightshade could be overrun by warriors by now. Grim could be in trouble. Oro wouldn't care about that; so she instead she said, "Lark has made it to this island. She's likely killing your soldiers right now, adding to her army."

His jaw tensed. "Just trust me, Isla," he said, and she would be a liar if she said hearing her name from his lips again didn't make her chest constrict. "We need to wait."

They did. And as they lingered at the front of the palace, she studied it more closely. The columns were made up of statues, a row of previous rulers. The pediments were filled with sculptural scenes showing a hunt. A wedding. A burial. All delicately crafted from the golden cliff face. Up above, at the very top—almost at the peak of the mountain—something flashed.

A flame.

Oro followed her line of sight. "That's the forever flame," he said. "It hasn't gone out in thousands of years. Kings have risen and fallen, curses have been woven and broken, and through it all, the flame has endured."

She watched it flicker. It wasn't huge . . . but it was mighty. Strong.

The darkness began to shift, and Oro stood straighter. He motioned for her to step inside the palace. *Finally.* She did and was plunged into darkness. Her energy was spent, but she reached for Oro's power, lighting the smallest of embers. His fingers curled over hers, snuffing it out.

"Unnecessary," he said. He turned back toward the door. Waited a second. Two.

Then light poured into the hall in a glittering line, like melted gold. As dawn rose, the slice of sun streamed across the floor, illuminating an intricate design beneath their feet.

It was beautiful. She turned to Oro, only to find him already studying her.

They stared at each other for a moment before following the sun-spun path down the long corridor and into a room that began flooding with light.

It was a tomb.

Oro moved carefully around the coffin. "Fire doesn't work in here. Any flame is immediately extinguished, which means this room is visible only in the winter, at dawn, for just a few minutes." It was aligned with the sun.

"We don't have much time, then." She took the tooth from her pocket. The moment it was freed from the fabric, it flew across the room, as if summoned, digging into the wall.

No, not a wall. A single page stretched upon it. The crimson red ink was faded, nearly illegible.

Carefully, she peeled it off the stone. Read over it quickly. Relief flooded her like an oasis in her bones.

"Does it have what you need?" Oro said.

She whipped around and nodded. "It's exactly what I was looking for."

The sunlight was already fading, its rays sweeping across the tomb. Beneath them, the metal glistened. *Shademade.*

Oro's eyes locked with hers. It seemed they were having the same thought. He didn't even know about Cronan, but he knew about Lark. "It can't be opened. Many have tried." Sensing her confusion, he added, "It's rumored Horus had a relic. A bone from the finger of a god. Many have searched for it."

The light was almost gone now. Isla didn't waste a moment before cutting a line down her arm and smothering her own blood across her palms. She barely felt the pain, barely heard Oro's yells in protest.

She pressed both of her hands against the tomb's wall and pushed it open.

Oro stood still as a statue.

A body sat inside. Not bones, a *body*. The man was whole, his skin intact. He looked to simply be sleeping.

Horus Rey, one of the three founders of Lightlark. He had Oro's golden hair. Sunlit skin. Straight nose. Sharp angles in his face.

"Is he . . . alive?" Isla asked. Was it possible all three founders hadn't perished at all?

The man's arms were folded across his chest, his hands stacked over his heart. Below them, gripped in his fingers, something was faintly glowing.

A bone.

Sunlight began melting from the room, as if drained. They didn't have any time; but still, Oro hesitated.

"Take it," Isla said. "It could help us against Lark."

It could help her.

A moment. Two. Then Oro slowly reached toward the bone. Gently lifted it.

The moment it was out of Horus's grip, his body became bones. The flesh turned to ash. He became a corpse.

He was dead, that was certain. Somehow, the power of the bone had preserved his body.

Quickly, before the light all but faded, they pushed the tomb's top back on. The room was quickly drenched in darkness, dust, and decay. Oro grabbed her hand, and together they found its exit. They slowly inched down the hall.

Just before they stepped back into the desert, the sand began to tremble. Rise.

Oro cursed. "Another storm."

They didn't have time. She had to go, *now*. Her voice was a frustrated growl. "They happen this often?"

He nodded. "It's why few have reached this place."

"What do we do?"

He looked around at the entrance of the castle and sighed. "We wait."

For an hour, they sat in near silence, staring at the raging storm. Slowly, Oro's eyes began to close. He must be exhausted. They had spent days walking. He hadn't slept the night before, and he had drained himself considerably to heal her.

His head leaned against the wall. His breathing evened.

She watched him, remembering what it was like to curl up next to him. He looked almost at peace now, across from her, one hand reaching in her direction, as if he was drawn to her even in his dreams.

Slowly inching forward, she ran her hand gently down his arm the way she used to, when they slept side by side. He groaned in his sleep, leaning toward her. He didn't even feel her grab the bone.

He was so content—so happy, so deep in sleep—that he didn't even hear her leave.

The storm bellowed around her. She had tied her shirt around her nose and mouth, remembering what Oro had said about inhaling the sand. She couldn't afford to lose herself to her emotions, not now.

Oro was right. Lark was all of their problem. But he might not agree with her solution. That was why she needed to leave him, even though it killed her inside.

The bone glimmered through the fabric of her pocket. She had read the missing page. It highlighted every instruction to open a

portal—and close it. It required multiple skyres, as well as powerful objects to draw from, and this bone would be central to her plan.

All she needed now was to get back to Nightshade.

When she couldn't see the palace any longer, she slipped her ring off her finger. A miniature storm swirled inside the orb, in sparkling gold.

She had to get back to Grim. She had to make sure Oro couldn't catch her before she got beyond the gates and their hold on her portaling.

She remembered what Azul had said about trapping storms. Shaping them.

With all the strength she could muster, she broke the stone between her fingers—

And the storm came tumbling out of it. *Her* storm. She kept her grip on it, as if it was still in an orb in her palm. Her teeth slid together as it fought against her hold.

Slowly, she gained control of its winds with Skyling power and hollowed it out into a vortex, piercing the other storm to form a tunnel for her to safely travel through.

Then she ran through it as fast as she could, knowing that soon, Oro would wake up and realize she was gone. Soon he would notice the bone was missing. He would suspect she had her own hidden plans.

And then he would chase her.

She pushed down the guilt, the lingering feelings, anything that would slow her down, because she couldn't afford to do anything but *move*.

Isla hoped he hated her. She hoped he forgot her. It would make things so much easier for all of them.

The miles were endless. Her limbs felt heavier and heavier. The roaring of the golden wind tunnel sounded like an ocean, one she would drown in if her control on the storm faltered for even a moment.

It wasn't long before the heat slowed her down again. Her eyes began closing. This time, there was no one to catch her when her step slipped. She barely maintained the tunnel while she shot back up, breathing hard.

You have to keep going, she told herself. *Trying . . . that's the hardest part.*

Isla remembered the bloodless soldiers, how they had cut down innocents and Grim's warriors with the same efficiency. Lark was nearly unstoppable. She would burn this world to its embers, stripping away everything that made it good. It wasn't perfect, but it deserved a chance to be better.

They had a chance. With this bone, and the skyres, and the instructions on the page folded in her pocket, they could send Lark away forever. But not if Isla died in this desert.

The heat and sand that had made it past the fabric messed with her mind. She saw the past like she was walking through memories.

She thought about her best ones. Running through the forest after training, smiling up at the treetops, singing with the birds. Finding her starstick below the floorboards. Portaling into her former friend's Starling castle for the first time. Seeing the world from far above, in the hot-air balloon with Grim. Walking through the fields of nightbane, their dark purple color like night being reflected up to the sky.

Azul, showing her the singing mountains here on Lightlark. Rebuilding Wild Isle with Oro, watching nature revive a dead place.

There were her worst memories too. So much loss, betrayal, and danger. But there was beauty here, in this world—more good than bad. And she was willing to fight for it.

With a groan scraped from the depths of herself, she gripped the storm harder—and felt it sweep below her feet, lifting her into its center, sand orbiting her body. *Higher.* Her arm trembled with effort, with control, her skyre setting her skin aflame, and the sandstorm

became a wave she rode across the desert. It rippled below, tearing across miles and miles. She knelt, her fingers running through it, feeling its power surging.

Oro won't catch up, she told herself.

She might reach the gates before he even knew she was gone.

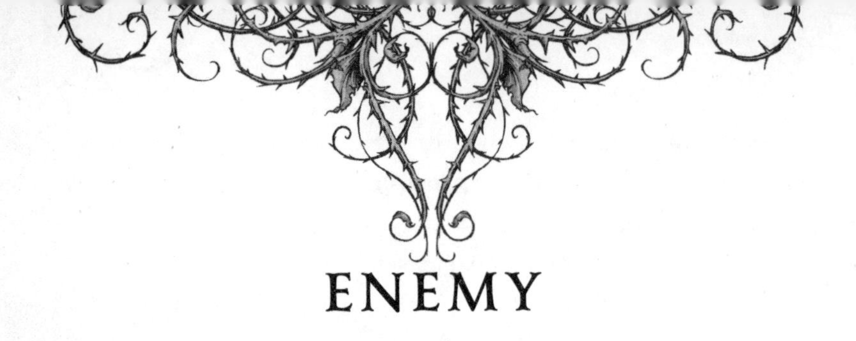

ENEMY

The gates loomed far ahead. The shred of storm she had stolen had long dissipated, melting down until she was back on her feet. She had been walking for hours in the open desert, shoes sinking into the sand. Now at least, she had reached the twisting canyons.

She was walking through one of the strangely shaped tunnels, hand dragging against the smooth rock, when she heard it. Something cutting through the air. Her breath hitched. She turned just in time to see a dagger pierce the stone wall inches from her face.

Her dagger.

One she had discarded on the journey. One that must have been picked up, by someone who would have known how much the blades meant to her.

Someone she had betrayed.

She ran.

Her legs felt boneless beneath her as she stumbled through the canyon, ducking, turning, barely missing the sides of the twisted rock that curved wildly under shards of sunlight.

Oro was the king of Lightlark. The ruler of Sunling. Even with the storm, she could not outrun him—not here in his own lands.

Another dagger. This time, just inches from her hip. She cursed. It seemed he had collected them all on his journey back. He had been right on her heels.

She tore around another curve of undulating stone, then stopped, breathing far too quickly. He was faster. Stronger here, in this heat.

Just before Oro turned the corner, she summoned any remaining energy she had—and used Grim's Nightshade ability to disappear.

It wasn't a power she had mastered. Her shadows were slippery in the heat, especially with her strength waning.

Still, she willed herself to keep a hold on them as Oro inched into her line of vision, another one of her daggers held loosely in his hand.

This wasn't the Oro from before the battle, the one who had called her his favorite everything. No, this was the coldhearted king she had met on the first day of the Centennial, his eyes narrowed in anger—in betrayal. His tall, muscular frame tensed with the practice of a hunter. He took a few more steps. Stopped. Looked up.

Then, very slowly, he turned.

And looked right at her.

He squinted. Isla's heart froze. She glanced down at herself. She was still invisible. She looked back up and found him in front of her.

She wasn't breathing. She didn't dare move an inch as he took a step. Then another. As he tentatively raised his arm. Reached for her.

It was a shame she hadn't learned to walk through walls, because when his fingertips brushed her cheeks, they both felt it.

And then, she became visible.

Before he could say a single word, her Starling shield rippled onto her skin, and she launched a wave of energy at him.

Oro crashed into the rockface with enough force to crack it. She turned to run, but Oro's hand shot forward. A sheet of stone from behind him ripped off the canyon, hit her hand, and pinned her against the wall. It curled around her wrist, trapping it above her head. With one more movement, her other wrist joined it.

His look was pure fire. Pure satisfaction.

He was using her own power against her.

They both knew what that meant.

He stalked over to her. A dagger of energy formed in his hand, and he raised it against her cheek. Isla glanced down at it. This was good, she tried to tell herself. This was what she wanted. For him to hate her. For him to resent her.

It was not all she wanted.

"You stole from me," he said, as if he still couldn't believe it. "You *left* me. You betrayed me."

She just stared at him, chest heaving.

"Did you think I wouldn't find you?" His face was just inches from hers, close enough to see the specks of gold in his amber eyes, simmering with fury. "Did you think I wouldn't catch you?" He leaned closer. "You can't hide from me," he growled. "Even if I can't see you, I can *feel* you. You are relentless. You are a gravity I've tried to escape, but I can't. I *can't*, Isla." His voice shook. He was one of the most powerful rulers in history, but his arm shook with restraint as he brushed his thumb against the wrists he had pinned above her head.

He looked like he hated himself, truly hated himself for his words. He looked like he hated that she shivered beneath his touch. He shook his head. "You chose someone else, you left, and still, I wait here like a fool for the day you might return."

He pointed just beyond the gates, close to the forest where he had found her.

"I go to that cliff, that beach, every single morning because the sea is the green of your eyes, and it's the closest I get to waking up next to you."

She shook her head. "Forget me," she begged. "I'm not good for you, Oro."

"You don't think I've tried?" He said, eyes blazing. "My love for you is like that forever flame, Isla. Relentless. Stubborn. Endless. Burning brightly, even if you're not around to see it."

A tear slipped down her cheek.

His anger abated. It was replaced by pain. "Come back," he said, his voice breaking, and she closed her eyes tightly. "Stay."

"Oro, I can't." He didn't understand. He didn't get it.

"You can," he said, and she opened her eyes to find his widened, desperate. "I've driven myself mad thinking about it. I understand why you left. You wanted to stop the battle. You wanted to stop the death. But I can't understand why you stayed. I kept . . . I kept waiting for you to come back. So I came to you, thinking there must be something wrong, that he was somehow keeping you there, but then," his voice broke as he cut off. He closed his eyes and took a breath, as if gathering strength. "Then you gave me *this*." He pulled the golden rose necklace from his pocket.

He carried it with him. He hadn't melted it down or thrown it into the sea, as she had imagined.

Oro must have sensed her surprise, because he said, "I wanted to destroy it. I wanted to burn it. But I couldn't." He shook his head. "Why, Isla? I would have thought the words you told me, the time we shared, had been a lie—but I could feel their truth. So why?"

He leaned closer, and she leaned away, her wrists still pinned above her. They were made of stone. She had energy left. She could remove them, but she didn't. She didn't, even as his lips lowered toward hers, as he said, just inches away from her skin, "Tell me you don't miss me. Tell me you don't think about me. Tell me you don't go back in time and change your mind." His lips grazed her cheek as he said, "Tell me that, and mean it, and I will leave you alone forever. I swear it."

She lifted her chin high and forced herself to meet his gaze. "I don't miss you," she said steadily. "I never think of you. I don't go back in time and change my mind."

His lips were just over hers. She felt his breath against her mouth. He leaned closer, like he might kiss her, like she might let him, and said, "Liar."

Then, he walked away, leaving her pinned against the stone.

He made it a few paces before he cursed. Isla wrenched herself from the wall and turned the corner.

The gates stood there, in view.

And an army stood beyond them.

Isla recognized the stillness of Lark's bloodless soldiers.

They were blocking their path, making exiting impossible, unless they wanted to risk getting cut down by dozens of blades.

Worse—they weren't just Nightshade. They were Skyling. Starling. Sunling. Some faces, Isla recognized from the battle, fighting on her side.

Now they stared blankly.

Oro's eyes were pure fire and fury, understanding coming over him. "I'm going to kill her," he said, his voice a dark promise.

Her words were barely a whisper. "She can't be killed."

He turned to her. "Then I will throw her into the forever flame and watch her burn until the end of time."

The bloodless soldiers watched them, waiting. Isla suspected what would happen, but she sent a spiral of flames through the gaps in the gates anyway.

They dissolved the moment they hit the gold. It was impenetrable, on both sides.

They were trapped. Only death awaited on the other side. The army could stand there forever if needed; they were already dead.

Without water, in this heat . . . Isla and Oro would soon join them.

They didn't have time for this. She needed to get back to Nightshade. She knew what she had to do. "I'm sorry," she told Oro.

Then, she pulled her necklace.

She could almost feel the air change around them, the sky going taut. His power cleaving through the world to get to her.

The ground itself shuddered as Grim landed just beyond the gates, in a scar of streaking shadow.

In an instant, the army of dead was ash. He walked over their sizzling remains, eyes never leaving hers.

Until they slid to Oro.

He looked between them.

Before she could blink, a shadow scythe was hurtling toward Oro, ready to cut him down. Only the gate stopped it.

Her look was crazed. “Don’t hurt him,” she said, stepping in front of Oro, even though she didn’t need to.

Grim just looked at her. Slowly, the shadows that had gathered in his hands withered. She turned to Oro. “You too.”

He glared at her as he cut his hand . . . and opened the gate.

She flinched, waiting for them to ignore her order, to fight each other until the death, like before. But they both stood very still. They both turned to her.

The army’s ashes swirled at her feet. They were just the beginning.

“Lark is here.” She looked at Oro, then at Grim. They were enemies. She could almost taste their hatred. But Lark would destroy them all if they remained on different sides. “We can’t defeat her divided.” She couldn’t believe the words that were about to leave her mouth. “The only chance we have is to work together.”

REMLAR

Enya spat at her feet when she approached. She looked at Grim and did the same. He didn't even acknowledge her.

Calder's normally jovial expression was cold. Wary.

Zed was missing. She remembered what Oro had said. He had imprisoned his friend.

They sat in the war room—the same place where they had planned Grim's death. Now, he leaned back in one of the chairs, glaring daggers at anyone that looked at him. Anyone but her.

"Lark means to kill both of you," Isla said, looking from Grim to Oro. "And me, likely. She won't stop until this world is leveled."

"Why didn't she just kill you when she had the chance?" Enya said, as if she would have really liked that outcome.

Shadows spilled across the table, ending in claws.

Isla ignored them. "She needs me to lead her to the heart of Lightlark. That's why she's here: to find it."

It only bloomed once a century, disguised as a living thing. The last time Isla had seen it, the heart was falling after Celeste into the center of the island.

"So, what do we do?" Calder asked, running a massive hand down his face. "How do we stop someone more powerful than any of us, who created the very island we're standing on?"

"We lure her out with the promise of the heart. Then, we attack."

Calder looked confused. "From what you're telling us, she's invincible. She can't be killed, or even injured."

"Perhaps," Isla said. "But if she can be stopped for even a few hours, one person on this island knows how."

"What then?" Enya said, leaning forward, elbows on the table. "Even if we can injure her, she's still unstoppable. We need a plan."

"I have one," Isla said.

Enya laughed without humor. "Why should we trust you?"

Isla let shadows engulf one of her arms. The other was wrapped in tendrils of ice, air, crackling energy, and fire.

"That proves nothing," Enya said. "Only that they both still love you, which is obvious." She glared at each of them, like loving her was a personal failing.

Isla looked at Grim. Begrudgingly, he made the tiniest of flowers bloom in his hand.

Then, Isla turned to Oro. It hurt to look at him. His eyes were not hollow, not lifeless, but full of pain. Fear. Determination. She remembered a time when they had only been filled with love.

Slowly, he uncurled his fingers. Petals dripped from them, onto the floor, roses tipped in thorns.

They both loved her . . . and she loved them. She wouldn't do anything to put them in danger, not right now, regardless of what the prophecy predicted.

It wasn't a guarantee . . . but it was something.

Enya looked unconvinced. "Why should we listen to you?"

"You don't have to," Isla said. "You can listen to his plan," she said, motioning toward Grim. "It involves using the portal on Lightlark, destroying the island, and sending all of Nightshade to the otherworld."

Grim nodded, looking as if that plan sounded perfectly fine to him. Enya glared at them both.

"My plan involves sending Lark away forever."

Silence. Then, Oro said, "We're listening."

She told them about the storm season. About the portal on Nightshade—and her plan to send Lark through it. She told them about the missing page she and Oro had discovered, detailing exactly how to do so.

Then, very slowly, she dropped the bone onto the table. Oro's jaw worked, watching it.

Enya turned slowly to face the king. "Tell me that's not what I think it is."

He remained silent.

She stood, fire flaring from her fists, scorching the floor. "That is our greatest relic. And you gave it to *her*? You—"

"He didn't give it to me," Isla clarified. "I stole it."

Enya whirled around to face Oro, speechless. His jaw tensed.

"I need it to create the markings necessary to close the portal," she said. "Its power is the best chance we have of defeating Lark."

Enya looked incredulous.

Grim said, "If you sun fools have a better plan, we're listening."

Enya's fire flared—before weakening. She slowly sat down. For a few moments, her anger heated the room. Then she sighed and said, "And what part do we each play?"

"You and Calder, gather up everyone left on Lightlark, all the remaining forces, then wait for me. We need to portal them to the newlands. Lark is here, and they're just more warriors to add to her army."

Enya begrudgingly nodded.

She turned to Grim. He waited, expectant. "Did you do what I asked with the sword?" *Cronan's* sword, the one they had searched for in the past, that controlled the dreks. She had asked him to return it to the thief's lair, but now she needed it.

He nodded.

"I need you to get it back."

"I can do that."

She turned to Oro. She opened her mouth, but he beat her to it. "No. Whatever you're doing, I'm going with you."

Grim's shadows sharpened.

Oro only looked between them. "You can't really expect us to trust you. Or that he won't use this as a distraction to go through the portal in the vault." The one in the Place of Mirrors, the one that would save her life forever.

The air seemed to shift as Grim began to stand. She gripped his wrist, and he stilled.

"Fine," she said. "We'll figure out how to injure Lark . . . together."

Enya left with Calder, without another word. Grim left too—and was back in just minutes.

"It's gone," he said simply.

Isla sat back against her chair. "What do you mean, *it's gone*?"

"The sword. The pile of relics. Even the damn dragon, it's gone." The pile of stolen enchantments had belonged to an infamous thief. They hadn't met her in all the time they spent trying to get past the dragon.

"She must have moved everything." Her nails dug into her palm as she regretted ever telling him to put it back. She had been trying to protect the world . . . now, this could put them in risk of losing it. The dreks were crucial to her plan.

Oro leaned back in his own chair, at the head of the table, and said, "I have an idea."

Zed was sitting against the back wall of his cell. He looked both bored and unsurprised to see both her and Oro.

He gave her a feline grin. "Brought me a cellmate?"

Oro glared at him. "Not quite. She's your ticket out."

Zed's smile didn't falter. "Oh, we both know I could have been out of this place weeks ago, if I wanted." To demonstrate his point, he slipped out of his binds, and kicked behind him. The stone went

soaring, taking half the wall with it, revealing a hole he could easily fly out of. "You seemed upset, though, so I felt it best to stay put."

"He's perfect," Isla said.

Zed narrowed his eyes at her. "Shameless of you to try to add yet another paramour to your messy situation, but you're not my type."

Oro sighed. "Have you ever heard of a thief better than you?"

That wiped the grin off Zed's face. "Only one. Why?"

"Do you think you can find her?"

"I can find anybody."

"Good," Isla said. "Make it quick. None of us have much time."

"I don't need much time." He reached his hand out, as if waiting to be portaled.

"Oh, no. I'm not going with you," she said.

Grim stepped from where he had been leaning against the wall, cloaked in shadows. He looked Zed up and down, unimpressed. "Why is he in prison in the first place?"

Isla's own grin spread across her face. "I'm sure he'll be happy to tell you all about it during your time together."

Grim glared at Zed, then reached down to brush his lips over hers. Heat spread behind her—anger she recognized as Oro's—but still, she went on her toes and said, "Come back to me," to Grim. Lark was out there somewhere. They were all in danger.

His hands were cold along the bottom of her spine. "You too, Heartеater."

Then they disappeared.

She was left with Oro next to her, radiating his undeniable tinge of fury.

"He's going to kill him once they find her," he said through his teeth.

She shrugged, trying her best to be casual. Trying to pretend Grim didn't just kiss her in front of Oro. "Zed's fast. He'll be fine."

Maybe.

Oro still hadn't looked at her. Perhaps he couldn't. He was likely disgusted by her, by the fact that she was married to the person they had once plotted to kill.

She turned to him. "Ready?"

Using Grim's portaling power was too much strain. She needed to conserve her energy for when her abilities would be crucial.

Her flying wasn't perfect. It would slow them both down. Reluctantly, Oro bent and took her into his arms.

She faced away from him, in a failed attempt to get her pulse to settle, as he shot into the clouds, toward Sky Isle.

The hive was empty.

They had portaled into the familiar lattice structure. The winged creatures were gone. Remlar was gone.

Oro frowned. "They were here."

Remlar was ancient. Could he somehow feel Lark's presence on the island? "They must have fled." But where?

"Is there somewhere else on Sky Isle they've been known to live?"

He shook his head. "Not that I'm aware of."

Great. She had been counting on the ancient being to help them. He had been born in the otherworld, and lived here, on Lightlark, since its inception. If there was a way to incapacitate Lark, he would know.

Oro looked ready to return to his friends, but she stopped him.

"We keep looking for him," she said.

He looked like he wanted to be as far away from her as possible, after seeing her with Grim, but he flew out of the hive, landing at its base.

She did the same, using his powers. His jaw worked as he watched her.

He could feel the bridge between them. He knew she still loved him. Yet, he had to watch her with *him,* his enemy . . .

"Oro—" she said.

He turned away.

For several minutes, they walked in silence. She wished she could fill it, tell him all her truths, the way she had before.

If only he could understand why she had left. Why she hadn't returned.

"How is he?" he finally asked.

Isla blinked. ". . . Grim?"

Heat flared through the forest. "No," he said sharply. "I don't give a damn how he is. I meant Lynx."

Oh.

Her leopard had always liked Oro. "He's fine," she said. "I think he misses it here. I don't think he likes the cold."

That was an understatement. Lynx slept exclusively next to the hearth in her room and had no shame in waking Grim up when the flames got too low.

"He could come back," he said. "No matter what . . . there would be a place for him here." She wasn't sure he was only talking about Lynx.

They sank back into silence. Any warmth he'd had toward her in the desert, any affection, was gone.

It pained her to see him hurt. To know that *she* had been the one to hurt him, betray him, again and again. All he had ever done was love her. After the Centennial, he had been patient with her as she recovered from Aurora and Grim's betrayal. He had helped her learn her powers. He had taken everything slow, which was what she'd needed in that moment.

She had ruined it. And he didn't even know why.

Her eyes stung. She couldn't take this. She continued forward, past him, desperate to be out of his orbit, his heat, his scent. She continued through the trees, remembering herself. She breathed deeply, needing

to focus, trying to bury her feelings for him down into the pit of her chest.

And then she was knocked to the ground with such a force, her breath left her.

Oro. He was atop her, shielding her. She looked up to see the spot she had just occupied was stabbed through with three lances, dug right into a tree.

She had stepped on a trap. It could mean Remlar and his Skyling sect were close.

Oro must have known it too, but they remained there, staring at each other.

Tears gathered in her eyes.

Oro blinked in confusion. "I don't understand," he said, sitting up, allowing her space to leave if she wanted. She didn't move an inch. "I can feel you still love me. It hasn't changed . . . not in the slightest. Tell me the truth. Please." He searched her eyes. "Is it what you did in the village? Do you think I can't forgive you? Nothing could make me stop loving you. *Nothing*. Let me in. I can help you, we can—"

"I'm going to kill you." The words were out of her before she could catch them. "There's—there's a chance I kill you."

Oro stilled above her.

Her mouth tasted of salt. Her voice was a rasp. "The morning of the battle, I went to the oracle. She gave her last prophecy." She had never wanted to tell him. But if marrying his enemy, if telling him about all the worst things she had ever done wasn't going to stop him from loving her, from putting himself in danger, maybe the truth would. "I will kill either you or Grim, with a dagger through the heart. It is certain. It is fated."

A crease formed between his brows.

"That is why I stayed away. Even though I wanted to, trust me, I wanted to come back."

He considered her. "You stayed because you believed it would keep me safe."

She nodded. "At first, yes. And then things changed. I love him, Oro. I'm . . . like him." Her tears dripped down her temples, into her hair. "Now you know the truth." She wriggled her way out from beneath him. "Now you know why you need to stay away from me. I'm dangerous. I'll be the death of you, if you let me."

"Isla," he said gently, standing.

"No." She shook her head. "It doesn't even have to be intentional. You've seen me lose control. I don't trust myself not to hurt you."

"*Isla*," he said again, stepping forward. She didn't know what he was going to say next, because before he could continue, there was a snap in the forest.

And a voice saying, "Look who it is. The traitor and the king who loves her."

Remlar stood before them, in the underground hideaway where he and his people had fled. Bright blue glow worms on the ceiling illuminated his skin of the same shade, his black hair glimmering beneath their light. It was part of the same cave system Isla and Oro had escaped to after the first time she had met the ancient, winged creature.

"I trust you've had your family reunion," her old teacher said, sneering.

He was aware of Lark's escape, then. "I have. You knew her, didn't you?"

Remlar grinned ruefully. "Unfortunately." His expression turned solemn. "I'm one of the few from the otherworld that wasn't killed to feed this land. I was useful to them, back then."

"I don't understand. Lark created Lightlark. I thought . . . I thought she wouldn't be . . ."

"Monstrous?"

She nodded.

He smiled sadly. "Those with godlike power usually turn out to be . . . There were gods in the otherworld. They ruled us all. They were worse than you can even imagine." He spoke of them with reverence . . . and fear. She didn't think she had ever seen him afraid.

She thought about the bone still tucked in her pocket.

"We're going to lure Lark out. I need a way to injure her, for at least a few hours. Do you know a way to do that?"

Mercifully, he nodded.

Hope must have bloomed in her expression, because his eyes narrowed. "She's far older than you, girl," he said. "She will be expecting you to do exactly what you're doing. She is many steps ahead of you already."

"I know." She was counting on it.

"There is metal that would leech her powers. You could find a way to get it on her."

"No. That's how she was trapped in the first place. She won't fall for that again."

Remlar looked pensive. "Then you'll need a curse. A strong one. Bound to something powerful."

She turned to Oro. "I don't know if Grim can spin curses." It was a Nightshade ability, but a specialized one. She had never heard him talk about it.

"The ruler cannot curse," Remlar said. "But I can."

She faced him. Remlar was partially Nightshade—she knew that—but his powers were mysterious. "You can?"

He nodded and pulled a blade from his pocket. It shone brightly.

"Shademade," she whispered, and he perked up.

"So, you have been learning," he said, grinning to reveal his crowded teeth. "I will curse this blade and bind it to myself. It won't take long."

They flew to the castle, where Enya and Calder had gathered all the remaining soldiers they could find—the ones that had agreed to leave.

She reached into the depths of Grim's power, across the bridge between them, and with effort that left her panting, portaled them away.

"Some were missing," Enya said when she was back. *Some had been killed.*

"Burn any remaining bodies from the battle," Oro said. Enya nodded. Calder followed her.

When they were gone, she turned to Oro. "I have to—"

"I'm going with you," he insisted. Fine. This time, she flew herself. They weren't going far. When she touched down at the Place of Mirrors, Oro eyed her warily. This was the home of the portal, the one that would doom him and Lightlark, should she use it.

"I just need to see something."

Walking into the glass castle felt like walking through a dream. She had spent some of her best and worst moments inside.

The vault sat in front of her, its door still open.

She stepped toward it. Oro was right behind her. She touched a palm to the metal. It glimmered in a way she hadn't truly noticed before.

Shademade. Of course. But Wildling power worked here. This metal had been infused with something that made their abilities slip through. She pressed her hand against it, feeling its power. Trying to sense the threads that it had been made with. Blood. Wildling blood must have been fused with it somehow.

"What are you doing?" Oro demanded. "Why did you need to come here?"

She ignored him.

"*Isla,*" he said. "What do you want with the vault?"

"Nothing you need to concern yourself with."

He caught her wrist. She had kept her markings shadowed before, but in the Place of Mirrors, they were on full display.

Oro stilled. "What are those?"

"Nothing."

"Isla. You saw what happens when you use shortcuts for power. Your soul—"

She shook her arm away and stepped out of the palace, into the forest. "My soul is already gone, Oro," she said.

He was relentless. "It isn't. How can you say that?"

She whipped around to face him. "How can you say it's not?" she demanded. "You know what I've done."

"It was an accident."

"And there are *more,* Oro. More deaths on my hands. And there will be *more.* Either you, or Grim, and—" she nearly choked on the words.

"And what?"

She threw her arms up. "There's another prediction. They said I'm going to either save the world . . . or end it." She closed her eyes. The truth, the truth she had started to hide from herself, spilled out. "I feel this . . . calling within me. To kill. It's gotten worse and worse. I told you before, I *like* killing people who I feel deserve it. But . . . even the ones that don't . . . even the ones that happen by accident . . . It affects me in a way I don't understand."

It was a relief to share the terrible truth with someone. Someone who had seen the good in her too.

"You think you might do it," he said softly. "You think you might actually end this world."

Isla nodded. "The bracelets stole away my power. They worked well. For a little bit, I almost felt like myself again. But then, I started killing. Something inside me started awakening." She felt tears like thorns in the corners of her eyes. "I'm afraid, Oro. I'm afraid of what I might do. I don't trust myself. I—I haven't had enough time with my powers, and they've been more of a curse than a blessing. *I've* been more of a curse than a blessing."

"That isn't true," he said, his voice steady. His amber eyes seared into hers. "You broke the curses. Don't forget that."

She often did. She often thought of even that act as something wrong. It had cost her a friend. It had been the worst day of her life to that point.

"I'll help you if you let me, Isla."

She wanted that. It was why she had told him, right?

It was easy, falling back into her past self here. Surrounded by this nature they had created together.

She wanted to let him in completely. She wanted to *stay*.

"Could you ever truly forgive me?" she asked. It was a dangerous question. "For killing all those people? For marrying Grim? For leaving Lightlark?"

Oro didn't even have to think about it. "Yes," he said, the word sharp from his mouth. "I've already forgiven you."

She and Grim . . . they understood the worst of each other. She was married to Grim—she loved him.

But she also loved Oro. Half of her belonged to him. Was that enough?

"I know you've made your choice," Oro said. "Don't change it for me. But you are my only choice. Forever."

They stared at each other. She reached for him—

A snap of a leaf, somewhere close by. She whirled around to face it. A woman stood at the edge of the forest, staring at her. She squinted. It wasn't just any woman.

It was Wren.

She stared at Isla . . . then she took off into the forest. Isla frowned. *What? Why was she here?* She had given her the starstick. *Was something wrong?*

Without another thought, Isla took off after the Wildling, Oro following closely behind.

"Wren?" she called into the forest. How did she know how to get to Lightlark, when she had never been here before? How did she know to find her on Wild Isle?

Just when she almost reached her, Wren ran down the bridge connecting the isle to the mainland. Isla followed, just a few steps behind. "Wren!" she yelled at the Wildling. But she didn't stop.

Isla crashed through the trees, clearing them with her power, but Wren remained just out of reach.

Enough. She burst forward with a shot of Starling energy and was nearly on her—but then she was gone. Isla stood in the clearing. Turned around.

"Where—"

And then there was a blade, stabbing toward her face. *Wren.* Isla barely got her own weapon up in time.

"What are you doing?" she screamed at the Wildling. She wasn't wearing her snakes. What had happened? "Where are the rest of the Wildlings?"

"Isla," a voice said. It was Oro's. He was standing a few feet away, looking unsure of what he should do.

She blocked another blow, her blade grazing down Wren's arm in the process. It was an accident. "I—"

Dread seized through her chest.

There wasn't any blood.

She looked up at an expressionless face. Glassy eyes.

"No," she said, or cried, she didn't know, all she did was block yet another advance. Another. Oro stood there, inching toward her, as if seconds away from interfering.

Tears swept down her jaw. "I—Oro, I can't," she said. She was gasping for air.

He seemed to understand, because before Wren could take another step toward her, she was covered in flames.

Isla watched her burn. Wren just stood there, expressionless, as the fire consumed her. As her skin separated from bone. As she burned until she was nothing but ash.

She sank to her knees. Wren was here, on Lightlark. Isla knew what that meant.

That was how Lark had gotten to the island so quickly. "She—she has my starstick."

Oro's features turned to stone. With portaling power, she could be anywhere at any moment. They needed to stop her *now*. They needed that cursed dagger. He pulled her to her feet.

Isla reached for Grim's portaling power to take them to Remlar.

But it was gone.

No. She reached again. Again. But it was like the bridge between them had been severed. It was like it had never existed at all.

Her heart was beating so fast, clawing up her throat. She couldn't breathe.

She reached. And reached.

Her emotions broke out of her chest, exploding from her ribs. "I can't feel it!" she screamed. She nearly sank to the floor. Only Oro kept her steady. "Oro—I can't feel him!"

He couldn't be dead. If he was, she would be too, right? Or was the heart of Lightlark keeping her alive for a few stolen moments?

Her scream was a guttural rasp; it didn't sound natural. Pain nearly ripped apart her chest. Power exploded, and Oro just barely shielded against it.

"Isla," he said carefully, "Grim is tough to kill. His power is likely blocked, like with your bracelets. You need to stay calm, or we won't survive this."

She couldn't. The idea that he was in trouble—that he had been captured. That he could be *dying*—

Oro grabbed her wrist, as if feeling something she could not. He threw up his Starling shield around them.

Seconds later, trees snapped in half as easily as matchsticks, as the forest was flattened.

Something roared.

A massive serpent broke through the remaining treetops, rising like a tower before them. The serpent-woman. The ancient creature that had fought beside her and Lightlark in the battle against the Nightshades.

Her scales were muted. She was covered in dirt.

Dead. She was dead and risen.

She launched at them with her tree-sized fangs bared, breaking through the shield.

Oro sent them hurtling back with a blast of power, and they rolled through the forest together, before hitting a tree that had been reduced to splinters. There was another roar as the serpent-woman made to strike again.

They couldn't portal away. They needed to run. Oro grabbed her hand to help her up, and she did not drop it as they tore through the forest, taking cover beneath any remaining trees, hiding from the massive serpent.

She couldn't think straight. Her head pounded and her breathing was uneven, but Oro guided them through the forest, running until they reached the cliffside. They stopped just short of the edge, rocks hurtling below.

The snake broke through, hissing. Curling. In a flash, she shot forward toward them, with nothing to stop her from swallowing them whole.

At the last moment, Oro grabbed her hand, and they jumped.

The snake followed, sliding right off the side—and crashing into the jagged rocks below, stabbed through. Pinned in place.

With Oro's power, they landed safely on the beach.

And were immediately surrounded.

Skylings, everywhere, with arrows drawn. Part of the legion that had fought in battle. There were dozens of them. Expressionless. *Dead.*

Arrows shot through the sky, right at Oro. Right at her.

She reached for Grim's power, hoping to find a thread, but there was nothing. *Nothing.* Fury gathered in her bones. Pain lanced through her.

I can't feel him.

I can't feel him.

I CAN'T—

Her vision went black as power exploded out of her. She could taste it, feel it slide against her skin like a blade, ripping the air itself into tatters, shattering everything in its path.

Her skyre burned. Her heart burned.

Mist rained down. She had boiled the sea behind her. She had turned the cliffs into a thousand daggers. All the Skylings were in pieces along the beach. Her breaths were labored from the effort. Her knees nearly buckled.

She turned slowly to Oro, only to see him clutching his chest. When he dropped his hands, she saw all the blood.

And the blade buried beneath it.

SACRIFICE

Oro was bleeding everywhere. His eyes were wide and unblinking.

Saltwater brushed against her legs as she kneeled beside him, hands shaking, rushing to apply pressure against his wound.

"I'm—I'm so sorry, it was—"

An accident. Just like before.

This couldn't be his end. This couldn't be the prophecy. She refused to let him die here, on this beach.

Water pooled in her hands, and she closed her eyes and forced herself to anchor through the panic, just like he had once taught her.

She didn't know how to heal, but Oro had trained her well. He had said that all powers were similar in their execution.

She heard his voice in her head—*Focus*. She did. She cleared her mind, even as pain and regret and shame raged. For him, she pushed it all away, until her mind was quiet.

The water was warm beneath her skin, prickling against places she had been cut. Threads appeared, waiting to be pulled. She reached for all of them and formed a bond. The water began circling beneath her hand, faster, faster. She opened her eyes to see it gleaming.

Slowly, she reached toward Oro's wound. She imagined it closing. She imagined the water soothing his pain, washing the blood away. Saving him.

It wasn't working. He was *dying*.

His hand inched toward her. Pressed against her heart. She knew him, knew what he was telling her.

It's all for you. All this time . . . I saved it for you.

She had access to his power. Lightlark wouldn't fall.

But he would *die*.

No. She refused. She thought of the beach he had promised to take her to, the one with water the color of her eyes. The one he visited every morning. She thought of the golden rose necklace. She thought of flicking his crown. She thought of him pulling the thorns from her back. She thought of crying in his arms and how he had held her, and comforted her, without having to say a word.

That sort of love didn't just die. He was right. This bridge between them was like the forever flame, relentless and unyielding.

If this was her fate, then she would fight against it. She would break it, the same way she did the curses.

Fate should fear her, should fear this clawing in her chest, this love that burned and burned.

She pressed harder. She poured power she couldn't spare into her palm, into him, and watched the sea shimmer. Watched as it twisted into his wound.

Watched as it stitched it together.

She didn't dare move, didn't dare break her focus, until his own hand came down over hers. She looked up, to see him staring at her. *Blinking.*

She choked out a sob. "I'm sorry, I—"

He reached up to cup her cheek. His hand wasn't nearly as warm as it usually was. She shook her head and sobbed again. "I'm a monster, I—"

"I love you," he said, even with the blade still in his chest. The one she was afraid to remove, for fear of doing more harm than good.

Her own words died in her mouth.

She shook her head. "You—you should hate me. Don't you see? I'll kill you, if you let me."

He just stared at her. "I'll never hate you, Isla. I'll love you until my final breath—even if you're the reason I'm taking it."

She didn't want to be the reason. He was conscious now but still bleeding. They were on a beach, far from help. He needed healing elixir. If only she could portal, to get it. If only she hadn't given up her starstick.

Slowly, Oro dropped his chin to stare down at his chest. "I'm assuming if I die from this, it won't fulfill the prophecy."

She shook her head. Her voice was a feeble whisper. "It's supposed to be my blade through your heart."

Clearly, mercifully, it had just missed it.

"Ah," he said. He winced. "Then this death won't do. It'll have been for nothing." The color in his face was fading. The water was working too slowly.

A sob spilled from her lips. She didn't know how to get help. She couldn't leave him here—without the pressure against his wound, he would succumb to his injury. She tried to keep him distracted, calm, hoping the water would be enough. "No. You can't die, because I don't know if I would ever be happy again."

"That's not true," he said. "You . . . you love him. I can see that."

She did love Grim. He did make her happy. Yet . . .

"My heart is halved, Oro. I love him . . . but I could never forget you. I could never not love you." She swallowed. "And even—"

"Even if you were with me . . . you would still love him."

She nodded. "You deserve more than that, Oro. Before I remembered my time with him, I loved only you. That was the truth. But now . . ."

Now, things were far more complicated. She felt torn between past Isla and the woman she was now. It was almost as if they were two separate people.

"I don't care what anyone thinks I deserve." His breathing was labored. The pain of the injury seemed to be catching up with him. "I want you. I still want you, even though you're a traitor. I still want you, even though you're my enemy. I still want you, even though you might kill me. I want you, I want you, I want you, and it is the most selfish thing I have ever felt."

His eyes fell closed.

She screamed. She pressed against his chest, tears falling against it. She begged the water to work faster. She pulled the bone from her pocket, but it was useless without the right skyre.

He couldn't die. She loved him. She felt their bond, felt it dimming, and would do anything to stop it. Give *anything* to stop it.

She pulled her necklace, reached for the other bond, cried out for anyone, anyone to help—

"Heart."

Isla whipped around to see Grim there, gasping. He was out of breath. Zed was there too. The Skyling rushed over to Oro's side and brushed her away, taking over the pressure on his wound.

She was in Grim's arms in an instant. "I—I couldn't feel you!" she said into his chest.

"I know," he said, holding up the sword he had retrieved. "We were imprisoned, we—"

He looked behind her. He saw Oro fading. She could see it, clear on his face. He wanted to let him die.

Isla forced him to meet her gaze. "Save him," she said, her voice a brutal command.

So Grim portaled them all away.

In the castle, she found Wildling elixir, a few leftover vials she had sent to the island. First, though, they had to remove the blade.

Grim roughly pulled it out, clearly taking some pleasure in the way Oro seized in pain. She shot him a look and applied all the elixir onto Oro's chest and waited. Waited.

When Enya entered the room, her fire-wings flared out of her back immediately. She rushed at Isla in a flash of crackling red, pinning her against the wall. Her hand was at her throat, and her eyes were brimmed in fury. "You did this."

Grim's voice was pure malice as he said, "Just checking, heart. You'd be upset if I kill her?"

"Yes," Isla gasped below the Sunling's grip, before Starling energy radiated off of her, sending Enya sliding back a few feet.

She couldn't blame the Sunling for her anger. It was her fault. Enya had been right about her.

The Sunling gave her a look that told her she knew that, before rushing to Oro's side. She grabbed his hand. Whispered a few words to him that she couldn't hear. They had been friends for centuries. She could see how much she loved him.

They all waited in the same room, watching as the elixir worked diligently. Oro had lost a lot of blood on the beach. It was a slow, painful process.

Zed was leaned against the wall, staring at the sword in Grim's hands.

"What happened?" Enya demanded.

Zed looked haunted. "I don't want to talk about it."

Isla glanced at Grim, who stood a few feet away, glaring at Oro, as if he could personally will him not to recover. He shrugged. "Not me. The thief. They had some sort of . . . quarrel."

For several agonizing minutes, she watched Oro, panic like claws around her heart, until his pulse began to stabilize again. Her relief was like ice through her veins.

"This ends now," she said, not wanting to wait a moment longer. Not when Lark had a chance at finding the heart.

"Stay here," she told Grim. "Make sure he recovers."

Begrudgingly, he nodded. Then, he portaled her to Remlar, to fetch the cursed blade.

The Skyling was still working on it. "Just a few more minutes," he said, before turning to her. His eyes glistened. "Now . . . tell me what you really want to know."

"I can wait," she said. "Until you're done with the curse."

"Don't insult me. I can do both at once." He sat cross-legged on the forest floor above the tunnels his people had escaped to, blade between his fingers. She sat in front of him, just like she had during their training. "What is it?"

The prophecy still existed. Lark's attack didn't change that. Its importance was clearer than ever, now that she had nearly put a blade through Oro's heart. "If one had to die—Grim or Oro—who would you choose? Whose death would do the most good?"

His answer seemed obvious, until he said, "Oro."

Remlar smiled at her shock.

"Why?"

He settled back. "Let me tell you a story."

Annoyance flared within her. "We don't have time for a story. People are dying as we speak."

He continued as if she hadn't said anything. "There was once a world with three gods. One that ruled the skies. One that ruled the dirt. And one that ruled the great below. All three stuck to their dominions and lived in harmony, until the sky believed it was more important. I have stars, the sky said. I have clouds. I have the sun. I have lightning. It decided it needed to be more powerful, and so it grew, and grew, until it ruled over both the dirt and below. It had children, and those children decided they needed to rule. Other children were born, from the sky, but also the dirt, and the below.

"The sky's original children decided they didn't like sharing power. So, they kept all their power to themselves. Anyone not in their family that had power was put to death.

"It wasn't until, one day, the children of the dirt and the below rose up and fought back for their power. It started a war.

“One of the princes of below and one of the princesses of the dirt dreamed of another world, where everyone would have power, not just the ruling line. They recruited a prince of the sky, and together, they lured their people to a new future.

“Oro, you see, is the last remaining part of this original ruling line. His bloodline has all power trapped within it. If he dies, that power is released. Given back. Nexus will exist no longer.”

Nexus was the curse that bound all rulers to their people. That made another form of rule nearly impossible.

“But nexus is a curse. Killing whoever spun it could end it too. Right? If it was bound to their life?”

“Perhaps . . . but Cronan is in the otherworld. And Oro is here.”

Cronan. Remlar had just confirmed he was the ruler who had created nexus. She should have known, but she had assumed he had been dead for millennia . . . now, she knew the truth.

The implication was clear. The only real way for her to end nexus was to kill Oro. It was what Maren had told her, long ago, with the rebels.

“You knew Cronan was alive,” she breathed.

He nodded. “I know a great deal more than anyone wishes.”

His eyes were wicked. His smile was sad.

“You must understand something else, my dear. You are the only person living who is of the sky, the dirt, and the below. You, Isla Crown, bring the gods to their knees.”

Right now, trapped between two unwanted fates, she didn’t feel powerful at all.

“You have been marked,” he continued. “The heart of Lightlark chose to mend your own. Its power was stolen from the otherworld, now it lives in you. No one can be sure how that might manifest.”

She didn’t know what that meant. She didn’t want to be marked or special. She just wanted freedom to do whatever she wanted, without her choices deciding the fate of the world.

But this was her role to play. So, she pulled the piece of parchment from her pocket, along with the bone, and asked him her questions.

"You'll need great power," he told her.

"I know," she said. She swallowed, understanding what she must do. "They'll never forgive me." It was a risk. Reckless.

"Then make sure," Remlar said, "it's worth it."

NO ONE

Lark wouldn't find the heart of Lightlark. Isla would make sure of it. The slice of power was warm and bright in her palm as she surfaced on Sky Isle, Remlar's instructions sharp in her mind.

She didn't even see the vines until they were wrapped around her and she was on her knees. A row of thorns forced her fingers open, peeling her skin in coils. She had no choice but to drop the heart.

Right into Lark's awaiting hand.

"Thank you so much for finding it for me," Lark said, her smile serpentine.

Isla bellowed as she fought against the restraints. Her anger exploded off her in waves of energy, sending the vines flying in pieces. In a moment she was on her feet, wiping her bloody hands down her clothing.

Lark frowned as she curled her fingers around the shining orb. Its light faded until it went dull and only an acorn remained. A very helpful illusion Grim had helped her master. "What is this?" she demanded.

"It's a trap," Isla said, and then the world exploded.

The acorn hadn't been an acorn at all, but something Zed had previously developed, an orb filled with their own concentrated power. It burst in Lark's hand, throwing them both backward.

Isla was caught by Grim's shadows, the cold darkness smoothing tenderly around her body and swimming across the skin torn by Lark's vines.

The Wildling landed on the other side of the clearing. Her body had been brutalized by the burst of energy, but she was healing quickly.

"Now," Isla yelled, and Oro was there, Remlar's blade in hand. The cursed weapon glistened. He didn't waste a moment.

Isla didn't dare breathe as he pulled back and stabbed the knife straight through Lark's heart.

Darkness seemed to swallow the world, blinding them for a moment before retreating. There was a gurgled scream.

The shard of ice came from nowhere. It struck Oro, and Isla roared. She broke free from the shadows and rushed forward but was thrown back by a sheet of water so concentrated, her spine hit the trees again.

Cleo stepped out of the woods. Isla should have known. Of course the Moonling was working with Lark.

Grim's shadows rushed forward; he would end her in half a second.

"Careful, Grim," the Moonling said. "Hurt any of us, and your wife's pretty little head will hit the ground."

That was when Isla felt a cold sword against her throat. "Hello again," a voice said. *Soren.*

The traitor.

Lark had mentioned someone had helped her surface . . . somehow, Cleo must have managed it. She wondered how that was possible, when only Grim's ability could free her.

It didn't matter now. Lark was cursed. Immobilized.

Even with the blade at her neck, Isla melted with relief.

Until Lark began to move again. To her horror, the Wildling stood, the dagger still sticking through her heart. *No. Impossible.* The curse was supposed to last at least a few hours, long enough to send her through the portal.

Slowly, Lark's skin began stitching around the blade, until the dagger was expelled and fell to the floor, as if it was nothing more than steel.

It didn't make sense; Remlar had bound the curse with his life.

The Wildling smiled again. "It seems we both planned traps today. You don't think I know where you went? *Who* you went to for help?"

She raised her hand, and the trees above shook. From its branches, a body dropped down, limp and dead. Eyes wide and pale blue throat slit.

Remlar.

"No!" she screamed, tears falling down her face and trickling onto the blade.

Lark only grinned wider. "What a curious being he was," she said. "Always had been." *He was a curious being,* Isla thought. *And a loyal one.* He wouldn't have told Lark anything useful, even while his life was at risk.

Oro was on the ground, surrounded by Zed and Calder, who were working furiously to close his new wound. Enya was in front of them, her wings of fire curling out of her back, balls of flames in her hands.

Grim was looking at Isla, eyes wide but focused, as if he was calculating the chances of being able to turn Soren to ash or portal her away, before her throat was slit. Soren's pressure against her neck was firm—portaling away could kill her.

But she wouldn't let anyone else she cared about die because of her failings.

Grim seemed to sense a shift in her emotions, because he stepped forward. "No—"

She was too quick. Using his power, using the strength of her anguish, she sent them all different places, far from each other.

Before she could think to portal herself, Soren pinned her against him, blade pointed right at her jugular. She didn't dare breathe.

All her focus shifted to holding on to her and Grim's bond, blocking his power, the same way Remlar had once taught her to, so he couldn't portal back to her. She immediately felt him fight against it,

the power pulsing, but she stood firm. Remlar would have been proud of her.

Lark looked surprised but not discouraged. "No matter. We will find the others later. And you will regret having ever wasted our time."

The hilt of the sword hit the side of her head, and the world fell silent.

She woke up bound. The air was stale and dry. She had been plunged into near-total darkness. She blinked and could just barely make out the figure of a woman in front of her.

Lark sighed. "Strange how easily mistakes are repeated . . ." she said. "How strange another Wildling ruler fell in love with her Nightshade counterpart."

Isla's grin was cruel as she spat at her feet. "Mine gave me his life. Yours locked you in a prison. We are not the same."

Lark just smiled back, but Isla could tell she hit a nerve. The Wildling still harbored deep resentment over Grim's ancestor. She could feel it.

"Let me give you some advice, Isla," she said. "Kill your heart before it kills you." She stepped closer. "The heart is always our downfall. No matter the poetry or the lessons about love conquering all, no—the opposite. Love conquers *us*. It is the true ruler. The true equalizer. The true weapon and scythe among men."

That, at least, was true. Isla knew it. Love had made her do the worst things she had ever done in her life.

But it had also made her strong enough to do the best.

"We could have been allies, in another life," Lark said. "You know what it's like to be locked away. To be betrayed by those you love." The side of her head ached where the sword had hit her. Her vision blurred, then returned. "Perhaps time will be what you need. Just like me."

It was then that Isla turned to see her wrists bound behind her, and what was around them.

Her bracelets, made into cuffs chained to the floor. The ones Lark must have found in the blacksmith's forge.

"No," she screamed, trying to break herself away from them. She summoned all her power—but it was gone.

Gone.

Lark sighed. "It's torturous, isn't it? Even worse after the first century. You'll see." She stepped closer to her. Isla lunged forward, but the chains dragged her back. Lark only smiled. "I don't need the heart of Lightlark when I have you. I'm going to find the Nightshade and Sunling rulers and send you pieces of them, until you comply. I'm going to kill every single person you've ever cared about." Isla raged against the bracelets, and Lark only smiled. "Goodbye, for now, Isla," she said, as the ceiling dropped to swallow her.

Isla's raging scream was heard by no one.

FED ON DEATH

Isla's wrists were raw from tugging against the bracelets. Blood dripped down her fingers and onto the floor.

Please, she said to herself, *please don't let her find them.*

If she did. If Grim and Oro were hurt—

She folded over and vomited.

She struggled against the restraints in vain.

Time passed differently underground, without the moon or sun to tell her how long it had been. She was slumped forward, having exhausted all her energy.

Damn her for having the bracelets made. She had done this to herself. She had sourced her own imprisonment, down to the metal.

Only Lark could remove them, which meant she would die with the bracelets still on her wrists.

No, that wasn't true. The only other person who could free her was the blacksmith, Ferrar. And she had plunged a blade through his chest.

All his work had been for nothing. The suit of armor and sword she had left in her bedroom. None of it mattered anymore.

What if I need you? She had asked him.

You've always had everything you needed, he had said.

If only that were true.

A day passed, it seemed, before a mindless soldier appeared in the cavern. His skin was leathered and far too cold as he roughly pulled her hair back and forced her to drink water. He shoved food down her throat, and she bit his hand as hard as she could, but he didn't even flinch as his fingers came apart in her mouth.

Isla folded over and retched, spitting wildly. And he repeated the process again, with his mangled, bloodless hand.

Another day. Another meal. Another guard, this time. She had been right. Lark might have summoned them from the dead, but they weren't whole. Lark was weaker here, in this world. Isla wondered, if, in the otherworld, she had been able to perform full resurrections.

What had she promised Cleo? Did the Moonling understand the limits of Lark's power here?

Isla wondered about Grim and Oro. She hoped they were safe and far away from the Wildling.

She felt around for the bond between them, like she did every few hours, but with the bracelets on, and this far down, she felt nothing.

The thought occurred to her later than it should have. Her necklace. If she could find a way to pull it—perhaps to trick the guard into doing it—Grim could find her. He had found her before.

The next day, Isla tried. She fought with the guard.

She folded herself over, in any attempt to tug at the necklace.

The day after that, she attempted to speak to him, to convince him to help her, but it was like he couldn't hear her.

Nothing worked.

Isla screamed again, as if her voice could cleave through the rock and alert Grim and Oro to where she was—

But no one came.

A week was a long time spent in silence. Her only company was her thoughts. There were only a few more days left of the storm season. A few more days before the augur said her body would perish. Perhaps Lark would find a way to keep her alive. Perhaps the Wildling planned to turn her into some sort of monster.

Ferrar's words were like a chant in her mind, an echo through the cavern.

Everything she needed . . . She began going over his words. Going over her research. Going over the events of her life.

The prophet-followers had been convinced she had been the curse born of life and death. That she would either end the world . . . or save it.

Sairsha's group had forced her to end them. They had believed they were giving her a *gift*. It didn't make sense—unless they thought by killing them, she would be taking something.

She thought about the thrill of killing Tynan. The surge of every death afterward. The beast within that was being satiated.

As her powers had developed, something dark had formed. It had started with using her blood and pain as power, on Lightlark. Then, on Nightshade, it turned into killing for power. Eventually, the skyres.

It was as if something within her was always taking. And always getting stronger.

Almost like another power completely.

That was impossible. She already her flair. She had her *father's* flair. She couldn't possibly have another one. Unless—

Unless she hadn't been born with her father's flair.

Unless she had taken it.

Isla began to shake.

We did not kill your parents. Terra had said those words, and Isla had been quick to dismiss them, even though doubt had harbored in the back of her mind. Then, using Oro's flair, she had confirmed it. Her guardians had no reason to take the blame of killing her parents. They had no reason to look fearful when she had returned from the Centennial, accusing them of that death.

Unless . . . unless they had kept it a secret. Unless they had been protecting her from the pain of the truth. Unless they had been protecting *themselves*, in fear of what she might do.

Tears welled up in her eyes, blinding her.

No.

Isla screamed at the top of her lungs.

She had killed her parents.

She had killed Aurora.

She had killed so many others since.

And it had made her stronger.

She *took*—she had taken the power of every single person she had ever killed. Shame consumed her, and she shook with rage. She fed on death. *Death.*

She was a monster.

But then realization washed over her like rushing water.

Because she had also killed the blacksmith.

You have always had everything you needed.

A primal sound left her mouth. The ground trembled in response to the force of her, because now that she knew the power she had—she could use it.

The blacksmith had put the bracelets on her before. He had always built a failsafe into his designs.

She had his power now.

Her focus unwavering, she remembered watching him in his forge. She remembered seeing him hammer, cleave, create. She imagined him taking his work apart, demolishing it forever. The metal bracelets at her wrists began to crack. Rocks in the ceiling began to fall like rain, shattering against the floor. And Isla just smiled.

She took, just like a curse.

And, as hard as she had tried, Lark would find that she could not be broken.

Isla dug it all up—the pain, the shame, the love, the hatred, the loss, the doubt, the fear, the life, the death, and wrapped herself in it, soaked in it. She scraped every ability from where it had been buried, every bit of power that she had ever taken, every strength she had been afraid to use. She filtered it through the skyre.

And she unleashed.

The world broke open around her. The ground parted like a screaming mouth in a roar that swallowed her senses, tearing through endless layers of dirt and rock until light rained upon her again. She blinked furiously against it, panting. Isla stood a mile down, in the new crater's center. The bracelets were just twisted scraps at her feet.

She had been buried deep below, where no one could hope to find her. She stared up at the distant sky, and the ground that had walled her in like a cage.

Lark would wish she had buried her deeper.

COST

Isla was filthy, bloody, and still shivering from the cold of the underground, but she needed to know for certain.

Terra and Poppy were guarding the door of the Wildling newland castle when they saw her.

Poppy's eyes went wide—not in fear . . . but in concern. "What happened? Are you alright? Let me see those wrists, they'll get infected."

Isla was too tired, mentally and physically, to refuse. She allowed her guardians to lead her to her old room. It took three baths and endless scrubbing to wash the blood and dirt from crevices she wouldn't have even thought of. Poppy brought healing ointments and wraps.

"Did she come for you here? Is everyone okay?"

Terra shook her head. "Wren portaled us here with the device, but she stayed behind, on Nightshade. She never came."

Isla closed her eyes against the memory of the burning Wildling. "Wren is dead."

There was just silence.

As Poppy finished the final set of wraps around her wrists, Isla couldn't take it any longer. She had to know for certain. "I killed them, didn't I? My parents."

Poppy looked at Terra. Terra only looked at her. She nodded.

Isla felt a part of her shatter again, but she didn't have time to break. She swallowed. "How?"

Terra sighed. "Your first cry . . . you brought the castle down. They were killed instantly. Only you remained. Her bonded . . . he shielded you."

Lynx. It was why he had hated her at first. He knew; he had been there. She had killed his bonded right in front of him.

"You were born with too much power," Terra said. "Your power threatened us all. Yourself, especially."

Isla didn't understand. It didn't make any sense. "I never had power."

Poppy's smile was sad. "We ensured that. There was a metal, passed down for generations. Rumored to suppress power. We never had much use for it . . . until you." The very metal that had just been tied around her wrists. But she'd never had bracelets like that.

"We ground it into your food. We laced it into your clothes and weapons," Poppy said. "Between that . . . and convincing you that you were born powerless, you never tried to use it. We knew the dose of stone wasn't strong enough. One day, you would overpower it. We trained you as best we could without it, hoping you would be able to control your abilities once they appeared."

Villainous from the first breath. The words she had once spoken in humor to Grim were very real when it came to her.

She fought against the tears. There wasn't any time for them now.

Poppy and Terra had brought her clothing. She slipped on her familiar brown training pants, long-sleeved shirt, and boots. Poppy silently braided her hair away from her face.

For the first time in months, she felt like a Wildling again.

"Things are going to get bad," Isla told them at the castle door. "Grim will come for you, if I don't." Terra nodded.

Poppy threw her arms around Isla. She held her guardian for just a moment.

She opened her eyes and found Terra watching her. Then, her former teacher said, "We trained you well. Now kill that murderous witch."

In her clean clothing, Isla used Grim's flair to portal into the clearing on Sky Isle. Leaves rustled across the forest floor, carried by the wind.

They had partially covered the body in the center of it, like a blanket.

She went to her knees and cried.

Remlar hadn't deserved this death. He had been alive thousands of years. He had helped her, when most wouldn't have dared.

He had become a friend.

She found his blade nearby. The one he had cursed. The one that held his power. It glistened beneath the light. *Otherworldly.* Shademade.

Isla remembered some of his last words for her.

You will bring the gods to their knees.

He had believed in her, when she didn't even believe in herself. She tucked his blade into her belt.

Then, she pressed a hand against his body, and portaled him to The Hive.

The winged creatures awaited. The woods shook with their sobs. He was carried on a scrap of wind, between his people. She watched in shock as they plucked feathers from their wings and put them upon his body, until he was coated in them.

She was the last in line. "I'm sorry," she said. "I'm going to do it. I'm going to do everything you taught me."

It was the last secret shared between them.

Isla stood on the edge of the cliff next to her father's estate, overlooking the cove where he had once tried to flee his destiny.

She clutched the large black diamond around her neck and pulled.

Within moments, the ground thundered as Wraith landed, his talons digging deep into the dirt. Grim was on his back. He wordlessly leapt to the ground. Isla's knees nearly buckled as he walked toward her. For days, she had wondered if Lark had found him. If she'd . . . if she'd—

"I thought you were—"

His lips covered hers, and she was engulfed in him—in storms and rain and shadows. "Don't you ever do that again," he said. And then, he kissed her more.

She wanted to capture this moment forever. But Lark was still out there. She still wanted all of them dead.

He hugged her to his chest. He was grasping her so closely, she could feel his heart beating wildly, right against her ear.

She looked up to see him studying her body, gaze snagging on her raw wrists. The shadows that had puddled at his feet now flared, eating across the cliffside. "What did she do to you?"

"She put the bracelets on and chained me a mile below the ground. She said she was going to kill all of you."

Grim's voice shook with rage as he said, "I'm going to rip that witch limb from limb and have her heal herself so that I can do it again and again until the end of time."

"And I'm going to help you," she said. "Where is she?"

"Astria saw her go underground a few days ago, and she hasn't surfaced since. The Skyling's blade might not have cursed her, but it was strong enough to have weakened her."

Good. His death was not for nothing.

Lark was strong. Soon, she would surface. There were only days left of winter. Their time was nearly up.

"This ends now," Isla said. She had everything she needed. "Get them all—Oro, Enya, Calder, and Zed—and bring them here. I'm going to Azul."

Grim nodded.

She left him on that cliff.

Azul was seated on his castle steps. He stood as she approached. "What's happened?" he said, as if he could read the pain and trials of the last few weeks in her features.

Energy simmered around her as she approached. Ever since she had discovered her true flair, it was as if part of her power had been

unlocked, and now it surged around her. "The storm to end all storms? It's happening tomorrow," she said.

Azul tensed. "How do you know?"

"Because I'm making it."

YOU

Tomorrow, she would face Lark. She would face her fate.

Her island was quiet. She could hear the waves wash ashore, could feel the forest breathe in and out.

She was on Lynx's back. She thought he might like to see it too. He had gone still beneath her, the moment they portaled here. His ears had sharpened.

"What do you think?" she asked him.

In response, he took off.

Isla was nearly thrown off his back. She had to press herself against his spine, fingers full of his fur, to hang on. "What are you doing?" she asked, as he crashed through the forest that she had come to know.

He didn't slow or waver. He traveled down paths she had never walked before, up hills, into valleys, with confidence.

As if he had been here before.

Isla slid farther up, to press her hand between his eyes. That was when she saw them. Flashes of memories Lynx gave her, melting into the present.

Her parents, here, on this island. Eating fruit from the trees. Riding Lynx. Building bonfires and—

The forest parted. Lynx came to a stop, right in front of a house that had been overtaken by the woods.

"No," she said, slipping off Lynx's back. She had come here dozens of times in the last few weeks and had never happened upon it.

He pressed his nose against her back, and she watched her parents build this place. Every bit of wood, every decoration, every rock. They portaled in some of their favorite things and made it a home. For the two of them. No . . . not just for the two of them.

In one of the memories, she watched her mom laugh, then turn toward Lynx. Her stomach was rounded, full. Her hands stroked down it.

Her. They had made it for her too.

Isla walked into the house.

In the last two decades, it had been overtaken. Vines crept inside, creatures scuttled in the corners. Cobwebs stuck against the ceiling. But parts of her parent's history had remained.

A lopsided table, with chairs that had clearly been made by hand.

Paintings of Lynx and her father . . . she recognized him from her bonded's memories. Her mother had been a painter.

On the center of the table, there was a piece of paper covered in a layer of dirt and yellowed by the air and time.

She froze as she read the familiar handwriting atop it.

Isla. Her father's writing. The same as his maps.

With trembling fingers, she unfolded the piece of paper.

My dearest Isla,

You will be born in just a few days, according to your mother. She has fallen asleep in the chair next to me, just minutes after she said she wasn't tired. I thought this would be as good a time as any to tell you just a little of our story . . . and yours.

Some of this, I'm told, you will know by now. Some might come as a surprise. Let me tell you all of it.

I was working with a man that hated the world, and himself. He sought to find a sword so he could overtake the land

his predecessors had lost. I helped him. I visited a blacksmith and gave my blood to make him an amulet that would allow him to walk in the night, like I could. In exchange, he had the blacksmith make me a portaling device so that I could better help in his mission to find the sword.

I found it, but I was injured in my efforts. I portaled to the Wildling newland, by accident. Your mother found and saved me. She told me that if I gave my ruler the sword, the world would suffer and countless innocents would die in a never-ending war. So, after much thought, I decided to make it seem as though I had been lost, the sword unfound, the portaling device destroyed with me. I left my old life behind, and it killed me. But your mother was a light in the darkness.

Her curse meant that the more time we spent together, the more my life was in danger. I decided to do something desperate. I used the portaling device to visit the blacksmith again, risking my entire plan. I begged him to make me another charm, for your mother, out of my blood. In exchange, he wanted death, but, because of his curse, I knew if I killed him, Grim would know I was alive. Instead, I gave him my armor, which had been passed down for generations. It had original power in it, and he accepted. He made me the necklace.

I wasn't sure if it was going to work, but it did. Your mother still needed blood to survive, but she could fall in love with me without feeling compelled to kill me.

I wish I could tell you every detail of our story, Isla, but it will have to be saved for a different time. I can tell you this, though. In the early days of meeting your mother, I could not stay on the Wildling newland. She was under near constant supervision, and my presence would have been noted. So, every night, I would return to a place I had discovered years before, when my ruler had first given me use of the portaling

device. An uncharted island so lovely, I called it by the name I always wanted to give my future daughter—Isla.

Each day before I left your mother, I would take one of her favorite flowers or fruits from her garden. It would annoy her endlessly. She thought I was doing it to be cruel, but I was planting it here. On this island. So that it would be made up of all her favorite things.

Every fruit, every flower, every animal, every insect on this island was loved by your mother, Isla. And she was loved, let me tell you.

When she was with child, your mother began having strange dreams. She started to believe that our child would be born at the cusp of a new era. And that she would either save our world . . . or end it.

Did you ever wonder what your mother's flair was? She never told her guardians, so I'm guessing you don't know.

Your mother could see the future, Isla. And that is how we know that your life will be a difficult one.

It is how I know you will read this letter on the eve of a day that will change your life, and this world, forever.

It is how I know what your flair will be.

It is how I know your birth will kill us both.

If you feel guilt for what you did, let me put an end to it. We knew what would happen if we chose to have you, Isla. We knew all that would occur. We made a choice, and we have never once regretted it.

You will have my flair. You will not know the pain of the curses. But you will not have your mother's, not yet. We took another trip to the blacksmith, and your mother told him he would die within the next quarter of a century. He was so pleased, he did us the favor of creating a vessel for your mother's flair. She wanted it to be your choice, to know the future, or not. She knows you will make many hard choices.

Your mother's flair is here. It's been waiting for you. Take it, and you will know everything.

You might be wondering how I can be so cavalier about my own imminent death. The truth is, my regard for my own life is nothing compared to my regard for your mother's. From the moment I met her, I loved her. From the moment we were married, I swore to protect her from anything that would ever cause her danger. I have killed anything that ever sought to harm her. There has only ever been one person I have loved more than your mother, Isla. Only one person I could bear losing her for.

And that is you.

Tears swept down her face, falling onto the page. They *knew.* They knew she would kill them, and they had her regardless.

They knew everything that would happen to her. And still . . . they believed in her. They believed she would make the right choices.

Beside the letter was a bracelet. She recognized the blacksmith's work. It had a tiny charm. A vial.

Somehow, she knew, breaking the tiny vial would mean claiming her mother's power. Knowing the future.

Knowing whether she would be able to change her fate. Knowing which of the two men she loved would live.

Part of her wanted to break it, take it, know immediately to stop the doubt and pain. Another part didn't want to know. Just wanted to stick to her plan.

She fastened the bracelet onto her wrist.

Then, she got on Lynx's back, pet him between the ears, and said, "Let's go home."

ILLUSION

Her plans were in place. Her hair was still wet, her arm burned, and her muscles were sore from everything she had prepared.

Everyone knew their orders. Grim was making sure of it now.

Lynx was sleeping peacefully in the middle of the hall of the winter palace. She heard him release a low growl and knew exactly what that meant.

She turned, nearly crashing right into Grim.

Isla hadn't seen him so exhausted in a while. His shadows were pulled in tighter than usual. His posture was slightly bent.

Still, he picked her up by the backs of her legs and set her on the dining table she had been pacing beside. "You're disappointed," he said, his cold nose running up the side of her neck, making her shiver. "Why?"

"Hasn't anyone told you it's rude to read someone's emotions without their permission?"

"Yes," he said into her neck. "My wife. Constantly." He looked up at her. "Why disappointment, heart? Did I do something?"

She shook her head. "No. Of course not. Did—did everything go well?"

He sighed. "Took just about all my power, but yes. We evacuated everyone on this side of Nightshade, split between every isle. Every newland. I've never portaled so much in one day in my life, but they're all safe."

Good. That was good.

Tomorrow, Nightshade would not be a habitable place. The storms would be worse than any of them had experienced before.

"And Oro?"

"Alive. For now," he said.

She gave him a withering look.

"He's ready."

"Lark hasn't surfaced?"

He shook his head. "No. Astria and Enya are taking turns on watch. I just saw them. Neither has spotted her."

Good. She sighed against his chest.

He looked down at her, expectantly, still not over the fact that she, for a fleeting moment, had felt disappointment. She shook her head. "It's nothing. With everything going on, it means nothing." He only continued to wait. "It's just—you look tired. And I had . . . I . . ." She made to move off the table, but he stopped her with a gentle hand against her hip.

"Ah," he said. "A final night together in case we all die a gruesome death tomorrow?"

"Something like that," was all she said.

His eyes darkened. "I'm never too tired to take my wife to bed," he said. "Unless you had planned something with portaling involved, in which case, you'll have to—"

She tried to pinch his stomach and found nothing but a little skin. Still, he feigned hurt. He smiled, and Isla died a little inside.

His grin withered. "What is it?"

"The storm . . . the portal . . . I worry it will destroy this castle." The entire back of the house was made of glass. She looked around. "This is the only real home you've ever had, and it could be destroyed. You must be devastated."

Grim nodded, understanding. "Of course I am," he admitted. "But I haven't lived here for centuries. I haven't felt as much of an attachment as you think." He dragged his fingers through her hair, his

palm cupped her face. "And this isn't my home," he said. "Not any-more. My home is wherever you are."

A tear slipped down her cheek, and before Grim could notice, she crushed her lips to his. At first, their kiss was gentle. Loving. Then it was desperate.

He parted her lips with his tongue, and she groaned as he tasted her thoroughly, stroking the top of her mouth, her tongue, her teeth. He nipped her bottom lip, then licked over the hurt, and a jolt of pleasure raced down her spine.

Her hips ground forward, desperate for any type of friction; and slowly, so slowly, his long fingers traced up the inside of her thigh, bringing her dress with them. His thumb made slow, teasing strokes, so close to where she needed him, before he pulled the hem of her dress up to her hip in one rough motion. Grim seemed to go preter-naturally still as he realized she wasn't wearing anything beneath it.

"Hearteater," he said, his voice strained. "Are you trying to kill me?"

"Yes," she said.

"Good. Now open your legs for me."

She did as he asked and arched as his knuckles brushed straight down the center of her, his touch featherlight, his skin cold against her heated skin. He growled at her want, at the way she clutched his shoul-ders like he was her anchor, at the way she tipped her head back as his fingers made long, languid strokes right where she needed him. At the way she cried out when he finally filled her.

"That noise," he said, his voice filled with such brutal want that she met his gaze again. His eyes had gone almost wholly black, dark-ened with desire, and he slowly leaned down, curled his hand around the back of her neck, and said right against her lips, "Make it again."

She did. Again and again as she shamelessly ground against his hand, chasing her pleasure with abandon. His thumb traced her pulse, then dragged down her neck to her sensitive chest. He caressed

it, back and forth, pace quickening. She panted into his mouth as she matched his pace with her hips; as she tensed, then broke, pulsing around him.

He gently removed his fingers, and she was left wanting—but not for long.

She was in his arms in an instant. He kissed her, dragging her swollen bottom lip through his teeth. His lips didn't leave hers as he ripped her dress off her, seams splitting, buttons flying, until it was just shreds of fabric on the floor. She didn't even yell at him. All she did was fumble with his clothes, before giving up and turning them to ash as he pressed her to the window. The glass was cold against her spine, and she gasped. Her ankles locked behind him.

Grim didn't waste a moment. Hands curled beneath her backside, he went in and in and in, and she didn't know if she would ever get used to the size of him, the feel of him.

"Wife," he breathed against her neck when he was fully in, his arms trembling with restraint as he waited for her to adjust to him.

"Husband," she said, right into the shell of his ear.

That one word seemed to be his undoing. He dragged his teeth down her neck as he drove into her in one brutal stroke, slow and deep, reaching a place that was all pulsing nerves. She made a sound she had never made before, and he laughed darkly against her throat. "There?" he said, and she nodded furiously. *There*. He hit that place again, and she buried her face in his shoulder, digging her teeth into it to keep from screaming.

More—she needed more, and he seemed to sense that, because his strokes became wilder, until he was moving so hard and fast, she didn't know how the windows didn't shatter behind her.

He held her close, one arm around her back and the other holding her hip, her sensitive chest dragging against his cold skin.

"I love you," she said in a quiet gasp in his ear.

"I love only you," he said. Then, both of his hands gripped her hips, and he took her harder, like he could fuse their very souls together, like he could show her his love with every movement. She clung to him through it all, meeting him stroke for stroke, spine sliding against the glass, their foreheads pressed together and gazes locked, until she clenched, and he cursed. He buried into her in one long stroke, and they crested together, holding each other through the pulsing, blinding pleasure.

Only later, when they were washing off, did he say, "We're infinite, heart. Never forget that."

She hoped he was right.

The skies were clear above the winter castle. That would change soon, she thought, as she stared out the windows.

She turned around to find Grim already dressed for battle. He wore sheets of metal and armor, with a sword on his back, its hilt peeking over his shoulder.

He looked like death itself.

She was in lighter clothing, fitted for the role she would play. Grim would be on the ground, with Lynx . . . she would be in the skies with Wraith.

Her leopard didn't seem too fond of the idea.

Grim had his instructions. "Look for my sign," she said.

He nodded. "I'll be there. So will Oro."

"Good. She's more powerful than all of us. We only have one chance at this."

She went on her toes to press her lips to his. He held the back of her head, fingers weaving through her hair, and kissed her like it might be the last time he ever did. When she finally pulled away and fell back on her heels, she felt breathless and even less willing to leave. But she had to.

They went outside, where a layer of fresh snow coated everything, even Wraith. The dragon flapped his wings, sending frost flying.

Lynx gave him a long-suffering look, which only intensified when Grim walked toward him.

Grim slowly offered his hand to Lynx's forehead—a truce.

The leopard huffed and turned away.

"Be careful," Isla said, squeezing Grim's hand, then looking at Lynx. "*Both* of you."

Grim portaled onto the leopard's back. He gave her one final nod that held all sorts of promises—that today wouldn't be their last, that they would repeat everything they had done the night before again and again, that they were infinite, and death didn't stand a chance—and then they left. Isla watched them go, fear and regret clutching her heart.

"It's just you and me, now," Isla said, rubbing the place between Wraith's eyes. They sharpened, as if he could sense battle was coming. Hot breath steamed from his nostrils. Then he leaned down, so she could climb atop him.

She settled in the place Grim had taught her. Curved her hands around the right ridges, and said, "Let's go."

An hour before, she had gone to Cronan's coffin. The portal was invisible, hidden, unreliable. Lark's power, she guessed, had torn the seam wider, her abilities calling to the otherworld. It, answering. They had fed each other.

But Isla had a piece of the otherworld too. *Two of them.*

Bracing against the pain, she had made her first skyre with the god-bone, right over her heart, where the heart of Lightlark had marked her.

The pain had been like swallowing a river of fire—power searing through her veins, desperate for an outlet. Soon, it would find it.

But not yet.

Her new skyre pulsed against her skin, the ink swirling, alive. The missing page had been right—bone held more power than blood. She

could feel the added strength in her bloodstream, heating it and adding yet another ability to her arsenal.

This was how she was going to open the portal. Closing it, according to the page, would require power from her, Grim, and Oro, along with enchantment.

First, they needed to send Lark away for good.

Wraith soared across the skies, and it wasn't long before she heard it—the marching of an army. Grim and Oro had been the bait, waiting for Lark to sense them. Bringing her out of hiding.

From high above the clouds, she and Wraith could barely see Grim and Oro—and the endless wave of bloodless soldiers that now surrounded them.

Isla swallowed, and a voice at her side said, "So. Which one's death would hurt you more?" The voice was angry. Mocking.

Enya. Her fire-wings spread long behind her, crackling.

Isla ignored the question. As easy as it would be to dislike the Sunling, she admired her loyalty to Oro. She was grateful he had someone like her in his life.

"Be careful," Isla said from Wraith's back, as the army below inched closer to the men she loved. Enya only raised a brow and said, "Worry about yourself, Isla. I do not die today." Then, with a wink, she plummeted, her fire-wings growing, expanding, blazing. Just before reaching the ground, she turned sharply to the side, and her wing dragged along the dirt, setting hundreds of bloodless soldiers aflame, scorching the world in a thick line as she shot forward.

She landed and turned sharply, wings curling, wrapping her in swirling flames. Isla watched from above, transfixed, as she tore through the army like a tornado, cutting them down with her fire.

"Impressive. You can say it's impressive," a voice purred right behind her. She jumped, nearly losing her balance, only to find Zed lounging behind her, hands resting behind his head, like there wasn't a battle beginning beneath them.

“Are they ready?” she asked. For her plan to work, everything had to be in place.

He nodded lazily. “Azul gave us everything we needed. And a few things we don’t.” He tapped his pocket, and she shook her head. He straightened and motioned toward the sea. “Calder gathered a few surprises too. You’ll see them.”

Then he fell right off the side of Wraith’s back, shooting across the clearing in a streak of blue. He landed in the center of a group of bloodless soldiers and cut them down with a curved blade crafted from a sharp wind. It was almost casual, the way he fought—never faltering, never looking like he was exerting too much effort.

Grim and Oro were the opposite. They stood back-to-back and raged. From above, all she saw was ruinous shadow meeting searing flame. Both extinguishing everything in their path.

She never imagined them working together, but Lark had made enemies into allies. She waited a moment, then two, for the signal.

It came in the form of a bell ringing. The same warning as the storm.

Astria had been watching Lark. She had emerged.

It was time.

Isla breathed in, and out. Wraith floated, barely moving his wings, keeping them very still, as she slowly rose to her feet.

Her power had been buried. It had been hidden. It had been forgotten. Now she reached into the deepest depths of herself, farther than she believed possible—

And called it all.

All that is buried eventually rises.

Her powers surged up with the force of a tidal wave, nearly knocking her off Wraith’s back, but she stood firm. Firm, as her power began to rise out of her, simmering, glittering green and red.

It formed a shield around her, a sparkling veil, and she could see all her powers swirling within it. Every person she had already killed. Every ability she had taken so far. It was all there, all within reach.

Her skyres burned, pleading to be used. The new ink, formed from bone and blood, swirled in anticipation, right over her heart.

It was time.

She called it forward and her chest glowed, the skyre's starlike pattern shining through her clothes, through the sky, like a beam of light. She was engulfed in power, brimming with it, like she had swallowed the sun and moon and stars and sky and all the universe between them.

Her back bent, her arms splayed out—and she launched it all toward the sky in a beam of unyielding, otherworldly strength.

She was the lightning.

The world thundered in response.

She could feel it across the island, the seam of the portal ripping open, called forward by its power, recognizing it.

From a distance, she saw clouds gathering, forming from nowhere, as if they had been portaled here.

They were dark, heavy, worse than any storm she had seen during the season.

And when they broke open, they did not rain water.

They rained creatures.

Scaled, clawed beasts fell from the sky in endless waves.

Grim saw them first. A stampeded of twisted creatures, with far too many limbs and necks and heads, barreling right toward them.

At first, his shadows killed them all. Oro's fire burned anything that hadn't become ash.

But then, the rain became droplets of metal. *Shademade.*

And all their powers—including Isla's—withered away.

The sky turned crimson. A wind toppled her over—she only escaped death by clinging to Wraith's ridges. She pulled herself up, flattened against his spine, and said, "Wait. Not yet."

The ground was overrun by snarling creatures, by boneless soldiers who worked as one, surrounding those she loved.

She watched, her skin itching to go there, to fight by their sides, to use her swords the way she had been trained.

But she stayed in the center of the storm as clouds began to circle her. It was quiet. Dark. She could barely see beyond the night-tipped clouds.

That was when a flash of lightning lit the skies for just a moment—revealing that they weren't clouds at all but shadow-shade beasts.

The light vanished. Isla trembled against Wraith's back.

And cries like a talon cutting across the night itself filled the sky. She gritted her teeth against the sound, and then Wraith was off—flying as fast as he could, away from the beasts that trailed them through the storm. He went higher, and higher, past the clouds. For a moment, she thought they had lost them.

Then fangs were illuminated by another flash of lightning, nearly closing upon Wraith's wing.

"Move!" she screamed, and the dragon ducked, turning, diving headfirst back into the storm. She held on for dear life, sweat-slicked fingers fighting to keep purchase.

The creature did not slow. It chased them through the storm with spiked wings and massive fangs that curled out of its leathery lips, mouth open, ready to swallow them whole.

Until it was devoured by a creature larger than a mountain.

The dragon shot back, just before it suffered the same fate. Isla swallowed.

The storm itself seemed to still, as the beast straightened to its full height—and roared from half a dozen mouths. It had wings that wholly blocked the sky, and six heads, each bigger than Wraith.

Slowly, very slowly, each of those heads turned its sights on them.

That's when she saw Lark sitting on the creature's back, watching her.

There would be no out-flying them. The creature was too large. Her powers didn't work up here.

Wraith trembled below, but his wings flared out. He didn't run. He was ready to look certain death in the face, with her.

She pressed a hand against his spine, remembering him as a tiny bundle of scales. Remembering him crying because of his injury. Remembering him healing. Getting stronger.

She was so proud of him.

So proud that when the beast lurched forward, he did not falter.

He shot toward it without slowing down, his head bent low. Determined. Brave. Knowing he didn't have a chance but trying anyway.

There were only yards between them.

That was when Isla dragged her sword from her scabbard and grinned wickedly at the look on Lark's face as she recognized it.

Cronan's sword.

She lifted it over her head and roared.

And the world itself seemed to tremble. Cries cleaved through the air, through the ground, a scar of land parting somewhere close by. Then, the sun was blocked out by a thousand pairs of wings.

Dreks.

They shot through the air like throwing stars, burying themselves into the creature. It bellowed. Its many heads tried to catch each drek, but they were too large, and the winged beasts were too quick. Too small. Soon, they swarmed the creature and Lark. They ate through the beast's flesh, infusing it with their poison, the same darkened veins that she had once seen on Grim. The wounds festered before her very eyes, and the creature dropped a few feet, off-balance, blinded by the rush of wings.

Isla stood on Wraith's back again and shot forward.

Some of the dreks surrounded her, like a legion, illuminated through the storm by the rings they carried in their talons.

Azul's rings. Hundreds of them.

Hundreds of storms. Power, trapped inside, that she could unleash, even in the metal. That she could *control*.

She lifted the sword again, in command, and the orbs all shattered.

Energy filled the sky, freed from the stones. Each storm orbited around her like rings of ability, so fast they became streaks of color. With a roar, she shot them all forward at the mountainous beast.

One head was slayed by a blizzard concentrated into a blade. Another by the force of a tidal wave she had morphed into a scythe. A third by a hurricane that went right through one of its throats. Storm after storm attacked the beast at every angle, until there was only one head left.

Wraith flew between two headless necks, turned sharply, and from her place standing on his back, the storm winds she now controlled keeping her balance, she made a blade of monsoons and floods and twisters, and chopped the final head off herself.

The beast dropped from the sky, taking Lark with it.

Her storms raged, painting it her own shade of oceans and snow and hurricanes and sandstorms and ice all controlled by her, all melding together to create the storm to end all storms. Arms shaking with strength and effort, she shaped them all into a single orb that she shrank down before adding it to her belt.

She turned Wraith around in a circle three times, marking the signal. Grim would get Oro. They would meet her at Ferrar's forge.

First, they needed Lark.

Calder was instructed to find Lark's broken body below and trap its pieces in ice, so she couldn't heal.

She needed to meet Oro and Grim at the forge. Their plan was almost complete.

First, though, there was something she needed to do.

Isla took off into the sky, on Wraith's back. She traveled to the winter palace for one final preparation.

She was walking by the wide windows of the dining room when she noticed the snow. It was increasing. Falling faster than usual.

Drops became a flurry, and then sheets, so white and thick she could barely see the gardens through them. It rushed downward faster and faster, and she took a step back, but it was too late.

The snow turned to water that broke through every pane of glass. The wave sent her across the floor, as she fought for purchase. She clung to the dining table, to chairs, to the window, but it was persistent.

It was no use fighting as it pulled her under.

She gasped as she crashed through the surface, desperate for air. She swallowed it in large gulps, her eyes blinking wildly, her body numb beneath her. When her vision cleared, she saw she was in the center of the long fountain behind the palace, in the middle of the garden.

Cleo and Lark stood before her.

The Wildling was supposed to be in pieces. She was supposed to be frozen solid.

Cleo. Isla bared her teeth at the Moonling. She hoped Calder hadn't been hurt.

Cleo responded by pulling Isla under again, and she thrashed against the water, fighting to summon some power—but she had been submerged for too long. Her body might as well have been ice. Her abilities had sunk to a place deep behind her ribs.

She broke the surface again, shaking wildly from the cold, coughing. Lynx roared from across the gardens. She heard him thrash, as if fighting against restraints, and her blood heated. Grim had left him here, tied, for her. He and Oro were waiting in the blacksmith's forge. They would be wondering what was taking her so long.

"You were right," Lark said. "She is a slippery one. In fact," she said, eyes flashing with anger, "I thought you were still in the center of the ground, waiting for me . . . imagine my surprise when I saw you in the storm, on the back of a dragon." Lark looked at her curiously. "How did you manage to get out of the bracelets, little Wildling?"

Isla spit in her direction and was dragged beneath the water again. She tried to fight against the liquid, to control it by using Oro's power, but it slipped between her fingers, as if Cleo had full control over all of it. She was a stronger Moonling. All water and ice and snow encasing the Algid was loyal to her.

"Not yet," she heard Lark say, and then she was gasping for air again. "I need her alive . . . for now." She grinned at Isla. Her eyes trailed to her heart and the scar on it that was just nearly visible in her now-sheer, long-sleeved shirt. It was faintly glowing. "Did you think your life was safe, because you hold a shred of the heart of Lightlark?" Her smile grew. "I don't need it. I just need you. I will drown you in my soil, and then you and your power will belong to me. I will raise you up just like the rest, and *you* will destroy this world, with all that great ability you hold. And then, with your bones, I will start anew. The world will be built off *you*, Isla," she said. "Find peace in knowing your death will have meant something."

The ground beneath the fountain began trembling. The stone around it fragmented, cracking along its veins. Isla lurched to the side, trying to avoid it.

Lark never took her eyes off her, a smile on her lips, her hand in front of her. Roots broke through the bottom, curling around Isla, pulling her, suffocating her. Dragging her down toward the water.

She would drown, then she would be buried below. She would rise. Lark would use her for her destruction.

She would become a weapon. She would either save the world . . . or end it.

Lark's eyes flashed with satisfaction as she watched Isla struggle against the vines. As she watched her try to summon her Wildling ability only to be overpowered. She smiled wider, baring her teeth.

She didn't even see the blade of ice until it was through her throat. Then it sliced through her chest, and legs, and arms. The ice kept shifting from liquid to solid, over and over, resisting Lark's healing.

"Thank you," Isla said to Cleo, and she broke free from the roots that had restrained her. Still on her knees, she thrust her arm into the water, until her fingers curled around the sword that she had thrown inside just minutes before. "Also—you almost killed me."

Cleo just shrugged a shoulder.

Lark watched, dying and healing, again and again, as Isla slowly rose from the water. She took a step, and metal flew through the garden, into the fountain, curling around her ankle. Then around her leg. The other. She outstretched her arm, and the pieces came together like puzzles, the armor Ferrar had made her from her father's own locking into place over every inch of skin, until she was luminous and warm. She had hidden it all. Everything had been planned.

She pulled Cronan's sword completely out of the water.

"I can't hold her for long," Cleo said. "Go. And don't forget your promise."

"I won't."

The night before, she had visited Cleo and made her a promise. The Moonling had freed Lark from the ice. She had brought her there.

Now was Isla's turn to follow through with her part of the plan.

She took off through the gardens, listening to Lark's gargled screams. The roots beneath her feet began to shift, and she knew she didn't have long as she tore down the path toward the maze.

A shot of blue sailed through the air, Cleo propelling herself toward the ocean in an arc of ice and water.

Her time was up.

She kept running, until she was at the maze's mouth.

And Lark was behind her. She was panting, healing, ice falling from her body and crashing against the frozen grass. She stepped into the labyrinth.

It was time.

Isla dug the sword into the grass. With shrieking cries, the dreks emerged and formed a barrier around the maze, encircling it, trapping them within. They moved in sync, as a single, giant being under her command.

Lark looked up at them, then at Isla. "Did you think they could stop me?" She took a step forward. And even though they were both within the maze, her wounds began to heal, flesh and muscle and bone rebuilding. Her face split into a smile. "Did you think my power would be nullified here? So close to a door to the place from which I came?"

"No," Isla said. "I didn't."

And then she portaled them both to the center of the maze.

ORO

He didn't know what was taking her so long. Grimshaw was pacing the forge, shadows eating away at the newly fallen snow, destroying everything in their path. That was what he did, it was what he was good at. Ruining all that was good in this world.

"Your acute hatred of me is flattering," the demon said, sensing his emotions. "But best to keep it at bay while we work together."

Speaking of working together, where was she?

The Nightshade seemed to sense his impatience, his concern, because he gruffly said, "She's coming."

"Let's go to her," Oro insisted. "She could—"

"She told us to wait here," Grim said, his anger making the shadows at his feet point like a dozen swords in Oro's direction. He could see it in his face, though, the concern they shared.

"For what, exactly?" Grim had barely told him anything.

"Closing the portal requires all our power. The blacksmith has enchantments here that can bind our abilities together. She's going to portal here, and we're going to send Lark through for good."

Oro frowned. He was just about to ask him what the hell kind of plan was that, when a screech clawed the air in half.

Dreks.

They were supposed to be gone now. The storm was over.

Oro stilled, as the realization dawned on him. "She doesn't need us to open the portal," he said. "She doesn't need an enchantment. She has our power. She can do everything herself."

Fear, potent as anything he had ever felt, filled his chest. "She has her own plan. That was why she only told you. I would have known she was lying."

Grim shook his head, still disbelieving. "Why would she lie? What could she possibly have planned?"

Oro tried to think, tried to put the pieces together. "I'm not sure, but she must mean to sacrifice herself in some way," he said, flames curling from his palms. "To try to get around the prophecy."

The Nightshade's voice seemed to shake the world as he said, very slowly, "What prophecy?"

PORTAL

The portal in the Place of Mirrors was crafted from shade-made metal . . . with Wildling blood infused. It had taken her time to figure out the technique, with the auger's help.

"It's like a shield with a sword-sized gap in it," he had said, musing.

That was how she had gotten the idea to come to the maze and infuse her own blood into the metal of Cronan's tomb. How she decided to create a new skyre, from the metal's blood.

They were one.

Her power slipped through the shield.

She unleashed that power right at Lark as they landed in the center of the labyrinth, sending her shooting back against the maze.

Lark recovered quickly. Her hands were out, and Isla was swallowed by the hedges. Their entire interior was made of thorns like pointed teeth. Without her armor, they would have ripped her to pieces, but this metal did not scratch, it did not falter.

Isla summoned her strength. She dug deep into herself, to the deepest springs of her power, and began to drag it out.

All the people she had killed, all the death, all the blood, all the dreks, all the things that made her a villain, instead of burying it down, she took hold of it and let it consume her.

Lark was powerful.

But so was she.

Isla stepped out of the hedges and felt herself glow, her abilities radiating out of her, circling her in a galaxy.

Lark forced the hedges behind her down—but they passed right through her: a Nightshade skill she had learned. The Wildling sent roots to chain her ankles and force her onto her knees, but they melted into nothing against her armor and the Starling energy she had coated across it.

The ground beneath Isla parted, attempting to swallow her, but she was faster, making her own tunnel down and appearing behind Lark. She whipped around, but Isla met her vines with a blade of shadow and watched them disappear.

She encased herself in shadows, and every bit of nature Lark threw at her withered away. Lark herself seemed to weaken the closer she got to her, as Isla grew and grew, until her darkness was taller than the hedges. This wasn't Grim's power. It was her own. Her father's. The one she had taken, the one he had willingly given her.

Isla allowed the darkness to claw its way through. She did not fight it, not anymore. It was part of who she was.

Every power she possessed emerged, melding, all six realms' abilities merging to form something else. Something different.

It was her distraction at finding something new inside that cost her.

Vines shot from the ground and wrapped around and around her head so that she couldn't see, couldn't hear, and couldn't move. Her senses were snuffed out one by one, and she roared just before her mouth was smothered as well, as she felt Lark press a nail into her chest. It was as if she meant to dig right through her flesh, to the part the heart had mended, and take it with her own hands. Isla tried to shoot her powers out into the world; but without most of her senses, she had no focus, no direction.

She whipped wildly around, and she couldn't breathe—couldn't think. She was suffocating beneath the vines. They belonged to Lark; she controlled them. Isla's arms went limp at her sides. Her chest constricted as she sought air.

That was when she felt it. *Them.* Oro and Grim. Their bonds to her. Getting closer.

No.

Lark grinned wickedly. "The most dangerous people are those who don't fear death, Isla." Lark didn't need to. She was impossible to kill.

"I hope you're right," Isla said, a smile spreading across her face. Her own body was smothered, useless—but her shadow was not.

It peeled off the ground, and she directed it as if it was another limb, just as Sairsha had. She instructed it to reach into her pocket and remove the feather hidden inside of it. The shadow began picking off the feather's barbs, and Isla found the restraints around her loosen. She found the nail that had begun digging into her chest retreating.

Isla took a breath in the space she was given, and unleashed. The vines splattered all around her, and her shadow dropped back onto the floor, but not before handing her the feather.

Lark was on her knees before her, panting, a hand against her chest.

"It took me a while to figure it out," Isla said. "But then I realized . . . Aurora must have tried talking to you. She must have found out about you somehow. She must have considered freeing you to get what she wanted. She was Starling. She wouldn't have put part of her soul in something like a feather . . . but you. You would. And you used her handwriting as your own. This was how you knew where I was. You were already rising, spreading poison through Nightshade, but you couldn't get out. My blood . . . it freed you, didn't it, when I pricked my finger?" Lark lurched, but Isla filled her palm with flames. She dipped the feather inside, and Lark twisted unnaturally, roaring. "This must hurt . . . right?" Isla said, barely recognizing her own voice, the beast within her preening at the sounds of suffering.

She blew the feather out, just halfway to burning. Lark heaved on the ground before her. And Isla took a step toward the coffin. She placed her hand against it, feeling its power rise and her own rushing

to meet it. She poured all of herself inside—the Nightshade, Wildling, and Sunling abilities she had gotten through both love and death. She had portaled hundreds of times with her starstick, and she summoned that ability, Grim's flair. She shook with her concentration, until she felt the world peel in front of her.

Clouds began to gather overhead.

With a flick of her wrist, the coffin exploded. Only a hole remained. It was dark and endless, a slice of sky breaking open, a burst of color at its center, as if a forever dawn bloomed inside.

"No," Lark said, still on the ground, choking on her words. "Foolish girl. Push me through, and I will find a way to return. I will come back."

Isla tilted her head at her. "No," she said. "You won't."

She slung the sword that controlled the dreks across her back. She could feel Oro and Grim fighting against the creatures. She could feel a break in their shield. At her command, they scattered, ordered not to hurt anyone anymore.

She hadn't had Zed and Grim steal the sword again to control the dreks, though they had been useful.

No, she needed it because it had been enchanted by Cronan himself. It contained his blood.

Which meant she could find him with it.

Remlar had explained the scroll. He confirmed what she had read in the desert—that a portal could only be closed on the other side.

It was why she had stolen the bone from Oro. Why she had started to shape her own plan.

She hauled Lark from the ground, snapping the vines and roots that sought to keep her. Sending Lark through the portal meant saving this world from destruction. But it also meant Isla's final chance at redemption.

Lark's power was bringing the dead back to life. Here, it meant little. It meant creating monsters. But in the otherworld . . . Lark

could fully resurrect people. Remlar had told her so. There, Isla could kill her. Isla could take her power.

And she could bring everyone she had ever killed back to life.

There was just one more thing she had needed, in order to use the portal. It was why she had visited the augur the night before.

"The prophet's scroll says to go to another world, I must know its name . . . but it's been forgotten."

The auger nodded. "It was on purpose, you see." He grinned. "But the prophet knew that . . . so he carved the name into himself before he came here, to ensure he never forgot." The augur had crawled to the back of his cave and returned with something gleaming white. Presented it to her. There, in scrawled script, was a word, etched against bone.

The otherworld's name . . . was Skyshade.

GRIM

She hadn't broken the curse on the maze; that was clear when his own power died before reaching the dreks. Instead, *she herself* had broken through it, somehow.

He had tried to claw his way through the creatures, stabbing them with his sword, but their skin was nearly impenetrable, and whenever one fell, it was replaced.

Oro battled next to him, roaring as the dreks tore him apart with their talons, but he did not falter, and neither did Grim.

There was a great crash and growl behind them. Isla's leopard had followed them. He ran toward the maze, toward her, as if he could feel something neither of them could see.

With his great size and might, he broke through the dreks, and Grim and Oro followed. With every turn, the leopard crashed into the hedges, cutting them in half, but the creature did not slow. He could smell her, and they followed.

Grim was powerless to portal. He was powerless to turn all the hedges to ash. All he could do was run as fast as he ever had in his life, next to his enemy, whose devastation he could see was as sharp as his own.

She had told *him* about the prophecy. She had trusted *him*. The pain twisted in his gut like a sword, because he only had himself to blame.

Now, for the only time in his long life, he was grateful for the king's presence. If he could help save her, then he would bow before him if he had to, he would do anything. He would do anything for her, and he was just at the beginning of proving it.

The leopard arrived first, and its roar shook him to his very core.

A streak of lightning cracked the sky in half, landing right in the middle of the maze. The force of it sent them all flying back. The land began to shake. All the windows in the palace behind them shattered. Grim was on his feet in an instant. He didn't slow. He didn't care at all about the palace. All he cared about was her, and—

He reached the center and sank to his knees. Where the coffin had once stood, just a charred circle and a burnt white feather remained.

Lark had gone through the portal to the otherworld.

And so had Isla.

ACKNOWLEDGMENTS

Every book in a series is its own journey, and I'm eternally grateful to everyone who has made putting *Skyshade* out into the world possible. Thank you to my editor, Anne Heltzel, for your endless championing of this series from the very beginning and for making so much possible. I am so incredibly grateful you took a chance on it and me. Thank you to Andrew Smith, for believing in these books, and for seeing their potential. Thank you to my literary agent, Jodi Reamer, for being my guiding star and for somehow having the time to talk to me almost every day. I am so grateful to have you in my corner. Thank you to my entertainment lawyer, Eric Greenspan, for taking me on before any of this, and for rooting for me every step of the way.

Thank you to Kim Lauber, for always listening to my ideas and for being an all-around superhuman. To Mary Marolla, for being supremely organized when I am not and for making magic happen. Thank you also to Megan Carlson, Maggie Moore, Josh Weiss, Taryn Roeder, Megan Evans, and Angelica Busanet for the incredible work you do to get this book ready to print and into readers' hands. And to Micah Fleming, Natalie C. Sousa, and Sasha Vinogradova for creating the snake and storm-filled cover of my dreams.

Thank you to Berni Vann, Michelle Weiner, and Annika Patton for everything. Berni and Michelle—I am so grateful to get to work with you. Annika—you are always the first person to read these books, and, first and foremost, I'm so grateful for your friendship. Thank you also to Denisse Montfort and Allison Elbl for all that you do, and to Anqi Xu, for giving me great notes.

Thank you to my love for your support over so many years. You make the real world better than a fictional one. I am so grateful I get to spend every day with you. I love you.

Infinite thanks to my family and friends for dealing with me and my lack of communication while I'm on what seems like a perpetual deadline. You know who you are, and I am so grateful to have you in my life.

Finally, and most of all, thank you, reader, for taking this journey with me. Your support for this series keeps me writing it—every book is for you. Thank you for everything.

Nightshade

The Newlands
Moonling Newland
Wildling Newland
Skyling Newland
Starling Newland

Wild Isle
Place of Mirrors
Forgotten Mine
Mainland Woods
Mainland Castle
Mainland
White Cliffs
Insignia

The Isles

Moon Isle

The Oracles

Broken Harbor

The Gates

Sun Isle

Singing Mountains

Agora

Hive

Sky Isle

Abbey

Bay of Teeth

The Last Tower

The Craters

Star Isle

Lightlark

NIGHTBANE

ALEX ASTER

LIGHTLARK #2

AMULET BOOKS • NEW YORK

PUBLISHER'S NOTE: This is a work of fiction. Names, characters, places, and incidents are either the product of the author's imagination or used fictitiously, and any resemblance to actual persons, living or dead, business establishments, events, or locales is entirely coincidental.

Cataloging-in-Publication Data has been applied for and may be obtained from the Library of Congress.

ISBN 978-1-4197-6090-7

Book design by Chelsea Hunter

Printed and bound in U.S.A.
10 9 8

Amulet Books are available at special discounts when purchased in quantity for premiums and promotions as well as fundraising or educational use. Special editions can also be created to specification. For details, contact specialsales@abramsbooks.com or the address below.

ABRAMS The Art of Books
195 Broadway, New York, NY 10007
abramsbooks.com

For Rron—
you make the real world better than a fictional one

My bane and antidote, are both before me.

—J. Addison, *Cato: A Tragedy,* 1713

VAULT

Isla Crown tasted death on the back of her tongue.

Moments before, she had unlocked the hidden vault in the Place of Mirrors. Inside, power churned, whispering in a language she didn't understand, calling to something deep in her marrow. It felt urgent, obvious, like the answer to a question she had somehow forgotten.

The rest of the abandoned palace was falling apart, but this door had remained closed throughout the curses. Her ancestors had fought to keep it a secret. Her crown was the only key and Isla thought, as she pulled the door open with a scream of a creak, that they must have hidden it away so thoroughly for a reason.

Her heart raced as she peered inside. But before she could get a look at anything good, a force battled through the gap, struck her in the chest, and sent her careening across the room.

The door slammed closed.

For a moment, there was silence. Peace, almost, which had become the most coveted and rarest of luxuries. It was all she dared wish for nowadays. Peace from the pain that pulsed through her chest, where an arrow had split her heart into two. Peace from the thoughts that ravaged her brain like insects feasting on decay. So much had been lost and gained in the last few weeks, and not in equal measure.

For that one second, though, she was finally able to empty her head.

Until it cracked against the stone floor, and her peace was replaced by a vision of carnage.

Bodies. Bloodied. Charred. She couldn't see what realms they were from; she could see only their skin and bones. Darkness spilled around the corpses like knocked-over pots of ink, but it did not settle, or puddle, or disappear.

No. This darkness devoured.

It finished off the rest of the bodies, then turned its attention to her. The tendrils climbed, cold and damp as lifeless limbs. Before she could move, the shadows parted her lips and forced her to drink them. She gasped for air, but all she tasted was death.

Everything went black, like the stars and the moon and the sun were just candles that had been blown out, one by one.

Then, the darkness spoke.

"*Isla.*" It had his voice. *Grim's* voice. "*Come back to me. Come back—*"

A blink, and she was back in the Place of Mirrors, all refracted sunlight and skeletal branches scraping against the remaining glass, reaching for her like hands.

And Oro. He was there in an instant, cradling her in his arms. He was not one for dramatic reactions, which only made his expression of horror more concerning.

Isla reached up and found blood running from her nose, her ears, her eyes, down her cheeks. She looked at the blood on her fingers, and all she could think about was what she had seen.

What was that? A vision?

A warning of what Grim would do if she didn't return to him?

She didn't know, but one thing was clear: as soon as she had opened that door, something had slammed it closed again. Something was in that room.

And it didn't want Isla to find it.

TRUTHS AND LIES

"It rejected me," Isla said. It didn't make sense. The power called to her; she could feel it. So why had the door slammed closed again?

The king's golden crown gleamed as he tilted his head back, studying her. He was standing as far from her place on the bed as the room allowed.

It didn't matter. Even from feet away, she could sense the thread that tied them together. Something like love.

Something like power.

Oro finally spoke. "You're not ready. I don't think your crown is the only key. If it wasn't meant to be easily opened, the vault's door could be charmed to admit only a Wildling ruler."

"I *am* a—"

"One who has mastered their abilities."

Oh.

Isla laughed. She couldn't help it. Of course the island would continue to come up with ways to make her feel inadequate. At this point, it was like a game. "If that's true, then I guess it will remain closed," she said, staring intently at a spot on the wall. The only Wildling masters still alive were her guardians—and if she ever set eyes on them again, she would kill them for murdering her parents. And for all the lies they had fed her.

Silence came to a boil and spilled over. She could almost *feel* Oro's concern in the air, a heat tinged in worry. She resisted the urge to roll her eyes. Of all the things she had been through, being swept across the room by a snobbish door was far from the worst.

She hated his concern, and she hated herself for the anger that had hardened inside her like a blade, that struck out at even something as innocent as worry. Lately, though, she couldn't seem to control any of her emotions. Sometimes she woke up and didn't have the energy to even get out of bed. Other times, she was so angry, she portaled to Wild Isle just to have a place to scream.

"I will teach you," he said.

"You're not a Wildling master."

"No," he admitted. "But I have mastered four realms' powers. The abilities are different, but the execution is similar." His voice was gentle, gentler than she deserved. "It was how I was able to use *your* power."

It was how he was able to save her. She would have been boiled alive by the core of the island if Oro hadn't used the bond between them to claim her powers in the Place of Mirrors. That had been the moment her feelings for him were revealed. The fact that he could access her abilities meant she loved him.

Though she didn't even know what that—love—was.

She had loved her guardians.

She had loved Celeste.

She had, at some point, loved *Grim*.

The vision. Death and darkness and decay. Was it a threat? A glimpse of the future?

The weight around her neck felt even heavier now. The necklace Grim had gifted her during the Centennial had been impossible to remove, and yes, she had tried. It had a clasp, but so far it had refused to open. It seemed there was no real way to take it off. Only she could feel it. Oro didn't even know it existed.

Isla wondered if Grim was like that necklace—insistent and refusing to let her go. Would he kill people just to have her?

"I have to tell you something." She considered keeping it to herself. If it had involved only her, she might have. She had broken the curses. She deserved more time to recover. Her cuts and bruises from the Centennial

had disappeared, but some wounds were invisible and took far longer to heal than broken skin and bones. "In the Place of Mirrors . . . there was a vision."

He frowned. "What did you see?"

"Death," she said. "He—" She found herself unwilling to speak his name aloud, as if that alone might summon him from the shadows, bring him to life in more than just her mind. "He was surrounded by darkness. There were dead bodies everywhere. The shadows were reaching at *me*—" She winced. "It looked like . . . war."

It looked like the end of the world.

Sharper heat swept through the room, the only sign of Oro's anger. His smooth face remained expressionless. "He won't stop until he has you."

Isla shook her head. "I chose *you* . . . He feels betrayed. He might not even care about me anymore." Oro didn't look convinced. She closed her eyes. "Even if he did, do you think he would start a war over me? Risk his own people?"

"I think that is exactly what he would do," Oro said, his gaze faraway, as if lost in thought. "Isla. You need to start your training, and not just to get into the vault."

Training. That sounded like far too much effort, she decided, for a person who had to bargain with herself just to leave her room every day. She didn't use to be like this. Training had been hammered into her like gemstones into a blade's hilt. It was part of her very essence.

Now, she was just tired, more mentally than physically. All she wanted was time to recover, and why did even thinking that make her feel like the most selfish person on Lightlark?

Luckily, she had an excuse other than her own unwillingness. "You know I can't." As king, Oro was the last remaining Origin who could wield each of the remaining Lightlark powers—Skyling, Starling, Moonling, and Sunling. It was supposed to be impossible for anyone other than his line to be born with more than one ability. According to

Aurora—whom she had once thought to be her best friend, Celeste—her Wildling and Nightshade gifts were tangled together in a way that made them largely useless unless a Nightshade released them. "My powers—"

"I have a plan for that."

Of course he did. Her teeth stubbornly locked together. "I don't have time to train. I have to get back to the Wildlings."

"They will need you to be at your utmost strength."

Why was he so set on her training? And why, truly, was she so against it? "It's a distraction," she tried. "I can learn later. After they're taken care of. After we've figured out the Nightshade threat, if my vision is even real."

"You have the power of a Starling ruler now, Isla," Oro said gently.

When Isla killed Aurora, she had used an ancient relic called the bondmaker to steal all the Starling's power. The action served as a loophole to fulfill the part of the prophecy that stated a ruler had to die to break the curses. A ruler's power functioned as the life force of their people. All Starlings would have died along with Aurora, if Isla hadn't stolen that power.

Now, she was responsible for two realms, when she wasn't even qualified to rule one.

"Your Wildling and Nightshade powers might have stayed dormant all this time," he continued, "but this will not. The abilities are too great. If you don't learn how to control them, they will control you."

That seemed unlikely. In the last couple of days, she had casually tried to use her Starling powers. To move a quill. To make a burst of energy off her balcony. Nothing. She would have doubted that the bondmaker had even worked if the Starlings weren't still alive.

"Isla," Oro said, and the tender way he said her name dulled the defensive edges of her anger and pain, just a little.

"Yes?"

He took a step, then another, until she was bathed in his warmth, even though he was still farther than she would have liked.

Oro studied her from the foot of her bed. "Say you'll train with me. And mean it."

"Fine," she said quickly, just because she knew it was what he wanted to hear. Just because nowadays, she would do anything to stop thoughts about the Centennial and what had happened. "I'll train with you. I mean it."

"Your excitement is overwhelming," he said flatly.

"I *am* excited," she said through her teeth.

His look sharpened. "You do realize I know you're lying?"

Of course he did. That was his flair, the extra power rulers often carried from distant bloodlines. She imagined fate laughing at the irony of their pairing: a liar loved by someone who could sense the truth.

Instead of glaring at Oro, she was happy to turn the attention back to him. Curiosity made for the best distraction. Wasn't that all life was, she reasoned, painful moments strung together by distractions? "What does it feel like?" she asked, sitting straighter on the bed.

The thin sleeve of her dress dipped down her shoulder. She watched him track its fall.

"What does what feel like?" he asked, eyes lingering on her newly bare shoulder.

Something thrummed in her chest. She hadn't often noticed Oro staring at her. Until the moment when Aurora confirmed the king loved her, she hadn't even thought he had *liked* her.

One of her bare legs ran the length of the bed, slowly, until her toe reached the floor. Her dress rode high up her thigh, and she could feel the heat of his eyes on her. She did the same with the other leg, until both feet were by the bedside.

He studied her, top to bottom, and suddenly the vault was forgotten. Her inadequacy—forgotten. The betrayals? Forgotten.

Part of Isla wondered if he was still just looking at her to see if she was okay, but no, no, it was far better to believe he was watching her for other reasons.

"When someone lies to you. What does it feel like?" She drifted over to him, barefoot, her back slightly sore from her rough landing. Her head pounded in pain, the wound just recently healed by her Wildling elixir, but she ignored it.

He remained very still as she stopped before him.

"Does it hurt?" She tilted her head. "Does *anything* really hurt you?"

The look he gave her made it clear he wasn't going to answer the second question, so she tried the first again. "Do the lies hurt?"

Oro was so tall, he had to crane his neck down to look her right in the eyes. He reached out and ran his thumb across the divots of her crown. "It depends on who's telling them."

Guilt sank its teeth into her chest. The idea that her lies had hurt him inexplicably made her hurt as well.

Was that what it meant to love someone?

She had lied to him throughout the Centennial, but he had never lied to her. She knew that now for certain. He was the only person she trusted in the world, though she realized trusting anyone after what had happened was astronomically foolish.

Was *that* love?

Isla placed her hand on his chest and felt him stiffen. He was warm in a comforting way that made her want to feel his bare skin beneath her fingers. He did not move an inch as she got closer—and closer still.

They had barely talked about the connection between them, the undeniable thread. He had let her have her space. She had wanted to take things slow. Not rush in, the way she had with Grim.

But at that moment, she didn't want any space between them.

She stood on her toes, wanting to bridge the gap between her lips and his, *finally*, but no matter how long she stretched her neck, she couldn't reach him.

Oro stared down at her and frowned. "Is this your attempt to distract me?"

Absolutely. She didn't want to master her powers. She didn't want to think about any of her newfound abilities. Once she started, she would have to think about things—and *people*—that had scarred her, perhaps beyond repair. "Yes. Let me?"

He lowered his head. His golden crown winked in the light.

Then his hands were on her waist. His fingers were long across her back; she arched into his touch. He grabbed her, so tightly she gasped—

But before she could wrap her legs around his waist, he carried her to the bed . . .

. . . and dropped her back onto the sheets.

By the time she made a sound of protest, he was at the door. "Rest, Isla," he said. "The dinner is in a few hours." She groaned. It was the first time representatives were all meeting, to discuss the aftermath of the curses. "Then, we'll begin our training."

FLOATING FEAST

Make me look like a sword," Isla had told the Starling tailor Leto. "One that's more blood than blade." A mixture of Wildling and Starling. That was what she wore as she swept into the dining room.

The Sunling nobles had arrived early with their ruler. They were already seated when Isla walked through the doors, and when their eyes went straight to her—sharp and hungry—she had the unnerving feeling of being the very thing they had come to pick at and consume.

Before, she might have cowered under their scrutiny, but now she strode to the table like she didn't notice. What could anyone on this island do or say to her that they hadn't already done? Moonling nobles had tried to assassinate her. The others had already judged her down to the bone. In the marketplace, most people avoided her, still hating Wildlings because of their bloodthirsty curse, even after it had been broken. Her new red, metal-woven dress whispered against the smooth floor, feeling almost like chain mail, fighting against the silence shrinking the room.

She quickly marked the Sunling nobles as she passed them by. A man with long golden hair tied into a braid and dark skin, wearing a solemn expression. A tall woman, made up of about a thousand freckles, her hair the color of rust. A man who looked old—remarkable, given that even Oro looked young, and he had been alive for more than five centuries—his spine curved toward the table as if emulating the top of a question mark. He smiled at her, light skin crinkling, but it tipped more toward amused than friendly.

Oro sat at the head of the table, and he was also watching. The king would have looked exactly like he did at the beginning of the Centennial, at that first dinner, if not for his eyes. Back then, his eyes had been hollow as honeycomb.

Now, they burned right through her with an intensity that made any previous thoughts unspool around her. He almost imperceptibly traced her with his gaze. Her bare, tan shoulders. The silk-and-steel corset. The slit in her dress revealing knee-high boots she'd had made, because they were more practical than her heels or slippers. Her long brown hair, with tiny red flowers woven through the ends. She watched him back, for just a second. His broad shoulders. Golden hair. The sharp panes of his smooth face. He had been paler before, after so many years without sunlight, but now he was glowing, radiant. He was so beautiful, it almost hurt looking at him.

She didn't remember noticing how attractive he was at that first dinner.

Was *that* love?

Oro looked away quickly.

As she took her place next to him, the doors opened, and a breeze blew her hair back, bringing with it the comforting scent of pine and the prickling chill of mountain air. Azul swept in with the current, feet never touching the floor. He was joined by two others, not nobles but elected officials. Skylings ran their realm as close to a democracy as was possible in a system where rulers were born with the bulk of the power, power their people's lives hinged on.

While Azul's hair was as dark as his skin, the woman behind him had hair the color of the sky itself, complete with a bit of white mixed in—a sign she was ancient, just like the curved-over Sunling. Unlike the old man's, though, her posture was perfect. Her skin was deep brown, and she was small in stature.

The Skyling next to her was built like a tombstone, as solid as if he were carved straight from the Singing Mountains. He was white as the

cliffs of Lightlark, and so tall Isla couldn't see the color of his hair from the way his face was angled as he stared straight ahead. He was large enough to carry three swords on his belt comfortably, and he dwarfed all of them. Isla had the unpleasant thought that her own sword would look something like a quill in the giant's grip.

Azul came around the table to greet Isla, though his seat was on the other side of Oro. "Your style has changed," he mused.

His, happily, had not. The ruler of Skyling was wearing a tunic with shards cut out of its sides and bulbous sapphires in place of buttons. He wore a ring on every finger.

It was her first time seeing him since the Centennial had ended. *You should have sought him out,* her mind whispered. Another failing.

She wanted to ask how he was doing after watching the specter of his long-lost husband disappear once the storm cleared. She wanted to apologize for believing even for a moment that he was her enemy. She wanted to ask him how the Skylings were faring in the aftermath.

Before she could get a word out, Azul said, "We could make time to meet, if you would like."

"I would like that very much," she said.

"Good." He dipped his chin and whispered, "Beware. Someone is always watching."

He was right. Conversation had started up, but she could still feel attention fixed firmly on her. In the days that she had spent in her room after the end of the Centennial, Oro had told the island's nobles and representatives that Isla had broken the curses and gained the power of a Starling ruler. The news had swiftly spread among the people of Lightlark.

The leaders sitting around her now had watched her stumble her way through most of the Centennial's trials. They must have wondered how she, out of all the rulers, had been the one to finally put an end to the curses.

Just as Azul was seated, the doors opened once more, and a single Starling walked through. She had light brown skin, dark eyes, and a sheet of shining black hair. Her clothes were faded silver, more storm cloud than freshly sharpened blade. She froze as everyone turned to face her. Less than a second later, she recovered, walking with her head high. Because of their previous curse, Isla knew for certain that the Starling was younger than twenty-five, close to her own age.

They locked eyes, and the girl frowned. Still, Isla felt an understanding pass between them. Two people who felt remarkably out of place.

"Maren," the Starling said simply before being seated, by way of introduction, and then she proceeded to focus very intently on the curved edge of the solid gold table.

Only one chair remained empty. Cleo's.

It didn't seem like the Moonling would be joining them. Chimes rang through the golden room, marking the hour. Oro stood. "After five hundred years of suffering, the curses plaguing our realms have been broken, thanks to Isla Crown, ruler of Wildling." She felt eyes on her again. "Over the last centuries, our priority was survival. Today, we meet to discuss how we move forward. I see an opportunity for growth in every sense of the word. To get there, we must deal with the aftermath of five hundred years of our people divided and our powers constricted in the face of new threats." He looked around at them all. "First, let us celebrate the end of much of our suffering by sharing a meal."

Oro was seated, and conversations began, but Isla focused only on her unsteady breathing. Nerves rolled through her stomach. The attention had already been turned to her. Soon, there would be questions. What if she answered wrong?

No one knew about her past with Grim. No one knew she was secretly also a Nightshade. If they did, they might have imprisoned her right then and there. Nightshade had been their enemy for centuries. They had been at war right before the curses. If her vision was to be believed, they might soon find themselves in another battle against them.

"We are monsters, Hearteater," someone said in her ear. "Or, at least, that's what they think."

Grim. He was here.

She startled. Her heart hammered. Her gaze darted around the table, expecting to find him close by or to see some reaction from the others.

But he was nowhere. Maybe he was invisible. Her eyes strained to see even the smallest ripple in the air that might give him away. She waited for him to appear before them. Her hand inched toward Oro to warn him—

Nothing.

She knew what she'd heard. Or did she? It could have been her own mind. Grim had said those same words more than a month ago, when he was still pretending not to know her.

The truth was, he had known *everything* about her. They had a year's worth of memories together that he had made her forget, to suit his own agenda at the Centennial. He had cut part of her life away as easily as Leto shearing excess fabric.

She didn't know what she would do if she ever saw him again, but she didn't need to worry about it at the moment.

Grim wasn't there.

She had imagined it, then. Perhaps her mind had made up the vision in the Place of Mirrors too. It couldn't be real. Grim wouldn't kill innocent people to get to her.

She saw flashes of that vision again. Death. *Children*—

"Breathe," she said to herself, before taking a deep breath, knowing how ridiculous it was that she had to remind herself, vocally, of a body's basic function. Her nails dug into her palms, trying to keep herself in the moment, as if she were clinging to an anchor instead of becoming unmoored yet again in the shifting currents of her mind.

"Don't forget to exhale too." Oro.

Under the table, he placed his hand on her knee. His thumb stroked the inside of her thigh. She knew he meant it as a comforting gesture,

but for a moment all her senses sharpened to his touch. Her eyes met his. He removed his hand.

A special drink was prepared, a Sunling specialty. Flaming goblets were served on floating platters by Starlings, who moved objects using their mastery of energy. Isla noticed they smiled at the Starling representative—Maren—in a friendly way.

Oro casually drank from the goblet, and the flames extinguished, not burning him in the slightest. The Sunling noble with the dark-red hair downed hers in an impressively short amount of time.

Would it burn her if she wasn't Sunling? No, of course not. Oro would never serve his guests something that would harm them. She was the next one to drink from her own flaming goblet.

It tasted of honey and burned like liquor. The flames licking the edge of the goblet stroked her cheeks as she drank, then sank into the dregs of the drink before simmering away completely.

The first food course was pure Skyling. It was a floating feast, served in a flowerpot—miniature vegetables still tied to the roots, flying about, that one had to pin down with their fork to eat. She couldn't place every food by name, but one had the familiar texture of potatoes, was violet in color, and had a surprising bite of sweetness. Some of the vegetables seemed to have minds of their own and playfully evaded capture, flying within the confines of their root leashes. Oro watched her try to pin down an especially active beet, amusement touching the corners of his mouth.

The second course was Starling. The fine silver plates contained a single orb. Once all were served, the Starlings snapped their fingers in unison, and the orbs exploded, revealing a cut of unfamiliar meat, carved into precise pieces. Large saltlike rocks formed a circle around the protein. Isla bit into one and startled when it burst like a firecracker in her mouth.

The Moonling course arrived last.

The Starling attendants mumbled apologies as they delivered the dishes, though they were clearly only following orders. Blocks of ice

were presented with live fish still swimming within them. Their eyes were wide as they tried to navigate their quickly melting confines.

Isla felt the heat of Oro's anger—almost enough to set the fish free—though his expression remained impassive.

Before Oro could say a single word, the doors of the room burst open. Isla expected to see a dramatic entrance from Cleo.

A Moonling stood at the entrance . . . but it was not the ruler. The man had long white hair that reached the middle of his torso, nearly the color of his skin, and a staff in his hand.

"Soren," Oro said. "How nice of you to join us. I presume this is your idea of a joke?"

The Moonling man—Soren—pursed his lips. "More of a statement. Excuse my late appearance, but I find I have no appetite when I consider the state of the island, not so unlike the blocks of ice before you."

That made them the fish.

"Cleo sent you in her stead?" Azul asked.

Soren nodded. He took the empty seat that had been set aside for the Moonling ruler.

Oro stood, and the entire center of the solid gold table dropped, forming a basin. The blocks of ice rushed to the middle, then melted, filling it. The fish swam in relieved circles.

With a look that was befitting of the cold king Isla had believed Oro to be before the Centennial, he looked at Soren and said, "Now that dinner has ended, why don't you begin by telling us where Moonling stands?"

The Moonling's longest finger slipped across the gem atop his staff. "You are of course aware that we have severed our bridge to the Mainland."

"Another statement?" Oro asked.

The Moonling shrugged a shoulder. "As well as a protective measure. The curses kept people in check . . . and we are aware we have enemies on the island." His gaze landed on Isla.

She almost wanted to laugh. *That* was the reason he was going with? *Her?* Moonling nobles had tried to assassinate her, and Cleo had, personally, nearly finished the job. She supposed it wasn't a leap to think she, with her newfound power, would be set on revenge.

It was still a ridiculous excuse.

Oro gave him a look. "And your armada of ships?"

The Moonling noble took a leisurely sip of the flaming goblet that had now been set before him. "So we can sail to the Moonling newland, of course," he said. "To unite our people once more."

That might have been partially true, but it wasn't the only reason, and Isla didn't need Oro and his flair to know it. Cleo had begun building her army of ships during a time when faraway travel was a death sentence for Moonlings.

"Unite them how?" Azul asked. "To bring those on the Moonling newland to Lightlark? Or bring those on Lightlark to the newland?"

The room was silent, charged with energy. This was the big question, she knew, from speaking with Oro. After the curses were cast, most of the realms had fled Lightlark to create their own newlands, hundreds of miles away. Some people had remained on the island. Would the rulers decide to move back, now that the curses were over? Would they leave Lightlark for good?

"My ruler has not decided yet," Soren said smoothly.

Oro turned away from the Moonling in dismissal to face Azul. "And the Skylings?"

Azul motioned toward his representatives. "These are elected officials Sturm"—the giant nodded, his eyes never leaving the opposite wall—"and Bronte." The petite woman gave the ghost of a smile.

"Every Skyling will have a choice," Bronte said. "To remain on the Skyling newland, or join us here on Lightlark."

That seemed in keeping with their realm.

Sturm nodded. "We have already begun teaching the newer generations the art of our flight, though the journey to or from the newland

is still too long. We have contraptions that offer flight by harnessing wind for that purpose."

Oro nodded. He made to face his own representatives when Azul said, "There is something else. Rebellion on the island is brewing. Our spies have heard the whispers, carried along the wind."

Oro frowned. "What do those whispers say?"

"The people are not pleased with how long it took to break the curses, or our decisions as rulers."

"Which realm?" Oro asked.

"All of them. The ones on Lightlark, at least," he said. His gaze shifted to Soren. "Yes, even Moonling."

Rebellion. Would the people of Lightlark really attempt to overthrow Oro, or any of the other rulers? Without heirs, their rule represented a total monarchy. Rebellion was futile, when killing a ruler would result in the death of everyone in their realm.

Their expressions were grave, but no one looked too surprised. It made Isla think rebellion was not a new concept on Lightlark.

"I plan to visit all the isles and newlands to address the people directly," Oro said, his eyes meeting Soren's. "Hopefully, it will give everyone a chance to air their grievances."

He nodded at his representatives. "Enya, Urn, and Helios join me," he said. Sunlings didn't have a newland—all of them had stayed, along with Oro, who was both ruler of Sunling and king of Lightlark. "As many of you know, they serve the Mainland court as well. We are focused on shifting our infrastructure and routines back to normal after being nocturnal for five hundred years." His eyes briefly met Isla's before he said, "We are also preparing our legion. With the curses broken, we can only assume Grimshaw will take it as an opportunity to attack."

This was in response to her vision, Isla knew. Oro was taking it seriously.

Soren frowned. "You believe he has the same ambitions as his father?" Grim's father went to war against Lightlark, Isla knew, decades before the curses. Nightshade wanted control of the island.

"Perhaps," Oro said. "All we know for certain is that Nightshade is more powerful than ever now that the curses are broken and our realms are divided. We must work together again to present a united front."

There were murmurs of agreement, and hushed whispers that sounded curious about the idea of a Nightshade attack.

"Speaking of working together . . ." Soren said. His attention turned to Isla. "All of the Wildlings fled Lightlark. How is your realm faring?"

After the curses, Isla had injected power into her lands, to save her people while she recovered. Late at night, with her portaling device, she had visited them in secret. "Wildlings have begun shifting their primary food source." She saw clear disgust on Soren's face, which she guessed had to do with the fact that her people had previously subsisted on human hearts. "My people have already started harvesting their own crops, but we will need aid to achieve an assortment of diet and agriculture now that they are dependent on farming. I—"

"How many of you are left?" Soren interrupted.

She frowned. "I'm not sure. As you know—"

"You're *not sure*?" Soren asked, eyebrow raised.

She could feel her face go hot. It was a reasonable question. The kind a good ruler would know the answer to.

"Do most of your people know how to wield power?"

"I don't know."

"How is housing? What has the rate of reproduction been in the last century?"

"I will have to find out," she said through her teeth.

"Do you—"

"Enough," Oro said. He turned to the Moonling. "Soren, I'm sure Isla would love to have you visit the Wildling newland if you are so curious about her people."

Soren looked like he would rather stick his fork in his eye, but he went silent.

Isla's gaze didn't leave the table. Her throat felt tight. Her breathing was constricted, as though her lungs had shrunk to half their normal size.

She didn't deserve to be a ruler. She had known that for a while, but Soren's line of questioning had thrown her lack of wisdom in sharp relief. Poppy and Terra had ruled the realm while she trained for the Centennial, and now they were gone. She had banished them.

For the first time, Isla wondered if that had been a mistake.

The Starling representative who had announced herself as Maren cleared her throat. There was an intensity to her, an energy that coursed through the room. "For centuries, we have been an afterthought. A blip in your ancient lives. We have been treated as disposable by many. Taken in the middle of the night. Subjected to labor, and torture, and sometimes worse." She looked at the king. "You executed those found guilty, but so many fell through the cracks." She grimaced. "Star Isle is in ruins. I can't imagine the newland is faring much better." She looked to Isla. "We need a ruler."

How could the Starling seriously be looking at Isla for help, after seeing how badly she had just recounted her own realm's condition?

Soren frowned. "What you ask is impossible. One cannot be the ruler of two realms."

"She did receive the full power of a Starling ruler," Azul remarked.

Soren barked out a laugh. "The girl can't even rule her own realm. Now you're ready to give her *two*?"

"The *girl* has a name—and a title," Oro said, his voice cutting through the room. "You will address her with the respect you give all rulers, or I will use you as kindling for the castle hearth."

Isla stiffened. Oro's defense had been sharp. She glanced at the faces around her, but they looked abashed rather than suspicious.

Soren's eyes flashed, but he bowed his head in respect. "Forgive me, King."

"Don't apologize to me," Oro told him.

Soren begrudgingly turned to Isla and said, "I apologize, Ruler." Isla just stared at him. He turned back to the king. "With respect," he said, his *s* pronounced in a particularly serpentine manner, "it does not seem wise to give a single ruler that much power . . ." He hesitated, considering his words. "*You*, King, are the only one meant to preside over multiple realms."

Oro's look at the Moonling was just one shade away from casting flames. "Azul is correct. She has the full powers of a Starling ruler, and, might I remind us all, is the sole reason any of the Starlings are still alive." He turned to Isla. "The responsibility is hers to accept."

Isla was silent. She couldn't decide like this right now. As much as she wanted to put a dagger through him, Soren was right. She had just demonstrated, very publicly, that she had no idea how to properly rule a single realm, let alone two. Two of the weakest realms, the most ravaged by the curses; the ones currently in need of the most support.

"How would that work?" the woman with the dark-red hair said. Enya. Her voice was raspy and deep. She carefully appraised Isla, tilting her head to the side. "Would she be coronated? Officially announced as ruler? She already has the power; it would simply be a matter of ceremony."

"The public will not like it," the Skyling woman—Bronte—murmured, though not unkindly. She was simply voicing a fact.

"Of course they won't like it," Maren murmured under her breath. "It would make it more difficult for them to continue to exploit us."

"What was that?" the old Sunling said, a touch too loudly, genuinely seeming as if he had not heard her.

"This is all going very well," Soren said offhandedly to the giant Sturm, who did not so much as blink in recognition that he was being spoken to.

"I said," Maren started, her voice growing in intensity, frustration and anger building in her expression—

"I'll do it," Isla said, standing, putting a bookmark in the plaited conversations.

Silence.

"Are you certain?" Oro said, holding her gaze. He looked at her like they were the only two people in the room.

"Yes," she said, not certain in anything but the fact that Maren clearly knew Isla was not the best leader . . . and she had asked for her help anyway. The Starlings must be desperate. She was not the right choice for this—of course she wasn't.

No, that wasn't right. She would *become* the right choice.

Isla couldn't deny them, especially now after she'd heard of the atrocities that had gone on for the last few centuries. Who was she, if she sat and did nothing after learning of that horror? What would be the point of killing her best friend and breaking the curses if Lightlark and its people descended into chaos soon afterward?

"I will officially become the new ruler of Starling," she said, meeting Soren's eyes. "I will have a coronation."

CHOICES

"I don't know how to rule," she admitted. Azul sat in front of her in Juniper's old bar. The spheres of liquor behind the counter were still filled. The curved chairs and tables hadn't collected even a spot of dust yet. The body and blood had been taken care of, but Isla was almost back to that day, weeks before, finding him dead. With Celeste.

Aurora.

The barkeep who kept secrets had died because of her. He had helped her. He was one of the *only* islanders who had helped her.

It made her want to be better—worthy of his sacrifice.

"A very dramatic declaration you gave. I quite liked it." Azul leaned back in his chair, a glass of sparkling water glittering in front of him, bubbles popping and releasing a berrylike scent. "Do you *want* to rule, Isla?"

No. That was her first response. But it seemed too selfish to say aloud, so she said, "Do I have a choice?"

The Skyling ruler raised an eyebrow. "You *always* have a choice."

Skylings valued choice over all else, as evidenced with their democracy. It was an alluring principle, Isla thought. What she wouldn't give to hand off all this responsibility to someone else.

"Do I?" she said, her voice more grating than she had meant it. "I have ruling power from Starling now, and Wildling. Who else could rebuild them?" Azul just looked at her, so she continued. His silence angered her for some reason, because all these questions were *real* ones, ones she wanted answers to. "Hmm?" she said. "Should I just go back to my room and let them all die?"

"You could," he said. Azul shrugged a shoulder, looked at a perfectly manicured nail. Every part of him was immaculate, as always. "But you're choosing not to." He met her eyes. "Right?"

She had requested he meet her. She had declared to the nobles and representatives that she would have a coronation. She had made not just a choice but *choices*.

"Right," she murmured.

He flashed his perfect teeth at her. "Good. Now that that's clear . . . Of course you don't know how to rule, Isla." The compassion in his tone caught her off guard. "When I was in my twenties, I was too busy flying off with boys and drinking every shade of haze to even think about anyone other than myself." His smile turned sad. "When you make the choice to rule, you are making a promise that you will put your people's well-being and happiness above your own."

Isla frowned. It shamed her how awful that sounded.

She didn't *want* to put others first, not after everything she had just been through. A person could only take so much. Her trust had been broken, along with her heart. There wasn't much left of her to give. She wanted to be selfish with the parts that remained. Didn't she deserve that?

"I see," he said.

"See what?"

Azul began humming to himself, and the wind seemed to mimic it. Somehow a current was moving through the room and jostling her hair, even though all the doors and windows in the bar were closed. "Of course."

"Of course *what*?"

The Skyling ruler folded his hands in front of him. "Are you close to your Wildling subjects, Isla?"

"No."

"They didn't know you believed yourself powerless?"

She shook her head.

"What was your relationship to them?"

Isla lifted a shoulder. "Nonexistent. My guardians made all the decisions. They ruled. Because of my . . . *secret* . . . I was kept far away. Only paraded on special occasions, at a distance." She bit the inside of her mouth, a habit that would have made Poppy flick her on the wrist with her fan. "If I'm honest, they are my blood, they are my responsibility, I would do anything for them . . . but they feel like strangers."

Azul nodded. "Of *course* they do," he said, and the way he validated her feelings . . . the compassion in his voice . . . it was beyond anything she had ever experienced. "And the Starlings here, they *are* strangers. You don't care about them." He shrugged. "You don't care about this island."

His voice was without judgment. His eyes held no disgust. Azul only shook his head. "How could you? You've only been here a few months. The worst moments of your life were likely spent right here on Lightlark. You don't have fond memories before the curses to look back on, and most of the people hate you, because of their perception of Wildlings."

Everything was said so matter-of-factly. Isla couldn't tell if his even tone made the words hurt less or more.

"Are you going back to the Wildling newland, Isla?"

"I plan to." She told him about her portaling device and how she had visited. She offered to portal him to the Skyling newland when needed.

Azul's eyes only glimmered with curiosity. "Charming," he said. "I appreciate your offer, but I meant . . . are you returning to the Wildling newland for good?"

For good. Before, when the Centennial had ended, Isla could not fathom staying on Lightlark. Now, things were different. *She* was different.

"No."

"Then this is your home now," Azul said. "Your *chosen* one." He stood, his light-blue cape billowing behind him in a breeze only he seemed privy to. "Learn to love it, and your two realms. It is up to the leader, not the subject, to connect." He outstretched his hand. "Come with me."

She took it without question, the rings on both of their fingers clashing together like wind chimes. "We're not flying . . . are we?"

Azul smiled. "Do you trust me?"

"I do," she said, and it was the truth. It was stupid, she realized, to trust anyone after everything. She knew that, but what was the alternative? Closing herself off forever? Ever since the end of the Centennial, she had felt a wall harden around her. If she wasn't careful, it would become impenetrable.

She had asked Azul for help. The least she could do was let him in.

They stepped out the back door of the bar, into an alleyway. He offered his other hand. "May I?"

She took his hand.

Then she was in the air. And Azul's flying was far smoother than Oro's had ever been.

In the aftermath of the curses, Sky Isle was transformed. The city built below had been abandoned for the one floating above, just as most of the Skyling people had promptly deserted walking in favor of flying. A castle sat nestled comfortably in the clouds, with spires pointing at the sky like quills ready to decorate a blank page. A waterfall spilled from the front of the palace in an arc that reflected every color imaginable, into a shimmering pool below.

And they were all *flying*.

It looked natural, like the air was so much empty space finally being put to good use. Isla had only ever seen Oro fly—and now, Azul. She hadn't expected there to be so much flourish. Flying seemed to be a bit like handwriting; everyone had their own signature. Some were graceful, like Azul, to the point of making it all look like a choreographed dance. Others were more like Oro, brusquely taking steps in the sky, as if walking on an invisible set of bridges no one else could see.

Some weren't really flying at all. They glided on contraptions with wings, using their control over wind to power the inventions.

Azul had wrapped her in wind. She floated right beside him—with her hand fully clenched around his wrist, just in case—taking it all in as best as she could.

"Your realm's curse . . ."

"Was one of the better ones," he filled in.

Not being able to fly for five hundred years certainly must have been terrible for a society that had clearly woven their power through the fabric of their day-to-day, but it wasn't nearly as bad as dying at twenty-five or eating hearts to survive. That didn't mean it wasn't deadly, though. "Azul. The day it happened—"

"We lost many of our people. They all just . . . fell from the sky."

Isla closed her eyes. The thought of them, without explanation, falling to their deaths . . . She clutched Azul's wrist harder.

"Flying comes naturally to us; even those with the smallest shred of power can do it. Those who weren't skilled enough—or quick enough—to use wind to cushion their fall . . . perished."

They had reached the castle. Instead of landing in the clouds—which Isla didn't trust in the slightest—they continued floating, right through the entrance.

The ceiling was nonexistent. One could float right in and through the palace in one smooth motion. The castle had hallways but no stairs. To get to the different levels and out of the main atrium, one had to fly. She could see why this palace had been abandoned after the curses.

Isla wondered how many important resources Skylings had suddenly had no access to, for years, because of their curse. The first time she had visited Sky Isle, she had marveled that the highest building in the city had a spire that reached the very bottom of the castle above it. Now, she realized that was the only way for them to reach what had been lost. They'd had to build to it.

The air felt thinner so high up, and it was cold enough to make her skin prickle, though the Skylings didn't seem to mind it. They all wore light blue in honor of their realm, in fashions with much more

range than she had seen from other realms. Dresses didn't seem to be so popular, which she imagined was a practical choice. Even now, Isla was grateful her dress and cape were heavy enough to keep her modest as she floated around.

Skylings nodded at Azul with respect, with joy, smiling, clapping him on the back as they passed him by. Most nodded at Isla as well. Some stared curiously. Others smiled openly.

They flew to the top of the castle and through its ceiling to view the palace and its floating city from above. He motioned toward the hundreds of people in a market that looked miniature from their height, then to a string of mountains miles away. Sky Isle went on and on, farther than she could see.

"They are my purpose," Azul said. "It was not easy to leave Lightlark after the curses, but my people voted, and most wanted to leave the uncertain future of the island. I'm proud of the Skyling newland, and all we created in the last few centuries, but there is no doubt that our power's heart is here." He took a deep breath, like he could smell and taste and feel that very power, thrumming across the isle. He looked at her. "I can't teach you how to rule, Isla. You must figure that out yourself. All I know is that I put their interests and well-being far above my own. Every day. They are what kept me going, even in my grief." He glanced at her sidelong. "Now that the curses are over, there will be pressure for you to have an heir."

Isla whipped her head to face him. "What?"

"Your people will want to secure their future." He sighed. "Many precautions were put in place in the last few hundred years to ensure the safety of rulers. My people voted for me to almost constantly be surrounded by a legion for protection. I was not permitted to travel to other newlands."

That made Isla's own travels with her starstick seem that much more reckless. For a moment, she began to understand why Poppy and Terra had been so strict.

Isla did not want to create an heir.

She wasn't ready. Did that make her horrible? Even more selfish?

She also didn't want to live the rest of her life insulated and heavily guarded, knowing her death would mean the end of all her people . . .

"There are other ways to have an heir, beyond the obvious," Azul said. "It is possible for rulers to transfer power, through a love bond, or special relics." *Like the bondmaker*, Isla thought. "The cost is high, however. Permanently transferring ability shortens a ruler's life significantly."

That didn't seem like a viable option either. She had barely had a life. She wanted to be able to live it.

"You look like you're about to be sick," Azul said.

"It's the height."

Azul made a sound like he knew the truth. "It is an honor to rule but not always a pleasure, Isla." He squeezed her hand. "Go, visit your people. Face them. Be honest with them. You are their ruler. Whether or not you have deemed yourself worthy, you are all they have."

That, Isla decided, was what she was most afraid of.

CORONATION

There were fewer Wildlings left than she thought.

Months before, she had addressed her people. Now, only a fraction remained. They looked weak. There were details she hadn't noticed before, when she had been so focused on her journey to the Centennial. Now, she saw the signs clearly. A woman with short hair, crudely cut, wore a torn top that revealed all-too-visible ribs. Another looked far too pale, lips chapped, face devoid of color. They had learned to make enough food; she had seen them. She supposed it would take some time for consistent nourishment to make them healthy again.

Some details were the same. A portion of her people had animal companions near them, just like the day she left. Wildlings were known for their affinity with creatures. Poppy had a hummingbird that flew around her hair. Terra had a great panther.

She had always wanted an animal companion. It would have made her life far less lonely.

Terra had always said no.

Isla opened her mouth to speak. Before she could, they did something she couldn't have expected. Didn't deserve.

One by one, they bowed.

"No, I—"

They had never done that before. Isla had never demanded it. It wasn't a custom she was used to.

She didn't like it. Anxiety thrummed across her skin, and she wanted to yell that they should be screaming at her, calling her names, telling her everything she had done wrong up until this point. They looked like they were still *dying*. She was a failure, not a hero.

Isla stepped back, words caught in her throat, when a woman with a capybara next to her said, "You broke the curses. You did what all other rulers for centuries could not."

She frowned. "How do you—how do you know that?"

"Terra told us."

Terra? The name was a dagger to the chest. How had her guardians even known she was the one to break the curses? Why had Terra told them, after being banished?

Had she defied Isla's order? Was she still here, on the newland?

"Where is Terra now?" the woman asked. "She was here . . . and then she vanished. And Poppy?" *No. Not still here.*

"I don't know," Isla said honestly. She thought about telling them about the banishment, but she needed to first get a sense of their allegiance. Would they be loyal to her . . . or to the guardians who had mostly ruled the Wildlings since her birth? "Please stand," she said. She told them everything else. That she'd believed she had been born without powers. That she had a device that allowed her to portal at will. That she now had Starling power. When she was finished, she said, "I have not been a good ruler. I don't know your struggles. Speak candidly, please. I know you must have questions. Ask them. Tell me what you need."

Something flickered in her vision. Isla turned, and for the slightest second, she saw Grim, standing among the crowd, watching her.

She froze. Panic dropped through her stomach.

A blink, and he was gone.

Someone asked a question, and she didn't hear it.

She shook her head. "Sorry, what did you say?" Her ears were ringing. First, the vision in the Place of Mirrors. Then, his voice in her head. Now, she was seeing him . . . What was next?

What was wrong with her?

"I asked what is happening on the island."

She wondered how much she should say. "There is uncertainty on Lightlark right now. The realms are divided. There are signs of rebellion. We also have reason to believe Nightshades might try to attack Lightlark, like they have in the past." She attempted a smile. "Once all of that is dealt with, I hope to have us all back on Lightlark one day," she said. "This has been our home for five centuries, but it is weakened. Lightlark is where we have always belonged."

There were some murmurs, but no one spoke out against her. She hoped that was a good sign.

She answered their questions as best she could, then sought out a woman who wore purple flowers through the ends of her hair, the color of leadership. She was tall, with light skin, dark hair, and sharp eyes. Her name was Wren, and Isla learned she led one of the larger villages on the newland.

"Why are some people standing apart from the rest?" Isla asked. Her people were not as united as they had seemed months prior. Some were huddled together, but others stood on the outskirts.

Wren looked at her for a moment. "I mean no disrespect," she said. "But you didn't have the curse. You don't know what it's like to have to kill others for food. To go hungry because there simply wasn't enough." She shook her head. "Most of us did things we're not proud of to survive."

Tears burned Isla's eyes. All her life, she had thought it a horror being locked in her room and training so rigorously. It was nothing compared to what her people had gone through; she knew that now. "What do you need?" she asked. "How can I help you?"

Wren pressed her lips together. "We have slowly learned to make food. It has been good for us, I think, figuring things out on our own. Any challenge now . . . it is a mere shadow of what we endured."

"You must need something," she said. "Some of you still look starved. I can bring more food. Bring people to help teach you to make other crops or help reconstruct houses." She had seen the state of the villages

during her travels with her starstick. Some buildings had stood the test of time, and others had fallen to pieces. "I can—"

Wren cut her off. "How are the Starlings?"

"I don't know. I've asked, but I haven't yet visited the newland or isle."

"Help them," she said. "We are resourceful. Older. They are so young. They need you more than we do." She smiled sadly. "It would help," she said. "With the guilt. To know in some way, we are aiding another realm, instead of . . ."

Killing them.

Isla nodded. "I'll be back," she said. "With help and resources, after my coronation."

Wren nodded. "We will be waiting."

Bells rang at a distance. The air was sharp with salt from the sea and burned honey from the fair that had cropped up at the base of the castle, all carts filled with varieties of roasted seeds and bands holding their instruments, but not playing them, not yet.

Isla stood at the top of the stairs, just beyond the shadow of the doors, just out of view of the thousands of people waiting below.

It was the day of the Starling coronation, and it seemed everyone on Lightlark was in attendance.

Well, almost everyone.

"No sign of Moonling," Ella said quietly behind her, because Isla had asked her to look. The young Starling had been her assigned attendant during the Centennial. Now, Isla employed her to be her eyes and ears wherever she could not see or hear.

The bells came to an end. It was time.

Isla stepped forward.

Strings of silver beads made up a dress like spun starlight. Her cape glistened in a ripple behind her as she walked down the stairs.

It was still a shock to wear a color she had only dared to use on her prohibited excursions beyond her own realm. It felt wrong, it all felt so *wrong*, like she had taken her friend's life, robbed her of her silver, and put it on herself.

Was that what these people thought? That she had killed Celeste—Aurora—for the power?

She looked to the crowd for answers, stomach tensed, braced. Their faces were a mosaic of surprise, curiosity, hate, disgust, trepidation, vitriol—

Breathe.

Isla took another step, and her foot nearly missed the stair completely. She briefly considered gathering her gown in her hands and running back upstairs, locking herself in her room and going anywhere, *anywhere,* with her starstick.

She wasn't worthy of any of this. She didn't deserve to rule anyone. She didn't even know herself. Part of her past was missing, and that person—the one who had supposedly loved a Nightshade—felt like a stranger. She was sad all the time, and there were so many emotions pressed down, in the deepest depths of herself, that she knew one day would overpower everything else and claw their way out—

She felt it: a thread of heat, steadying her. It was honey in her stomach, a beam of sunshine just for her.

Him. She met Oro's eyes. The king was her destination. He stood tall and proud and golden, at the very bottom of the steps. There was a silver crown in his hands.

He looked at her like it was just them, no crowd, no crowns.

She took another step. Another. Until she was standing in front of him.

Oro didn't say anything. He didn't have to. She could read a thousand words in his amber eyes, like *you can do this. I'm here for you.*

The past few days, she had been avoiding him, knowing he would want her to begin her training. She felt ashamed. Her people needed her to be strong. He just wanted to keep her safe.

He raised the crown high above her, not wasting a moment, knowing she wanted this to be over as soon as possible.

"As king of Lightlark, I name you, Isla Crown, the ruler of Starling." He placed the crown on her head. It was done.

There was a rumbling.

Oro had turned to address his people, but he paused, his brows coming together slightly.

Nervous murmurs spread through the crowd. There was a second of stillness, the island righting itself, and the people silenced, their momentary curiosity instantly forgotten. But Isla watched Oro, and his expression remained the same. Her hand inched toward the blade at her side.

Before her fingers reached the hilt, the island broke open.

The ground beneath her feet parted like a screaming mouth. She would have been swallowed if she had not been on its edge, on a part that rose like a sharpened tooth. Her body soared back with the force; she closed her eyes. Pain across her side was the only sign she had landed.

Screaming sliced the air in half as a scar tore across the castle steps in a rippling sweep, stone crumbling and falling away.

Both were drowned out by the screeching.

Winged, monstrous creatures howled as they barreled through the open fissure.

Their necks were short, their limbs long. Their tails were nearly nonexistent. Their anatomy almost resembled people, except for their faces—which were pure reptile—their black scales, and, of course, their wings.

In a few moments, they were everywhere.

Dozens of the creatures dropped down, aimed at the crowd. Isla put a hand above her, as if it would be any type of shield against the teeth that curved out of the beasts' mouths like slanted blades.

Before the beasts could reach them, a blanket of flames erupted into a barrier. *Oro*. The heat was scalding, steaming Isla in her clothes.

When the fire was pulled away, the creatures were gone, reduced to ash that rained upon them. Dozens were killed.

Before anyone could run for shelter, more creatures emerged.

The scar had to be closed. The beasts were rising in endless sweeps, squeezing through the gap. Groaning, Isla pushed herself up to her arms.

Oro was leaned over his knees, clutching his side. Any injury to the island hurt him as well. It must have felt like he was also being peeled open. Face twisted in pain, he lifted his hand and created another barrier, but the creatures closed their wings together in response, making themselves into sharpened arrows, talons at their fronts like blades. With cries that threatened to crack the sky into shards, they barreled through the protective sphere—

And feasted on them all.

Bones crunched, blood splattered, limbs were torn away. The beasts crashed down, undisturbed by Sunling flames, Starling sparks, or Skyling wind. Their talons tore through flesh as easily as swords through sand.

Azul shot up into the air, with a legion of Skylings surrounding him. They fought with bursts of wind, shooting the creatures down from the sky or slamming them against the island until they went still. Sunlings wielding swords covered in flames guarded people huddled behind the carts in the fair. All the islanders fought back, but many were no match for the creatures, whose hides resisted most uses of power. Before their strategy could be changed, most of them were torn in half by powerful jaws. Some islanders stopped using their abilities altogether, as it marked them as targets, and pressed themselves to the ground or ran.

Just like at the ball months before, Isla watched it all unfold, a helpless spectator. No. They might hate her, this might never feel like home, but she had to do something.

Isla stood on weakened legs, blood hot on the side of her face. She placed a hand over her heart. The heart that had been torn in two by

an arrow. The one that was healed by the heart of Lightlark itself, the one that was linked to Oro's own ability.

A heart that had, more times than not, failed her.

"Please," she whispered, eyes on Oro, who was oscillating between killing swarms of beasts attacking his people and trying to close the scar the winged creatures were still flying through in droves.

She could help him. Wildling power included controlling rock and land. If she could manage to grasp some of that power, she could help all of them.

Isla closed her eyes. She focused on her breathing.

Nothing.

She stretched out her trembling hand. "Come on."

Nothing.

The powers she had been born with were twisted together, making them harder to access. Her Starling abilities were not, however. They were there, just below the surface. She summoned them.

Nothing happened.

Perhaps she could focus on the link between her and Oro instead. Use *his* power. She looked at the king, whose arms were both shaking with effort, one outstretched at each side.

She felt it. Tried to grasp it. *Nothing.*

She shook her hand toward the cut in the ground, picturing herself sealing it shut with ice or burned rock or energy, willing with every bit of her being for it to close. "Come on!" she bellowed.

Nothing.

Her yell had attracted the attention of the closest winged creature. It opened its mouth, and a severed arm fell to the ground.

Then, it lunged at her.

Isla didn't have a chance to scream or attempt to use power again. With just a flap of its wings, it was right above her. She saw the creature bare its teeth, open its massive jaw.

An inch from swallowing her head whole, the creature froze. Its wings moved slowly as it closed its mouth and lowered its face, as if to inspect her.

Isla didn't know why, but she reached toward it, until the very tips of her fingers grazed the space between its eyes—entirely too aware eyes.

The beast blinked. Then, it opened its mouth again—

And screeched. The sound nearly popped her ears, and everything around her muted. She gritted her teeth, readying herself to be eaten alive.

But the creature only turned its head and left, with another screech.

The rest followed.

Isla watched them flee to the horizon, calculating the direction they were going. Nightshade. They were going toward Nightshade.

No. She remembered her vision in the Place of Mirrors . . . Grim attacking with shadows that killed everything in their path. She had convinced herself it was a figment of her imagination, but—

Maybe it was real.

By the time the beasts were just a smudge in the distance, Oro had closed the opening in the ground. Screams still pierced the air, along with the metallic scent of blood. The back of Isla's throat burned with inhaled ash. The injured . . . their wounds didn't look normal. Their skin looked ravaged by shadows. The lesions were growing, moving, slowly decaying everything in their path.

"You did this."

The voice sounded smothered, faraway. Isla turned. A woman was standing in a sea of bodies, not far at all, pointing a finger right at her.

"It didn't attack her. She was communicating with it!"

She took a step backward. "What? I didn't—"

A man joined the woman. "I saw it. She's allied with the Nightshades, isn't she?" Isla shook her head. "This ceremony was a setup, so we could all be here at once. So the beasts could attack us."

"No, of course not," she said, barely hearing her own voice, taking another step back.

No one was listening to her.

Isla's heart was beating too fast; she was hyperventilating, and still none of the air seemed to be reaching her lungs, and she was suddenly light-headed—

"Enough." The word was an order and silenced the crowd. Azul dropped down from the sky, landing in a crouch that shook the ground with power. He had one of the creatures' heads in one of his hands, cut neatly by the sword on his waist, dripping in dark blood. He turned to look at Isla for just a moment, and she worried his face might be full of suspicion, but he only looked curious.

A hand hot as fire gripped her shoulder. She turned to see Oro, searching her face, looking her over, checking for serious injury. Only when he seemed satisfied did he turn and begin yelling orders. Isla could barely hear a word that came out of his mouth. The world had started tilting. In response to one of Oro's dictations, Azul flew from what was left of the steps in the direction of the isles.

"Wildling elixir," she said to herself, knowing this was how she could help. People were dying all around her—they needed to be healed. She had never seen injuries like this, but the healing serum had never failed her. If she could get to her starstick, she could portal to the Wildling newland and get more. She made her way up the steps, narrowly avoiding the closed scar, walking over corpses of the creatures that Oro had killed. They sat charred and steaming.

She didn't even make it to the doors of the castle. At the top of the steps, Isla fell to her knees. Her legs had gone numb. Panic closed in around her. She couldn't breathe. Blood. Everywhere. So many dead. She hadn't been able to save them.

If she hadn't been so selfish, so weak; if she had started training like Oro had insisted, she could have helped, she could have been more than just a blight.

She thought of her vision again and Grim's voice. *Come back to me,* he had said. That was what he wanted.

The creatures were clearly summoned by Grim. There was a reason they hadn't hurt her.

Her breathing was labored. She heard Ella saying her name, attempting to pull her up. Her eyes closed, and all she saw in her mind was the woman pointing at her, declaring her the cause of all their suffering.

Isla couldn't help but think that maybe she was right.

INSIGNIA

The Insignia glowed faintly as if whispering a welcome. Isla hadn't stood on the marking since the day she had first arrived on the island. The symbol was simple—a circle that contained illustrations representing all six of the realms. This was a neutral place to meet and speak on the Mainland, with the castle standing watch, a beast of stone, towers, and fortress walls.

Isla shifted on her feet, over the rose of Wildling. Oro was across from her, on the sun. Azul stood on the bolt of lightning.

Cleo emerged in a crashing wave, straight from the ocean. Seafoam still puddled at her feet.

The last time Isla had seen her, Cleo had tried to kill her.

The Moonling turned to look at Isla, and her eyes gleamed, as if she was relishing the same thought. Her white dress had a high neckline and sleeves that ran all the way to the floor, covering the etching of the moon.

Whatever she hoped to find in Isla, she was clearly disappointed, because Cleo frowned and turned to Oro. "How, exactly, did she stop it?" Her voice sliced through the silence and a wave crested high behind her as if to meet it. She commanded the seas. All the water in the world bowed before her.

"I'm standing right here," Isla said. She was more than capable of speaking for herself.

Cleo only slightly shifted direction to face her again. She smirked. "How did *you*, once supposedly powerless, now all-*powerful*"—the ruler made even the word *power* sound pathetic when related to Isla—"stop the dreks?"

Dreks. Was that what they were called?

How did Cleo know what they were?

She probably should have come up with a response to the question if she was going to insist on being the one to answer it. She swallowed. "I—I don't know. I touched it."

Cleo said every word like it was its own sentence. "You touched it."

"Yes," Isla said through clenched teeth.

The Moonling turned back to Oro. "How many more do you want us to heal?" she asked the king, and Isla understood that she had been dismissed.

Forty-five people were dead. More were still fighting for their lives. She had gotten Wildling healing elixirs from the newland, but they needed more help. Oro had summoned Cleo through Azul, and she had taken her time arriving to the palace.

"Fifty-four are critically injured," Oro said.

"We will provide healers."

Oro nodded. "You've visited the oracle, I presume. Were you able to wake her?"

The oracle was on Moon Isle and only rarely chose to unthaw. The Moonling shook her head no.

Oro would know if she was lying. "We all know this was likely an attack from Nightshade. We need our realms united. Where do you stand?" he demanded.

"I haven't made my decision to stay or to leave."

Oro's expression did not shift an inch. He had been expecting this. "What is the true purpose of your army and ships?"

"To protect Moonling's interests when I do make my decision."

"Make it soon," Oro said. "This is not the time to flee to your newland."

Azul spoke up. "Cleo, you aren't actually considering leaving."

Cleo whipped to face him, her dress a white puddle beneath her feet that shifted, liquidous. "We have long been too dependent on this land.

The curses are broken. It could be an opportunity for more. Perhaps the island should fall."

Azul stared, unbelieving. "If Lightlark falls, the realms will follow. Our power is strongest here. Our future is here."

Isla remembered what Azul had told her during the Centennial—Cleo hadn't attended the previous one.

This was not a sudden decision. Cleo had thought about leaving for a while. Why? It didn't make sense.

Oro's eyes were pure intensity. "If we go to battle with Nightshade, which side will you be on?" Leaving Lightlark for the Moonling newland was one thing . . . choosing to stand against it was another.

Cleo raised her head. Her chin pointed in the king's direction, sharp as her tone. "The winning one."

A hundred-foot wave crashed against the cliff, spilling onto its lip, right over the Moonling ruler.

When the water pulled back, she was gone.

The Moonling healers had never seen anything like the drek wounds. They were able to slow the decaying of the skin, but, in the end, her Wildling elixirs were what was able to remove the marks completely. She portaled back to her newland several times throughout the night, and her people had willingly given their own stores of the elixir. They were down to just a small patch of the rare flowers.

Most people were saved. The rest had succumbed to their wounds. Isla walked to her room slowly, Oro at her side. The moon trailed them both through the windows as they made their way up the castle stairs.

She leaned against her door when they reached her room. "Cleo called them dreks. Have you heard of them before?"

"No. Moonlings have always prized their histories and historians. She might have read about them." He was studying her again. She had caught him doing it, every few minutes, since the attack. It was as if he needed to constantly reassure himself that she was uninjured.

"I'm fine," she said gently. She looked down at herself and winced. She was covered in blood, after helping the healers. It wasn't hers.

"I know," he said, but his brow didn't straighten. Worry was etched into each of his features, and not just for her, she knew.

"You did everything you could," she said, reaching up to touch his face, because she was known for giving far more grace to others than to herself. Her fingers were covered in blood—she dropped her hand before it reached his cheek. "Those creatures . . ."

Oro closed his eyes. She would bet he was replaying the events in his mind. When he opened them, she saw guilt in his expression. He blamed himself for every single death.

She wanted to take that pain. She wanted to think of anything that could make him feel better.

Before she could say anything else, he brushed his lips to the crown of her head and said, "Goodnight, Isla."

RISING UP

It was the middle of the night when the balcony doors to Isla's room burst open. The ocean rose like a hand, and it dragged her out of bed.

She gasped in shock, salt water scorching her throat and nose and lungs. Her shirt scrunched up, her stomach raked against the stone terrace, and she had enough good sense to cling to the balcony pillars, but the sea was too strong. It pulled her hundreds of feet down, straight to its depths.

She choked on lungsful of water, sure she was going to die, until her vision went dark.

When it returned, she was on her knees, hearing the word, "Now," and then the water was being pulled back out of her as quickly as it had been inhaled, salt scraping against her throat.

The high ceiling was stone. Stalactites hung from the top, sharp as icicles. She was underground. No one would hear her screams. Her eyes still burned from the sea, but she blinked frantically past the sting, looking for a way out. Shadows glinted all around, and suddenly her captors came into focus. They were wearing masks—monstrous red masks that hid their faces completely.

Her kidnapper and the one who had revived her were clearly Moonling; they had to be, to use the sea to their advantage as they had. The rest were not.

Isla spotted the blue hair of Skyling. The gold and red tresses of Sunling. No Starlings she could see. Their clothes were all the same shade: beige. A color that had not officially been claimed by any of the realms.

"Are you sure?" She could just make out the words of a muffled voice. "Perhaps if we waited—"

"There's no time," another, louder voice said. "The drek attack is just the beginning. This happens now."

At first, Isla's mind had gone straight to Cleo, but now she wondered if the rebels were behind this, the ones Azul had mentioned at dinner. Did they think she was responsible for the dreks? Is that why they were hurting her? Isla opened her mouth, to say anything, but her throat was raw. Nothing came out.

She had no weapons. She was already covered in blood, the skin of her stomach scraped clean. Salt stuck in the wounds. If her hands weren't tied together behind her back, she could have reached for her invisible necklace, clutched the stone, and watched Grim turn all of them to ash.

Should you ever need me, touch this. And I will come for you, he had said when he had given it to her.

The fact that she was even considering it worried her.

Isla should have listened to Oro from the beginning. Her life was not her own.

Were none of them Starling? Why would they want her to die, when it would mean the death of so many others? She heaved again.

"Don't move," someone commanded as some in the group inched forward. She watched them approach and counted her last moments down in her mind.

Cold hands gripped her raw skin—

The world exploded.

At their touch, energy rippled out of Isla like the consequence of throwing a stone in a still pond. Power burst in every direction, sending everyone around her soaring. She heard the crunch of bones as some were catapulted against the stone walls. Screams. She saw the red of the masks mixed with blood.

Someone had been thrown directly into a stalactite, pierced right through their skull.

"I didn't—" Her voice was barely a rasp. She hadn't tried to hurt them, even though they'd clearly intended to hurt her.

She didn't wait to see if they recovered. The energy had torn through her restraints. Isla ran.

The tunnels were dark and musty; she heard the crash of the sea somewhere nearby. There were multiple directions, but she made a choice and kept going, eventually on an incline. She needed to reach the surface. The rebels—were they right behind her? She didn't stop to listen. Sharp stones stabbed her bare feet until everything began to go numb. Her clothes were drenched in blood, fabric stuck against her wounds.

Just when she wondered if she would be trapped forever beneath Lightlark, there was a path so vertical, she had to climb it on her hands and knees. A wooden door, barely the size of a cupboard, was at the top.

She burst through, into an abandoned shop, covered in cobwebs, dust, and broken glass. Some of it cut her feet as she ran through the door, right into one of the forgotten corners of the agora. The harbor was to her left. She saw the broken ships, some on their sides, some no more than a pile of wood.

Down. She needed to go down to the heart of the market. For a moment, her fingers inched toward her necklace, her mind going there again.

The rebels could be chasing her. Grim would end them all in a moment.

A shiver snaked down her spine. That was the problem.

What was wrong with her?

Isla dropped her hand and raced down the narrow stone road, past shops long closed.

It was late, and the streets were empty, except for a patrolling Sunling guard. When he saw her, his eyes went wide in alarm, and Isla wondered if she should be afraid. Could he be working with the group that had taken her? Some of them had been Sunling, after all.

Before she could worry too long, the guard swept off his golden cloak and draped it over her shoulders. Only then did Isla realize she was in her soaking nightclothes, her body nearly completely visible beneath them.

The cloak was warm, and Isla sank to the ground wrapped inside it while panic spilled around her as more Sunling guards were called. Someone shouted to alert the king.

She knew Oro had received the news when a tidal wave of heat raged across the island.

When Oro had found Isla, shaking and raw skinned, he had looked like he wanted to bring the entire island down. The very ground beneath their feet had shaken as he had said, very calmly, "Who did this to you?"

By the time he had ripped the abandoned house to pieces, the rebels were gone. He had ordered his guards to search the tunnels, and they had found hundreds of passages that no one officially knew existed.

Now, in the throne room, everyone was quiet with fear. Isla had never seen Oro so angry. The only person who dared even look at her was Soren.

"Treason has been committed," Oro said, his eyes pure fire. His voice thundered through the room. He was standing in front of his throne, addressing a hall filled with all the nobles and representatives across the island. Azul stood down the steps, to his side.

Isla was next to him. Her skin had been scraped away; parts of her stomach had needed Wildling elixir to piece back together. The salt water had made the pain unbearable. Every sweep of the fabric of her dress even now was torture, but Isla wanted to stand here, in front of them, as a demonstration of strength.

"A ruler was attacked. Let it be known that anyone who is found associated with this group of rebels will be strung across the cliffs in the Bay of Teeth." It was a torturous death, according to Azul. Sea creatures as large as entire parts of the castle lived there, in waters so deep it was

rumored no one had ever seen their bottom. "Any ill will toward the Wildling realm stops now. A Wildling broke your curses. *This* Wildling is the reason Lightlark still stands. You will treat her and her realm with respect, or you will find another place to live."

The representatives quickly filed out of the throne room when the king was finished. Soren was last to leave, and Isla had the unsettling feeling that he was going to talk to her. In the end, he simply turned and left.

Azul approached, with two guards behind him. "This is Avel and Ciel," he said. "Two of Sky Isle's best warriors. They have volunteered to be in your service for as long as you require them." Guards. They wanted to keep her safe. Avel was a towering blond woman, with her head shaved nearly all the way down. Ciel was the same height, with the same color hair, though his grew long. Their features were almost identical. Twins, she assumed.

The idea that someone outside of her realm, who had no link to her at all, wanted to help her . . . it made her eyes burn with emotion. Not everyone on this island hated her because she was a Wildling, she thought. Not everyone wanted to hurt her.

"Are you sure?" Isla asked them.

In unison, they knelt in front of her, bowing their heads and offering their sapphire-tipped daggers. "You broke the curses, Ruler. We are forever in your debt."

Isla shook her head. "No. No—you are *not*," she said. She thought about the rebels and their attack. "But I will accept your services, at least for the time being."

She thanked Avel and Ciel, then asked them for privacy. They stood watch outside the doors of the throne room.

Only she and Oro remained inside. By the time she walked up the steps to Oro, he was sitting slouched over, his head lowered. One of his hands dragged down his face. He startled as she knelt before him, so their gazes could be level.

His eyes were bloodshot and devastated.

"I will find them," he said.

She put her hand on his cheek. For a moment, he stiffened, like he wasn't used to being touched—who would dare touch the king?—but a second later, he leaned into her palm. "I know," she said.

"If they had *killed* you, I—" He closed his eyes, and the heat of his anger was like a wall, mixed with the tinge of something heavier. Sadness.

"I know," she said again, because she would feel the same way if something happened to him. Their love was a shining link between them. She felt it, lustrous, as she leaned her forehead against his. "I'm here. We're both here. We're both fine."

His eyes dipped to where her dress had partially fallen open, showcasing some of her remaining scars, including the one over her heart, where an arrow had pierced her during the Centennial. No amount of elixir had been able to fade it. She leaned back so the dress fell closed again.

"The healers said I won't even have a mark from the attack by the end of the week." She had been treated by some of the Moonlings who had remained in the castle with those injured by the dreks.

"You shouldn't have a mark to begin with."

"Oro," she said. He didn't meet her eyes. He was looking past her, likely imagining the dozens of ways he was going to torture the rebels once he finally found them. "I want to start my training."

That got his attention.

"With the dreks, I tried—" She winced against the memories of limbs being torn away, of screeches blowing out her eardrums. "I attempted to use the powers. I really did. Even with people dying around me, I couldn't summon my abilities. I couldn't save them." She grimaced. "But then, underground . . . I didn't even try, I didn't even *think* about it, and I became a weapon. I'm glad I did, but you were right. I want to learn to control my powers so they don't control me."

He nodded, looking determined, relieved, like she had given him something to do to help keep her safe.

"You said you had thought of a way to attempt to untangle them?" she asked.

His relief faltered. "Yes," he said. "But you're not going to like it."

UNLEASHED

Remlar was grinning like someone who had boldly declared the future, then watched it come true. Oro's glare did nothing to dim that smile.

"I told you she would return willingly," the winged man said. During the Centennial, he'd told them, *I want the Wildling to visit me. Once this is all over . . . she will come willingly, I assure you.*

He had known, Isla realized. Back then, when he had said that she was *curious . . . born so strangely*, she had believed Remlar was talking about her secret, her powerlessness, but now she understood. He had known then she was Nightshade.

"Tell me, King, you weren't that naive," Remlar said. "She is so very clearly touched by night."

"Enough." Oro's voice was sharp. "Can you unravel her powers?"

Remlar nodded. He was an ancient creature. Isla didn't know the extent of his abilities, but she sensed he was older than she could even imagine. He had dark hair, like Grim's. Was he truly a Nightshade? How was that possible?

"Do it," Isla said.

Oro looked at her. "You have a choice. You don't have to—"

"I know," she said. Then, again to Remlar she said, "Do it."

Before Remlar could move an inch, Oro took a step toward the winged figure. "If you hurt her," he said, voice lethally calm, "she will kill you. And then I will find a way to revive you so I can kill you again with my own bare hands."

The threat made Isla's own mouth go dry, but Remlar, who clearly had put a very low value on his life, just grinned wider. "I would expect nothing less, *King*," he said. "But she has nothing to fear from me. She's one of us."

Us.

It was foolish, but something in her swelled at the word. When so many had rejected her, someone—even someone like Remlar—claiming her . . . it felt good.

He walked over to her, clicking his tongue. His wings twitched as he studied her, mumbling to himself. His skin was the blue of a bird's egg. His stride was feline, graceful, and his eyes were as sharp as his teeth.

His grin became wicked. "You might want to run," he said casually to Oro. "Or, better yet, fly."

Isla didn't know if Oro heeded his warning. With one rapid motion, Remlar placed one hand against her forehead and another against her heart, and her vision exploded.

Pain tore her in two. Her scream was a guttural rasp; she could hear it even above the ringing in her ears. Tears swept down her cheeks.

She fell to her knees.

Her left hand struck the ground, and darkness erupted from her fingers. It ate through the nature in its path; everything living became cinder. Trees fell and disappeared; the air went gray with swimming shadows.

Her right hand landed, and from it a line of thousands of flowers billowed, rising from the ground in waves, blossoming in rapid succession. Roses, tulips, marigolds—they made a blanket across the forest, color streaming.

The world died and came to life in front of her, and she kept screaming until her voice disappeared in a final croak. It might have been seconds or minutes, but eventually, everything settled, and she stood.

One side of her was total desolation—the other the very definition of fertility.

Oro was in front of her in a moment. "Isla," he was saying, but it was just a whisper at the end of a tunnel.

She took one step forward. Teetered.

"Look at me, love," he said.

Love. She held on to the word like an anchor, but the thread between them slipped through her fingers—

Darkness won the war and swallowed her whole.

BEFORE

Isla took the steps two at a time—she really shouldn't have come. How had she been so foolish?

Terra had always warned about Nightshades. They were the villains in all her stories. The monsters.

She really hadn't meant to. She had meant to portal somewhere else entirely, but one thought, while her puddle formed—

Here she was, in the most dangerous place in the world. Running from a group of guards, around dark stone corners, in halls that echoed and closed around her in cavernous arches.

Isla turned into a narrow hallway and crashed to her knees. "Come on," she growled, pressing her starstick firmly against the ground.

No puddle formed.

Isla didn't want to wonder what would happen if she wasn't able to travel home. Nightshade lands were thousands of miles away from the Wildling newland . . . It would take *months* to return by ship, and how would she even pay for passage? She didn't have any jewels on her. Now that she thought about it, no one in their right mind would agree to take her anywhere, anyway.

If anyone figured out who she was . . . she was dead.

The Centennial was just a year away. The Nightshade ruler was a monster. He had been invited to attend the event for the first time, according to her own invitation.

What would he do to her if he found her? Kill her immediately as the first step in breaking the curses? Imprison her? Torture her?

She swallowed. She had thought of her own room as a prison . . . how foolish she was. There were much worse places to be trapped.

Yells. Steps. The clatter of armor.

Instinct took over. She lunged for a door—and it was unlocked. Before the guards could spot her, she threw herself inside.

Another hallway.

Voices outside. Already. There were several more doors. She tried all of them.

Locked.

Locked.

Locked.

Locked.

The voices were closer. Without thinking, she started pounding on the last door, desperate, frantic—

It opened.

A woman stood there. Her arms were crossed.

"You're late," the woman said. "Put this on and join the rest."

Isla had no idea who the woman thought she was, or who the rest were, but she knew luck when she saw it.

The woman all but shoved her into a different room. And Isla was so grateful, so afraid for the guards to find her, that she stripped off her clothes in the dark and put on whatever the woman had given her—fabric that was tight against her body. All Isla cared about was that it would make her look like the rest of the Nightshades. Even if the guards *did* find her here, she would blend in. Especially if she was joining people wearing the same thing.

The door swung open, and Isla nearly brandished the dagger she had kept strapped to her thigh, alongside her starstick.

It was just the woman. She had paint on her finger, and before Isla could object, she unceremoniously smeared it across her mouth.

"Go," she said, pushing her toward another door.

A dozen other women were waiting on the other side. All dressed like her. She nearly sighed in relief. She blended in perfectly . . . especially with the red on her lips.

All she had to do was find her way back outside, where she could try her starstick again—

"Into position!"

Position? The women suddenly straightened into a line, one she quickly joined, wondering what in the world was happening.

Was this a fighting legion?

If so, why were they wearing dresses?

Was this some sort of rehearsal?

She swallowed. If it was, she would be found out momentarily. She obviously wouldn't know any lines for a play, or choreography for a dance . . .

"I hope I'm chosen," a woman to her left whispered to someone who seemed to be her friend.

"I hope *I'm* chosen," she replied. "This is my fourth time hoping to get noticed. It would be an honor to be part of the ruling line."

Ruling line?

Isla turned to the women to ask them what was happening, and why they looked so excited, when the door in front of them opened.

He walked in.

Isla froze.

She knew who he was instantly. Something about the way the air moved around him, about the resonance of his step. He was the tallest man she had ever seen, a foot and a half taller than her at least. He had relatively long black hair like spilled ink, falling across his forehead, curling around his ears. His mouth seemed set in a permanent frown. Unimpressed.

He was the king of nightmares, a demon.

The ruler of Nightshade.

She was dead. He had found her out. They had trapped her; the woman must have recognized her somehow, alerted the guards—

What an idiot. Poppy and Terra had taken such great pains to keep her safe, and she had disobeyed their orders, for what? To experience something new? How selfish she was.

Her fingers inched toward her thigh. She wouldn't have a chance against the ruler of Nightshade, against *any* ruler—no matter how well she could handle a blade, power was power—but she would die with dignity. Fighting.

Just as her pointer finger found the smooth metal, his eyes met hers. She stilled.

His look was strange. There was no hint of fury, or even satisfaction. Just a slight widening of his eyes—a curiosity.

That didn't make sense. If he was about to kill her, wouldn't he announce his intention? Slay her where she stood, in front of all the others?

"You," he said.

He was staring at her. He meant her.

She didn't move a muscle. His eyebrows rose just a fraction of an inch. Surprise. Another unexpected emotion.

The woman from before all but shoved Isla forward, toward him.

The Nightshade ruler stared down at her. She didn't breathe. Then, he turned and walked back through the door.

She was expected to follow him. She knew that for certain when the woman from before gripped her wrist and said, "*Follow*," so fiercely that she actually did.

Her steps echoed through the empty hall. His were almost silent in front of her. All she saw was his back. Her own shoulders were small—tiny slopes.

His were wide cliffs.

He had perfect posture. The posture of a warrior. She swallowed. How many thousands had he single-handedly taken down? Even in her

glass room, she had heard whispers about his malice. Some Nightshades could kill with a single touch—wasn't that the rumor?

A shiver worked its way down her spine . . . and turned into a pit in her stomach when he led her into a dark room.

Was this where she would be executed?

She tugged her dress up while his back was still turned and risked a look at her portaling device. It was still dark, lifeless.

No.

Isla needed a plan.

The voices in her head crowded, wicked, quick to attack. What plan could she possibly come up with to have a chance against him?

She was a fool. A powerless fool.

The door closed behind her, and she jumped.

The ruler of Nightshade—*Grimshaw*—turned to face her. He looked her over quickly. Was he sizing her up? Deciding how he would make her suffer?

She swallowed. Took a step back.

He lunged for her.

Isla should have grabbed her dagger, but she was more shocked than she had ever been in her life, so she froze.

Froze as he pressed her against the wall, and—

He . . . he lowered his face until his lips were mere inches from hers. His eyes were hungry, full of desire. He wanted to kiss her. That didn't make any sense.

Suddenly, all the pieces came together. Why the women in line looked so excited. Why they were speaking of hoping *to be chosen*. Becoming *part of the ruling line*. They had all clearly volunteered to be presented in front of the Nightshade ruler. He thought she wanted this. He thought she had *signed up* for this.

He didn't know who she was.

She could have pushed him away. Told him the truth. But she didn't. She was a fool. That had already been established, hadn't it? Her entire

life, she had been locked up. She had never been this close to a man before. She had never *felt* this way before.

His hands, so large, so callused, gripping her so strangely. His *height*. His eyes, dark and gleaming. *Hungry.* His hard body, pressed against hers, his muscles and her curves lining up so naturally. Those seemingly unimportant things—much less important than who he was, and what kind of weapons were inches away from her—became all she could think of. She went very still.

For a moment, she forgot herself. And him. She forgot everything she had ever been taught.

"Is this okay?" he asked, looking down at her. He was leaning lower, his breath grazing her lips. A shiver worked its way down her spine.

This was her chance to say no. Instead, she found herself saying, "Yes." And meaning it.

Then, his lips were on hers.

Isla had never been kissed. Didn't *want* to be kissed by her enemy, her rival, the filthy, deadly—surprisingly attractive—Nightshade. Then why had she said yes? She should push him, say something, but his lips were a key, unlocking things she had never felt. Heat, pulsing everywhere. Sparks, dancing across her skin, as his thumb pressed against the palm he held against the wall. As his teeth skimmed her lips, as his lips dipped down her neck . . .

She kissed him back. She held him just as tightly as he held her.

Her hands ran through his hair, and it was so much softer than she would have imagined. She felt her way down his neck, his chest, and he felt hard and cold as stone. His tongue swiped against the hollow of her throat, and she made a sound that shocked her.

Sensing her excitement, he made some sort of growl and hauled her up, against the wall, as her legs locked around his middle. She gasped, because in this position, she could *feel* him . . . *all* of him. Right against her. Right against her—

All at once, she remembered herself.

Remembered who he was, how she needed to get out of there *now*.

He was her enemy. The moment he found out who she was, he would hurt her. This could be a trick. Surely, he was going to attack her at any moment.

She needed to strike first.

Just as he deepened their kiss, she grabbed her dagger from where it was holstered on her thigh. Gripped its hilt.

And stabbed him through the chest.

There was a moment of quiet. The Nightshade ruler met her eyes, right before his chin dipped, and he slowly looked down to his chest, where the dagger still stuck out, inches from his heart.

Then, he released her.

There was no time. No time to turn around, to check if the warmth across the front of her body was shame or fear or his blood.

She ran out the door, grabbed her starstick, which somehow, mercifully, now glowed.

She drew her puddle of stars—

And was gone.

FAVORITE

Isla awoke soaked in sweat and panting. Oro was there, hand behind her head. The rest of her was draped across his lap. They were still in the forest, framed by life and decay. She imagined Remlar was lurking, watching.

She pressed her forehead to Oro's shoulder and cried. Her Nightshade powers had been awoken, and they had begun to unravel her mind. Undo what had been done. She thought of what Grim had told her, weeks before, after the Centennial.

Remember us, Heart. You will remember. Then you will come back to me.

She would never go back to him. Nothing would change his betrayal. Nothing would change the fact that Grim seemed intent now on killing innocent people. One thing was for sure, however.

She was starting to remember.

Her powers were detangled, and Isla wondered if they would have been better left alone.

She had been going in and out of consciousness, but now all her senses came flooding back, far too sharply. They were in the Mainland woods. Oro must have flown them here. Her memory still clung to the corners of her vision, as if it had claws.

A blink, and she saw Grim again, his hands curled beneath her—

No. She pushed the image away. She wouldn't tell Oro about it. It was the past. It didn't matter. She had been vulnerable while her power had been unleashed, she told herself. It wouldn't happen again.

She felt Oro's hands smoothing down her back. "There you are," he was saying, meeting her eyes, frowning as he checked her temperature with the back of his hand. "How are you feeling?"

Her head pounded like the sea against the cliffside, and there were *voices*. Whispers everywhere, from every direction. Something had filled her body to the brim. She was an overserved goblet, wine spilling down the sides.

"I feel everything," she said. Tiny threads all around her, waiting to be pulled. Whispers from the vines beneath her hands, from the towering trees around her, from the shadows beneath them. "There are a million voices, all fighting for my attention." Power was like a seed in her chest she had swallowed whole, and it was growing roots within her.

All her life she had wondered what it would be like to have power. All her life she'd had it, hidden deep inside. Now, it was free.

"We can find you a Wildling master," Oro said, his voice a blade through the chaos. "I can get your portaling device. We can take you to the Wildling newland." It made sense to train there, with her own people, but—

"No," she said quickly. "I don't want to risk harming them. I—" Her touch had killed an entire forest. It was just like her Starling power exploding out of her. She had no control. Panicked, her eyes darted around. "Take me somewhere else. I don't want to hurt anyone."

With three separate powers—Wildling, Nightshade, and Starling—the abilities seemed to be battling. When she had gotten her Starling abilities, she had felt strange but nothing like this.

In an instant, she was in Oro's arms, and they were in the air. When they landed, she immediately stumbled away, afraid that if he touched her for too long, she might hurt him.

"You can't kill anything here," he said simply. "Everything is already dead."

He was right. They were on Wild Isle. The voices had quieted, just a little. Still, the skeletal trees called to her, the dirt beneath her

feet hummed, and she could still hear the Mainland woods even from far away.

She needed those voices out of her head—it was already a crowded place to begin with. She needed to stop feeling pressure against her ribs, like the seed of power was going to burn right through her chest. "It's too loud," she said. "I can't—I can't escape it."

"When you gain a hold on your power, you won't hear them anymore," he said. "Right now, you are inadvertently summoning everything—the world is simply answering your call. It will get better as you begin to gain control."

She shook her head. How long could that take? "I can't, I can't—"

One more step, and she sank to her knees and said, "I think I'm going to be sick," before she did just that. Her throat was still coarse and sore from the ocean water; it burned like a skinned knee.

He was behind her, his heat a welcome warmth, his hand gathering her hair in a single fist. "It's going to be a rough few days as your body adjusts," he whispered. "I'll be right here with you."

"Please don't leave me," she said, her voice frail and pleading. For just a moment, she wanted to cry out for Terra, her teacher for her entire life. *She* was the one who should have been teaching her this. But Terra had betrayed her, and besides Oro, she was alone.

"Never, Wildling," he said.

She retched again.

The Place of Mirrors became their temporary home. Avel and Ciel moved in as well. They helped coordinate getting furniture, food, and supplies, alongside Ella, who brought clothing and Starling soup. The Skyling twins took turns guarding the entrance to Wild Isle. No power other than Wildling could be used in the Place of Mirrors; she had learned that during the Centennial.

It gave her an added layer of protection. Isla was more vulnerable than ever, but she felt safe here against the rebels—and with Oro sleeping right beside her.

She wished she could enjoy that fact a little more, but for the next few days, she was always either clenching her teeth against pain, being sick, or sleeping.

A fever turned to chills. She felt nauseous all the time. Oro fed her pieces of bread and soups and got her to drink water even when she cried, because everything hurt, and would he please make it stop?

He looked as pained as she felt.

She fell asleep holding his hand every night, and every morning when she awoke, with a headache worse than the last, he was already there, looking like he hadn't slept at all.

"You can go," she said weakly one night, as he very badly attempted to brush her hair and tie it with one of her ribbons. Ella typically helped her, but she had sent the Starling home early that night, since she had been working around the clock for days. "I'm sure you're needed elsewhere."

Oro just looked at her, the corners of his lips twitching in amusement that didn't reach his eyes. "I was given strict orders not to leave your side."

Isla managed to smile, before grimacing as a new wave of pain washed over her. "Oh? I didn't know the king of Lightlark took orders from anyone."

"Not just anyone."

She stared at him, her pain abating just a little. A wavy lock of hair came loose, and Oro cursed, starting over.

"You have many skills," Isla said, a faint laugh escaping her even as every part of her ached. "Doing hair isn't one of them."

Oro began to smile in earnest. "Here I thought I had another talent." He brushed through her locks again and said, "I like your hair."

"You do?"

He nodded. "It . . . shines nicely in the sun. I didn't know that until after the curses." She smiled, despite the pain. The fact that he noticed something that specific about her, that he was paying that close attention . . . it made her feel warm inside, for just a moment, before the nausea returned.

"I like your eyes too," he offered, studying her face, as if wanting to make her smile again. He quickly returned his attention to her hair. "They're my favorite color."

She raised an eyebrow at him. "My eyes happen to be your favorite color?"

Oro paused, looking a little like he regretted starting this conversation in the first place. He stared intently at the ribbon between his fingers, and it looked almost physically painful for him to get the next few words out. "No. It . . . it *became* my favorite, after . . . after—"

He was flustered. Isla couldn't believe it. The king of Lightlark, the cold ruler of Sunling she had heard about her entire life, was *flustered*. It was adorable. Isla's chest felt like it was being cracked in half, but she couldn't help but tease him. "Really?" she said. "Please. Tell me everything you like about me, slowly, in detail."

Oro gave her a look that made her certain he knew she was reveling in his discomfort.

She pressed her lips against another smile. "Do I encompass any other favorites? Am I your . . . favorite liar? Favorite incapable ruler?" Her tone slowly became bitter, because in truth, she couldn't imagine being anyone's favorite anything. "Your favorite weakling who can't go a few hours without retching?"

Oro turned to her, then. He looked her right in the eyes as he said, "Isla. You are my favorite everything."

Her lips had been parted with another self-deprecating and annoying statement, but she closed them.

That couldn't be true.

What was there to like about her? She was weak. Foolish—

She looked away. Suddenly, she was the one who was uncomfortable. Oro didn't lie, but she couldn't imagine anyone saying good things about her, when her mind told her the opposite. "I feel better," she lied. "You can leave for a bit, if you want."

"Is that so?"

"Better than ever, actually."

"Right." He lightly brushed away another strand that had come loose—because he was truly hopeless at tying her hair—and she knew he was also subtly checking her temperature. "Well, Wildling, even if I couldn't naturally tell that you're a liar, your skin is so warm, you could pass for Sunling."

Oro should be with a Sunling. Someone more like him. Someone who wasn't such a mess. "Do you wish I was?"

"Sunling?"

She nodded, and it didn't do anything to make her head feel better. Before he could respond, she added, "Do you wish I wasn't . . . everything I am?"

He was quiet for a moment. Her eyes slowly began to close, suddenly heavy. Fighting against sleep was useless in this state. "No, Isla," he finally said. "It's the parts you don't seem to like about yourself that I love the most."

Love—

She wanted to accept it, savor it, clutch it, let the word swallow her whole and make her happy. But instead, she drifted off, into the waiting arms of sleep.

BEFORE

She was kicking off her shoes, rubbing her toes. No matter how many times Poppy made her stride in straight lines, or even forced Terra to make her train in the ridiculous heeled shoes, she would never get used to them.

And the *dresses.*

The ones with all the ties and buttons hell-bent on not letting her breathe. Each stitch and clip of her corset was conspiring together to suffocate her, she was sure of it.

Your face and words will be just as important as your blades and swords during the Centennial, Poppy said.

Isla highly doubted it.

She had all the buttons down the back of her dress undone when she noticed a shadow in the corner of her room. A shadow that *flickered.*

In a moment, the dagger she kept hidden beneath her vanity was in her fingers, and she whirled around, only to be face-to-face with the shadow now as it rippled then settled.

Grim was standing over her, eyes trained on the dress that hung from her shoulders, not her blade.

"Hello, Hearteater," he said.

He had found her. She had foolishly hoped it would take him longer to figure out her identity. Or that her stabbing had wounded him enough to buy her a few weeks to figure out a plan. She knew it wouldn't kill him. She had just wanted to incapacitate him long enough to make her escape.

Now here he was.

Impossibly, in her room, in the Wildling newland. Here to kill her.

Before she could breathe, his hand was wrapped around hers—the one that held the dagger—so painfully that she flinched.

Isla grunted, adrenaline rushing through her, as she tried to wrestle herself away. That only made him angry. He growled and shoved her against the glass wall of her room. It felt nothing like before.

No, this time he twisted her arm painfully, so that her own knife was at her throat.

She writhed beneath him, heart pounding, arm flashing in pain. All he did was frown down at her, eyes fixed in a glare.

"You cursed hearteater"—he spat the word like it disgusted him—"dare to come to *my* realm, disguised, to assassinate me." The blade dug against her neck. She had sharpened the tip herself; it was so sharp that it immediately cut into her skin. She smelled her own blood. He was going to kill her, stab her just like she had him.

She wasn't like him. She didn't have power that would delay her death.

Isla flicked the wrist that he wasn't holding. The weapon disguised as a bracelet unveiled its spike. She stabbed it through his thigh.

The Nightshade ruler roared, and her dagger dropped to the floor—but before she could take her chance to escape, the blade to her neck was replaced with an invisible grip.

She choked as she floated in the air, clawing at her throat. He stood there, focused, as she was hauled farther up the wall.

Isla gasped for breath, but the grip didn't loosen. She saw stars. Could barely hear him as he said, "Was this your plan to keep me from the Centennial? To try and break the curses? Did you mean to make a fool of me?" The pressure gripped even tighter, and her vision went white. "Who are you working with?"

Isla tried to speak, but her words sounded like whimpers.

"How did you travel to Nightshade so quickly?"

At that, Isla glared at him, enraged, exasperated. How was she supposed to answer all his questions when he had her throat in an invisible fist?

Like he could read her thoughts, he bared his teeth—

And released her.

Isla fell to the floor in a heap, gasping, her fevered forehead and hands flat against the cold ground. Her unbuttoned dress slipped down her shoulders.

It took what seemed like a lifetime to catch her breath. Once she did, she gripped the dagger from the floor, scuttled to the corner of her room, away from him, that monster, that filth—

He had almost killed her.

Across the room, Grimshaw frowned. *Frowned.*

It was her turn to bare her teeth at him. She lifted the dagger in his direction, with a shaking arm. "Monster," she said, her voice just a rasp against the back of her throbbing throat. She spat at him.

He had the nerve to laugh. He took a step forward, and she had to force herself not to flinch.

"*I'm* the monster?" he said. Another step. "When Wildlings eat the hearts of men?" He looked down at her with disgust.

He didn't know, then, that the curse didn't apply to her. That was good.

Her hand went to her neck, and she winced. The skin there was tender.

Grimshaw followed the trace of her fingers. "Do I need to remind you that you *stabbed* me?" With a furious motion, he tore his shirt up to reveal an angry scar just inches from his heart.

Isla swallowed. Stabbing him had been a mistake. She had been panicked, acting on instinct.

Now she knew how foolish it had been. If he hadn't been her enemy then, he certainly was now. Grimshaw would be at the Centennial if he decided to accept the invitation. He would kill her.

The Nightshade ruler took a step closer. Prowled, really. His chin bent low, he looked at her with eyes dark as charcoal, squinted into a glare.

She scuttled back an inch. Another.

"How did you get into my realm?" he demanded.

Panic spiked through her chest. She forced her eyes not to dart to the floorboard where she hid her starstick. Her spine was drenched in fear, but she used all her strength to sit up straight, to meet his gaze.

The Nightshade ruler's voice became eerily calm. "How," he said, taking another step. "Did." Another step. "*You.*" The word held the same poison as his look as he regarded her, splayed against the greenhouse glass like a weakling. "Get. In."

He bent down low, eyes never leaving hers. By the time he was almost nose to nose with her, she used that fear as a cover. As she cowered beneath his shadow, she gripped the blade still in her hand.

Before he could take another breath, its tip was resting just below his chin.

Her nostrils flared. Her voice shook, out of not just fear now but anger. Anger at herself for being so weak.

"Get," she said, matching his tone. "*Out.*" Something in his expression flinched at the spit flying from her mouth, from the intensity of her words. Good. "Of. My. *Room.*"

She pushed the blade into his skin for emphasis, waited to feel the heat of his blood on her hand.

But before she could apply enough pressure, he vanished.

She collapsed fully against the floor, shaking like a child, wondering how the Nightshade seemed to have the same portaling ability as her starstick.

KEY CLICKING INTO A LOCK

Isla startled awake. *No.* Oro was still clutching her hand, but he was finally sleeping, head leaned to the side. She didn't want to wake him.

A single memory was one thing. *Two?*

She had been so weak. Cowering. Now that her abilities were unraveled, she refused to ever feel that way again.

That day, Isla left her bed. She bathed in the small tub Ella had set up. The water was freezing, as Oro couldn't use his abilities in the Place of Mirrors to heat it, but she gritted her teeth against the chill. She put on the dark-green pants, long-sleeved shirt, and high brown boots Leto had made her.

Isla began her training.

The dirt was dead in her hands.

Isla sat in the middle of Wild Isle, fingers curled into the soil. The headache and voices hadn't gone away, but she forced them to the corners of her mind. She had been trying and failing to use her powers for nearly an hour.

"I don't understand," she said. "Before . . ." All she'd had to do was place a hand on the forest floor and it had exploded with life and color.

Oro was standing a few feet away, leaning against a half-rotted tree. "Raw power is like a beast. Without mastery, it lashes out unpredictably. Not always when you want it to." The memory of the rebels touching her skin flitted through her mind. "That's why learning control is so important."

"And difficult?" she asked, finally pulling her hands from the dirt.

"And difficult," he agreed. "Using it in a directed way requires intense focus."

Focus.

Her mind was filled to the brim, a thousand thoughts running rampant. She couldn't focus on a single thought if her life depended on it.

"It might," Oro said, and only then did she realize she had said part of that aloud. He bent down and grabbed a rock. He placed it in front of her. "Instead of just trying to force your power out, focus all of your mind and energy on this," he said. "Move it."

He got up and left.

She whipped around. "Where—where are you going? I thought you were going to train me."

"I am," he said.

She watched him walk back to the Place of Mirrors.

Her first impulse was to yell at his back that he had promised not to leave her, but no. She could do this.

Isla dug her fingers into the dirt again. She took a deep breath. Dropped her shoulders. She tried to focus on the sensations around her. The dryness of the ground. The heat of the sun warming the crown of her head. The slight wind making the loose hairs around her face go wild.

It took only a few moments for focusing to feel almost physically painful. Then it slipped, and thoughts poured into her mind like high tide. Worries. Anxieties.

Him.

No. She shut him out, closed her eyes tightly. Dug her fingers deeper into the ground. "I will get this," she said. "I will forget, and I will focus."

Would she, though?

Her powers needed a strong vessel. She was a half person. Walking through life carrying the weight of her past around with her.

She tried to force it all away. She sat and curled her fingers even deeper, until dirt ran far up her fingernails.

Nothing happened.

For days, she sat in silence, then went to bed frustrated. Some hours, she could hold her attention in small spurts. Others, distractions would dive in like vultures. Sometimes, the voice in her head was cruel. It was like there was a blade in her mind, feeling around for where it could hurt her the most.

The rock never moved an inch.

When Oro came to meet her that night, she was exhausted and frustrated. "I cannot just spend days staring at a rock," she said.

"Learning to wield takes time."

"How long did it take you?"

Oro raised a brow at her. "To master? Years for each power."

Years. She didn't have years. Her vision of Grim's destruction could happen at any moment. She wondered if she should have told the other representatives and rulers about it. Would they trust her at all? Would they believe she was working with Grim, like the woman after the drek attack?

He must have seen her face drop because he said, "It won't always be hard. One day, something will give. Some of a ruler's mastery of power is like a key clicking into a lock."

Breath caught in her throat. So far, she had felt no such key. It was another rejection. First the vault. Now this.

"Isla," he said, coming to stand in front of her. "What's wrong?"

"You don't get it," she said quickly. "Control was probably easy for you. You never knew what it was like to be *alone* in your incompetence, to not be in total and complete control of—"

"I killed someone," he said, and his voice was so serious, she tensed. "By accident, with my abilities. When I was a child."

"What?"

"Power usually develops later in life, but I set my crib aflame when I was just a few months old. My mother found me sitting in the center of the flames, just staring at her. They were forced to train me as soon as possible, as they feared I would destroy the castle with a tantrum. I was far stronger than I was supposed to be, as a second child."

"Stronger than Egan," she said, speaking his brother's name. The former king, who had sacrificed himself, along with all other rulers, for the chance of a future.

Oro nodded. "I was sent to the isles every few years, to master each ability. Control was the first lesson I ever learned as a child. Control your emotions, or you could bring the palace down. Control your heart, because allowing anyone access to that power would be ruinous. Control your tongue, because you are not the firstborn, and your opinions don't matter."

Isla's heart broke for the little boy Oro had once been. She took his hand.

"I did all of it," he said, staring at the ground. "There was another ability, though, that hadn't manifested in centuries." His eyes met hers. "Since I didn't know about it, I couldn't control it. I had been playing with my friends, having too much fun, and, before I knew what was happening, I turned an attendant to solid gold." His voice had become lifeless. The mistake still seemed to haunt him, centuries later.

Isla couldn't imagine the pain. If she killed an innocent person by accident, because of her lack of control, she would never be able to forgive herself.

"I felt such guilt and shame, even as my parents celebrated my power. The only thing that got me through my training were the people I met. I had—*I have*—really good friends."

He did? Isla felt ashamed that she had never even asked him much about his life before the curses.

"For years, I didn't wield," he said. "I was ashamed of my abilities. The guilt ate at me. I hated myself for a long time."

Tears stung her eyes. He couldn't know how similar she felt now, for different reasons.

"It was only after I was able to forgive myself for the mistake I made as a child that I could start living again." His thumb grazed the back of her hand. "You will get this, Isla," he said. "It might not be today, or tomorrow, but I will be here with you until you do. You are not alone."

You are not alone.

It was early the next morning when she snuck out of the Place of Mirrors, shoes crunching on the leftover glass on the floor.

She took the rock to the edge of the isle. Legs hanging, she watched the sun climb from the horizon like a phoenix, dying every day, only to rise again.

She closed her eyes.

For once, instead of trying to keep everything down, Isla dared her mind to do its worst, and it did. Her pain came flooding through the walls she had put up, and it hurt, *it hurt so much,* but it was almost a relief to have her emotions spilling out of her, instead of keeping them all pressed down.

She thought about her parents. Born enemies. A Wildling and a Nightshade. Life and death. They really must have loved each other, she thought, to not only get together . . . but also have a child.

Would they be ashamed of her? Would they think her weak?

She allowed herself to grieve the little girl who had grown up locked away like a secret. The one who had bled countless times to be the best possible warrior. Terra had taken the approach of breaking her first, so that the world would not. All she had ever wanted was to be accepted. To be good enough. To be *loved—*

It had made her the perfect person for Celeste—*Aurora*—to target and take advantage of. That name in her thoughts made her ache. Her *friend*. She had been her best friend.

Finally . . . she thought of him. *Grim*.

The memories were like pulling the stitches of a wound, making it bleed again.

After hours of letting her thoughts go wild, Isla took a breath and began to forgive herself for some of her mistakes. She pictured the little girl, sitting alone in her room, and thought, *She doesn't deserve this*.

When she focused on the rock again, she realized that besides her crown, her powers were the only thing that connected her to her ancestors. To her *mother*.

She closed her eyes and found the incessant, anxious, cruel thoughts weren't so strong anymore, as if letting them run wild had caused them to lose their energy.

Isla had never known her mother, but she wanted to make her proud. She wanted to help her people. She wanted everything that she had already been through to be worth it.

She wanted to be better, for that little girl sitting in the glass room.

Her arm lifted, her gaze trained on the rock.

Something in her chest thrummed, coming to life, then caught—a key clicking into a lock. She didn't dare blink as she outstretched her hand.

The rock began to vibrate. It squirmed beneath her gaze.

She reached back, then threw her arm forward.

It moved—

Along with the five feet of island beneath, which was carved out like a giant had dipped its finger into Wild Isle and dug a path right across it. Isla now had a clear view all the way to the water from where she stood. She was covered in dirt.

Isla was breathless. It was sloppy, and far from controlled, but she'd done it.

. . .

From then on, they trained from the first sunlight to the last. In the mornings, she and Oro ran on the beaches below the Whitecliffs. He said it would help clear her mind, and it did.

She practiced moving large and small objects. She practiced manipulating the dirt and rocks around her. Every day, he came up with new tests, new ways to sharpen her control. In the evenings, they had dinner together, just the two of them. Afterward, they would sit on the floor, drinking tea, trading stories about their childhoods, until Isla inevitably fell asleep. She always woke up in her bed, though, meticulously wrapped in blankets.

Since she hadn't been able to visit the Starlings after the coronation, Isla asked Oro to station guards at the Star Isle bridge, to prevent the attacks, and to provide any immediate assistance they might require.

"Consider it done," he had said, and it made her feel a little better about committing all this time to training.

Little by little, control became natural. The power within her, unruly and vast like the sea, began to sharpen into a single stream of ability.

Today, Oro pulled a blindfold from his pocket. "Is this okay?" he asked.

She nodded, and he tied it tightly around her head. "Bring back any memories?"

He laughed, the sound low and scraping the back of her mind.

"Did you want to kill me that day?" she asked, remembering how she had knocked the crown from his head with one of her throwing stars. How it had clattered noisily in the shocked silence.

"No," he whispered somewhere close to her ear, the shade of his voice making her arms prickle, even though it was scorching outside. "Quite the opposite."

"Really?"

"Really. That night, all I could think about was your annoyingly smug face when you took off the blindfold."

The corners of her lips twitched. "I was pretty impressed with myself." She frowned. "Though my demonstration wasn't nearly as impressive as your gilding." She said the last word carefully. With what he had shared with her, she imagined his ability to gild was still tinged with pain. Tainted. Hundreds of years had gone by. She wanted to take the pain associated with the ability away.

Was *that* love?

She reached up and moved the blindfold so she could see him. "You know," she teased, "for someone who can make anything into gold . . . I would think you would have already gifted someone you love at least a golden apple. Or a golden . . . blade of grass."

Someone you love . . . She surprised herself with the boldness of her words.

He tensed. She only got a glimpse of his surprise before he tugged the blindfold down over her eyes again. His hand did not leave her face. His thumb slid down her temple, and it sent shivers through her body. He sighed and leaned down to whisper in her ear, "When all this is over, I'll gild you an entire castle. Is that sufficient?"

"That's a little excessive."

Another sigh.

He stepped away, and his voice became serious. "Wielding power means feeling it around you, not simply seeing it. Even with your back turned, or eyes closed, you should be able to sense a threat."

A rock hit the side of her head, and she whipped around, baring her teeth. "Really?"

"It was a pebble. I'm reaching for a rock now. Focus."

Isla couldn't see a thing behind the blindfold, but she focused, and the tiny threads that had annoyed her so much previously began appearing, a million little links around her. She had blocked them out the last few weeks, but now they all came rearing back, especially since one of her main senses had been taken away. The more she mentally searched her

surroundings, the louder everything became again. It was like endless noise; she couldn't focus on anything—

By the time she sensed the rock, it had already hit her shoulder.

She winced. The bruise was sure to look like a storm cloud.

"Focus."

"I am," she said through her teeth.

Another rock hurtled at her. She sensed it and shot out her hand but missed. It hit her hip.

Isla felt something rising through her ribs, uncurling in her chest.

When the next rock hit her in the stomach, it unleashed.

"Put your arms down, Isla."

Were they even up? She ripped the blindfold off, only to see sharp blades made from branches, dozens of them, levitating in the air, all pointed at Oro. Rocks hovered between them, vibrating with intensity.

Isla gasped, and they fell to the ground with a lifeless thump.

She took a step back. "I—I'm sorry." She hadn't even realized what she was doing. Her power had taken over.

Oro stepped toward her. "I was never in danger."

But what if she *did* hurt him one day? When he was asleep? When she wasn't paying attention?

"You need to work on controlling your emotions when using power," he said. "But." There was a but? "That was impressive."

"It was?"

"It was focused, at least. A lot more controlled than when Remlar initially released your powers," Oro said.

"So, what you're saying is, I am getting more efficient at trying to kill you," she deadpanned.

"Precisely." His expression turned serious. "Emotion undoes control," he explained. "When you're emotional, your power has no constraint. It might seem like it makes you more powerful, but it can be dangerous. It can drain you completely until there's nothing left."

Isla trained harder. She tested the limits of her control, working to keep her emotions steady. Her life narrowed to just her, Oro, and her Wildling power. For over a week, there were no more memories. No more voice inside her head. No sightings.

The shadow of Grim had disappeared, and Isla hoped she never had to see him again.

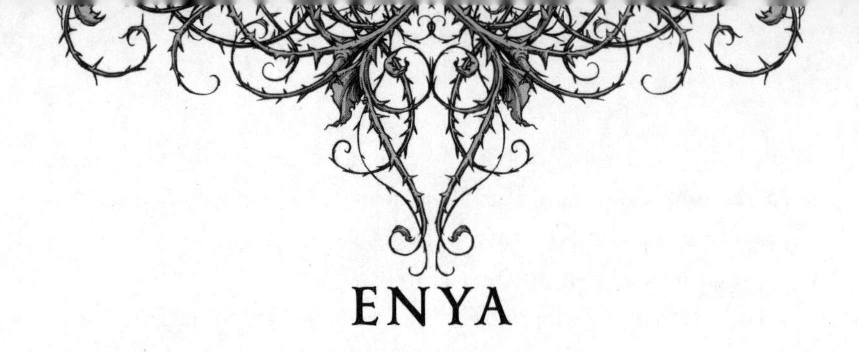

ENYA

"I want to continue my training on the Wildling newland," Isla said.

They had worked together for weeks. She was still far from a master, but she felt in control enough that she wouldn't be a danger. It had been too long since she had visited her people. She needed to make sure they were taken care of, then she needed to start preparing for the inevitability that Grim was coming for her. He had likely orchestrated the drek attack.

What was next?

"And I need help. I don't just want to bring them provisions. If it's possible . . . I would like to see if anyone would volunteer to teach them skills they didn't need before. How to prepare different types of foods, for example, and a dozen other things I can't think of. I don't really . . . I don't really know—"

"I know someone."

"What?"

"I know someone who will know some of what they will need," Oro said.

Her brows came together. "Who?"

"Do you remember Enya?"

Isla remembered the tall Sunling at the dinner with the dark-red hair and freckles. She hadn't looked unfriendly but not exactly friendly, either. Appraising, maybe.

"She taught Sunlings how to survive in the dark, after the curses. How to set up systems that allowed for crops to still grow, and life to still happen, even though we couldn't be outside in the daylight. She's good at coming up with solutions for problems that don't even exist yet."

That person sounded perfect. "It sounds like she has been a great Sunling representative."

"More than that."

She raised an eyebrow at him.

"Remember I said I had friends?" Oro said.

"It was the shock of my life."

He gave her a look.

"She's one of them?" she asked, incredulous. They hadn't seemed that close at the dinner, but she supposed it had been a serious function.

He nodded. "She's one of them."

The Sun Isle castle looked dipped in a pot of gold. Enya sat at the head of a long dining table, with her feet propped up on the chair beside her. Her red hair was tied into a braid. She had an orange peel and a knife in front of her.

They had met before, but Isla was suddenly nervous. She hadn't known that she and Oro had been friends. Would the woman judge her? Did she know about Oro and Isla's . . . connection?

He placed a gentle hand against her lower back, as if sensing her nerves. His touch was fire. It was such a simple gesture, but it immediately made her feel better. She looked up at Oro and found him watching her. His fingers flexed against her spine—

"It's a wonder either of you train at all, with how much you look like you want to bed one another."

Her eyes snapped back to the woman sitting across the room.

"Enya . . ." Oro said smoothly. "At least give Isla a few minutes before she's wishing I hadn't brought her to see you."

Enya shrugged and swung her legs around. She wore dark-gold—almost brown—leather pants, and a gold metal corset over long-sleeved

chain mail. Armor, it looked like, though somehow casual. Her metal-plated boots clanked against the floor as she walked over, beaming.

"Well, you look different," Enya said. Isla was wearing her training clothing, instead of her usual dresses. Her crown was in her room. Before Isla could say a word, Enya pulled her into a hug. Into her ear, she whispered, "He's almost intolerable, isn't he?"

"I can hear you," Oro said.

"Of course you can, that's the best part," Enya said.

"How—how do you know each other?" Isla asked. They bickered like siblings. But no . . . Oro's entire family was dead.

"Our mothers were best friends," Enya said. She stepped to stand next to Oro. Her height was impressive, but she was still short enough to lean her head against his shoulder. He did not so much as move a muscle in response. "Whether he liked it or not, that meant I would be by his side forever."

Oro sighed, but Isla could see fondness there, beneath his frown. "Enya has been one of my Sun Isle representatives since before the curses. She often acts as my proxy, and attends meetings in my stead."

"Like Soren," Isla said, almost to herself.

Enya made a gagging noise. "Nothing like him, Isla. But yes, a similar role." The Sunling got straight to business. "I hear you need help on the Wildling newland. Volunteers. Infrastructure. Some organization?"

"Everything."

"Good. I've taken the liberty of, and I hope you don't mind"—she looked to Isla like she really did care if Isla had an objection to what she was about to say—"rounding up a group already. All of them are respectful of all realms, including Wildling. They don't know what it's for, in case you don't approve, but—"

"Once she gets something in her head, she is relentless," Oro said.

Friendship, for more than five hundred years. Since childhood. Part of Isla wondered if she should be jealous, but she just . . . wasn't. Isla

was grateful that Oro had had someone he could count on when he lost his family. Someone he could trust.

Enya shrugged, not even trying to deny it. "I can get obsessive. At least I know that about myself . . ." She shot a wicked grin at Isla, then turned to Oro. "*Some* people are far less eager to admit their faults." She led them through the palace to a room that looked like it was used for strategy. There was a circular table inside, decorated like a sun. At its center was what looked like a pile of ash.

"Would you mind sketching the Wildling newland for me? I already have a rough idea of how many people we will need, and where, but it would be helpful to see."

Isla just stared at the pile. She turned to Oro, and he smoothed the ash into a thin layer. "Here," he said. He traced lines in the ashes with his finger, and a moment later they hardened, becoming three-dimensional figures. Interesting.

She dipped her finger inside and felt like a painter, with a canvas and paint that both came to life. There was a time when Isla hadn't known much about her lands, but she had explored them through portaling many times since.

When she was finished, Enya reached over and grabbed the map. It came off in her hands. She looked at it from all angles, then set it down again.

"Very well. We'll be ready in three days. I've organized my schedule so I can stay there for a week, to make sure everything goes smoothly. Does that sound acceptable?"

Acceptable? Isla wanted to bow at the woman's feet.

"It sounds perfect," Isla said.

"Oro tells me you have a portaling device?"

She nodded.

"How many people can it transfer at once?"

"I'm not sure. The most I've tried is two."

Enya waved away any worry. "No matter. We will go in small groups. We'll make it work."

Isla believed her. She would believe anything that came out of her mouth.

"Thank you," Isla said, and, unexplainably, her eyes stung. She felt such gratitude . . . Enya didn't even know her, and she was helping her. Her people.

"Thank *you*," Enya said, and her eyes sparkled mischievously. "For showing us that our dear Oro does indeed still know how to smile."

Enya had gathered a dozen volunteers. They all stood together on the Mainland, with supplies between them. She quickly explained the usage of the starstick, and the volunteers looked curious, but no one questioned it.

Isla drew her puddle of stars as big as she could, and they all barely fit inside. Then, they were in the Wildling newland.

One of the volunteers was immediately sick. "Sorry," she said. "I should have warned you about the nausea."

Isla had portaled them to Wren's village. The tall Wildling stepped out into the street within minutes. At first, she looked alarmed, but slowly, her expression calmed. She dropped the hand that had instantly gone to her blade. Isla realized then that she hadn't properly prepared her people for visitors.

"This is Oro, king of Lightlark," Isla said. By then, a few Wildlings stood in the streets, watching the volunteers warily.

At once, they bowed their heads.

Isla introduced Enya, then Ciel and Avel, who rarely left her side, then the rest of the volunteers. Her people stared at them with varying levels of wariness.

The volunteers looked a little frightened too. The Skyling to her right was smiling, but her gaze kept darting to the monstrous hammer one of the Wildlings carried on her back.

Isla stepped between her people and the visitors. "We are here to help," she said. "*All* of us."

She worked with the volunteers to hand out supplies from the Mainland castle stock. They would need more for the rest of the newland, but this was a good start. Wren proposed the Wildlings be temporarily consolidated into a few key villages, so help could be centralized. A vote was conducted, and every person agreed to host their neighbors for the time being. Many Wildlings gave up their own homes to the volunteers for the week they planned to stay. Lightlark chefs began teaching Wildlings how to safely prepare meat.

"I'd like to do this for the Starling newland too," Isla told Oro. "If Enya wouldn't mind." She had portaled there a few times, to check on them, in secret. They could use this just as much as the Wildlings.

Isla stayed up until the early morning speaking to her subjects, learning their names, their habits, their lives. She fell asleep on a bench in the middle of the modest village square to the lullaby of laughing, building, and sizzling cooking. Oro must have flown her to bed, because she woke up in her old room a few hours later and startled.

She gasped, tensed. She was back in this prison, this glass cage—

"Breathe, Isla."

Oro was leaning against her doorframe, nearly filling it with his height. His golden hair was slightly damp from rain, like he had only just walked back inside. Something about the sight of him made her feel like she couldn't breathe properly.

It felt criminal for someone to actually look good with limited sleep. Had he even slept at all?

She assumed he had just been at the village. "How are they?" she asked, her voice a little strained.

"Good. Enya has a new system for storing water and food and tracking who can wield."

"Of course she does," Isla said, not unkindly. She was in awe of the Sunling's organization.

It was hot and humid in the Wildling newland, and Oro had placed her in bed wearing her clothing from the day before. She began to peel off layers, without really thinking, until she looked up, and found him watching her, eyes slightly wide.

Isla held his gaze as she slowly removed her long-sleeved shirt, leaving her in just the thin sleeveless fabric she wore beneath. It clung to her skin, outlining her every curve.

She could have sworn she felt the room get even warmer, as he lost hold of his Sunling abilities. His control slipped, for just a moment.

Oro stared at her, and she watched him swallow—

He was the one to look away. "Are you ready for training?" he asked the wall.

She sighed. Training was the last thing on her mind at that moment. She wanted him in her bed; it would be so easy to just let the world disappear for an hour—

"Isla?"

Her name on his lips made her burn even more, but she said, "Yes."

"Good," he said. "Today, we're growing something."

POISON

Oro made an orange rose sprout from his palm. He reached over and put it in Isla's hair. "Your turn."

Isla sat and stared at her own hand for several minutes, without any results.

They were sitting at the edge of a stream. The sound of water rushing over rocks was a balm rubbing against some quiet corner of her mind. The stream was framed by hill faces on either side, some parts jutting out more than others, creating a curved, somewhat narrow river, making it impossible to see exactly where it led. Thin waterfalls fell off some of the cliffs, sheer and frayed like curtains of hair.

Isla had always wondered what it might feel like to swim here but had always feared Terra and Poppy seeing her wet clothing or hair and not being able to explain it. Visiting the stream at night might have been an option—her guardians at least gave her privacy when she was supposed to be sleeping—but then she would have been at the mercy of a forest draped in darkness that she had learned the hard way had no mercy at all.

The woods had not hurt her when she walked through it this time. No, the nature had leaned down toward her, as if the trees had wished to whisper their secrets into her ears.

"Close your eyes," Oro said. "Let your mind go still. Find nature in the world around you. Form a connection to it. Siphon that energy exactly where you want it. Think of the rose, blooming in your hand."

She followed his directions, but her heart was beating too fast. Her lids fell closed far too easily. She wasn't sleeping more than a handful of hours a night, and she was starting to feel it.

"Breathe, Isla," Oro said.

She breathed and started the process again, focusing her thoughts. When her eyes opened, she found the smallest of flowers blooming in her palm.

Before she could smile, the rose shriveled up and died, as if poisoned.

She was the poison. For she was born not just with the power to give life . . . but also to take it away. "I cannot be Wildling without Nightshade," she said, her voice brittle. "I will always be death. I will always be darkness."

"You decide what you are, Isla," Oro said. "No one else."

It might have been a comforting thought, if Isla didn't immediately think that she would only have herself to blame for her own mistakes, should she make them.

No one else.

Tears streamed down her cheeks, shocking her.

Oro was instantly inches away. "What is it?" he asked, fire already flaming in his palms, as if he was ready to reduce anything that made her upset to ash.

What was wrong? Why was she crying? All she knew was that now that it had started, she couldn't stop. A sob scraped the back of her throat.

Oro always demanded the truth. She gave it to him.

"I . . . I don't want to rule. I don't want my life tied to thousands of others. I don't want to have all this responsibility." She shook her head. "And I know that makes me selfish and awful, and I have no right to be so upset, but I am. I want a life, Oro. Worse than all that is I don't deserve any of this power. I am no one."

"You are not no one," he said steadily. "You are Isla Crown, and you are the most powerful person in all the realms."

She choked out a laugh that sounded more like a sob. "I am *a poison*," she said. "I have almost no control of these powers. They are wasted on me." She shook her head. "Take them. *You* take them, Oro. I'm serious. Use them. Steal them, with the bond. You open the vault."

Oro frowned. His anger seemed to burn through his previous hesitance at giving compliments, because he said, "Love, you seem to be under some delusion that you are anything less than extraordinary. Who did that to you? Your guardians? Did they make you feel like nothing you did would ever be good enough? Or was it him?" *Grim*. The woods heated with his anger. "Tell me, Isla. Did someone else break the curses? Am I mistaken?"

She clenched her teeth. Tears swept down her jaw, getting lost in her hair.

"Damn the vault," he said. "Damn the powers. You had nothing, and you broke the curses. *You* are the key. You see that, don't you? We were broken before you came. With you, we were saved. You are not a poison, Isla," he said, his voice filled with intensity. "You were the cure."

Isla shook her head. "I shouldn't have won," she said. "It should have been someone else."

Oro cursed. He knelt before her and gently took her face in his hands. "Is this what's been worrying you? Is this why you haven't been sleeping?" He had noticed, then. Ever since she'd had the second memory, she had tried her best to hold off on deep sleep. She rested only a handful of hours a night, not long enough for her to slip into another memory. So far, it had worked.

She didn't respond, and he studied her expression. Sighed. "I wish you could see yourself the way I do. You would never doubt yourself again."

Isla closed her eyes.

What if she tried to believe him? What if she put the negative thoughts to rest once and for all?

He was right. She had survived the Centennial. She had *won*. She had defended herself against the rebels. This power was alive, somewhere inside her, and she was going to claim it fully. She wasn't going to let anyone—or *anything*—use her like a puppet again. She had saved everyone else. Now, she just needed to save herself.

"Isla," Oro said.

He was looking down at the hands in her lap.

In them sat a blooming rose. Minutes passed, and it did not die.

For the first time, Isla sneaked out of the Wildling palace through the front door.

She had woken up early. It had been like almost every other morning in her life before the Centennial. Taking a bath. Tying her hair back into a braid. Strapping herself into her light-brown fighting clothes, fabric wrapped around and around her arms. She slipped on simple shoes.

Before she could lose her nerve, she stepped into the forest. Oro was right. She was more capable than she gave herself credit for.

She refused to be the person who believed in herself the least. She refused to keep being her own worst enemy, letting her own mind get in her way. It stopped now.

The weak girl who had been raised here, who had feared the forest, was gone. It was time to bury her for good.

These woods had never felt like home. She had trained around these same trees for years, her own blood had been shed here, but never had she felt any sort of attachment to it.

Until now.

Isla leaned down and took off her shoes. She took a step forward. The moment her bare foot hit the ground, a shock went right through it, up her leg, her spine, into the crown of her head and up toward the sky.

Oro had spoken about forming a link with her power source. A trust. A connection clicked into place. The woods knew her.

There was no wind, yet the trees rustled in greeting. She took another step, and the dirt trembled around her toes, as if power surrounded her. All thoughts drained from her mind.

She placed a hand against the nearest tree, and moss flowed from her fingers, rippling down to the grassy forest floor. The grass grew to a wild height that reached a branch that sprouted bright-purple wisteria. The flowers spiraled down the branch in bunches like bracelets, until the end, where an acorn grew, drooping like an earring. It became so large that it fell, right into Isla's palm.

This was what it meant to be Wildling.

She took off running. The world stepped to the side to let her through. Trees moved their branches, vines on the ground curled back toward their roots, animals waited for her to pass. A group of birds followed her path, their chirps sounding like encouragement. Flowers sprouted as soon as her feet left the soil, filling her footprints. A blanket of marigolds and roses bloomed in her wake.

She jumped into the air, hand outstretched, and a vine soared to meet it. She swung, careening through the forest, landing in a tree. She didn't stop, she kept running, and a bridge of branches formed before her, spanning across the top of the woods in a pathway.

It was a flow, a heightened state, a different awareness. She tasted the forest on the tip of her tongue, moss and dew and pine. A warmth traveled through her bones, as if parts of her that had been dormant were now awakening, a flower in her chest finally blooming under the sun. The woods uncurled at her proximity.

The forest was alive—she could see it now as she ran across its back. It was on her side. It would never hurt her again.

It was part of her.

She ran and ran, climbing higher. Nature raced to meet her every need, without her even having to think it. Her focus was complete, she had given all of herself to the woods. In that moment, they were one entity—she could feel it around her, a heartbeat, an ever-changing and flowing force.

It felt like nothing could break that concentration, until she looked down and saw Grim standing far below, watching her.

Isla gasped. Her focus fell, and her pathway along with it. She crashed through the treetops. A branch hit her back, stealing her breath. Her vision swam with shadows. Her head knocked against another branch, and the pain was blinding. She reached for anything to hold on to, but her fingers were sweaty, and she couldn't get purchase.

The forest would save her, wouldn't it?

Her connection had given out. She was a stranger, yet again.

No. Her powers would lash out. Surely, they would save her. Her Starling abilities. Wildling. Even Nightshade.

They wouldn't let her die—

She gasped, watching the ground rush up to meet her.

Just before she hit the forest floor, two strong arms caught her.

Avel was panting over her. Her pale face was flushed red and sweat dripped down her cropped hair. "You fall fast, Ruler," she said, out of breath.

Isla's eyes were wide. "You were there?" She had thought she had sneaked out of her quarters successfully.

She was such a fool. One drop, and her people would have been dead. How could she be so careless?

She had felt so in control. So powerful.

Control was fickle, she realized.

"We're always here," she said, and Ciel came crashing through the trees to land next to them. His face was flushed too. In that moment, they looked identical.

"Thank you," she said, though those words would never be enough.

Avel and Ciel took her back to the Wildling palace, and Isla watched the forest floor for any sign of Grim.

LYNX

By the time the volunteers left, the Wildlings had their homes fixed, a steady food supply, new skills, and resources. Isla decided to stay behind for a couple of days, to spend time with her people. She sent Ciel and Avel back to Lightlark, to help in Azul's search for the rebels. Oro had insisted on staying, not wanting to leave her alone, but she knew he had spent too much time on her already. She told him to trust her, and he did. On the Wildling newland, she felt safe.

She got to know each of the Wildlings in the village and ventured to other settlements close by. Wren took Isla into the forest and taught her a few Wildling wielding techniques, including stances, arm movements, and uses of ability. They spoke for hours.

At the end of one of these lessons, she caught Wren studying her, and said, "What is it?"

Wren shook her head. "It's just—we always wondered why you never came to see us," she said. "I know why now, but before . . . we were confused. Your mother is the only other ruler I've ever known, and she was always there. Playing in the village. Talking to us. She knew everyone. Everyone loved her."

Her mother.

"What—what was she like?" Isla asked, her voice small. She felt like a child again, clinging to any mention of her mother. Terra and Poppy almost never spoke about her.

Wren smiled. "She was extraordinary," she said. "Fearless. Reckless, at times." Her smile faded. "We grieved her immensely and hoped to

know you too. But . . ." She shrugged. "I suppose we did know something must be going on," she said. "We were curious . . . when you didn't take a bonded."

Isla's brows came together. "Take a what?"

"A bonded," Wren said. She lifted her arm, and a massive hawk with a stripe of orange on its back came soaring down from the treetops, landing on her sleeve. The bird blinked at her with its sharp eyes.

"Oh, an animal companion," Isla said.

"A *bonded*," Wren repeated. Isla didn't know why it seemed to be important to Wren, but if taking one showed that Isla was a Wildling, even though she hadn't had their curse or powers up until recently—

"I'll take one," Isla said. "If it's not too late." It might be a pain to transport the creature with her everywhere, and she didn't know how Oro would feel about an animal residing in the Mainland castle, but she would figure that out later. Gaining her people's trust was more important.

Wren seemed surprised. "You would do the ceremony?"

Isla didn't know anything about a ceremony, but she said, "Of course."

Wren smiled. "Then I will announce it," she said. She looked around, felt a leaf between two fingers, and studied the treetops. "Tonight is a good night . . . yes, tonight will work."

Tonight.

Okay. Isla could do tonight. "So . . ." she said. "I can pick anything? An insect"—that would be easier to carry around—"a bird"—could be useful to transport messages—"a . . . butterfly?"

Wren shook her head sharply. "A bonded reflects the disposition of a person. For *rulers*, it represents their power and strength."

So, Isla would be expected to bond with a larger animal. Great. That would make things more difficult, but she couldn't very well back out now.

"And *you* don't pick your bonded," Wren continued. "It's the other way around." Her eyes were fierce. "The bonded chooses you."

. . .

Isla was wading in water up to her knees. The ceremony, it turned out, was far more complicated than she had anticipated. This was a sacred part of the newland, Wren told her, the oldest part, born of seeds and creatures taken straight from Lightlark. It was a swamp, with grass that grew taller than her, water lilies as large as rugs, mud that seeped between her bare toes, and slick creatures that moved below the dark water, smoothing around her ankles.

She was at the very front, a leader who had no idea where she was going. She should have asked more questions, she thought bitterly, though they would have revealed how little she knew about her people and their customs.

She risked a quick look over her shoulder and saw the Wildlings silently wading behind her, faces illuminated by the fireflies they held in their palms. Their bonded were with them, swimming alongside, flying above, or watching from the thin strips of bare land at their sides.

One of them caught her eye, and she whipped back around. Her head was beginning to itch. She scratched just below the crown of flowers her people had made her for the occasion—purple larkspur, in honor of her ancestor, Lark Crown, one of the three original creators of Lightlark. She had spent hours sitting still as her people made bracelets down her arms from the rare varieties of larkspur, its color so concentrated, it stained parts of her skin purple, an honor reserved for a ruler. It was a valiant color. The color of a leader and warrior.

Isla didn't feel like either as she carefully stepped across the muddy ground, wincing anytime her foot sank too deep or connected with something solid. She was so focused on stepping around a strange clump of rocks that it took her a while to notice the wading behind her had all but quieted.

She turned to see the Wildlings were retreating, the light of their fireflies getting dimmer and dimmer.

Only Wren approached. "This is where we leave you," she said. Perhaps it was Isla's eyes widening, but Wren seemed to sense she needed more instruction. Her head dipped low. Her tone was sharp. "You don't come back until the morning. You don't come back without a bonded." Isla swallowed. What if none of the creatures wanted her? Wren handed her a bow and a single arrow.

"What is this for?"

"It's tradition, for a ruler's hunt for their bonded. For the rest of us, we simply must catch our animals, to show our worthiness. Rulers must put an arrow through theirs." Wren's eyes darted around nervously, and that's when Isla's stomach began to sink in earnest. The Wildling looked afraid.

Of what?

"I thought—I thought you said the creature chooses me."

"It does," Wren explained. "The creatures out here . . . if you're able to wound one . . . it's because it *allows* you to."

Isla took the bow and single arrow with trembling fingers. As soon as they were out of her hands, Wren gave a sharp nod, then began to hurry away, toward the others.

She watched them go, her confidence shrinking along with their silhouettes, until she couldn't see them anymore.

With a shaking breath, she turned around to face the heart of the swamp.

The swamp turned back to forest, though none of it was familiar.

She climbed out of the water and stilled—the trees lining the marsh . . . they were in the shape of people. Their arms made up the main branches, green sprouted from the crowns of their heads, their bodies formed the trunks, and their legs, the exposed roots that went straight into the dark water. They were frozen in strange movements, their faces carved into the wood. Some had mouths stretched far too wide, like they had been screaming.

Isla swallowed and kept moving. Wren had been clear. She couldn't return without a bonded. It would make her look weak, unworthy of ruling her realm.

The forest was quiet. She walked until she reached a massive tree that had tipped over on its side. Its branches were large enough to be entire pathways, rising into the air, going as far as she could see. They were covered in a thin layer of moss. She jumped, gripping the soft edge with her fingers, then pulled the rest of her body onto the lowest one. With a quick assessment of her surroundings, she followed the path, into the core of the tree.

It was far too silent. Isla had the uncomfortable feeling that there were eyes everywhere, watching her, yet every time she turned around, she was alone.

Alone. No one understood her, not really. Oro tried, he really did, but there were parts of her she would never let him see.

She wondered if a bonded animal would be able to sense every aspect of her—the good and the bad. The potential. The idea of someone or something seeing her for what she could be, instead of what she was . . .

Or maybe the creatures of the forest had already assessed her, and rejected her, just like the vault. It wasn't enough for *her* to feel the connection. According to Wren, the animal decided.

For now, it seemed, they had decided against her.

A rustle, and she turned to find herself facing a wolf, covered in moss and greenery instead of fur. Its tail was made of long reeds. Isla raised her arrow. Hope built in her chest. The wolf wasn't large, but at least it was something.

Before she could let her arrow loose, the wolf was gone.

Her fingers curled painfully around the bow. Slow, she had been too slow. Is that why it had run away?

What if she didn't see another creature?

Moments later, she realized that wouldn't be an issue. A spider with legs as tall as trees walked by, its body casting a thick shadow around

her. Isla didn't even raise her weapon. The spider was massive, but she felt no connection to the creature whatsoever.

She just needed to keep going, she told herself. There was a bonded for her here. She just needed to find it.

Her bare feet were soundless against the moss of the branch. Tiny flowers bloomed with her every step, painting the greenery. The occasional bird swooped down to study her, before flying away. She walked down the path as it curved into a forest floor shaded by a massive canopy of treetops. A giant rib cage greeted her, with flowers growing out of its bones—the remains of a creature so large, she couldn't even imagine what it had looked like alive.

Just then, a stag with branches for horns stepped into her path. It stared at her, tilting its head in wonder.

It was beautiful. Something in her chest thrummed to life as if welcoming the connection. She slowly raised her bow, clicked her arrow into place—

The stag stepped toward her, then froze. Its eyes focused on a place behind her. It shuffled back in fear.

What was—

A deafening roar shook the trees at her sides. Birds flew away, in the opposite direction. Hot breath heated her body as she was covered in spit.

Slowly, arrow still raised, Isla turned around and looked up. And up. And up.

A giant bear stood on its two feet, with a crown of horns that could skewer her in a moment.

Was this her creature? It would certainly mark her as a strong ruler. Isla released the arrow, trying her chance, but the bear knocked it away with a paw, breaking the wood in two.

Her only arrow, gone.

Isla wasn't thinking about the fact that she wouldn't be able to find a bonded now. Panic had taken over. She dropped the bow. The bear

roared again, getting close to blowing out her hearing, and Isla realized why Wren had seemed so intent on leaving the swamp.

Venturing to this area of the newland was a risk. Her people were endangering their own lives by letting her complete the ceremony.

This was the first step in them trusting her, she realized. A leap of faith. They believed she was strong enough to survive it.

So, she would.

The bear was too large, there was no hope in outrunning it. Just as it reached back its clawed hand to rip her to ribbons, she darted between its feet and ran up into the treetops. The bear couldn't climb; it was too heavy, it would break the branches. That was what she told herself as she climbed as fast as ever, purple rings of flowers down her arms seeming to glow in the dark.

She scurried up, higher and higher, and risked a look behind—

Only to see the bear's horns inches away, as it climbed after her.

Nature. She was in nature. Her heart was beating too wildly to form a connection to the woods the way she had before. She gritted her teeth, trying to focus. Her arm shot out, and she managed to make a few smaller branches fall in the bear's path, but it did nothing to slow it down.

She needed to break the branches below the bear. That way, it would fall through the treetops. She threw her powers out, but panic had clouded her mind, weakening her hold on her abilities. The branches creaked but did not crack.

The bear growled, and Isla began climbing once more. Heart echoing through her ears, she squinted through the night and saw that the branches became much thinner farther up the tree. She threw out her power, and one broke. It would have to be one of those, then.

Isla reached for the next branch—and roared as the bear's horns flayed the back of her calf open.

Her scream echoed through the woods, and she continued to climb, dragging herself up, one of her legs now useless, fighting her way to the top. If she could just make it a little higher. A little—

A crack. The first crack beneath the bear's weight as they traveled up to the thinner branches. It didn't seem to notice as its horns broke through the foliage, as it bared its teeth, chomping at the air.

Her leg was on fire; she couldn't think around the pain. She felt her grip on her powers almost completely slipping. She didn't have the strength left to break several branches. It would have to be one strategic cut. She stopped climbing and watched the bear get closer. Closer. She took a breath. In. Out. Attempted to focus as much as she could. Narrowed all her energy to one spot, one particularly thin branch, right in the bear's path. It kept going. It was just feet away. Then inches. She outstretched her hand. Nothing.

Come on.

Nothing.

She felt its breath on her face, saw its tongue in its mouth as it parted its teeth and roared—

Snap.

Her power split the branch in half, and the bear immediately fell out of view. Cracks sang through the woods as the bear broke everything in its path, and then there was a final thunderous echo as it landed.

Silence.

Isla panted. Too close. She risked a look down at her leg and tensed. The skin was split and she could see muscle. Blood was smeared across the tree. Other creatures would find her—

Just as she had the thought, two large eyes glowed through the night, in the tree across the way. They were looking at her. She scrambled back on her branch, arm raised, willing any of her power to rise.

The creature stepped out of the shadows, and Isla gasped.

It was a massive black leopard. Standing, she wouldn't even reach the top of its leg. It had bright-green eyes and teeth the size of her skull.

She looked down at her calf, then at the creature. It had smelled the blood. She was injured, an easy target.

It stalked toward her, head bent low, assessing. It looked ready to lean back on its haunches and strike.

She tried her best to focus on the forest, to form a connection, to beg it to protect her, but the pain in her leg had become a complete distraction.

The leopard should have been too heavy for the branches, but it leaped gracefully until it was right in front of her.

Isla's entire body shook as it leaned down far too close—and sniffed her.

She swallowed, hoping for the life of her that she smelled unappetizing. It opened its mouth, revealing its monstrous fangs. Then, it did something unexpected.

The leopard begrudgingly leaned its head down, as if bowing before her.

Isla blinked. Had it . . . had it accepted her?

She didn't have her arrow . . . the bear had split it into two. She couldn't—

The leopard made what seemed like an annoyed sound as it waited. What did it want? It leaned down lower, and no . . . it couldn't . . .

Did it want her to get on its back?

She was bleeding too much; she needed the wound closed soon. She fought to stand, gritting her teeth against the pain, and limped over to the leopard's side. She tried to climb up its fur, but she kept slipping, her blood getting everywhere. Eventually the leopard seemed to get tired of waiting, because it gripped the back of her shirt with its frightening teeth and flung her over. She landed painfully on its spine and fought for purchase, gripping its dark hair in her fists.

The leopard didn't give her even a second to get used to it. Before she could test her position, it leaped off the branch.

Her stomach was in her throat, her eyes burned against the air, she was floating off its back—then roughly landing again, her leg roaring in pain.

With a few jumps that made her want to retch, the leopard finally landed on the forest floor. It stalked around, head bent low, as if looking for something. Finally, it paused and tipped over to the side. Isla slipped off its back in the most undignified way imaginable.

Exasperated, the leopard motioned with its head toward something on the ground. Her arrow. Half of it, at least.

It was telling her to complete the ceremony. Somehow, it knew that to claim it, she had to shoot it.

The bow would be useless now. She leaned down, grabbed the broken arrow, and approached the creature.

It watched her warily.

"This is . . . this is going to hurt . . ." she said.

The leopard regarded her in a way that hinted at disdain. Great. Her own bonded didn't seem to like her.

Then why choose her? Why let her do what she had to do next?

Isla winced before reaching her arm back and putting all of her remaining strength into stabbing the leopard in the leg with the arrow.

It didn't even move or make a sound. It simply reached down, grabbed Isla by the back of the shirt again, and threw her behind its head.

"Hey!" she said, wincing. "Stop doing that! It—"

Before she finished her sentence, the leopard took off. She yelped and held on tightly, ducking her head down, lest a branch behead her. The leopard raced like lightning, jumping over roots, traversing around trees. The world moved so quickly around her, she buried her face in its surprisingly soft fur, until the leopard finally slowed.

It had brought her to the center of the village. She sat up as the leopard walked down the streets and watched as her people left their homes, staring at her in clear wonder.

It stopped in front of Wren, whose eyes were wide. Her voice was thick with emotion. "I wondered . . ." she said. "I—I didn't dare hope."

Isla slid off the leopard's back and nearly collapsed on the road, her leg covered in fur that had stuck to the blood. She looked from the animal to Wren. "Wondered what?"

"Isla," Wren said. "Lynx was your mother's."

REFLECTION

Her mother. This leopard . . . was once bonded to her. Isla was losing a lot of blood, but she turned and looked the creature right in the eyes. For a moment, the disdain faded, and she saw only unfiltered sadness.

The cat grieved her mother. That was why it had chosen her.

"We need to get you healed," Wren said. Other Wildlings rushed forward. There were calls for the healing elixir. "He'll follow, don't worry."

Wren was right. Lynx remained by her side. He was so large he couldn't fit through the doors of the palace, so she used her starstick to portal him into her room, which he didn't like one bit. He made a disgruntled noise before he went to the corner, curled, and sat down, making the ground tremble and taking up a large portion of her space. Wren pulled the arrow out of his leg, then put healing elixir on it. Everyone left her to rest.

Through the darkness, Isla saw his bright-green eyes gleaming. Then, as they closed, the world went dark again.

The next morning, Isla portaled to Oro and said, "I need to show you something." She took him back to the newland with her.

He now stood in her Wildling room, staring at the creature that was staring back, many feet above his head, baring its massive teeth.

"You have . . ." Oro was saying.

"An animal companion," she said. "A bonded." She motioned toward the great leopard. "His name is Lynx, apparently."

"Right." He reached out a hand, not seeming too concerned that the leopard could tear it off, and Isla watched as the leopard sniffed him. Tilted his head. Then leaned down, allowing himself to be petted between the eyes.

Isla was outraged. "He likes you more than he likes me!" she said. The leopard's eyes slid to hers, unimpressed, before looking at Oro again.

Oro smiled, and the sight was so beautiful, her hurt all but shriveled up. "What an impressive creature," he said. "I've never seen anything like him."

She frowned. "Not on Lightlark?"

He shook his head. "We have lions and tigers on Sun Isle, but none remotely this size."

That seemed to please Lynx. He made an approving sound, and Isla shot him a glare. "I told you this morning how impressive you were, and you turned your back to me," she said.

Lynx didn't even bother looking at her.

She sighed. "He was my mother's bonded, according to Wren."

"Ah," Oro said. He pressed his hand against Lynx's lowered head. "You must miss her," he said to the cat, and he made a thrumming noise.

Isla's throat worked. She wished the cat could speak, so she could ask him all about her mother. Now, though, she had to think of the practical. "I don't know what to do," she admitted. "There's nothing like these woods on Lightlark. I don't want to trap him in a castle . . . if he even fits in the hallways."

Lynx gave her a scathing look.

Fine. If he could understand her, let him decide. She stood in front of the leopard and said, "I can take you back with me, to the castle. Or I can leave you in this forest and come back to visit soon. I can start making a place for you on the island."

Lynx stared at her for half a second, before turning toward the window. His choice was clear.

A pang of disappointment shot through her chest, though she understood it was the right choice. She didn't know why she was so surprised. Lynx had clearly chosen her out of obligation, not fondness.

Oro rubbed his hand down Lynx's lowered head again before turning back to Isla. She watched him study the circles under her eyes. She had only slept a handful of hours last night. He sighed and said, "There's something you should know."

Upon their return to Lightlark, Azul and her Skyling guards were waiting.

"The rebels were spotted," he said.

Isla's chest tightened, remembering the pain of that night, being swept away under the water, so helpless—

Never again. She could use her Wildling power now. She might not be invincible, but at least she had a fighting chance.

She also wasn't alone. Ciel and Avel moved to her sides immediately.

"Where exactly?" Oro demanded.

"Their whispers were heard by our spies, coming from Star Isle. We tracked them down from the sky, but they just . . . vanished. Underground. We found more tunnels, but they all had dead ends."

Ella spoke from her place at the back of the throne room. "It's true," her attendant said. "I saw them for a moment. There are Starlings among them, I'm almost certain."

"Who?" Oro demanded. Isla remembered his threat. He would string any of them up across the Bay of Teeth. "Give me names."

Ella did not hesitate. "I didn't recognize anyone specifically. They wore masks. They must have Starlings among them, though, because no one else knows about the tunnels in the crypts."

Oro frowned. "Crypts?"

"They were built during the curses. To house the many dead. And hide us from the rest of the island." Anger curled in Isla's stomach as she remembered hearing about the abuse of the Starlings. "We kept them a secret, because of that. They're the only reason some of us are still

alive . . . and they're the only way to get past the creatures that took over the east side of Star Isle."

"What do you mean, creatures?" Isla asked.

"Monsters. No one goes there anymore, except through the tunnels to gather supplies. Anyone who goes too far . . . never returns."

Guilt swirled in Isla's stomach. She had been so focused on her powers and the Wildlings, she had abandoned the Starlings beyond asking Oro to send guards and provisions. She should have gone to Star Isle sooner. She should have made sure they were okay.

She wouldn't waste another moment. "Ella. Will you send word to Maren? I'm going to Star Isle."

"I'm going with you," Oro said.

She turned to face him and said in a low voice, "I need to go alone."

He frowned.

"Not alone," she clarified. "Ciel and Avel will be there." Her Skyling warriors inched closer.

Isla imagined Oro would demand to speak to every Starling and interrogate them over any information about the rebels. That wasn't what they needed. That wasn't the way Isla wanted to first address her new people.

Oro nodded, but he didn't look happy in the slightest. He turned to Azul. "Did your spies hear anything else about the rebels? Has anyone else been attacked? Threatened?"

Azul shook his head. "No one else."

That couldn't be true. Why only target her?

If what Ella said was correct, that there must be Starlings among the rebels . . . that didn't make sense. They had hurt her. They could have killed her, which would have led to the deaths of all Wildlings *and* Starlings.

Something wasn't adding up.

Isla caught up with Ella before she left the Mainland castle. She felt awkward asking her these questions, but she had to know. "Are the

Starlings . . . are they disappointed that I'm their ruler now? Are they angry that I still haven't visited?"

"No. They know you were attacked and that you've been busy since."

Isla frowned. "They must resent me, though. They must—"

Ella laughed. Isla didn't think she had ever seen the Starling laugh before.

"Isla," she said softly. "All of us grew up accepting that our lives would be short and likely miserable. Few of us had any dreams. Or goals. Or hope. *You* gave us a chance to live. To most of us, you are a god. A savior."

As she walked back to her room to change into her training clothes, Isla repeated the words she had told herself in the Wildling newland woods. She was strong. She was the ruler of Wildling.

And the ruler of Starling.

Isla closed her wardrobe after getting a dress and froze.

In the mirror, there was Grim, standing in a full suit of armor. He held his helmet loosely in his hand. Ready for war.

She spun around and shot her arm out. A branch from the tree of her room snapped off, then sharpened into a blade. It stabbed right through the room.

But it was empty.

CINDER

Star Isle was in ruins. Its castle looked long abandoned. Towers lay in the sparkling silver dirt. Windows had been blown open. The pathways were covered in rocks and trash. Ciel and Avel flew above, circling so high up she had to squint to see them. Ella was at her side.

Maren, the Starling representative from the dinner, met them at the entrance of the crumbling castle. There was a little girl with her, with the same shining dark hair, wide eyes, and light-brown skin. "My cousin," she said curtly. The cousin stared at Isla and opened her mouth to say something a few times, but Maren gave her a look, and the little girl went quiet. "They're all in the throne room."

"Is everyone all right?" Isla asked. The Sunling guards at the bridge hadn't seen the rebels. There were Skylings in the rebel group—they must have flown in from another isle. Their motivations were a mystery. Why only target her? "Did the rebels . . ."

"We're safe. Thankfully, it seemed they were just recruiting. Or, perhaps, looking for something."

She frowned. "Why do you think that?"

Maren raised a shoulder. "Why else venture through the crypts? They're dangerous. All Starlings know that. No one goes inside them unless they're desperate."

When she walked into the castle, Isla's stomach plummeted.

Much of the room was empty, and everyone was breathtakingly young. Children, mostly. Only a few dozen looked to be around her age.

They watched as she walked through the crowd, to the front of the throne room. There were no seats, and because they were all standing, so did she.

"I don't know what I'm doing" was the first thing that came out of her mouth, and she almost instantly regretted it.

They just stared at her. There was just silence, until a voice said, "No one here does," quite cheerfully.

"Cinder!" Maren said, shooting her cousin a look. "Forgive my cousin, Ruler." The girl couldn't be more than eight years old, and she didn't stop beaming, even when Maren elbowed her side. Some people around her nodded.

"It's okay," Isla said, smiling at Cinder. She felt a little better . . . and worse. It might have been a relief to get here and see that someone had everything taken care of. "How many Starlings are left on Star Isle?"

"There are a hundred or so more," a man closer to her age said. He looked to be one of the oldest among them, with a strong jaw, messy silver hair, and white skin. "Give or take."

She frowned. "Did they know about the meeting?"

The man smiled without humor. "They knew." There was something in between his teeth that he was chewing, long and glimmering.

"Okay." Isla wove her fingers together and drew in a breath, straightening her spine. She wouldn't let opposition deter her; it was to be expected. First, then, the simple questions. "Where do you all live?" She waved a hand around the throne room. "Here? In the castle?"

There was a bubble of laughter somewhere in the crowd.

"*Some* of us do," Maren said, looking pointedly at a group of Starlings Isla could now tell apart from the others. Their clothes were nicer. They wore fine strings of constellation-like diamonds around their necks and wrists.

The nobles. Of course. She recognized some of them from the Centennial. There were eight of them in the group, all with different features, hair textures, and skin tones. Unrelated, it seemed. The last of their lines?

She turned back to the group. "And the rest?"

The man with the reed between his teeth lifted a shoulder. "We can show you."

Yes. That would be better. She still had so many questions. How did they source food? Did most of them know how to wield power?

Celeste—*Aurora*—had demonstrated her realm's capability for making weapons during the Centennial. Did they have stores of them?

Before she ended the meeting, there was something she needed to say.

"Your ruler was my friend, I thought. I took her power to save this realm." She lifted her palms. "I didn't want to be your ruler. But I will be what you need me to be," she said, surprising herself with her words. "Right now, things are difficult. Starlings died in the attack of the dreks. We are preparing for the possibility that it was one of potential future Nightshade attacks. Rebels were spotted just yesterday." She looked around. "I am here for you now, and together we will navigate this new chapter. Your ruler's death will not be a waste. Tell me what you need."

There were whispers. No one spoke up, though, not for a minute.

Then, Maren said, "What we need most is for you to stay alive. You gave us a chance at a long life. We intend on using it."

Isla asked Ella to stay behind and write a list of any immediate grievances and necessities. She figured the Starlings would be more comfortable telling someone familiar what they needed.

Maren and the man chewing the reed between his teeth—Leo—led her to where they lived. They were bickering in front of Isla in a familiar way.

Maren's cousin fell back to walk by Isla's side. She could feel Cinder's eyes on her, and after a few minutes of clear staring, Isla finally turned to look.

"Yes?" she coaxed gently.

"What's the king like?"

Isla blinked, startled. It wasn't the question she'd been expecting. No one on the island knew that they were . . . she didn't really know what they were.

Of course, the little girl didn't know that. As a ruler, Isla would obviously have been in contact with him. She was just curious.

"Brooding," she replied, giving Cinder a wink. Maren must have heard, because she snorted in front of her, unexpectedly. Within a moment, she was back to her rigid posture.

The little girl's eyebrows came together. "What's brooding?" she asked. Before Isla could respond, she yelled to her cousin, "Maren, what's brooding?"

Her cousin ignored her and started fighting with Leo again. "He's just . . . serious," Isla explained. There were a thousand other things he was that she wouldn't tell the little Starling girl. "Haven't you seen him?"

She shook her head so hard, her short, wavy hair hit the sides of her face. "No. Maren doesn't let me go on the Mainland and keeps me inside when he visits. What's the Mainland like?"

Isla frowned. "What? Why—"

Maren turned around and said, "That's enough, Cinder. Stop bothering our ruler," before taking her wrist and pulling her ahead.

They led her to a row of abandoned buildings composed of towering silver columns, broken stairs, and missing cobblestones.

Isla watched as Starlings darted into different structures, walking expertly over the smashed steps.

Maren, Leo, and Cinder turned into one of the buildings, and Isla followed, careful of her footing. Silver vines and leaves curled through every gap in the place. The ceiling was high and vaulted. Centuries before, it must have been a royal assembly hall. Now, it housed dozens of makeshift houses. Some were built of wood and stone. Most were a mixture of different fabrics and hides, pulled taut.

Isla stopped in her tracks. "This is where you live?" She couldn't keep the shock out of her tone.

Cinder studied her face a moment, then said, "What's wrong with it?"

"Go find Stella," Maren said, motioning an unwilling Cinder away.

"But I don't *want*—"

"*Go*," Maren said. Cinder pitched her shoulders back and walked away in slow, dramatic despair.

Maren turned to Isla. There was a sharp look in her eyes, as if she might scold her, if she wasn't her ruler. "Two years ago, a fire burned down where we used to live." She looked quickly over to where Cinder had wandered off to, still slowly making her way to wherever she needed to go. "This is where we went."

"This is where *some* of us went," Leo clarified. "Others went their own way." Someone called his name, and he nodded at Isla before jogging over to the other side of the structure.

Isla shook her head. "I don't understand. Star Isle is massive, and there aren't many of you left. Why didn't you simply go to a different set of houses? Or live in the castle?"

"The castle belongs to the nobles," Maren said. Isla was about to object to that when she added, "And the specters. They're too troublesome to live among . . . dangerous too." Isla remembered the specter that had entered her body, and had wanted to stay in there forever, and immediately understood. "Most of the residences are on the far side of the isle, and we don't go there anymore."

"Why?"

"Creatures took over, centuries ago. Anyone who goes east of the forest never returns."

The creatures Ella had mentioned.

Anger surged in Isla's chest. Aurora had visited the island every hundred years for the Centennial. She had known about all this and had done nothing. Of course she hadn't. She'd clearly never cared about anyone but herself.

Isla shook her head. This isle needed far more help than she had realized.

A thought prodded at her. "Why haven't you let Cinder leave Star Isle?"

Maren looked at her with what could only be described as contempt. "I told you all during the dinner. During the curses, the other isles treated Starlings as disposable. Our lifetimes are—or have been—just a blink compared to others'. We were often taken. Abused. Killed, even. Especially since many of us haven't learned to wield . . . there's not much in the way of protecting ourselves."

"Not anymore," Isla promised. "I won't let anyone harm any of you," she said, and she meant it, though she didn't know how she was going to keep that promise.

Maren smiled, but it was tight, like she didn't quite believe her.

When she returned to the castle, Oro was waiting for her. His posture was rigid, as if worry had hardened his body into stone. His eyes lit in relief when she approached. "How did it go?" he asked.

She let him into her room and told him everything. He listened and asked a few questions, but she could feel him studying her. Finally, he took her hand. Smoothed his thumb across it. "I'm worried about you," he said.

Isla frowned. She motioned toward herself. "Oro, I'm fine—"

"You're not sleeping well . . . it doesn't seem like you're eating well either . . . You seem haunted," Oro said. "What is haunting you, Isla?"

Her mouth fell closed. She wanted to tell him. She really did. But part of her thought if she said the words aloud, it would make the memories more real, and they would come at her at full force. She didn't want to remember. She just wanted them to stop.

Oro was right, though. She was being haunted.

It wasn't what was haunting her, but who.

She didn't want to think about Grim right now. The only time her thoughts of him stopped was when she was with Oro.

She took a step toward him, and she changed the subject. "I missed you, the last few days," she said, and it was the truth. Spending time with the Wildlings was important, but she had started to expect Oro's presence. He was always there for her. So patient when they practiced. Even now, he recognized the signs that she wasn't fine, when no one else did. He knew her.

Isla wanted to know him.

"I missed you too," Oro said, looking surprised the words had fallen out of his mouth. He frowned, clearly frustrated that she had shifted the conversation.

She stared at his mouth. *That mouth*. How was it possible that they both knew they loved each other, yet they hadn't so much as kissed?

Her heart began beating unsteadily. She wanted to know what it was like to touch him. She wanted to feel his heat against her bare body as they explored each other's every inch in the dark.

Before she could say or do any of the things that had raced across her mind, Oro pressed his lips against the top of her head, said, "You need to rest," and left.

She might have been more annoyed if he wasn't right. Her body felt like it weighed a million pounds.

That night, she was so exhausted, she fell into her deepest sleep in weeks.

BEFORE

Isla was a fool.

That was what her own mind told herself, anyway, repeatedly, its favorite lullaby. Terra might have judged her harshly, but Isla was her own worst critic.

She was trying to be nicer to herself lately, so she might have convinced herself she was *not* a fool if she wasn't objectively doing something astronomically foolish.

Her puddle of stars rippled before her, a slice of midnight. Her guardians were away for the day, visiting a local village. This was her chance. Before she could stop herself, she threw herself through, right into the Nightshade ruler's room.

It was just how she remembered it.

Black marble floors. High, vaulted ceilings. A bed with simple black sheets.

Only one thing was missing: the towering ruler who had pressed her against that very wall, and—

She shook the thought away and gripped the vial in her hand. She was here for a very specific, *very stupid* reason. A few days prior, the Nightshade had appeared in her room and tricked her into revealing her portaling device. Before he could take it from her, she had cried and begged him to let her keep it. It hadn't been one of her proudest moments.

Grim had called it his, and after witnessing his portaling power, she could only conclude that he must have enchanted it. Objects could be infused with power, she knew. It had a cost, though, shortened life, depending on how much ability was given.

Why had Grim made a portaling device? And how had it ended up in her room?

In the end—shocking her and likely him—he had disappeared, without taking it . . . which made her feel inexplicably guilty about having stabbed him in the chest. She didn't like to be in someone's debt, so she had brought something for him, as a peace offering.

So where was he?

Isla stood in the center of his room for half an hour, pulse racing, expecting to find a blade against her throat at any moment. Every minute that passed convinced her more how foolish this errand was. The starstick was *hers* now, but somehow she had convinced herself that him not stealing it from her was something to be thankful for.

Stupid. The more she thought about it, the more ridiculous it seemed. She was just about to form her puddle of stars and retreat to her room when she heard his voice.

It was joined by another. A man. She could barely make out their words. They were discussing some sort of strategy.

And both were getting closer. Closer.

Her starstick was lifeless in her lap. Of course it was. Of *course.* No time to try to coax it into working. She had to hide.

There was barely any furniture in the room. No desk to duck beneath. The bed didn't have enough room under it.

But there was another door. She threw herself through it just as the men entered the room.

A bathroom. All black as well, though here the black marble floor was threaded through with silver veins. A massive onyx tub sat at the center. Its spout was located on the ceiling, twenty feet above. Under normal circumstances, Isla might have marveled at it—it truly was a beautiful concept, a stream of water falling from such a height into a tub, like a miniature waterfall—but right now, it was her hiding place. She tucked herself into the basin and brandished the starstick.

It was dead in her hands. Something about this place must make it difficult to use, she thought, which she probably should have considered before portaling herself here.

"Stupid," she called herself as she willed the starstick to glow again. "Not you," she whispered. "You're brilliant." The enchantment still didn't light up. "Unless, of course, you don't work—then you're stupid too."

The starstick was still dim when the bathroom door suddenly creaked open.

Isla didn't dare take a breath. She closed her eyes tightly. Listened.

Leave, please leave . . .

The opposite of leaving. The sound of something light hitting the floor. A pause.

One step. Another.

Then, the stab of something sharp right through her chest—

Isla screamed.

Her dress was soaked through. But not with blood. She had been pierced by the cascade of water.

The stream abruptly shut off, and Isla sat up, only to come face-to-face with a ruler with a horrified expression on his face.

"Have you lost your mind?" he asked, the words sharp and filled with malice. He was shirtless.

Isla quickly looked away. She held something out toward him, palm open. "I—I came to give you something. As a thank-you—" No, she had already decided she didn't need to thank him for not taking the thing she held most dear away from her. "—I mean, a peace offering. Here."

She threw it in his general direction, and the only indication that he had caught it was the fact that no glass shattered against the smooth floor. After a few moments of silence, she dared look back at him. He was frowning down at the vial, which looked laughably small in his hand.

The elixir was something the Wildlings had been developing. The bud of a certain rare flower, when extracted correctly, produced an

elixir that healed all wounds. There were only two problems. The first was that each flower produced only a tiny amount of useful nectar. The other was that the serum did nothing to remove pain.

"It's a healing ointment. For—" She motioned toward his chest and winced. "For that." Silence. He looked like a sculpture she had seen in a Wildling garden, perfect and almost scarless except for that massive cut right next to his heart. It was clear he had a Moonling treating him, or that would have been impossible. So, why hadn't he fully treated this one yet? "For the scar," she clarified, thinking he must be confused. "Listen. I didn't mean to portal here before; it was a mistake. I didn't plan on stabbing you. It was just—an instinct?" She spoke too quickly, trying to get the words out. "I came to offer peace. We don't need to be enemies."

I don't need you as an enemy was what she didn't say. *The Centennial will be hard enough for me as it is.*

The Nightshade didn't say a word as he dropped the vial into the sink. She winced as the glass shattered.

Then he said, "Get out."

The venom that filled his voice . . . He was disgusted by her. So disgusted, he had refused her gift. No, he had *ruined* it.

This was her fault. She was a fool to have wasted it on him.

She wanted to follow his command, get out and never come back. But, as insufferable as he was, she needed him to agree to peace. She didn't want to live looking over her shoulder, waiting for the Nightshade to exact revenge. "What do you want, then?" she asked. "What can I give you?"

He paused. He was already halfway to the door, and she watched the muscles in his back tense. Without turning around, he said, "You are incapable of giving me anything of value."

His words were like a slap to the face, because they were true. She was a powerless ruler of a steadily dying realm. But he didn't know that.

"Then let's settle it with a duel," she said, the words tumbling out

of her before she could stop them. "If I win, all ill will between us is forgotten. We can begin anew at the Centennial."

That made him turn around. He was glaring at her. "Only a fool would believe they could best me in a duel." He looked her up and down, his distaste only deepening.

She glared back at him, even as her confidence wavered. He was right. Why did she suggest this? It seemed impossible to beat him, but now, she had to try. "Wildlings are warriors, just like you."

His lip curled with humor. "No, Hearteater," he spat. "Not *just like me*." He picked up his shirt from the floor and slipped it back on. "Fine. When I win, you will never return here again. I've tired of you."

Demon. An easy promise to make. She slowly climbed out of the tub, and walked with as much dignity as she could muster in a wet dress, until she was right in front of him. He roughly took her hand. His hands were freezing. Enormous.

"My swords are in my room," she said.

A moment later, she was back in the Wildling newland.

Impossible. He really did have the power of her starstick. That was how he had appeared so easily in her Wildling palace, twice now.

"How—" she said, but he was dropping her hand like her touch was poison.

"I have more important matters to attend to," he bit out.

She didn't need to be told to hurry. Isla reached for her favorite sword.

"Let's go into the forest," she said. It was still day. She estimated they had about an hour of sunlight left until the Nightshade had to be indoors again.

He walked steadily toward the glass wall, toward the woods—then walked *through* it. Another rare Nightshade ability she had heard about but that seemed impossible until she had seen it with her own eyes.

What would she do with a power like that? She would never be trapped in her room again. She wouldn't need to sneak through the

very inconvenient and nearly too-small window like she did now, on her stomach, the bottom of her still-wet dress catching and ripping on the way out.

Grim stared down at her, unimpressed, then walked into the forest like it wasn't a mess of vines and roots that could suffocate him if they wished.

With every step the Nightshade took, the shadows in the woods seemed to lengthen toward him.

If Isla had Wildling power, would the plants reach toward her the way the shadows did for him? Did he notice that they didn't?

Grim whipped around and struck.

He would have sliced her right across the middle if she hadn't practiced every day for nearly two decades for the Centennial. It was one of the few times she was let out of her quarters and permitted to enjoy the castle grounds. She had thrown herself into it, relishing the way her body moved more and more deftly at her command.

Instinct made her own sword—her favorite, a blade half the size of the one the Nightshade was using—meet his own.

A clash, another, and the Nightshade advanced so forcibly, Isla wondered if he was trying to ensure she would never bother him again, not by winning the duel but by killing her. She was forced to retreat farther into the forest. Only knowing the maze of this slice of the forest kept her from tripping over vines. This was where she and Terra trained, almost every day. The forest might not listen to her, but she knew its every detail.

Grim frowned as he followed her. "This is a duel, not a scenic stroll," he said.

Isla tried her best to stand her ground. At the force of his next hit, she dug her heels into the dirt instead of retreating. She felt the strength of his blow in her teeth.

Maybe she wasn't as good at swordplay as she thought. What was she thinking, suggesting a duel?

He'd had five hundred years and active experience in battle to perfect his fighting. Where Isla had to think about each move, his every advance seemed mindless, simple, natural. She gritted her teeth, but he was expressionless, like this wasn't taking even a scrap of his energy.

Her skill was nothing.

A sharp sting across her arm—she'd been cut. She didn't dare look down at it; she couldn't afford even half a second of distraction.

You need to win, the voice in her mind said. *Grim is too strong to be an enemy at the Centennial. Or an enemy at all, really.*

But winning seemed impossible.

No—not impossible.

She knew the forest. That was her advantage.

Isla's mouth twitched. This forest was dangerous. And Grim was about to find out how.

"You look far too confident for someone with such a lack of skill," he said.

And he looked far too smug for someone who was about to be flat on his back, Isla thought.

Renewed with determination, she matched each of his blows, again, again, again, their swords clashing together like lovers, the sound of metal against metal echoing through the forest. The Nightshade didn't even seem to notice that they were moving in a specific direction. He didn't even look at the ground until it was too late.

Isla swept around a tree, inviting him to lurch forward in attack—

Straight into a slice of bog sand.

It decorated this forest in patches, strong enough to trap animals in its clutches.

And, apparently, surly Nightshade rulers.

Once he was in it to his ankles, Grim couldn't move his legs. He made to move, then startled, staring down at his feet and still annoyingly blocking her advances. He wasn't even looking! When he realized he would no longer be able to move his feet while they dueled, he bared his teeth at her.

"You know I could portal out of this," he said. "If I believed it would in any way impact my chances of winning."

"I believe that would be considered cheating."

Grim gave her an incredulous look. "And trapping me in this vile substance isn't?"

Angry, he swung his blade harder than ever, and she met him stroke for stroke, her feet just inches away from the bog sand's clutches. The tree hunched above them was trimmed of some of its leaves as their blades clashed at an impossible speed. Isla was afraid to blink lest she miss one of his blows, and by the set of his eyes, Grim almost looked . . . *impressed* that she could keep up.

Then, without warning, he reached his other hand between their blades, grabbed her by the front of the shirt, fell back, and pulled her atop him.

She would have been skewered on his sword if he hadn't been holding her up with a firm hand against her chest. His blade's tip was positioned right against her heart.

He had won.

"I don't ever want to see you in my lands again," he said.

Then, he vanished, leaving Isla to fall face-first into the bog sand.

GOLDEN ROSE

Isla awoke on the floor, having fallen out of bed. Sunlight streamed through the gap in her curtains.

No. Another dream had turned into a memory. They were getting stronger. Longer.

They had dueled. The match they'd had during the Centennial hadn't been their first. Grim's skill hadn't been nearly as impressive then. She'd been so pleased with herself, being able to best an ancient warrior. But no . . . she knew now he had clearly been holding back. He'd wanted her to look strong in front of the others, so they would think twice about attacking her.

Her hands curled into fists as the realization settled into her mind. "The demon let me win."

If Isla couldn't stop the visions, she could at least replace them—make new memories to erase the past. Erase *him*.

Oro and Isla had just finished training. She had managed to roll a boulder across a field without touching it at all. The heavier the object, the more concentration it required. She'd rushed to move the rock, to finish the lesson early. Because afterward—

It was time to do something bold. Make clear exactly what she wanted.

She had just taken a shower. Her hair was still damp. She had summoned Oro to her room, and when she stepped out of the bathroom, he was waiting, freshly showered himself.

Isla might have laughed at the expression on Oro's face if she wasn't so nervous. She had never seen him go so still. She wasn't sure he was even breathing.

His gaze was a brand as it traveled up her bare legs, to the red lace that left little to the imagination.

Oro rose from the seat he had been waiting on, his movements slow, like he was using every ounce of his well-practiced control. He walked one, two, three steps, eyes never leaving hers, until he was before her. "Are you trying to torture me?" His voice was thick.

She repeated the same words as before. "Yes. Let me?"

He didn't even smile at her attempt at humor. He just stared, then closed his eyes tightly. "*Isla,*" he said, her name a prayer.

She waited for him to sweep her off her feet, to crush her against the wall, to feel every part of him against every practically bare part of her.

But he did not move an inch.

Isla shook her head. "I don't understand. I can feel it. You love me. Why—why won't you touch me?" She had tried to touch him multiple times—had tried to kiss him, to get close to him, to make clear what she wanted. Every time, he had rejected her. The realization came at her like a sword hilt to the temple. "Are you—are you not attracted to me?"

He said nothing, and she suddenly felt ridiculous. Of course he could love her without wanting her in that way. Various shades of love existed. She was so stupid, so foolish for just *assuming*—

"I'm sorry, I—"

Oro had her pressed against the wall before she could say another word. He was looming over her, eyes filled with a burning intensity that made heat pool everywhere. "Isla," he said. "*Attracted* does not begin to describe what I feel for you."

She swallowed, and his eyes went to her throat. He reached out a tentative hand and traced a line over her collarbone. Lower. Down her chest, across the mark where an arrow had pierced her heart.

"Every time I see you, I think the gods must play favorites. Every time you're near me, I am overcome with the urge to bed you, to have you, again and again. I want to devour every inch of you, until you're all I taste, until you are shaking with pleasure in my arms. *That* is what I want."

Isla had never wanted a person more in her entire life. She pressed against him. "Then do it. All of it."

She glanced down, and the evidence of his want was clear. It made her heart race to an impossible speed. With shaking hands, she unbuttoned the clasp of her top until it dropped. He looked at her like he wanted to spend a week with her, locked in this room.

But he only closed his eyes and said, "Isla. I want everything with you. But not now."

"Why not?" she asked, tears hot behind her eyes. She willed them not to fall, knowing she looked pathetic enough already.

His expression softened. "You're struggling, love." He took her hand. "I feel like I'm watching you fade, day by day, and I don't know what to do." He surprised her by going down on one knee, his gaze never leaving hers. The king of Lightlark was kneeling before her. "Tell me how to help you. I'll do anything. Give you anything. Just tell me."

The tears fell freely now. "I can't," she said.

He rose and cupped her face, smoothing her tears away with his thumbs. His palms were hot as coals, and she leaned into them. "Whatever it is, you can tell me. You are not alone. You do not face the world alone anymore."

Isla closed her eyes. It was hard to swallow; it was like her throat was swollen and raw, trying to keep the words down.

This secret . . . It was too much to bear. The memories were trickling in against her will; she was defenseless against them. Isla had told Oro she trusted him. That was true, wasn't it? If she couldn't tell him what was happening to her, then who?

Her eyes were still closed as she said, "I'm starting to remember."

She felt him stiffen in front of her. She opened her eyes, and Oro . . . his gaze was fire. He was angry, so angry—

Isla squirmed beneath his hands. Was he mad at her? She suddenly felt deeply ashamed for some reason, laid even more bare than she already was. "I'm sorry," she said, and she wasn't sure why.

Oro's eyes softened immediately. "Isla, don't ever apologize for something that isn't your fault." A muscle in his jaw shifted. "This is his fault."

She understood now. Oro looked murderous because he wanted to kill Grim. He was the reason she was suffering.

She nodded. She agreed, and she hated him, *hated* him. She needed Oro to know that. "I despise him," she said, words shaking in her mouth. "He is a monster, and I . . . I don't want to remember." She shook her head. "I'm trying my best to block them out, but with my powers untangled . . . I tried not to sleep, and it worked, for a while. But . . . I think things are starting to remind me of him, unlocking those memories. He went into my room during the Centennial; I don't think that helps. He was in my *mirror*. It's driving me mad. All I see when I close my eyes is *him*—"

"Move into my room," Oro said immediately.

Isla blinked. "What?"

"He's certainly never been there." Lest she suggest moving into any other room that wasn't his, he added, "It's the most protected place in the castle, should he be trying to reach you through other means. You can take it. I'll stay somewhere else."

Isla didn't want him to stay anywhere else. The fact that she was wearing only lace in front of him was proof of that. But Oro wouldn't hear of it.

By that afternoon, Oro had her stuff moved into his chambers and his moved out.

The memories stopped after Isla moved into Oro's room, and she was able to peacefully sleep through the night. It was as if the proximity to

the king's belongings, sleeping in his *bed*, was enough to smother all thoughts of Grim. She found a drawer that had been forgotten, filled with his clothes, and claimed one of his shirts. Then another. And another. They were massive and comfortable, and wearing them to bed helped her feel less alone.

At training, she was better able to focus. Every day, she grew stronger, her power inching forward, the blade within her sharpening.

What had started as a reaction to an attack, a desperation to open the vault and prepare against the next crisis, had started to become . . . fun.

They were sitting in a forest on the Wildling newland, Lynx watching them as they trained. She visited the leopard often, bringing gifts, all of which he rejected. She would wait at the edge of the forest surrounding the Wildling castle, offering in hand. Eventually, he would prowl out to meet her, sniff what she had brought, and walk back into the woods.

She was convinced the only reason Lynx had stuck around this long today was because Oro was here.

They were telling each other what to make, back and forth.

"A yellow rose," Oro said, and she made it bloom in front of them.

"A sunflower," she told him, barely containing a smile. He rolled his eyes and made it.

"A twenty-foot vine," he said, and she made it hang from a tree, so long it wrapped in spirals on the ground.

Her lips twitched.

"What?" he asked, voice flat.

"A—a—" She couldn't say the words before bursting into laughter. And it really wasn't that funny. Truly, it wasn't funny at all.

But she didn't know how long it had been since she had truly laughed. A week had gone by without any memories. She felt lighter. Freer.

Oro seemed to like her laugh. He tried not to smile and failed, until his face was overcome with it. And she was no match for the brightness

of that smile, like sunlight was filtering through his skin. His warmth grew, engulfing her like a blanket.

"What is it, Wildling?" he said, shaking his head as he watched her try to regain her composure.

She closed her eyes. Looking at his face would just make her laugh more; she was suddenly stuffed with joy. With happiness. With . . . love.

Sitting here, in front of him. Sharing a power between them. His patience, as he had helped her learn.

She breathed slowly, trying to stop herself from going into a fit again, and said, "A—" She laughed silently, shoulders shaking. "A golden blade of grass."

She heard Oro sigh in his long-suffering way. She heard shuffling in front of her.

Her eyes were still closed when he lifted her hand, opened her fingers, and left something in her palm.

It was not a golden blade of grass. Or a golden apple.

It was a tiny rose, turned into solid gold. Petals frozen. Bulbous and beautiful. It was perfect.

Her lips parted as she looked up at him. He was smiling.

Isla had never seen him look so happy.

"Oro," she said.

"Yes, Isla?"

Emotion made her throat go tight. Her voice was thick. "Everyone I've ever loved has betrayed me—"

His eyes gleamed with flames, the heat of his emotions burning the space between them.

"Except for you."

She stood and walked in front of him. For the first time, she was towering over him from his place on the ground. He looked up at her, the sun illuminating the sharp panes of his face. He was beautiful. She'd known it from the first time she saw him—though she wouldn't have admitted it to herself back then—but now she saw more. The set of his

eyebrows, the way they were always straight, unless he was smiling. The way his frown seemed deep-rooted, his mouth nearly perpetually turned down. Except when he was with her.

"I want to burn all of them alive," he said simply. "Everyone who ever hurt you. I want to watch them go up in flames."

She raised an eyebrow at him. "That's not very noble of you."

"I don't care."

By the set of his jaw, she knew he was thinking about one person in particular.

"Ask me," she said.

"Ask you what?"

"Ask me if I still love him." During the Centennial, she had developed feelings for Grim. When it mattered, though, he couldn't access her abilities. Still, Oro knew she was starting to remember their history. He must have wondered if it had changed anything.

Oro grimaced at the ground. "It isn't a fair thing to ask."

"Ask me anyway."

He paused. "You don't have to answer."

"I know."

"Do you love him?"

She didn't hesitate. "No."

Isla could see the little signs. She recognized them now. His shoulders settling. Jaw loosening. Relief.

She was telling the truth.

Isla didn't love Grim. Perhaps she had, at one time. But that was in the past. Now she was completely focused on the future.

He was her future. He was her friend. The person she trusted. The person she was happiest with.

He finally stood, towering over her. She looked up at him and said, "Oro. Oro—I love you."

He knew that. He had known for months, thanks to the thread between them. She had almost said the words before.

He went very still anyway.

Then he broke out in the most beautiful smile she had ever seen. "Say it again," he said. "I missed it."

"You did not," she said, laughing. Then she took a step closer to him. "I love you."

He closed his eyes, like he was taking every word in, committing this moment to his mind. "Again," he said, like they were in training.

She took a step closer and whispered it right in front of him. "I love you . . ." she said. "Even though you've never taken me on a date . . . even though you've never so much as kissed me."

Oro opened his eyes and peered down at her. "You want to be kissed, Wildling?" he said.

She shrugged. "Among other things."

He shook his head at her, but then he raked his long fingers through her hair, cupped her by the back of the neck—

And kissed her.

His lips were hot as flames. Their first kiss was soft. Loving.

Their second was not. He pulled back to look at her for just a moment, then seemed to forget they were in front of Lynx, who made a sound of distaste. In a quick motion, he lifted her to his height by the waist, turned, pressed her against the closest tree, and kissed her desperately.

He parted her lips, and she could taste him—he was summer and heat and fire, and when he bit her bottom lip, she groaned into his mouth. She couldn't get enough of this; her heart felt like it might burst inside her. Her chest tightened as she felt his warm, muscled body pressed against hers.

His grip kept her firmly against the tree, but his thumbs swept under her shirt, making circles against her lower stomach.

Fire flowed through her veins at his every touch. She lowered her head and brushed her lips against his neck and kissed against his pulse.

It quickened—his hands suddenly curled beneath her, and she locked her legs behind his back.

Want bloomed deep within her. His eyes were rooted to hers, flashing with intensity. She reached for his shirt—

Lynx growled in warning.

Oro laughed silently, then carefully took the hand that had tried to undress him in his. He pressed their intertwined knuckles against the tree, next to her head.

His lips swept down her neck. "I love you too," he said against one of her collarbones, and then he kissed her again.

WILDFLOWER

The kiss had been its own sort of key. It unlocked emotions she had pressed down deep within her soul. Positive ones, for once. She hadn't realized how much good had been buried beneath the gloom. Love was a wildflower, she realized. It grew best in secret.

Love made her bold. "I have an idea," she told Oro the next morning. "Two ideas, really."

"Tell me."

"First—I want to celebrate Copia. Here, on Lightlark." She imagined Oro had heard of it when Wildlings lived on the island. It was a day of celebrating abundance and creation. Isla had only ever seen the celebrations from far away, as a figurehead, but even with her people in a weakened state, she remembered flowers in hair, trees growing fruits, music, and dancing. "Not to the full extent, of course. But just with a dinner. Here, in the castle gardens." She shrugged. "It seems like a good way to introduce the people here to the idea of Wildlings potentially coming back. And to showcase my powers in public. Show the rebels that I'm not afraid of them."

"Would you want to bring your people here for the celebration?"

Isla had considered it. None of the Wildlings alive had ever stepped foot on the island. And the people here were . . . unwelcoming, to say the least. She didn't want to bring the Wildlings to a place where they would be ogled, and judged, and potentially harmed. Especially with the rebels still at large. "No. Not yet."

"What is your second idea?"

She smiled. "When my people do end up being ready to come

back . . . I want them to have a place to come back *to*. I want to make a place for Lynx, if he ever decides he likes me."

Oro flew them to Wild Isle. She started with a hand against the ground. A rosebush, blooming from the dead dirt. "I want us to bring it to life again," she said. She reached for his hand. "Together."

Using her power, Oro made an oak. Another. Isla turned to a mummified tree and ran her fingers up its peeling bark. At once, it exploded in color and leaves. She went around, painting Wild Isle in vibrant hues, shades of green and red and purple and blue and brown. Flowers, everywhere, in every shape. Trees, huddled together like gossips, their branches scraping in the wind.

By the time the sun came down, part of the isle was alive, so alive.

She beamed.

Isla had created hundreds of little lives, little threads, all reaching toward her, glimmering, shining.

And—as if it had never happened before, like the Nightshade power in her had withered away—nothing died.

Every time Oro used her power, she felt it, like a hand stroking down the rivers of her ability. It was an intimate experience. He had used her power before but never for this long. Today, they had worked for hours. By the time they reached his room, she had never felt closer to him.

"Tonight . . . stay with me," Isla said.

Oro looked down at her, and she didn't think he had ever looked so exhausted.

"Nothing needs to happen," she said, her voice a smooth whisper. "We can talk. We can sleep. We can dream, side by side. That's all, unless you want more." And, even though she wanted him now more than ever, it sounded like more than enough.

"This is what you want?" His eyes searched hers. "This will make you . . . happy?"

She nodded.

He entered.

Isla went to the bathroom to change. She wore what she had been wearing to bed every day for the last week or so: one of Oro's shirts. He had a lot to spare. They all smelled like summer, and soap, and faintly of citrus.

She didn't even really think about it until she stepped out of the bathroom, and Oro looked at her as if she had stepped out naked.

He looked almost horrified.

"I—I'm sorry." She moved one foot back into the bathroom. The marble was cold beneath her feet—everything was cold compared to him. "I found them in your room. I didn't think you'd mind. I can change."

Oro laughed.

He *laughed*.

His hand slid slowly down his face, then curved to the back of his neck. He groaned. His voice was dark as midnight as he said, "Don't you dare. Don't you dare wear anything else." She had never heard him so . . . possessive before. It made the bottom of her spine curl, made her think about them, and the bed, and the fact that they would soon be in it, together—

Any hope that something would happen between them died when Oro changed and slipped beneath the covers before she could diligently study what he wore to bed. Then, the flames of the room were extinguished.

She squirmed beneath the covers. Her nerve endings were on fire; she felt *everything*. The sheets against her legs, her shirt against her chest, prickling with need, the fabric of that shirt riding up, nearly showing the lace she was wearing underneath.

Oro was silent behind her. Warm, as always. She tried to even her breathing. Suddenly her heart was beating far too quickly.

Isla slowly smoothed a leg across the sheets until it met his, scalding her in heat that dropped right through her.

He was there. He was always there for her, wasn't he?

"Oro." The word was swallowed by the dark silence of the room. Seconds passed.

"Isla," he said, his voice free of sleep, like he had been awake this entire time as she had shifted uncomfortably with need. Need for *him*.

She turned around to face him. "I—" she said. She closed her eyes tightly. What was she doing?

He reached a hand to her shoulder, likely to comfort, but she wanted more than *comfort*. She immediately placed her hand over his.

She found his amber eyes in the darkness, clouded with concern. No, she wanted them to be filled with something else. She looked him right in the eye as she said, "I need you."

Oro stilled. He swallowed. His gaze sharpened, suddenly on high alert.

"Isla—"

"No." She shook her head. "Please, don't tell me that it will confuse me, or it's the wrong time." She shifted closer. "I want you. Right now. I *need*—"

Intimacy. Pleasure. Those were the words she didn't say, but the way his eyes closed for just a moment, his jaw clenched, told her he knew her meaning.

Her body shifted closer, until the hand that he had placed on her shoulder fell to her hip. She slid the sheets down, so he could see her, all of her, in his shirt.

He took in her every inch, and his hand clenched the excess fabric at her side, as if he was physically stopping himself from touching her skin.

"Touch me. Please," she said.

His own rules were forgotten.

She wasn't sure she was breathing as his fingers slipped up her leg, then beneath the waist of her underthings. His hand curled around her backside, his thumb stroked the inside of her thigh, so close, so *close*—

Isla looked from the sight of her body nearly exposed, his hand on her, to him, now just a few inches away. In his eyes, she saw torture.

She frowned. "Oro, if you don't want—"

Before Isla could finish, he flipped her around and gripped her hips. She gasped as he pulled her toward him, up against him and the proof that he wanted this just as much as she did. The pulsing heat within her became a wildfire. She arched her back and ground against him, making him curse.

Oro slid his hands up to her waist. He leaned down to whisper in her ear, in a deep voice that scraped against the back of her mind. "Knowing you've been wearing my shirts to bed, Isla," he said, "it drives me mad." His lips touched the edge of her ear. "That's what I'm going to think about when I'm alone." He pulled the shirt up, exposing her underthings. He looked and drew a sharp breath, taking in the lace. "You. In my clothes."

Her heart was going to break out of her chest. They both watched as his fingers slowly, slowly, too slowly, slid their way down to where she wanted him most. Finally, he reached her, and she closed her eyes tightly as he found the proof of her own desire. He stilled, his hand right there, right *there*—

She froze too, wondering if she should be embarrassed. . .

"Do you want this?" he asked.

She looked over her shoulder at him. She had never wanted anything more. "Yes."

He was a man unleashed. Suddenly, his shirt and her underthings were on the floor, and his hands were on her chest. In the dark, all her focus narrowed to the heat of his touch as his calluses lightly brushed across the most sensitive parts of her skin. She seemed to melt against him, making all sorts of sounds as he swept his knuckles down her bare stomach and murmured in her ear. "Tell me what you like, love," he said. "Show me."

“Here,” she said, squirming. She found his hand and started to guide it down again. “Please.”

But his fingers were long and practiced and needed little direction, even though he seemed to enjoy the sight of her hand over his. When he was right where she needed him, she reached back to weave her fingers behind his neck and said, “Don’t stop. Don’t you dare stop.”

His lips were right over hers; his breath was hot against her skin, and he groaned as she began moving on him.

Her head fell back and she made a sound that he seemed to like, because he kissed across her pulse. He knew where to touch her, where to linger, where to explore.

It only took moments for her to be panting and at the edge of the world, and nothing had ever felt this good, this sweet. “Oro, I—” she said, because she could feel sparks traveling up her spine.

“Not yet,” he said. He kept going, and she gasped as his teeth scraped lightly up her neck, until he reached her ear. “I want you so much I think it might actually kill me,” he whispered, before he curled his fingers, and the world shattered around her. He held her close, both arms tight around her body. “Never doubt that.”

She never would again.

ILLUSION

Isla fiddled with the petals on her bodice. That night was Copia. She had helped the Starling tailor make her dress. For fabric, she had bloomed hundreds of flowers, weaving their stems together, blanketing them across his shop floor.

A hand covered her own to stop the picking. It swallowed her own and pressed against her chest in a way that made her suddenly forget whatever errant thought was circling in her mind.

"Flowers don't pick themselves, remember?" he said, repeating her own drunken words from the Centennial. She hadn't known he had heard that part.

She smiled and turned to face him. He was golden, in his most official of outfits for the occasion. Isla smoothed the silk of his shirt that required no smoothing whatsoever. "What about kings? Do they pick flowers?"

Oro's expression was pure promise when he leaned down to say right into her ear, "Only when the flower picks them."

"Good," she said. "Because I'm pretty sure you're going to have to cut me out of this dress." She turned for him. "See? No strands. No buttons." In fact, she had molded the dress to herself. With Leto's instructions to his design, she had woven the dress around her, the flowers coming together, clasping tight, their stems locking her in.

Another fact was that she could certainly undo the dress herself as well, but the alternative was so much more enjoyable.

"Hmm," Oro said, his voice getting deeper. His mouth brushed against her bare shoulder. His fingers trailed down her spine, where corset ties might have been were this a traditional dress. They did not stop. She felt the heat of his hand sweep across the base of her back before gripping her hip bone. "That shouldn't be a problem," he said.

"Are you sure?" She blinked innocently at him over her shoulder. "If you're too busy with your kingly duties, I can ask someone else . . ."

He took her chin in his hand. Tilted her head up to his, so he could say right against her lips, "Tonight, my only *kingly duties* involve my mouth and whatever you wear beneath a dress like this."

Isla's eyes were still the height of innocence as she said, "So, your mouth and . . . nothing?"

Oro cursed, and heat filled the room. They were standing in front of a mirror. She turned her head and watched him look at her like she was the most precious thing in all the realms. And she . . .

She looked happy. She *was* happy. Her mind had emptied of most of its anxious thoughts. How had that happened?

Oro had happened. He had taken all her broken pieces in his hands and vowed to one day make them whole. He had been patient. Kind. Loving.

Inside, Isla now had a pocket of peace. A slice of sunlight. It was an anchor. If her thoughts ever spiraled, in her darkest hours, she would return here, to this moment she tucked away in that pocket.

Before, she had felt unmoored, betrayed, like she didn't truly have a home.

Now, *he* felt like home.

"Look," she said, fishing a thin golden chain from beneath her dress. The small golden rose hung there, in the center of her chest. She'd made a necklace of it. "It's heavy, but—"

"You kept it," he said, almost in awe, his brows coming together. Oro swept his fingers over it, and it became lighter, as if hollowed.

"Of course I kept it," she said. "It's us. A rose surrounded in gold."

Oro didn't seem to care that he was disrupting all the petals on her dress as he lifted her up.

Isla thought, as he leaned down and kissed her, that she had never been happier in her entire life.

The Mainland gardens were decorated with flowers Isla had bloomed herself. She'd spent all afternoon crafting the decor. The event was meant to showcase her abilities. It only made sense to have her power on display everywhere.

A hundred islanders and newlanders had been invited—not just nobles. In fact, some nobles would find that they were left off the list. People of every realm sat at the tables, and Isla had seated them all together, not separated, as they so often were.

The most surprising guest of all was Cleo. She had accepted her invitation, and Isla could only hope that it meant the smallest of peace offerings. The Moonling ruler sat perfectly postured, her chin as high as always. Her white hair was tied into a single long braid behind her. Her face didn't betray a single expression.

Oro squeezed Isla's hand under the table. *You can do this*, he seemed to say.

She could.

Isla stood. She was barefoot. Flowers bloomed with her every step to the center of the celebration.

She did not have to tell them to fall silent; they did that themselves. "Thank you for attending this banquet in honor of my realm," she said. "This day is meant to celebrate growth." Her voice sharpened with meaning. "Growth is not limited to our plants, or our realms, but *ourselves*. No matter what happened before, we can change. Our opinions can change. Hatred can become hope. And I sincerely hope, one day, Wildlings can return to Wild Isle, the way they lived for thousands of years." There was murmuring, but no one dared say a word against the idea to her face. Isla had to think that was some sort of progress. "On behalf of our realm, we wish you a season of growth . . . in the right direction."

This was it. This was the moment.

Everyone knew she had been powerless. They knew she didn't know how to wield.

Isla unraveled her hand, revealing a rare seed she had gotten from the newland. She tossed it in front of her, to the ground below, and everyone watched as it was sucked into the dirt. A moment later, the ground rustled, and a tree formed in front of them, years of growth in just seconds. The bark layered over itself, the branches thickened, leaves decorated, and then fruit blossomed. "This tree has not grown on Lightlark in centuries," she said. "Its fruit is often called enchanted because of its sweetness." She turned in a semicircle, and arches of vines and thorns and roses sprouted around the gathering, one after the other.

Whispers. Murmurs. Wide eyes. Curiosity.

Her demonstration worked.

Oro's hand was on her knee as soon as she sat down. His thumb rubbed down her thigh, and she was suddenly flushed, remembering his promises for that night.

The clatter of silverware against glass plates was a welcomed symphony. At first, conversations at tables between realms seemed quiet, perhaps even tense, but by the end of the dinner, there was laughter. Conversation. Joy, even.

Then, far too soon, everything went silent.

It was as if all noise had been plucked from the island. The candles lining the garden began flickering. Dimming.

Before them, Isla's tree wilted, branches dehydrating, until it was just a pile of dead leaves.

Then, in an instant, darkness smothered them all.

Everything in the garden turned to ash. Tables were toppled over. Shadows shot down from the sky like strikes of lightning, then raced across the Mainland like tornadoes that had fallen over, erasing everything in their path.

No screams, though mouths were open. No cries, though tears slid down Isla's cheeks.

She shot out her hand, but no power came out. It was as if everything within her had been extinguished.

No, no—

A blink, and everything returned to how it was.

Isla remembered Grim's demonstration of power at the Centennial. An illusion. This was an illusion.

Then, his voice was in her head.

It was in all their heads.

"Consider this a warning," it said. "A glimpse at the future. You have one month to vacate the island. In thirty days, I am coming to destroy it."

Shouts. Screams.

"Nothing will be left. You can choose to flee to your newlands . . . or join me in a new future. The choice is simple. Fighting is futile. The ruin coming is inevitable."

HISTORY

Isla flew down from the sky, carried by Ciel and Avel, who each gripped her beneath a shoulder. Before, she would have been afraid of the height. Now, she didn't have room for such a simple fear.

She landed on Cleo's castle steps and within minutes was surrounded by white-wearing guards. They had sloshing water pouches along their hips, water ready to wield into weapons.

Cleo came sweeping down from one of the highest balconies of the castle, on the back of a waterfall. When she landed, the water froze, a wide white halo around her feet. "The brave little Wildling," she said. "What have you come to crow?"

"Stay," Isla said.

The Moonling looked intrigued. "Here I was, thinking we were enemies."

"You're not my enemy," Isla said. "I've watched your every move. You always do what's best for your realm. Leaving Lightlark would be a mistake."

"Would it?" she said, seeming bored.

"Lightlark is the base of your abilities. If you leave and Lightlark falls, your people won't last."

Cleo almost smiled. Surprisingly, it didn't look cruel. Her expression, more than anything, seemed sad. "You know so little," she said, her voice empty of any contempt. "You assume you know my motivations. You assume your facts are truth."

Isla narrowed her eyes. "You found something out before the last Centennial. That's why you didn't attend. That's why you've been

building ships. That's why you are considering evacuating your people from Lightlark. Isn't it?"

Cleo said nothing. The Moonling only tilted her head at Isla, as if appraising a dull rock, searching for any hidden glint.

Isla took a step forward. "Answer me," she yelled, and thorns grew around her wrists, out of nowhere, trailing down to the floor.

A dozen Moonling guards surrounded her in seconds. Avel and Ciel were at her sides, each of their hands on her arms, ready to fly her to safety. She had her starstick just in case. She felt invincible.

The Moonling frowned at the thorns dripping from Isla's palms. "What a waste," Cleo said, then she turned toward the massive, frozen doors of her palace.

"We could work together," Isla said.

That made the Moonling stop in her tracks. She turned around, the hem of her white dress hissing across the iced-over stone.

Isla took her chance. "Wildlings and Moonlings are more similar than you might like to imagine," she said. "You have frozen, infertile lands. We have started to learn how to grow crops again. We could help you, so you don't have to rely on fishing. You can vary your diets." Lately, Moonlings weren't seen in the markets. They had almost completely cut themselves off from the other realms.

The Moonling's expression remained as still as the frost beneath her feet. Unconvinced.

"We are also healers," she said. "The elixir I demonstrated during the Centennial—we know how to make it. Between your people's natural healing abilities and the ones we can extract from nature, we could mend almost anything."

Cleo stared at her for a moment. Another. Then, she turned away again.

"What happened?" Isla asked. "What happened a century ago? Why didn't you attend the fourth Centennial?"

At that, ice swept across the isle. It rippled in every direction and hardened beneath Isla's feet. She had to sprout vines from her hands to root her in place, to keep from slipping. Ciel and Avel braced her sides, wind circling around their bodies to keep them still.

Cleo turned. "You dare ask me a question like that?"

Isla took a step forward, beyond her Skyling guards, her roots digging into the ice, keeping her grounded. "I do," she said. "Something happened. What was it?"

For the fraction of a second, Isla caught a sliver of real emotion that made its way past the Moonling's normally icy mask. *Pain.*

Cleo could feel pain?

"We both want the same thing. For our realms to survive. We can help each other." Cleo looked doubtful, and Isla growled. "I know you hate me, but you love your people. Do it for them."

To her immense surprise, the Moonling smirked. "I don't hate you," she said. Then she turned, and the ice around her retracted, curling back to its source.

Only when she was almost at the palace's front doors did Isla hear the Moonling ruler say, "I'll consider it," before sweeping inside.

Grim was coming to destroy Lightlark in twenty-nine days.

From her vision, she had figured an attack was inevitable, but that didn't help the pain of knowing someone she once cared about was set on destroying everything she now loved.

Oro was irrevocably connected to Lightlark, as king. If the island fell . . . so would he.

All representatives were called for a meeting first thing the next morning. Isla hadn't told Oro about her visit to Cleo the night prior. As she watched the door, her hope the Moonling would stay withered. Grim's declaration of an attack was the perfect excuse for Cleo to leave Lightlark once and for all, on her ships. The Moonling newland was well

established and not under threat. It would be so easy for Cleo to take her people and flee.

They couldn't leave. If the other realms went to war with Nightshade they would need Moonlings and their healers more than ever.

Enya was at her side, curling and uncurling her fingers. Anxiety spiraled through the room. The same people from the dinner were present now, but this time there were no floating foods or flame-trimmed goblets, or fish trapped in ice.

This time, instead of whispers, there was only silence.

The clock began to chime, marking the hour.

Just before the last ring, Cleo swept into the throne room, and Isla tried her best not to fall out of her chair in surprise. The Moonling ruler had listened.

She had stayed.

Soren's cane cracked against Cleo's icy wake as they both made their way to their seats.

Oro did not waste a moment. "We have twenty-nine days before Lightlark is under siege. Twenty-nine days to figure out how to stop Grim."

Silence broke open, and questions spilled over.

"Can he even do that?"

"Does he control the winged beasts from the coronation attack?"

"It's five realms against one; we can protect the island, can't we?"

"What did he mean 'new future'?"

One of Isla's necklaces sat heavy against her throat as she swallowed, seeing flashes of her vision.

Grim could do it. Grim could destroy them all.

She blinked and found Cleo watching her intently. The Moonling wasn't focused on the lively debate around her. She was just staring at Isla, the specter of a smile on her mouth, the look of someone who knew a secret.

"Yes?" Cleo said suddenly, responding to Oro, because apparently, she had been listening. Her eyes remained fixed on Isla's.

"Is the oracle awake?" Oro asked.

She shook her head. "I visited the moment I returned to the isle, and she refused to thaw."

There was muttering. Heat flamed from Oro, but he moved on to his next question. "How many healers do you have?" Oro asked.

"Nearly a hundred on Lightlark. Triple that on the newland," Cleo answered.

Isla jumped in. "Combined with our healing elixirs, we'll be able to heal almost any injury. We'll start producing more right away." Her back was straight. She glanced at Soren, daring him to question her the way he had at the last dinner. He said nothing.

"Both will be critical," Azul said. He trailed his gem-covered fingers across the table and shook his head. "If Grim is taking on all other realms, he must be well equipped, and determined. He must want something. This isn't just about destroying the island, or he would have done it during the curses, when we were most vulnerable."

For a moment, Oro's eyes flicked to Isla. She knew what he thought.

Grim wanted her.

No. If this was about wanting her, he could have appeared at this very moment and taken her. She agreed with Azul. There was a purpose for Grim's destruction. If they knew what it was, perhaps they could stop him.

Oro's gaze was pure fire. "Whatever he wants, his intent is clear. He is coming to destroy us. We need to use every resource we have, every bit of ability." He addressed them all. Heat scorched the room. "This is our home. It is our future. Our power lives here. Without the island, our realms will die. We have twenty-nine days to either save Lightlark . . . or lose it forever."

That night, Isla curled against Oro's chest and traced him in the darkness. His cheeks. His lips. She touched him gently, just the slightest brush of her fingertips, and felt him shiver. "Oro," she said. "Growing

up, I didn't experience seasons. It was always warm. But there were a few weeks in the middle of the year when everything felt the most alive. I called that summer, and I used to wish that it would last forever." She frowned against the memory of her vision. "You and me . . . we built an endless summer. And I won't let anyone destroy it."

The next morning, he was gone when she woke up. The clock had started counting down, and chaos ensued. Word of Grim's warning had spread, and people rushed the castle, frantic, looking for answers.

Every willing and able adult was expected to begin training.

It had been centuries since war. Many of the best fighters had died during the curses. Oro went off to Sun Isle, with Enya, to get their forces together. Azul assembled his flight force, a legion in the sky.

Isla felt uncertain about asking any of the Starlings to fight, given most were barely older than children. A few people on the Starling newland volunteered to fight, and the rest who could wield would make weapons and provide energy for a shield that could be used to protect parts of the island.

That night, before going to Oro's room, she went to her own. She didn't make it past the entryway before pausing.

There was a flicker of curling white fabric on her balcony.

Cleo.

The Moonling ruler stood there, hands gripping the ledge, facing the sea. Her white hair cut through the night in sharp strands. Her dress was a pale puddle across the stone floor.

Isla swallowed. She wondered if she should be afraid. She waited for the fear to come . . . but it didn't.

A greater danger was coming. *Grim* was coming. Fears were relative, she realized. They could feel smaller when placed next to bigger ones.

She wasn't afraid of Cleo. Not anymore.

The door creaked as it opened. From this angle, the full moon looked like a halo around Cleo's head. It lit her white dress and skin—she was

a candle without its wick. The Moonling didn't even turn around as she said, "It was a night just like this." Isla eyed the pool of water around Cleo's dress. "The worst night of my life. It was a full moon . . . just like this one."

Isla leaned against her door. "What do you want, Cleo?"

Cleo almost smiled. It was a sad expression. "Tonight? It might surprise you . . . but I want to help you."

Her eyes narrowed. "That does surprise me," Isla said. Vines crawled up the cliff, until they reached her balcony. They didn't stop until they wrapped around Isla's arms and down her palms. "Considering you tried to kill me."

Cleo looked from the vines dripping down her fingers to her face, and smirked. "Wildling," she said. "If I had wanted to kill you, you would be dead."

A massive wave crashed against the balcony, and Isla felt the force of it in her knees. Freezing water soaked her legs, and she tried her best not to shiver.

"I heard you were locked in a glass box of a room. Is that true?" Cleo asked. Where was she going with that? How did she even *know* that? Isla nodded warily and watched as Cleo turned back toward the moon. She stared at it as she said, "You are a young fool, but you remind me so much of him." Isla could have imagined it, but Cleo's voice cracked with emotion, splitting from its normal coolness. "My son."

The sea that had made its way through the teeth of the balcony pillars froze over. It nearly reached Isla, though she didn't move a muscle.

Son? Cleo had an heir . . . ? That couldn't be right; heirs weren't allowed at the Centennial—

"He died. The curse took him." Cleo looked down at the sea, sloshing and churning, and Isla saw a hatred there. "I did everything I could to protect him. I locked him up just like you, and I failed."

Isla would have thought it impossible to ever feel some sort of hurt for Cleo, though her eyes burned as she thought of her son, locked in his

room, and the mother who just wanted to keep him safe. "That's why you didn't attend the fourth Centennial," Isla said. "You had an heir."

"Our curse was well managed by then. It was more important to secure my realm's future. I had an heir, because, like you said, I do *everything for the good of my realm.*"

It wasn't just Isla who thought that. She remembered Oro during the Centennial saying Cleo was the most dedicated ruler of all of them. Though she'd had relationships with both men and women before the curses, she hadn't formerly been with anyone since becoming ruler. She put her realm's safety above all else.

"Something unexpected happened, though," Cleo said. "I . . . loved him. I had forgotten what that felt like . . . to love someone so much, it feels like drowning." She turned to fully face Isla, and the ice around her turned liquid, before crackling once more. Cleo had always worn dresses with a high neckline, but tonight she wore something more casual. Because of that, Isla was able to see a necklace: a simple ribbon with a light-blue stone that glistened in the moonlight. "I attended the last Centennial for him, so no one else would be taken by the curses." She looked Isla up and down, her expression still dripping in dismay. "And because of him, I'm helping you."

Isla didn't know why Cleo had told her all of this now, when she had been so defensive just days before.

Cleo wanted something from her. She just needed to figure out what it was.

"The oracle," Cleo finally said. "She's awake and has a message for you. You'll want to visit her soon."

The oracle was awake. They needed her now more than ever. Hope sprouted, but was tinged with suspicion.

The oracle was on Moon Isle. Cleo could keep Isla from accessing her if she wanted.

"Why . . . why are you telling me this?" Cleo said it was because of her son, but that didn't make any sense. Her son was dead. "Are you

agreeing to be loyal to Lightlark?" She needed confirmation before she could take anything the Moonling said seriously.

Cleo looked at her and frowned. "I'm loyal only to myself," she said.

She did not look at Isla again before a wave rushed up and took her away.

This time, Isla told Oro about her conversation with Cleo. They were rushing down the castle steps the next morning, on their way to the oracle, avoiding the craterous fissures from the drek attack, when Azul crashed in front of them with the force of a lightning strike. He was crouched, a jewel-covered hand balanced in front of him.

Ciel and Avel came down a moment later, flanking Isla.

Azul straightened, and for the first time, she could see traces of his true age in the heaviness of his expression.

"What's happened?" Oro asked, stepping forward. He reached almost absent-mindedly toward Isla, in a protective motion, and Isla watched Azul track it.

"See for yourself," the Skyling said, his voice grave.

In an instant, Ciel and Avel lifted Isla up, and the five of them shot into the sky. Azul's expression was serious, but he glanced down at her as he flew above, knowingly. Warily. Then, his gaze went back to the horizon.

Isla saw it before they landed, and her mouth went dry.

A fleet like dozens of swans, positioned in the shape of a diamond, cut through the ocean, riding against the current. These ships did not have or require sails. They made currents of their own. The sea parted from their path.

The ones who controlled the decks moved in unison, in practiced motions. They had been preparing for this. Training, just like her.

Cleo was on the front-most ship. Her white dress billowed, puffed up, the only thing resembling a sail on those vessels. She turned, staring right at them.

They were not the only ones watching. She heard the islanders on the beaches below and by the Broken Harbor witnessing history unfold. Moonling was leaving Lightlark.

"They're fleeing," Azul said, his voice still nearly unbelieving.

"No," a voice said, and they all turned around to find Soren standing there, watching the Moonlings fade away. "They're joining Nightshade."

PROPHECY

Moon Isle was melting. The previous labyrinth of ice and snow had lost its bite. The ice sculptures that had lined the walkway to the palace for centuries were nothing more than puddles. The woods were carved open, no snow to hide their inner workings. It was like the Moonlings had taken the cold with them, packed it in their ships.

Cleo had told her the night before to visit the oracle. Now, with Oro next to her, she needed to find out why.

The oracle was already thawed. She floated in the water of her glacier, edges melting.

Isla remembered what the oracle had told her and Oro months prior. *So many secrets, trapped between you. But, just like this wall, they too will one day give way and unravel and fall . . . leaving quite a mess and madness.*

Back then, there had been three women trapped in the glacier. Three sisters. Oro had said the other two had allied with Nightshade and hadn't thawed in over a thousand years. Now, they were gone.

"You're dying," Isla said. The oracle's power—a force in the air that Isla could almost taste now that she knew what to look for—was dimming. "Cleo injured you."

"Don't look so dour, Wildling. I'm ancient. We tend to die slowly. She left me alive long enough to tell you what you need to know."

It didn't make sense. Why would Cleo help her, then join her enemy? The oracle's white hair floated around her face, curling in the water. Her voice was a thousand voices braided into one, echoing, smothered

slightly by the wall of ice between them. "Though . . . you are the one with most of the answers this time. Not me."

"What do you mean?" Oro demanded. Isla wasn't sure if they could trust the oracle, but he would know if she was telling the truth.

"Her memories are the key. They unlock the world. Everything—why they are coming, what they will do with Lightlark, the weapon they already have, how to stop them—is in her mind. All she must do is remember. *Everything*."

No. The memories had only just stopped again, and she was happier than ever. She swallowed. "And if I can't?"

"Then Lightlark will fall. Forever."

Oro frowned. "Is the future not solid?"

The oracle's gown floated in the slight current of the water, her sleeves going far beyond her arms. "No, it is not. Not all of it." She looked beyond them, at the woods that had been far whiter the last time they had visited. "This much is clear: they are coming. If they succeed, there will be nothing left. And by the time they step foot on the island, I will be gone."

The ice started hardening again, and Isla pressed her hand against it. "I need to know. Is my vision real?"

The oracle nodded. "Very."

Chills snaked down her spine. That level of destruction . . . the death in her mind . . .

She had one more question. "The vault," Isla said. "Is it important?" Even though it had rejected her, she knew it was crucial. She could feel it calling to her, the connection stronger as her powers intensified.

"More than you know," the oracle said. "The vault will change everything . . . if you can find the strength to open it for good." The woman tilted her head at Isla for just a moment—and in that second, somehow, she spoke directly into her mind. The oracle said, "Before Nightshade arrives, you will visit me. Alone. Only then will I give my

final prophecy." Isla wasn't sure if it was an order or yet another telling of the future, but it didn't matter.

As soon as Isla nodded—the most imperceivable lowering of her chin—the oracle fell back into the last remaining ice and froze over.

"I don't want to remember," she told Oro as she sat at the foot of their bed.

They had shared it for over a week now. During that time, her mind had been blissfully clear of any memories of Grim. Oro had banished his presence. She was happy.

She should have known happiness was only ever temporary.

Oro shook his head. "There has to be another way."

"There isn't. The oracle was clear. I have to remember everything . . . and somehow find a way to open the vault."

Her knees were pulled to her chest. The memories she'd had so far were useless. Her being foolish enough to portal to Nightshade. Stabbing him in the chest. Grim nearly choking her. Their duel.

"I hate him," she said. "Not just for taking the memories away. But in the memories themselves. The ones I've already remembered."

Isla had already made up her mind. Of course she would remember. Of course she wouldn't put her own happiness above the safety of all Lightlark.

It didn't mean she was happy about it.

Tears streaked down her face. "I hate him, and I hate myself for even having these memories in the first place."

Oro's arms went around her back and under her knees. He hauled her against him. "This is not your fault, Isla. Whatever happened a year ago . . . you were not the person you are now. Do not judge yourself. Do not hate yourself."

After Oro was asleep, Isla sneaked into her room. She found a parchment and quill and wrote herself a note. No matter what she remembered. No matter what had happened in the year before the Centennial—

You hate him.
You hate him.
You hate him.
You hate him.
You hate him.
You hate him.

That very same night, Isla used her starstick to portal to the only person who might be able to get her memories back faster.

Remlar did not look surprised to see her. He was standing outside his hive. Isla didn't know if he ever slept. "Welcome back, Wildling," he said, purring the last word. He was surrounded by the other winged beings who lived in the hive. Their skin was light blue, and their wings were thin and silky behind them. Before, they hadn't worked. Now, they stood perched high over their shoulders.

"If my memories were taken by a Nightshade, how would I remember? Can you give them to me?"

The others flew away, up into holes in the giant wooden hive behind them, clearly not wanting to be involved in this conversation.

Remlar pursed his lips. "No. Memories are difficult to uncover. A skilled Nightshade could return them . . . but doing so all at once could be dangerous. The mind is so easily fractured . . ." He sighed. "The far better option is that they be restored by you." That, at least, explained why Grim hadn't simply given her memories back at the end of the Centennial. He had seemed so confident she would remember . . . and she had.

"How do I do that?"

"Assuming they weren't meant to be erased forever, the stronger your Nightshade powers become, the more the veil that has been put on them will weaken."

Isla frowned. "So, the more I master Nightshade power, the more I will remember."

He nodded.

Great. Now, she needed to learn yet another ability? She didn't want to wield death and shadows. She had been suppressing it. She didn't have time.

But if this was the way to save Lightlark . . . she had to try. "Fine. Teach me."

Remlar raised his brow at her.

"Please."

He shrugged a shoulder and pointed to the grass before them. "It's simple. Summon, Wildling."

"How?"

"Just try it. Focus. Reach, just like you do for your other abilities. But this time . . . look for the shadows."

Isla placed a hand in front of her. She could feel the Wildling ability inside, humming, ready to be used. Familiar.

Then, there was its umbra. It was harder to grasp—slippery, temperamental. The roots of her hair became sweaty as she focused, using all her usual rituals and tricks. Her mouth was a line. She reached for the power, over and over, until finally, she clutched it, for just a second—

Her hand pressed against the ground. Whatever her skin touched died. When she removed it, there was only her imprint, dark and sizzling.

"Is that good enough?" she asked.

Remlar didn't answer.

She turned—but she wasn't in the Sky Isle woods any longer.

BEFORE

She was in a market.

It had been a month since Isla had dueled with the Nightshade in the forest. She hadn't expected to see him again, of course. He was repulsed by her.

She was repulsed by *him*.

Her days were spent training with Terra and Poppy and meeting Celeste in secret.

She had a million things to think about, but sometimes, her thoughts would drift to the Nightshade ruler.

Grimshaw. In her mind, she called him Grim. It seemed fitting, given the dread his memory caused. Losing the duel meant Grim could slay her the first chance he got at the Centennial. It pained her to think one mistaken visit to Nightshade could cost her years of training and preparation. Especially since she was working with Celeste.

Isla had spent the last three weeks looking for an object that was central to her and Celeste's plan to survive the Centennial: a pair of gloves made of flesh that would allow them to absorb a whisper of power. She had searched every dark market in every newland, without success.

Except for Nightshade.

It had a famed night market that now operated during the day. A place where ungodly things were sold and traded. She had heard whispers of it in the darkest corners of the other agoras, which had been a bit like monsters whispering about even bigger monsters.

Skin gloves had to be made while a person was *alive*—they couldn't be taken from a corpse, which might have made attaining them slightly easier. According to the few merchants she had trusted enough to ask, they used to be far more common years before, when more power could be absorbed. Nowadays, after the curses, the amount of ability the gloves could muster was useless.

In most cases, anyway.

If any last pair of skin gloves still existed, they would be on Nightshade. She had promised herself she would never return, but—

Isla drew her puddle of stars, then it was done.

With mastery, one day, she might be able to portal anywhere she wanted. For now, she could only return to places she'd been before. The moment she landed in Grim's castle, she imagined he might step out of a wall and put his broadsword to her chin. But the hall was empty.

She didn't linger or explore—that was what had gotten her found out last time. With quiet steps, she made her way out of the palace and into the busy streets. Women wore clothes she had never seen in other realms' lands—boots that reached their thighs, dresses with chain mail woven through, pants that were glossy and shimmering. Compared to them, Isla was wearing far too much clothing. She kept her head down and her hood—a black one she had procured in another market—buttoned at its front, so as not to show what she wore beneath, the only other dark-colored clothing she owned, a deep-plum silk dress meant for sleeping.

Get the gloves and get out, she told herself.

The night market smelled of rotting flesh and boiled blood. Her black hood dropped so low it almost obstructed her vision as she wove through the crowds. No one paid any attention to her. She was the least interesting thing in the market.

One stand exclusively sold teeth. There were barrels of them—most looking distinctly human.

Another had skulls tied on strings. Some were small as fingernails, others as large as boulders—*what creature could possibly have such a large head?*

"Nightbane," someone whispered from a stall. She slowed in front of it, curious. There were small vials of something dark. The seller's face lit up at her attention. "Takes away all troubles and pain . . ."

Nightbane. She had never heard of it.

The seller reached for her, as if to place the vial in her hand, eyeing the gems she wore on her fingers, and she kept moving.

Crimson wine filled a cauldron a woman with fingers that looked suspiciously like claws stirred with what looked even more suspiciously like a femur. Poison. It had to be poison. The woman met her eyes, and Isla quickly looked away.

Gloves, gloves.

She looked for flesh, and—*gulp*—found it rather quickly.

A stand had skin spread out across racks, some still in need of more thorough cleaning. Isla nearly gagged. She parted the curtains of the shop and entered, sinking her face into the folds of her cape to try to mute the smell of decay. Disgusting. She couldn't fathom the type of people who could regularly visit the night market, let alone work here.

Gloves. Gloves. She searched, hoping to find them. If no shop sold them, she would have to find someone she could pay to *make* them for her. That possibility made bile crawl up her throat. No, the best thing would be to find some already made, preferably from the skin of a child murderer, or someone equally as deserving of such a cruel, torturous death.

She parted another wall of curtains. The shop was like a labyrinth, and some of its sweeping walls felt too thick—*skin?*—and she was suddenly sweating beneath her cloak. She tried to hold her breath as much as she could as she scoured the shelves and racks for something resembling human hands . . .

Until she did find human hands.

Or, rather, they found her.

Before Isla could scream, someone placed their fingers over her mouth and pulled her backward, straight through another set of curtains.

Into an alleyway.

She was shoved against a wall, her hood falling, the back of her head colliding with wet bricks. Something dripped against her forehead from far above and slid down her cheek.

A man whose flesh hung off his bones like the skins in the shop towered before her. He looked old, which meant he either had generations of children or had been alive more than a millennium.

Or . . . by the crazed look in his eyes and the faint yellowing of his skin, he had dabbled in something dark enough to have leeched away his life.

With a motion quicker than his appearance suggested he would be capable of making, he wrapped her hair around his other wrist and pulled.

Isla cried out behind his filthy palm. The man ignored her, inspecting her hair like it was a treasure.

"Yes . . ." he said, eyes sparkling. "This would fetch a pretty price . . . Wildling hair. Shiny temptress locks. Must get the root . . . that's the best part. The whole scalp, that will do nicely." He pulled a long, curved knife from his pocket.

Isla had a blade through his chest before he could point it in her direction.

It shocked her. The only other person she had stabbed was Grim.

The man's mouth turned into a curious shape, and his eyes were not on her but her hair as he crumpled to the ground.

A group of guards chose that exact moment to walk by the entrance of the alley. One stopped. Took a look at the man bleeding at her feet. That didn't seem to disturb him that much.

He might not have pursued her if she hadn't taken off, wielding the ruby blade she had just fished from the man's rib cavity. It was an admittance of guilt. But she couldn't stop herself.

She bolted, and he followed.

The group joined him.

Isla hurtled back into the market. She ducked and wove herself into the crowd, not turning around to see how close they were to catching her. She pulled her starstick out of her pocket and saw it was faintly glowing.

Thank the stars.

All she needed was to hide long enough to draw her puddle, and she would be gone, gloves be damned.

She ducked beneath a low-hanging row of axes, jumped over a tangle of snakes sitting in front of a shop—fangs not even removed—and tried to find a place to hide.

By now, everyone was watching.

Risking a glance behind her, she realized why. Many, many guards had joined the pursuit.

Did they have no one better to chase in this wretched market? she thought.

Then, she remembered what the old man had called her. *Wildling.* He'd still been alive when she left him. Had he told the guards?

Wildlings weren't supposed to be here. There weren't laws against it, but who would be foolish enough to travel to the infamous Nightshade lands? Her. She was foolish enough.

She ran faster. They were on her heels.

The boiling blood—she tipped the cauldron over onto the streets, and it sizzled as it burned their feet. They cursed, and she was off again.

She turned a corner, into another branch of the market, and searched desperately for another path, but they were too quick, right behind her.

Her blade gripped in one hand and starstick in the other, she wondered which one she would have to use as she turned and climbed up a short wall. She ran as fast as she could, turned again, and found a nearly empty part of the market, half abandoned. Without risking a glimpse behind her, she fell to her knees.

Mercifully, though her starstick seemed temperamental on Nightshade, it worked. It was a simple, practiced movement. Drawing her portal, watching it ripple, preparing to jump through—

Before it fully settled, she heard footsteps in front of her. The puddle shrank and disappeared.

She looked up, only to find Grim standing in the center of the road.

"You," he said.

You.

The guards caught up to her then. She was roughly hauled to her feet, against one of them. He smelled of smoke and sweat. Before she could reach for her dagger, a dozen blades were at her throat.

Grim's eyes did not leave hers as he waved his hand and said, "Take her to the cells."

Her wrists were shackled to the ceiling. It had been hours, and her arms ached. The guards had taken her cloak, as if it had disgusted them that she dared wear their color. They had taken her starstick too.

Grim appeared in front of her cell and frowned. "Is that supposed to pass for black?"

He was looking at her silk dress.

She hadn't intended for it to be seen. She wasn't wearing anything beneath it. Her hands weren't available to cover up parts that she didn't want him to see, but he didn't even bother looking, giving her body the most cursory of glances before meeting her eyes.

"Demon," was all she said.

"Fool," he responded.

That she could not argue with.

She was the biggest fool in the realms for returning to this place when something bad happened every time she did.

With barely a move of his finger, the chains holding her to the ceiling melted into ash.

She fell to the ground in an undignified heap.

Grim studied her while she clutched her wrists, both raw and red. "You swore not to return."

Isla looked up at him. "No."

"No?"

"The promise from the duel was that I wouldn't return *here*, which, in the moment, meant your *bathroom*. Which I have no intention of ever doing again, don't you worry."

He looked at her with unfiltered disdain. "What are you doing on Nightshade?"

She said nothing.

Grim turned to go, and she rose to her feet. "You're keeping me here?"

He looked over his shoulder. "You appear in my realm, using a stolen relic. You stab me in the chest. You return and hide in my chambers. Then, you return yet again and attack an innocent man in the middle of the street."

She made a sound of indignation. "Innocent? He wanted to scalp me and sell my hair by the strand!"

Grim's eyes narrowed. "What type of people did you expect to encounter at the night market, Hearteater?" he asked. That last word dripped with mockery.

"My name is Isla," she said through her teeth, stepping closer to glare at him right through the bars of her cell.

"I will never call you that."

"Why?"

He looked down at her. "Calling someone by their first name is a sign of familiarity. Of respect."

Her nostrils flared. "You don't respect me?"

"You don't seem to respect your own life. Why should I?"

She scoffed. "Fine. Don't respect me. I don't care. You weren't why I came here."

"Clearly. Why *are* you here?" he demanded.

Isla crossed her arms, both in annoyance and to cover up her chest, inconveniently prickling in the freezing prison. "Why are *you* here?" she asked. "You clearly would love to see me rot. And it would benefit you at the Centennial." As soon as she said thc words, she regretted them. What if he turned away and never returned? What would she do? Escape was impossible without her starstick. She would waste away far beneath Nightshade. Even Celeste wouldn't be able to free her. She didn't even know Isla was venturing here for the gloves, didn't know she had met the Nightshade ruler before—

"I believe . . . we might be able to help each other," Grim said.

Shock rendered her silent.

"We are looking for the same thing."

Isla frowned. "You're looking for skin gloves?"

He looked at her strangely. "No. You are looking for a way to survive the Centennial, are you not?"

Of course she was. She didn't say a thing.

"I have a deal for you, then."

"A deal?"

He nodded. "I'm looking for a sword. I believe you can help me get it."

"What sword?" And why would he possibly think she could help him?

"A powerful one that very few people know exist," was all he said.

"What exactly does it do? What does it look like?"

He bared his teeth. "Do you think I'll tell you so you can rush off and try to find it yourself?"

"I wouldn't do that." That was exactly what she was planning to do. "So, I help you get the sword. What do I get out of it?"

Grim looked pointedly at the bars. "For starters, you wouldn't freeze to death in this cell, in that flimsy dress." Isla had dropped her arms, but she covered her chest again. "And, if you can help me, I will not only agree not to kill you at the Centennial, but I will also be your ally."

"You—you've decided to attend?"

"Only if you help me find the sword."

His aid would be invaluable. With Grim by her side—along with Celeste—she might really have a chance of surviving the hundred days on the island.

Still. Grim couldn't be trusted. She and Celeste had a plan. She would find a way to get the gloves. "No."

Grim's shadows flared around him. "No?"

She shrugged. "No."

His fingers twitched, as if desperate to turn her to ash, just as he had done with the shackles. Instead, he said, "Very well," and turned to leave.

He made it to the end of the hall before she said, "Wait. You wouldn't leave me here, would you?"

"I would."

Her eyes bulged. No, no, he wouldn't.

Who was she kidding? He was the ruler of Nightshade. Famed for his cruelty. He had killed thousands in his lifetime.

His steps retreated once more, before she said, "Fine! Fine. But only if you return my starstick."

His lip curled back in disgust. "Your *what*?"

"My portaling device."

With a flick of his wrist, it was in his hand. "I feel strongly that I will regret this," he said, eyes narrowed, as he slipped it to her.

She grinned, cradling it in her arms. It was her most prized possession. Grim just frowned at her.

That was how she made a deal with a demon.

REVELATIONS

"There is a sword."

Isla recounted her memory to Oro. It was the first one that seemed remotely helpful. "He said I could help him find it. He said it was powerful."

Oro's brows came slightly together. "Do you know anything else about it?"

"Not yet. But it might be the weapon the oracle says he has."

Oro nodded. "Then we need to find out what it does."

By the end of the day, Oro had dozens of people in every library and archive, searching for records of important swords.

Isla knew the answers would not be found in books but her own mind.

She just needed to remember.

The Wildlings didn't seem surprised at the idea of war.

"This is what we've always trained for," Wren said. There were nods around her.

"You—you want to fight?" Isla asked, doing her best to siphon surprise out of her tone. This was not really their battle. Wildlings hadn't been on Lightlark in five hundred years. None of her people had been alive before the curses. They had never even stepped foot on the island.

Asking them to potentially die protecting it seemed like a stretch.

"Are you giving us a choice?" Wren asked.

Isla hesitated. *Choice*. She was their ruler. She could have ordered them. *Should have*, probably. Now, Grim had Moonling. Cleo had been

building a legion. She had seen it herself during the Centennial, sneaking around the Moon Isle castle.

To defeat them, they would need as many warriors as they could get. Still . . .

"Yes," she said quickly. Once the word was out of her mouth, she couldn't take it back. "You have a choice." Isla studied her people. Some looked determined. Others looked wary. "I hadn't been to Lightlark until a few months ago," she said. "I could have returned here and ignored the threat on the island, but I know if Lightlark falls, so do we. Eventually, without that power . . . we will cease to exist. I see a future where we return and claim our isle again. I see a future where we use the power of the island to help regain everything we lost." She paused. "Who will fight alongside me for that future?"

For a moment, no one moved a muscle, and Isla's heart sank below her ribs. Wildlings were known to be among the best warriors. Without them—

One woman stepped forward. She had long hair tied into a braid and wore bracelets made from thorny vines.

Another.

Another.

Then, an entire group.

Isla wanted to smile, she wanted to cry, but she did neither. She nodded sharply and thanked them.

"For those who will not fight, I ask for something critical." She was honest with them. "Moonling joined Nightshade." There were a few murmurs. "They took their healers with them. To keep this war from destroying us, we need as many healing elixirs as possible."

"It's not something that can be rushed," Wren said. "We only have one small patch of the flower left."

Isla knew that. "We'll need to find more," she said. "We will need to search every inch of the isle for it." She sighed. "The elixir will be

the difference between life and death. We need everyone available to learn how to extract it."

Wren nodded.

She faced the rest of her people. "Grim is coming to destroy Lightlark." Her vision echoed in her head, and her heart started beating faster, each beat like the chime of a clock. "We are in a race to save thousands of lives."

Lynx was waiting for her in the woods outside the Wildling palace when she was done. Now that part of Wild Isle had been restored by her and Oro, she had contemplated bringing him to Lightlark.

With Nightshade approaching, however, she didn't know if it was the best idea.

"War is coming," Isla told him, wondering if he really could understand her. "I . . . I saw a vision a while ago. Of someone I used to care about, destroying the world . . ." She swallowed. "He's Nightshade, like my father."

Lynx's gaze sharpened.

"You must have known him, right? My . . . dad?"

The leopard blinked, and Isla didn't know if that was confirmation.

"The oracle said I'm the key. I'm the only one who can remember why he wants to destroy Lightlark, and how. I'm the only one who knows about the mysterious weapon he has. Some sword." She sighed. It was nice talking to someone, even if she wasn't sure he was listening. "I'm the only one who can open a door that has rejected me already, that is apparently extremely important in all of this." She laughed without humor, and Lynx just stared at her. "You know what? After the Centennial, I truly believed things could not get any worse. I was wrong. I . . . I was wrong about a lot of things."

Lynx didn't care. She knew that. She made to turn around, to leave him to his business, when he stopped her, with a quick nuzzle of his head that nearly sent her off-balance.

She turned around and found his head bent low. She reached out with careful fingers, and he allowed her to pet down his nose. His eyes closed, and he made a thrumming sound in his chest.

Her bonded didn't hate her. That was a relief. At least, he didn't hate her today.

Perhaps, Isla thought, it meant she had proven herself as a Wildling. Perhaps it meant she could finally open the vault.

Isla stood outside the hidden door. Voices echoed inside. It reminded her of being in the forest when her powers had first been released, a thousand mouths calling her forward. They were almost clear but muffled in meaning, like speaking underwater. She took another step and tried to listen. They became louder, more insistent.

A spark traveled up her spine, and she didn't dare move too quickly, in case it broke the connection. This was it all along, she thought. All she needed to do was connect to the vault, the same way Oro had taught her to form a link to her abilities. The same way she had begun to form a connection with Lynx.

Something in her recognized something in the hidden door. It pulled her forward, a hand gripping a thread behind her navel. It all felt so natural, so right, so fitting, just like the crown clicking into the lock, every twist and ridge lining up. Just like turning it, and pulling it—

Closed. It remained closed. It didn't move an inch, not even a sliver of an opening, like before. No force threw her across the room.

Just . . . nothing.

Isla ripped her crown from the lock and almost hurled it across the room. They had twenty-six days. Twenty-six days before—

Her vision flashed in front of her eyes, and she could almost smell the burning. She could almost feel the ashes landing on her bare arms as they swept over her in torrents. She coughed like the cinders were in her throat again, choking her. Screams sounded in her ears, followed by howls from dreks—

Dreks. That was new. She hadn't seen them in her vision before. They had suspected the drek attack was from Grim, but this was confirmation.

"We were right. He has dreks," Isla told Oro. She could still hear their howls in her head. "Last time was a bloodbath. How could we stand a chance against that many? Their skin is nearly impenetrable."

Oro sighed. "Ever since the first drek attack, I've had my best team looking for a special type of ore. It was mined a millennia ago and requires Sunling and Starling power to turn it to metal. When weapons were made from it, it's said that they could pierce even the thickest hides."

"Have any of those weapons survived?"

He shook his head. "If they did, none of us know where they are. We've already checked the castle's reserves."

So they would have to make new ones. "Who's looking for the ore? Have they had any progress?"

He looked at her. He seemed . . . almost nervous. "You've met Enya. Now, it's time for you to meet the rest of my friends."

Just an hour later, Oro led Isla into a room located in a turret at the back of the Mainland castle, with massive, curved windows overlooking the sea. A round table sat in its center, crafted from solid gold. It was a war strategy room. Oro walked to the windows and looked out at the horizon, in the direction of Nightshade.

Enya swept into the room at that moment. Her expression was pointed in concentration.

Two men who could not look more different walked in behind her. The only thing they shared was their significant height.

The much larger of the two was a Moonling. He had brown skin and a shock of white hair. His eyes were bright blue, framed by thick, dark lashes. He wore a sleeveless white tunic, and had the most muscled arms she had ever seen.

The other was Skyling. He was tall—though still shorter than the

Moonling—and lean. He had dark hair that tinted blue in the light, pale skin, and sharp cheekbones.

He narrowed his eyes at Isla and said, "So. You're the reason Oro doesn't see us anymore."

Enya gave him a look. "No, the reason he doesn't see us anymore is because the last time we got together, you called him an uptight wretch and asked when the last time he bedded someone was."

Isla raised an eyebrow. She glanced at Oro, who was glaring at his friends.

The Moonling sat down at the first available chair. "Well, he *was* dying," he said, shrugging. "He gets a partial pass on being a wretch."

"How generous of you," Oro said. He sighed and turned to Isla. "This is Calder."

The Moonling spoke up. "Cal, mostly." Despite looking like he could snap the table in half with his bare hands, there was something gentle about his demeanor. He had the kindest face she had ever seen.

"And Zed." The Skyling glared at her. He was studying her far too intently. Far too suspiciously.

Calder beamed. "Pleased to finally meet you." Isla took the hand he offered, her fingers laughably small next to his, and smiled weakly.

She shook her head. "I don't understand. I thought—"

"All Moonlings were like Cleo?"

She shrugged a shoulder.

He laughed, and it was a pleasant sound. "I can't blame you, after everything that happened, but . . . some opposed her. We are few, but some of us stayed."

"Like Soren."

There was a collective groan at the sound of his name.

"Cleo never trusted me in the slightest, of course. I moved to Sun Isle just before she cut the bridge."

Isla looked at the group and almost frowned. Enya was Sunling.

She understood how she and Oro had become friends. But from what she had seen, realms didn't often fraternize together. How—

"Wondering what we all have in common?" Enya asked casually.

She nodded.

"Him." Enya motioned to Oro.

Isla turned to him as he made his way to the front of the table. "You know that I was sent to train for years on each isle." He nodded at Calder. "He was the first in his class—in most subjects, anyway." He looked at Zed. "And he was the worst."

Zed grinned as if relishing the fact.

"He would have been the best, if the lessons were on anything he was remotely interested in," Enya muttered.

"What—what are you interested in?" she asked Zed, almost afraid to hear the answer.

"Thieving, for one," he said.

Isla frowned. "Who do you steal from?"

Zed nodded at Oro. "Him, mostly."

Oro sighed. "Zed likes to prove the supposed inadequacy of my guards every few years. He started breaking into the castle when he was a child. My father would have banished him from the island if he hadn't been my friend."

"No," Zed drawled. "He would have banished me, if he had actually been able to capture me."

Enya rolled her eyes. "He's the fastest Skyling in recent record, and rest assured, he will find an excuse to mention it at least three times during this conversation."

Isla raised an eyebrow at Oro. "Even with five hundred years of extra practice, you still can't beat him?"

Zed's eyes sparkled. "Perhaps he could. Let's check, Oro, shall we?"

Cal leaned back in his chair, making the wood groan. "You'll learn this, but they are annoyingly competitive."

Enya shook her head. "They are both annoying period, but Cal here has always preferred playing peacemaker to beating them both, even when they have definitely deserved it."

Zed raised an eyebrow. "To beat me, Enya, he would have to—"

"Catch you, we get it," she said, muttering something else under her breath. She shot a look at Isla. "See? I don't exaggerate."

By the time Zed turned back to face her, any amusement in his face had withered away. "So. You're Nightshade."

The air seemed sucked out of the room. Isla turned to Oro, who was staring at Zed like he was an enemy and not seemingly one of his oldest friends. "Zed," he said darkly, the word a warning.

"He didn't tell me," Zed continued, ignoring Oro. "A forest turned to ash on Sky Isle. The place next to it looked like a damned palace garden. It wasn't hard to put together."

"Zed—" Oro said.

"I am Nightshade," she said.

The room went silent.

Zed leaned back in his chair and stared at her. For a moment, he almost looked impressed. "I wasn't expecting you to admit it."

Isla sat straighter. "It is what I am. I can't control it more than you can control your dark-blue hair, or he can control the fact that he was born in a realm ruled by a witch." She motioned to Calder.

Enya nodded. "It's true," she said, looking at Zed as if to scold him. "All of us were born different, in one way or another. It's what brought us together."

Calder shook his head. He tried to smile at Isla. "Ignore him. He's just moody that Oro hasn't been joining our weekly games. The teams aren't even."

"Games?" Isla wondered.

Calder's grin grew. He opened his mouth, excited, but Oro stopped him.

"Enough interrogating Isla and talk of games," Oro said, setting his hands on the table. He looked pointedly at his friends. "We are at war, or have you all forgotten why I asked you to meet?"

That sobered the room.

Enya's expression became focused again. "Oro and I have the Sunling forces set up. Most are rusty, but our numbers are strong, and they are training as we speak."

"Do they need weapons?" Zed asked.

"No," Enya said. "All can wield. It's better they're not weighed down by swords or armor."

"Same for the flight force," Zed said. He glanced at Oro. "Is Azul coming?"

Oro nodded. "He's in a representative meeting, but he'll be here soon." He looked at Isla.

"Wildling warriors have volunteered. They can all wield and are training now. We have our own weapons." She looked at Calder hopefully. "Are you a healer?"

Enya made a choking noise, and Calder gave his friend a look. He smiled sheepishly when he turned back to Isla. "Currently the best on Lightlark."

"Because all the other healers are on Nightshade," Zed said smoothly.

Isla's smile faltered. Great. "We have healing elixir and are trying our best to make more of it. Starlings have volunteered to fight, but we see their best contribution as creating a shield around parts of the Mainland."

Zed nodded. "Smart," he admitted.

"I'm still trying to figure out how many talented wielders are on Star Isle, but I'm going to assume they're limited." She had asked Maren to get back to her with a list of the best, but so far she hadn't received it. "So, the shield will be small, but it might mean we can reduce where Nightshade can attack."

Calder nodded. "I can freeze parts of the sea around the island to limit where their ships are able to land too."

"He's not coming from the sea." Dread churned in Isla's stomach.

Calder frowned. "You think he'll arrive from the skies?"

"No."

That was when she told them about Grim's portaling flair. He and his army could appear anywhere, at any time. There would be no warning except for the one he had already given them.

Silence.

Zed paled even more. He bit out a curse word that almost perfectly encapsulated the situation.

"Exactly," Oro said. "To have any chance at winning, we need to be smart. We need to be ready."

"We need to find out why he's coming to destroy Lightlark in the first place," Zed said.

She agreed with him. All she had to do was remember. "Until we figure that out, Wildlings can work with the island's topography," she said. "We can cover the Mainland in barbs, or thorns, or poisonous plants, so they are forced to appear exactly where we want them." She remembered a grain of something helpful from her memories. "Bog sand, even. It . . . traps anyone that steps in it."

Oro nodded. He looked impressed. "We can fence them in."

"Exactly."

Zed leaned back in his chair. "That won't stop the winged beasts, though. We can only assume Grim will bring them."

Dreks. Her gaze met Oro's.

She knew she should probably tell them about her vision, but they were strangers. She couldn't trust them with the knowledge of her and Grim's history, or their memories . . .

It was a good thing Zed brought the creatures up first. He was right. She and the rest of the Wildlings could use nature to make the Mainland as uninhabitable as possible, but none of that stopped creatures that could fly.

"You haven't been able to locate the ore yet?" Oro asked.

Zed shook his head. "We're working on it, but the Forgotten Mines are tough to navigate, and the ores are almost impossible to extract. We should be able to get some soon, though."

"We need that metal," Enya said. "Making arrows for the Skylings should be the priority. They'll be crucial in the air, so those creatures don't pick us all off."

Yes. The Skylings would be critical. Without them at the coronation, many more people would have died.

Just then, Azul rushed in, wind on his back. "Apologies. The meeting went . . . longer than anticipated." Isla noticed Azul's typically jovial tone was completely missing. His expression was grave. He didn't even bother sitting down, before saying, "We have a problem."

"My people want to leave Lightlark," Azul said.

The world came to a halt. No one moved a muscle. Isla remembered how silent the Skyling representatives had been during their meeting.

No. They had already lost Moonling. They couldn't lose another realm. Wildling and Starling were the smallest; even with her people fighting, it wasn't enough—

"It's decided?" Calder asked.

"Not yet. But there will be a vote soon, and it isn't looking good."

Oro's eyes were raging amber. "We need you in the skies." His hands were pressed firmly against the table.

"I know," Azul said. "I want to fight. It is not my choice, however. My realm—"

"The island will fall," Oro said, his voice rising. "You understand that would be the end of your people. One generation, maybe two, and then the power you draw from would dry up."

Azul sighed. His eyes were bloodshot. He looked tired, like he had been up all night arguing with his representatives. "I know that, Oro," he said. "I do. But in the end, it will be their decision."

"How do we change it?" Enya said. "There has to be something they want. Something your realm needs."

Azul shook his head. "I spoke to them for hours. I don't think there's any changing their mind. There will be debates. Then, a vote." He didn't look hopeful. Azul's eyes were burning then, filled with meaning he hadn't put into words, as he looked at them. "I'm sorry," he said.

He left the room, and there was silence.

Heat swept across them all. Oro's brow was pinched. He ran a hand down his face.

"If we lose Skyling, we lose the war," Enya said. Her eyes were on the table. She was leaned back in her chair. "The winged beasts will decimate us, if Grim brings them, even if we do manage to find the special metal."

"Then we can't lose Skyling," Zed said.

She threw her hands up. "You heard him, Skylings cannot be bought or bartered with. Nothing we have could convince them."

Oro pressed two fingers against the side of his head. "The Skyling vote will take time. We have to operate under the assumption that we will lose the flight force and a large part of our legion."

"We need more soldiers, then," Zed said. He leaned farther back in his chair. "Calder and I already went to the corners of Lightlark. Gathered all the outside communities. Most have agreed to fight. Without Moonling and Skyling, it's still not enough though, and we've exhausted our allies."

A thought occurred to Isla. Oro's eyes met hers as she said, "Then what if we turn to our enemies?"

"Which enemies?" Enya asked.

"The Vinderland." The violent group they had encountered on their search for the heart of Lightlark.

"Absolutely not," Oro said.

"We're desperate, Oro," she said. "We just likely lost another realm."

"We're not that desperate," he said through his teeth.

"We need more warriors. *They* are warriors."

Oro shook his head, unbelieving. “Do I need to remind you that I watched them put *an arrow through your heart*?”

He didn’t need to remind her. She saw the angry mark in the mirror every time she got dressed. If it hadn’t been for the power of the heart of Lightlark, and Grim saving her, she would be dead.

Isla shrugged a shoulder. “That’s in the past. We need them now. And we have a common enemy. They already hate Moonlings, right? They’ll likely hate them more now that they’ve teamed up to destroy their home.”

“Who they hate most is *Wildlings*,” Oro said pointedly.

Isla knew that. Oro had told her during the Centennial that the Vinderland used to be Wildlings, far before the curses ever existed. She stood from her chair without breaking his gaze. “But I am not just Wildling,” she said. She was also Nightshade. The Vinderland were not the only people who lived in the shadows of the island. There were other night creatures they had encountered during the Centennial. Perhaps she could convince them to fight.

Remlar had said it before—*she’s one of us*. She had pushed her darkness down. Perhaps she could use it.

“No,” Oro said.

Isla stood her ground. “Are you telling me I can’t?”

A muscle in his jaw worked. “You are free to do as you wish,” he said. “But this is reckless.” His face softened. “We have time. We don’t know if we’re losing Skyling yet.”

At the end of the meeting, Enya stayed back with Isla. When Oro was out of earshot, she said, “He is blinded when it comes to you. He forgets his duty.” She placed a hand on her shoulder. “If you decide to go to the Vinderland for help, I will go with you.”

With Skyling likely gone, Isla’s memories became more important than ever. She trained with Remlar any chance she could. He taught her use of her shadows.

Now, he stopped in front of a tree. It was so wide five men would not be able to link hands and reach around it.

"This is a kingwood," he said. "It takes hundreds of years for it to get this big. This one has seen all the Centennials, Egan's rule, and even that of his father."

Isla pressed a hand against it. The thread between it and her was clear. Shining.

"Kill it."

She blinked. "What?"

Remlar's expression didn't change. "Use your Nightshade powers. And kill it."

"No." Her answer was immediate. She was the ruler of Wildling. Her allegiance was to nature, not the darkness. She was here only to pry the memories from her mind.

Remlar raised an eyebrow. "Have you killed people before, Wildling?"

She thought about the Moonling nobles, blood puddling on the abandoned docks. Countless others who were hazy in her mind . . . almost masked. By time. By *him*.

"Yes."

"Yet you won't kill a tree?"

Isla glared at him. "The people I killed deserved it. This tree has done nothing. Who am I to end it? For the sake of . . . practice?"

Remlar frowned. "Practice? I thought you needed answers. Answers to how to save thousands of people. A tree is but a small sacrifice."

"No," she said again.

Remlar grinned. "You have killed countless plants. When I untangled your powers, you destroyed an entire forest."

"That was an accident!"

"Does it change the fact that you are responsible for killing the woods?"

Isla closed her eyes tightly. No. It didn't.

Remlar sighed. "Nature is a flowing force," he said. "You destroy one tree, you create another. Pick one flower, plant another. The ash it turns into becomes fertilizer for another. It is a never-ending turning of a wheel, and there is no ending, or beginning, just constant turning, turning, turning."

"You're not making any sense."

"The tree does not care if you kill it," he said. "It will return as something better, something different. Everything that is ruined—especially by your hand, especially *here*—is reclaimed, remade."

Could that be true?

Remlar said it again. "Kill the tree. Leech it of its life . . . then create something new."

Create something new. If Remlar was right, she wasn't truly killing it . . . just turning it into something different.

Isla placed her hand against the tree.

Shadows curled out of her chest, flowing through her, turning liquid. They unfolded, and expanded, until she tasted metal in her mouth, and then, through her fingers . . . there was energy. Not only pouring out . . . but pouring in. Something vital, flowing out of the tree, and into her.

It was delicious.

Like gulping water after a day in the desert, Isla was suddenly desperately parched. The bark cracked beneath her fingers, split, shriveled. Branches and leaves fell and were ash before they hit the ground. By the time she was done, all that remained of the tree was a skeleton.

Isla was gasping. She was too full, a glass overflowing. She made it one step before falling to her hands and knees.

Life exploded out of her.

Dozens of tiny trees, just saplings, burst from the ground, breaking through the dirt.

She flipped over to her back, breathing like she still couldn't get enough air. Just a moment later, Remlar's head and the tops of his wings were blocking her view of the sky.

"I was right, Wildling," he said, sounding quite pleased with himself. She heard his voice before falling into another memory. "You are the only person living who is able to turn death . . . into life."

BEFORE

She was doing it. She was really going to work with . . . him. The Nightshade appeared in the corner of her room, as if emerging from her thoughts, shadow melting into a ruler dressed all in black.

He didn't say a word. He just looked at her, frowning, as though he found every part of her disappointing.

Isla glared at him. "You do know *you* asked to work with me," she said.

Grim frowned even more. She hadn't known a frown of that magnitude was even possible. "I am aware," he said curtly.

With about as much revulsion as possible, he outstretched his hand. It was gloved this time, as if he couldn't bear having his skin touch hers.

He hated her. She didn't really understand why. Was it because she was Wildling? Was it because she had seriously injured him during their first meeting?

It didn't matter. She had been raised to hate him too. Nightshades were villains. Theirs was the only realm that drew power from darkness. Their abilities were mysterious, intrusive, vile. They had the power to spin curses. Most people thought *he* was responsible for them.

She reminded herself that working with him meant he wouldn't become her enemy during the Centennial. He could be the only reason she actually survived it.

"Wait," she said. "If my guardians come in and see I'm gone—" They usually granted her privacy after training, but it wasn't night yet. They could very well check in on her while she was away.

"I'm going to set an illusion in your room."

Oh. She supposed he had thought of nearly everything.

So why did he need her? It didn't make any sense.

"Great. Let's get this over with," she said, taking his hand.

Before the final word left her mouth, they were gone.

They landed on the edge of a cliffside made up of lustrous black rocks, crudely puzzled together. Ocean crashed hundreds of feet high, so close she could smell the sea spray. Rain instantly flattened her hair against her face in wild strands. It soaked her to the bone. She shivered immediately.

Isla heard the unforgiving sound of iron banging against iron, far above. They were on a ledge.

"Where are we?" she asked, gasping through the wind and cold. She wasn't sure where she was expecting Grim to take her first on their search, but it wasn't here.

"Before we look for the sword, I need to pay a little visit to its creator," he said simply. "The blacksmith."

From Grim's mouth the title sounded ancient.

"We'll have to climb the rest of the way to his forge," Grim said before stepping in front of her, toward the next wall of dark rocks. He didn't offer an explanation. Could he not use his abilities close by? Did he not want the blacksmith to sense him coming? With one gloved hand on the rocks, he suddenly turned as if in afterthought and said, "Don't let the rocks cut you."

Grim started up the wall. She reluctantly followed.

The rocks were slippery in the rain. Isla grabbed one and had to strain the muscles in her fingers just to hold on. By the time she moved a few feet, she looked up to see that Grim was already almost halfway up. Demon. He would leave her if she wasn't quick enough.

She squinted through the rain as she fought to grasp the next rock. The next. Her shoes were made with special bark at the bottom that had a good grip, at least. She climbed higher. Higher.

While she moved her feet into their next positions, her fingers

suddenly slipped, and her heart seemed lodged in her throat in the slice of a second it took to find another hold. She grabbed it desperately, without caring about the sharp corners.

Blood seeped down her hand, warm against the freezing rain. So much for not cutting herself. The rocks were sharp as knives. She risked a quick look down and swallowed. From this height, scraping against them would disembowel her before the fall would kill her.

Her gaze traveled up. And up. She was less than halfway done. There was no way she could make it, not without slipping again.

Isla closed her eyes. Her mind was running wild with fear and a thousand stressful scenarios that hadn't happened yet, so she focused on her breathing. This was unfamiliar terrain, but she had climbed her entire life. Terra would have told her that any climb could be broken into smaller steps. She started up again, concentrating only on the path right in front of her. And breathing.

She inched up the rock face, fingers carefully dodging the sharpest points of the stones. They were each long and narrow, a thousand giant crystals crushed together to form a wall. Her hand screamed in pain, and red kept streaming, even after the rain cleaned it, again and again. She would need to use her Wildling healing elixir when she returned to her room.

Almost there.

Before she could reach for the final few rocks, strong arms pulled her up the rest of the way, careful not to drag her against the cliffside. Then she was unceremoniously discarded on the ground. Mud squelched below her. She imagined she was now caked in it.

She glared at Grim, hovering above. His dark hair was plastered down his forehead, over his eyes, down half of the bridge of his nose. Even without his armor, he looked terrifying. She thought about the rumor that he had killed thousands with his blade, and the fact that this might have been their last sight. A towering shadow. "You are an exceptionally slow climber," he said. "I should have left you behind."

He turned on his heel and continued the rest of the way.

Isla muttered words that Poppy and Terra certainly didn't know she used as she followed him.

The banging of steel now rang through the rain, so loud, Isla winced as they got closer. Thunder rumbled above as if warring with the sound. The very ground seemed to tremble.

They climbed at a sharp incline, until finally, at the top of the hill, a structure came into view. Grim paused, his black cape whipping wildly in the wind.

The blacksmith's house was no more than a shed. It was made of the same stone that had cut her hand, and she could only imagine the type of tools necessary to be able to not just forage those rocks . . . but build from them.

The door was open, and flashes of red flickered through the entrance. Sparks from the molten-hot flames.

Abruptly, the banging stopped.

Grim slowly turned to face her. His eyes found her hand, still dripping in blood. "You fool," he muttered. "He will try to kill you."

Then Grim vanished.

Isla was alone. She looked down at her hand. It had already dripped a small puddle of blood below her. Could the blacksmith sense blood?

Was he a creature?

Her eyes searched through the rain, but she couldn't see anything. There was only one thought in her mind, carved from basic instinct and training.

Run.

She took off down the side of the hill, into a forest. She didn't know if nature was dangerous everywhere, but she would rather take the risk of the woods hurting her over a blacksmith who sensed blood.

Her heart drummed in her ears as she fought her way through the thicket. The branches cut through her clothes. She used her arms as shields, barreling her way through.

She felt the moment the creature entered the woods. All her senses seemed to heighten in warning. The forest itself seemed to still. Chills swept down her spine. It was as if her body knew there was a predator. And she was being hunted.

There was the crack of splitting bark as an arrow lodged itself an inch to her right, into the tree at her side. It was metal tipped. It would have gone right through her neck, with better aim. She gasped and took off again.

Another arrow whizzed by, and Isla didn't even bother to look where it went. She just ran and ran, crashing through branches and jumping over snaking vines.

The forest dipped low, and she lost her footing.

Suddenly, she was falling. She screamed out as her shoulder crunched painfully, her elbow scraped against a rock, her leg moved in an awkward direction. Her body tumbled quickly, only stopping when she hit a tree.

Then, silence as the world stilled and her pain caught up with her. She screamed soundlessly against the back of her hand. Dirt and mud caked her every inch. Her shoulder—something was wrong with it. Her entire body felt like a bruise.

Get up, that instinct in her mind said.

It was too late.

Footsteps sounded close by. Heavy steps that she heard even through the rain. Isla didn't dare move a muscle as the predator inched closer. Closer.

He stopped right in front of her.

The blacksmith leaned down, crouched to look upon the heap that was her broken body.

That was when she struck. She gripped the dagger she always kept on her and stabbed the blacksmith right through the eye.

He roared, and Isla scrambled to her feet. It took one step to realize something had happened to her ankle. She couldn't move—

She *had* to move.

Isla spotted a fence and limped forward. It was high. The gate was open. If she could just get through, maybe she could get it closed. Maybe she could figure out a plan.

She could hear the blacksmith getting up. He roared words into the rain that she didn't understand. She didn't dare turn around.

The whistle of an arrow, and she ducked low. It skimmed right above her head. She leaped to the side—her shoulder and ankle screaming in pain—behind a tree, and another arrow flew past.

She ran the last few steps, dragging her foot behind her, until she was past the fence. Her shaking hands hauled the gate closed and she collapsed against it.

Her teeth gritted against the pain. She closed her eyes as her body trembled against the gate. Hopefully it would hold. Her hands ran down its strange pattern. It was so smooth. Made of mismatched parts. So—

She opened her eyes. Looked behind her at the gate. And found that the entire fence was made of melded skulls and bones.

A yelp escaped her throat, and she scrambled back on the muddy ground, her fingers sinking into it. Her back crashed into something solid, and she screamed again.

Just then, the entire gate ripped off its hinges.

The blacksmith stood there, her dagger still lodged through his eye.

He was the most muscular man Isla had ever seen. His arms were enormous. He was holding a massive hammer that looked like it would go right through her body if she was hit with it. He had long, flowing black hair. Skin the pallor of a corpse.

Isla scrambled back against the other wall she had hit, a scream lodged in her throat.

The wall spoke. It sounded bored. "You can't have her, Baron. At least . . . not yet." She looked up and saw Grim frowning down at her. Not a wall. She had crashed into his legs. He raised an eyebrow. "I told you not to cut yourself, Hearteater."

The overwhelming urge to put a dagger through *his* eye filled her, but she couldn't stand again if she tried.

The blacksmith—*Baron*—hissed and returned the hammer to a holster on his back. "Ruler," he said, bending onto a knee. "To what do I owe the honor?"

"Black diamond hilt. Twin blades. You know the sword."

The blacksmith smiled proudly. Isla wondered if he was ever going to take the blade out of his eye. "I do. A very special weapon indeed. Among my best work."

Grim motioned toward her. "You've sensed her blood. Can she help me find it?"

The blacksmith pursed his lips. Considered. "She can."

This was why he needed her. Isla was trembling on the ground, but she found her voice long enough to say, "Why can't he find it himself?" She wondered if the blacksmith would answer her after she stabbed him in the face. Or if Grim would even allow him to.

The blacksmith met her gaze with his now single eye, and a shiver snaked down her spine. After a moment, he said, "The sword was cursed so no Nightshade ruler can claim it. If the sword so much as senses his ability, it will disappear."

So Grim couldn't use his powers to find it. This was why he needed her . . . though that didn't make sense.

Why not force one of his people to search for it? Why choose one of his rivals in the Centennial?

Before she could ask anything else, Grim said, "Do you know where it is?"

"Decades ago, I heard it had been stolen from a Skyling market. I sensed it return here, to Nightshade. Since then, nothing." He frowned. "I can't feel it anymore. Wherever it is . . . it's slumbering."

"Is there anything else we should know?"

The blacksmith opened his mouth again. His eyes darted to Isla. Then he closed his mouth. "Nothing else," he said.

"Good. Now, return the dagger. We'll be going."

The blacksmith roughly pulled Isla's weapon from his eye. What was left . . . Isla looked away to keep from retching.

He bent low to return it to her. Isla reached out with shaking fingers. Dark blood coated her blade. The rain only partially washed it away.

Before he handed it back, the blacksmith said, "You weren't supposed to be able to do that."

Then he walked back up through the forest to his forge, and Isla was left with burning questions.

And anger.

She turned on the ground to face Grim. "You *demon*. You almost got me killed. You—"

He rolled his eyes. "I was there. You were never in any danger."

Isla's entire body shook with her fury. "Never in any danger? My ankle—something is wrong with it. And my *shoulder*." She shook her head. "Why? Why let him hunt me?"

Grim shrugged. "I wanted to see how you would fare without me. Call it curiosity."

"Curiosity? Curiosity?" She attempted to stand, dagger gripped tightly in her hand, but her ankle rolled, and she nearly fell over.

Grim caught her beneath the arms. She tried to shake herself away, but it was no use. His grip was hard as marble.

"Why didn't you use your Wildling powers in the forest?" he asked.

The lie came easily. "You didn't portal directly to the house. You didn't use your own powers. I figured . . . there was a reason."

He just stared down at her.

She tried to move away again, then grimaced as pain shot down her shoulder. Grim held her still. He frowned. "It's out of its socket. I have to right it." Grim twisted her around, so her back was to him. He leaned down and said, "This will hurt."

Before she could object, his hands twisted, and she screamed so loudly, it hurt her own ears.

"Done," he said. "Now, there's nothing I can do about that ankle."

"Just—just portal me to my room," she said. The Wildling healing elixir would take care of the swelling, but it would be weeks before she walked the same again. She would have to come up with an excuse for Terra and Poppy. Pretend she had sprained it in training, or something else.

Her teeth gritted against the pain that roared again with their landing. She looked down at herself. She was a mess. Covered in dirt and mud. She would need about a thousand baths, and a quarter vial of healing elixir.

Tears stung as she closed her eyes. Was this what it would be like working with the Nightshade demon? Getting hurt? Running for her life from an ancient being for *curiosity's* sake?

She opened her eyes again and was surprised to see the Nightshade was still in the center of her room, leaking darkness everywhere.

"Can you not do that?" she snapped, watching the shadows uncurl, spreading themselves all over her stuff, only to return and repeat the process.

The shadows twitched, as if they had heard her and were offended.

Stupid. A shadow can't have its feelings hurt.

Grim looked appalled. "You do not give me orders, witch."

She glared at him. "I thought I was *Hearteater*," she said, in about the most syrupy tone she could manage.

He glared back.

This was her chance to get answers. "Why did he have so many bones?"

"The blacksmith kills people with unique abilities and makes weapons from their blood and bones. He senses blood close by and kills anyone he can find, on the off chance they are useful." So why had he seemed desperate to have her blood?

Isla swallowed. She could have very well joined the fence of bones and skulls. Her people would have fallen. The blacksmith was ancient.

He'd seemed surprised that she was able to harm him. She had never been more grateful to have her dagger.

"So you can't use your abilities during our search. You will have to be powerless."

Grim said nothing.

Why was Grim the one looking for this sword? Not using his powers seemed like a massive inconvenience. Didn't he have people for that? Didn't he have far better things to do? She asked all these questions, in quick succession, and Grim's annoyance grew.

"You talk too much," he growled, and, for some reason, that stung.

Isla's chest felt as if someone were sitting on it. "I don't usually have people to talk to," she murmured.

His tone didn't get any gentler as he said, "This is too important for me to tell anyone in my court. I can't risk sending someone else or trusting them with any of my information." He hesitated before saying, "I've been betrayed in the search for the sword before."

Someone betrayed him? Why?

Would he betray her?

Isla turned to him, an eyebrow raised. "But you trust me?"

"Absolutely not." He took a step toward her. Another. "If you have any desire at all to survive the Centennial, you will not tell anyone in your court either."

Her court. She didn't even know what that was. Celeste didn't have a court, just her string of guardians who died every few years and were replaced, an endless cycle. Terra and Poppy were the only people Isla saw regularly.

As if she would ever tell any of them. They would all call her a fool for working with the Nightshade. They would ensure she could never leave her room again until the Centennial.

"What about the blacksmith? He knows we're looking for it."

Grim shook his head gruffly. "He won't remember."

She tilted her head at him. "Why?"

"Few people are foolish enough to visit him in the first place. But, in an abundance of caution, I took his memories away."

Isla blinked. "That's something . . . you can do?"

He nodded, as if it were not the cruelest power in the world.

"It's . . . permanent?"

"If I want it to be."

She shivered. There were still so many unanswered questions. If he needed the sword so badly, why didn't he look for it before? Why now? What had changed?

Isla wondered if she should back out. Grim was clearly using her. Now she wasn't even sure if what he had promised was worth the risk.

She and Celeste had a plan for the Centennial. She hadn't managed to find the skin gloves, but there was still time. Almost a year.

Isla looked around her room. The glass cage. Grim was insufferable, but the search for the sword promised something she had longed for since she was a child. Freedom. Escape, for just a while.

"So . . ." she said, wondering if she was making a huge mistake. The blacksmith had said the sword was stolen and last sensed on Grim's territory. "Who are the best thieves on Nightshade?"

PREMONITION

There was still no word on the Skyling vote. It had been pushed back, after much debate. Most Wildlings trained for war, and the rest worked nonstop to make more healing elixirs. Starlings on the newland were creating special armor for them, infused with energy.

Now, she needed to focus on the shield. Maren had promised Isla a list of the greatest wielders on Star Isle, to determine how large it would be.

Days had passed without her request being fulfilled. It was unlike Maren, who had managed all other aspects of preparing for the incoming war and evacuation with ease. Enya had helped Isla provide direct aid to Star Isle in the last few weeks—food, resources, guards at their bridge—and Maren had managed everything without issue.

She was clearly surprised to see Isla when she stepped foot on Star Isle.

"Isla," Maren said. "I wasn't expecting you today. We can get—"

"Who is the best Starling at wielding?" Isla asked. "Just—just take me to them." Her tone was harsh, but Grim was coming in only twenty days. They couldn't waste a moment.

Maren didn't meet her eyes. It took her several seconds to even say a word. "There are a few who are skilled. I can take you to them."

"No," Isla said. "Who is the best?" She frowned. "Is it—is it you?" Was that why Maren had been evasive?

Maren shook her head.

"Then who?"

The Starling met her eyes. The intensity there took Isla aback. "The king hasn't changed his mind about taking fighters who aren't volunteers?"

"No. No one is being forced to fight. We just need energy for the shield."

"Can . . . can the pooling of energy be anonymous?"

Anonymous? Isla was getting irritated. "I suppose so. Why?"

Maren's expression became more intense than usual. "Promise me," she said. "If I tell you, promise that you won't tell anyone."

Isla frowned. She was her ruler. She didn't have to make promises in exchange for information. Still, she saw the fierceness in Maren's face and nodded. "I won't tell anyone but the king."

Maren considered. She closed her eyes. "I will show you," she said.

She took her to a field of craters. They were holes in the isle like stars had fallen from the sky and left their marks. Someone stood in one of the craters' center.

Streams of silver shot from their hands in glittering ribbons. They whipped against the sides of the crater, piercing the rock, slicing through it like butter. Creatures formed from the sparks, and they slithered, jumped, flew around the crater, contained only by its perimeter. It was a dazzling display of power.

It was Cinder.

Isla's mouth had dropped open watching. Cinder wielded power like a master. Her stances, the liquidous movements of her arms—everything was so natural, as if she'd been alive for many multiples of her actual age.

She jumped down into the crater, and the little girl whipped around. A smile transformed her features. "Isla!"

"Who was your teacher?" she asked in lieu of greeting. "Are they still living?"

Cinder regarded her strangely. "Teacher?" She looked to Maren,

who had carefully made her way down one of the crater's edges. Maren only shrugged a shoulder.

"Who taught you to wield this way?" Isla shook her head in disbelief. "I was told there weren't any Starling masters left. How many can wield like you? You must have started training before you could walk! You must practice every moment."

Cinder laughed. "No, not really." She shrugged. "I'm just good at it, I guess."

I guess?

Isla looked to Maren, who seemed wary. She stepped to the opposite side of the crater, away from Cinder, and Isla followed. "When she was two years old, I heard her laughing in a room all alone. I came in to find her playing with a perfect ball of sparks. One she had created herself."

Isla's brows came together. "But that . . . that shouldn't be possible, should it? Someone who isn't a ruler being that powerful?"

"It is certainly unusual. She is the best wielder on the isle." She lowered her voice. "And she is the only reason any of us survived the fire that destroyed our homes."

Cinder was laughing as she created an animal with a crown of antlers out of sparks. It hopped on its haunches, jumping around her in a circle. Isla understood now. "That's why you've never let her leave," she said. "You don't want anyone else to know."

Maren nodded. "She is more a sister to me than a cousin. Having any family relation is rare for Starlings. She is my responsibility. She is everything to me."

Cinder blasted over, propelled by Starling energy shooting out of both of her palms. "Your turn, Isla! The crater is so plain and boring. Paint it with flowers!"

Maren gave her a look. "She is our ruler, Cinder. You do not command her."

"It's all right," Isla said, smiling. She raised her hand, and flowers bloomed across the ground.

"Pretty! Make a beast next! Make one like I do, but out of plants and sticks and stuff!"

Her expression faltered, just a little. "I—I don't think I can, Cinder."

Cinder frowned. "Why not?"

"I'm only now learning to wield. I'm not a master. Not yet."

Cinder tilted her head, her dark hair falling across her forehead. "You can't fully wield power?" A little crease appeared between her brows. "But . . . it's so easy."

"Cinder."

"Especially for a ruler. Right?"

"*Cinder*."

"And you have *so much*, you—"

"Cinder!" Maren took her hand and began leading her away. "That's enough. And enough of this," she said.

Isla had the impression that Maren had restricted Cinder to use her power only during certain time frames and within the confines of this crater.

"Maren," Isla said, stepping forward while Cinder collected her things. Her voice was low. "We need her to provide energy for the shield." And possibly, Isla thought, to turn ore into the essential metal, if Zed and Calder managed to extract it. Maren looked from Cinder to Isla warily. "We're going to cover most of the Mainland with thorns and bog sand, but walls of energy will be critical to limit where Nightshade can strike."

Maren closed her eyes. "You promise to keep it anonymous?"

"I give you my word. She can form her part of the shield with no one else around."

"Fine," Maren said. Then, she called Cinder to her in a sharp tone. "We're leaving," she said. As she was taken away, Cinder looked over her shoulder and smiled. With a flick of her tiny hand, she sent a flurry of sparks to Isla that fell from the sky like glitter.

. . .

Isla told Oro about Cinder before bed. She was walking around the room, speaking with her hands, trying to demonstrate what the little girl had done.

"What do you make of it?" she asked, turning to face him when she was done.

"I think Cinder sounds like a very special child."

"Have those existed?" she asked.

"A few, over the centuries. There have been non-rulers born with flairs, even. Unfortunately, their tales often end in tragedy. Maren is right to keep her hidden."

Isla frowned. "But you're the king. Couldn't you protect her?"

"I could order an army to stand around her at all times. I could send for her to come live here, in the castle. Would you like that?"

"No," she said. Cinder's life seemed difficult, but in many ways she was free. The castle or legion would just become a thicker prison.

She took a step toward the bed, exhausted, when her vision suddenly went dark. Her limbs went numb—her body folded over. Before she hit the ground, she was in Oro's arms. Physically, warmth surrounded her.

Mentally, all she felt was cold.

It was her vision again, clearer than ever.

Darkness fell from the sky, night cut into pieces. It pressed onto her skin, got stuck in her eyelashes. Howls. Dreks.

Screams. People dying all around her.

Through it all, she saw Grim. The darkness touched everything but him. He was its source.

He was looking at her. He didn't look at the dying around him, he just looked right at her and stalked toward her with a concentration that cut through her like a blade.

Run, a voice inside her head said. *Leave. Save yourself.*

She either couldn't or didn't. She stayed there as darkness parted her lips and forced her to drink it.

She tasted death on the back of her tongue.

Then, in her chest.

Something was wrong. Something was very wrong.

Isla tried to fight it, but it was no use. In her vision, her organs began to shut down, one by one.

She felt it, as every part of her withered away.

She felt herself die.

Oro was cradling her in his arms. Apparently, she had been screaming. Tears choked her words, as she tried to explain what she had seen. Her vision, but more. It was clearer now. Longer. Before, she had seen only Grim's darkness and destruction.

Now, she knew how it ended.

"He kills me," she said. "In the future, he kills me."

Heat nearly set the room aflame. Oro's lip curled over his teeth. She had never seen him more murderous than she did now. "Then we will kill him first."

Her eyes rolled to the back of her head as she fell into another memory.

BEFORE

Poppy and Terra had sealed the loose pane in her room. She'd had to tell them about it in an elaborate story to explain her sprained ankle. For hours, Terra had screamed at her about how foolish she was.

Poppy wrapped her ankle in medicinal bark, and as punishment, Terra trained her harder in ways that didn't require putting weight on her legs. It took ten days for her to walk close to normally again. She wondered if Grim would look for the sword without her, but he waited until she was almost fully healed.

He didn't do it out of the kindness of his heart, she knew. It was because he needed her. She was integral to his search. She just needed to figure out how she fit into his plan.

Grim appeared in her room. He had a hold on his powers. The shadows that typically leaked from his feet were gone. His crown and cape were missing. He might not have worn his emblems as a ruler, but he was still unmistakably terrifying.

The blacksmith had told them the sword had been stolen, and, according to Grim, there was a notorious thieving group on his lands. They had a base on the other side of Nightshade. He wordlessly took her arm.

They portaled to the edge of a fishing town. The air was thick with salt and rotten catch. The streets were empty. Every curtain was closed. Of course, it was night—

Isla tensed. Panic gripped her chest.

"*Your curse,*" she said, words sputtering out of her. She pointed at the moon, like a fool, then, at him. "You can't—"

Grim wore a bored expression. "Go outside at night?"

She nodded.

"That won't be a problem." Then he turned back around.

Not a problem? "Even *you* are not powerful enough to escape the curses."

He sighed in clear irritation that she kept insisting on speaking to him. "No," he admitted. "But someone else was, and they made me this." He clutched at something below the collar of his shirt, some sort of charm, then instantly turned his attention away from her.

That didn't satiate her curiosity or confusion at all. How was it possible that a simple strand allowed Grim to be immune from his curse? It didn't make any sense. It should be impossible—

"While I am flattered by your concern about my well-being," he said, in about the most pompous tone possible, "focus on finding the sword. Not me."

She shut her mouth but wondered about the charm. Why didn't he make one for every Nightshade? Was it rare? Did he want his people to stay cursed?

A small boat with paddles floated at the docks, waiting for them. Grim couldn't portal them to the thieves, lest the sword be there and sense his power. Isla had asked if she could use her starstick, and he had said no.

She tried to grab one of the paddles, but he snatched it out of her hand. She sat behind him, watching his back as the muscles rolled. The sight should have disgusted her.

She wished it disgusted her.

It was miles to the isle. His paddling never weakened.

"It's surprising," she said, staring at him. The ocean was dark as ink around them. The moon was a paltry crescent.

She thought he was going to ignore her, but after a few minutes, he said in an annoyed voice, "What, pray tell, is so surprising?"

He was facing the opposite direction. She couldn't see his expression, and perhaps that made her bold. "Your flair is portaling. You can go

anywhere without lifting a finger. Yet . . . you climb quickly. You can paddle well. You are . . . muscled."

"Ogling my body, Hearteater?" he asked.

Isla's cheeks burned. She was suddenly extremely grateful they weren't facing each other. "Only in your dreams," she said.

He sighed. "Is there a question?"

"Yes. It's been hundreds of years since war. You can portal anywhere with half a thought. Why keep up with your . . . fitness regimens? Why . . . when you have so much ability?"

"I have never relied solely on my powers," he said. "A person's mettle is determined by who they are beneath them." He turned to look at her, lip curled in disgust. "And only a fool waits to prepare for a war until one is declared."

She was silent after that, until the boat roughly washed up onto the pebbled rocks of the isle.

He turned to look at her. "I won't save you," he warned. "If it's you or the sword, it will not be a difficult decision. I will find a way to get it without you."

"I am aware," she said through her teeth.

"Good."

The thieves' base was a tall structure with long and rectangular windows, all covered with thick fabric, which made their approach much easier.

"We look for the sword. If we don't find it, we get information," he said.

The first window they approached was unlocked and unguarded. Grim opened it from the bottom, and they slipped through without issue. Isla supposed the thieves weren't worried about any Nightshade visiting their isle at night. Who would be able to?

Inside, there was only silence.

"I'll search the top floors," Grim said. He swept past her, leaving her alone. The room was unremarkable. Just a place to store supplies,

by the looks of it. She removed the top of a barrel and found some sort of alcohol. Before she left, she listened.

There wasn't any noise in the hall either. Maybe the thieves were asleep?

She crept along the first floor, going from room to room. One looked like a kitchen. One had a few tables. The walls were stone. Wind whistled through large cracks. It was freezing.

Isla finally reached a hall, lined in windows. She carefully pulled part of one of the curtains away. The sea crashed nearby. The slice of moon illuminated the water. She saw its reflection in the waves.

She pushed the curtain back into place, then walked backward, admiring the high ceiling. Wondering if Grim was almost done searching the top floors.

She didn't even hear them coming until a blade was already against her throat. "I wonder what you might go for," the voice in her ear said.

Training overruled panic. In a flash, she grabbed his arms with both hands and pulled, giving some distance between the blade and her neck. She curved her shoulder up, bent under his arms, hands still gripped on his wrists, twisted to his side—and stabbed him with his own dagger, over and over and over. Terra had tested her in this exact scenario.

The man slumped to the ground. He looked surprised to see blood puddling next to him. He was still alive, just in shock. She couldn't afford to be. She took a step, and two more Nightshades were on her.

She reached for her blade, and they reached for theirs.

They struck first. Isla dodged the first man's blows, steel echoing through the room. More would come. She knew that.

Where was Grim? Had he searched the floors already? Had he run into his own trouble?

She remembered his words. He wouldn't save her. She needed to save herself.

The next man struck, and Isla raced to defend from both sides. Sweat shot down her temple. She had never fought like this before. Training was one thing . . . real fighting was another. One of the Nightshades aimed for her head and just barely missed.

Her fingers felt around the side of her pants, slipping into the specially designed pockets that held her throwing blades. It wasn't her dominant hand, but Terra had ensured she was proficient in both. She gripped the blades between her fingers and threw them at one of the men, just as he was going for another blow.

One landed in the middle of his chest. The other landed in the middle of his throat. He looked down briefly before falling forward, accidentally impaling himself on his own sword.

Nausea rolled through her stomach. She had just killed her first person that she knew of . . . Should she feel guilty? He had been attacking her. But she had invaded his home . . .

The blow came out of nowhere. The other man struck the side of her head with the hilt of his blade, and she immediately fell to the floor. Her ears rang. Blood dripped down her temple.

He could have killed her, but he didn't. Which meant he was thinking of other uses for her. Anger and fear made her breathing uneven.

In the fall, she had dropped her sword. The Nightshade approached. He kicked her weapon out of reach, and the metal clattered against the marble floor. He smiled as he walked toward her. His eyes roamed down her body in a way that made her want to retch.

"I think I'll keep you for myself," he said. "I like them with a little fight."

Grim. Where was he? Was he coming?

The man stepped forward. From this angle, he was framed by the window curtain behind him. He grinned as he approached. He wanted to be closer to her. He wanted to be pressed against her.

She decided to give him exactly what he wanted.

Before she could have second thoughts, Isla rushed to her feet and shoved herself against him with a roar, his blade slicing her arm in the process. He tensed in confusion. She pushed as hard as she could—

And sent them both crashing through the window. The curtain ripped away. Glass shattered.

The man screamed for half a second before his entire body melted into ash beneath her. She gasped and accidentally inhaled some of it. The rest stuck to the blood on her arms and face.

Isla stood on shaking legs, caked in what was left of the man. She turned very slowly to see Grim standing in the hall, staring at her through what remained of the window.

She bent over and retched.

Grim just watched her as she walked through the open hole in the wall. She used one of the other curtains to try to get the ashes off her. "Did you find it?" she asked before heaving again.

"No," he said. "But I found him."

That was when she noticed the Nightshade on the floor, bound and gagged. "I've asked you three times about the sword," Grim said. "I've described it in detail. You know what I am referring to. Now, for the last time. Where is it? Is it here?" He ripped the fabric from the man's mouth.

The Nightshade made a sound like a whimper. He shook his head.

Grim sighed. "I really didn't want to get my sword dirty," he said.

Then he cut off the man's hand.

The Nightshade screamed a wild sound. She watched the man's hand spasm on the ground and felt like she was going to be sick again.

"It's already dirty now," Grim said, frowning down at his sword. "Your limbs are next."

He lifted his blade, and the man said, "Wait. Wait." He trembled. "If I tell you, will you let me go?"

Grim considered. He nodded.

"Do you swear it?"

"We swear it," Isla said, eyes darting to the man's injury. He needed to cauterize the wound soon, or he would bleed to death in front of them.

The man swallowed. His words came out in just a rasp. "It hasn't been here in decades. We stole it, but one of us went rogue. He took the sword and lost it to someone else. Only he knows where it is now."

"Where can we find him?" Grim demanded.

"His name is Viktor. He's been seen near Creetan's Crag."

"How will we know it's him?" Isla asked.

The man let out a wheezing noise. He was pressing his wound against his body to try to stop the blood. It was getting everywhere. "He has . . . he has a snake. Takes it with him everywhere." A snake?

"Thank you for being so helpful," Grim said, sounding genuinely sincere.

Then he slit the man's throat.

Isla gasped. She watched the man choke on his own blood before he collapsed on the floor.

"You promised," she said, turning to him.

Grim frowned down at her. "No, Hearteater," he said. "You promised." Tears stung in the corners of her eyes. They swept down her cheeks. He looked at her with disgust. "Don't tell me you are crying for that filth's death."

"Filth?" she asked, incredulous. "He is one of your people."

"Don't speak about my people when you don't know the first thing about your own. Locked in a room with the glass painted over . . ." Grim bared his teeth at her. "He was a thief and sold much more than just rare objects," he said. "He deserved to die, and I was happy to be the one to end him."

Isla swallowed. She turned to the other dead body in the room. Then to the man she had stabbed in the side with his own dagger. He was dead now too. And the man who was now no more than ashes . . . A sob scraped against the back of her throat. "I—I've never . . ."

Grim just stared down at her. His expression did not soften in the slightest in response to her tears. He watched her cry for a few more seconds, before saying, "It gets easier."

Then he took her arm and portaled them back to her room.

She had to close her eyes against the sudden rush of nausea. She didn't want to retch again. She didn't want to think about what she had just *done*—

"There is a celebration on Creetan's Crag in two weeks," he said. "That's when I'll return."

Her eyes were still closed when he left.

I DO NOT DIE TODAY

The outcome of the battle was not set in stone, that was what the oracle had said. Those were the words Isla clung to as her own death replayed in her mind, over and over again, and as she watched Oro rage against the vault.

He had tried to use her power to open the door, but it remained closed.

"Oro," she finally said, placing a hand against his tensed back. Only then did he stop.

He pulled her into his arms and said, "He isn't going to kill you. I will rip him limb from limb before he ever hurts you."

The floor seemed to tremble with his promise. She had never seen him so disheveled, so . . .

Afraid.

She was afraid too. "I need to know. You and me . . . we have a love bond. Does that mean if I die . . . you can take my abilities? You can save the Starlings and Wildlings?"

Oro's eyes flashed with fear. "You're not going to die, Isla. But yes. I should be able to."

Her relief must have been visible because Oro became more distressed. She placed her hands against the sides of his face. "You aren't going to lose me," she said. "I'm not going to die." She would make sure she kept that promise.

Which meant they needed to make sure they won the war.

"I'm going to see the Vinderland with Enya," she said. "And you need to be okay with that." The Sunling was waiting for her now. They were going immediately.

More fear and pain had hardened in Oro's eyes, and she understood, she really did. If he was set to do something reckless, she would feel the same way. She thought of her guardians then, and Cleo with her son.

It was possible to love someone too hard. It was possible to turn love into a prison.

He finally nodded. "You're right," he said. He walked her over to Enya, who was waiting beyond the Mainland woods. Before they left, he pressed a hand against her arm. Sparks erupted from his touch, shimmering, covering her entire body from the neck down. It formed onto her as closely as her clothes. Besides the faint sparkle, it was nearly invisible.

"It's a Starling shield," he said. "Like the one you're creating for the battle, but smaller. Can you take it over?"

She focused on the energy. Breathed in and out. Slowly, under her command, it dripped down her fingers, past her skin. Keeping the shield in place took effort, but she was grateful for its protection.

"It's not invincible," Oro said, "but it will stop an arrow."

"Thank you," she said, before lifting on her toes to kiss him. At first, it was soft, but then Oro grabbed her like he was afraid she wouldn't be able to keep her promise, like she might be gone any day now. His fingers ran through the back of her hair, tilting her head, giving him a better angle. His other arm curled around her waist, and she felt her shield ripple there. She pulled him closer.

Enya cleared her throat, and Isla tore herself away. The Sunling shook her head at them while Isla drew her puddle of stars and portaled them to the people who had split her heart in two.

Wind howled in her ears. Her cheeks went numb. The air was white, coated in a thin layer of snow. They were on flat land, yet fighting against the current of the snowstorm made every step forward feel like climbing up a mountain.

"What a charming place to live," Enya bit out, before her body was coated in reddish gold. It wrapped around her like Isla's Starling shield, then spread beyond, warming the air around them until Isla could feel her nose again. "That's better, isn't it?" she asked. The snow below the Sunling's shoes melted and sizzled.

Isla searched the blank horizon. There were a few monstrous mountains, covered in sharp panes of ice that looked like scales. "I don't know how they survived out here," she said. She remembered coming to Vinderland territory with Oro, during their search for the heart. It was hard to imagine, but back then, it had been colder. Ever since the Moonlings left, Moon Isle had increasingly gotten warmer.

"Are you . . . are you afraid?" Isla asked, wondering if she sounded like a fool.

Enya only glanced over at her. "No. Not at all."

"Why not?" she said. "The Vinderland are warriors. I've seen how well they fight"—which was why they so desperately needed them in battle—"They don't just kill their enemies . . . they *eat* them." And not because of a curse. Simply for pleasure.

Enya stared at her for a long while. "I'm going to tell you something only Oro, Cal, and Zed know."

Isla blinked. She was surprised Enya would tell her anything personal. They weren't necessarily friends. It had been clear from the beginning that Enya was like a shield around Oro, protecting him at all costs. Her loyalty was to him, not her.

She waited.

"I know exactly when I will die," Enya said.

Isla stopped and was instantly drenched in cold, now outside of the dome of warmth Enya had created.

She thought of her vision. Her own death.

"What? How—how could you know that?"

Enya motioned for her to keep moving, and she did. "The day I

was born, a Moonling sent for my mother. The oracle wanted to see her. She hadn't thawed in a while, so it was considered important. She visited her, holding me. The oracle told my mother she had seen my death."

Isla realized they had more in common than she'd thought. For a moment, she wondered if she should tell Enya about her vision. Who else would understand?

In the end, all she said was, "That's . . . awful."

Enya shrugged a shoulder. Bits of snow fell above them and melted inches away, raining onto their heads. "Most mothers might think so, but mine wasn't like that. She said, 'Well, are you going to tell me?' The oracle did. When I was old enough to understand, my mother gave me the choice. Know how and when I will die . . . or don't. I've been told I'm a lot like her . . . and you already know which choice I've made."

"Does Oro know?"

"When I die?"

Isla nodded.

"No, though he used to ask me incessantly when we were younger. I think he wanted to know so he could somehow keep it from happening. He's like you, in that way. He carries guilt around that doesn't even belong to him." She lifted a shoulder. "I think of it as a gift. I know when I die, so I can spend every day until then living to the fullest. You and Oro seem to get lost in your minds, thinking about the past, future—I spend most of my time in the present." She sighed. "The reason I'm telling you this is to explain why I'm not afraid. Not even in the slightest."

Just as the words left her mouth, a legion of Vinderland appeared on the horizon, wearing metal helmets with massive tusks, fur around their necks, and intricate armor. They were holding swords and axes longer than her limbs.

Enya casually turned to Isla, winked, and said, "I do not die today."

. . .

A flurry of arrows struck Isla and ricocheted off the Starling shield glittering along her skin, humming with energy. It took every ounce of focus for her to hold it in place, and she winced with every hit. They might not have pierced her skin, but they would certainly leave bruises.

At her side, Enya formed a wall of fire, charring the arrows before they reached her. Her movements were smooth, casual even, as she melted all ice and snow around her and turned their weapons to ash.

There was a battle cry, and Isla leaped to the side as an axe was thrown right at her body. Its blade missed her by inches, and then the warriors descended.

They bellowed words she didn't understand and rushed forward, moving surprisingly quickly with the heavy armor they wore. Thick furs peeked through the gaps in the metal.

"Red hair," one of them yelled, staring at Enya. "You're going to make a lovely stew. Charred and zesty." He smiled, revealing teeth sharpened into points—better to tear flesh with.

"And you're going to make a lovely pile of ashes," Enya replied, her fire bursting forth, burning his beard. The man screamed as the rest of him caught fire. He rolled onto the snow.

A sword came for Isla's neck, and she ducked, then hit the man in the temple, knocking him out. They needed these warriors—they were worthless in battle dead.

Enough.

She flung her arms to either side, and trees sprung up from the lifeless land, breaking through the ice.

The Vinderland went still. If they didn't recognize her before, they certainly did now.

One towering man stepped forward, his armor clanking. He took off his horned helmet, revealing a sharp face with a

diagonal scar across it. "How dare you come here, after killing so many of us?"

Isla bared her teeth. "You all almost killed me. You tried to eat me. You put an arrow through my heart."

His eyes narrowed. "Yet here you are. Do you think you'll be so lucky to escape death a third time?"

She almost smiled. *Escape death*. That was exactly what she was trying to do.

"With your help, I hope so," she said.

The man laughed. It was hoarse and made her skin crawl. The rest joined him, their laughs echoing in their helmets. "We would sooner die than help any of you."

"Then you will die anyway," she said, stepping forward. "Nightshades are coming to destroy Lightlark. There will be nothing left. Every inch will be decimated. Everyone will perish, including you."

The man's eyes narrowed at her. "Lightlark has survived thousands of years, several wars—"

"Not like this one," she said. "I know the future, and it is destruction."

"The oracle—"

"She says Lightlark's fate is in the balance. Everyone must protect it." She curled her lip in disgust. "I hate you," she said. "And you hate me. But we have a common enemy, and that is anyone who would destroy Lightlark. I'm sure you've noticed Moonling has left."

He nodded.

"They have joined Nightshade."

The warriors behind him began talking to each other.

"We need you," Isla said. "We need every warrior on this island to defend it. Say you will fight alongside us. If we can make peace, then there is hope for the future of Lightlark."

The man considered. She waited. Finally, he put his helmet back on and said, "No."

Then, he gripped his battle axe and aimed for her head.

Her focus wavered; her shield fell away. Time seemed to slow down as she watched the axe swing toward her face. Her hand instinctively raised to block herself, fingers half an inch from the metal. In her mind, she knew, logically, her hand would be cut in half, and the axe would bury in her brain. She would die.

But that's not what happened.

The moment Isla touched the blade, the axe turned to ash.

BEFORE

Isla counted down the days until her visit to Creetan's Crag. She often waited up past midnight, in case Grim might make an appearance. Maybe there would be a change in their plan, another place to go.

He never came. She started to turn their last conversation around in her mind. *Don't speak about my people when you don't know the first thing about your own.*

He was right. All she knew about the Wildlings was what Terra and Poppy had told her. Her people were strangers. She only ever saw them during ceremonies.

That night, so late that she was sure Poppy and Terra were sleeping, she grabbed her starstick and portaled to the other side of the Wildling newland. Before, she'd never dared. The cost of getting caught was too great.

Tonight, she just wanted to see them. Understand them.

She had been to one of the villages before, for a short, closely monitored visit. That was where she went.

The forest scraped against her skin as she landed, purposefully trying to mark her. She stayed on its outskirts, eyes on the village. From here, she could see the backs of houses. They were worn and leaned together like a group of old friends.

Something in her burned. Her only friend was Celeste, who was currently angry at her. Since Isla had started working with Grim, her visits had become more infrequent. Celeste had noticed. Isla had made excuses, of course. Lies. With each one that slipped out, they got easier to tell. Just like Grim said about the killing.

A light burned up ahead. Someone was awake. Isla wondered if she could creep around the edges of the village, just to overhear a conversation. Just to watch. She wondered if perhaps she could try to blend in. Maybe they wouldn't recognize her. The dress she wore was not elaborate. The only times they would have seen her would be in full costume, barely recognizable as a person underneath so many flower petals.

Just one step out of the woods. Just a few minutes walking around the village. It couldn't hurt, could it?

She was very close to taking a step out of the forest when the choice was made for her.

"Now," she heard, and she turned around, in time to see the hilt of a sword before it hit her forehead.

When Isla awoke, she was bound. Her hands were tied behind her, at the base of her back. Her ankles were roped together.

There were voices.

"I don't recognize her. Do you?"

"No."

"Good. Get your dagger."

There was a pause. Then, "She's Wildling."

"So? We're starving. There haven't been hearts in weeks."

Isla's vision was still blurry, but she regained consciousness quickly. *Starving*.

She didn't understand. Terra and Poppy hadn't mentioned a shortage of hearts. She knew her people were steadily weakening since she was born powerless, but she was under the impression they still had a decently steady supply.

The women left the room she was being kept in, and Isla saw her chance. She wrestled with the restraints, but they were tied tightly. With a roll of her spine, she realized they hadn't found her starstick. It was still tucked into the back of her bodice.

She stretched her fingers up as far as they could go, twisting her wrists painfully, seeing if she could reach it. But there were still a few inches between them.

And the women were back.

"She's awake," one said uncertainly. There was regret in her tone.

"Doesn't matter," the other replied.

The one who had reservations was her last chance. "You don't have to do this," she told the woman. Her vision was still blurry from the hit, her forehead pulsed in pain, but she could make out the Wildling's features. Large, dark eyes. Small nose. Long limbs, and hair down to her waist. "I'm Wildling. Please."

She turned to the other woman, as if to say, *See?* but the second one simply stuck something firmly in her mouth. A gag.

No.

Then she produced a dagger.

What a fool. She should have used her few words to tell them she was their ruler. Then they would understand her death would kill them all. She had been too worried about revealing her identity—

Too late now. With little ceremony, the woman ripped her bodice down the center. Then she began to carve through her chest.

Isla screamed an animalistic noise that made it past even the gag and scratched the back of her throat like sharp nails. She was on fire. The pain was a flame consuming her, eating her from the inside out. She could smell her own blood, and the Wildling kept sawing, through skin and tissue—

When the blade went deeper, Isla arched unnaturally, and that was when her bound fingers grazed her starstick. She screamed to the heavens, wondering if it might make it across the realms to Grim, not even knowing if that was possible.

With renewed hope, she fought against the restraints, the rope burning her wrists, until she could finally grasp the device. She wrestled one hand free, then drew her puddle behind her. She hurled herself off the table and was gone in an instant.

She couldn't go home. Terra and Poppy couldn't know about this. With this pain, it would be almost impossible to keep quiet. One moment she was being carved. The next, she was bleeding out in the middle of Grim's room. He was standing in its corner, without a shirt on, clearly getting ready to sleep.

Shadows raced across the floor. He pulled the gag out of her mouth, and his eyes widened at the state of her chest.

"Sorry. I shouldn't have . . . I didn't—I didn't know where else to go, I couldn't go home," she said, and then his arms were lifting her from the floor. "My guardians—they can't know I—"

He made a sound like a growl and said, "You are a fool."

"I am very much aware."

"Who am I killing tonight?"

"What? No one."

He looked down at her. "I don't know how you're still conscious," Grim said like an accusation. Then, "Why won't you stop bleeding?" almost to himself. The remaining rope around her wrists turned to ash.

"I just need you to do one thing for me," she said. "Well, two." Her breathing was labored. "I need you to get my healing elixir from my room." She described it to him, and he was gone. A moment later, he returned with it. With a shaking hand, she poured the liquid over her chest.

Her scream would have woken up the entire Wildling castle. She shook as she applied more, until the skin began to slowly grow back. It did nothing for the pain. Grim silently offered her a roll of bandages, which she took and wrapped around herself, making a makeshift top. It soaked with blood immediately, so she added more. When she peeked over her shoulder, she saw the Nightshade was gone.

That was fine. She knew he didn't care about her injury, so long as she lived.

He returned a little while later and all but shoved a mug at her. "Here. Drink this."

She winced as she took it from him. "Medicine?" she asked.

"No. This has sugar that will keep you conscious. It . . . helps." She glanced down and saw it was dark brown, and thick. Was he lying to her?

Isla dipped her nose to it to smell.

"I could kill you a thousand different ways, Hearteater," he said flatly. "Poison would not be one of them."

True. She took a sip, and he was right. Pain still consumed her, but this made her feel the littlest bit better.

Chocolate. It was melted chocolate and tasted like molten divinity, poured into this stone mug. The best thing she had ever tasted. She'd had chocolate a handful of times in her life, from the chefs in the Wildling palace during special holidays and from the Skyling market. But not like this. Not in a *drink*.

"So, I take it you like chocolate."

"Yes," she said, voice coming out like a croak. "Do you have something else for the pain?" she asked, desperate. "How about that Nightshade substance?" She remembered the vials in the night market. The seller had said it would take away all pain. "Nightbane?"

Grim went still. In a voice that chilled the room, he said, "You will never know nightbane."

"Why not?" she asked. Why did he get so upset about it?

"It's a drug."

"What does it do?"

He frowned. "It makes you the happiest you've ever been and takes away all suffering."

She blinked. "I want it."

He gave her a scathing look. "It kills you slowly, methodically, efficiently, until you die with a smile on your mouth. With continued use nightbane is a death sentence, and everyone who takes it knows it."

Never mind. "So why take it?"

Grim shrugged a shoulder. "I will never understand. I suppose they feel the pleasure . . . however short-lived . . . is worth it."

Isla moved, and pain ripped down her middle. "Alcohol. Do you have . . . alcohol?" She had never tried it, but it was rumored to help with pain.

In a moment, a bottle was in her hands, and she drank a large swig.

She immediately choked. Her throat burned. It was as if the liquid was eating through it. It turned out alcohol tasted exactly like it smelled. "Why don't you have anything but alcohol in your room for pain?"

"Pain is useful," he said quietly. He didn't elaborate.

"It doesn't feel very useful now," she mumbled.

Grim looked down at her. It seemed to surprise them both when he said, "When I was seven, my training consisted of being cut and skinned until there was barely any flesh left on my back."

Isla's jaw went slack. Her training could be painful . . . but to do that to a child? "That is barbaric."

He only lifted a shoulder. "It was a custom here, for a very long time. Meant to toughen the body and mind at the height of its growth. The place I trained as a warrior . . . we were punished for the smallest of infractions. In public. Shadows can turn into the sharpest, thinnest blades."

"That's humiliating."

"It wasn't. It was a chance to prove we didn't react to the pain. Standing there, being cut, and not moving a muscle in your face . . . It was seen as strength." His eyes weren't on her when he said, "My father would come and watch. It was an honor to show him that I had no reaction to the pain."

She crinkled her nose. "You know how awful that sounds, right?"

He nodded. "It's why that doesn't happen anymore. Our training is still ruthless . . . but not as cruel."

Isla swallowed. What he had said about the punishment . . . "But . . . you don't have any scars." He only had one. And she had given it to him. "You have a Moonling healer, don't you? Or Moonling healing supplies?" It didn't make sense. "Why is Cleo helping you?"

Grim just looked at her. After a few moments, all he said was, "You should leave."

She felt a bite of hurt and didn't know why. He was asking her to leave his quarters, when she was injured. Why was she shocked? He didn't care about her.

The second thing she needed from him. Isla collected her torn top from the floor and said, "Can you . . . destroy this? I can't bring it home. All the blood . . ."

A moment later, the top was only ash.

She grabbed her starstick and, without another word, portaled back to her room.

In the middle of the night, she woke and almost screamed.

Grim was sitting across from her bed, watching her.

"What are you—"

"I'm making sure you don't bleed out in your sleep," he grumbled.

Isla looked down at her bandages. Blood was already peeking through again. She got a few rags she used to clean her swords and pressed them to her, so she wouldn't stain her sheets. She would need to ask Grim to destroy them before he left.

"I'm fine," she said, though she certainly wasn't. All she could do was hope the bleeding stopped by the time her training started. "You can leave."

Grim gave her a look that made her think he didn't believe her for a second. He leaned back in the chaise he had decided to sit on. It was decorated with roses, and far too small, but he made himself comfortable and stretched his long legs out in front of him. "Your death would be most inconvenient. I'll stay a little longer."

"Inconvenient?" she said, scoffing at him.

He didn't look fazed. "Inconvenient," he repeated. "You are an investment."

Her voice raised to a high pitch. "An investment?"

He continued as if she hadn't spoken. "My time is valuable. I have a lot to do. Choosing to work with you . . . fitting you into my plan. You are an investment. You're no good to me dead."

She glared at him.

Fine. Let him stay. If he wanted to watch her sleep, that was his decision.

She made it ten minutes this way, willing sleep to come down and find her again. It did not, and the only thing more uncomfortable than having him sit and watch her was the pain pulsing like a second heartbeat in her chest.

When she carefully sat upright and pulled her knees to her chest, she found him still watching her.

"I can't sleep," she said.

His chin rested on his hand. "Clearly." He studied her. "If you weren't going to sleep, I suppose I could have allowed you to stay at my palace. Let you heal there."

"I hate your palace," she said.

That seemed to surprise him. "Why?"

"Besides the fact that you live there?" Grim looked faintly amused. "There's no color. It's so . . . dark. I could never live in a place like that." He said nothing. "You know," she said, staring at her glass wall. "My guardians closed my window because of you."

He raised an eyebrow at her.

"There was . . . a loose pane. You saw it when we dueled. It was the only way I could sneak out. I had to tell them about it, to explain my ankle injury."

"Can't you use your portaling device to go outside?"

Her eyes found the floor. "I—I'm awful at traveling short distances with it. And I can only reliably go places I've been before."

The portaling device was born of his own power, which he clearly had complete mastery of. She wondered if he would think less of her than he already did.

"I'm sorry," he said suddenly. Her eyes abruptly met his again. "About the window."

Isla asked a question she'd had for a while. "If you created my device, then how did it get to Wildling?"

"I'm not entirely sure," he said.

All at once, a thought gripped her mind and chest. "Did you . . . did you know my mother?"

Grim frowned. "No. I haven't met a Wildling since the curses," he said.

So how had her mother come to possess the starstick?

They just stared at each other. Isla watched him watch her and wondered if he would be the first to look away.

"Do you always play with your hair when you're uncomfortable?"

It wasn't until then that she realized she was raking her fingers through her damp hair like they were two combs. She immediately put her hands in her lap. "No."

"Liar. I've watched you do it on no less than three occasions."

She narrowed her eyes at him. Without breaking his gaze, she made her way to the end of the bed, so she was sitting right in front of him. "Here I was thinking that you couldn't even bear to look at me, and you've apparently been studying me quite carefully."

Grim's expression did not change. "You are my enemy. Of course I study you carefully."

"Right. Tell me, Nightshade," she said. "What do *you* do when you're uncomfortable?"

"I rarely am."

"You seemed pretty uncomfortable when I stabbed you in the chest."

Grim looked bored. "I'm used to being stabbed."

"By someone you were trying to bed?"

That got a reaction from him. His jaw tensed. "You tricked me. Had I known who you were, I never would have touched you." The disgust in his tone was clear.

Isla scoffed. "Had *I* known what was about to occur, I never would have joined that line."

"Why were you there, then?" he snapped.

She recoiled, taken aback by his sudden rush of anger. "I accidentally portaled there with the starstick. It wouldn't work, and I was chased by your idiotic group of guards. The head woman grabbed me, and the next thing I knew I was in that line."

Grim crossed his arms. "I should take that thing away from you. All it's bringing you is closer to death."

"You could try," she said, her voice as threatening as she could make it.

Grim looked at her and said nothing.

"So. You have a harem?" she asked. Since that night, she had wondered who those women were. Their function was clear.

"No."

Isla laughed, disbelieving. "So, women just line up to sleep with you? They volunteer for the honor?"

Grim glared at her.

He had the reputation of an accomplished killer. There was no way the women didn't know about it. "Who would want to sleep with you?"

Grim stood from the chair, until he was right in front of her. He towered over her, his shadow even bigger behind him, filling her wall. "I don't know, Hearteater," he said. "You seemed pretty willing."

Isla swallowed. He was so close. She was breathing too quickly, and it only made her wound more painful. "No. I was disgusted."

Grim grinned. "Is that so?"

She nodded, even as he placed his hands on either side of her on the bed and leaned down so his face was right in front of hers.

"I can feel flashes of emotions," he said. *He could?* Now that she thought about it, it was a rumored Nightshade ability, one only the most powerful possessed. The blood drained from her face. "And yours were very, *very* clear—"

She wasn't breathing.

"—just as they are now."

Her heart was beating wildly. She told herself it was because she could feel the power rolling from him in waves. She told herself she was afraid. "Your powers are wrong."

He tilted his head at her. She watched his eyes move from her collarbones to her neck to her lips. "No. I don't think so."

Then he went back to his chair. "Go to sleep," he said.

She crawled back to her place and covered herself in bedding so he wouldn't see the heat of her face.

LINE BETWEEN LIFE AND DEATH

Isla blinked. She had just had a memory. It didn't seem as though any time had passed, however.

Was it because her Nightshade abilities were getting stronger? Had it always been this way?

The Vinderland warrior was frozen in front of her. She had just demolished his weapon with a single touch. "What are you?" he asked. "You're . . . Wildling."

"I'm more than that," she said, stepping forward. Suddenly, she had Enya's confidence. She had seen her own death too.

She would not die today.

"You are going to join us in battle, or we are going to all perish," she said, her voice taking on an edge. "It's as simple as that."

He looked down at the pile of ashes that had once been his weapon. They mixed with the snow, then blew away in a flurry. The warriors at his sides spoke to each other in low voices. Their eyes were wide. They looked stunned.

"A Wildling who is also Nightshade," the man in front of her said, his tone completely different than before . . . almost reverent. He seemed to turn the words around in his mind before he reached for another weapon—a sword this time—and held it high in the air.

Isla might have been afraid that he would try to behead her, but she knew the positioning of his sword. She raised her own, and the swords clanked together loudly—a warrior's handshake.

"Singrid," he said, sheathing his weapon.

Isla shot a look at Enya, who shrugged.

"You . . . you will fight with us?" she asked.

He shook his head. "No. We will fight with *you*."

Isla should have celebrated, or left while she was ahead, but she didn't understand. "You . . . you tried to kill me. Just moments ago."

Did her being Wildling and Nightshade really mean that much?

"Apologies," he said, looking like he truly meant it. "I should have known. You survived an arrow to the heart . . . we have stories about people like you. Those who stand on the line between life and death."

Isla shifted in the snow. If only he knew that she had seen her own demise.

She wasn't about to tell him that. Instead, she said, "How many of you are there?"

Their numbers didn't seem significant the last time she had encountered them, but she hadn't seen their base or full population.

"Hundreds," he said, and hope swelled. "Most cannot fight, however."

Hope withered. "Why?"

"They have a sickness," he said. "The last few decades, it has spread. Incapacitated most of us."

A sickness? Isla almost asked why they hadn't seen a healer, but she stopped herself. No Moonling would ever treat part of the Vinderland. They were known for their viciousness and appetite for human flesh.

"What if we could heal them?" Isla asked.

She felt Enya staring at her.

Singrid took a step forward. "You have a healer?"

"Yes," she said, avoiding Enya's look. "If they could recover in time . . . could they fight?"

Singrid nodded. "We are all trained."

Good. "I'll be back, then," she said. She raised her sword and clashed it with a weapon from every one of the Vinderland in front of her.

She had a legion, she thought. If she could just find a way to heal them.

"Please tell me you can help," Isla said to Calder. The Moonling frowned as she told him about the sickness. "You . . . you *are* a healer, right?"

He gave a weak smile.

"The worst," Zed said. "He's the *worst* healer."

Enya shot him a look. She turned to Calder. "We know you're not the best . . . but you're who we have. And Isla here might have exaggerated your skill set."

She had a thought. "Oro's a healer, isn't he?" He had healed her injuries before, during the Centennial.

Enya moved her hand back and forth in front of her. "He can heal physical wounds, but only straightforward ones. As far as I'm aware, he's never tried sicknesses." She looked at Calder again. "You have, though, Cal. Right?"

Calder swallowed. "I . . . I *have*, but—"

"I'll bring you to the Wildling newland," Isla said. "Our healing elixir is made from a flower. Perhaps if it was boiled, made into a tea, that could help them as well. I can show you."

Calder agreed, and that was when she told him and Zed about her starstick. The look the Skyling gave her could only be described as withering.

The three of them went through the puddle of stars.

At Isla's request, Wren showed them the patch of flowers where the healing elixirs came from.

"These are magnificent," Calder said. Isla hadn't ever seen them in their original form before. They were deep violet in color, with sharp petals. Beautiful. Vicious.

"The flowers are so rare, we use them only in emergencies. We've never tried them for sickness," Wren said. Her eyes darted to Isla. "We . . . we have only been able to find a few more additional patches."

They didn't have many to spare.

Isla sighed. This was the hard part of ruling, she decided. Was it better to use a portion of the flowers now, to ensure the help of the Vinderland warriors, knowing there would be less healing elixir later, which could save lives?

Though . . . having more warriors would save lives too, wouldn't it?

She closed her eyes tightly and decided. "Let's test with just a few flowers. If we see meaningful results . . . we can determine how many we would need to heal all of them."

Calder nodded. Wren began to pluck the flowers. The moment they were pulled from the ground, the color became darker, almost black.

There was a rustling in the woods by the patch and Zed froze. He looked up, and up. His hand inched toward the weapon on his belt.

"Don't you dare," Isla bit out, before breaking into a smile.

Lynx. She had missed him.

He bowed his head begrudgingly, as if acknowledging he had maybe missed her too.

She jumped as high as she could and threw her arms around his neck. That was apparently taking it too far, because the massive leopard shook her off.

When she turned around, Enya, Calder, and Zed were gaping at her.

"That is the largest cat I have ever seen," Enya said.

Lynx uttered a sound that made it clear he did not like being referred to as a cat. She placed her hand against his side. "He's a leopard, thank you very much," she said. Lynx didn't even acknowledge her.

Zed narrowed his eyes at Lynx. "I . . . I don't think that's a leopard."

"Of course he is," Isla said. "Look. If you squint, you can see the patterns."

Calder stepped forward to get a closer look, and Lynx bared his massive teeth. The Moonling held his hands up. "Never mind. I can see from here. Very pretty."

Zed just shook his head. "Are there more of them?" he asked.

"More of what?"

He motioned at Lynx. "Your *leopard*."

She looked at Lynx, whose eyes slid to hers. Somewhere deep inside of herself she knew that meant no.

Was that part of the connection between Wildling and bonded?

"No. Why?"

Zed shrugged. "We could use creatures like that. The Skyling vote's in a few days. I'm not holding my breath."

He was right. Isla wanted to bring Lynx to Lightlark for the battle. If she could manage to ride him, it would be a considerable advantage.

When they returned to Lightlark, Calder joined Isla to visit the Vinderland, with the flower. If it worked, she would be adding hundreds of skilled, ruthless warriors to their army.

The next day, she would visit Cinder on Star Isle to begin practicing the walls of energy that would keep the battle enclosed. She had already started learning to create the defensive nature that would cover other parts of the Mainland. Confined, the Nightshade soldiers would be easier to defeat.

They had a plan.

As Isla fell into another memory that night, though, she couldn't help but think it still wasn't enough.

BEFORE

Grim was gone in the morning. Her chest still burned in pain, but the healing elixir had worked. Her skin was nearly completely healed.

That night, after her training, he appeared in her room again. Any trace of humanity she had seen from him the night prior was gone. He looked furious.

"If you are going to insist on keeping my device and portaling anywhere you wish, I will teach you how not to be an idiot."

Isla glared at him. "Or what?"

"Or I will take it back," he said, eyes darting to the floorboard where she kept her starstick.

Her hands clenched. She knew he wasn't kidding. "Fine," she said. "When are you going to teach me?"

"Now." He grabbed her arm, and the world turned. When it righted itself, they were in a long hall.

"This . . . is in your palace," she said, looking around.

"It's a training room," he said.

"I didn't bring anything," Isla said. Grim made a motion, and her starstick fell through the sky, right into her hand.

"How did you—"

"The first thing you should know is your device is unreliable," he said. "I did not pour much power into it. Around other portaling ability, it won't always work." That explained why it had failed her during their first meeting. "Portaling power is all about visualization. That is why you believe you can't go anywhere you haven't already been."

"So how do I go somewhere I can't visualize?"

"Maps help," he said. "It's easier to go places when you have a sense of the distance and relation to other locations." Grim clearly didn't rely on maps anymore. Hundreds of years of mastery seemed to mean he could travel nearly anywhere he pleased. "Now," he said. "About the short distances."

Grim was there. Then he wasn't. He appeared right behind her.

"It requires far more control. And control is developed through practice." He nodded at her starstick. "Try to portal across the room."

Isla planted her feet firmly against the ground. She drew her puddle and focused on the small distance. Visualized the other side of the hall.

She landed on dark volcanic sand. The tide washed in, soaking her hands and knees. She heard a tsk above her. She looked up to see Grim standing there, frowning. His castle was a monstrosity above, overlooking the beach. "You overshot by a bit," he said.

He portaled them back.

"Again."

The next time, she landed in the night market. Grim swept her away before anyone noticed.

The time after that, she appeared in his bedroom. It was immaculate. Grim sighed. "You are, surprisingly, getting closer."

After five more disastrous attempts, she appeared in a throne room. It was long as a field. The throne was made up of what looked to be calcified shadows, melted together, moving.

"The training room is the next one over," he said behind her.

She turned around to face him. "Where are your people? Your attendants? Your nobles?"

"In other parts of the castle," he said. "Most parts are restricted only to me."

Grim was free, but he seemed almost as enclosed as she was. "How often do you see them?"

“Whenever I command it.” He motioned behind her. “Close your eyes.” She did. He took a step forward. He was so close she could feel his breath on her cheek. “Focus.”

It was hard to focus on anything with him this close to her, but she tried. She made a map in her mind of all the places she had mistakenly portaled to. The distance between her and the training room became clearer. She kept her eyes closed as she reached for her starstick and formed her puddle. She fell through.

“Good,” Grim said, her only indication that she had done it. She opened her eyes. She was in the center of the training room. “I was beginning to think you were incapable of being trained.”

Isla glared at him.

“Now,” he said. He made a motion, and one of her favorite swords fell through the air. She caught it. “You are tolerable at swordplay, but your defense needs work.”

She scowled at him. “My guardian is an excellent teacher.”

He raised an eyebrow at her. “Has she seen war? Has she encountered creatures who could swallow her whole?”

Isla flattened her mouth into a line. Terra and Poppy had both been born after the curses were spun. As far as she knew, they had never left the Wildling newland. “No,” she said through her teeth.

“Then it seems I have a few more lessons to teach you,” he said. In an instant, he had his own blade in his hand and he was on her, sword moving so rapidly, she could barely keep track of it. He grunted commands while he fought, criticizing her technique, chastising her every move.

“Dead,” he said, slicing the thinnest of lines across her chest with his sword. It cut through the fabric of her shirt but did not pierce skin. That kind of control was extraordinary. One inch off, and her insides would be spilling out. She reached out to block him again.

His blade sliced against her stomach, forming another slash in her clothing. “Dead,” he said again.

She tried her best to cut *him*, but no matter how hard she fought, how much she tried to trick him, his blade was always there, sending hers away.

Isla gasped as his sword swept across her throat. This time, he *did* cut her. The smallest drop of blood dripped down her neck. "Very dead," he said, his voice just a whisper, far too close.

A growl sounded deep in her chest. The demon could have killed her by accident. Enraged, she fought harder, advancing, cutting the air between them to pieces. She wanted to cut *him* to pieces.

He blocked every blow, but there was an opening. She saw it, and took it, and cut the smallest rip in his shirt.

Isla grinned and was unceremoniously knocked on her back. He had kicked her feet out from under her.

She made an awful sound as she fought for breath. Grim leaned over her. "Another lesson. Sometimes your opponent will let you get a hit in, as a distraction." His blade traveled up her chest, right to the center of her breast. He tapped once and said, "Dead."

Isla glared at him. "I get it. You could kill me any number of ways, including with a sword. Teach me to be better."

He did. They spent the rest of the night dueling in that room. He taught her moves that were ingenious. He taught her how to fight without a sword as well.

"Always go for the nose," he said.

By the time the sun came up, and Isla was due in her quarters for even more training, she was dripping in sweat. "Thank you," she said, even though she knew he wasn't training her for any other reason than because he needed her to find the sword. *You're no good to me dead*, he had said.

"The celebration on Creetan's Crag is in three days," he said. He stepped close, narrowing his eyes. "Before then, do me a favor, and don't die."

CREATURES IN THE WOODS

Grim had taught her to defend herself. She blinked away tears as she wondered if he would ever guess he would become her greatest threat. In the future, he killed her. She saw it clearly.

Why would he hurt her, after taking such pains to keep her safe? It was counter to everything she knew about him.

Though, perhaps she had never truly known him at all.

When Isla crossed the Star Isle bridge, the air felt taut with energy. It smelled faintly of metal. Just like when Celeste used to get worried and upset.

She ran the rest of the way to the ruins where the Starlings lived, and there, she also smelled blood.

"What happened?" Isla demanded.

"The creatures," Maren said. "A little girl . . . about Cinder's age . . ." Her voice cracked at the end.

Leo was there, a reed sticking out of his mouth. He chewed it with nervous fervor. "She went into the woods, and this is all we found."

A cloak sat on the floor. It was soaked in blood. Someone cried out. A sister, or friend, she didn't know.

Isla shut her eyes tightly. She had promised to protect them.

She looked around at the Starlings. They were young. Scared. They were staring at her, and she remembered what Ella had said. *You gave us a chance to live. To most of us, you are a god. A savior.*

It was her duty to see if she could possibly save the little girl.

With more resolution than she felt, Isla asked, "Where can I find these creatures?"

None of the Starlings would walk beyond the first silver stream of water that cut the isle in half. It looked like a piece of ribbon, glittering below the sun.

Everything was silent.

Ciel and Avel circled above. She told them to keep their distance. Surprise would be an advantage.

"If you see them, you're already dead," one of the Starlings offered, and she expected fear to curl in her stomach.

It did not. She had seen her own death in her head. She had faced many dangers already. Those thoughts kept her moving forward, through the stillness of Star Isle.

A bird with silver wings cut through the sky like a pair of swords. She recognized it immediately. Celeste—Aurora—had told her about the bird. A few of them had made it to the Starling newland. It was a heartfinch, named so because they always traveled in pairs and often leaned their beaks together in a manner resembling a heart.

This one was alone.

Isla's fingers slipped down the hilt of her blade at her waist, by habit. The ability in her chest thrummed, as if in warning, and she let it warm her, like drinking a hot cup of tea.

The crumbled wall is your last chance to turn around, Leo had told her around his reed. *After that . . . you belong to them.*

They looked nervous that Isla was going to confront the creatures. She would show them she was capable of protecting them.

The wall was no more than a few scattered silver stones, with an arch that had partially collapsed. There was a puddle of something at its entrance. She leaned down and dipped a finger inside.

She didn't need to smell it to know it was blood. It had gone cold.

Just as she straightened, squinting behind her to see Ciel and Avel circling in the distance, it began to rain.

Of course, she thought, glaring up at the sky, wishing she was a Moonling so she could at least direct the water around her. She was no such thing, so she shook her head and resigned herself to being soaked. Water splashed in the puddle of blood, overflowing it, making it run down the mossy cobblestone, through the gaps between them in lines like veins. She studied it for a moment, her stomach turning, then stepped through the remaining half of the arch.

Isla walked for nearly an hour without incident. She had reached the forest where the creatures were said to live. It was nothing like the other Star Isle woods she had visited during the Centennial. Where that one had been sparse, this one was overgrown. Wild. The silver trees had leaves sharp as blades. Their trunks were braided together into thick knots, their roots were the width of her arms. Thorned brambles made up much of the space between them. She would have exerted much of her power to clear a path, but she didn't need to. She happened upon a wide, clean pathway cut right through the forest, as if made for her. There were no roots or errant flowers or weeds on it. It was smooth. Recently used.

That didn't make sense. Was there a community living out here? Were they like the Vinderland? Outcasts who had renounced all realms a millennium ago?

Isla gripped her sword hilt again.

She felt little connection with this place. It seemed defensive, a fortress. Lightning struck, slicing the sky in half. Thunder clapped, and more rain showered down, pelting her through the treetops.

She whipped around.

Out of the corner of her eye—she swore she saw movement, far above. Her sword made a high-pitched scratch as she unsheathed it and leaned into her stance.

Seconds passed. Nothing moved. The flash of motion she had seen had been high above her, past even the treetops . . . She squinted through the rain, but the trees were empty. The leaves were too sharp, she reasoned. No people or animals could comfortably climb them. They would cut themselves. Right?

She did not re-sheathe her sword as she stepped forward, into a clearing. A massive lake sat in its center, a slice of silver in the shape of an eye. Its surface vibrated with a million raindrops, tiny circles everywhere, overlapping.

As she walked toward it, she tripped. A root—how did she miss it? No. Upon closer inspection, she saw it was not a root. It was a snake. Its metallic scales shined brightly. It writhed below, lifting its head as if to strike her. She took a step back and noticed a new shadow, casting long in front of her, all the way across the lake. It was too large to be a tree.

It hadn't been there before.

Chest constricting, Isla slowly turned around.

Lightning struck again, reflecting off the scales of a coiled, hundred-foot-tall serpent.

Isla resisted the urge to scream.

There was the creature. One of them, at least. It was large enough that it could swallow her without any trouble at all. It could swallow a *tower* without any trouble. She took a step back—

It struck.

At the last moment, Isla rolled to the side, and its fangs sunk into the wet, silver-speckled ground.

Move. She needed to move. Avel and Ciel weren't far behind, but by the time they got to her, it would be too late.

Before she could react, the serpent recovered and reared back, ready to strike again.

It launched into her, throwing her into the lake.

For a moment, there was silence as she fell through the ice-cold water, a thousand needles through her limbs. Bubbles exploded from the surface—

Then, there was the snake head. She cut her hand as she gripped both ends of her sword in front of her body, to keep it from swallowing her whole. The snake's massive jaw only widened. Her arms shook as she struggled against its strength, as it pushed her farther and farther down into the water.

Her vision began to lose its sharpness. Her hands and feet began to lose their sensation. The options were clear. Either the serpent was going to eat her, or she was going to drown. Potentially both. She called to her power, but there was no foliage here, in the center of this lake. She tried her shadows and watched them dissolve in the water, useless.

Without warning, the serpent pulled back and she heard a muted roar through the water.

Mind spinning, chest pulsing in pain, lungs begging for air, she crashed through the surface, only to see that Ciel had dug his sword through the space between the serpent's thick scales. It roared and raged, striking at the Skylings in the sky, as they battled with torrents of air.

She raced out of the water, dripping, freezing, in time to see the snake spin and strike Avel with its tail. She fell from the sky and landed in a heap on the ground. Her twin cried out, distracted, and the snake took that opportunity to attack—

It hit a wall of thorns instead.

Slowly, very slowly, the serpent turned around. Isla stood there, panting, arm raised. She had power.

She would use it.

Isla kicked off her shoes. She dug her feet deep into the muddy ground and focused. Found her center. Cleared her thoughts. The connection clicked.

She had been practicing.

Her eyes opened, and the forest raged. The woods rose around the serpent, so quickly it was trapped before it could move an inch. Thick roots acted as chains, tree trunks curled around its body, vines pinned it in place. By the time Isla was done, it couldn't wriggle even an inch

out of its prison. She expected the serpent to roar again, or try to strike, but it just watched her.

She was panting. Her chest felt hollow. Too much power had been used in too short of a period. Her gaze shifted to Ciel, who was cradling Avel's head. Relief rained down her spine. The Skyling was awake.

Isla was about to tell Ciel to get his sister help, when the serpent suddenly slipped out of its confines. She watched, frozen in place, as the snake shrunk, turned, and uncoiled—

Until it became a woman.

She easily walked through the tower of restraints Isla had made, tilted her head, and said, "Wildling?"

Isla didn't breathe as the woman stepped forward. She was wearing a long dress that trailed across the floor, made up of the same scales she had just worn across her body.

As a *snake*.

"What are you?" Isla demanded. She had never heard of a person being able to change into an animal before. It was an impossible ability.

The woman tilted her head at Isla, the movement purely serpentine. "You don't recognize your own people?"

She . . . used to be Wildling? Had she somehow, like the Vinderland, abandoned her realm?

How was that even possible? It clearly wasn't anymore, or most people would have abandoned their ties to their realms during the curses.

The woman nodded. "You're putting it together, I can see it . . . your face is very expressive . . . not a very good trait as a ruler, is it?" She stepped forward, and it took everything in Isla not to recoil.

"The little girl," Isla said, her voice shaking. "Is she—"

"She's gone," the woman said quickly. "Not me . . . but . . . all the same, there's nothing left."

Isla's bottom lip trembled. Her eyes stung. Poor girl . . . she should have been here to protect her. "You . . . you kill children," she said, her voice full of disgust.

The woman's lip curled away from her mouth, baring teeth that were far too sharp. "Oh, and other Wildlings didn't?" she took a step forward. "We have done what we needed to survive. We needed food. We're no different from you."

We. Were there more like her? Serpent-people? Or were the other ancient, deadly creatures different?

"It ends now," Isla said. "I rule Starling, and you will stop killing them."

The woman just looked at her. "Tell them to stop coming to this part of the isle," she said. "We never hunted; we simply took whatever came wandering in. We could have killed them all, you know."

Killed them all.

Isla wanted to kill the serpent-woman right then . . . but she thought about Zed's words. They could use beings like her in battle.

"Nightshades are coming to destroy the island," Isla said. "You will fight with us." It was a command.

The woman looked at her. Then, she laughed. It was too loud, like the roar of the serpent, like the clap of thunder that sounded above. "Now . . . when you asked that, did you really believe I would say yes?"

Isla stepped forward. She worked every bit of command into her voice as she said, "You are Wildling. I am your ruler, and I am ordering you."

The woman bared her teeth. Before Isla's eyes, her dress became a tail. It took her half a second to be upon Isla, growing larger and larger, rising, serpent part piling beneath her. "I *was* Wildling," she said. "I will not fight for you or anyone else on this island." She leaned back as if to strike again. "I will let you live today, and you should take that as a gift."

Avel was on her feet. Blood dripped down the side of her head, but she looked capable of flying. Before Avel and Ciel lifted her between them, Isla said, "You will not kill another Starling."

She could hear the woman laughing as they took to the air and left.

It was only once she was in bed that night that Isla remembered a very different encounter with a snake.

BEFORE

Music thrummed through the day. Drums, everywhere. Laughter. Jeers. The sharp smell of alcohol that was so concentrated, it burned her nostrils.

Some people walked through the streets nearly naked, covered only in scantily used body paint. There were designs painted across their chests, their legs, their stomachs. Others lined the sides of the road, shouting. They all had blades on their belts and drinks in their hands.

Everyone was wearing masks.

Her own was tight to her face, but she reached to put her hair behind her ear, just for an excuse to touch its edge, to be sure her mask was secure. Grim had thrown the mask and a scrap of fabric at her the second he had appeared in her room.

"Today's the longest night of the year. There's a celebration at Creetan's Crag. During the day, obviously."

She had caught it and frowned. "Masks?"

"Everyone wears them."

Isla had scowled as she let the dress unravel in front of her. "Does everyone wear *this*?" It was black and gave her Wildling clothing competition for impropriety. It hung by two thin straps that looked one wrong move away from snapping, had the lowest-cut bodice she had ever seen and a slit so high, there was very little fabric in the middle holding it all together.

Grim didn't meet her eyes. "Most people do choose to wear little clothing, yes. At least, at celebrations like this. Some just wear paint." He stared at her then, an eyebrow raised. "Would you prefer I get a pot of ink and a brush?"

That had sent her behind her dressing curtain without another complaint. She didn't have a full-length mirror in there, so it wasn't until she was in front of him that she saw herself clearly.

Her breasts were pressed together and spilling over the top. The slit was so high, she'd had to forgo underclothes altogether.

Grim stared at her and looked, more than anything, horrified.

"Do I look Nightshade?" she asked, a note of panic in her voice. She smeared bright paint across her lips, the same way she had the first time she had met him, which seemed to be a Nightshade fashion. Then she put on her mask. He hadn't answered, so she turned back to him, only to find his eyes still on her. "Hmm?"

"It'll do," he had said gruffly and extended his hand.

Now, as they walked through Creetan's Crag, Grim looked straight ahead. Even if he wasn't looking at her, others were. She felt their gazes on her and resisted the urge to press her hand against the slit, to ensure it didn't expose more than her leg.

Grim seemed more on edge than usual. He couldn't use his powers, on the off chance that the sword was close by. They'd had to portal far away and walk for nearly an hour as a precaution.

"How does it feel?" she whispered.

He looked over at her. "How does what feel?"

"Not being the scary, all-powerful Nightshade ruler anymore. In a crowd like this."

Grim gave her a look. "I could still kill everyone here with my sword."

"Not me."

His eyes were back on the street. "Are you forgetting the results of our duel?"

"I didn't hate you as much as I do now. I'm sure that very fact would help me win."

"Is that so?"

"Absolutely."

Speaking of the crowd . . . "How do you know a celebration like this will draw him out?" The mysterious thief. The one with the snake who had been seen nearby.

"I don't. But if he is here, all this . . . distraction will be useful."

Distraction was one word for it.

Thousands of people made currents through the streets and filled each shop to the brim, so much so that she watched someone fall through an open window in a bar and land right in a pile of vomit.

Demonstrations, shows, and betting rounds were going on. Cards were being played. By the sounds coming from alleyways, every type of desire was being fulfilled.

"We know he has a snake. How else are we supposed to find him?" She looked over at him. "Do you know how to get information without cutting off hands?"

Grim glanced over at her. Not a minute later, he stopped in front of a woman. She had five drinks in her hands and looked about to take the order of a group of people sitting outside a bar.

Isla watched the woman's entire face change as she took him in. His wide shoulders, his height. Her expression went from annoyed to curious in an instant. Even from a few steps down the street, she couldn't hear what they were saying over the music and drunken jeers. The woman was saying something, and then she placed a hand on his arm, and he *let* her. Something uncomfortable that she didn't want to name curled in her stomach.

When Grim returned, he looked far too smug. "I know where to find him."

Isla didn't give him the satisfaction of looking surprised or impressed. "Good. Lead the way."

They didn't have to walk far. Minutes later, they entered a massive tent. "That's him." The *him* was a man wearing his shirt completely open, revealing a muscular chest. He had pale skin, hair cut close to his head, and, most remarkable of all, a viper wrapped around his shoulders.

The thief was with a group of people—his collaborators, no doubt—sitting front row at a very . . . interesting show.

People with fabric draped over them—and little else underneath—danced in front of bright lights, turning the sheets they held completely sheer. Every inch of their bodies was visible. Some wore nothing underneath; others wore limited underclothes. The man was watching them intensely, elbows on his knees.

All right. There he was. Somehow, they would have to get information from him. "He seems preoccupied. How are we—"

Grim looked from the dancers to Isla. Then back again.

She scoffed. "Absolutely *not*, you cursed demon—"

He shrugged a shoulder. "Then we'll find another way. I just thought, you being a temptress and all, you could use *your* powers, since I'm unable to use mine."

Powers. She was supposed to be a cursed hearteater, able to tempt a person with a single look. Capable of bringing anyone to their knees with her seduction. Somehow he hadn't seemed to notice her powerlessness, beyond a few pointed statements. He couldn't find out she didn't have ability. What if that was why he was working with her in the first place? Would he rescind his offer to help her during the Centennial?

Roaring began filling her ears. They hadn't found the skin gloves. She and Celeste needed him. *Her* people needed her. They were suffering.

"Can't you just torture the information out of him?" she asked. Suddenly, that option sounded a lot more appealing.

Grim looked amused. "Of course I can, Hearteater. But one of the most infamous thieves, one of the only people who knows about the sword, turning up dead in such a violent fashion? It would be suspicious . . ." He shrugged a shoulder. "I suppose, if you are unable to actually *use* your powers—"

"Of course I can," she said quickly.

Grim looked unconvinced. "It's fine. We'll find another—"

“No.” She was suddenly intent on wiping that look off his face. She reached back into her dress and shoved her starstick at him. “Take this from me, and you’ll see my *other* Wildling curses in action,” she said.

Then she turned on her heel, toward the tent behind the stage.

All her previous bravado was gone. She had traded one of the girls in the show a ruby from her necklace in exchange for her extra set of clothing. Now, she stood just offstage, trembling. Her chest was covered only by a thick strip of black fabric. Her other parts were covered only by a skirt that truly had not earned that description, for it barely concealed anything.

The sheet was over her, but she had seen it at work in the light. Everything would be revealed. *She* would be revealed.

Get it together, she told herself. Her people were starving. The mark above her heart was only the faintest scar now, but the encounter had left more than torn flesh behind. She had seen the women’s desperation. They looked guilty, but they were hungry. She was their ruler. It was her responsibility to do whatever she could to survive the Centennial and break their curse.

With her people in mind, a stupid dance in front of a thief seemed easy. She had a plan. Seduce him, bring him to a private place, and feed him the bottle of liquor she had also bought off the dancer.

“A drink of this, and any man will be flat on his stomach,” she had said. “Lets us accept payment without doing most of the more unsavory acts.”

Finally, Isla had asked for advice. “Do you know the man with the serpent?”

She had rolled her eyes. “We all do, unfortunately.”

“How do I get him to notice me?”

“Easy,” she said. “He likes attention.”

All she had to do was dance in front of him.

How hard could it be?

She was wearing a mask. Anonymous. No one knew her here—except for the cursed demon, who she doubted would even be watching.

With a burst of confidence, Isla stepped onto the stage, wrapped in the cloth she knew was made completely transparent by the lights behind, casting her body in full shadow.

Gazes were brands searing her skin. At first, she rejected it, felt disgusted, but then . . .

This was a choice. She was not being forced. They were here to watch, and she had agreed to be part of the entertainment.

She positioned herself right in front of the man with the snake, making sure to give a smile just for him, and she began to dance.

The music was a rush of drums and strings so fast and intoxicating that her body moved to its rhythm, matching the routine of the others. Her hips swayed, dipped, her arms reached above her head, she ran her fingers down her stomach, touching her body through the fabric . . .

And met his gaze. *Him.*

Grim.

He was watching her like she really had power and could seduce a man with one look. He was staring like a man entranced, standing predatorially still. She met his eyes, and he did not look away—no, if anything, he looked more intensely. His eyes swept down her body, and up, and lingered, and she felt it in her blood, in her bones, *him*—

His gaze broke away, narrowing on something right in front of her, just a half second before she felt a pull on her fabric.

She heard a hiss.

The thief. The snake around his neck flicked its tongue out. The man offered his hand, which was full of coins she had never seen before. "Might I have a private show?" he asked.

Bile worked its way up her throat. She gave her most convincing smile. "Of course."

The man helped her off the stage, and she led him to the back of the tent, where she had watched other dancers take their clients. Before going into one of the private areas, she scooped up her bottle of liquor.

"For you," she said reverently, and he smiled. The snake hissed again, and he petted its head. "Apologies—she is a jealous woman," he said about the serpent.

The curtains made a scratching sound as she opened them. They were in a building now, with stone walls. The sounds of music and yells were muted here. In their room, there was only a chair, some candles, and a table with awaiting goblets.

She uncorked the bottle and poured him a glass.

He took it immediately, and Isla thought he was a fool for not even smelling it before gulping it down. He must not have viewed her as a threat.

Perhaps this was how he'd lost the sword.

"More," he said, offering his goblet. She happily obliged, and he downed the drink again, before loudly leaving it on the table. "Now," he said, smiling, teeth shining in the limited light of the few scattered candles. "Dance."

Isla did. She danced in front of him, smiling coyly when he made to reach for her, turning around strategically, so he didn't think she was denying him.

When she turned around again, she saw his eyes were drooping. He fought to stay awake, his head lolling, then straightening, again, and again.

This was her chance.

"Come here," he said, patting his leg. She felt a bout of nausea but complied, sitting on his lap, far from where he wanted her.

The snake lunged for her, and Isla startled, but the man just laughed, head lolling to the side. "Don't worry, she doesn't bite," he said. "I had her fangs removed." Though she was grateful for it now, Isla thought that was very sad. For a moment, she felt pity for the snake.

"I'm looking for something," she whispered.

"Are you?" he said, his voice slurring.

"A sword. The one your group stole from the Skyling market and that you stole from them. Where is it?"

He laughed, his eyes rolling back. "That sword ruined my life," he said. "It's nearly killed anyone who's tried to use it. I suppose none of us were powerful enough for it." He laughed some more.

She leaned closer, clutching both sides of his open shirt in her hands. "Where is it?"

The man smiled. His eyes were nearly closed now. His very pale cheeks were now flushed. Perhaps the drink had worked too well. "A thief stole it from me. Ironic, isn't it? Some call her the best thief in all the realms."

"What's her name?"

"No one knows."

"Where can I find her?"

He lifted a shoulder.

That wasn't helpful. She shook him by the sides of his shirt. "Where do you think the sword is now? Would she have traded it? Sold it?"

"Oh, I *know* where the sword is."

Isla stopped shaking him. "You do?"

He nodded as much as he could manage. "The thief has a favorite hiding place."

"Where?"

"Here, on Nightshade."

Hope bloomed. "Close by?"

He shook his head. "No, no. Far."

"Where?"

"The Caves of Irida."

Isla stopped breathing. That was a very specific location. She didn't know where it was, but Grim would.

Suddenly, her hope began to deflate. "Wait. If you're so sure you know where it is, why haven't you stolen it back?"

He laughed, but it sounded faded. He was moments from sleep. "Besides the fact no one will go near it? Because it's impossible," he slurred. "The thief has a monster."

"Monster?"

"It guards her bounty."

"What kind of monster?" she demanded.

But the thief had succumbed to the liquor. She let him go, and he crumpled against the chair, making a snoring sound. The snake slid across his face, as if trying to wake him.

Isla only realized that in her fervor to get information she had climbed atop the man when Grim opened the curtain to the room. She stood quickly, grinning, mouth opening, ready to tell him everything they now knew, when she abruptly shut it.

Grim looked furious. He looked at the man, sleeping peacefully, then at her.

"Don't kill him," she said.

He gave her a look.

"You look like you want to kill him."

"I want to kill a lot of people," he said, like that made things better. He looked her dead in the eyes. "I *kill* a lot of people."

She swallowed, and his gaze went straight to her throat.

He stalked toward her, and Isla backed away. Her spine hit the wall. Her heart seemed ready to beat out of her chest, but she smirked. "I got the information. I know exactly where the sword is. Seems like I'm a perfectly good temptress." In the most mocking tone that she could manage at the moment, she said, "Tell me, nonpowerful Nightshade. Was I able to tempt you?" He frowned down at her, and she grinned. She stared up at him through her eyelashes. "Did I make you fall hopelessly in love with me?"

Isla gasped as he pinned her against the wall. His hands were rough against her hips. His fingers traveled up the sides of her stomach, to her ribs, to her breasts. She arched her back, groaning as his thumbs made wide sweeps across them. She knew he could feel her emotions, her want.

"No," he said against her parted lips. "You are not something special to me. You are not something I want to love." He reached up to her lips and smeared her red lipstick with his thumb. "You are something I want to ruin."

Then he ducked his head to her throat and bit her.

It was a light bite, just a scraping of his teeth, but Isla gasped, which turned into a moan as his tongue swiped across the same spot. She wanted him so much—she wanted everything.

In a single motion, he turned her around, so her chest was pressed to the wall. His hands raked up her thighs, until he gripped her hips.

Before she could move against him or do any of the millions of things that were racing through her mind, he made a portal with her starstick against the wall in front of her and pushed her through it.

SPLIT

She woke up next to Oro and couldn't even look at him. When she was in her memories, it was as if everything was happening to her, *again*, and—

It felt like a betrayal.

Oro would tell her it wasn't her fault. That these things had already happened, months before she ever met him.

But now, reliving them . . . sleeping next to someone else . . .

It was a poison she was feeding herself. Forcing herself to swallow it down, even though it was killing her inside.

She felt like she was being split apart. Past Isla, a person she barely even recognized. Current Isla, who had slipped back into pain, into anxiety, into hurt, due to the memories.

A person could take only so much.

Midnight was a comforting time of action. Perhaps it was the quiet, or the fact that the chances were low that someone would stumble upon her, or the indulgence of patting herself on the back that she was going above and beyond by even being awake at this hour, let alone working, or maybe it was all of that encapsulated into one.

Maybe it was because she was part Nightshade.

She used her starstick to portal herself to Wild Isle. There, she went through the Wildling movements. She began practicing forming the types of defensive, thorned plants that she would create across the Mainland. She made patches of bog sand.

Isla visited her room before she went back to bed and watched herself in the mirror. There were dark circles beneath her eyes. Her lips

were raw and chapped. Her skin was rough in some places where it had been smooth. She looked too thin.

Her eyes slid to her neck. It looked bare.

It was not.

She touched a hand to the necklace, which only she could feel, and anger built inside. Of course Grim would gift her a necklace impossible to take off. Of course he would make sure she couldn't forget him, even though she *wanted to*.

She remembered his words when he had gifted it to her, at the ball. *Should you ever need me, touch this. And I will come for you.*

Enough. Isla got one of her blades and positioned it precariously against the necklace. One slipup and she would be dead, but she would not slip. She began trying to cut the damned thing off.

The blade didn't even make a mark. She tried pulling the back, nearly choking herself in the process, but the necklace stayed firm, undisturbed.

She tried wrapping Wildling power around it. Sawing it. Burning it with her fireplace poker. Even summoning a handful of Nightshade shadows and sharpening them into weapons.

Nothing worked.

Thirteen days before Grim was set to destroy the island, the Skylings finally held their vote. The meeting on Sky Isle was well underway. For hours, different sides had debated the issue. Isla, Oro, Enya, Calder, and Zed sat watching as they discussed the very good reasons why all Skylings should leave Lightlark.

She had seen it in her vision—dreks were coming. Without Skylings in the air to fight them, it would be another bloodbath. Hundreds of Skyling soldiers had been trained in the flight force. They made up a large part of their numbers.

"We can't lose them," Enya whispered, almost to herself.

The sides were almost evenly matched—just a few votes were undecided. Still, it seemed clear that it would tip toward leaving the island.

Before the final vote was cast, Oro stood to address them. "We all know the value of your flight force and numbers in this battle. You might believe you can flee the danger, but it will follow. If Grim wipes out Lightlark, what is to stop him from taking out the Skyling newland as well? For all we know, he wants to wipe away the world." There were whispers. A few people nodded. "Regardless, without Lightlark, Skyling will fall. Every generation will become weaker. People will die. Power will dwindle. Your ruler's ability and your own stem from the power that is buried deep within Lightlark. If the island is destroyed . . . so are we all."

Oro sat down. It was a good speech. There was murmuring. Still, something in her chest said it wasn't enough. Something told her how the vote would go—

She stood, and the whispers quieted. She looked at Azul, who had organized the meeting. "May I speak?" she asked.

Azul nodded.

"This isn't just about the battle," Isla said. "This is about *after*. The future we build after saving the island. Building a better Lightlark." She looked at the committee, including Bronte and Sturm. Then, at the Skylings sitting in the room, watching her.

She needed to offer something to the Skylings. They didn't value much . . . but they did value something above all else.

She hesitated, before saying, "If we survive this attack, I plan on implementing a democracy for Starlings." Murmurs. Zed shot her a look. She straightened her spine and continued, "I will hold a vote, and if someone else is more capable of being ruler, I will step down." She meant it. She had always admired Azul's rule, and the truth was, the Starlings deserved to be ruled by one of their own. Maren, for example. "Anyone who stays and fights is battling for a better future. One where more people have choices and rights. We need Skylings, or we will lose, and that better future will have been just a dream, extinguished."

Oro placed his hand on hers for a split second as she sat down, and she felt better, knowing he had agreed with what she had done.

She didn't think it would shift the vote, but it could encourage some Skylings to stay and fight. She only knew she'd had to try.

Azul's voice thundered through the room as he said, "We will now conduct our vote."

Isla waited for the results with Enya and Calder, in the war room. Oro was at the vote. Zed was casting his own.

At first, the group used the time to catch each other up on their progress. Enya determined the Lightlark civilians would have to be evacuated between the Skyling and Starling newlands. She was preparing infrastructure and supplies for them to be able to comfortably live there for however long the war went on.

Calder had been visiting the Vinderland every day, tracking their progress. So far, the flower wasn't working. Perhaps their preparation had been wrong. They would have to figure out another way to heal them.

Then, there had been hours of quiet, as they waited.

The moment Oro walked through the door, Isla knew it was bad news. She could feel it in her core. Zed was right behind him.

"We lost Azul," Oro said. Enya gasped. "The Skylings voted not to allow him to fight." His eyes found Isla. "Part of the flight force made their own choice, though. If you pledge to make Starling into a democracy, they will stay."

"How many?" Enya asked.

"One hundred."

Mixed emotions battled within Isla. Azul was the strongest of the Skylings, a ruler. He held most of the ability in his realm. Losing him would incapacitate them significantly.

Zed shook his head. "It's not enough. It's not nearly enough."

Azul walked in, then. He looked devastated. He closed his eyes and said, "I do not agree with this choice. I—I am truly sorry."

Zed turned to him. "I'm staying here. I've made my choice. Yet you're leaving us. For what? Democracy? Does democracy even matter, if we're all dead?"

"Zed," Oro said steadily. The Skyling sat down, but his glare did not diminish.

Azul shook his head. "I am truly sorry." He looked at Isla, and she remembered the words he had once told her: *It is an honor to rule but not always a pleasure.*

She didn't want to be mad at him. She *agreed* with his way of ruling. How could she fault him for upholding his people's wishes?

Their wishes, though, meant she and the people she loved most might die.

Later that day, she portaled to a deserted part of the Wildling newland and raged her shadows across the dirt, letting her anger scorch the world, until she collapsed into another memory.

BEFORE

It had been a month since Grim had pushed her through the portal, along with her starstick. He hadn't followed her into her room, so she assumed he had portaled himself back to the castle after taking the thief's memories of their meeting away.

She had been left feverish, wanting, consumed by need—

Now she just felt empty.

Why had he left? At a time when she had most wanted him to stay?

Isla might have assumed he had gone off to find the sword without her—if he hadn't left before she could tell him where the sword was. She knew exactly where to find it now. He *knew* she knew.

So why had he gone weeks without seeking her out?

Her confusion and anger soon turned to dread. What if Grim had . . . died? Word wouldn't reach the Wildlings of Nightshade's demise for weeks. Months, maybe.

It was this thought that made her do something careless. That night, she finally reached for her starstick, intent on finding Grim herself.

His room was empty and just the way she remembered it.

Part of her itched to draw her puddle of stars and leave again, but she decided to wait. It had been a *month*. She was tired of staying up late at night, wondering about his absence.

An hour became two. Then three.

Finally, the door to his room opened.

It was not Grim.

It was a woman.

Isla stood from the chair she had been lounging in, and the woman froze. Then, her eyes narrowed. "Who are you?" she demanded.

Who was *she*?

The woman, mercifully, closed the door, as if she had walked in on something private, and Isla portaled away.

Isla felt inexplicable rage. Had he decided to start looking for the sword with someone else? Had he cut her out of his plan? No. She wouldn't let him. She needed him to fulfill his side of their deal.

She knew where the sword was. She would find it herself, and he would be forced to help her at the Centennial.

Isla put on the only black clothing she had—the unfortunately flimsy dress from Creetan's Crag, with her black cape atop it, which conveniently covered the sword strapped to her back—and portaled away.

Grim's lessons had been useful. She needed a map to find the Caves of Irida. Then she could work on trying to portal there.

That was how she ended up in the night market.

It was less than an hour to sunset, and the place was still surprisingly busy. A few carts began packing up for the night. Some people ventured inside large buildings that looked mostly abandoned.

They made a good vantage point. All she needed to do was spot a map shop from above and wait until sunset to sneak inside and find what she was looking for. That way, she wouldn't risk running into trouble again.

She left the market and entered the closest building. The ground floor seemed to be an extension of the shops, a place to trade when the sun went down. It was bustling with the sounds of carts being pushed inside from out, haggling, and whispers.

No maps sold, though. Higher. She needed to go higher and get a better view of the market outside.

The stairs creaked but were empty. So was the second floor. There were just a few boxes and barrels lining the large room, all the way to

windows caked in dust. She rubbed her cape against one and peered outside. Shops were folding closed.

In the corner of her vision, she spotted it. A stall with elixirs sold at the front and parchment in the back. A large map took up its entire back wall—

Footsteps sounded behind her.

Then, "What do we have here?"

Isla turned to see the room was now quite occupied. A dozen Nightshades stood around. Had they been invisible when she walked in? Or had they soundlessly followed her?

She drew her sword. One of them laughed. Her own shadow behind her whipped like a viper and knocked her blade away.

Shadow-wielders. Her chest filled with dread.

Isla quickly turned, deciding to take her chance on the window. She was only on the second floor—

Before she could break through the glass, shadows wrapped around her ankle and dragged her across the room.

Her cheek hit a snag on the floor and tore open. Broken glass stabbed through her hands and her thin dress.

When she was forced to her knees, blood dripped down her chin and chest. She couldn't even move her fingers.

Her cape was ripped away from her by invisible hands, and she gasped at the cold. The man was circling now, a predator leering at his prey.

"Who are you?" he asked.

She spat at his feet, and one of his shadows slapped her in the face. Blood trickled down the corner of her mouth.

"I'll ask again," the man said. "Who. Are. You."

Why did he care? Why was he doing this to her?

She didn't say a word and cried out as another shadow struck her. It was sharp as a blade. Blood dripped down her shoulder. If she didn't heal her cheek soon, it would scar. Another hit sent her crashing to her

glass-filled hands in front of her. She screamed as the glass embedded itself deeper. Another flash of shadows, and she gasped for air.

The man bent down and grabbed her face roughly in one of his hands. Her entire body was shaking. She was going to die. She was such a fool. Hadn't she learned her lesson with the Wildlings who'd tried to carve out her heart? Why had she believed that she could do this herself?

Tears blurred his face in front of her. "You shouldn't have been able to cross the threshold," he said very carefully. "You're going to tell me who you are, or I'm going to skin you alive."

Her blade was on the other side of the room. She hadn't brought any of her daggers or throwing stars with her. The man's shadows were creeping toward her again, across the floor.

She remembered what Grim had said—go for the nose—and head-butted him in the face with her forehead.

He staggered back and called her an awful word, but Isla didn't look to see if she had broken his nose.

She pulled her starstick from her leg holster and drew the puddle of stars. It formed.

Just before she could dive through, the man dragged her away by her hair. She cried out. He ripped her portaling device from her hand and shoved her against the back wall.

The puddle sat there, rippling, in the center of the room. A few of the other Nightshades inched closer to it, murmuring.

"It's . . . a portal," one of them said in awe. More of them rushed to get closer.

The man frowned. Blood got into his mouth. She had broken his nose. "Go see where she was running off to," he ordered.

One of the Nightshades fell through her puddle. It closed after him.

Her only escape, gone.

The only relief was that she hadn't been trying to portal back to the Wildling newland. No . . . she had been trying to portal somewhere else entirely.

"The rest of you," the man yelled, "get out your blades. Let's see how quickly we can skin her. Make sure she stays alive. I want her to feel every inch of this."

She tried to run, but the shadows behind her became restraints around her legs and ankles. One tied around her mouth, muting her screams.

Some of the Nightshades laughed at the sight of her struggling. She heard the scrape of metal as they took their daggers out of their holsters. Some were caked in rust. Others in dried blood.

The man in front of her plucked even more shadows from the room. They inched up her neck, then sharpened into knives.

"Let's start with your face, shall we?" he asked.

Isla winced. Braced herself for the first strike of pain.

His shadows fell away.

The man frowned. He tried his shadows again, but they didn't cooperate. The Nightshades went suddenly quiet.

They slowly turned around. Isla looked through the gaps between them.

Grim stood there, holding the Nightshade who had gone through her puddle by the neck, high above the ground. Her portal had led to Grim's room. There was a crack, and he released him. The man fell in a heap at his feet, dead.

He looked murderous.

In front of her, the man's trousers turned dark, dripping down his leg.

Grim wore his crown and armor. He looked like a demon come to life, spikes on his metal-covered shoulders. Shadows leaked from his very form, snaking through the room. Some of the Nightshades scrambled to kneel. Others tried to flee.

At once, they all jerked high into the air, feet dangling, clawing at their throats.

Grim's eyes never left hers as he stalked over to her. He scanned her body. The cuts across her chest. Her ripped-open cheek. The long marks across her shoulders. Her hands covered in glass.

Grim's voice was lethally calm as he said, "Which one?"

She opened her mouth, but no words came out. Her eyes darted around the room. With them all floating at this angle, she couldn't see their faces clearly. Which body was he? Tears blurred her vision.

"Isla," he said carefully, like he was trying very hard to keep all of himself reined in. He had used her first name. "Which one did this to you?"

She didn't know what he would do, or if she wanted to be the one responsible—

"Fine," he said. "All of them, then."

There was a chorus of cracks as all their necks were broken in tandem. They all fell to the floor. Grim opened his hand, and her starstick flew into his grip.

"You idiot," he said before reaching down and taking her into his arms.

He was furious. He had portaled them into his room. He set her down on a couch and growled, "I'll be back," before vanishing.

Her head fell against the back of the chaise, and she groaned. She had truly believed she could find the sword herself. How wrong she had been.

He reappeared, holding about a dozen different types of bandages and a bowl. He motioned for her to lie down, then went to work, placing the gauze over her shoulders, where she had been injured. They were cold as ice. At their contact, she bucked, cursing.

Grim kept her down with a firm hand on her lower stomach that made her feel shockingly feverish.

"These are Moonling," he said. "They're good at healing cuts."

She was right. Cleo was helping him. Or, at the very least, he was stealing from the Moonlings. "Do you . . . trade with them?"

Grim didn't answer.

His brows were drawn in focus as he plucked pieces of glass from her chest. She closed her eyes tightly against the pricks of pain.

"Let me see your hands."

They were a wreck. She didn't even want to look at the damage. She held still.

He snatched one himself and cursed under his breath. "This will take a while," he said. She imagined there were dozens of pieces buried deep beneath her palm and fingers.

Without warning, he lifted her in his arms again. And set her on his lap.

Isla tensed. She was still in her far-too-revealing Nightshade dress. "What are you doing?"

"You need to keep still," he said. "Or the glass is going to move while I'm working and make removing all of it almost impossible. I can make you pass out if you prefer."

Isla balked. "I most certainly do not prefer that."

He looked down at her, waiting for approval to continue. She gritted her teeth and said, "Fine."

"So charming," he said coolly. Then he snaked his arms around her, pinning her in place, while he gently opened her fingers.

She wasn't breathing. She was engulfed by him. He was cold as bone. She shivered.

He plucked the first piece of glass from her hand, and she bucked again. This time, though, his arms were around her, hard as iron, keeping her in place. She breathed too quickly, pain shooting up her arm. She watched him expertly remove piece after piece.

She gasped at an especially deep incision. He was tall enough that he rested his chin against the top of her head, and said, "There are about a dozen more on this hand alone, so I would find a way around the pain."

She peered up at him. He glanced down at her for half a second before focusing back on her hand.

"Where were you?" she demanded.

A muscle feathered in his jaw. It had been a month since she had seen him. "I was preoccupied," he finally said.

"With what?"

He said nothing.

She scoffed. Unbelievable. "What could be more important than finding the sword?"

"Not more important, simply more . . . pressing." He had hinted at trouble in his realm. Was that what he was referring to?

"You could have told me. You could have visited at least once . . . allowed me to tell you what I had learned."

He raised an eyebrow at her. "Miss me, Hearteater?"

She huffed. "No. Every time I see you, I get injured, or insulted."

Grim frowned, just the smallest bit. He focused solely on her hand. "What were you thinking?" he said harshly.

She sighed, wincing at another shot of pain. "I was thinking I could find the sword without you," she said honestly.

Isla leaned against his chest, gritting her teeth against the pulling of the glass. Some shards were small, but others felt like knives being plucked from her palms. She tried to breathe past it. The same pain, over and over, she could almost get used to. She had learned that during the hours she had spent preparing for specific Centennial ceremonies.

"I went looking for you, before," she said, voice just a rasp.

"I know."

The woman must have told him. Her cheeks suddenly heated with embarrassment. And . . . something else. Her next question bubbled out of her. "Who was that woman?"

"She's my general," he said.

His general. "Does she suspect . . . ?"

"I told her you were someone I had found to bed from another realm."

Isla swallowed. He said the words so simply . . . was that what she was to him? A girl from another realm he had clearly, at Creetan's Crag, wanted to bed?

Inside, she felt like shattered glass, but she closed her eyes and said as smoothly as she could manage, "I know where the sword is. The thief in Creetan's Crag told me."

"Where?"

"The Caves of Irida."

"I know it."

She expected him to look happier about this development; they were so much closer to finding the sword, but his focus was still pinned on her hand. The last piece of glass on that hand clinked against the bowl. He leaned down and whispered right near her ear, "This is going to hurt," before he poured alcohol over her hand.

Grim pressed his palm against her scream. She was grateful. It was an anchor in the sea of pain.

It was blinding. She writhed against him, and he cleared his throat. One of his hands pressed against her hip, holding her still.

"If you can help it," he ground out, "please stop that."

Oh.

She froze.

She was suddenly far too conscious of his body pressed against her as he reached for her other hand and began again.

Underneath her, Grim had tensed completely. His eyes were trained on her palm. He looked intent on his task.

She was not. What was wrong with her? The pain slowly muted as she focused on every graze of his callused fingers against hers. Every part of her was too sensitive. She was now very aware of every place they were touching. The chin against the crown of her head. The muscled torso behind her, hard as rock. Beneath her . . .

She drew a shaky breath.

Grim seemed to rush, because just a few moments later, he said, "Done." This time, he easily lifted her off him before pouring the alcohol on her hand. She closed her eyes tightly and didn't open them again until the Moonling remedies began to reduce the pain.

He was staring at her.

"Thank you," she said.

He said nothing.

"When can we go to the caves?"

"Once you can properly hold a sword again." It wouldn't be long. By morning, with her Wildling elixirs, most of her wounds would be healed. They would still hurt, but not enough for her to want to delay their search.

"Tomorrow," she said.

He nodded. He reached to portal her back to her room, when she said, "Wait. There's one problem."

"Problem?"

She told him about the monster supposedly guarding the sword.

His eyes narrowed. "What kind of monster?"

"I'm not sure."

Grim didn't look too worried. Monsters weren't scared of other monsters, were they? He offered his hand again to portal her back to her room. "Then I guess we'll have to find out."

ASKING FOR HELP

"We found the ore," Zed announced during their next meeting. He had been searching the Forgotten Mines for days, with Calder, navigating through their dangerous tunnels. Most of the passages had collapsed over time. His face turned from smug to wary as he looked at Isla. "We need your help," he said simply.

Enya was peeling citrus fruit, the smell brightening the room. She raised an eyebrow, and Zed shot her a look.

He didn't particularly like Isla. That much was clear.

"With mining it?" she asked.

He nodded. "I tried using air, but the ores are almost impossible to move. But you . . ."

Control rock. Isla almost smiled, thinking how far she had come from glaring at the stone Oro had placed in front of her on Wild Isle. "Lead the way."

Breathing was difficult in the mine. Zed kept having to move fresh air down deep into the tunnels, which only barely muted the smell of dirt, dust, and sulfur.

She held the fabric of her shirt over her nose. Zed walked in front of her, carrying an orb of fire he had gotten from Enya.

"I would say you get used to it," Zed said. "But you don't. Just feel lucky you haven't been trapped down here for weeks."

She suddenly felt extremely lucky.

They were mostly quiet as they walked. It was a mutual silence—both were happy not to speak to each other. After several minutes, though, she had a thought. "Why does everyone hate Soren?" She remembered how he had questioned her in front of the others, seemingly intent on proving her unworthy of being a ruler. "Beyond the obvious, I mean."

Zed chuckled lightly. He looked over at her. She bet she looked ridiculous, half of her face hidden in her shirt. "He thinks Moonlings are superior to all other realms, and he acts like it. Under his guidance, healers closed their shops in the agora. Less Moonlings started visiting the Mainland at all. They became more closed off and guarded. He used the curses as an excuse to isolate their realm from the others."

He was more awful than she had previously given him credit for. "If he believes that, then why did he stay? Wouldn't he be happy to leave?"

"Perhaps he hates Nightshade more than he hates all of us," Zed mused. He shrugged a shoulder. "Or he stayed behind as Cleo's spy."

She didn't trust Soren in the slightest, but something occurred to her. "Is . . . is Soren a healer?"

Zed nodded, and hope felt like sparkling wine in her chest. He frowned. "You're not seriously going to ask him to help you with the Vinderland."

"That's exactly what I'm going to do," she said.

Zed finally stopped. He motioned to a wall, and all the rock looked the same, save for a tiny flicker of color. She pressed her hand against it and closed her eyes. Beyond, she could feel it—ore buried deep within the wall. It would take concentration to ensure she wouldn't completely bring the entire mine down atop them, but she felt confident she could extract it.

"You might want to make a shield with your wind," she said, before her hand burst through the rock wall.

The entire tunnel trembled—rock fell from the ceiling and was deflected by a stream of wind above them. She felt around in the wall, looking for the bundle of ore. Her fingers broke through stone like a blade through butter. She finally gripped it and pulled her hand back through. "I think this is what you're looking for," she said. It was the first of many. It didn't look very special, but Zed had explained that

with a Starling's energy and Sunling's flames, it could be turned into the drek-defeating metal.

Zed stared at her, the wall, then the ore, eyebrow slightly raised. "That's one way to do it," he said.

Isla found Soren on Moon Isle, looking quite comfortable roaming the palace. She didn't know if he was a spy or had his own agenda, but she would soon find out which side he was on.

He seemed pleased to see her, which only made her more suspicious. He scraped his ice cane against the floor with a sound that stabbed through her brain. She got straight to the point. "Which side are you on? Ours? Or Nightshade's?"

Soren blinked at her. "I assumed it would be obvious by my presence, here on Lightlark."

"Good," she said. "Then you wouldn't have any problem healing potential warriors for our fighting effort?"

Soren's eyes narrowed. She tried to look as innocent as possible. "I . . . suppose not," he said.

She smiled sweetly. "Great. Because . . . if you had said no . . . I would have had to assume you were a spy for Cleo, or somehow working against us."

Soren smiled in the least friendly way possible. "Who am I healing?"

Isla found particular pleasure in his expression after she said the words, "The Vinderland."

The hardest part about getting Soren to heal the warriors ended up being convincing the Vinderland not to kill him.

He showed her how to correctly steep the Wildling flower for tea without losing its healing properties, then began healing their sickness in conjunction with the elixir. The results weren't immediate, but Isla was hopeful that enough of the warriors would be doing better in time to join her in battle.

She had extracted several ores for Zed. Later that night, Isla visited the Wildling newland and found Lynx waiting outside the woods for her.

Her lips twitched. "If I didn't know any better, I would think you were worried about me," she said.

Lynx made a sneezing sound that felt like a denial.

She stood in front of the creature and offered a slab of meat she had gotten from the kitchens.

He sniffed it . . . then, for once, accepted her gift. Progress, she told herself. It was progress.

When Lynx finished eating, she asked, "I've told you we are going to war. Will you fight with me?"

She searched his eyes for a response.

He bowed his head, almost all the way to the ground, and something inside her chest constricted at the clear *yes*.

So often, she had been betrayed. Put her trust somewhere dangerous. The fact that Lynx, who liked to pretend he didn't care for her much, was willing to go to battle with her . . . it meant everything.

She threw her arms around his neck, and he let her hang there. He lifted his head, and she held on, legs dangling.

"We'll get you armor made." She was floating just inches from Lynx's eye as she said, "First, though, I need to learn how to ride you."

As the days before war dwindled, it became clear that there was not enough of anything—time, soldiers, resources, energy.

They sat at the round table again and planned their strategy. They had limited everything, which meant they needed to figure out how to be strategic—how to force Grim and his soldiers to fight exactly where they wanted them to.

They had crafted a map of the Mainland with the mysterious ash Isla had used before, on Sun Isle.

Oro and Zed had been arguing for hours about where they would have the best advantage.

"Here, over the mines," Zed was saying. "We can have warriors in the tunnels. It could work as a trench."

"It would work well for the Nightshades, who could demolish the ground and bury our forces alive," Oro said.

"How about between the Singing Mountains? Nightshades don't know how to fight in mountainous terrain."

"Sunlings don't either."

In the end, they agreed the best place to fight was on the west side of the Mainland, in the space between the agora and Mainland castle. That way, the Mainland woods would naturally frame their fighting area, along with the Starling walls and Wildling defensive nature.

"Can you manage to cover that much territory?" Zed asked. "In nine days?"

"Yes," she said, because there was no other option.

At night, she practiced riding on Lynx. She fell off so much, they had started moving their lessons to the river. The leopard was tall enough that he could easily walk through even its deeper parts, and Isla wouldn't risk a serious injury every time she fell.

She fell a lot.

Each time, Lynx looked at her in a way that could only be interpreted as unimpressed, and then he would fish her out of the water with his great teeth and throw her on his back again.

If only they had more time, she thought. The days were slipping through her fingers.

She needed to get the Wildlings on Lightlark, to start coating its surface in poisonous plants. She needed to start portaling civilians onto the newlands. That alone would take days and much of her energy.

She needed a shortcut.

She needed to remember something useful.

BEFORE

Monster was a kind word for the creature that lived in the cave, housed at its mouth.

It was a dragon.

When Isla was a child, Poppy used to tell her stories of beasts large as hills, with scales like peeling bark and claws at the ends of wings so large they blocked the sun. Isla used to be afraid one might find its way to the Wildling palace and break her room apart with a single shrieking cry.

Don't worry, little bird, Poppy had said. *All the dragons are gone.*

No. Not gone. Just hiding.

"It's asleep," Isla whispered. The dragon was curled in the mouth of the cave, its head facing the opposite direction. Its body rose and fell in a steady rhythm.

She squinted. The cave was not deep. There was a sliver the dragon wasn't covering, and she could see behind it, farther inside—

"No," she said, blinking quickly. "That can't be—no, that's too easy, it can't—"

"It's the sword," Grim said.

Just behind the dragon, the sword was sitting on top of a pile of other relics. It was made of two pieces of metal, braided together like lovers, until they formed a single joined tip.

She made a sound of relief. "We just have to sneak past it without waking it. That's it."

Grim didn't look convinced. "And if it does wake, it will char us alive," he murmured.

They approached the cave slowly, silently, keeping to its very edge.

This would be easy, she reasoned.

The dragon was sleeping soundly. The sword was *right there*; she could *see it*.

The moment Isla stepped foot inside, something flew through the sky. She felt a howl of pain in her leg.

Grim moved fast as lightning. He knocked her off her feet and pinned her against the ground, hand coming down behind her head to soften the fall. Less than a second later, half a dozen arrows went right through his body.

Isla opened her mouth to scream, but before she could make a sound, Grim's other hand smothered her lips. It stayed there, cold and solid as ice. Her eyes were wide, and they stared at each other, faces inches apart, as more arrows stabbed him through his arms and legs. His body lurched with every new hit until they finally stopped.

There was a moment of tense silence, both waiting to see if they had awakened the dragon. She was panting, her chest nearly meeting his own.

No movement.

Her eyes dropped to his wounds. Twelve arrows. It was a wonder none of them had gone through his heart. Blood soaked his clothing, dripping onto her body.

He had shielded her from the attack, without a moment's hesitation.

She dragged his hand down from her lips. "Portal away," Isla mouthed, lips shaking around the words.

Grim shook his head.

If they used his power or the starstick, the sword would disappear. They might never find it again.

Somehow, Grim had to make it out of the cave.

Isla wasn't even sure how *she* was going to make it. The one arrow that had pierced her before Grim had made himself into her personal shield had gone straight through her shin.

With more strength than she could imagine, Grim somehow got to

his feet. She quietly stood too and had to bite her hand to keep from screaming from pain. She tried to walk a step and nearly crumpled back down to the floor.

With one quick motion, she was off her feet. Grim, twelve arrows still sticking through him, held Isla in his arms and somehow walked steadily out of the cave and through the field until he could portal them away.

The moment they landed in his room, Grim collapsed, sending Isla sliding across the floor. She gasped as she made her way to her feet, toward him. No. To the cabinets. She opened them all, hurriedly looked for healing supplies, and found Moonling gauze. She used her starstick to portal back to her room, grabbed an entire vial of healing elixir, then returned.

Before she could help him, her own leg needed to be dealt with or she would lose too much blood and pass out. Bracing herself for just a moment, she snapped the end of the arrow and pulled it out. She screamed against the back of her hand. Her wound stung as healing elixir dripped onto it. Her fingers trembled as she quickly wrapped her leg with the bandage.

No time to wallow in the pain. She limped over to where Grim had barely managed to sit up and knelt before him.

"I'm going to—"

"Do it," he said, his breathing labored.

She snapped the first arrow, and he swore. She slid the first arrow out, and when she poured healing elixir over the wound, he bellowed. "Well, you have about another dozen of those, so you better toughen up," she said, partially echoing his own words, only because she knew it would bother him enough to stay awake. "Or did you forget that pain is *useful*?"

"Don't mock me," he said, teeth bared. "It's true."

She rolled her eyes.

"I'll tell you a secret, Hearteater." He flinched as she removed the next arrow. "Pain makes you powerful."

Isla let out a sound of disgust. "It does not," she said. "Though I suppose that's a very Nightshade thing to believe."

"No," he said, mouth curling in amusement even as he suffered. "It isn't an ideal. It's truth. Emotion feeds power. And pain is the strongest."

Isla frowned. That couldn't be true.

"It is true," he said, likely sensing her doubt.

If it *was* . . . "Have you . . . have you ever *purposefully* . . ."

"Yes," he said quickly. "I have purposefully caused myself pain to access deeper levels of power. That was a long time ago. Now, it isn't so necessary." As if in afterthought, he said, "And . . . there are many different kinds of pain."

Isla still couldn't believe it was real. Did every ruler know about it? Why wouldn't it be widely used, then?

No. It couldn't be.

Grim shook his head, reading either her face or her emotions. He tsked, then braced himself as she pulled another arrow out. "Still doubting me," he said. He looked her right in the eye then. "How, Hearteater, do you think I am so powerful?"

That made her hands still around one of the arrows for just a moment. He had experienced deep pain. That was what he was telling her.

It surprised her, but . . . she wanted to know what had made him this way. Who or what had hurt him.

He stared at her. She stared back.

She removed one of the arrows from his chest, and he roared.

By the time all the arrows were out, she'd heard every curse word she knew and over a dozen she didn't. He helped her get his shirt off so she could apply the healing elixir. She caught sight of the small charm beneath his clothing. The one that kept him immune from the Nightshade curse. When his chest was bare, she winced at the sight of the dozen wounds.

Grim laughed darkly.

Laughed.

"I've never had a woman wince at my naked body," he said.

She shook her head. "It must be exhausting carrying around such a magnificent ego."

He laughed faintly as she began applying the serum. The first press of the liquid to his skin, and he hissed. His normally cold body was feverish.

"Your leg," he said, even as he was bleeding from a dozen places.

"Is already bandaged," she said before moving on to the next wound. She worked quickly and diligently, brow creased with focus as she made sure all the splinters were out of his skin and that each place was thoroughly cleaned. Through it all, she could feel him studying her.

"What?" she finally said.

Even in what must have been knee-wobbling pain, the demon still managed to sound pleased. He smirked. "I just think it's ironic that the hearteater who stabbed me through the chest is now tending to my injuries."

She gave him a look. "*I* think it's ironic that the demon who claims he has no shred of humanity left used himself as a blockade against an army of arrows to save me."

He said nothing.

When she was finished with the last injury, the healing elixir was halfway gone. The gauze was on its last few rounds.

Now that he was taken care of, Isla looked at the mess in front of her: his blood-soaked shirt, the pile of broken arrows. She threw up her hands. "Seriously. Why did you *do* that?" she said, exasperated.

Grim's head was lolling to the side. He looked half a moment away from passing out. "That's an interesting way of saying thank you," he drawled.

One of his bandages was already soaked in blood, so she moved to make it tighter, to stop the flow. Once she got it in the right position, she went to remove her hands, but one of his own came over both of hers, pressing her fingers to his chest. “The cold, Hearteater,” he said before closing his eyes. His head fell back against the wall. “It helps the pain.”

She sat like that for a few minutes, the only movement the steady beating of Grim’s heart somewhere near her hand. His eyes remained closed the entire time. After her hand warmed against him, she took it back and sat against the wall next to him.

“What happened?” she asked. The arrows had come from nowhere. “I didn’t see anyone, or even where they were coming from—”

“It wasn’t a person; it was a weapon. A mechanism designed to go off against intruders. I’ve seen it before.”

“Where?”

“My own castle.”

Isla turned to look at him. His eyes were still closed, and the crown of his head was still leaned against the wall. “You believe the thief stole it from your castle?”

Grim shrugged a shoulder. “If she did, she really is the best.”

“I take it there aren’t any ways around it.”

He shook his head. “Infallible, unfortunately.”

She sighed. “What do we do now?” There had been yards between them and the sword. Even if they could lure the dragon out of the cave, who knew how many other enchantments the thief had protecting her bounty?

Grim groaned as he straightened himself. “Tonight? I drink my entire store of liquor. Later? I suppose I continue to play shield until we get past all the protections.”

PAIN

Power was metal in her mouth, in her nostrils, down her throat, in her stomach. It lit every inch of her up and through; she was a shining beacon, a blade of power carving the world to her desired shape and measurements.

In her memories, Grim had taught her something no one else had bothered to. To win, she needed more power.

Grim claimed *pain was the strongest emotion.*

Pain could be useful.

Trees rose from the soil in bursts of dirt. Ground broke and built until it formed the beginnings of mountains. Flowers blanketed in front of her, so many, so quickly, they fell right off the side of the island.

More. She needed *more.*

Barbed plants, the same ones that had stabbed her everywhere during the Centennial, rose up in thick brambles. Plants with poisoned leaves sprouted. She painted the Mainland in them both, all the parts they needed to block off.

Isla sank her hands into the dirt, fingers in wild shapes, and bellowed, until the ground broke open and more plants formed all around her. Thorn-covered, monstrous plants that would fight back and defend themselves.

It might have been minutes or hours later, but she felt him, a ray of sunlight landing behind her. "Isla?" he said. Her name was a question.

"I finished it," she said. It had seemed almost impossible to create so much nature in nine days, but she had done it in a single night. "Look,

I made walls to block their paths. I covered all the open spaces. Grim can only portal them where you and Zed decided." She was beaming.

He did not look proud.

He looked . . . horrified. She didn't think she would ever forget the way he now looked at her. Like she was something wrong.

Like she was a monster.

"What have you done?" he asked.

She tracked the direction of his gaze and saw it. Blood dripped down the front of her dress. Her hands reached up and touched it, coming from her eyes, her nose, the sides of her mouth, her ears.

Power . . . tasted like blood.

It tasted like blood.

She was saying it over and over, or maybe it was just in her head, or maybe she lived in her head, maybe she never had to leave, maybe she should open herself completely up to the world and let everything in her finally pour out—

"*Isla.*" His hands were rough against her shoulders. He was shaking her. He looked angry. Upset.

Disappointed.

She ripped her power back into herself, and the world steadied before her.

The voices stopped.

It was only her and Oro. And still . . . he looked displeased.

"What did you do?" he said again. His voice was harsh. It was the voice of the king, not of the man who slept beside her, who swept his hands along her back to help her sleep.

"I found a shortcut," she said. "And tested it."

Oro studied her hand, and she winced at what she had done. She had carved a thick line through its center. That was the shortcut. Doing what Oro had warned against, months before.

Using emotion to spur power.

Pain can be useful.

Pain makes you powerful.

"It's fine," she said, fishing her healing elixir from her pocket. She put a drop on her injury and watched the skin grow back. "Look. Like nothing happened."

"Isla," Oro said carefully. "I told you. Wielding power through emotion is dangerous. The power might be immediate, and strong, but it comes at a cost." His hands were in fists; he was practically shaking. "I told you that this could kill you! It *is* a shortcut," he said, spitting the words out. "A shortcut to death."

Heat blanketed the air. It was suddenly sweltering. Then, it was all ripped away.

Realization made him predatorially calm. "He taught you this. In your memories."

Isla did not deny it.

Oro looked at her . . . and shook his head. He studied her face, covered in blood, then her now healed hand, and said, "I don't recognize you, love."

Her hands trembled. She didn't recognize herself either. She didn't recognize the girl in her mind, the one who had made decisions she didn't understand . . .

"I know you want to get into the vault. I know you want to defeat Grim. I know you want to save yourself and everyone," he said. "But this isn't the way." He looked at her. "Promise me you won't try this again. Please, promise me."

"I promise," she said, because he looked so concerned. Because he was just trying to protect her.

She didn't want to tell him that though she was bleeding, she felt stronger than she had in a long time. She felt in control. Transcendent.

The blood tasted like power, she wanted to say. Power—

It tasted like blood.

. . .

Over the next few days, Isla did not sleep. She began portaling all the civilians to the newlands. She recognized some of them.

None of them sneered at her or called her names. Not when she was their only quick way off the island before the attack.

She was about to leave the Starling newland for the tenth time that day, when she did something she had been avoiding for far too long.

She stepped into the room almost as familiar as her own. She almost expected Celeste—*Aurora*—to be waiting there, braiding her silver hair, just to do something with her hands.

The room was empty.

Memories were everywhere. The pile of silver blankets in the corner that they always used to bundle themselves in. The peeling paint that revealed another color beneath, left over from a previous era. The stone floor in front of the fireplace that had been worn over time, soft enough to lie across. They used to joke that the Starlings before Celeste had loved that spot just as much as they did. Now, Isla supposed, it had always been Aurora, sitting in front of that fireplace. Changing the room color. Alone, until Isla came along.

The flames were gone now. Only cinders remained.

A collection of orbs sat on a shelf. They were some of Celeste's most prized possessions. Each held something mysterious. Celeste had claimed they had been passed down through generations and she didn't know what each contained.

Liar.

Isla grabbed the largest and threw it to the floor. It shattered, glass going everywhere. Angry tears prickled the corners of her eyes. "You must have thought I was such a fool," she said.

She hurled another against the wall. "Did you laugh when I left your room? When I told you my greatest secrets, and all you gave me were lies?"

Another orb hit the door. "Was any of it real?" She threw another. She thought of the little Starling girl who was killed by the creatures. All the people who had died in the last five centuries. Her voice shook as she said, "I killed you, and it wasn't enough. The curses didn't die with you. They are still felt." She clenched her hands in fists. "Did you know you were going to kill thousands of people? Did you even care?"

Shadows exploded out of her, tipped in claws. Gashes ran down the walls, cutting through the paint. There was a halo of black around her feet.

Isla panted, the anger and sadness stuck in her chest. She closed her eyes tightly as tears swept down her cheeks. She flung her arm to the side, and shadows destroyed the rest of the orbs.

All were empty, except for one. When it shattered against the wall, something slowly floated down to the floor.

A single silver feather.

Isla stepped forward. She leaned down to take it between her fingers. It had a sharpened tip, almost like a quill for writing.

Why would Aurora put a quill in an orb?

There wasn't any ink on its bottom, but Isla tried to write on a piece of parchment anyway. Nothing.

The room was in ruins. It looked like a giant beast had broken in and tried to claw its way out. It pleased some part of her to see it destroyed.

"I hate you," Isla said to what was left of the bedroom.

She took the feather with her.

It was late afternoon, when shadows were the longest. The ones the trees cast were uniform, and pliable under her command. Remlar sat on a high branch as Isla turned in a circle, roping them all together. Once they were tied, she flicked her wrist and snapped them like a whip. Their sharp edge cut a row of trees down.

"Learn that in one of your memories?" Remlar called from above.

Isla ignored him. She replaced the trees that she had destroyed with new ones. That was her rule. Replace everything she ruined.

"Now that war is almost here, I feel the need to remind you that not all life can be restored," Remlar said. "At least, not on Lightlark."

Her teeth came together. She was aware of that fact, and it ate at her.

If Oro was right, and Grim really was declaring war over her . . . that would mean every death would be on her hands. She couldn't take it—couldn't live with it.

She still didn't understand. In her memories . . . they didn't love each other at all.

Darkness pooled out of her as she flung her hand out. It shot through the forest, destroying everything in its path. Something about using her Nightshade abilities was therapeutic. It was like letting the worst part of herself out.

Remlar floated down from the tree, landing firmly in front of her. He looked pleased. "Your darkness is blooming," he told her, eyes trailing over the path her shadows had made. She had obliterated part of the forest.

"It is," Isla agreed. She had felt it, inside. Uncurling. Awakening. She was remembering more and more. "That's what I'm afraid of."

"You shouldn't be afraid," Remlar said. "You should use it."

"Use it how?"

"War is days away. Me and my people"—he nodded at the hive—"plan to fight. There are other creatures on Lightlark touched by night that would join you, if you asked."

She shook her head. "No, they wouldn't. I *have* asked." She thought of the serpent-woman on Star Isle.

"Have you asked all of them?"

No. She hadn't.

"How would I convince them?" she asked. "What would I offer them?"

"You," he said simply. "You would offer you."

"Me?"

Remlar nodded. "It has been thousands of years since a single person wielded both Nightshade and Wildling power. You cannot begin to understand what that means." It reminded her of the reverence with which the Vinderland had treated her.

"Tell me what it means," she almost begged.

"You don't need me to tell you," he said. "You will see yourself." He motioned around him. "The creatures as old as me on the island will join you. They will immediately understand what you are."

"And what is that?" she asked.

He looked at her, and she saw a gleam in his eye. "Hope."

"Hope?" she asked, before turning toward a sudden trickling sound. A column of water was impossibly falling from the sky.

She blinked, and the rest of the forest fell away.

BEFORE

The bath was almost full. The water was murky, darker than a bog. She could see the pillar of water from his bedroom.

"Medicinal," Grim said gruffly. "Helps with healing." He began to shed his clothing, revealing deep gashes that would have been deadly for anyone without a ruler's power.

They had visited the cave five times. Each visit, they uncovered another enchantment designed to keep thieves out. Grim always took most of the impact, but that day, when a million ice chips had rained down from the ceiling, some had cut down her arms, face, and back before he'd pulled her out of the way.

Isla winced as she reached to pull her starstick from its place against her spine. Her skin was coated in blood. Her vial of healing elixir was steadily running out. She would have to sneak into Poppy's quarters while she was sleeping if she wanted to get more.

"Stay."

The word was followed by silence. It was said matter-of-factly. Flatly.

"Stay?"

Grim was down to just his pants. His chest was a canvas of gashes, blood, and, of course, the mark oh so close to his heart. "The bath is big enough for two. It will help you not scar."

Isla just stared at him.

He didn't leer or make a suggestive comment. It seemed he was too tired to even say anything worth glaring at him over.

"I'll face the other direction."

Isla found she was too tired to turn down the offer of a warm bath with healing properties. But . . .

"I can't," she said. "Remember?" It seemed like years since they had dueled.

Before she could say another word, Grim said, "I take back my win. You're welcome in every part of my palace."

Isla told herself it was shock that made her step into the bathroom. True to his word, at least this time, Grim turned around. She did too.

The sound of his pants being discarded seemed to echo through the vast bathroom. Then, the sound of water parting, letting him in, settling around him.

She didn't check to see if he was facing away as she peeled her own clothes off. It was a painful process. Fabric stuck to her wounds, blood making a most inconvenient adhesive. She made a small sound of pain and hoped he didn't hear it, though she knew he heard everything. The shuffling of her pants being rolled down past her ankles. Her fingers unraveling her braid.

The groan as she placed a leg into the tub, chills sweeping up the back of her calf and up her spine, burrowing into the crown of her skull.

Grim was very still as she lowered herself completely. All she saw was his back, tight in its rigid posture, his shoulders nearly as wide as the tub itself. Everything else was hidden beneath the dark water, swirling with healing enchantment.

"You can turn around," she said. He did not move an inch. "The water . . . it covers everything." It was true. The only part of her that was visible was her head, framed by wet hair, her shoulders, and collarbones.

Seconds passed. Tripped over themselves. Finally, though, he turned.

She was pressed against one side. He was pressed against the other. The tub was enormous; they might as well have been on opposite sides of the room. They just stared. No words were exchanged, but she saw an understanding there. Two people who had fought back-to-back for something they both wanted more than almost anything. A chance to save their people.

The water became clearer and clearer, the medicine dissolving, until Isla crossed her legs, pressed them to her chest, and looked away when Grim did no such thing.

Isla was still looking away as she heard him stand, the water scattering just like anything in Grim's path always did, and he left.

ARMOR

It was time to have armor made for Lynx. She had practiced riding him in the forest, up hills, down steep cliffsides. With every session, his disdain for her dimmed, little by little. He almost seemed pleased that she was now able to stay tethered to him, no matter how fast he ran.

"See?" she had told him the last time. "I can hold on now."

He had promptly taken a hard turn, which had her falling straight into a stream.

As long as he wasn't intentionally trying to throw her off, she felt confident she could bring him into battle.

Wren was training with the other Wildling warriors when she found her.

"I want to have armor made for him," Isla explained. "I was hoping to get your advice on what that would look like."

Wren frowned. "You don't need to have it made," she said.

"I—"

"Lynx already has armor."

Isla slowly turned to look at the leopard, and he just blinked at her.

"He does?"

Wren nodded. The light in her expression suddenly dimmed. "He fought bravely. With . . . your mother."

"Fought who?" she asked, bewildered.

The Wildling smiled. "It's quite a story. I would be happy to tell it to you."

She wanted to hear it more than anything . . . but not now. Not when every hour mattered. Less than a week remained before the battle.

"Another time, I would be very grateful to hear it," she said. "Do you know where the armor is?"

Wren led her to a store of weaponry. There were dozens of swords, sets of armor, and shields. In the very back were enormous sheets of metal that could only fit a very specific, easily annoyed creature.

Isla had to focus for several seconds before she was able to shakily use her Starling energy to move the armor onto Lynx. It included iron plates down his sides and around his front and neck. It even had small holes for his pointed ears and a place for her to sit. Wren helped her put the piece together, and once they were finished, Isla took a step back.

"Don't you look menacing," she said.

Lynx made a sound of approval. He seemed to like being back in his armor. He lowered his head, motioning for her to get on his back, and she did.

"Thank you!" she told Wren, as Lynx took off.

He raced out of the structure, into the forest. Isla gripped the strange saddle, finding it made holding on infinitely easier.

She bent her head down low as they shot through the brush. The first few times, she had felt afraid of being so high up, but now she felt safe. Protected.

Lynx slowed in the middle of a clearing. He bent his head, his silent request for her to jump off. She did.

There was nothing around. What did he want to show her?

Usually, Lynx would have straightened by now, but his head was still bent. She touched between his eyes, silently asking what he wanted, and went rigid.

Her sight was taken away. No—replaced. She was in the same clearing, but it looked different. There were more trees. The grass looked healthier.

There was a girl. Her? It looked just like her. But she didn't have those clothes . . . she didn't often walk with her hands on her hips.

The image became clearer, and her voice shook as she said, "Is that—is that . . ."

Her mom.

She had never seen her mom before. There weren't any paintings of her. Terra and Poppy hadn't given a description, beyond once commenting that she had her mother's face.

Now, she saw it clearly. Lynx was *showing* her.

Her mother was far more beautiful. She had tanner skin and thicker hair. It was shinier. Her eyes were a lighter green. They had the same lips, though. Same high cheekbones. Slightly different noses.

"Lynx, come on," her mother was saying. "Terra's going to have both our heads."

The image disappeared, and Isla started to protest, until it was replaced by another one.

It was her mother again, but this time, there was someone else too. A man with black hair and lighter skin. He was looking at her mother the way Oro looked at Isla. Like he would gladly lay his life down for hers.

The image shifted, and there was crying. Her parents were holding a little bundle between them, looking like they might burst from happiness.

Isla fell to her knees. Tears streamed down her cheeks, into the grass in front of her. She could barely speak. "You—you met me," she finally said.

Lynx had seen her as a baby.

That was right before her parents were killed. He must not have been there, because Isla knew for certain that he would have done everything he could to protect her mother.

Did he feel shame? Guilt? Had he partially blamed Isla for her mother's death? Or did he blame her father?

Lynx made a soft sound as he bent down and wiped her tears away with his fur, on the parts that weren't covered by iron. He ended up swiping his wet nose across her face, and she sputtered.

"Thank you for showing me," she finally said. She wasn't sure how exactly the bonded connection worked, but she felt grateful for it. "I never knew her, but . . . I think this would have made her happy. Us . . . finding each other."

Lynx closed his eyes for a long time, and she could feel his grief like it was her own. She pressed her cheek against his and for a while, it was just them, in the clearing, sharing a memory between them.

When the sun went down, Isla portaled them back to her room. Lynx sat curled in his favorite corner as she stared at her swords, contemplating which ones to bring into battle. There was a whisper of movement behind her, and she turned, mid-sentence.

Only to see that Lynx had been replaced by someone else entirely.

BEFORE

Grim was standing in front of her. She was ready to go to the cave again, but he said, "Not tonight."

"Why not?"

"I have a commitment."

She frowned. "What is it?"

"A ball." He said it with venom.

Isla laughed. "A *ball*?"

"Is that amusing to you?"

She lifted a shoulder. "*You* hosting a ball? Decorations? Dresses? Clinking wineglasses?" Isla had never actually been to a ball, but that was the picture painted by Celeste and the books she'd read.

"Hardly," he said coolly. By his reaction, he made a ball seem like a death sentence. "I would cancel it, but it is a good distraction."

"From?" she asked.

He didn't answer, but she imagined he meant whatever danger was threatening Nightshade. The threat that could mysteriously be solved by the sword. The reason there were often long stretches between his visits. The *more pressing* matter he often needed to attend to.

"Can I come?" she asked.

He looked at her as if she had asked if she could have his throne. "Absolutely not."

Then he vanished.

Late that night, Isla was bored to death on her bed, reading her latest book for the tenth time. She had already filled the margins with notes.

With a sigh as dramatic as she could manage, she flipped onto her back and flung the book to the other side of her bed. She wondered what the ball was like. Were women throwing themselves at Grim? Of course they were. And he was probably accepting them with open arms. The thought made her more than a little nauseous.

She had already changed into her pajamas and was ready to go to bed when her starstick glimmered from beneath her floorboard. It was almost like an invitation.

One she accepted.

A quick, thieving trip to the night market later, she was dressed in about as little fabric as possible to still be considered clothed.

She doubted Grim would even see her. She would stay out of sight. Even if he did see her, so what? He would have to pretend not to know her, to keep up appearances. It was late enough into the night that most of the people at the ball were probably too intoxicated to notice. They couldn't leave until daytime. The party was meant to last until the morning, she realized.

Isla portaled to the Nightshade castle.

If the word *debauchery* had been a place, Isla was looking at it.

The halls of the castle were filled with music so loud and fast it drowned out the moans she could hear only when she passed by the dark halls, people moving furiously in the shadows. Inside the ballroom, all pretense of propriety was abandoned.

People danced with long ribbons of black silk, on platforms lining the room between full suits of armor. In the darker corners of the rooms, couples were coupling, not seeming to care in the slightest that they had hundreds of people as their witnesses.

Before, Isla had felt embarrassed by the amount of skin she was showing, but now she saw she was wearing almost the most fabric in the room. Her dress was black gossamer, with a dipping neckline, two

pieces covering her breasts, then coming together in the middle. It had a slit up to her hip.

Eyes were on her immediately. At first, she panicked, wondering if they somehow recognized her.

No—their gazes were not threatening. They were hungry.

Tonight, she embraced it. It felt good to be seen and wanted.

Isla assumed the party would be crowded and raucous enough that she wouldn't even see Grim, but—

He found her immediately.

She felt his gaze like a brand, and when the crowd naturally parted at the sound of a new song, there was a direct path, across the room, from him to her.

Even from far away, she could see he was furious. Women fought for his attention, barely clothed, but he was watching her, eyes blazing with so much anger, he looked ready to wage a war.

Isla did the most foolish thing possible in response to his anger, which was smile and blow him a mocking kiss.

Immediately, he stood, knocking over some of the goblets that the women had placed around his throne. He didn't even look down; all he did was take a step forward, as if he was going to portal to her and send her straight back to Wildling.

No. She knew it wouldn't do much good if he really wanted to find her, but she ducked into the crowd. In the center of so many people, Grim wouldn't dare appear and whisk her away. She was unknown in the court—it would lead to too much notice and too many questions that Grim had gone to great lengths already to avoid.

That was what she told herself, at least.

The music seemed to get louder, and Isla danced, just one person in a crowd. She met gazes that looked her up and down and seemed to like what they saw. One pair of eyes never left her as she moved until the song ended, and the man walked over.

He was tall and had a scar across his cheek and hair cut short to his head. He wasn't shy with his notice. "You are the most beautiful creature I have ever seen."

Creature seemed like a strange term, but she had never been spoken to so boldly, and she felt her skin prickle. "I am?"

He took a step closer to her. "I've never seen a face like yours," he said. "Not ever."

Isla could feel herself blush. It was so stupid, but the compliment made her feel like a puddle.

"Would you dance with me?"

The crowd behind the man shifted, and Isla saw Grim clearly, sitting back on his throne. His gaze was set on her, expression fuming. His eyes narrowed, as if daring her, just *daring her* to say yes.

She smiled. "I would love to," she said, watching as Grim's grip on his throne tightened.

The dance started off innocently enough. The man stood a respectable distance away and led her through a series of moves that corresponded with the quickening beat of the drums. Then the Nightshade offered her a drink, and she swallowed it down in a single gulp, hoping it would give her the nerve to have the night of her life while she still could. Within moments, she felt light as a feather, and the beat of the music seemed to be synchronized to the beat of her heart, both quickening.

Keeping her eyes right on the Nightshade ruler, she stood in front of the man and danced. Grim's knuckles became skeletal white as he gripped the sides of his throne.

He watched her like he could see right through her, like he was a moment away from turning the entire crowd of people before her to ash.

Still, he did not move to stop her. When the man asked her if she wanted to go into the hall—and Isla had seen *exactly* what happened there—she said yes and let him lead her there.

Isla expected Grim to follow, but he did not. Just a few steps out of the ballroom, she shifted her focus to the man leading her away.

She decided she was going to kiss him. Grim was the only person she had kissed before. Every time she was near him, she felt covered in sparks. Even when they were apart, she felt somewhat empty, like he had taken a part of her with him.

Maybe that was what it was like with every man. Maybe she would kiss this one and see that it felt the same. Better, even.

It would be a relief. Grim was her enemy. She *shouldn't*—couldn't—be attracted to him.

They found an empty corridor, and the man didn't waste any time. He pressed her against the wall, and his mouth went straight to hers.

Nothing. Her skin didn't prickle. She didn't feel heat traveling through her core. He tasted of smoke and alcohol, so she turned her head, not wanting to taste him anymore. He took that as an invitation to continue a path down her neck.

Maybe she just needed to get used to him. She stood still as he explored her, hoping a connection would click.

It wasn't like with Grim at all. The man palmed her chest in a way that should have made her groan. She felt nothing.

His hand started making its way down her stomach, and she watched it, knowing she could stop it but wondering how it might feel. He was so close. Maybe, if he touched her there—

Just as he reached the bottom of her stomach, he froze. He did not blink. His shoulders were hiked up in shock.

That was when they both looked down to see a sword sticking straight through his chest, its tip an inch from her own. The blade was quickly removed, and the man crumpled to the ground, revealing Grim, standing right in front of her.

"Don't worry, Hearteater. He's not dead. I will make sure of it," Grim said in response to her expression of horror. He leaned down to whisper, very slowly, "Because I'm going to bring him to the brink of death a thousand times before I will finally allow him the mercy of dying."

Isla stared at him in shock. "Because . . . he kissed me?" she asked, chest still heaving.

Anger flashed in his eyes, then disappeared. "No, Hearteater," he said. "Because he poisoned you."

She shook her head. "What?"

"The drink he gave you. A few minutes more and you would find yourself paralyzed, a motionless vessel for his pleasure."

Even as he said the words, Isla felt her muscles tightening, like every part of her was hardening into bone.

"How do you know?"

"I didn't until you were leaving. Your face and chest are flushed scarlet. It's a sign." He tilted his head at her. "You feel it, don't you?" he said. He offered her a small vial. An antidote? She swallowed it down. "Better?"

Better. The tightening loosened.

All softness left his expression. He looked down at her, at every inch of her dress, the fabric wrinkled in the places that had been gripped by the man now gurgling on his own blood at her feet.

"Hearteater," Grim said, voice mocking, "who knew you were so desperate for pleasure?" She glared at him, and he only grinned. "If you wanted someone to bed you so badly, all you had to do was ask."

She took a shaking breath. "I would rather die than have you touch me, demon," she said.

He frowned down at her. "Is that so?" He dipped his head, so his cold breath was against her mouth. "All right. I will not touch you again until you ask me to. I won't touch you again until you *beg* me to."

"That will never happen," she spat. "I hate you."

"You can hate me, Hearteater, and still want me in your bed."

She laughed in his face. "In your dreams, demon."

"All of the best ones," he agreed. His eyes seared through her as he looked her slowly up and down. "We do such depraved things, in my dreams."

Isla opened her mouth. Closed it.

Grim leaned closer, so they shared breath. “When you finally do beg me to touch you—and you will—you won’t want anyone else to touch you ever again, Hearteater.” His voice was a dark whisper against her ear. “Late at night, you will think of me touching you. With my hands. My mouth.” Isla’s chest went tight at his words, his proximity. Her insides puddled; she was hot everywhere. “And you will dream of me too.”

Isla closed her eyes tightly, trying to force herself to be repulsed by his words.

When she opened them, both Grim and the Nightshade who had poisoned her were gone.

NEXUS

Five days remained. Isla was back on the Wildling newland. Enya was helping her make the final arrangements for the warriors to travel to Lightlark. The Sunling had already found space for them in the castle, close to Isla. They catalogued the healing elixirs that were left, after she had given a great portion of them to Calder and Soren. Reluctantly, Soren had agreed to let Calder shadow him as he treated the Vinderland. Calder was an eager learner, writing notes, which only seemed to annoy Soren.

Every remaining drop of elixir was crucial.

They both worked without speaking, exhausted, but there was no time to rest. She finished her remaining tasks and, at the end of the day, portaled them back to Lightlark.

In Isla's overstuffed chairs, they were finally still. After a few minutes of companionable silence, Isla asked, "Do you have anyone? Anyone you're . . . worried about, beyond Oro, Zed, and Cal?"

"You mean, do I have a partner?"

She nodded.

"Not at the moment. I've loved many women through the centuries, but it always seemed selfish to take a wife, knowing . . . what I do." Knowing when she would die.

The Sunling tilted her head at Isla. Her red hair was vibrant against her pale skin. "You are different than I thought you would be. I like you, Isla, I really do," she said, and Isla felt the same way. She wanted to tell her, but in the same breath, the Sunling said, "But I don't like you for him."

For him.

For Oro.

Isla's previous love for the Sunling woman hardened into rock. "What do you mean?" she said slowly.

Enya sighed. "May I be honest with you?"

Isla nodded, even though her teeth rubbed together, painfully, behind her lips.

"Oro is king of Lightlark. His duty, from the moment his brother died, was to his people. Not himself. Not me. Not anyone he cares about. I used to hate it. I used to hate that one of the people I loved most would never truly know happiness. Now, I accept it. Because his happiness, and mine, are not more important than the happiness of everyone else on this island."

Enya filed her fingernails against her pants. "He loves you, and that love is making him weak. If he's not careful, it will be the death of Lightlark."

Isla felt her face twist. "How can you say that? How can you paint love as the enemy?"

"Because I've watched thousands of people die, I've watched devastation for five centuries—all in the name of love." *The curses.*

"This is different," she said.

Enya smiled, and it was sad. She didn't look cruel, or mean, and that made her words sting even more. "I believe those words have been spoken by every person in love since the beginning of time."

You don't know anything about us, Isla thought.

It would have been easy, so easy, so *convenient,* to ignore Enya's words as jealousy or misguided advice.

Deep inside, if she really thought about it, she knew Enya was right.

Isla was almost done portaling the rest of the civilians. By tomorrow, only warriors would be left on Lightlark.

She was walking across the Star Isle bridge when she got the feeling she was being followed.

She focused on the ground beneath her, and she could sense the footsteps far away. Walking. Waiting.

She was about to be ambushed. She knew it, and she understood that only one group of people would be so bold, so close to the day of battle.

Isla let them capture her.

She braced herself, and the strings on the other side of the bridge snapped. It swooped down like a pendulum, and a force plucked her from the air, into a carved opening in the side of the Mainland cliff. The ones who had been following her swung in after her.

She rolled inside, her ribs screaming in protest as she tumbled before nearly hitting a wall.

When she opened her eyes, a dozen red masks looked back at her.

She smiled. "I don't think this is going to go the way you're hoping," she said. Then, she twisted her fingers, and the ground grew teeth, trapping them all against the ceiling. She hadn't killed them.

Not yet.

"Wait," someone said. One of them fought to get their arm out between the ceiling and rock, to remove their mask. "Before you kill us, please just listen."

Isla didn't listen. She lashed out, the ground beneath her shook—

The person got their mask off, and Isla went very still.

"Maren," she said.

Isla imagined she look crazed. Another Starling she had trusted, betraying her—

"How could you?" she asked, voice shaking. Maren had Cinder. She was a *leader*.

She had tried to kill her—

"We didn't mean to hurt you before," the Starling said quickly. "The Moonling who performed that did not consider the fact that you might . . . drag across the balcony. It was supposed to be simple—"

"What do you want?" Isla demanded. "You have five seconds to explain before I bring this cave down all around us."

"Do you agree with the system of rule, Isla? You each make decisions that affect us all, whether you intend them to or not. The system of rule is a curse. Our lives being tied together is a curse."

"No." Her answer was immediate. She didn't think it was fair that rulers were born with the bulk of power. "That's why I'm implementing a democracy on Star Isle."

Maren nodded. "We heard, and we appreciate it," she said. "But the current system of rule goes beyond just votes and voices. We have all historically been tied to rulers' lives, because of the power they alone channel. Do you know why, Isla?"

She shook her head.

"Because thousands of years ago, the king's ancestors had a Nightshade create a series of curses called nexus, designed to keep the people weak. Everyone—except for his line—was cursed to only be born with a single ability. And people were cursed to be tied to their rulers, so power could never be overthrown. Nexus was meant to keep us all weak. Subservient. Loyal."

Nexus? She had never heard of it. "How do you know any of this?"

"History was buried. It took centuries for our group to finally gather this information. It started during the curses. You six were the stars of the Centennial, but we regular islanders also worked to break them. We learned that it used to be possible for a person to denounce their power and leave a realm."

Isla thought about the Vinderland and the serpent-woman, who had left Wildling many centuries ago.

"We believed that if we could figure out how they did it, we could give up our powers and not be bound to the curses. It was a sacrifice many of us were more than willing to make. That led to researching why the ties between the people and their rulers existed in the first place.

"We failed to figure out how to properly denounce our realms, but, after you broke the curses, we realized you could be the answer to all of our problems. You could break the current system of rule."

Now, Isla was lost. "How could I possibly do that?"

"We believe you have a flair, Isla."

She didn't. If she did, she would know it by now, wouldn't she?

"We believe you are immune to curses."

"What?"

"You were not cursed, even though you did indeed have power. And you were born with two abilities, Wildling and Nightshade."

Isla took a step back. How did they know—

"We have members in Skyling," Maren said. "You practice in the woods." She should have been more careful. "If we are correct, then you have already inadvertently freed two realms from being tied to your life. Wildling. And now, Starling."

Her death wouldn't be the death of everyone she ruled.

She shook her head. She wished more than anything that it was true . . . but none of this made any sense. "Why wouldn't you just tell me then? Why kidnap me? Why be so secretive?"

Maren glanced at the others. They were all still crushed against the rocks, and Isla loosened her hold on them, just a little. "Because to free all the realms from nexus would require the death of the king. We needed to talk to you without him finding out."

Isla laughed. She actually laughed. "No," she said, the word final.

"We haven't even told you how—"

"I don't care," she said, baring her teeth. "I won't do anything that requires the king dying."

Maren just looked at her. "Even if it means potentially saving thousands of people?"

She knew how it looked. How could she possibly choose one life over thousands?

Perhaps she wasn't as good as she thought she was, because she said, "Yes. Even then."

Without another glance at the rebels, she carved stairs out of the side of the cliff with her power and climbed out of the cave.

That night in bed, Isla wondered if she should tell Oro about them, or ask about the nexus. She quickly decided against it. They were days away from battle. There was enough to deal with.

Isla shifted in the bed and startled when a loud thud broke through the silence.

BEFORE

The noise had come from the center of her room. It was the middle of the night, and something heavy had just thumped against her floor.

She was up in an instant, the long dagger she kept between her bed frame and mattress fisted in her hand.

Squinting through the darkness, she found someone slumped over in front of her bed, their blood staining the stone.

"Hearteater," he said.

She threw her dagger down and rushed to his side. "Grim?" It had been days since the ball.

He grinned. "I believe you'll be pleased," he said, his words labored.

"Will I?" she said, eyes searching his body for where he was bleeding the most, for signs of what could have possibly happened.

"Something got very close to killing me."

The sinking feeling in her stomach was like a boulder dropping into a river. This information did not please her at all, and she knew he could feel it. "Oh? That is wonderful news," she whispered.

He nodded. "It is with great regret that I share it did not succeed."

She shrugged a shoulder. "Not yet, at least."

He barked out a laugh, then groaned.

Her arms circled his body, and she pressed him against the floor with all the strength she could muster. Shaking hands—from worry, of course from worry—began unbuttoning his shirt.

He made half-sensical comments about her undressing him, but she shushed him, eyes studying the constellation of wounds across his torso. They weren't like anything she had ever seen before. His skin had turned ashen; the marks were dark. Black veins like roots from a decaying tree wove across him.

"What is this?" she asked. He glanced down at her hands pressed against his chest, and she slowly removed them.

Grim ignored her question. "The elixir, Hearteater. The Wildling flower," he said.

Then his head fell into her lap and he ceased speaking.

Isla tried to undress Grim properly, but he was too heavy to move all that gently. Instead, she took her knives and cut the clothes off him. She could only imagine what he would say about that.

She nearly gagged at the sight of him. The wounds were eating through his skin and bone, ruinous and sinuous. It was as if the darkness was still feasting, even now.

"What is this?" she said to herself. And why wasn't Grim healing quickly, the way he did with typical injuries?

Isla hoped the elixir would help. If it didn't, would the shadows spread until Grim was nothing more than ash? Was the entire fate of the Nightshade realm in her hands right now?

With determination, Isla applied the elixir to every wound. On his neck. His chest. His stomach. His arms. His thighs. When she was done, her vial contained only a few more drops.

She sat next to him as he slept and was there when he gained a sliver of consciousness. "Isla," he said.

She nearly jumped, looking to see what he needed. But his eyes were closed.

It was only a little while later, knees to her chest as she watched him, that she realized what he had called her. *Isla.* He had sworn never to call her by her first name . . .

Yet there it was again, falling so effortlessly from his lips.

. . .

Isla portaled them both to his room, where he soon dozed off again. Luckily, she was able to transport them to his bed in his groggy state, or he would have woken up on the floor. His ruined clothes were a tattered pile nearby. Isla toyed with the idea of dressing him again as he rested but settled on simply covering most of his body with one of his dark sheets.

Slowly, like clouds clearing after a storm, the elixir had eaten through the wounds. His skin had grown back. He still wasn't in perfect condition, but he would live, and for that, Isla found, she was grateful.

Strange. Months ago, she'd wished him dead.

Now, the thought of him dying—

She was sitting at the edge of the bed, legs crossed in front of her, when his eyes snapped open. This time, they were more alert and found her immediately. "You healed me."

Then he studied himself. Lifted the sheet. Raised an eyebrow.

"It isn't the first time," she said. "And . . . you have healed me too."

"Thank you," he said then. He leaned forward before she could stop him, wincing from the effort . . . and did something so unexpected, she didn't move a muscle. He kissed her on the forehead, then leaned back against the pillow.

Watching him shift uncomfortably, her expression turned serious.

"What happened?" she asked. Then, her eyes narrowed. "Are you—are you looking for the sword without me?" Were those somehow wounds from the dragon? Had he awakened it?

"I'm not," he said. She must not have looked convinced, because he added, "I am the ruler of Nightshade. Do you truly believe working with you is the only opportunity I have to be wounded?"

"Yes," she said. "Because only in the cave can you not use your powers. With them, you just do . . ." She waved her hands in front of her face dramatically.

Grim raised an eyebrow at her. "I do *what*?"

"You know what I mean," she said, shaking her head. "Shadows. Death. Stuff. You know."

He sighed. "Well, the creatures I face often are mostly immune to *shadows. Death. Stuff.*"

Creatures? "Grim. What is going on in Nightshade? What could possibly be strong enough to wound you like this? Why do you need the sword?"

There were too many questions spilling out of her mouth, but she couldn't push them down any longer. Things between them had changed. Before, she'd agreed to work with him only because of his promise to help her during the Centennial.

Now . . . she wanted to help.

He studied her. It was a minute later when he looked down at his hands, still partially covered in marks from the attack. "It is treason if I tell you. It is one of the greatest secrets of our realm."

Isla just looked at him. "Everything about this is treasonous."

He frowned. "I suppose you're right." He shifted his position and winced. "Centuries ago, after the curses were spun, a scar opened up across Nightshade. Winged beasts began escaping from it. They look like dragons, but smaller, and their scales are nearly invincible. They're called dreks, and they have already killed thousands."

They sounded terrifying. "Do people live near the scar?"

He nodded. "Near the parts that are inactive. The attacks have been concentrated to one area in the last century."

Grim rubbed a hand across his forehead. He looked exhausted.

"Dreks used to be people, millennia ago. My ancestor Cronan cursed his warriors to become unbeatable beasts. He had the blacksmith make him a sword, imbued with his power, so his later generations could control the drek army. Also . . . so they could make new ones. After his death, one of his descendants predicted the dreks would lead to the end of the world, so she cursed the sword to be unusable by a Nightshade ruler." How was he going to get past that curse? Was he hoping *she* would use it for him? "Dreks had ravaged both Lightlark and Nightshade. After Cronan's death, they were all banished below. Now . . . they've started rising up again."

"So . . . the sword controls the dreks. That's why you want it? To stop them?"

Grim nodded.

"My father was obsessed with finding the sword," he said, seeming to surprise himself, because he frowned.

"Why?"

"He wanted to use it to invade Lightlark. It would have been easy, with the dreks."

Grim's father sounded awful. Good thing it seemed like Grim was nothing like him.

She wondered . . .

"What was your mother like?"

He seemed shocked by her question. She was shocked she had asked it. Eventually, he said, "I wouldn't know."

Her brows came together. "She—died? In childbirth?"

Grim frowned. "No. On Nightshade, rulers don't take wives," he said. "They don't ever even bed the same woman twice. Or, at least, they're not supposed to."

"What? Why?"

"A precaution," he said simply. "Love makes our power vulnerable. It is a weakness."

She just stared at him. "You don't actually believe that, do you?"

"I do. If I love someone, they have access to my ability. It's a liability. My ancestors never cared to take the risk."

Pieces came together. "That's why you had the line of women," she said. "The volunteers. To make sure . . . to make sure you never sleep with the same person twice."

He nodded. "Not that I would remember them, but the palace has records. It's a precaution. It's been that way for generations."

Isla realized something. "You're trying for an heir, aren't you?" She remembered the women talking about being involved with the ruling line . . .

Grim did not deny it.

She swallowed. "I'm guessing . . . it hasn't worked?"

He shook his head. "Bearing children as a ruler can take time." He looked at her. "No, I haven't continued since we made our agreement."

Good. If he created an heir, he couldn't attend the Centennial. Still, there was only one reason why he would want to have a child that she could think of. "You think the dreks will eventually kill you," she said. "You want to ensure your realm survives."

If he was dead, he couldn't help her at the Centennial. It was in her best interest to not only help him find the sword . . . but also help him use it.

Grim nodded, just the slightest bit. "It's my duty."

"And if you did eventually have a child, after the Centennial, you wouldn't want to know the mother? You wouldn't . . . allow her to help raise the child?"

"No," he said.

A precaution. Love makes our power vulnerable. It is a weakness.

"That sounds . . ." she said, "very lonely."

Grim made a face. "I've never felt lonely in my life," he claimed.

The way he said it made her feel like he really believed it. Still—everyone got lonely. "Maybe you just don't know what it's like to miss someone, then," she said quietly. "Because you don't open yourself up long enough to let them in."

He shrugged a shoulder. "It doesn't matter," he said. "Love is for fools, anyway. It makes people do foolish things." He looked at her and said, "I do not intend to become a fool."

She was the fool, she knew. Because something about him saying that made her heart break.

LOYALTY

"I know what the sword does," Isla told Oro. He immediately called a meeting.

Azul was not fighting with them, but he had remained on the island, to help in any way they needed him.

He was there, in the war room, when she told them everything. Her history with Grim. The oracle's words. The fact that she had important memories. Azul looked pensive. Zed looked furious. Enya looked curious. Calder looked from Oro to Isla, then back again.

They might have been angrier if she hadn't immediately told them about her latest memory.

"Dreks used to be people. Cronan made a sword that controls them and can make more." She pressed her lips together. "I believe Grim now has that sword."

Heat flooded the throne room.

"It's done, then," Zed said. "It's—"

"Wait." Azul held up a hand. "You don't remember finding it, though, right? Perhaps you never did."

It was a good point.

Zed laughed without humor. "The oracle said Grim has a weapon. The dreks flew toward Nightshade after the attack. It's obvious he controls them. And now, with the sword . . . perhaps he has created more. We must prepare to face an army of endless dreks."

Calder was the one who said what they must all have been thinking: "How do we possibly prepare for that?"

Even before learning about the sword's use, winning seemed impossible.

Now, she wondered if it was foolish to ever think they could stand a chance against Grim.

"We're dead," Zed said, after a few moments of silence. "If he really has that sword, and can create dreks at will . . . we're dead."

Enya stood. "No. Not yet. What we are now is desperate. We need to find more power. We need to find another way to win."

"We only have four days left, Enya," Calder said.

She whipped around. "So, we give up? We let this army destroy our home? The one our own parents loved and protected?" She shook her head. "No. I refuse." She took a step, and wings of flame burst forth from her back. They curled open, sizzling behind her. She looked like a phoenix. "I didn't live five hundred years in the darkness, dreaming of the day I got to feel the sun on my skin again, to have my home taken away."

Enya was right. They couldn't give up.

And she was right about something else. They *were* desperate. Which meant Isla was about to make a very bad decision.

Grim was coming with an endless army of dreks. Loss felt almost certain, but she couldn't give up.

There had to be a way to save the island. There had to be a way to save Oro and herself.

Isla used her starstick to portal to the edge of the Star Isle forest. It didn't take long for the serpent to find her.

She watched as the snake turned into a woman and walked toward her, her long green scale dress trailing behind. "I let you live last time," she said. "It seems you have rejected my gift."

Isla didn't have time for games. "We need you," she said. "The destruction coming . . . We have no chance against it. Not without you and the other ancient creatures."

The woman glared at her. "We are outcasts. No one has ever cared about us. How dare you ask for our help?"

Isla let her shadows loose. They swept across the silver ground, swirling like ink. "Because I'm an outcast too," she said. She stepped forward. "I understand if you can't trust anyone on this island. I understand what it's like to be hated and abandoned." She took another step. "Don't trust them. Don't believe in them. Believe in me."

The serpent's eyes sharpened.

"I will not abandon you. I will fight by your side, and when all of this is over, I will make you a place on Wild Isle. You won't have to hide or kill innocent people for food. You will be part of the island again. I promise. I extend that promise to whatever else lives in this forest."

She meant it. With every part of her, she meant it.

The serpent rejected her anyway.

Isla didn't let the rejection stop her. There were other night creatures on the island. She went to each isle and sought them out.

Remlar was right. Most, when she showed them who and what she was, bowed their heads and joined her.

Her. Their loyalty was to *her*.

All this time, she had rejected the darkness within her. Now, she wondered if it was her greatest strength.

By the time she left the last isle, the shadows of the island tilted toward her, as if called by her presence.

She took one in her hands, felt it glide across her fingers. It slipped away, and she turned to grab it again—

But she wasn't on Lightlark any longer.

BEFORE

Grim had made her an illusion of the cave. They had gotten past every single obstacle until the last—the dragon itself. Its tail now sat between them and the sword, too spiked to climb, and impossible to get through without power. If they couldn't get past the dragon, they would have to lure it out.

They were thinking of ways to do that when Grim suddenly said, "I want to show you something."

She took his hand, and they were off.

They landed in a field of flowers so beautiful, they looked like melted night. Deep purple, with five sharp petals. Stars.

Grim picked one and gave it to her. At first she was surprised, and touched, but he said, "Smell it, Hearteater."

She did and frowned.

"Familiar?"

She would know the smell anywhere. "It has the same scent as the Wildling healing elixir," she said warily. It smelled sweet. Syrupy.

"I think they're the same flower."

What? That didn't make any sense. Isla turned around in a circle, eyes focused more closely around her. There was supposedly only a small, coveted patch of the flowers that produced the healing elixir in the Wildling newland. There were entire rolling hills of these here, a sea of nighttime sky. "What even is this?" She didn't know the name of the flower that produced the serum.

"It's nightbane."

Nightbane. The drug he had talked about. The one that made people endlessly happy while killing them from the inside out. She felt like an idiot shaking her head so much, but none of this was adding up. She felt the need to spell it out clearly. "But the Wildling flower doesn't kill . . . it *heals*."

"We extract the same nectar. In Nightshade hands, under our own extraction process, it turns into a drug that produces euphoria," Grim explained. "I suspect under a Wildling's touch it turns into a healing elixir instead."

She stared down at the flower Grim had given her. Her fingers ran across its petals. They were as soft as velvet and didn't fold beneath her touch.

Both poison and remedy. Opposites, like her and Grim. The ruler of life and the ruler of shadows.

The flower connected them.

"We can make a deal," Isla said quickly. "We—we don't have much of this flower. If you can give us some of yours, we can provide healing elixirs." Isla said it and wasn't sure how to even make that happen. Terra and Poppy had no idea she had spent the last few months with Grim. It wasn't as if she could tell them out of nowhere that they were making a trade agreement with Nightshade, but her people were dying and desperate. "In exchange, we need hearts," she added. "From . . . from people you are already going to kill. And other stuff I can't think of right now that we need."

Grim stared down at her. The corner of his lips twitched in amusement. "It's a deal, Hearteater," he said. He held out his hand, and she took it. They shook on it. By the third shake, he had portaled them back to her room.

He didn't drop her hand. She didn't drop his.

Isla swallowed, and his gaze traveled down her throat. Lower. Lower. She took a step back, and her spine hit the wall. He stepped forward.

Grim had told her more about himself than ever, the last time she saw him. He'd let her look beneath the mask of death and darkness. Underneath . . . there was a man. Someone who had been through pain.

Someone she had started to understand.

Their gazes were locked. Isla had the sense that the room could come crashing down around them and they still wouldn't break eye contact. Grim stepped and stepped, until he was right in front of her. She had to crane her neck to watch him.

He leaned down. He dipped his head slowly, tentatively. He was the greatest warrior in all the realms, but Isla could have sworn he was trembling. She felt his breath against her face. His breathing was labored.

"Please," he said, sounding pained. "Please, tell me you want this." He waited for her to nod. He traced her body with his eyes and said, "I know if I touch you again it will kill me . . . but I think I might die if I don't."

She didn't dare move as he gathered her in his arms and ducked to meet her.

An inch from her lips he stopped. Cursed.

She straightened. "What is it?"

"There's been a breach in the scar," he said.

Then he vanished.

GONE

When Isla awoke that morning, she startled out of bed. Oro was next to her in a moment. "What's wrong?" he asked.

"Not wrong," she said, frowning. "Just . . . a development. The Wildling healing flower, the rare one?"

He nodded.

"It's *nightbane*." She said it like it was the biggest news in the world, but Oro just looked at her.

"What's nightbane, love?" he asked.

Oh. She sometimes forgot that he wasn't in her head. There was an entire life she was currently living internally that he didn't know about.

She closed her eyes. Breathed. "Nightshade has fields of the Wildling flower." Isla didn't know what to do with this information; she just knew it was important. "I—"

Suddenly, her head was pounding. She bent over and felt Oro race to her side. She blinked, but she wasn't seeing in front of her.

No. She was seeing a forest.

She knew that forest. It was right outside Wren's village. There was a pull in her chest, a desperation, a call.

Lynx.

Somehow, she was seeing what he was seeing right at this moment.

Just as she wondered about the connection between bonded, she saw him.

Grim.

He was in the Wildling village. *No*. Fear gripped her chest.

Lynx leaped forward. He raced through the trees, to the village. Before he could reach any of the villagers, though, the vision vanished.

"I need to go to the Wildling newland," Isla said, her voice just a rasp, her hands shaking.

"I'll come with you."

She portaled her and Oro to the village, the same way she had done almost every day for weeks.

Silence.

Isla portaled to another, smaller village, which had been filled with singing and laughter and the snap of weaving with wood and vines the last time she visited.

It was empty.

She went to another. Empty.

Every house was vacant. Crops that should have already been collected that day remained untouched.

She portaled back to the outskirts of Wren's village, where the small patch of deep-purple flowers had been planted and extracted. It was where she and Enya had just finished cataloguing it all.

The healing elixirs that they had spent weeks producing were gone.

Gone.

"Isla," Oro said, putting a hand on her arm. Lynx broke through the brush. His eyes were wide, angry.

No.

She'd finally faced her people, gotten to *know* them—

And they were gone.

It was in her room in the Wildling palace that she finally found a note. Its seal was as black as melted-down night sky, and bile rose up her throat. It confirmed what Lynx had shown her.

I've brought them to Nightshade, it said. *They're waiting for you, heart. We're all waiting for you.*

A chill dropped through her stomach. Darkness bloomed.

The paper disintegrated in her hands, blowing away in a few pieces of ash, and she raged. The stone in her room rippled with her anger. Her wooden door flew off its hinges, collapsing against the opposite wall. The spot beneath her was tinged with darkness.

Lynx made an angry sound as Isla broke down completely in front of Oro, sobbing into his chest. "He took them," she said. "They're gone. They're all gone."

BEFORE

Grim was gone. One moment, he was there, so close to her, and the next, she was alone. There had been a breach in the scar, he said.

How did he know? Could he feel it?

It had been hours since he had vanished, and she began to worry.

A part of her, a whisper in her mind like a shot of ink tainting all other thoughts, imagined the worst. It spun possibilities. What if the dreks had defeated him? What if he was stuck on the battlefield, slowly being consumed by the darkness that only her elixir seemed able to heal quickly?

What if he needed her?

She told herself she was worried because if he died, he couldn't help her at the Centennial. Only for that reason.

Night bled into early morning, and Isla decided she couldn't sit in her room and wait. She had to do something.

She was wearing one of her nightdresses. Isla considered changing, then forgot it. Grim could be dying. He could be in his room, bleeding out, not able to portal to her . . .

She portaled in secret to Poppy's room to steal more serum and drew her puddle of stars.

Isla had been waiting in his room for half an hour, sitting perched on the edge of his bed, when he finally entered.

Relief filled her, then rushed away.

He looked like a demon.

Grim wore a helmet with spikes that curved down over his nose, his temples. His shoulders had barbs like blades. Touching him anywhere would draw blood. His armor resembled dozens of scales, plated together. He looked like a creature of the night, a monster in the dark. Shadows puddled at his feet, circling.

Isla didn't dare breathe. She told herself she should be afraid. If she had met him like this for the first time, she might have been.

But when the demon shed his layers, there was a man beneath. His helmet cracked against the floor when he dropped it. He stripped the armor off, with the tiredness of someone who felt suffocated, who wished to be free.

His shirt beneath was black and tight, fabric wrapped around and around. Isla didn't know how he hadn't noticed her yet.

All she could do was sit in shocked silence as he took off his shirt. Only when the fabric was over his head did his back tense.

And he slowly turned around to face her.

Isla felt her face go scarlet. He was unharmed. She felt foolish. Of course he was unharmed. Last time must have just been a fluke. He was the ruler of Nightshade; he knew how to defend himself. He didn't need *her*, of all people, looking after him.

Stupid. She felt her face heat. She stood from his bed—*why had she decided to sit there?*—and smoothed her hands down her silk dress. Grim's gaze dropped. She felt it like a flame, heating her from her collarbones, down her chest, her stomach, to places that made her dress suddenly feel too thin. "I—I just wanted to make sure you were fine," she got out.

He motioned toward himself. "I'm fine," he said.

Isla swallowed. "I can see that." She straightened. Opened her mouth. Closed it. Her gaze slipped down his bare chest. She had seen him without a shirt before, of course she had, but she hadn't ever allowed herself to truly study him this way. Now, she took all of him in.

He looked etched out of marble. Every muscle was defined by

training, cut perfectly. His shoulders were wide. She studied him, and part of her ached to keep watching, to get closer, to touch him—

His words from the ball were right. Late at night, she sometimes thought of him, of his hands, rough against the softest parts of her.

In her imagination, she followed the muscled lines of his stomach, lower, lower, only to awake gasping.

Now he was right here, and he wanted her. She could see the evidence of it, right there in front of her.

She looked away. Suddenly the wall behind him looked very interesting. There was a mirror there, and she saw herself, standing very stiffly in her red dress. She studied her reflection, wondering what could have possibly made him want her in that way when she wasn't doing anything special, she was just standing there, in a dress she often just wore to sleep.

The straps were thin; the bodice was overflowing. Her dress clung to her. It was more revealing than she had previously realized.

Isla looked to Grim. He was looking at her like she was the world, and he wanted to conquer it. For a second, she felt brave. Powerful, in a strange new way.

She stepped toward him.

Grim stood unnaturally still.

Her hand pressed against his chest. Her fingers were trembling. His skin was cold and hard as stone. Isla wasn't sure if he was breathing. His eyes were hungry, devouring her, taking in every inch of skin. She bit her bottom lip.

He studied her mouth, and she didn't want him to keep looking, she wanted him to *do* something.

She stepped forward, until every part of her pressed against every part of him. Her fingers did not shake any longer as she traced the large scar in the center of his chest. His reminder of her. Her hand ran lower. Lower.

Lower.

"Hearteater," he said, voice strained. The word was a warning.

She met his gaze. His eyes held all sorts of dark promises, and she wanted them all.

He was too tall. Too far away. She went on her toes to reach him, but she still could not.

She frowned and fell back onto her heels. He desired her, that much was clear. She felt like a flame, like she might just simply burn away if he didn't extinguish this feeling building inside her, this insatiable want—

Grim had told her he wouldn't touch her unless she begged. Back then, she had promised herself that wouldn't happen.

Now, she was ready to go on her knees before him.

"Touch me," she said, her voice just a whisper. "*Please*."

Grim didn't move an inch. He stood almost impossibly still.

Isla frowned. Did she have to say it again? She ran her hands lower, as if to show him exactly what she meant. Until she could almost feel all of him. "*Please*, Grim, would you just *touch*—"

Before her sentence was over, his mouth was on hers. The kiss was punishing, exploring, unrelenting. He tilted her head back, hands cradling her neck, thumbs brushing across her throat.

She made a sound into his mouth, and he seemed to like it, because he growled and bit her bottom lip before swiping his tongue over the hurt. She was on fire; everything burned, some places more than others, and she needed those hands, that tongue, everywhere. Now.

He broke their kiss and looked down at her. She looked down too. Her nightdress was pulled so low, she was nearly spilling out of it. Her chest was heaving.

Grim looked at her body like he was committing it to memory. "You know, I really like this dress," he murmured. He traced the neckline. His fingers slipped beneath the fabric and Isla gasped at the cold, then moaned as he traced every inch of her chest. "But it's in my way."

He gripped the silky fabric with both hands. He paused, looking

at her as if for approval, and when she gave it, he ripped it right down the center. Stitches broke; fabric was torn.

He kept going, until her nightdress was nothing more than shreds of fabric on the floor.

And she stood naked in front of him.

No one had ever seen her this way. Isla was burning, ready.

But all he did was look at her. For far too long, he just stared.

Was something . . . was something wrong with her? Was he not attracted to her? Had they gone too far already?

Isla began covering her body with her hands. She sat on the bed and crossed her legs, embarrassment heating her face.

"Is . . . something wrong?" she finally asked.

Grim laughed. It made her want to crawl into a hole. But then he said, in a tone so earnest and gentle that she believed him, "Nothing, absolutely nothing, is wrong with you, Hearteater."

He removed her hands covering her chest and replaced them with his own. She stood and groaned as his calluses stroked against the softest and hardest parts of her skin, as his hands pulled and explored. Then, he lowered his head and did the same thing with his mouth.

Isla's head fell back. She had never felt so sensitive, all her senses zeroing in on the strokes of his tongue on the peaks of her chest, on his mouth taking everything in.

His hand traveled down her stomach. Before he reached the place she wanted him, he paused, again waiting for her approval.

She parted her legs, giving it, then gasped as his fingers finally touched her *right there*—

He felt her own want for him and made a deep sound that rasped against the back of her mind.

"Are you always like this around me?" he asked.

Isla gasped again, then glared at him. He only grinned.

"You certainly think highly of yourself," she said, breathless. Grim explored her with his hand, and she moaned.

"It's hard not to, when I can feel the effect I have on you. Tell me, Hearteater, has anyone ever touched you like this?"

He knew the answer. He must. The demon just wanted to hear her say the words. She ignored him. Her eyes fluttered closed, as he pressed—

"Is it just me who elicits this response?"

Her head fell back as he kept circling. Her chest was bare to him.

"No need to reply," he said. "The sounds you're making are all the confirmation I need."

She scowled. "You just like to hear yourself talk, don't you?" His fingers slid lower, and her breath hitched.

"I do. But I like to hear *you* talk more. So, tell me." He stopped suddenly. Withdrew his hand. "Are you always like this around me?" he repeated.

She scoffed at him. "Are you always this desperate for validation?"

"No. Not from anyone. Only you."

She blinked, surprised by the admission.

"If you want me to continue, answer my question," he said. He was breathing just as quickly as she was, chest heaving. "Please," he added.

Isla knew he wasn't used to saying that word at all. Yet, now he had said it to her multiple times.

Part of her wanted to portal away. Leave them both unfulfilled. But right now, the way he was looking at her . . .

She felt truly powerful for one of the first times in her life.

"Yes," she said, and took great pleasure in watching his eyes burn even brighter in intensity. She wrapped her arms around his neck. Leaned in until her lips brushed his ear as she said, "Always."

Grim was unleashed.

His hands gripped her waist, lifting her into the air with little effort. He hooked her feet behind him and brought them to the bed. Her back hit the sheets, and his hand returned to where it had been. Their chests were flush, just as they had been when he had shielded her from the arrows. He leaned down and looked her right in the eye, like he wanted

her to hear every word. "Next time, I'll use my mouth," he said. "And then, after that—"

She needed to feel him. Her hand shifted below his waist, to the evidence of his desire, and all thoughts eddied away.

He filled her with all sorts of want, and she didn't know what to do, didn't know how to make him feel as good as he was making her feel, but just having her hand on him made his breath catch.

At least, until he gently removed her hand and laced their fingers together. He pinned her hand above her head. "Let me focus on you," he said. "I don't want to miss a moment of this."

He filled her more than she ever thought possible, and she met him movement for movement, eyes fluttering closed. "That's it, Hearteater," he said. "Make it good for you."

"*Grim*," she said. His name caught in her throat and she clutched his shoulders.

He looked her right in the eyes and said, "Remember this, Hearteater, the next time you want to stab me through the chest."

He swallowed her final moans with his mouth and pulled her into him, lifting her to his chest with a hand against her lower back. He held her closely, so closely. Only minutes later did he set her down.

Lost for breath, lost for sanity, she managed to say, "I'll remember."

REUNION

Isla didn't want to remember anything else. He had stolen her people. He had forced them to his territory. How afraid they must have been. How unwilling.

It was time to bring an end to this.

At midnight, Isla sneaked back to her room. Oro would hate her if he knew what she was about to do. Everyone would. None of them would trust her again, because what she was planning was so traitorous, so foolish—

She stood in the center of her room, the moon wide as a judgmental eye through the window in front of her.

She pulled her necklace.

If she had feared he wouldn't come, that he wouldn't drop anything he was doing and rush to her, she was wrong.

Barely a second after her fingers left the black diamond, she heard a step behind her. Then, "Hearteater."

She turned and he immediately swept her into his arms. He looked crazed, hungry, relieved, *so* relieved. He was an inch from pressing his lips against hers, and she was an inch from letting him—*she was confused*, she told herself, *the memories were messing with her*—before he saw her expression. Sensed her emotions. There was no thread between them. From her side, anyway.

He went still.

"You heartless *demon*," she said.

Grim's eyes had been pleased, delighted, but now he looked devastated. "You don't remember."

"I remember plenty," she said, stumbling away from him. Her eyes glimmered with tears. Angry, angry tears. "How could you?"

"You got my note."

"Yes, I *got your note*," she said, spitting the words out with disgust. "How could you take them? How could you *make them* go with you?"

Grim raised a hand. "I didn't *make* them do anything," he said. "They chose to come with me."

No. Liar. "Why would they ever go with you?"

At that, Grim went silent.

He wasn't telling her something. But he didn't have to. Pieces came together, questions finding answers.

She shook her head, unbelieving. Hoping she was wrong. "You have Poppy and Terra," she said, her voice a whisper. "You took them in."

Grim nodded, and her tears fell freely now. The betrayal . . .

"You know what they did to me. What they did to my *parents*—"

"It is unforgivable," he said. "But you need them. You need—"

"I don't need anyone!" The words exploded out of her. The vines on her balcony rushed through the open door, spreading like fingers, devouring the room. Shadows leaked from her feet, from her hands.

Grim's face broke in half, into the biggest smile. "Heart, you are radiant," he said.

Her shadows lunged at him, but he stopped them with a simple wave of his hand.

Her voice shook. "You are a monster."

Grim frowned. "Am I?" He took a step forward. "Tell me why I'm a monster. Because I brought your people to a place with more comfort, more options, more chances of survival? Because I have them all waiting for your return?"

Her return. He made it sound like a certainty, and she nearly laughed in his face.

"Because I helped them forget what they did?"

Isla froze. "You . . . what?"

"Some of your people were suffering from endless guilt. They couldn't get past the actions they had committed during the curses. I . . . took their memories away."

Shadows exploded out of her. She heard the mirrors in her room shatter, but they were just white noise compared to the anger that surged through her. "How could you? Haven't you learned?"

"They asked me to," he said. "Are you denying your people their own choices?"

She shook her head. "Why would anyone ask you to do that?"

His face hardened. It seemed he wanted to tell her something, but instead, he changed the subject. "We made a deal . . . remember? Wildling help with nightbane, in exchange for a very vague assortment of whatever your people needed." He shrugged. "I was simply making good on it."

Isla curled her lip in disgust. "I suppose you think that makes you generous, don't you? Helping my people? You are not. You are a monster. You portaled the dreks here. They killed *dozens* of people, innocents—"

Grim bared his teeth. "I did no such thing. I told you before, dreks were buried below Lightlark and Nightshade. They must have started rising up, the same way they did on Nightshade."

"They went to your land, like they were called—"

"I didn't call them. They must have sensed their kind."

"You control them," she said. "I know you have the sword."

At that, Grim studied her. "I do. But I did not order them to attack Lightlark. I swear it."

Her mouth went dry. There it was. Confirmation that Grim had gotten the sword. And, somehow, he had found a way to use it.

Even if he didn't order the attack, she had endless reasons to hate

him. "You are coming to kill everyone on the island. You will murder thousands of innocents just to get it. You sent a message of ruin, of destruction—"

"No. I'm not. I warned everyone here, which is more than they deserve. They can either leave . . . or join us. It is their choice. No one has to die."

It was almost heartbreaking how he really believed this. If only he knew what she had seen. All the death that would result from his own hand.

Her own death.

"Do you really think anyone would give up their home without fighting?"

"When fighting is futile . . . I do."

Isla was filled with rage. Hurt.

"Heart," he said gently. "If I wanted to take the island by force, I could. Right now. Destroy all of it and everyone, in a matter of seconds. The curses are over." She could feel the power of him, especially now. Every ounce of it, so much waiting to be unleashed.

His eyes dipped to her neck, where her necklace had become visible, where her fingers had instinctively gone, and she ripped her hand away. "Take this off," she said.

A wicked grin spread across Grim's face. "You remember, do you? No . . . No," he said. He prowled closer. Closer. "If you did, you would know I cannot."

Talking to him wasn't working. She could see in the set of his mouth, his eyes, he was intent on invading Lightlark. She shook her head. "Grim, *please*. If you care about me at all, please don't do this."

Grim smiled softly then. He reached out. "Heart," he said, his voice as gentle as she had ever heard it. His fingers traced her cheek, from her temple to her lips. She was trembling—why was she trembling? "It's *because* I care about you that I'm doing this."

And then he was gone.

. . .

Isla knew what she needed to do.

Remlar was having tea in his hive. A tree grew beneath her, taking her to its highest floor, and she walked through the gaps, right to his makeshift throne. Vines were crawling in her wake, mixing with shadows.

"You look determined, Wildling," he said, putting his cup down. "You look ruinous."

"I want you to train me in something wrong. Something treacherous."

"Oh?"

"I want you to teach me how to cut off someone's power through a love bond. At least, for a few moments."

Remlar's lips crawled into a wide, wide smile. "It would be my pleasure," he said.

Grim had the Wildlings. Three days remained. She convened everyone in the war room once more.

"I summoned him," she said, and Oro turned to look at her. His expression was unreadable.

Zed stood roughly. "You what?"

"I thought I could reason with him," she said. She knew it was risky. Stupid. Still, at any moment he could have portaled into her room and taken her. He hadn't, which meant Grim wanted her to remember everything. He wanted her to go back to him willingly.

And he needed something from Lightlark, beyond her. She just needed to figure out what it was.

Zed's look was incredulous. "That . . . that's treason," he said. "You summoned our enemy to the Mainland castle. The person who is hell-bent on destroying all of us." He looked to Oro, whose expression had hardened.

"Let her speak," he said, though his voice did not have any hint of the warmth it had developed over the last few months with her.

"When I was with him, I could feel . . . I could feel that he still loves me."

Azul leaned forward. "You felt the connection?"

She nodded.

Zed still glared at her. He wouldn't ever trust her, she knew that. If she were him, she wouldn't trust her either.

Still, he was wrong about her. She loved Oro. She was loyal to Lightlark. She closed her eyes and said, "I know how we can win." They waited. No one moved an inch. "Grim is too powerful. It makes him nearly impossible to defeat. Especially with the sword. But he loves me—I can use the link and take away his powers long enough for us to overpower him."

Silence.

Enya was the first to speak. "Have you ever tried doing that before?" Isla shook her head. Not that she remembered. Yet. "Have you ever tried . . . even accessing his powers?" Again, she shook her head. Not that she remembered.

Yet.

She turned to face Oro. "But I've done it before . . . Accessed powers through the link."

It wasn't easy to do. Especially for someone like her, who had only recently wielded power at all.

"It requires an intense . . . connection," Oro said. He wasn't looking at her. He shook his head. "It would be too big of a risk. If you couldn't steal his powers immediately, he would know what you were trying to do and would portal away."

Calder said, "Oro. This could change everything. It could change the entire tide of the war. Though . . . we would be sentencing all Nightshades to death."

"Maybe not," Enya said. "If Isla took all his power, it would spare his people, wouldn't it?"

"It should in theory, though something like that has never been tested through a love bond," Azul said. "This is a very . . . unique circumstance." Azul studied her. "You would be willing to kill him?"

The words hit Isla like a stone in the chest, even though she had been the one to suggest it.

Kill Grim.

The thought sounded poisonous in her mind, but she remembered her vision in front of the vault. If she didn't stop Grim, he would kill innocent people. He would kill her. Oro had been right. Grim's words in her room had confirmed it. *It's because I care about you that I'm doing this.*

Grim was really going to war because of her. She didn't know his main reason for destroying Lightlark, but his purpose was clear. Which meant every death would be her fault.

He had stolen her people. Her memories. Her happiness, the last few months.

She wouldn't allow him to steal anything else.

"Yes," she said.

Oro met her eyes. She expected to see relief, but all she sensed was concern. He reached across the table for her. She watched Azul track the exchange. By now, he must have known. Oro didn't seem to care that everyone else was watching as he said, "You don't have to do this."

Isla remembered Enya's words. She saw her meaning clearly now. Oro was putting her own well-being above that of the entire island.

She wouldn't let him. "Yes," she finally said. "I do."

She was going to kill Grim.

Remlar taught her the basics of taking power. It required a complete hold. Pinching the thread between her and Grim between her fingers and being strong enough to stop the flow of power within him.

"It will be painful," he warned. "And difficult. Grimshaw is a most talented wielder," he admitted. Isla wondered if Remlar had ever met him.

They had almost run out of time. Only two days remained. Grim clearly needed something on Lightlark. If she could remember what it was, they could shift their plan to make sure he didn't get it.

She just needed a shortcut.

"I need you to help me speed it all up," she told Remlar. He had warned her it would be dangerous to force the memories. It could break her, mentally. At this point, she didn't care.

"Are you sure?" he asked. "Even knowing the risks?"

"I'm sure."

Remlar began making tea.

Isla's mind was a battleground.

She didn't want to remember—*she had to remember.* She didn't want to feel anything but disgust at the Nightshade—*she had felt* everything *with the Nightshade.*

The more she saw, the more she knew . . .

"What is the opposite of night, Wildling?" Remlar said, as he poured the tea into her mug.

Isla frowned. She was convinced Remlar just liked to hear himself talk. "Day?"

Remlar shrugged. "If you say so."

Isla narrowed her eyes at him. "What do you mean? What's the answer?"

Remlar took a sip of his own tea. It looked scalding. "Very few questions in this world have only one answer."

Isla wondered what the point of this conversation was.

"What is *your* answer?" she asked. She watched as her tea became more saturated in color.

He didn't say a thing. These were mostly one-sided conversations. "What does power feel like to you?"

She lifted a shoulder. "Like a seed. Behind my ribs."

Remlar nodded, excited by her response. "A very pretty way of seeing it," he said. "Very fitting, for a Wildling."

"What does it feel like to you?"

This time, he answered. "Like nothing," he said. "I've been alive for so long that my power is as much a part of me as my blood and bones."

She dared ask a question she had wondered since the first moment she had seen him. "Are you truly Nightshade?"

"Labels are so unproductive," he said. "Though, I suppose you would call me a Nightshade. In terms of my power."

"You wield darkness?" Isla asked. "How have the islanders not banished you?"

"They fear me too much," he said.

"Why?"

"Because my knowledge surpasses theirs. I have survived when kings have risen and fallen and died. I have remained. We, the ancient creatures, remain. And some of us remember."

"Remember what?" she asked. She finally took a sip of her tea. That was all it took. Within seconds, her mind began to slip away from her. The past bled into the present. She blinked and watched Remlar fade far away.

The last thing she heard him say was, "Home."

BEFORE

They had a plan to get past the dragon. Grim would lure it out of the cave, and Isla would get through all the protections herself before the dragon returned. She practiced going through each one, with the help of Grim's illusions. He watched as Isla finished the entire circuit for the tenth time successfully. She turned to face him when she was done, and he actually looked impressed.

They were standing in his training room. She leaned against a stone wall and slid all the way down it. "I'm exhausted," she said.

"I can imagine."

Grim had clearly just come from the scar. He was covered in ash. "You look awful."

"*That* is harder to imagine, but I will take your word for it."

Magnificent ego, indeed. She sighed. "I'm ready. Why don't we celebrate?"

He lifted an eyebrow at her.

"Tonight is the Launch of Orbs in the Skyling newland," she said. She had attended the previous year, but only barely. She had hidden in the shadows, watching. Wishing to be part of it all. "It's to celebrate the new season of hot-air balloons being unveiled."

Grim scowled. "They are always finding an excuse to celebrate. I bet they celebrate tying their own shoes."

"I've always wanted to ride in one," she said. She looked pointedly at him.

His eyes slid to hers. He looked like he would rather do absolutely

anything other than be launched into the sky in a balloon. "Don't you have anyone else to go with?"

Isla stood. She gave him a withering look. "You know what? I'm sure I can find someone else to spend the evening with me," she said. She turned on her heel, but before she could take a step, he was up in a flash, holding on to her wrist, stopping her in place.

"Don't even think about it," he said, his voice a growl in her ear.

She turned to face him and found him towering over her. His shadows were spilling everywhere. She lifted her chin in defiance. "Let go of me," she said.

"Never."

Isla was breathing too rapidly. He was too close. Her voice came out brittle. "Might I remind you that there is nothing between us. I do not belong to you. And you do not belong to me. If we decide to have . . . fun . . . then that is all it is. Momentary entertainment. Nothing more."

Grim's grin was wicked. "Oh, Hearteater." He leaned down, until his lips were pressed right against her ear as he said, "If we do decide to truly have fun, there will be nothing momentary about it."

Isla swallowed. He traced the movement. His lips were dangerously close to her neck. "Take me to the festival," she said, her request breathless.

"Fine. Get dressed."

Grim was right. Skylings did truly seem to think up any excuse to celebrate. She loved it.

At the Launch of Orbs party, everyone wore glitter. In their hair, on their outfits, dusted upon their shoulders. She asked Grim to buy her a few things in the market to wear, and—with more than enough complaining—he surprisingly complied.

She got ready in her bathroom, and, after an hour, there was a loud knock against her door. "Are you preparing for battle or for a foolish party, Hearteater?" he asked.

"Both, if you're going to be so insufferable," she said before she opened the door.

Grim went silent.

Her dress was tiny, sky blue, and strapless. She had glued little gems around the sides of her eyes. Glitter dusted her collarbones and shoulders. He had bought her each of these items—with very specific instructions—but he still looked surprised.

They were about as mismatched as possible. She was glittering, and saturated, and he wore his typical all black, cape and boots included.

"How do I look?" she asked, smiling, turning to see herself in the mirror.

Grim frowned. "You look like a Skyling."

"Good. That's exactly what I was going for."

The sky was filled with balloons. Light-blue baubles floated close to the stars, looking like daytime sky peeking through the night.

"It's beautiful," Isla said, smiling.

She could feel Grim's eyes on her. He was looking at her face, not the sky. "No," he said. "It's not." She frowned and moved to turn his head toward what they were here to see, but he didn't budge an inch. "When you've seen something truly beautiful, everything else starts to look painfully ordinary."

Isla took his hand. His fingers immediately tensed, as if he was about to recoil. Then, after a moment, he gingerly cupped his hand around hers. "Come on," she said. And he did.

Crowds were stopped, listening to something. A speech. She heard a rich, pleasant voice, moving airily through the crowd, as if his voice had grown wings. When they got closer, she saw a dark-skinned man dressed in a thousand glimmering jewels. He wore a crown.

"Azul?" she said, and Grim grunted in response.

She was suddenly grateful that he had formed an illusion around them, disguising them—even if she had spent an hour getting dressed.

What would Azul, ruler of Skyling, think, seeing the ruler of Nightshade and the ruler of Wildling here, in his territory . . . *holding hands*?

Truly . . . what was she doing?

The thought made her drop his hand. Grim frowned and immediately grabbed it again, locking her fingers in his. The action made her inexplicably warm everywhere, made her remember how he had touched her—

Grim glanced at her, and she knew he could feel her emotions. She swallowed and quickly changed the subject. "What do you think of Azul?"

"He runs his realm as a democracy. Everyone has a say. It's foolish."

Isla's brows came together. "That doesn't sound foolish to me."

Before Azul's speech was over, he led them toward where the balloons were taking off. There was an entire field of them, all painted slightly differently. All magnificent.

"Choose," he said.

Isla frowned. "I don't think we can choose, and I think there's a line—"

He followed her line of sight, to the one she thought was the prettiest. It looked like a light-blue egg, with a white swirl in the center.

In less than a moment, they were standing in its carriage. Somehow, he was starting it up. And then they were flying.

Isla gasped, watching the ground suddenly push away from them, and she stepped back. Right into Grim's chest.

He looped an arm around her waist, tethering her. It made her feel safer. Grim—for as much as he had claimed he had no interest in riding in the hot-air balloon—was peering over the edge, watching the newland with interest. Isla looked too, but she suddenly felt afraid.

"I don't think I like heights," she said. Her stomach shifted uncomfortably. Her heart was in her throat.

Grim made a calming noise that couldn't have possibly come from him. He leaned his head down, so his chin rested where her crown would have been if she had worn it. "I can portal us anywhere, remember?" he said.

It did make her feel better. She took a step toward the edge and leaned over, just a little. The world was beautiful. It was mountainous and wide, and she felt suddenly free. For nearly half an hour, they just watched the world in comfortable silence.

As she moved back again, her foot knocked against something she hadn't noticed before. It must have been included in each of the carriages for the night. A bottle, with transparent liquid filled with bubbles. Water?

"Skyling wine," he said, frowning. "Disgusting."

Isla uncorked the bottle and tentatively sipped it. She grinned. "This is the best thing I've ever tasted."

Grim sighed.

It was sweet, and sparkling on her tongue, and—

Grim plucked the bottle out of her hands after her second sip. "You might want to wait a little while before drinking more," he said. "Unless you don't want to remember the night." He offered her the bottle, letting it be her choice.

She shook her head. No. She didn't want that at all. She wanted to remember all of this.

Isla turned to face Grim and tilted her head.

"Can I say something honest?"

He looked taken aback. Nodded.

"You are the most unpleasant person I've ever met."

Grim raised an eyebrow at her. "And you are the bane of my existence."

She took a step toward him. "I was disappointed when I didn't kill you."

Grim ran his hand up her thigh, taking her dress with him. She bristled at the cold, at the fact that soon, if he continued, anyone around would be able to see her undergarments . . . but they were in the sky. The next balloon was yards away. "And I'm disappointed you haven't tried again."

His hand curled around her waist. His lips traced her neck. Her back arched, and she moaned as he began kissing her across the glitter on her shoulders, her chest, as he started licking it. "I don't think it's edible," she said.

"I don't care."

And then she was kissing him. Their lips crushed together, and his hands were instantly everywhere. He swept his tongue into her mouth, and she groaned. With one rough motion, Grim lifted her into the air, then placed her on the edge of the basket. Isla's eyes flew open, wind dancing behind her back, roaring in her ears.

"Relax, Hearteater," he said, and his breathing was uneven. Her legs widened, and he settled between them. His hand gripped beneath her knee, and she wanted more, more—

"Portal me to my room," she said.

Grim pressed her fully against his chest—and pushed her over the edge.

Before she could scream, the world tilted, and she landed on Grim. He was on her bed. She was straddling him.

A thousand violent words in her throat, but all of them withered and died when she felt him—every inch of him—against her. Her hips rocked back and forth, ever so slightly, and the friction made her head fall back, her shoulders hike up.

Grim laughed darkly beneath her. "The sight of you, on me . . ." He stopped her, with two hands curved under her backside. He lifted her off him.

She was desperate for his touch, aching—

He gently set her down next to him. He seemed faintly amused by her bewilderment.

"Not tonight, Hearteater," he said, tucking hair that had fallen across her face behind her ear. "Sleep."

Isla was flushed with need, with want—

He was too.

Grim chuckled into the darkness. He pulled her toward him, tucking her into his side. "Remember to dream of me," he said lightly, and she wondered if he knew how often she did.

BEFORE

They stood just out of view of the cave.

"Are you ready?" Grim said.

"Yes. Are you?"

He nodded. While she trained, he had researched the dragon. He had a plan for distracting it.

All Isla had to do was make sure she made it through the trials and to the sword without dying. She crept silently toward the entrance of the cave. The dragon was curled, asleep. She waited, at the edge, for Grim to wake it.

There was a noise outside. The dragon opened an eye and roared.

A massive leg peeked out first. She didn't even look at Grim or what he was doing. She focused on the thin sliver of opening the dragon offered.

Another leg.

Then the dragon shot out of the cave like a strike of lightning.

Now, her mind said, and she leaped into the cave.

First, the arrows. The ones that had wounded Grim in a dozen places. As soon as she triggered the trap, she moved, hurtling for the opposite side. She watched arrows pierce the ground, exactly where she had been.

Isla swallowed. So close. No time for fear. The dragon was still distracted, but who knew how long it would take for it to realize it was being tricked?

Boulders fell from above, and Isla rolled out of their path. A thousand shards of ice were next, too many to miss, so she lifted the metal shield she had brought with her over her head. It made a torrential sound, and Isla winced, knowing the dragon would hear it.

Faster. She had to be faster. As she hunched over, waiting out the last of the hail, she locked eyes with the sword.

It was sitting in a pile of spoils. Just one of hundreds of relics. She didn't even look at any of the rest; she just focused on the blade, shining, as if winking hello.

Only a few more steps.

Isla leaped to the side, just missing a hidden pile of spikes.

A spear flew, aimed at her side, but she was faster. She ducked, missing it.

Just two more steps.

A foot before the pile, a tunnel of wind suddenly burst through the cave, a storm blasting. That, she could not duck to avoid. She faced it, full-on, shield in front of her, jaw clamped tight, fighting against its current, barely making it an inch forward. Another inch. She gritted her teeth, groaned, fought forward—

Until it stopped, and she went tumbling. The sword was in her reach.

Just one more step.

She heard a great roar behind her.

Now. It had to be now.

Her hand reached for the sword. The moment she had it in her grasp, they could portal away. The dragon was coming. Her fingers brushed its hilt. It felt cold under her touch, before warming. Waking up. She turned around, to see where Grim was, to tell him that she got it.

Only to see a flood of fire filling the cave.

It was too late. She wouldn't reach her starstick fast enough. Flames poured in to the brim, hurtling toward her. There was only time to turn her head. The sword sparkled prettily. She hadn't even gotten the chance to fully grip it. Isla prepared to be burned alive.

Before the flames caught her, shadows filled the cave. They wrapped around her, shielding her. Saving her.

The fire cleared. The shadows fell away.

And Isla watched the sword vanish.

. . .

Grim had saved her. He had used his powers, knowing it would mean giving up the sword. And it had disappeared.

"Why did you do that?" Isla said. She had bathed and changed into one of her dresses. Grim had gotten changed in his own chambers and returned here, to her room in her castle.

She was grateful he had . . . but it didn't make any sense.

Grim's eyes locked on hers. "You think I would watch you die, for the sword? Did you think I would make any choice that wasn't you?"

"Yes," she said, incredulous. "You said so."

He just looked at her. "Things changed."

She realized then that she would have done the same. She would have chosen him.

"But your realm . . . you said you need it. For you, it's the most important thing in the world."

"My realm does need it," he said. He traced his fingers down her temple and said, in the quietest of voices, "But it is not the most important thing in the world."

She looked at him, really looked at him. Saw pain in his eyes, as he assessed her for any injuries, even though he had already done so before she had bathed. Saw patience as she scowled and told him again that she was fine.

She didn't see regret.

"I touched it. For a moment, I touched it. Maybe I'll be able to find it again now that it knows me."

"Isla," he said gently. "I don't want to use the sword anymore."

Her brows came together. "What? Why?"

"Its cost is too high," he said thoughtfully.

It seemed Grim had changed his mind about the sword in the time between entering the cave and saving her. It didn't make any sense.

"How are you going to save your realm now?" she asked. "How are you going to stop the dreks?"

Grim lifted a shoulder. "I'm going to use my power, the same as always. Use myself as a shield." He grinned, and she knew it was solely for her benefit, to make light of a devastating situation. "I make a decently good one, wouldn't you agree?"

The thought of him, shielding his entire realm from the dreks. Only his power against theirs . . .

"Will you still keep your promise?" she asked, attempting a smile back. "To help me at the Centennial?"

Grim grinned wider.

"Of course, Hearteater," he said. "It's going to be fun pretending not to know you. To introduce myself to you."

He was right. No one could know they were allies. No one could know they had known each other for months. They would have to pretend to be strangers.

"To pretend I don't know that you love chocolate, and touching your hair, and that you blush when I look at you for more than a few seconds. Or that you hate the cold and love to dance and you frown when you lie." His words were so soft. So unlike him. He tucked her hair behind her ear. "You really do, by the way," he said. "You should work on that before the Centennial."

She blushed, because he had been looking at her for more than a few seconds. She felt tears stinging her eyes, because he knew her.

He really knew her. He'd been paying attention.

What a thing, to be known.

Isla's voice was thick with emotion when she said, "And it will be fun pretending like I don't know the shadows at your feet puddle when you're happy. Or that, for some reason, you've had healers remove every one of your scars, except for the one I gave you. Or that you have a magnificent tub in your bathroom, and an even more magnificent ego." She bit her lip. "And that, even though I hated you, *really*, really hated you . . . whenever I'm not with you, whenever I'm with anyone else, I feel hopelessly alone."

He took her hand, and she said, "At the Centennial . . . we're going to be strangers."

"No," he said. "We could never be just strangers."

"So what are we then?" she asked. "If not strangers? If not . . . enemies?"

"I don't know," he said. "But I want to be the only person you glare at, Hearteater. I want to be the only person you insult. I want to be the only name you speak in your sleep." His eyes darkened. "I want to be the only person who knows how to make you writhe against a wall." He studied her. "You know what? I want everything. I want to be greedy and selfish with you. I want all your laughs. All your smiles too." He frowned. "I would rather die than watch you smile at anyone that isn't me." Grim closed his eyes slowly. He looked almost pained.

Why pain? It didn't make sense.

When he opened them, he said, "There's something I need to tell you."

"No," she said. "There's something *I* need to tell you."

He had saved her life. She hadn't ever trusted anyone this much, other than Celeste. For some reason, she wanted him to see all of her. She didn't want to hide it any longer.

She swallowed. Her guardians would have her head if they knew she was about to tell the ruler of Nightshade her greatest secret. "I—" she said. "I'm—"

Grim watched her struggle to get the words out, and he grabbed her hand, to keep her from touching her hair. "Hearteater," he said, the word so gentle now in his mouth. "I know."

Her brows came together.

What did he think he knew? What did he think she was talking about?

"I know that the curses don't apply to you," he said. "I know that you have never wielded power."

She stepped back. Time had been wounded; it wasn't moving, it was dead—

Part of her wondered if she should run, or hide, or be afraid—

"I've known for a while."

He's known for a while. And he hadn't tried to kill her. He hadn't shared her secret. He'd continued to work with her. He knew how meaningless her life was, how weak she was, how in trouble her people were, and yet . . . he hadn't used it to his advantage.

"Nightshades can sense curses. I didn't realize it at first, but I couldn't sense yours. Then, when the Wildlings were able to attack you in the forest, to try to get your heart . . ." Of course he would have questioned why Isla hadn't fought back. Why she hadn't used even a drop of power the entire time they were working together.

Tears fell freely now. "Grim . . . what—what is wrong with me?"

He took her face in both his hands. "Nothing, absolutely nothing, is wrong with you, heart." He said it for the second time, and it directly contradicted everything she had ever thought about herself.

She went on her toes and kissed him. It was clumsy and too forceful and caught him by surprise. She fell on her heels, wondering why in the world she'd done that, but she didn't wonder for long.

Hands still pressed to her face, he ducked and parted her lips with his own, kissing her like she might be leaving, like he might never get to do it again. His tongue swept across the roof of her mouth, and she groaned. This was impossible—it was impossible to feel this good.

She was a burning flame, and there were too many clothes, too many layers between them. She had always been told that her body didn't belong to her, it belonged to the realm, but *no*, right now she wanted to feel everything that was possible. She wanted Grim to *show* her.

"I want you," she said, breaking their kiss, breathing too quickly. "I want everything."

Grim looked like he might be losing his mind. Like he couldn't have

possibly heard her correctly. His chest was heaving. He blinked. Again. Said, "Are you sure?"

"Yes," she said, and she meant it more than she had ever meant anything else.

Grim swallowed. "I'm not gentle," he said gruffly.

Isla opened her mouth. Closed it. The thought of him not being gentle . . . it unexplainably made her feel hot everywhere.

"Could—could you be?"

He hesitated. Then nodded.

The way he carried her to the bed . . . it was as if she were made of glass. He laid her on her sheets like she was mist and might just slip away if he wasn't careful. Isla's eyes darted to the closed door.

"We're hidden," he said. And Isla had never been so grateful for his illusions.

He was over her now, completely clothed. No. She didn't want anything between them.

She yanked his shirt up, and it didn't move at all. But Grim reached back and tore it over his head in one smooth movement, making his shoulders flex, and Isla couldn't see enough of his body, couldn't touch enough.

"You are perfect," she said, and she couldn't believe the thought had reached her lips. "I didn't know—I didn't know someone could look like this. It's unfair, really."

Grim only laughed. "You're doing very little to discourage my *magnificent ego*."

Her hands stroked down his hard chest. He radiated pure power, strength. She traced the scar just half an inch from his heart, and his eyes fell closed for a long moment. She could have sworn he shivered. The shadows in her room melted across the floor, puddling.

His gaze locked on her chest, prickled with need, aching like every part of her, and the silk of her dress did nothing to hide it. His hands

went to the bodice, to rip it like before, and Isla made a sound of protest. "Demon," she said. "I'm not going to have any dresses left if you keep destroying them."

"I'll buy you new ones. I'll buy you a market. I'll get you your own tailor."

"Fine," she said, and the dress didn't stand a chance. It was ribbons in a second, and then his mouth was on her chest. He bit her, lightly, and she made a rasping noise, her back arching.

His hand trailed down her stomach, below her underthings, and when he touched her, he cursed. "*Isla,*" he said against her chest, "you are truly going to kill me."

"I will," she said, "if you don't keep touching me."

She was burning, aching, desperate for more.

"Please," she said. "I want everything."

Grim took the rest of his clothes off, and Isla went still. She had felt him before, but now . . .

He climbed over her again, his hips settling between her legs, and her breath hiked. He pressed his lips against her shoulder, her chest, her neck, her cheek. "I think you'll find we fit perfectly," he said, as if reading her thoughts.

Then he looked at her and asked one final time. "Are you sure?"

"Yes," she said, and he reached down between them.

For a while, there were just their shared breaths, his forehead pressed against hers. He was leaning on his arms, holding himself over her, shaking slightly as he exercised every ounce of control.

At first, there were flashes of pain. She winced, and Grim always stopped. Always waited for her to tell him to go farther.

He went farther. And farther. *Farther.*

Her nails dug into his shoulders, and she breathed through it as her body got used to him. He was gentle, so gentle, fisting the sheets in his hands, cursing words into the place between her neck and shoulder.

Suddenly, it all seemed to go so much easier. Suddenly . . . Isla's head was falling back as she groaned, and Grim was making a sound like a growl. His arm curled below her spine, and he hauled her fully against his chest. Her legs locked behind him.

Isla saw stars, gasped his name, said all sorts of ridiculous things, and then she was whimpering, because she had never felt this good, this close to the stars—

She pressed her cheek against the sheets, and he kissed up the length of her neck, until he gently turned her head, fingers curled around the back of her neck, until their eyes locked. He seemed fixated on her every expression, the way she drew breath when he reached down to raise her hips higher, the way she bit her lip to keep from making more noise.

He tugged her bottom lip from between her teeth and kissed her.

She cried out against his lips as she shattered, and Grim kept going, and going, until he joined her over the edge.

For minutes, he just held her, tightly, as if someone might take her from him. Then, he rose to look at her face, emotions battling across his own. Unexpected ones. She wanted to tip his mind over and play with the contents.

"Hearteater." He leaned down and pressed a kiss to her lips. "You are both curse . . ." he whispered against her skin, lips traveling down her neck, to the center of her chest, ". . . and cure."

After the first time, she didn't want to stop. It was as if an entirely new world had been opened, and she wanted to explore every inch of it.

Hours later, she woke up sprawled on top of Grim. Her cheek was against his chest. One of his arms was wrapped around her, the other was hanging off the bed.

The things they had done in this bed . . .

She lifted her head, to look at him, and found him already awake. He met her eyes and smiled.

Smiled.

She had never seen him smile, not like that.

"You have a dimple," Isla said in disbelief. It made him look boyish, and adorable, and she couldn't believe it.

"Do I?" he said.

He didn't even know.

She crawled up his chest, to rest her chin on her arms, right below his face. She just looked at him, up through her lashes.

Suddenly, something occurred to her. He had told her Nightshades didn't keep the same partner for long. Soon, would he leave her? Would he forget her, like the rest?

Grim sat up. "What's wrong?" he asked, expression filled with worry.

"You—you aren't going to disappear, right? Now that we . . . now that we—"

He laughed. He folded over, shoulders shaking with it. She pinched him below the ribs, and he kept laughing. "Hearteater," he finally said, breathless. "I said Nightshade rulers are typically forbidden from bedding the same person more than once. Last night alone . . ."

Multiple times. Relief filled her. It didn't look like Grim was going anywhere. She rose until she was straddling him. She ducked her head, so she could say right into his ear, "Good. Because I want to do it all again. Immediately."

Grim groaned. His head fell back, and he closed his eyes again. "Hearteater," he said. "You are a bane." She remembered his words from before: *You are both curse and cure.* "It's never . . ." He sighed. "For me, it's never felt like that."

She wondered if he really meant that. He was her first; she didn't know what it felt like, other than last night. And last night . . . "So, you won't be entertaining other women lining up for the privilege of sleeping with you anymore?"

She expected Grim to make a joke, or at least look amused, but his expression turned serious. "No." He shook his head. "You have

ruined me." He swallowed. "I have a thousand things to do, but all I want is to lock us in this room . . ." He traced his hand down her spine, and she shivered. "All I want is to claim you so thoroughly, that there won't be a part of you that doesn't have a memory with me."

Isla was going to burst into flame. "Do it," she said. She was ready, she wanted it—

Grim closed his eyes again. His chest quivered with restraint. "A curse," he said.

Then he took her into his arms.

And he did.

She portaled to Grim's room a few days later. Within a moment, she was in his arms. He kissed her like he hadn't seen her in years, even though they had seen each other that morning. He leaned down, slid the bridge of his nose down her neck, and whispered in the place between her neck and shoulder, "You are an addiction." He bit her lightly, and she gasped. "You are my nightbane."

Isla was glad he was in such a good mood. "Don't be mad."

Grim immediately tensed. It took him a moment, but he eventually stepped away from her. "Why would I be mad, Hearteater?" he asked. His eyes were studying her, as if searching for injury.

"I went back to the cave—"

His eyes widened. He took a step toward her. "Are you—"

"I'm not hurt," she said. "But . . ."

He crossed his arms across his chest. "Yes?"

She tried to give him her best smile. "It's nothing bad! Don't get upset."

His expression didn't change. He looked down at her and said, "Hearteater, what is it?"

She opened her mouth. Closed it. Then, she said, "I should probably just show you." She pulled out her starstick, but before she portaled

away, planning to bring her discovery to his room, Grim grabbed her arm, taking himself with her.

Which meant he portaled right to the tree where she had leashed her—

"Dragon," Grim said, staring down at the little bundle of black scales. "Hearteater . . ." he said. "You didn't."

Isla knelt next to the little dragon. She had found it wandering alone, near the cave. "I think he was abandoned by his mother," she said. "Because he's small. Or injured. I'm not sure yet."

The dragon was small enough that she could hold him in her arms. His black scales glimmered like a collection of dark gems. His head was rounded. She hadn't seen him spread his wings yet.

"Think of him as . . . a pet." Her eyes darted to him and back to the dragon again. "For you."

He looked at her like he was trying to evaluate her mental condition. "You think I am going to keep this creature in my quarters?"

"Yes," she said. "I think you are. Because I am asking you to."

His eyes flashed with disbelief.

"Please, Grim," she said.

Isla knew he would refuse. Her mind sifted through different places she might be able to take the dragon on Wildling. Maybe she could hide it in the forest and visit between trainings? Maybe she could find someone who would make a good caretaker?

But without another word, Grim frowned, picked up the tiny dragon, held it as far away from his body as he could manage, and portaled them away.

"We need a name," she said after a week.

"A name? It should be grateful it has a home."

"Grim."

"Yes, Hearteater?"

"Stop being so cruel. Look, it just dipped its head. You made it sad."

Grim whipped around to face her with a look of pure incredulity. "You think that animal can speak?"

She glared at him. "No. I think just like another *beast* in this room, it might be able to sense emotion. Or, at the very least, tone." Isla sat down and scooped the dragon into her lap. She stroked a finger between its eyes, and it sighed. "It's okay," she cooed. "He's mean to everyone."

Grim raised an eyebrow at her. "Is that what we're calling what I did to you last night? Mean?"

Isla felt her cheeks flush. The dragon tilted its head at her in curiosity, and she wondered if it really did understand them.

"That thing keeps flying into my bed at night," Grim said.

"That's adorable!" Isla exclaimed.

Grim looked at her in a way that could only be described as a fusion of disgust and horror. His favorite expression. She looked at him and thought she had never been happier.

FORGIVE ME

It hadn't worked. None of those memories had been useful. If anything, they had been ruinous. Now Isla felt far more conflicted about what she had to do.

Oro met her in the Mainland woods. She had practiced dipping her hand into the link between them and attempting to hold his powers. She could only ever do it for a moment at a time.

"It will only take me a moment to kill him," Oro said. "You won't have to hold for long."

Kill him. Some echo of her past screamed against the words. She pushed the doubt away.

"You must hate me," Isla said.

Oro's brows came together. "Hate you?"

"Yes," she said. "I summoned Grim. It—it was reckless."

"It was," he agreed, "but it helped you come up with your plan. It could save us, if it works."

She looked at him, incredulous. He *should* hate her. His endless patience and forgiveness was infuriating, because it couldn't possibly be real.

Enya was right. Oro deserved better than her. She wasn't good for him.

"I'm broken, Oro," she said. "You should really—you should really find someone else to love."

He raised an eyebrow at her. "Do you think that's how this works?" he asked. "Do you think love is something you can control?"

She put her hands up. "I'm a mess. I see the way you look at me. I can imagine the things you want. A future. What if I—what if I'm not ready for any of that?"

His gaze did not falter. "I have waited hundreds of years for you," he said. "You have no idea how patient I can be."

Tears burned her eyes as she looked at him. "I don't deserve your love."

"Is that what you believe?"

She nodded. She really did. "You don't know," she said. "I—I'm awful inside. My mind is a mess. *I'm* a mess." She shook her head. "One day I'm going to do something, and you're going to see. You're going to see me. The real me. The worst me."

"I see everything, and I love you. Is that what scares you?"

"Why?" she demanded. "Why do you love me?"

He looked at her. "For hundreds of years before I met you, I don't think I smiled or joked or laughed more than a handful of times. Nothing excited me. Nothing made me feel *anything* anymore." He took her hand. "Meeting you was like remembering what I was like before the curses," he said. "Loving you is remembering what I once loved about me."

He leaned in closer.

"You feel so strongly. You *care*. I went centuries without feeling a single thing. Until you. Don't you see? You brought me to life."

Isla pressed her hand against his chest, over his heart. She heard it beat under her palm. The love between them was a bridge. It went in both directions. She could feel where their forces met as much as she could feel his heartbeat.

She dipped inside the bridge. She felt Oro there. His power. Sunling. Starling. Moonling. Skyling.

She gripped a bit and opened her palm. Fire curled out of her fingers. It was tinged in blue, just like his flames.

She had never felt closer to him. Sharing power was intimate, she knew that.

Darkness had clawed its way into her heart, but for this moment, all she could see was light.

All she could see was *him*.

She went on her toes and kissed him. He startled for just a moment before kissing her back. She clung to his neck, nails digging into his skin the same way they had the first time he took her flying.

"I'm not going anywhere," he whispered against her lips. "My heart is yours for as long as you want it."

"I'm not going anywhere either," she promised.

Isla told Oro she needed to train alone for a while, in preparation for the battle. She asked him to supervise the Starling barrier being built. Earlier that day, Cinder had started the shield, summoning enough energy to make an entire shining wall herself. The rest of the Starlings were now going to build a second one, on the other side, securing their position.

When he was gone, and she couldn't feel the connection between them at all, she sighed.

Remembering hadn't worked.

She walked to the Wild Isle bridge. Crossed it. Made her way to the Place of Mirrors. She stopped in front of the vault and produced a blade.

"Forgive me," she said to Oro. Then, she broke her promise to him. She sliced a long line across her palm. The skin parted, blood flowed, pain bellowed—

She turned it into strength.

All the Wildling power within her—the seed—melted down, dripped through her bones like liquid gold.

Isla stuck her crown into the lock, turned it—

And forced the door completely open.

No surge stopped her.

She took a step into the vault.

UNLOCKED

The vault was starless black.

And it was empty.

No. That was impossible. She could feel the power everywhere, metal in her mouth, enough to nearly bring her to her knees.

Where was it coming from?

Blood from her hand dripped onto the smooth stone floor. Her bare feet slid across it as she desperately searched every corner.

Nothing.

Roaring filled her ears; the world seemed to tip to the side.

There were footsteps behind her.

Isla whipped around and nearly dropped to the floor.

Terra said, "Hello, little bird."

Her guardian stepped forward. "Do you feel proud, little bird?" she said. She smirked at Isla's hand, still bleeding profusely. Isla didn't even feel the sting of pain any longer. Power was still gathered in her bones; it still honeyed everything it touched. "Do you feel proud, when you should feel ashamed?"

Grim must have portaled her here. It was the only way. He must be watching her.

Did Terra steal whatever was inside?

No. She couldn't have. Isla's crown was the only key.

So why was she here?

Isla laughed without humor, the shock slowly wearing off. *Ashamed?* "You, who lied to me my entire life. You, who trained a girl to fight but

planned for her to seduce a king." She took a step. "You—" Her voice began to shake uncontrollably. "Who *killed my parents* in cold blood." Another step, until she was out of the vault and standing in front of her old guardian. Her old teacher. Her old *friend*. "You, who warned me my entire life about Nightshades and have now joined them."

Terra stood and listened, chin raised, almost in challenge. "I did what I needed to in order to protect our realm. To protect you. And I will continue to." She outstretched her hand. "Come with me, little bird," she said. "Before you make more of a mess of things."

A mess?

She spat at Terra's feet. "You are a traitor," she said. "Don't speak to me about making a mess."

The vine came out of nowhere.

Isla was slapped across the floor. She slid for a few feet, then stopped. Her shoulders curved. She panted. Then she smiled.

"I'm not the powerless fool you raised anymore," she said. Then she brought the entire force of the forest through the ceiling of the Place of Mirrors.

Trees blew through the remaining windows, and branches snapped, twisting into mangled shapes.

Vines lunged at Terra in every direction, enough to drown her in their grip, but the fighting master sliced her arms through the air in practiced movements, and they were all cut down.

Isla's power was everywhere; it flooded her every thought, every sense, the pain in her hand feeding its frenzy. She bellowed, and the stone floor shattered as spiked trees erupted from below, right where her guardian stood.

Terra leaped from side to side, just barely missing every one right before it impaled her on its thorns. She tsked. "Little bird, your form is dreadful." She shook her head, moving effortlessly to the side as a boulder broke through the ceiling, cracking into a thousand shards. "And far too predictable."

Predict this, Isla thought before sharpening the trunk of a massive tree into a blade. She flung it at her old teacher, the drumming in her ears, her power, eager to see her cut down. She wanted to see her dead, bleeding out on the floor.

Power tastes like blood.

Before her sword could skewer Terra against the wall, her teacher made her own blade, cut from the side of a cliff. It raced through the broken windows of the Place of Mirrors. Both of their weapons now floated between them, two massive swords ready to duel.

Isla grinned. "Just like old times," she said through her teeth. She tasted metal. She tasted blood.

She attacked.

Their blades crashed together, making a sound that rumbled across Wild Isle. Isla wielded hers with her mind, faster, faster, using all the techniques her teacher had taught her. But now, she was stronger.

She was a ruler. She ruled over *everyone*, not the other way around. Not anymore.

And Isla didn't care about playing fair.

She created another sword, this one crafted out of a thousand gems. She made them from thin air, her power hardening into crystal and ruby and diamond. It took so much effort, enough that she felt her power scraped to the very bottom, getting every last shred. It was her anger, hardened into a blade, glimmering, remembering, about to make her guardian pay.

It sliced through the air behind Terra, ready to plunge through her back, to destroy everything she ever was.

But before it could, Terra turned her hand into a fist, and it all shattered.

Isla was sent backward, flying. She hit the ground with a crack. She slid until she hit the wall.

Her power had been drained to the ashes. All her fury and sadness and pain had lashed out—and had been defeated.

She was powerless to move a muscle when Terra walked over and frowned down at her. "Little bird," she said, "your emotions always were your greatest weakness. You are still so foolish. Have it your way." She bent down to say, "Thank you for opening the portal for us." Her footsteps echoed as she left the Place of Mirrors.

What? What portal?

Terra's last words were a key, unlocking a memory.

BEFORE

Isla was polishing her throwing stars after training with Terra when she felt it. Something calling to her from the forest.

She frowned. It didn't make a noise, but it was like it was tapping her on the shoulder with its presence.

Grim was supposed to meet her soon. She should wait for him.

But the calling beckoned, more desperate now.

She tucked her throwing stars and daggers into her pockets and used her starstick to portal into the woods.

The sun was getting close to setting. Gold peered through the tops of the trees. It was a dangerous time to be in the woods. They were bloodthirsty and known to lash out.

Still, she followed the call.

She followed it until she reached a spot the eldress had shown her before she died. A river framed by cliffs, and waterfalls that fell in transparent sweeps. Stones larger than her skull lined the edge, smoothed over time.

And sticking out of the dirt, as if thrown down from the heavens, was the sword.

The sword's double blades refracted light in twin shimmers. A bright-red stone sat buried in its hilt. It was heavy in her hand.

Grim portaled into her room and paled.

"Hearteater," he said. "Where did you find that?"

At first, she was happy. Excited, ecstatic that the sword had presented itself. It would help *Grim*. He would help *her*.

Then she began to ask questions.

"You said you had something to tell me," she said, remembering the night he had first taken her to bed. "Before I interrupted you. What is it?"

Grim swallowed. He looked almost . . . afraid. He took a seat in one of her chairs and beckoned for her to sit across from him.

"I'll stand," she said sharply, already feeling betrayal rooting itself inside her chest.

Grim was silent for a few moments, eyes on the hands in front of him, and then he spoke. "More than twenty years ago, I began my search for that sword," he said. He looked at it for just a moment before bringing his eyes to hers. "I had help. My best general. One day, he went to follow a lead, taking my relic I had made to get there." *Her starstick.* "Then . . . he was gone."

She remembered Grim saying he had been betrayed before, by someone else he had hunted the sword with. It was why he had always been so secretive, so stingy with information.

"I assumed he died in the attempt to get the sword. For over two decades, I believed that to be true. Until you portaled into my palace."

What did his general have to do with her?

"Guards found your clothes, the ones you had left behind. When I discovered you were Wildling, I knew there was only one way that you could have gotten to my palace so quickly. Then . . . when I realized you were uncursed, everything made sense."

Isla took a step back. The tip of the sword shrieked against her floor. "Wh—what do you mean?"

His eyes softened. "It's rare, but non-rulers can have flairs," he said. "My general had one." His voice was gentle. "He was impervious to curses."

The one who had made his charm.

Tears stung her eyes before she even knew what he meant, like her body had put everything together before her mind could process it.

"He was your father, Isla," he said.

"No."

That would mean—it would mean—

"I'm not Nightshade."

Grim smiled. "But you are. You *are*."

She shook her head. "That doesn't make any sense—"

"I believe your father did find the sword. But he always feared I would one day share my father's ambitions and use the dreks to conquer Lightlark." He frowned. "He must have met your mother. And clearly . . ."

"Why would he think that?" she demanded. Her father had gone to great lengths to make sure Grim couldn't get the sword. He must have had a good reason. She remembered what Grim had told her. "Why did your father want Lightlark so badly?"

"Lightlark is a miniature," Grim said. "The creators of the island fled a world made up of different countries. Moonling, to the very north, buried in the ice. Sunling at the center, where the sun shined brightest. Wildling close by. Skyling, then Starling, then Nightshade at the opposite end, where it was darkest and coldest. They took thousands here, to another world, and created a smaller version of the one they left behind."

She had never heard of that. It sounded impossible.

"Cronan, my own ancestor, wanted to go back, after he was cast out from Lightlark. But the portal is built into its foundation. Using it successfully would mean destroying the island."

"Why doesn't anyone know about this?" she demanded. Poppy and Terra had never mentioned any of it in her history lessons.

"Only the ancient creatures remain from that world. Over time, the information was lost, but not by Nightshade. Though, my people never attempted to try to seek out the portal again until I was born."

"Why?"

"I have the same flair as Cronan. Portaling. The portal doesn't work on its own, it requires someone with my skill."

The destruction of Lightlark . . . it would doom thousands of people to death. "Why would anyone ever want to go back to that other world?"

"I don't," he said. "We went to war over the portal, but after the curses, when my father died, I abandoned the search myself. I only needed the sword after the dreks became a problem, to stop them."

"Does anyone else know about the portal?"

Grim nodded. "Only one other ruler that I know of. Cleo. She is . . . very interested in using it."

That was how Grim had the Moonling medicine. Cleo was helping him for a reason. She was trying to persuade him.

"Why would she want that?"

"I don't know," he said. "She wants to go to that world, for some reason."

"You won't do it, though, will you?"

"No. Even if I wanted to, I couldn't. The portal is in the Wildling palace on Lightlark. Only a Wildling ruler can open it."

She would never do that. Tears stung her eyes. She would never doom an entire island of people.

Her throat felt tight. She finally had answers. Though, part of her wished she hadn't asked any questions. She was happier, she thought, living in ignorance.

"Here," she said, flinging the sword at him. She wanted to stab him with it.

Grim caught the sword and leaned it against her wall. "I told you. I don't want to use it anymore."

"Right," she said, her voice cruel. "The cost is too high. Tell me the truth now," she demanded. "What was the cost?"

"Your life."

He said it so matter-of-factly, all she could do was stare at him as tears slowly fell down her cheeks. "My . . . *life*?" Her voice broke on the last word.

"I needed you to use your flair to break the curse on the sword," he said. "It was an ancient curse. Breaking it would have either killed you on the spot, or significantly shortened your life."

Her world had just smashed against a rock. Everything she thought she knew was shattered.

"You knew from the very beginning," she said. Tears were hot down her cheeks. "You knew when we made the deal. *That's* why you made it. You knew it might kill me. You probably weren't even planning on going to the Centennial at all."

He didn't try to deny it. "That was before I knew you," he said. "Before . . . all this happened."

She didn't care. She could barely even see; her tears had made everything look distorted, and she didn't mind, because she didn't want to look at him. "Goodbye, Grim," she said. "I never want to see you again."

Silence.

"You mean that?"

"I do."

He closed his eyes against the words. For a while, he didn't say anything. Then, very slowly, as if he was still trying to make sense of his own emotions, he said, "I've been stabbed a thousand times . . . but none of that hurts more than hearing you say goodbye."

And then he vanished.

PORTAL

Oro didn't say a word about the cut on her hand. He didn't get angry. All he did was scoop her from the ground of the Place of Mirrors and bring her back to their room. He cleaned her wound, and fed her broth, and brought her medicine. Ella was in the Skyling newland now, almost everyone was, so he went down into the kitchens and made everything himself.

Oro had found her through their link. She had called to him, her essence just a whisper . . . and he had answered.

He had always answered.

He deserved so much better. Enya was right.

Why didn't she ever listen? Why didn't she ever learn?

When she was back to her previous strength, she said, "I need to tell you something."

The castle was empty. The attack would happen the next day. Azul, Oro, Isla, Zed, Calder, and Enya stood on the stairs in front of it for their meeting. The legions had their orders. They had their plan.

But something had changed.

"I know why he's coming," she said. She told them everything. About the other world. The portal. The fact that using it would completely destroy Lightlark.

"Why would he want to go to a different world?" Azul asked.

Isla didn't know. That part didn't make any sense. In her memories, he had told her about the other world without showing any interest in visiting it.

What else wasn't she remembering?

Zed paced up and down the stairs. "Whatever his reason is, we have to make sure the portal stays closed," he said. "We must—"

"It's already open," she said, tears streaming.

A storm cracked the sky in half. Wind howled around them. "What do you mean, it's already open?" Zed demanded.

She felt everyone's eyes on her.

Terra was right. She was still so foolish. She had been so blinded by her need to get the vault open, by her desire to prove herself as a true Wildling, that she had given her enemy the key to destroying everything she loved.

Her voice was just a rasp. "I opened it for him."

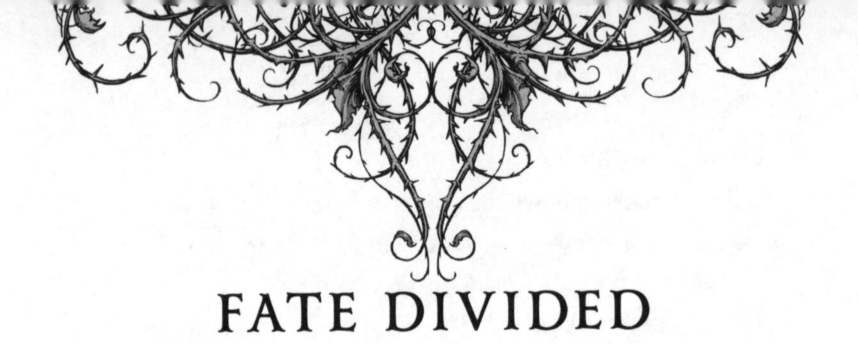

FATE DIVIDED

It was the morning of the war. The oracle was leaning against the ice, as if she couldn't hold herself upright. She smiled when she saw Isla.

"You left it until the very last moment, didn't you?" she asked, her voice echoing. "My very last prophecy, the most important yet . . . and you almost miss it."

Tears were dried on Isla's cheeks. She was numb. She had ruined everything. The oracle had demanded she return. "What do you want?"

The oracle hummed against the ice. "My desires matter very little, actually," she said. "Yours, however . . . Yours will decide the fate of the world."

Isla shook her head. "Fate has already been decided," she said. "I opened the portal." Her voice shook. She had tried to close it again, but the door had not moved an inch.

Wrong. She had done everything wrong.

The oracle looked at her curiously. "Fate has not been decided," she said. "The battle hasn't even begun."

No. That couldn't be true.

"Wildling," she said. "You need to understand, the future is split in half. There are two possibilities, not one greater than the other. I see you choosing each path. It changes almost every minute."

"What paths?" Isla asked.

"Your heart decides the future of the world," she said. "Your choice decides."

"What choice?" she practically screamed.

"Oro and Grim."

Isla froze at their mention.

"You will kill one of them. That much is certain. Which one lives, and which one dies . . . that has not yet been decided."

She planned to kill Grim that very day . . . but the oracle said it was just as likely she would end up killing Oro.

It couldn't be true.

Now that she had most of her memories back . . . she didn't want to kill either of them.

"*Nothing* is decided," the oracle repeated. "Both possibilities are just as likely. You *will* kill one of them, with your own hand."

This couldn't be her fate. She couldn't be the one to decide the future of the world. Why her?

"You, whose heart has been split in two in more ways than one, are capable of both life and death. You are both curse and cure."

Grim had said those same words to her—

Isla sobbed into her hands. Her mind was at war. The more she remembered—

"They're almost here," the oracle said. "Go, now. Make your choice."

The oracle smiled, one last time, before the wall of ice cracked and fell, water forming a wave that Isla only missed by rising above, using her Wildling abilities.

When the water cleared, the oracle was gone.

Isla raced across the Mainland on Lynx's back. He was wearing his full armor, scuffed with marks from previous battles with her mother. Lynx hadn't needed much time to get used to the island. She held tightly as he expertly avoided the brambles she herself had set up, to block the Nightshades. Wind whipped her face. Tears were briny on her cheeks.

You will kill one of them.

No. Days before, she had declared she would help kill Grim. She

would put a hold on his powers. But now . . . she remembered so much more.

He was her enemy. He was coming to destroy the island. He was going to kill innocents, kill *her*, if she didn't stop him. So why did the idea of hurting him hurt so much? Why did it feel like she was being torn in two?

Their army was lined up and ready, spread across the only clearing left on the Mainland. Skyling warriors glimmered like ornaments, armor shining as they waited above. Ciel and Avel were among them. Each were supplied with dozens of metal-tipped arrows. Zed and Calder had worked hard to make sure of it.

Before Azul had left, hours before, he had given them a gift. A violent storm raged high above the island, contained between rows of clouds, as a fence to keep the dreks from being able to escape once the Skylings began using their special weapons.

Azul had looked devastated to leave. He had clutched her hands in goodbye and she had slipped one of her rings onto his finger, the same way she had the first time they ever saw each other. "Keep it safe for me," she said. "Until we see each other next."

Lynx came to a sudden halt in front of Oro. The traitorous creature greeted him with about ten times more fondness than he had greeted her.

Enya stood next to Oro in rose-gold armor, looking determined. She nodded at Isla, then at Lynx, who tipped his head in greeting.

A Sunling called to her, and she excused herself. Isla watched her go and—

"Be—be careful," Isla said, surprising herself. She didn't realize how much she had come to care about the Sunling, even after what she had told her.

Enya grinned over her shoulder. "Don't worry about me, Wildling," she said, winking. "I do not die today."

Isla wondered if she could say the same.

She slipped off Lynx's back and landed in front of Oro. She couldn't meet his eyes, after what she had just learned. "They'll be here soon," she said. She wouldn't tell him how she had visited the oracle. How could she explain that the woman had predicted she had just as much chance of killing Oro as Grim?

No. Impossible. She would kill Grim today and end the prophecy. There would be no chance that it could ever be Oro.

"Are you okay?" he asked. His hand was warm against her arm.

"No," she said. "I'm afraid." She had never been in a true battle before. And certainly not one of this scale. "I'm afraid I've already ruined everything."

Oro shook his head and pulled her fully to his chest. "We have a plan," he said, lips pressing against her forehead. "The portal being open doesn't change that."

No. But it certainly made the stakes higher.

Their plan had slightly shifted, now that they knew Grim was targeting the portal in the Place of Mirrors. Nightshade power didn't work there, which meant Grim couldn't portal directly inside. Isla had covered every inch of the isle in poisonous plants. The closest he could get was the bridge, where she would be waiting.

That was where they would battle.

"Isla," Oro said softly. She looked up at him. He traced her lips with the tip of his finger and smiled. Then his face became serious. "If something happens to me, I want you to leave. I want you to take all my power and leave."

She frowned. "Oro, *nothing* is going to—"

"Love," he said, smiling again. He looked almost happy . . . almost at peace. He tucked away a stray hair and said, "It's all for you." He took her hand and pressed it over his heart. His eyes closed, for a moment, and he kept smiling. "All these years, I saved it for you."

Isla didn't know why she was crying.

"It's yours. It will always be yours. Protect the people of Lightlark."

No. She didn't know why he was talking like that. All she could say was the truth. "I love you."

Oro smiled wider, and this was too perfect, too much joy to fit in a person, too good to be true, like a sunny day right before a storm. He produced a rose in his hand and said, "I know."

She reached beneath her shirt and showed him her golden rose. The necklace she wore below the one she couldn't take off.

He took her into his arms and kissed her.

That was when she started to worry.

His kiss was desperate, like it might be one of the last things he would ever do. He leaned down and whispered in her ear, "One day, I'm going to take you to my favorite place." She remembered him telling her about it. A beach on Sun Isle with water the green of her eyes. "And I'm going to lay you upon the rocks." Her pulse quickened. "And I'm going to make it your favorite place too."

Isla smiled. She wanted that, desperately. She could see it so clearly—Oro pressing her against the sand, waves washing around them while he wrung pleasure from her, the same way he had in their bedroom.

And she could see beyond that too.

"Tomorrow," she said. "We're going to do that not *one day* but tomorrow. We're going to win, everything is going to be fine, Lightlark is going to survive, and we're going to go to the beach tomorrow."

Oro smiled. Nodded. But she knew him now. She could see the tiny signs.

He didn't believe her.

One moment, the Mainland was empty, save for their own soldiers.

The next, Grim's army was everywhere.

Isla's blood went cold. Grim had portaled them all—*thousands*—at once. She knew how much power that required.

Shadows and ash erupted across the Mainland and were met by lashes of fire. Wind swept down from the sky. Metal clashed against metal. Screams, cries, bellows—

"Tomorrow," Oro said, pressing one final kiss to her lips. Then he jumped into the air, straight into the battle.

His effect was immediate. Isla watched in awe as Oro's fire became a wave that washed over dozens of Nightshade soldiers. As he pulled water from the sea and flooded an entire unit, washing them right off the side of the island. He made a sword of Starling sparks and began fighting, and anyone who dared approach him died.

Lynx knelt, and Isla pushed the ground beneath her to propel her onto his back. She slipped into her saddle. "Let's go," she said, and he raced forward.

A group of Nightshades stepped into their path, but before they could draw a single shadow, Lynx plowed through most of them and tore the rest apart with his mighty fangs.

From his back, Isla had the perfect vantage point. She turned in both directions, her arms moving wildly, burying some Nightshades in the ground, and covering others in a sea of poisonous plants. The flora she had created previously also fought back, almost extensions of herself, stabbing with their barbs and thorns.

Near the coast, Isla saw what looked to be a moving wall of water. It was Calder. He swept across the land inside a massive wave with a dozen serpent heads coming out of it. They each lashed out, swallowing Nightshades, drowning them. Calder looked deep in meditation. It seemed contrary to his peaceful nature to kill, and she knew every death would haunt him afterward.

Nightshades fought back with relish. Unlike Calder, most of them seemed to enjoy the killing. Darkness was everywhere, ink turned over, just like in her vision. She watched a Sunling turn to ash. A Skyling was sliced in half by a ribbon of umbra. His pieces fell from the sky, landing amid the barbed brush.

She shot her arm to the side and sent a line of Nightshades hurtling toward one of the Starling shields. Their bodies broke against it. She propelled another group into the center of her poisonous plants. Their screams quickly turned to silence.

No sign of the dreks. Not yet.

Perhaps she had been wrong. Maybe Grim hadn't found a way to use the sword. Maybe the dreks wouldn't be a threat. They would be in battle by now, wouldn't they?

In a flash, the world went sideways as Lynx was struck. Isla just managed to encase them both in a shield of energy, and together they slid across the Mainland, raking through all the plants in their path.

"Lynx!" she yelled as soon as she was on her feet. She raced to the leopard. He was on his side. He wasn't moving.

She threw herself atop him, guarding him with her power.

No. If he was hurt, if he was—

He made a sound of irritation below her, as if annoyed that she was scrambling to feel for his heartbeat.

She buried her face in his fur, relief cold through her blood. Shadows had eaten through part of his armor. If he hadn't been wearing it, that would have been his skin.

They could have killed him.

Rage shot through her veins—energy filled her limbs. Oro's voice was in her head, telling her to calm down. Telling her that being emotional would make her lose control.

She tried to breathe through the anger, but it only intensified, until her power was so saturated, she could feel it like a weight in her chest.

Before she could stop herself, her hand struck the ground before her, and the island shattered. Its terrain rippled, swallowing any Nightshade in its path, until they were buried beneath rock. More of them rushed forward, and she almost smiled, something wicked uncurling inside her chest.

They called their shadows?

She called her own.

They streamed from her fingers, and she gathered them up just like she had in her training with Remlar.

"Get down," she told Lynx, and he ducked just as she turned her stream of shadows into a scythe that cut all the Nightshades around her down.

She was panting. She had used too much power too quickly.

But all the enemies around her were dead now.

More were joining them.

Skylings shot powerful gusts from above, forcing Nightshades toward the center. Sunlings created walls of flames. Grim's army was slowly being boxed in, Lightlark's legion advancing from all sides.

Now, she thought, grabbing her starstick from its place along her spine. "I'll be right back," she told Lynx, who bowed his head, before she portaled to Sky Isle, where her own legion was waiting.

"It's time?" Singrid asked as soon as he saw her, grinning, clearly eager to join the battle. The Vinderland stood ready behind him, hundreds of warriors clattering their weapons together. Nearby, Remlar watched with curiosity, along with his people and the other night creatures she had recruited.

Their plan was simple. Oro's armies would surround the Nightshade forces. Trap them. Keep moving them to the center of their battlefield. Then, Isla would portal the second wave of warriors right into the middle, so Grim's forces would be enclosed in all directions.

"It's time."

Isla drew her puddle of stars as large as she could make it. And, with all her remaining strength, she kept it open as the hundreds of soldiers rushed in. She was the last to fall inside.

Battle cries pierced the air. Nightshades were now being smothered. Sunlings, Skylings, Vinderland, and night creatures all fought side by side.

Isla marveled at them. Enemies, united.

She was lifted off her feet by Lynx, who threw her onto his back without stopping. She gripped his saddle and joined the fighting.

The Nightshades didn't stand a chance. They were almost easily overpowering them.

Then a woman came from the sea, on the back of a swell that dwarfed even the Singing Mountains.

The water crashed across the Mainland, and soldiers were covered, then frozen where they stood. They couldn't move their legs. Lynx only avoided the ice by jumping at the last moment. His paws cracked as they landed on the frozen ground.

Suddenly, Cleo was right in front of her. She wasn't wearing a dress. No, now she wore a fighting suit that covered every inch of her body except for her hands and face. It was white, with dark-blue detailing. She frowned at Isla and Lynx. "What a pleasant . . . pet," she said, tilting her head. "You're on the wrong side, though, Wildling. You said you wanted your realm to live, didn't you?"

It wasn't lost on her that Cleo hadn't killed the Lightlark soldiers. She could have frozen them solid, but she didn't. There was still a chance she would change sides.

Isla understood her now more than ever: A woman who had dedicated her entire life to leading her realm. Who had allowed herself one happiness. Who had lost it.

"Why are you doing this?" Isla asked.

"For him," she said. *Her son.*

"I don't understand."

Cleo reached down into her collar and pulled out the necklace she wore. The blue stone shimmered. "The other world has power we can't begin to fathom. Souls can rise once more."

She understood now. Cleo believed there was a chance to see her son again.

"I can't let you use the portal," she said.

Cleo frowned. "I hoped you would see reason," she said. "We really do need you."

The Moonling raised her arms, and the ocean rushed to wrap around her body, curling, alive, forming her shape. She rose into the air, on a swirl of sea.

She shot her watery hand out, and her arm became a rope of water that sent Isla flying back, right off Lynx. Her leopard roared. Before she cracked her head against Cleo's ice, a bed of flowers bloomed behind her, bursting through the frost, breaking her fall.

Cleo laughed, the sound muted and distorted by the water surrounding her. "Flowers won't help you."

Isla slowly rose. She took a step, and the ice broke. Flowers sprouted in her wake. Vines formed down her arms, long thorns growing against her knuckles.

She had been watching the Moonling fight. She used her hands. She needed them to wield water.

It was impossible to grip Cleo's wrists in her water-covered form. Isla's restraints would slip right off the sea.

Cleo was too busy staring Isla down to notice that Enya had become a living flame behind her. An understanding passed between Isla and the Sunling.

Isla charged. Cleo watched her, water swirling, towering.

So did Enya. She jumped, wings made of flames uncurling from her back and wrapping around the Moonling ruler.

Cleo was quick—she sent Enya backward with a thick stream of sea. But, for just a moment, Cleo's water shield had melted, weakened by the flames.

It was all Isla needed. Roots flew up from the ground and tied around the Moonling's wrists in seconds. They trapped her legs next. One wrapped around her neck for good measure. Flowers bloomed on the restraints. Isla plucked one.

"The flowers helped," she said.

Isla didn't see any more Moonlings. Cleo had a legion. Was she saving them for after Grim's own army was finished?

Part of her feared that Wildlings might fight alongside Nightshade . . . but her people were nowhere to be found.

Isla wondered if that was better or worse.

She was back on Lynx in a moment, hurtling through the battle. Hope bloomed once more. Much of the Nightshades were dead.

They had a chance, Isla thought. It looked like they could win.

Until a crack sounded through the world, and dreks filled the sky. There were hundreds of them. So many, they looked like nighttime sky ripped to flying shreds.

They were everywhere. Skylings fought back, with their metal-tipped arrows, and some of the creatures were shot down, but they were quickly replaced.

A flash like a bolt of lightning shot above her—someone was twirling a special metal-tipped sword and traveling so quickly, they went through one of the dreks. The creature died instantly and fell, crushing a group of Nightshades.

Zed.

He really was that fast.

Isla breathed in and out, trying to focus her energy to the sky. She had one of the metal-tipped blades in her belt. With a shot of power, she might be able to take one of the beasts out. Just as she was about to try, a drek dipped low, and she was knocked off Lynx with the force of its wings. She hit the ground, and the air was stolen from her lungs.

Lynx lunged for her but was immediately surrounded by Nightshades. She gasped for breath, watching helplessly as he was surrounded in shadows.

No.

Two figures came crashing down from the sky.

Ciel and Avel.

Relief rained down her spine. "Thank you," she croaked as Ciel reached a hand to help her up.

Even now, they were still watching out for her. Even—

Ciel's kind face twisted in shock as a drek's talon went clean through his stomach.

Avel's scream shattered the world. She rushed to catch her twin in her arms, her hands shaking as she tried to keep all the parts that were falling from him together.

No. With a roar, she turned the drek to ash. She fished in her pockets for one of her last remaining vials of Wildling healing elixir. She poured it all over Ciel's injury, hand shaking.

It was too late.

His eyes were cold and unblinking.

Avel cradled her brother in her arms and screamed.

This was her fault. Ciel was trying to help *her*.

Dreks landed all around, tearing limbs.

"You need to get up," Isla told Avel. "They're going to—they're going to—"

She refused. She cradled her brother and wouldn't even look at her. Tears swept down Isla's face as she created a small dome of Starling energy around them both, hoping it would hold.

She heard a growl. Lynx. He was fighting off too many soldiers. Isla gathered her power and raged against all of them, until they were nothing but dust.

Her energy was drained. She fell to her knees, and Lynx shielded her with his body.

Through his legs, Isla watched, helpless, as death drowned everything around her. The dreks were endless. Grim must have made more.

It was just like her coronation. Limbs being torn. Screams turning to silence. Bodies fell from the sky more than dreks did. The flight force had been reduced to just a few units.

They didn't stand a chance.

The island would fall. Oro would die. She would die.

A deafening roar sounded across the Mainland. Even the Nightshades stood still. They watched as a serpent with its jaw pulled all the way open swept across the land, swallowing all the Nightshades in its path.

The serpent-woman. *She came.* She stood on her massive tail and picked dreks off from the sky, stabbing them through with her fangs.

The dreks attacked the serpent, but their talons could not penetrate her scales. The storm Azul had created kept the dreks flying low, and she took out a dozen in a few seconds, hitting them with her tail, piercing them with her teeth.

Oro fought nearby, charring the skies with his flames. Zed sped through multiple dreks. Enya was a phoenix, fire-wings curling behind her as she fought.

It still wasn't enough.

Isla looked around. The dead were everywhere, from both sides. Grim still hadn't revealed himself, but this had to be put to an end.

Lynx helped her onto his back, and they raced across the Mainland, passing battling Vinderland, and Remlar, who had been fighting near the woods. He brought dreks down with the smallest movements. They shared a look.

The forest flew by in a flash, and then she was at the bridge. She slid off Lynx.

He would come to meet her. She knew he would. Isla waited for minutes, wincing as she heard the battle raging, willing Grim to come find her.

When more minutes passed, she almost pulled her necklace.

Then, the woods filled with shadows.

At once, the bridge was blocked by a new wave of the Nightshade army. They drew their shadows. They were everywhere.

A howl broke the air in half.

"Even think about touching her, and I'll kill you," a voice said. Steps sounded behind her. "Hello, heart."

BEFORE

When Isla finished training, Grim was waiting for her in her room.

It had been weeks since he had told her the truth. She hadn't sought him out, and he hadn't returned.

"I told you I never wanted to see you again," she said. The betrayal was still raw.

She didn't mean it. She had missed him so much, but she needed time before she could think about forgiving him.

Grim tried at a smile. "I might have good news for you, then," he said.

"What do you mean?"

He looked so serious.

Grim swept across the room and took her in his arms, and she let him, because she knew something was wrong. He studied every part of her face, as if trying to commit it to memory.

Her starstick was hot against her back. It was glimmering in his presence, as if in warning. *Something isn't right*, it was saying. She gripped his chest and said, "What's wrong?"

"The scar has opened. In a place it never has before. A place previously deemed safe." Isla's stomach sank. He had told her about the scar, about how he didn't think Nightshade could survive much longer. "Hundreds of people live near it."

Isla gasped. She opened her mouth, but he beat her to it.

"Whatever happens to me, heart, I want you to know something."

"What?" she said. She tried to shake out of his arms. "Grim, nothing is going to happen to you, nothing—"

“Let me talk, heart,” he said, pressing a finger against her lips. “Interrupting is very rude.” She could tell he was trying to distract her. Trying to make her smile. She did not.

“I need you to know that you changed everything.” He ran his thumb down her cheek. “The gods don’t listen to people like me, but I would go on my knees and beg them to let me keep you. You were once the bane of my existence . . . and now, you are the center of it.”

He couldn’t possibly be saying this, not him, demon in the shadows, ruler of darkness. Not him, looking at her as if she was the answer to all his dreams. “My entire world was night, and you lit a match. No matter what happens to me in this life, I’ll find you in the next one. I’ll always find you. What I feel for you can never be extinguished. Like the nighttime sky, it is infinite. You and me . . . we’re infinite.”

Tears streamed down her face. Why did it sound like he was saying goodbye forever?

“No. Don’t go,” she said. “I can help you. We can figure this out, whatever it is, Grim, *together*. Let me go with you. We can try the sword. Let me go.”

“Okay, Hearteater,” he finally said. “You can come.”

He kissed her. It was quick, and brutal, and then soft—

She didn’t even notice when he slid a hand down her spine. By the time she did, it was too late.

He had taken her starstick and vanished, making sure she wouldn’t be able to follow.

DAY AND NIGHT

Grim stepped onto the bridge. Exactly where they needed him. He was wearing his full armor, the one she had seen in her memories. Spikes everywhere. On his shoulders. On his helmet. He looked the part of a demon. Shadows swirled and lashed out around him.

But the ones at his feet puddled. "This is obviously a trap," he said, taking a step forward. "You knew I'd find you." He smiled. "You knew nothing could ever keep me from you."

"Even certain death couldn't keep you away?" she asked, voice trembling.

He smiled wider. "Oh, Hearteater," he said. "You and me . . . we're infinite. Death doesn't stand a chance."

Isla couldn't breathe. She was drowning from the inside out, knowing what was about to happen. Knowing what she must do—

Oro landed in front of her, and power rumbled across the island.

Grim only smirked at the king. "And neither do you."

And then he struck. A burst of shadows erupted from him, right at Oro, but the king shielded it with a covering of flames so saturated, they were tinged in blue.

Isla prepared to block herself from the shadows too, her Starling shield forming, but they moved around her almost gently, like extensions of Grim himself.

Oro burst forth with a thick cord of power—a mix of silver energy, water rushing from the sea, and flashing flames. Grim met it with a chain of pure darkness.

Their powers clashed and reverberated in waves. The bridge below them shook. Isla barely kept herself on her feet. She felt the force of their strength in her bones.

Both were too powerful. They roared, fighting, each with equal hatred clear on their faces.

Grim was gone—then, he was right behind Oro. He hit him with a wave of shadows, and Oro only just barely blocked it with a shield of crackling Starling energy. Still, the impact knocked him onto his back.

Before Grim could take another step, Oro's arms went wide, and the sea rushed from hundreds of feet below. It hit Grim, then hardened, then cracked as he fought to melt through it with his shadows. He couldn't move his arms. Oro shot enough fire to char Grim through the ice, but, at the last moment, he portaled away, leaving the frost behind. It fell back onto the bridge and shattered.

"Behind you!" Isla shouted, and Oro turned just in time to block Grim's blade. Oro created a sword out of Starling energy, and they dueled across the bridge.

Grim grinned as if he was having the time of his life. "It's been a long time since we fought, Oro," he said, advancing. "What a shame that it will also be the last time."

Oro let his sword disappear and shot up into the air.

Grim followed. He portaled so quickly that it was as if he were also flying, appearing then disappearing in wild spurts. They dueled in the sky, this time with streams of power.

Isla watched from below, finding herself cringing at every blow the other landed. She bit the inside of her mouth, dread churning in her chest.

There was no winning.

A rumble sounded before the sea below spiraled up, becoming a massive snake that lunged at Grim. In response, he spun a wolf formed of shadows. The creatures battled, mauling each other, protecting their creators.

Oro shot out his hand, releasing a dozen throwing blades made from flames. Grim blocked them with a dark curl of smoke before that shield became a dozen arrows all aimed at Oro's chest.

They ricocheted against Starling sparks, and both of their attacks quickened. Grim was portaling so fast, she could barely track him in the sky, and Oro was creating so many weapons, she missed half of them by blinking.

Finally, Oro paused for a moment, as if gathering his energy. This was it. It was about to be over. The air seemed to go taut in anticipation before he shot out his hand—and released a strike of lightning. It raged across the sky, charged with energy, a combination of his abilities.

It all happened so quickly.

Before the lightning could hit Grim, he was gone, then replaced—

With Oro.

Grim had portaled him there, using his power, in that fraction of a second. Isla watched helplessly as Oro's own lightning struck him.

And then, he was falling.

He landed on the bridge with a force that threatened to make it crumble away beneath them. She raced forward, but Grim landed between them.

"No!" she screamed.

Shadows burst forth from his palm, but before they turned Oro to ash, he came to and lifted his own hand. Fire, energy, and wind wrapped around and around. Their powers met in the middle.

Oro was injured. He looked like he could pass out at any moment. She knew what she had to do.

It was time.

Don't do it. The voice was firm, speaking from the past. Her own voice.

She didn't want to. But the oracle had made it clear—it was either Grim or Oro. Her choice would define the world.

She had to decide. As Grim and Oro dueled, so did past and present Isla.

Don't do it—

She had to do it.

DON'T DO IT—

Her fingers shook. Tears blinded her. She closed her eyes and followed Remlar's instructions.

She reached for the link. The one between her and Grim. It held every memory of them together, like beads on a bracelet. She saw them in her mind. The first time they met. The first time they kissed. The first time they were one. The first time she made him smile. A sob scraped the back of her throat, and Grim's eyes went to her. A stream of power was hurtling toward him, and he didn't seem to care. He looked at her.

It nearly broke her to reach for their thread. To reach for his power.

And take it.

BEFORE

No.

Isla's chest was ripping in two. She was helpless. Stuck here, on the Wildling newland. It would take months to sail to Nightshade, and even then, even if they let her in—

It would be far too late.

No. This wasn't happening. She hadn't finally found someone who understood her only to lose him.

Tears and salt and gasps turned into a predatorial silence. All her senses sharpened like a dagger.

Grim was a demon. He was the feared ruler of Nightshade.

But he had become her friend. They had faced countless challenges together. He had touched her in ways that made her feel alive, and like the space between stars, and she had felt, for once, that her body belonged to her. Not the realm. *Her.*

For all his remarks and attitude, he had believed in her. He had trusted her.

And she trusted him.

He had saved her.

She was not going to give up on him.

Thousands of miles were no space at all, not for them. He was right. They were infinite. She reached out, looking for her demon, for *him*. The one who had pressed shapes against her skin, the one who didn't know he had a dimple because he so rarely smiled.

Her mind emptied of anything other than him. She could see him in her head, could smell him, could feel him.

She reached out with every ounce of herself, threw her marrow through the world—

And found him.

When everything else cleared away, the universe fading like ash and smoke, only a link remained. She could feel it now, tying them together.

Isla didn't think about what it meant. Not then. The thread was wrapped in power, and she didn't know how to use it; it slipped through her fingers, but she had one ask—one request.

Take me to him.

With the sword in her hands, she grasped Grim's power to portal with every inch of herself and vanished.

She landed on her knees.

Dreks were falling from the sky like pieces of night smelted into rain. Hundreds. Thousands. Grim had told her about them, but nothing could prepare her for seeing them—hearing them.

They were far smaller than the dragon, but whereas the creature was graceful, these were like throwing stars, shooting across the sky, falling to the ground, talons first.

Grim was at the center of it all.

There were others. They did not last long. She watched Nightshade warrior after Nightshade warrior be plucked up and away. Some were torn in half in the sky; others were eaten whole. Blood, everywhere, screams, men twice her size yelling for their lives.

Grim. He was rumored to be one of the strongest rulers.

Shadows erupted from him, and where they struck, everything died. He was seeping, everywhere, roaring—

It was not enough. The curses had dimmed his power. There were too many. And some seemed immune to even his shadows. They barreled toward him, and Isla knew how these injuries worked. They rotted flesh and bone and did not heal. How many times had he already been struck?

The scar ran across the ground, for as far as she could see. Grim said it went across all of Nightshade. Right there, so close, was a village Grim had told her about—the one that had been deemed *safe*. Dreks swooped down into the streets. Cries. *Children.*

Grim looked up, as if sensing her. And Isla had the feeling that no matter where they were, even on a battlefield, he would always be able to find her.

Horror. Pure, unfiltered horror, and devastation, to find her here, in a place where everything would soon be dead.

Then—surprise.

Understanding. He had taken her starstick. There was only one way she could possibly be here.

They stared at each other, and for just a moment, it was like no one else was there. Just them. No dreks. No soldiers.

He looked at her like she was the beginning and end of his world, and he *smiled*—smiled because he had found love, even if it was just before he died.

Grim closed his eyes, and she knew what he was going to do. He was going to portal her away. He was going to *die*.

Before he could, a drek pierced his chest. Its talons went right through him.

She screamed, and it didn't sound human; it sounded like scratching the night sky with a blade, like pain spun into a sound.

Other dreks shot down. Grim roared, and they all descended, seeing their chance. They gripped him by the shoulders, and his head went limp. They were going to tear him in two—

No.

No.

Isla didn't hesitate before she took the sword in her hands—and dug it deep into the ground before her.

Nothing happened, not right away. She didn't know how to break the curse, she didn't know what to do, but she was desperate.

And there was something there. Something strange and twisted.

Isla grabbed it.

Her pain provided passage. Everything she was made of spilled out. The sword shook beneath her hands. Then, her fingers slipped, and when her hands hit the ground, death was unleashed.

From her poured an endless wave of shadows. The dreks shriveled and died. The soldiers became clouds of blood. Everything that wasn't him disappeared.

Her darkness ate the world, and it had no limit. It kept going.

You and me . . . we're infinite.

She felt infinite.

Power poured out of her like the ocean tilting itself to the side, unstoppable, uncontrollable; it raged and raged, and Isla kept screaming until it finally ran out. Because her love might be infinite, but her abilities were not. Her life was not.

It felt like she was saying goodbye, but she didn't really care. Because he was there, and he would be okay, and she loved him, she loved him so much, she just hoped he would take what she was offering, all of the Wildling power she wasn't supposed to have, because she knew he would take care of her people. Just like he had taken care of her.

Grim roared, and Isla sent her Wildling powers across the thread that bound them together. It was the last thing she did as she stumbled and fell.

Into his arms. He had portaled and caught her, and she knew he would survive his injuries, but he was searching her face like he was the one dying, and he was yelling at her, but all she could do was smile.

"Isla, come back to me. Come back."

He shook her, and she could barely feel it; there was barely anything left.

Her body stiffened. Her breathing stopped. Grim roared.

"Wake up," he said. His voice was thick with desperation. He was *crying*. "Stab me through the chest again if you have to, just wake up."

She wanted to. She really did.

"Grim," she said to him, the last of her life leaving her. She remembered what he told her. *Pain could be useful. Pain was the strongest emotion.* "Pain is not the strongest," she said.

Then, her heart went still.

SACRIFICE

Isla took his powers. Grim's shadows ceased, and he was hit by the full force of Oro's fury. He landed on his back. Isla didn't know how he wasn't immediately killed.

Or how he slowly inched up, gasping for air. His hand lashed out as he tried to summon his shadows once more. He could not.

He frowned and turned to look at her with an earnestness that made her want to sink to the ground. "What is this, heart?" he asked.

She was sobbing, and he didn't look betrayed—he looked devastated that she was crying. He was *upset that she was upset at the fact that she had stolen his powers, readying him for Oro to kill—*

She couldn't do it. Her concentration wavered.

Still, she didn't stop her hold on his powers.

Oro made a sword out of Starling energy. It crackled with strength, and he lifted it over his head. Grim wouldn't be able to defend himself. She had weakened him. In one moment, he would be dead. He would be dead. *He would be dead.*

That was the first moment she had ever seen Grim afraid.

Just before the blade found his neck, he bellowed, "If I die, *she dies*."

It wasn't even his death that he feared. It was *hers*. Her death was what made him rabid, shaking, yelling, eyes wide and desperate.

Oro froze, just an inch from ending the Nightshade. "No," Oro whispered, disbelieving. Furious. Understanding something Isla still hadn't. "You didn't."

BEFORE

This is wrong, was Isla's first thought. She shouldn't be alive. Her body recognized it. Its life force had been drained away completely.

She opened her eyes, and Isla had never heard such a sound of relief.

Grim was kneeling in front of her. Her hand was in his. "Heart," he said. "You're here, heart." It was like he still couldn't believe it.

She had been somewhere else.

Now, she was back.

"How?" she asked.

His head lifted, and she saw tears in his eyes. His face was covered in dirt and blood, but he was here, kneeling before her, like she was something to worship. "You died," he said, the word cracking. His voice was raw, like he had been screaming too. "You died in my arms."

Grim closed his eyes, and tears fell. They made lines in the dirt and crusted blood. She reached for him on instinct, clearing them away. She *had* died. Were her people okay? Had giving her power to Grim through the thread that connected them worked?

She couldn't cheat death. Grim couldn't either. It didn't make sense that she was still living.

"How?" she asked again.

MISSING PIECE

"You bound her to you," Oro said, voice shaking with anger. With shock.

She remembered now. Grim's explanation in the past. She knew binding someone to oneself meant sharing a life. Not just powers, but life itself.

One could not die without killing the other.

That was why, when the arrow had split her heart in two during the Centennial, she hadn't died immediately. Not just because of the power of the heart of Lightlark . . . but because Grim was keeping her alive.

"It was only a temporary solution," Oro said, voice shaking with anger, but also fear.

Grim nodded. "The other world offers a permanent one."

That was the reason for this war. That was the reason for all this death. She remembered what Cleo had said. In the other world, *souls can rise once more.*

He wanted to open the portal to save her life.

Oro hesitated, sword still in his hand. If he killed Grim, she would die too.

"Do it," Isla said, because she was willing to die if it would save everyone else. Even if most of them still hated her and thought she was a blight on the world. The same way Oro had said he would give her his power, she would give him hers, in case the rebels were wrong.

Oro looked at her, and she saw fear and fury and disappointment—disappointment in *himself* for not being strong enough to make the right choice for his people. Enya was right. Isla had made him weak.

"I can't," he said, the words so soft.

"*Kill him*," she said, her voice getting hysterical. "He's going to kill innocent people. I told you about the vision. He's going to *kill children*. He's going to kill me."

Grim looked at her. "Heart . . ." he said, so gently. "What do you mean?"

She saw flashes of her vision again. The darkness, eating everything. Skin sliding from bone. Bone reduced to ash. Death, everywhere, and Grim standing in the middle of it—

It looked familiar now.

Isla started sputtering. "The village. The people. Their skin melting from them, the shadows. Then the—the darkness came into *me*—"

No.

The world went silent.

The vision was not a look at the future. Not an example of the lengths Grim would go to get her.

It was a memory.

And Grim wasn't the one who had summoned those shadows, wasn't the one who had killed those hundreds of innocent people.

"It was me," she said. "It was me."

She saw herself, returning to the place where it had all happened, where she had offered all her power she didn't know she had to save Grim. She saw the village, on the outskirts of the scar. Charred. There were only shapes of people—of children—where they once stood.

She saw herself collapsing on the ground, sobbing. Screaming, "I did this. I did this."

Oro was in front of her now, hands pressed against her face, taking her out of the memory. "You are not a monster." Was that what she had been saying over and over? "You are not defined by one mistake."

But it was not *one mistake*.

Isla had used emotions to wield her power multiple times. Recklessly. Even after Oro had warned her, she hadn't been able to help herself, she had done it again and again.

She was not to be trusted. She was reckless, dangerous, a *monster*.

Enya was right. Oro deserved so much better.

"Get away from me," she screamed. She tried to step away, but Oro took her hand. "Let me go."

She understood now how it was even a possibility that she might kill Oro. Just by *proximity* to her, he was in danger.

She had no control of her emotions. Of her powers.

She would kill him. One day, she would be overcome with emotion, she would lose control yet again, and she would kill him. She saw it so clearly now.

"Let. Me. Go," she bellowed, her voice thick, tears falling into her mouth.

She tried to wrestle herself away, but Oro didn't budge. He didn't understand; he didn't know how much of a danger she was to him—

Grim's voice seemed to rumble the world as he said, "Let go of my wife."

There it was. The final missing piece.

BOUND

That word, *wife*, unlocked a door in her mind that had been stubbornly jammed.

She saw it. Hands joined together, before an altar. Then, against a bed frame.

She saw months of suffering with guilt for having killed so many innocent people. She saw herself begging Grim to take the memory of what she had done away. She saw him refusing.

Memories fluttered, until they snagged on one last moment. She saw herself wearing her Centennial dress. She watched Grim take a necklace out of his pocket and present it to her. One with the biggest black diamond she had ever seen. "In Nightshade, instead of rings, we give necklaces," he said. "I should have given this to you before. It's a sign of our commitment. Once I put it on, it is on forever. Only with your death will it be released."

She saw herself smiling and telling him to put it on her. She saw her move her hair, clearing the way.

Instead of clasping it forever, she saw him slip it back into his pocket.

She heard him say, "Please, heart, forgive me for this."

She watched understanding come over her face as she said, "Grim, no—"

But it was done.

She watched him take her memories away, return her starstick, and send her back to the Wildling realm.

Isla knew what happened next.

TRUTH

Oro let her go. Out of shock, or disgust, or because he was finally listening to her, she didn't know.

You will kill one of them. That much is certain.

Screams sounded from the battleground; power rippled through the air. Out of nowhere, more dreks appeared, screeching. Arrows shot through the sky, and the creatures fell, but there were too many. They picked Skylings off, one by one. She watched helplessly as more Skylings dropped from the sky, limp or in pieces.

Death, so much useless death. Pain and blood painted the island. It made her remember what she had done. What she had done—

Her voice was trembling. "If I go with you, will you leave? Will you stop the attack?" she asked.

"*No*," Oro said, the word a plea.

Grim's answer was immediate. "Yes."

He held his hand out, the same way he had countless times before, and the echoes of it reverberated in her mind.

Isla reached for Grim's hand. She was a monster, just like him. She needed to get away from Oro and this island. She looked at Lynx, and Grim said, "Don't worry, he's coming too." She watched her leopard vanish.

"Don't," Oro said. His voice broke on the word. She knew he wouldn't let her go. He didn't understand; he didn't know about the prophecy. He would think there was another way.

So before Grim could portal them to Nightshade, she turned and said, “I love you, Oro.” She closed her eyes tightly. Felt tears sweep down. She took Grim’s hand. “But I love him too.”

And, because of his flair, he knew it was true.

ACKNOWLEDGMENTS

I want to start by thanking you, the reader, for supporting this series. When I wrote *Lightlark,* I never could have imagined that people around the world would love this story and these characters as much as I do. Your excitement for this book got me through every deadline. I am endlessly grateful for you. *Thank you.*

I have many people to thank for helping to get *Nightbane* out into the world. Thank you to Anne Hetzel, my editor, for believing in *Lightlark* before everything, for your editorial guidance, and for your infinite championing of me and this series. Thank you to Andrew Smith, who saw *Lightlark*'s potential, and has made so much possible. Thank you to my literary agent, Jodi Reamer, who read too many versions of this book, and was my guiding star during this entire process. I am so grateful to have you in my corner.

To everyone at Abrams, including Megan Carlson, Micah Fleming, Maggie Moore, Marie Oishi, Ashley Albert, Abby Pickus, and Angelica Busanet, for all your hard work on this series. To Chelsea Hunter and Natalie Sousa, for designing the book covers of my dreams. To Kim Lauber and Hallie Patterson, for everything you have done for me and *Lightlark*—it is truly a joy to work with both of you.

To my incredible team, who has made all this possible. To my entertainment lawyer, Eric Greenspan, for taking a chance on me. You have been one of my biggest supporters from the very beginning—thank you. To David Fox, Chris Maxwell, and Debby Sander. To my Film/TV agents at CAA, Berni Barta and Michelle Weiner, who have made some of my wildest dreams come true. Also, to Ali Ehrlich—thank you for

everything. To Denisse Montfort and Allison Elbl, for all that you do. To Cecilia de la Campa, for everything to come. To Katelyn Detweiler—I am so grateful that you believed in these books first. Your kindness and sincerity are a gift. To Sam Farkas, who has made it possible for *Lightlark* to be published around the world. Seeing the foreign editions of *Lightlark* has been one of my greatest joys—thank you for everything.

To Anqi Xu, for reading this book early and for giving me great notes. To Sean, for being one of the first to read all my books, including the early drafts, even when you're busy—I really appreciate your help. To Kaitlin López for your last-minute assistance that saved the day. To Annika Patton, who has become one of my dearest friends. You were the first person to read this book, back in January (and the first to react to the ending!).

To my heart, Rron, for supporting me, even when I had to write through the holidays and weekends. Eight years together means you knew me as a teenager writing books and dreaming of becoming an author. This book is for you. I love you. To your family as well, for their love and support, and for bringing me snacks while I worked on this book.

To my parents, who always encouraged me to chase my dreams. Mom—I hope one day I can be as strong as you. Dad—thank you for teaching me that the harder you work, the luckier you get. To my twin, Danny, who used to sit with me after school in the bookstore as I looked up literary agents to query. I am so proud of you. To Angely, a second mom to me; Carlos, who is always there for me; and JonCarlos and Luna, for being the lights of my life. I can't wait to watch you both chase your dreams. To my grandma Rose, for telling me stories before bedtime and inspiring me to become an author. To my grandpa Alfonso, for teaching me resilience and a strong work ethic. To Maureen, Uncle Buddy, and Aunt Patty for always believing in me. To Leo, Bear, and Truffle, for bringing me so much joy.

To my author friends, who have helped me navigate all of this. To Adam Silvera, who always answers the phone, even when he's on

deadline, and is the Honest Friend. To Chloe Gong, who doesn't get mad when I talk more than I write at "writing sessions" in coffee shops and is the fastest reader I know. To Dustin Thao, who is always there for all of us. To Sabaa Tahir, Marie Lu, Brigid Kemmerer, and Zibby Owens, for your support. I am so grateful to know you. To every other friend—you know who you are, and I am so lucky to have you in my life.

Finally, thank you to everyone who follows me on social media, or has ever recommended my books. Your messages mean more to me than you will ever know.

Nightshade

The Newlands
Moonling Newland
Wildling Newland
Skyling Newland
Starling Newland

Wild Isle
Place of Mirrors
Forgotten Mine
Mainland Woods
Mainland Castle
Mainland
White Cliffs
Insignia

ALEX ASTER

AMULET BOOKS • NEW YORK

PUBLISHER'S NOTE: This is a work of fiction. Names, characters, places, and incidents are either the product of the author's imagination or used fictitiously, and any resemblance to actual persons, living or dead, business establishments, events, or locales is entirely coincidental.

Cataloging-in-Publication Data has been applied for and may be obtained from the Library of Congress.

ISBN 978-1-4197-6086-0
ISBN (B&N/Indigo edition) 978-1-4197-6667-1

Vine artwork courtesy STOCKMAMBAdotCOM/Shutterstock.com
Book design by Chelsea Hunter

Published in 2022 by Amulet Books, an imprint of ABRAMS.

Printed and bound in U.S.A.
20 19 18 17 16 15 14 13

Amulet Books are available at special discounts when purchased in quantity for premiums and promotions as well as fundraising or educational use. Special editions can also be created to specification. For details, contact specialsales@abramsbooks.com or the address below.

Amulet Books® is a registered trademark of Harry N. Abrams, Inc.

ABRAMS The Art of Books
195 Broadway, New York, NY 10007
abramsbooks.com

For Rron. I couldn't write our love story if I tried.

CHAPTER ONE

ISLA

Isla Crown often fell through puddles of stars and into faraway places. Always without permission—and seemingly on the worst occasions.

Even after five years, portaling still made her bones groan. She held her starstick tightly, her breath bottled in her chest like the rare perfumes on her vanity, the glass room spinning and fractured colors bleeding together, until gravity finally pinned her down like a loose thread in the universe.

And it was safely tucked down the back of her dress, along her spine, by the time the door swung open.

"What happened to your hair?" Poppy shrieked so loudly, Terra came rushing in behind her, the many knives and swords at her waist clanking together.

Her hair was the least of her worries, though she didn't doubt it resembled a bed of moss. Traveling between the realms' newlands with her starstick had the habit of undoing even Poppy's most tightly wound coils and firmly made braids—an unexpected perk, really.

Isla didn't pretend to be an expert at using the device. In the beginning, the puddle of stars took her unexpected places. The snow villages of the Moonling newlands. The airy jubilees of the Skyling newlands. A few lands that hadn't been settled by any of the six realms at all. Little by little, she learned how to return to locations she had been to before. And that was the extent of her mastering of the starstick. All she knew for certain was that somehow the mysterious device allowed her to travel hundreds of miles in seconds.

Terra sighed, hand dropping from the hilt of her blade. "It's just a few loose strands, Poppy."

Poppy ignored her. She rushed over to Isla, wielding a brush and a vial of syrupy leaf oil the same way Terra had taught Isla to brandish weapons years before. Isla grinned at her fighting teacher over her charm teacher's shoulder and cried out as Poppy roughly removed the pins. Poppy shook her head. "Have to start from scratch." She stuck the clips between her lips and spoke around them. "I leave you alone for an hour, and you're a mess. Even locked the door for good measure! How in the realm did you manage to mess it up in your own room, little bird?"

Own room. Her room was not her own. It was an orb of glass, the remnants of an ancient greenhouse. But the panes had been painted over. The windows had been sealed. All except one door had been removed.

She was a little bird, just like Poppy and sometimes even Terra called her.

A bird in a cage.

Isla shrugged. "Just some swordplay." Poppy and Terra were her only family—though they weren't family at all. Everyone who shared blood with her was long dead. Still, even they didn't know about the starstick. If they did, they would never let her use it. It was the only key out of the bird's cage. And Isla had been locked inside not just for her own safety—

But for everyone else's.

Terra eyed her suspiciously before turning her focus to the wall. Dozens of swords hung there in a shining row, a makeshift mirror. "Pity you can't bring any of them," she said, a finger trailing across the wall of blades. She had given Isla every single sword, presented from the castle's ancient store. Isla had *earned* them after each training achievement and mastery.

Poppy scoffed. "That's one Centennial rule I agree with. We don't need her reaffirming all the other realms' horrible views of us."

Nerves began to swirl in Isla's stomach, leaves dancing in a storm.

She forced a smile, knowing it would douse Poppy's frustration—her guardian always *was* telling her she didn't smile enough. Isla hadn't met many people, but the ones she had were simple to figure out. She just needed to uncover their motivations. Everyone wanted something. And some things were easier to give. A smile for a charm teacher who had spent nearly two decades teaching her student manners. A compliment for a woman who prized beauty above all else. "Poppy, pretty as you are, all of their horrible views are true. We *are* monsters."

Poppy sighed as she slid the last pin into Isla's hair. "Not you," she said meaningfully.

And though her guardian's words were wrapped in love—*good*—they made her stomach pool with dread.

"They're ready," Terra said. She took a few steps toward the vanity. Isla watched her through the mirror, its edges spotted with age. "Are you?"

No. And she never would be. The Centennial was many things. A game. A chance at breaking the many curses that plagued the six realms. An opportunity to win unmatched power. A meeting of the six rulers. A hundred days on an island cursed to only appear once every hundred years. And for Isla—

Almost certain death.

Are you ready, Isla? a voice in her mind said, mocking and cruel.

Her fear was only tempered by her curiosity. She had always longed for more . . . everything. More experiences, more places, more people.

The place she was going—Lightlark—was made of more. Before her guardians had discovered it and had it sealed, Isla used to sneak through a loose pane of glass in her room and down into the forest. It was there that she met an Eldress who had once lived on Lightlark, the way all Wildlings used to before the curses were spun. Before most of the realms fled the island to create new lands in the chaotic aftermath. Her stories were fruits in a tree—sweet and limited. She spoke of kings who could grip the sun in their hands, white-haired

women who could make the sea dance, castles in clouds, and flowers that bloomed pure power.

That was before the curses.

Now the island was a shadow of itself, trapped in a forever storm that made traveling to it outside the Centennial impossible, by boat or even by enchantment.

One night, Isla had found the Eldress at the base of a tree, on her side. She might have thought the woman was sleeping, if her tanned skin hadn't become bark, if her veins hadn't turned to vines. Wildlings wielded nature in life and joined it in death.

But there had been nothing natural about the Eldress's passing. Even at over five hundred, even away from the strength of Lightlark, she had died too soon. Her death had been the first of many.

And the fault was Isla's.

Terra repeated her question, dark-green eyes the same color as the leaves and ivy that wrapped around the Wildling palace, a skin over everything. The same color as Isla's. "Are you ready?"

Isla nodded, though her fingers trembled as she reached for the crown in front of her. It was a simple gold band, adorned with golden buds, leaves, and a hissing snake. She placed it atop her head, careful not to interfere with the clips that kept her long, dark-brown hair out of her face.

"Beautiful," Poppy said. Isla didn't need to hear the compliment to know it was true. Beauty was a Wildling's gift—and curse. A curse that had gotten her own mother killed. Which only made the fact that she supposedly had her mother's face all the more unsettling. Poppy met Isla's eyes through the mirror and said fiercely, "You are enough, little bird. Better than any of them."

If only that was true.

Isla could feel a jolt of panic breaking her features in half. What if this was the last time she ever saw her guardians? What if she never returned to her room? Her hands acted on instinct, reaching for each of her guardians, wanting to touch them one last time.

Before she could, Terra gave her a stern look that made her go still.

Sentimentality is selfish, her stare seemed to say.

The Centennial wasn't about her. It was about saving her realm. Her people.

Chastised, Isla straightened her spine. She stood slowly, the heaviness of her crown far greater than its weight. "I know what I must do," she said. Each ruler arrived at the Centennial with a plan. Terra and Poppy had hammered theirs into Isla since she was a child. "I will follow your orders."

"Good," Terra said. "Because you are our only hope."

The Wildling castle was more outside than in. The halls were bridges. Trees extended their arms into the corridor, branches catching gently on her dress as if to say goodbye. Leaves rustled at Isla's sides as she walked through the endless chambers she wasn't allowed access to, Poppy and Terra right behind her. Vines crept across walls. Birds flew in and out as they pleased. Wind howled through the halls in a breeze that made Isla's cape billow behind her. She wore deep green to honor her realm, a fabric that clung to her ribs, waist, knees, and pooled at her feet. Her cape was made of gossamer, sheer enough to make its traditional purpose for modesty obsolete. And that choice represented her realm just as much as its color.

Wildlings had always been proud of their bodies, beauty, and ability. They had always loved wildly, lived freely, and fought fiercely.

Five hundred years before, each of the six realms—Wildling, Starling, Moonling, Skyling, Sunling, and Nightshade—were cursed, their strengths turned into their own personal poisons. Each curse was uniquely wicked.

Wildlings' was twofold. They were cursed to kill anyone they fell in love with—and to live exclusively on human hearts. They turned into terrifyingly beautiful monsters with the wicked power to seduce with a single look.

Thousands of Wildling men and women had been killed off since.

Love became forbidden. Reckless. Fewer children were born . . . and daughters had always been more common for their realm. Though love had various forms, men were killed more often when the rules were broken, and they had slowly become a small community of mostly warrior women. Feared. Hated. Weak, since fewer people meant less power. The Centennial was the only chance to end their curses, to return to their previous glory again, to regain the power they so badly needed. *Isla* was their only chance.

You are our only hope . . .

She heard them before she saw them. Chanting their ancient words, clashing their blades together like instruments. Wildling control over nature was on full display. Flowers bloomed and spilled over the balcony, down into the hall, not stopping until they reached her feet. They grew exponentially, doubling over themselves in a puddle of petals and rising to her ankles. According to lore, a thousand years before, Wildlings had been able to grow entire forests with half a thought, move mountains with a flick of their wrists.

Now, hundreds of years after the curse and just as much time away from the island's power, their abilities had dwindled to barely more than party tricks.

Isla walked carefully over the flowers until the castle walls ended and she faced hundreds of cheering Wildlings.

The trees above bloomed cherries and berries and bloodred blossoms, which fell onto the crowd in a colorful rain. Animals crept from the woods and into the group, sitting beside their companions. Wildling powers varied in their mastery of nature, but they often included affinity with animals—Terra had a great panther named Shadow she spoke to as easily as she communicated with Isla. Poppy had a hummingbird that liked to nestle in her hair.

When Isla nodded, the crowd fell silent.

"It is my honor to represent our realm this Centennial." Isla's pulse quickened, a drum along her bones. She looked across the crowd, at

stunning, hopeful faces. Some Wildlings wore dresses made from bits of fabric woven through with leaves and vines. Some wore nothing at all except for the swords draped down their backs. Some had clearly just fed, their lips stained deep red. Isla looked and tried her best not to tremble. Not to let her voice crack, or stumble, or make them question for a moment why their ruler often hid behind the thick walls of her castle. Why attendants were banned from entering her quarters. She tried not to wonder how many of these Wildlings had heard this same declaration a hundred years before, from a different ruler—how many of them were even left, after the recent string of deaths. She made a promise, because that was what her people were looking for. Reassurance. Strength. "I vow to shatter our curse once and for all."

They would have every right to be worried. Isla's failure would doom them all for at least another century. And there had been four failed Centennials already. Isla clenched her back teeth together, waiting for them to see right through her—waiting for her perception of what they wanted to be wrong.

But the morning air ignited with yells and blades raised high overhead. Birds screeched from the treetops. Wind rustled leaves into a roar. Relieved, Isla walked down the stairs, smeared in petals, nature blossoming at her feet as the crowd parted, making a path toward their most ancient twin trees.

Their roots crested into the air, then braided together, forming a towering archway, round as a looking glass. The other side of the forest waited beyond, safe and familiar. But that wasn't where she was going. Isla swallowed. She had been preparing for this moment her entire life. Terra's and Poppy's hands found her shoulders.

Isla walked through the portal that only worked once every hundred years, her last words to her guardians fresh in her mind: *I will follow your orders.*

And wished they hadn't been a lie.

CHAPTER TWO

THE ISLAND

The portal rippled closed behind her, choking the cheers into silence. Only Isla's ragged breath remained. She took a single step forward, and light like a thousand dying stars and suns blinded her.

She teetered to the side. An arm reached out to steady her.

"Open your eyes," a voice said, dark and striking as midnight.

Isla hadn't even realized they were closed. With a blink, the world stumbled then steadied, this portaling far worse than using her starstick.

The face belonging to the man looking down at her was amused. And familiar, somehow. He was so tall Isla had to tilt her chin to meet his eyes, black as coals. His hair spilled ink across his pale forehead. Nightshade, no question. Which meant . . .

"Thank you, Grimshaw," Isla said firmly. She quickly straightened and looked around, hoping no one had seen her stumble. She could practically hear Poppy and Terra in each of her ears, scolding her.

But besides Isla and the Nightshade, the cliff was empty. She turned, and a tiny choking sound rasped against the back of her throat. The sea raged angrily hundreds of feet below. She had almost joined the jutting rocks and ended her plans at saving her people before the Centennial had even started.

Ended *all* her plans.

"That would have been inconvenient." The Nightshade ruler grinned, revealing a single dimple, completely out of place in his cruelly cut face. "Call me Grim, Isla."

Grim. What a terrible word, Isla thought, worn with pride. Still, the name suited him. There *was* something grim beneath that grin, a faint shadow that might become monstrous in the dark.

"Have we met before?" It wasn't that he knew her name, no. That was expected. It wasn't even that he pronounced it perfectly, like a snake's hiss, with all the letters sounded out. There was something else . . .

That grin faltered. "If we had"—his eyes dipped for just a moment—"it wouldn't have been just once."

Isla could feel her face get hot beneath his gaze. Other than rare, closely monitored interactions or her secret travels to the other newlands with her starstick, she hadn't spent much time with men.

Especially men who looked like him.

Especially men who didn't seem to be terrified of her and her Wildling curse.

She frowned. He *should* be afraid. If a Wildling wished, they could make a person fall off a cliff in pursuit of them. Their power to beguile was impossible to resist—though forbidden during the hundred days. The Nightshade must have thought he was safe.

He was not.

Each Centennial was a giant game, a chance to gain unparalleled ability. It was said that whoever broke the curses by fulfilling the prophecy would be gifted all the power it had taken to spin them—the ultimate prize.

Was his flirting meant to distract her?

Isla glared at him.

And Grim grinned even wider.

Interesting.

Every hundred years since the curses had been cast, the island of Lightlark appeared for just a hundred days, freed from its impassable storm. Rulers of each realm were invited to journey from the new lands they had settled after fleeing Lightlark, to try to break the curses binding each of their powers and the island itself. Every realm except

for Nightshade, that was. Nightshades had the power to spin curses, making them prime suspects for having created them in the first place, though they denied it. This year, it seemed as though the Lightlark king was desperate.

It was the first Centennial Nightshade had been invited to.

Grim took her arm once more. Before Isla could object, he gently moved her to the side. A moment later, the giant marking on the edge of the cliff—an insignia representing all six realms—glowed gold, and someone else appeared from thin air, right where Isla had been.

A pale-blue cloak cracked with wind before settling against bare, very dark shoulders and muscled arms. The man had eyebrows larger than his eyes, a sculpted chin, and perfectly coiffed stubble that framed his pink mouth. Azul, ruler of Skyling. Isla had known their names since the time she could talk. Azul and Grim were both ancient, more than five hundred years old. Alive the day the curses had been cast. They were legends—compared to them, she was no one.

Centuries were apparently not enough time for Azul and Grim to have become friends. The Skyling nodded curtly at the Nightshade, and Grim's smile turned wicked. Mocking. Azul turned to Isla and bowed fully, reaching for her hand.

"Nice to have new Wildling blood this Centennial," he said. His bright eyes met hers, then studied her fingers, each covered in rings with gems as big as acorns. Though the rest of the realms liked to view Wildlings as savages, their wealth was unquestionable. Control of nature had its advantages. "Clouds, I've never seen a diamond that big."

To Isla, it was just a rock. Pretty, of course, but nothing in spades ever seemed too special. Jewels were made when great power was wielded over nature, and over the centuries the glittering gems had bloomed beneath the ground in the Wildling newland, rising up eventually, blossoming like flowers. It was difficult *not* to trip over some sort of precious stone in Isla's lands, which she only knew from texts, and certainly not from personal experience.

As far as Terra and Poppy were aware.

Terra always said those glittering rocks were the reason they had such a steady supply of hearts. Thieves from other realms, foolish and bold and wicked, sneaked onto their territory for the diamonds.

Isla smiled. So, the Skyling liked jewels. She slipped the ring right off her own hand and onto Azul's longest finger without missing a beat. "It compliments you much more than it does me."

Azul looked like he might object—but didn't.

Someone else appeared, stepping easily past them, as if walking through portals was as seamless as the tide coming in. She turned to Isla. Her frown seemed to come as easily as most people's smiles. "So, this is the new pet?"

An ember lit in Isla's chest. The rest of the realms viewed the women warriors as savage temptresses, predators that lured lovers, then feasted on their hearts.

And Isla really couldn't blame them. Because that was very nearly the truth.

But Wildlings were so much more. At least, they had been. And still could be.

Though part of her wanted to say something she would likely regret, Isla knew the ruler *wanted* her to bite back. She was trying to tempt the monster out of Isla, to show the rest of them she was nothing more than a bloodthirsty beast. Instead, Isla bowed. "An honor to meet you, Cleo," she said, nodding her head in slight reverence. Cleo was the oldest among them, even older than the king of Lightlark, who also ruled over all Sunlings. Her age was at odds with her perfectly smooth, youthful face. Though most of the rulers were hundreds of years older, it was almost difficult to tell the difference between them and Isla. Almost.

Instead of making another insult, Cleo simply raised her chin at Isla and sneered, looking at her green dress as if she had stepped onto the island naked. Compared to the Moonling's clothing, she might as

well have. Cleo's white gown had long sleeves like milky beams of moonlight, a neckline that reached her chin, and a cape that completely covered three-fourths of her body. The skin Isla *could* see was so fair, her veins shined through, blue streaks on a slab of white marble. She was not only many shades lighter than Isla but also far taller. Her face was long and pointed in three places, cheekbones and chin, sculpted like a diamond.

The insignia glowed a final time, and a girl stepped forward, stumbling ever so slightly. She was the silver of stars, from her long, straight sheet of hair to her twinkling dress to her gloves, which reached her elbows. She smiled sheepishly at them, heart-shaped face going wide, then stood tall. "I suppose I'm the last to arrive?"

Cleo channeled her distaste right at the girl. The ruler of Starling, like Isla, was new. Starling's curse had been one of the cruelest. No one in their realm lived past the age of twenty-five.

Isla stepped forward and offered her hand. "Celeste, is it?"

The Starling smiled warmly. "Hello, Isla."

"Enchanted," Grim said, offering a bow that seemed to mock the one that Azul had given just moments before.

The Skyling frowned for just a moment before he offered Celeste his own fingers, now glimmering with Isla's diamond. "More new blood. I have a good feeling about this Centennial."

Cleo raised an eyebrow at him. "She better hope so," she said, nodding at Celeste. "She won't be here for the next one."

The Starling's face fell. And the Moonling simply turned around, her white cape floating slightly behind her.

"Don't feel too special," Azul said with a wink. "She's this unpleasant to everyone."

The rulers began the path to the palace, and Isla's heart tripped in anticipation. She had been so focused on them, she hadn't gotten a chance to truly take in her surroundings. The rest of the century, the island was encased in its storm. But now the clouds had cleared.

Lightlark was a shining, cliffy thing. Its bluffs were white as bone, and sunlight rained down in sheets of misted gold. One of the original sources of power, its ground still thrummed with it, singing to Isla in a humming siren song. She could feel its force with each step, each breath. She drank the island in greedily, like the wine she was never allowed to touch. Equally addictive and dangerous.

Poppy's lessons ran through her head, facts on paper that were now real and solid before her.

Thousands of years ago, the island was cut into several pieces, so each realm could claim a shard. Nightshades left the island shortly afterward to form their own land. Wildlings left after the curses. The pieces that remained were Star Isle for the Starlings, Sky Isle for the Skylings, Moon Isle for the Moonlings, and Sun Isle for the Sunlings. Then, there was the Mainland, where all the realms had traditionally gathered together. It was the Centennial's base.

It was also historically home to Lightlark royalty.

The Mainland castle loomed nearby, set high on a cliff like a crown jewel, jutting precariously out over the sea. Large enough to be its own city. Which was good, considering its main inhabitant could not leave it.

Not during the day, at least.

Isla must have been staring at it, because Celeste sighed next to her. "Do you think he's watching us?" she said quietly.

He. The Sunling ruler and king of Lightlark. The last remaining Origin, with blood from each of the four realms that still had a presence on the island. He could wield each of the four Lightlark powers.

And, by all accounts, he was insufferable.

On Lightlark and beyond, love had a price. Falling deeply and truly in love meant forming a bond that gave a beloved complete access to one's abilities. They could do whatever they wished with it. Wield it, reject it. Even steal it.

Knowing very well how many people wanted access to his endless stream of power, the Lightlark ruler was untrusting. Paranoid. Cold.

Isla dreaded meeting him. Especially given the first step of Poppy and Terra's plan for her.

She stared back at the castle and resisted the urge to flinch. Instead, she broke through her mask of charm and made an obscene gesture at the palace.

The game had officially started.

"I hope so."

Crowds awaited them at the castle doors. Starlings. Moonlings. Skylings.

On the night of the curses, five hundred years before, all six rulers perished. Their power and responsibility were transferred to their heirs, and all of them except for the new king fled the island's instability to create the newlands, hundreds of miles from the island and each other.

Some subjects had remained on Lightlark.

Once, Isla had asked the Wildling Eldress why anyone would stay in the near constant cursed tempest that had overtaken it.

Power is in the island's blood and bones, she had said. *Lightlark lengthens our lives, gives us access to a power much greater than our own. And more than that, to many . . . Lightlark is home.*

No Wildlings remained. She would get no aid from her people.

She was alone.

"Don't worry," a deep voice said mockingly at her side. "I don't have any adoring fans either."

The crowd watched Grim with a healthy mix of fear and disdain—Isla studied their reactions carefully. He looked like night come to life, his clothing shadow spun into silk. If Wildlings were looked down upon on Lightlark, Nightshades seemed to be outright hated. And, according to Terra and Poppy's lessons, never fully accepted on the island. They had their own land, a stronghold they had maintained for thousands of years.

The war between Nightshade and Lightlark hadn't helped either.

Isla didn't meet his gaze, though she felt his eyes all over her. It was unnerving. Her skin felt inexplicably electric. "I'm sure you get more

than enough attention back home." She smiled politely at the crowd, testing their own reaction to her. Some of them returned the gesture warily. Others visibly recoiled from the sight of her, the heart-devouring temptress. She wasn't surprised. Everything she represented was forbidden. A Moonling woman covered her child's eyes and made a figure in the air, as if warding off a demon.

"I do," he admitted. "Yet, I'm left . . . unsatisfied."

Isla ignored him. She wasn't going to play this game with him, whatever it was. She had her own game to play.

The interior of the castle looked like a sun had burst inside and bathed the walls in its glow—an ode to the Sunlings who had built it. Everything was gold. Buttery sunlight spilled from long windows, coating the foyer in glittering light that reflected off the smooth, shining floor. Isla squinted as if she was still outside. A raging fire burned in a ring high above them on a chandelier, flames peaking in place of crystals.

The Sunling ruler was not there to greet them. He couldn't be, even if he wanted to, which Isla truly doubted. Sunlings had been cursed never to feel the warmth of sunlight or see the brightness of day—forced to shun that which gave them power. The king of Lightlark was trapped in the darkness of his chambers, only able to surface at night. In that, Isla supposed they were similar. She had spent a lot of time trapped inside too.

A woman in Starling silver bowed before them. Behind her, a small group of staff echoed her movement. Each ruler received an attendant for the entirety of the Centennial. "It would be our pleasure to escort you to your chambers."

Each ruler was led away to completely different parts of the castle. Far from each other. Isla didn't know what to think about that. Intentional—every detail at the Centennial was intentional, that was what Terra had taught her.

A young Starling girl walked toward her slowly, slightly sideways, the way a child might approach a coiled snake. "My lady," she said,

voice so soft Isla had to lean in to hear her, which only made the girl flinch. Isla resisted the urge to roll her eyes. Did the girl actually think she would feast on her heart in the middle of the foyer? Her kind was wild, but they weren't *animals*. "Follow me."

"Isla," she said at the girl's stiff back as she raced away with a noticeable amount of trouble. Isla would likely need the girl's help during some point—which meant she would need to earn her loyalty somehow. "You can call me Isla."

"As you wish," the girl murmured.

She led Isla up a sweeping set of stairs that ran through the center of the castle and down an impossible tangle of hallways that jutted over and across each other like bridges. But, unlike her palace in the Wildling realm, this one became more and more enclosed the deeper she went. It reminded her of a maze in a cave. Or a prison. She suddenly imagined the king as an ancient beast, trapped in the dark. Lost in the labyrinth that was his castle. They reached a stretch without a single window. The halls grew colder, the walls thicker.

The girl stopped in front of an ancient stone door. With about all the strength it seemed she could muster, she pushed it open.

Someone had managed to plant a tree right in the middle of the room, an oak with blush-colored blossoms and blooming fruit Isla didn't recognize, its roots dug right into the stone floor. Ivy crept across the ceiling in a pretty design, leading to the wall her bed rested against, which was covered in leaves down to the floor.

There was more. Isla walked across the room and onto a wide, curling balcony that jutted right over the sea. Dangerously so. Waves churned below. The castle was a curious child perched at the top of the mountain, leaning way too far over the edge.

Isla frowned. "How sturdy is this?" It seemed like the balcony could break off at any moment, or that the castle itself could simply slide off the cliff during a storm.

"As sturdy as the king himself, I suppose."

Right. Isla knew that from her lessons. The king of Lightlark didn't just control its power—he *was* its power. If something happened to him, the entire land would crumble away, and every Lightlark realm would fall. That was why he trod so carefully. Not in fear of being killed, but in fear of someone stealing that terrible power right from under him.

Another similarity. Isla couldn't fall in love either.

Well, she *could,* but everyone lived in fear of a Wildling loving them. Their curse made love a death sentence.

Not exactly the fodder for romance, admittedly.

It hadn't been an issue so far, in Isla's relatively short, halfway-contained life. Yet—

How cruel would a king who had been afraid to fall in love for more than five hundred years be?

It seemed she would soon find out.

"Dinner is at eight chimes," the Starling girl said before beginning to stoke the already monstrous fire burning in the hearth across from her bed.

"It's hot enough," Isla said. "Don't trouble yourself."

The Starling continued, moving the coals around in a practiced way. "The king has given strict orders for the fires to remain burning constantly."

What a strange command, Isla thought. Before she could ask why, the Starling was across the room. She bowed once before quickly closing the door behind her.

Isla was just finishing surveying her bathroom—more spacious than the one back home, even, with a tub she could do laps in—when a knock sounded on her door.

She tentatively opened it.

And found Celeste standing there.

Isla immediately threw her arms around the Starling ruler. They jumped in a tiny circle, embracing and laughing so hard, Isla kicked the door closed to keep it from echoing down the hall.

Celeste raised an eyebrow. "Celeste, is it?" she said, doing a shockingly good and unflattering impression of Isla. She threw her silver head back and laughed.

Isla's smile strained, wondering if she hadn't been convincing enough. "Do you think they—"

"They don't suspect a thing," Celeste cut her off. She clicked her tongue and reached to pull a lock of Isla's hair. "I thought you were going to cut this."

Isla sighed. "I tried. One look at the scissors, and Poppy almost stabbed me with them. She confiscated every set in my chambers."

"Confiscated?" Celeste raised an eyebrow. "Do I need to remind you that *you're* the ruler of your realm?" Isla laughed without humor. She turned to walk deeper into her quarters, and Celeste's hand went straight to her back. "You brought it?"

She caught her reflection in the mirror. Something along her spine was faintly glowing—it must have been Celeste's presence. She cursed, hoping no one else had noticed, and pulled the starstick out. "I couldn't leave it behind."

Celeste frowned. "It's risky. Hide it well." She was right. If anyone found out Isla had the enchantment, their secret alliance would be compromised.

Isla had found the starstick in her mother's things, five years prior. More desperate for freedom than fearful of being portaled somewhere dangerous, she had traveled the realms' newlands with it for months before finally coming across Celeste. That was the first time they had ever met.

Celeste had instantly recognized the starstick as an ancient Starling relic. Isla had no idea how her mother had gotten her hands on it before her death. And, since Celeste's own family had died long before, thanks to the curse that killed all in their realm at twenty-five, she didn't know either.

Though it belonged to the Starlings, Celeste had never asked for it back. That had marked the start of their friendship—two rulers of realms, their lands separated by hundreds of miles, with one thing in common: they both desperately needed to break the curses *this* Centennial.

For Celeste, breaking her curse was the difference between life or death. Not only for her, but for all her people.

For Isla . . . things were even more complicated. No one realized how small their realm had gotten. Many more Wildlings had died than been born. Their powers had gotten weaker with every generation. Forests had shrunk. Wildlife had gone extinct. At the rate her lands and people were deteriorating, there wouldn't be any Wildlings *left* by the next Centennial.

Isla had never agreed with Poppy and Terra's plan. It was too complex. Too demeaning.

So, she had created a new strategy with Celeste.

"I should go," her friend said after fully appraising Isla's room. "For the record, your quarters are nicer than mine. Though my room isn't in such a drafty old corner of the castle."

Isla rolled her eyes. "I'll see you at dinner."

Celeste turned on her way to the door and formed a wicked smile. "So, it begins."

CHAPTER THREE

BLOOD

The sun had fallen. It was just a yolky thing, halfway consumed by the horizon, when Isla opened the double doors and stared up at the incoming moon. She was in the middle of getting ready, just in her slip. The gauzy white curtains blew back in the breeze, trailing her arms, falling against her bare knees, her toes. She crept out onto the balcony, the stone cold beneath her feet. Breathed in salt and brine.

She carefully climbed onto the wide stone ledge, knees to her chest. And just like she did back home when she was alone in her room, whenever she felt anxious and lonely and trapped, she began to sing.

Singing was a Wildling thing, a temptress thing. Just like their sisters, the sirens of the sea. Isla's voice was unnaturally good, like silk and velvet and deep dreams. She knew it and liked the sound. Liked how her voice could be as deep as the ocean floor and as high as wind chimes. She didn't need music. The sea below was instrument enough, its waves crashing roughly against the island's harrowing white cliffs as if trying to get a good look at her.

She sang and sang, meaningless words and melodies, letting her voice ripple and peak and dip, like drawing on an endless canvas. She sang to the sea, to the moon, to the rising darkness. All things she hadn't been able to see from her painted-over windows in the Wildling realm. Finally, she ended on a high note, letting it drag out as much as she could without taking another breath. She smiled to herself, always surprised by what came out of her mouth. Always relieved by how it put to rest even her darkest thoughts.

And there was clapping.

Isla whipped around to see a man on another balcony yards away, tucked so far back into the castle she hadn't even noticed it. Practically in her underclothes and caught completely off guard, Isla gasped. She whirled too quickly, startled. Her arms pinwheeled at her sides, but it was no use—gravity was too great.

She fell straight back, clean off the ledge.

Her breath spooled out of her chest, and she screamed soundlessly as she fell, grasping at the night air like the stars were footholds.

But only air passed through her fingers, and she fell, fell—

Until the sea roared below, and her head cracked against its surface.

Isla sat up so quickly she retched sea water. Her throat burned with it. She blinked and blinked. Wiped her mouth with the back of her hand.

And found that she was back on her balcony, in a puddle of water. Her hair was dripping wet. Her slip clung to her body, completely soaked through. Her head pounded in pain from its very crown. When her fingers gingerly ran over the spot, she expected there to be blood. There wasn't.

She was very much alive. Not drowned, the way she should have been. That person, the one who had been watching her . . . he must have saved her.

Then dumped her here, not even bothering to see if she would wake up.

Who would do such a thing?

The more surprising part wasn't that he had discarded her . . .

But that he had *rescued* her.

After the curses were spun, there was chaos. That same night, the six rulers of realm sacrificed themselves in exchange for a prophecy that was promised to be the key to breaking the curses. Terra and Poppy claimed her own ancestor had been the one to lead the sacrifices, the first to die.

True or not, Isla could never imagine the strength it must have taken to give up their lives for the chance at their people's salvation. The power

the six injected into the island and transferred to their realms made the Centennial possible. Every hundred years, for a hundred days, the six realms were given a chance to save themselves, because of that sacrifice.

The prophecy to break the curses had three parts, which had been interpreted in several ways throughout the centuries. One was clear. For the curses to be eradicated, one of the six rulers had to die. It was why the Centennial was such a risky affair, feared and prepared for, why Terra had trained Isla to fight since the time she could walk.

Isla's sudden death by drowning might have been the first step to fulfilling the prophecy. But for some reason, the person on the balcony wanted to keep her alive.

Why?

Bells rang through the castle, making Isla almost jump out of her skin. She counted them, then cursed.

For the first dinner, she was supposed to have spent an hour on her hair, arranging it in a complicated design atop her head. She was supposed to choose the perfect gown, rub rose-scented lotion on her skin until it gleamed, and apply her makeup with precision, using tools she had learned to wield just as expertly as her throwing blades. All things Poppy had drilled into her.

Instead, she combed her wet hair with her fingers and almost slipped in the trail it made, threw on the first gown she could get her hands on, put on a pair of silk slippers, and grabbed her crown at the last moment, placing it haphazardly on her head as she tore through the door.

And almost ran into the same Starling girl as before. Her tiny mouth was open in shock, and she put her hands up on instinct, shielding from an attack. "This way . . . Isla."

A dozen hallways later, the doors to the dining hall opened, and everyone turned to look at her.

Isla wished she was a Nightshade, just so she could disappear.

Celeste sat back in her chair, eyebrows raised.

Azul put down the goblet he was holding.

Cleo regarded her with even more disdain than before. In her rush, Isla had grabbed one of her most brazen dresses, one she had been instructed to wear far later in the game. The bones of the bodice were visible, the panels nearly sheer. The skirt had a slit that ran up her leg, to the top of her thigh. Her cape was green lace, attached to a dipping neckline.

Grim looked amused, eyeing her every step in a way that made her flush, mortified.

There was someone else at the head of the table. The same person who had been watching her sing—who must have both saved her and abandoned her.

Oro, king of Lightlark, ruler of Sunlings. He had hair like woven gold, eyes as amber and hollow as honeycomb. Mean eyes that pinned her in place. He frowned and nodded curtly at her in welcome, purely out of obligation.

Why had the king saved her?

Only to regard her so dismissively.

She returned the cold nod and took the empty seat at his side, cursing whoever had placed her there.

Isla's wet hair draped over her arm, dripping down her skin and onto the floor beside her in a puddle. Her body shook slightly, freezing, the flimsy, practically fabric-less excuse of a gown doing absolutely nothing to warm her.

The taunting voice was back: *Are you ready, Isla?*

Of course she wasn't. How had she been foolish enough to accept the Centennial invitation? To walk directly into such a deadly game?

One of the six rulers had to die. As the youngest and least experienced, she would be a fool to believe it wouldn't be her. Especially when she had nearly died twice already, less than a day into the ceremony.

If she was smart, she would leave that night, using her starstick.

If she wanted to live, she would abandon the island, her realm, her people, her duty, and never look back. Lands beyond Lightlark and the newlands were largely unexplored. She had always wondered about them. It would be risky traveling beyond them, but certainly not more dangerous than the Centennial . . .

She couldn't. Not if she ever wished to be truly free. Her curse would never allow her to have the full life she wanted, with the people she cared about most. Terra. Poppy. Celeste.

If all went to plan, she would never have to be hidden away like a secret again. She would never feel ashamed about who she was. She could lead her people to prosperity and travel the newlands at will, visiting Celeste whenever she wanted to.

Isla had spent countless hours of her life studying other people, guessing at their motivations.

Freedom was hers.

Oro studied her dripping hair, and he had the nerve to smile. "I know our seas are irresistible . . . but please, in the future, do limit your swims to earlier in the evening so as not to keep the rest of us waiting." He raised his chin slightly. The crown atop his head was gold and gleaming, its spikes sharp enough to draw blood. "Very rude—though perhaps my expectations of your realm were too high to begin with."

Cleo's eyes glittered with amusement, relishing the red that Isla could feel spreading across her cheeks. "A swim in *that* sea, at *this* hour? She certainly is a wild pet. Even a Moonling wouldn't think to do such a thing during the Centennial. Only a fool would."

Wild. Pet. Fool. The Moonling had managed to insert multiple jabs in just a few short sentences.

"Certainly not on a full moon," Isla said smoothly, the words slipping out before she could stop herself.

Silence.

Silverware clattered together somewhere across the room.

Moonlings' curse meant that every full moon, the sea claimed dozens of lives from their realm, drowning anyone who found themselves too close to the coast. It made faraway trade nearly impossible, made living near the ocean a danger, and had completely crippled the Moonlings' economy.

Isla regretted her words immediately. The way Cleo's eyes narrowed, right at her, like an arrow marking its target, made her feel like she had just officially made her first enemy.

Before anyone could say another word, a plate was placed in front of Isla. On it sat a bleeding heart.

"Sourced from the worst of our prisons," Oro said smoothly. "A murderer of women."

It took all of Isla's will to smile warmly at him. "How kind of you. However, I prefer to eat in private. Some find it . . . disturbing." She looked around for the Starling who had led her to the dining hall. "Could I have this sent to my room for later?"

"Nonsense," Oro said. He stared down at the heart, then at Isla. "Eat."

She could feel everyone's gaze on her. It had been a while since they had encountered a Wildling. Isla carefully took her fork and knife, nodded graciously at her host, and cut a piece of the heart, blood pooling out of it, filling her plate. She breathed in the metallic sent.

Then she took a bite.

Grim roughly placed his goblet of wine down onto the table. "Isla, as much as the blood on your lips suits you, I sense my good friend Azul's distaste for Wildling . . . pleasures." Indeed, the Skyling, though clearly trying to be polite, looked ill. Grim motioned for the staff. "Please send this to her quarters."

He spoke as if this was his castle, not Oro's. The Sunling ruler blinked but did not stop the Skyling boy from taking Isla's plate away. "Weak stomach, Grimshaw?"

The Nightshade grinned, the dimple returning. "We all have our weaknesses, Oro," he said. "I'm counting on them."

Somehow, Isla made it through the rest of the dinner without having to excuse herself.

Then she spent the night retching blood.

CHAPTER FOUR

RULES

Isla had been born without the Wildlings' curse—or their power. Since birth, she'd lived locked away, protected by Poppy and Terra, in fear that her realm would discover her secret.

Her mother was to blame. She broke the most important Wildling rule—she fell in love. Then she failed to kill him. Terra and Poppy always said there were consequences to breaking rules . . . and that, no matter what, curses always found their blood. Isla's father had murdered her mother moments after Isla was born, and their spawn was powerless—her own curse, as a consequence of her mother somehow thwarting the first. Isla's malediction was not eating hearts or killing a beloved. But being a ruler born without powers was just as deadly.

Rulers were expected to inject their power into their lands to keep their people strong. It was why Lightlark was so engorged with energy, and how the realms had survived in the newlands they had formed after they had fled the island. Without power to give, her realm was steadily dying. So far, her people had blamed their curses and length of time away from Lightlark for the deaths. But some were beginning to become suspicious of Isla.

It was her greatest secret. One that would be a death sentence at the Centennial.

One of the six rulers had to die to break the curses, according to the oracle's prophecy. But it was worse than that. A ruler's power was the life force of their people. So, if one died without an heir—

All their people would die along with them.

Those were the stakes of the game. Breaking the curses meant eliminating an entire realm.

The first Centennial had been a bloodbath. All the invited rulers set out to kill each other, and many of the islanders were caught in the cross fire. But the heads of realm were too skilled, too ancient already. The hundred days ended with all of them alive and the curses intact. It was decided that future Centennials would have order.

It was decided that there would be rules.

Oro stood on the steps in front of his golden throne, instead of on it. That was the first thing Isla noticed as she entered the grand hall. Leaders seemed to be constantly reminding people around them of their authority. During the few times she had visited the Moonling newland, she had seen countless ice statues carved in the likeness of their ruler, heard Moonlings speak of paying their monthly dues, saw the patrol Cleo kept constantly roaming the streets.

Was there a reason the king was hesitant to sit on his throne?

The next thing she noticed were the half dozen chandeliers of fire, overlapping across the ceiling. They echoed the flames of four hearths, burning brightly. She thought back to her attendant's comment. The king never wanted any of the fireplaces going out.

Why not?

The rulers gathered in a circle, and Isla stood tall, ignoring the pang of hunger in her stomach. She had sneaked into the kitchens early that morning, but all she had been able to procure was some stale bread, fruit that vaguely resembled mura from the Wildling newland, and a cup of milk. A longer-term solution to her food problem would be necessary.

Celeste, across the way, looked well rested, her skin vibrant. Isla imagined her friend had visited Star Isle for the first time that morning. Perhaps there had been a ceremony honoring her. Without regular

access to their leaders, the Skylings, Starlings, and Moonlings who had remained on Lightlark had created their own subgovernments. Their rulers had become seen as almost gods, figureheads they deferred to and only saw for a few months every hundred years. All rulers traditionally spent most of their time on the Mainland during the Centennial. But there were occasional exceptions.

Isla had always wondered what the different isles that made up Lightlark looked like. She longed to ask her friend all about it, wishing she knew how to work her starstick between small distances so that she could simply appear in Celeste's room whenever she wanted. Instead, they would have to rely on using the hallways for that. And meeting up often, this early in the game, was too great of a risk.

She turned and accidentally put herself in Cleo's path. The Moonling eyed her with too much interest. There was a sharp gleam in her gaze—a predator sizing up its prey.

Isla would pay for her comment the night before. She was sure of it.

Oro finally spoke. "Let us begin by stating the rules of the Centennial."

The air was electric, buzzing with energy.

"The first rule. A ruler may not assassinate or attempt to assassinate another ruler until after the fiftieth day." The rule was a relief to Isla. For at least half of the Centennial, powerless or not, she would be safe. Which was why she and Celeste planned to be off the island before the ball on the fiftieth day even took place. "And, when pairs are decided on the twenty-fifth day, a ruler may not assassinate their partner."

After the chaos of the first Centennial, the hundred days became more structured, split into parts. The first twenty-five days were dedicated to demonstrations hosted by each ruler, designed to test one another's strengths—and worthiness of staying alive. Each test had a winner. The ruler who won the most trials would decide which pairs the rulers would split into for the remainder of the Centennial.

"The second rule. All rulers must attend and participate in every Centennial event." That rule seemed innocuous but was dangerous, depending on what it was.

"The third rule. To participate, no ruler can have an heir." So, their death would successfully eliminate their familial line and break the curses, according to the prophecy. It would also mean the end of their realm forever.

Each ruler received an invitation to the Centennial containing these rules. Acceptance of it meant acceptance of the three ordinances.

But every good promise was sealed in blood.

With a flick of the king's wrist, a fire erupted in the middle of their circle. Isla knew exactly what was to happen next.

Poppy had made her practice the act, over and over—*again, until you don't flinch!* Her wound would be stitched up, only to be sliced open again and again and again, until she had no visible reaction to the pain.

In sync with the others, Isla removed the crown from her head—and used its sharpest point to form a deep cut across her palm.

She did not flinch. Poppy would be proud.

Before she offered the stream of blood to the flames, there was another part to the ceremony that she had practiced. Each ruler's blood had special properties, in accordance with their abilities. Wildling blood was supposed to bloom flowers.

Isla was prepared, petals hidden between her fingers. When her blood finally dripped down her palm, it held a miniature rose.

Cleo's blood hardened into ice before being seared by the fire. Grim's blood became dark as ink. Azul's blood suspended in the air, separating into parts, before finally falling. Celeste's blood burst into a mess of sparks. Oro's blood burned brightly before even reaching the flames.

The fire turned crimson, stained with their blood—then vanished.

Now, they were bound to the rules. Breaking them had consequences. For Isla, Celeste, Grim, Cleo, and Azul, it meant forfeiting claim to the

Centennial's prize: the unmatched power the oracle said would be gifted to the one responsible for breaking all the curses. Oro, as king and host of the Centennial, was bound to the rules with his life.

Was that why Oro had saved her? Did he have a responsibility to? It was unclear how accidental deaths factored into the prophecy.

What *was* clear was that the king of Lightlark had a plan. And it apparently involved Isla staying alive.

At least, until he wanted her dead.

CHAPTER FIVE

GRIM

The next morning, when Isla's attendant knocked on her door, she was ready.

She hadn't been allowed weapons, but she *had* been allowed a trunk of belongings. She applied kohl to her green eyes, in perfectly arched streaks. Her lashes were already thick and long, but she curled them even more. Spread a balm across her full lips that brightened their natural shade. Her skin was naturally tan, but she still looked too pale for her liking, having spent far too much of her life inside.

That would be easily remedied. Now that she was free to explore, she had no intention of locking herself in her room.

The few dresses from her trunk looked more like a collection of sewn-together ribbons. Sheer, bare, and so smooth they looked liquid. In the Wildling realm, in the constant seclusion of her chambers, she could get away with wearing loose, soft clothes. But this was the Centennial, and Poppy had chosen these gowns for a reason.

A reason that made Isla want to throw them all into the closest fireplace.

That day, she chose a dress the pink of tulips, with a plunging back and fabric that clung to her like it was wet. It was tradition to wear the color of one's power source. Starlings wore silver, Sunlings wore gold, Skylings wore light blue, Nightshades wore black, and Moonlings wore white. Because nature was multicolored, Isla was not bound to one shade, as long as she did not infringe upon anyone else's.

The Starling girl startled when Isla answered the door so quickly.

Isla did not waste a moment. "What is your name?" she asked.

"My name?" the girl said with such confusion, Isla couldn't help but laugh.

"I'm assuming you have one?" she joked, hoping her smile made it seem good-natured, not mean.

The girl smiled back tentatively. *Good.* "Of course. It's Ella, lady." She shook her head. "I mean, *Isla.*"

Isla dipped her head, the way she had watched people do when they were about to speak in confidence. She had heard many a secret whispered in a back alley, or on the outskirts of a village, thanks to her starstick. Over time, she had learned how to go undercover, to blend into a crowd so seamlessly that no one would guess she didn't belong. "I notice you walk with a limp, Ella," she said.

The Starling girl looked taken aback. She took a shaky step away, and Isla wondered if she should have waited longer . . . or if she had been too direct. The girl's hand went instinctively to her leg. "My—my bone," Ella finally said. "It broke a while ago and never healed right."

Isla frowned. "Aren't there Moonling healers here that could help?" Their skills were legendary. Beyond controlling water, healing was their power.

"At a cost," Ella said, smiling weakly. "If at all, lately." Isla wondered what she meant, but before she could ask, Ella added, "Also . . . I'm not so far from twenty-five. It wouldn't, it wouldn't—"

Be worth it. Isla winced. Even with Celeste as her best friend, sometimes she forgot about the cruelty of their curse. No Starling had lived past twenty-five in hundreds of years.

"Well," Isla said, reaching into the pocket in her dress. "This should help." She handed over the tub of paste, a Wildling healing elixir made from specially grown flora. The same potion that had healed the cut on her palm from the ceremony the day before.

Ella just stared at the tub placed in her hand until finally Isla curled the Starling's fingers around the container and gently pushed her hand away, signaling for her to take it.

"Now," Isla said brightly. "I need something from *you.*"

With the means to getting regular meals delivered settled, Isla set off for the marketplace, an invitation from the tailor that Ella had brought in her hands. Before participating in any of the six demonstrations, she needed new clothes. There were only so many outfits one could pack in the allotted luggage, so each Centennial, every ruler was gifted a custom wardrobe.

Today was Isla's appointment.

She heard Poppy in her ear.

Your dresses are your armor—your jewels are your weapons. They were the tools of a seductress.

It was the role Poppy had trained her for, as the first step of her guardian's plan—which Isla had no intention of following. She might not have powers, but that didn't mean she was *powerless.*

She could blend in. Listen. Hide. Strategize. All skills her and Celeste's plan required.

Ella had insisted on escorting Isla to the agora at the center of the Mainland, where the tailor operated. The Wildling Eldress had mentioned it in her stories, as *an enchanting place that blooms at night, like a flower facing the sun.*

Isla had insisted on going alone. It would give her a good opportunity to scope out this part of the island, to watch the islanders from a distance, unnoticed for as long as possible.

With three words, that plan went out the window.

"You're up early." *Grim.*

Isla swallowed, suddenly too aware of how tightly the fabric of her gown clung to her as she turned around.

Only to find him inches away.

Isla stumbled back. It took her a moment too long to find her voice. "So are you."

Grim lifted a broad shoulder, looking down at her just as she was forced to crane her neck up to maintain eye contact. "I like to take advantage of any time I can be out."

Right. His curse was the mirror of Oro's. Nightshades could not feel the energy and calm of night. Though they used to be nocturnal, choosing to live in darkness, that all changed five hundred years before.

"And I have business in the agora."

"As do I," Isla said.

Grim grinned. "Good. I hate walking alone."

Guards stood along the entrance and noticeably stiffened as Grim passed. Isla tried not to think about all the terrible things she had heard about Nightshades. About *him.* She tried and failed, and though her chin was held high, her legs went boneless beneath her.

Terra always said they were the most dangerous of the realms. Nightshades drew power from darkness, while all others drew from light. Rumors of their abilities abounded—the power to disappear, move through walls, spin nightmares, wield darkness itself.

Grimshaw had a reputation. There had been a war between Lightlark and Nightshade, just decades before the curses were spun. He had been the most fearsome warrior. It was rumored that by the end of a battle, his cloak was always soaked through with the blood of his enemies. Which only made his clear discomfort at Isla eating the heart at dinner more confusing.

Despite Grim's skill, Lightlark won the war, and a treaty was made. There was peace between all realms for a while.

Then the curses were cast, and most were convinced Nightshades had spun them in revenge.

Isla didn't know what to think. Nightshade had suffered a great loss thanks to their curse. Their realm's leader, Grimshaw's father, had died for the prophecy. His son had come into power immediately, back

when having an heir was the norm. They weren't allowed anymore. Rulers attended the Centennial at their own realm's risk.

Isla knew why *she* was on the island. Grim's reasons were more of a mystery. If the rulers of realm wanted anyone dead more than Isla, it was Grim. He would find no allies during the Centennial. Winning the prize of the power promised would be nearly impossible without true partnerships. So why attend—why take the risk?

What did *he* want?

A knowing grin overtook Grim's sharply cut face as he studied her right back. His black hair was smooth down his pale forehead, ink across a page. "Deciding if I'm a villain?"

Isla narrowed her eyes at him. "Can you . . ."

"Read minds?" His head knocked gently from side to side. "Not really. I can read flashes of emotions. Fear. Anger." His lips raised into a half smile. "Curiosity."

Isla's next breath was as unsteady as if rocks had been piled in her lungs. She was an impostor, a powerless ruler in a pack of wolves. She was skilled at playing the part of a Wildling ruler, of keeping up the facade, but her emotions were far harder to control. This power of his could be her unraveling if she didn't learn to manage her feelings around him.

Mind abilities were common in Nightshades. It was part of what made them so dangerous. Rulers also often had one additional ability—rare powers carried through bloodlines, popping up generations later. They had nothing to do with the stars, moon, sun, nature, darkness, or sky.

Isla wondered if on top of this, Grim had one of those.

"You're nervous now." He stopped and looked at her. "Why are you nervous?"

Nervous wasn't something a powerful Wildling ruler should feel, even around the Nightshade ruler. She looked up at him, into eyes so dark they seemed endless, two galactic black holes, and pulled herself together enough to boldly ask, "Do you have a flair?"

Grim's head tilted back in understanding. "You're worried I have an ability I'm not telling you about. One I'm using against you at this very moment."

No use in hiding it. In her hundred days on the island, she would have to lie, steal, and possibly kill.

Grim wasn't part of the plan. Not yet.

Isla nodded.

He raised a shoulder and started down the walkway once more. "I do. But it's something I'll keep to myself, for now." Grim glanced at her. "It's not mind reading, however. Or anything else I could secretly use on you."

The hill ended, the grass stopped—and below, in the valley between two mountains, sat a marketplace.

Grim sighed. "Five hundred years, I haven't been back. And nearly nothing has changed." He turned to her, a gleam in his eye. "Hearteater—can you have chocolate?"

Isla tried to keep the hunger off her face. "I can eat my weight in it."

Islanders flooded the marketplace, pockets clinking with coin. The hubbub was unnerving. The Centennial was a deadly game. Didn't they understand that if the rulers were successful, one of their realms would perish? Weren't they afraid?

It seemed the hundred days of sunshine, outside of the storm, outweighed any terror.

The agora was made up of tiny houses, all pushed together and different as each of the realms. One shop resembled a turned-over teacup, its walls made of frosted glass. Another stood tall as a redwood, smoke spilling from a chimney like a string of storm clouds. The next was held up on stilts. Yet another resembled a star roped down from the heavens, silver and glittering.

The one they entered was shaped like a winter ornament, painted bright blue. "Skylings make the best sweets, I'll admit it," Grim said over his shoulder before opening the door with so much force its hinges

screamed. The moment Isla walked inside, she groaned from somewhere deep in her chest.

Chocolate—velvety, nutty, sugary, silky cocoa.

She had only tasted chocolate on her forays to Skyling villages on their newland, during their quarterly celebrations. Skylings made constant excuses to host parties—before storms, after storms, even *during* storms. But nothing like this. Nothing like the thick slabs of fudge she watched a Skyling slice into rounds with a long knife.

Grim glanced at her, amused.

The man behind the counter paled at the sight of him. He shot a look over his shoulder at his associate, who had conveniently slipped into the back room. He didn't even register Isla.

Interesting. Being around Grim was like being a slightly smaller lightning rod in a storm—all wrath went to him.

Though he was one of the most powerful rulers, and she didn't have *any* power, in the islanders' eyes, they were both villains. Isla knew how important this was. Though, if they were successful, the rulers would decide which of them would die to fulfill part of the prophecy, the islanders' opinions and actions could shift the course of the Centennial. Their help—or lack of it—could mean the difference between life or death, especially for Isla, who didn't have any of her own people on the island. They were also typically invited to witness all six demonstrations.

Grim didn't seem to notice the way they all looked at him. Or, if he did, he didn't seem to care, unnervingly willing to play into the villainous role.

Though maybe he wasn't playing at all.

"Two of everything," he said lazily, pulling a handful of coin from his pocket and not bothering to count it. He set it on the counter and didn't wait for a reply, didn't look the man in the eye as he found a seat.

It was laughably small. His knees bumped against the top of the table. Isla slipped slowly into the chair across from him. "That's a lot of chocolate."

He shrugged. "You said you could eat your weight in it. I'm taking that at face value."

Soon, the owner of the shop placed a monstrous silver tray on the table. He bowed quickly, once at Isla, then at Grim, before hurriedly joining the rest of the staff in the back room.

Isla raised an eyebrow. "Did you set fire to the agora the last time you were here?"

Grim's knee bumped into her own, and she pulled her legs back so quickly, he grinned. "Let's just say the islanders' memories are long."

Before she could ask for clarification, he plucked a truffle between two enormous fingers. "Try this one first."

She tentatively took it, chewed it—and her eyes bulged.

"Divine, isn't it?"

Isla sank into her chair, her head lolling back. She shouldn't be wasting precious time on a chocolate tasting. But getting to know the Nightshade—perhaps getting him to trust her—could be useful. She closed her eyes, caramel on her tongue. "Wake me up when all of this is over."

A chuckle. Eyes still closed, she felt something rough against her lips.

"Open."

She did, and Grim dropped another truffle against her tongue. This one had a berry cream filling. A hard outer shell.

Isla tried every single one he offered. The fudge, the mint thins, a banana butter bar. Everything except for the chili pepper–powder praline.

"It's not that spicy," Grim said, throwing one carelessly into his mouth. He shrugged. "A hint of heat, nothing more."

"I like my tongue *functioning,* thank you."

Grim strung his long fingers together and rested his chin on the bridge they made. "So, you'll devour hearts and blood, but not a chili-dusted chocolate?"

A joke, but dangerously close to the truth. "Fine," she said, mumbling something else under her breath that made him grin wickedly.

Isla put the chocolate in her mouth and instantly regretted it. Her eyes watered, her mouth burned, her tongue immediately swelled. She spit it out, forgetting every manner, not even caring that the shop owner was peering at them through the kitchen window. Her nostrils flared. "*You,*" she said between deep gulps of water that made the pain even worse.

Grim laughed and laughed and laughed, that stupid dimple bright on his face. He tried to say something, then laughed some more, not stopping even when he got up, even when he used his Nightshade abilities to walk *through* the counter as if it was nothing and helped himself to a jug of milk. Not even when he placed a glass of it in front of Isla and said, "Drink."

She stared daggers at him the entire time she gulped it down, so desperately it dripped down her chin and the front of her dress. Villain indeed.

"Demon," she said meanly.

He raised an eyebrow at her. "Not quite." He frowned at her dress. "We'll have to replace that. You're headed to the tailor now?"

"And you know that how . . . ?"

He only answered once they were out of the store. "I was also offered a consultation with the Lightlark tailor."

"I'm guessing your wardrobe doesn't have much range."

Grim frowned down at his black shirt, black pants, black boots, and black cape. "I told them I'm capable of dressing myself."

The streets were filled with dozens of torches dug into the stone, burning even though the day was warm and the sun was out. Sunling guards seemed to be in charge of keeping them lit, flames curling from their palms.

They reached a shop with crystalline glass windows, each pane cut in an emerald shape. Inside sat a rainbow of Wildling colors—spools of fabric, ribbon, thread, and piles of pins.

All for her.

"Enjoy," Grim said mockingly, and then he was gone.

Vanished. There one moment and gone the next. A chill tripped down her spine.

What would it be like, having a power like invisibility?

She entered the shop.

A bell rang, announcing her presence. A young Starling man with pins stuck into a cushion on his wrist froze. Isla waited for his eyes to widen in disgust or fear.

But the tailor bowed gracefully. "Isla, ruler of Wildlings. Pleasure. What happened to your gown?" Before she could respond, he lifted a hand. "Not to worry—*I* only use giant spider silk in my shop . . . Doesn't stain . . . strong as steel . . . and the fit is unparalleled." He motioned for her to step onto the platform.

"Preferred colors?"

The answers that came out of her mouth might as well have come from Poppy's, hundreds of miles away in the Wildling realm. Isla had been taught exactly what to say.

"Green. Red. Purples and pinks, on occasion."

"Preferred fit?"

"Tight."

"Length?"

"Long."

He examined her. "How attached are you to this dress?"

She looked down at it and shrugged. "Not especially."

"Good," he said, and snapped his fingers. At once, everything in the shop floated. Thanks to Celeste, Isla knew this realm's powers well. Starlings channeled energy from the stars, allowing them to move objects. He pointed a finger, and a spool of rich, bloodred fabric flew across the room, wrapping around Isla in a flash, so fast that it replaced the pink she had been wearing before, and she only realized it when she saw her old dress in ribbons on the floor. The red wrapped breathtakingly tightly around her waist; floating scissors made rough slices; flying threads and needles sewed at an impossible speed. The tailor directed it all like

leading an orchestra, hands moving gracefully in front of him. Another sheet of fabric formed a silky, gauzy cape. A bodice was expertly crafted around her, and she was tied tightly into its corset, sucking her breath.

In seconds, she was in a new, beautiful gown.

She turned to face the tailor and found someone else sitting in the shop, elbows on his knees.

"How did you get in here?" she asked incredulously.

Grim looked bored. He raised an eyebrow at her, as if to say, *Is that a serious question?*

The tailor eyed him—remaining surprisingly calm compared to the other islanders they had encountered—and turned his attention to Isla. "How does it feel?"

She regarded herself in the many mirrors. "Like water. The fabric . . . it's smooth as a rose petal."

"Giant spider silk, Ruler. I'll get to work on your wardrobe."

Keeping her voice as low as possible, and shooting another look in Grim's direction, she said, "If it isn't any trouble, in addition to the dresses, I require something more suited for fighting. Pants. Armor." *Those* instructions came from Terra. As the tailor wrote down some notes, she peered behind him, getting a good look at the back room . . . and the lock on its door.

The tailor placed his hands perfectly together, as if in prayer. He *did* seem to worship clothes more than most people did their rulers. "My pleasure. I will have everything sent to the castle shortly."

Isla thanked him and glared daggers at Grim as she left the shop, knowing he would like it. Sharing chocolate had seemed to put some of her fears about Nightshades and their powers to rest. Part of her was surprised that she felt so comfortable around a man after only a few days of knowing him. And perhaps that was just what he wanted—for her to let her guard down. "Could you be less of a creep?" she said.

Grim's expression turned serious. "If you would like me to leave you alone, I will. Say the word, and I'll vanish."

Isla said nothing. She wondered what Grim was playing at. Whether she could use him, and this, to her advantage.

He started walking, and she fell by his side. Islanders turned to stare as they passed and looked at her for just as long as they did Grim. She supposed she stood out in her red dress, so bright against the light blue, white, and silver the day-dwelling islanders wore. Like blood spattered in the marketplace. "You're curious again, Isla."

She didn't meet his gaze. "Don't read me. It's rude."

He laughed. "It's not like I can help it."

Isla gave him a look. "The famed, all-powerful Nightshade ruler can't control his own abilities?"

The corners of his lips turned deviously. "Famed? Well, at least I know rumors of my greatness have reached even the Wildlings." He looked down at her, and the smile faded. "I'm glad you are having armor made," he said, pulling something from his pocket. It was a sheet of gold foil, the same paper her Centennial invitation had arrived on. "My demonstration is first," he said, returning the card to his black cloak before she could make out the words. He leaned low, lips getting dangerously close to her ear. "You will also need a sword."

By the time Grim's words sank in and the chill from his proximity had disappeared—so had he.

And Isla was left alone in the market, wondering why the ruler of Nightshade was helping her.

CHAPTER SIX

BONDBREAKER

Isla threw the weapon at Celeste, who caught it in the air, in her power's invisible grip. "What is this?"

"A sword," Isla said, pulling her own from behind her spine, where she had smuggled them both into the castle. "And an expensive one, at that."

Celeste gave her a look. "I *know* what it is, Isla," she said. "What I'm wondering is why you've brought the ghastly thing into my quarters."

Isla had long ago learned that the Starling didn't have the same appreciation for weapons, though her realm was famous for making them with their proprietary techniques and metals. Why would she? Celeste had the power of energy at her fingertips—she could wound an enemy from across the room. In her eyes, a sword was a clunky misuse of iron.

Which, Isla imagined, was exactly why Grim had chosen a duel as his demonstration. Well, he hadn't said the word *duel,* but with his clues, he might as well have.

"Our first trial is a duel," she said. "We'll need these."

Celeste crinkled her nose as if she had smelled something foul. "And who told you that?"

"Grimshaw."

Celeste blinked. "Is that who you were with this whole time?"

"No, just for a bit. Why?"

Celeste gave her a look. "Really, Isla?" She didn't need to say anything else. Grim was bad news. Dangerous. Untrustworthy.

"I know, I *know.* But I got this information, didn't I? Don't you think he could be useful?"

Celeste shook her head firmly. "No, Isla. I think, if anything, he'll use *you.* Us."

Was that what their trip to the agora had been? Just strategy by the wicked Nightshade ruler?

Of course it was. It would be foolish to believe it to be anything else.

Isla started to wonder if Grim's heads-up was even accurate. Maybe it *wasn't* a duel, or any type of demonstration involving a sword, and he was just trying to fool her into thinking so.

She frowned.

Celeste sighed in a long-suffering way. She placed both of her delicate hands upon Isla's cheeks and said, "My lovely, lovely, *naive* friend." Isla would have balked if it had been anyone other than Celeste saying those words. But even though they were practically the same age, Isla had learned priceless lessons from the Starling. Celeste had taken her under her wing when she had no one other than Poppy and Terra. "You will stay away from him," she said steadily, a sister warning a misguided sibling who should know better.

Celeste was right. Grim was a distraction. She wouldn't be the fool who fell for his tricks. Especially when her own mother had died because of her affection toward a man.

Especially when she had made it her mission to prove she was more than the temptress her guardians had trained her to be.

The first step in Terra and Poppy's elaborate plan was to seduce the king. Steal his power by making him fall in love with her. Without this step, the rest of their strategy was useless. And Isla was willing to do many things to save her realm. But that wasn't one of them.

Luckily, her friend had thought of another way for Isla to get everything she wanted.

"Good. Now. Even though we haven't started the demonstrations, the sooner we start preparing for finding the bondbreaker, the better," Celeste said.

The bondbreaker. That was their plan. In a room full of manuscripts taken from Lightlark, Celeste had discovered a text speaking of an enchanted relic. A giant glass needle with two sharp points on either side that could break any bond that imprisoned a person and their family line—including curses.

But everything on Lightlark had a cost.

The bondbreaker's cost was blood. Enough to kill even a ruler. That was why, to their knowledge, it had never been used before. On Celeste's chamber floor, they had come up with a plan to split the cost between the two of them.

And hope it wouldn't kill them both.

According to the text, the bondbreaker was hidden deep within a library on Lightlark. They didn't know which one, and each isle had its own. So, they would have to search them all.

Celeste would search Star Isle's library first. Hopefully, it would be there. If not, the Starling would have to go to great lengths to procure the tool Isla would need to access the rest of the libraries.

And, with their tight timeline, Isla needed to operate under the assumption that she would have to.

The bondbreaker would only break *their* realms' curses, not the rest. They wouldn't win the prize of the power promised in the prophecy. But Isla didn't care. By breaking the curse of being born powerless, she would finally receive the Wildling ability that had been denied to her at birth. And her realm would be rid of its suffering.

She could return to the Wildling newland free at last—no need to hide in her room any longer. She could inject power back into the land and make it prosper once more. She would have the life of an immortal ruler, centuries to explore the world with Celeste.

Everything she wanted hinged on finding the bondbreaker and its ability to break all the curses that affected her and her realm.

"I'll start tonight," Isla said.

To secretly search the libraries on Sun Isle, Moon Isle, and Sky Isle, Isla would need to blend in.

Her dark hair would be the first giveaway to her identity. But she had arrived prepared. Before leaving for the Centennial, she had sneaked into Poppy's quarters. Wildling elixirs ranged from healing remedies to enchantments to beauty products. Creams that tinted one's lips, or cheeks, or even, temporarily, *hair.*

She would have to mix the right color herself, which would be its own challenge, but at least she had the materials.

Clothing was the other problem.

Far past midnight, she crept out of the castle. She committed landmarks along the way to memory. The abbey with a giant single stained-glass eye. The insignia she had arrived upon just days before. A pile of ruins that she liked to think might have once been a lighthouse, powered by Sunling beams. She had read about those in one of the few books she was allowed a year.

Terra learned early on that she liked to read. So, she used books as incentives. If Isla didn't complain about her split knuckles or sore muscles during training, if she mastered a certain fighting technique, if she threw her throwing stars right at their marks, she was rewarded with a trip to the library.

Isla cherished them, wrote her favorite lines down on paper. Felt pangs of grief when she was forced to give them away in exchange for another.

Only one book at a time, her guardian told her. *Don't be greedy.*

She stopped just short of the agora, surprise making her still.

The marketplace transformed when the sun went down. Most shops were closed, their windows dark, but the ones that were open were . . . *open.* Just as the Wildling Eldress had described.

Somehow, some of the stores had been turned inside out, their walls completely folding out into the streets, no doors to be seen, the ceiling stretched out and wide like a fan. Patrons walked freely inside pubs and, moments later, out, holding foaming, overflowing drinks. Skylings danced in the middle of the road to music that spilled into the night, drums and guitar and voices that forced the darkness to obey its wild rhythm. Sunlings were specks of gold everywhere, enjoying the hours they could be outside.

The agora was lively, disorienting, but Isla remembered the roads from earlier. She took a back way, choosing alleys instead of main streets, following the lines of lit torches until she ended up at the back door of the tailor.

Every light was off. Every window was locked.

When she was sure there was no other way inside, she got on her knees and pulled out her pins. On one trip to the Skyling newland with her starstick, she had trailed a group of thieves, curious. She had watched from the shadows as they used pins and curved needles to work their way into a lock.

A useful skill for breaking into Poppy's and Terra's rooms later. For breaking out of her own room too.

The door popped open, and Isla gathered her tools, careful not to leave anything behind. She squinted through the darkness, not daring to turn any of the lights on. A tailor wasn't typically a place prone to robbery, therefore guards wouldn't be focusing on this street, but who knew how long it would take someone to stumble into the alley and see her through the window?

Quickly. Her eyes zeroed in on the colors she needed—every Lightlark realm's hues other than Starling, which Celeste would take care of.

White. She grabbed a simple long-sleeved and high-necked Moonling dress.

Light blue. She took a dress with pants that were supposed to be worn underneath, a fashion she had seen a few Skylings in the market wearing.

Gold.

There was no gold. Come to think of it, she didn't remember seeing the color in the store during her appointment.

Did Sunlings not use the same tailor as the rest of the realms?

Why not?

A voice at the window sent her to the floor. Two friends were leaning against the store, laughing merrily, clinking glasses together. She crawled to the wall and put her back against it, determined not to make a sound.

Half an hour passed before the men moved along, and Isla was gone moments later, careful to close the door on her way out, hoping the tailor would assume he left it unlocked by mistake.

With an armful of silk, she returned to the castle, one step closer to the bondbreaker.

CHAPTER SEVEN

DUEL

On the fifth day of the Centennial, the invitation to the first demonstration arrived. The paper was charred, black, burned. Only a few words were visible, carved into the page with a knife.

Be ready to duel.

Isla couldn't help but smile. Grim *had* helped her.

But why?

The time of the event was scrawled at the bottom—in one hour. Instead of having to scramble for a weapon, Isla had already purchased the ideal sword. One that was light enough for her to wield almost weightlessly, but sharp and firm enough to strike true. It had taken hours to choose the right one in the Starling weapons shop. The realm's metalwork really was unparalleled . . . though she longed for the familiar feel of one of her own blades from home.

The tailor's wardrobe had arrived the day before. The man worked at a remarkable speed. His commitment to his craft only made Isla feel worse about stealing from him.

By finding the bondbreaker, I'm saving him and his realm, Isla convinced herself to counteract the guilt.

One gown was the dark blue of sapphires, with crystal-shaped shards cut out of its sides. One was the purple of fresh lavender with an eye-rollingly low-cut bodice and skintight pants, finished with a glittering cape that tied around her waist, creating the illusion of a skirt. One, the green of emeralds, was tight and light and sheer enough to make her blush. Another, she discovered, had pockets.

For this demonstration, she wore the armor. Ella helped tie the many pieces together, grunting as she lifted the metal.

To Isla, it was a second skin. Terra had made sure of that.

How many times had she been left abandoned in the middle of the woods, or in the center of a rain forest storm, with fifty pounds of chain mail and armor on her? Getting back took more than a day. Without water, without food, with the howls of wolves and patter of panthers at her heels.

The last half mile was always done on her stomach as she dragged herself back to her room, nails digging into roots and dirt for purchase.

In comparison, the smartly made Starling fabric and thin sheets of iron were nearly weightless. They had been fashioned into parts that accentuated her figure while also protecting it—metal shoulder pads, chain mail sleeves and tights, metal-plated boots that ran up to the top of her thigh, a sculpted breastplate.

"Done," Ella said, slumping over after the last of Isla's outfit was assembled.

"Thank you," Isla said before taking a bite of the vegetable skewer and grains Ella had brought her for lunch. In exchange for the healing elixir, the Starling girl brought Isla regular meals, believing them to be indulgences, in addition to the hearts she planned to secretly throw off her balcony. "For *everything*."

Ella bowed her head and gently tapped at her leg. She walked almost evenly now, and her brow wasn't set in its constant tension at the pain. "Thank *you*," she said.

The duel took place at an arena in the farthest reach of the castle, one that used to be open but had been covered with a dome after the curses. It made the crowd's cheers echo and braid together, forming a single taunting voice from a thousand mouths. Rulers controlled many

variables about their trials—what it would test, where it would take place, if there would be any advance notice, and who was allowed to witness it. Grim had invited all islanders. They sat separated by realm, filling every seat, rows lined by dozens of lit torches. Starling in their glittering silver. Skyling in their bright blue. Moonling in their immaculate white. Sunling in their polished gold.

Demonstrations were a spectacle. She knew that. Meant to test different skills. Meant to manipulate favor. Meant to decide who deserved to die.

Or, at the very least, who would determine the teams they would break into, which would, in some way or another, change the course of the Centennial by forcing alliances.

Each trial was also a risk. Though killing was not permitted until after the fiftieth day, Isla's own ancestor had lost one of her hands during a demonstration. It had weakened her ability to wield power significantly, and she was forced to have a child after the Centennial ended, as a better representative for the next one.

Grim's voice rumbled through the applause, silencing the room.

"Welcome to my demonstration," he said, somewhere. She couldn't place him—it was as if his voice was coming from everywhere at once. "You are all very menacing *with* your endless powers . . . but how will you fare without them?"

He announced the first pair—Oro against Azul.

The king's sword was made of solid gold to match his priceless armor. Isla wondered if the duel would end up embarrassing the king in front of his people, and the thought nearly made her smile. She had never heard anything of the king's fighting abilities in her years of lessons, which might mean he relied heavily on his fire instead.

Azul's own weapon was covered in precious jewels, sapphires mixed with diamonds. He didn't wear armor at all; much of his chest was exposed. But he *did* wear the ring she had gifted him. Was he so good he didn't require protection?

Both of Isla's assessments were wrong.

The duel finished within seconds. The king struck so quickly, she almost missed it. One moment, the tip of his sword was dug into the gravel of the arena—the next, it was at the Skyling's throat.

Azul only smiled graciously and bowed, admitting defeat.

Sunlings were on their feet, roaring in approval, waving long lengths of golden fabric above their heads.

Celeste and Cleo were next.

Isla's manicured nails dug into her palm, watching her friend enter the arena. The Moonling wore a serpentine grin. She didn't wear armor either, but she had opted for pants. Her weapon was long and thin like an ice pick.

Celeste held her sword steadily. Isla had chosen a lighter one for her friend, one that would be easy to maneuver by someone who didn't have extensive training. Her silver hair was plaited, stuck firmly to her scalp.

At the bell, Cleo lunged—

"Nervous, Hearteater?"

Grim's voice was at her ear. She didn't dare take her eyes off the action. Cleo had missed Celeste's arm by inches, and her friend had just unsuccessfully struck back.

"Don't call me that," she said quietly, wincing as Celeste nearly tripped right into Cleo's blade.

It was like she could hear the grin in Grim's words as he said, "Is that the thanks I get for my help?"

She spared him a quick withering look, retort on her tongue, and—

Froze. Grim was a fearsome warrior. He wore a helmet of spikes like daggers that shot from the crown of his skull. One dipped between his eyes, shielding his nose. His shoulders had the same sharp metal points that ran down the lengths of his arms, spikes everywhere.

He was a demon, death itself.

She swallowed. He watched the movement, staring at her neck far too intently, before almost absentmindedly baring his teeth,

like he wanted to bite her there. Her skin inexplicably prickled at the thought.

No, that's disgusting. Isla forced herself to get it together. He didn't want to bite her. That was just in her head.

Why was that in her head?

The ringing of a bell tore her attention away, back to the arena.

Celeste's sword was on the ground. Cleo's blade was tapping recklessly against the Starling's heart. Then, it too dropped to the floor.

Relief washed over her. Celeste had lost, but that didn't matter. They both planned to perform adequately. Not badly enough to be marked as weak, but not strong enough to be chosen as a partner. While they couldn't control the pairings that would be decided on the twenty-fifth day unless they won the most trials—which would instantly identify them as competition to be potentially eliminated—they were relying on the fact that whoever *did* win would pair the youngest, most inexperienced rulers together. It would be the smartest choice, they reasoned, tying the weakest links together as easy prey for the rest of the matches.

Don't draw too much attention to yourself, Celeste had warned.

"Our turn, Hearteater," Grim said before strolling past her into the ring.

Oh.

Somehow, Isla hadn't put together that *they* would be dueling. She had been too distracted by Celeste's battle.

She didn't move a muscle, watching the center of the arena as Grim reached behind him for a broadsword thicker than her thigh.

Her throat was suddenly too dry. Grim chose the matches. This was his demonstration. He must have paired them together for a reason.

A theory formed in her head, pieces coming together. They were the only two rulers without their people present. The two most hated. Did he purposefully match them to show his superiority over her? To make sure, from the very first demonstration, that the island rooted for *him* over her?

Celeste was right. She couldn't trust him.

"*Go,*" her friend whispered sharply, suddenly at her side.

Right. Isla stepped into the exposed center on legs that weren't as steady as they had been a few minutes before.

Not one person cheered. When Isla's sword knocked into the metal plating her long boots, feeling uncharacteristically off-kilter, the sound was projected through the silence.

Get yourself together, she told herself, thinking of her training. Of Terra.

The Nightshade might be plotting against her. All she could do was ensure his plan was foiled before it even began.

With a steadying breath, Isla drew her weapon and took her stance. It was second nature, like tumbling into sleep or taking a breath. The only time she ever felt like she had a whisper of power. Part of her still wanted to cower. But Isla knew how to handle a blade better than a quill.

The bell rang out, loud and clear.

Grim struck first.

Isla twirled to the side, fast as the wind. His blade met air. She pivoted on her heel and aimed for his chest.

Grim was too quick. He dodged the blow, then struck again, only for his blade to meet hers. Her arm shook for a moment from the sheer strength of it. Quickly, she regained her balance and slid her sword right down his, the metal against metal making her wince, slicing through the room.

His eyes widened in surprise as he shot backward, barely missing the tip of her blade.

See? Maybe you should have chosen a different opponent, she thought.

"You're feeling confident, Hearteater," Grim purred. He advanced, and she blocked his blow. Tried again, only to meet steel. For a few stumbling, dizzying seconds, their blades met over and over and over,

touching, skimming, clashing. Somehow, he was at her ear. "Tell me, how will you feel when you lose?"

She swallowed and whipped around—then ducked, air shooting out of her nostrils as he went for her neck. And barely missed. *Too close.*

She shot up and forward, one arm completely outstretched, the other tight behind her back. She was light as a dandelion on her feet but strong as the steel of her blade with every advance. It was a part of her, a fifth limb, a beautiful, gleaming thing. Each of her motions was faster than the last as she slipped into her rhythm, her flow. Her dance. She felt the room like she was barefoot, the air like it was electric. A growl sounded from the back of her throat as she pushed Grim farther down the arena, toward its wall, at the crowd sitting high above.

His mouth was a line as he focused; she could have sworn a bead of sweat shot down his temple.

"You're feeling surprised, *Grim,*" she said, her voice deep and raspy.

His eyes were fierce, no gleam in them anymore.

Isla grinned, spun fast as a maelstrom to gather more strength, and struck like a cobra—so hard that Grim stumbled, just the slightest bit.

It was all she needed. She leaped off the floor with a warrior's cry and landed right in front of him, pinning him to the wall.

Her blade was at his throat.

His clattered to the ground.

She was panting, right in his face. He was looking at her like he hadn't ever seen her before.

"Everyone seems to forget," she said, not breaking his gaze, even though it meant tilting her head. They were both panting, their chests flush with every breath. "That Wildlings are, above all, warriors." Isla might not have had powers. And she might have been trapped like a bird in a cage her entire life because of it. But she could fight as well as any ruler—Terra had made sure of that. She dropped the blade from his throat.

And there was clapping.

Isla whipped around, stunned by the sound, the only cheer in the room of hundreds.

The king. He was clapping for her.

Again.

She turned back to the Nightshade ruler, expecting him to hate her. But he was grinning, his eyes filled with something like delight.

He was *thrilled* that she had beaten him.

Which made no sense.

Her eyes narrowed at him, trying to read him. Never had anyone's motivations been more of a mystery.

What did Grim want?

What game was he playing?

Spurred by their king, a few claps sounded in the crowd, then spread like wildfire until everyone was cheering, celebrating her victory, the lesser of two evils overcoming the other.

Still confused, Isla made her way to the sidelines, only to find a concerned Celeste. Her friend couldn't say anything, not in front of the other rulers, but Isla knew she had made herself stand out too much. Her job was to skate by, mostly unnoticed, so they could hopefully be paired together.

The islanders and rulers were certainly noticing her now.

Cleo and Oro dueled next, as winners of their pairs. The Moonling put on an impressive display. In less than a minute, the king succeeded, however. But not before Cleo was able to tear a line down his arm. The skin flayed open. Blood stained the arena, sizzling. He did not make a move to heal himself before moving on to the next duel.

Part of Isla wondered how the Moonling dared wound the king. Nervous energy seemed to swirl through the arena, some of the islanders perhaps thinking the same thing.

Oro did not even bother leaving the ring. He stood, blade dug into the ground before him, hands resting on its hilt. Still bleeding. Staring at her. His final opponent.

His eyes were hollow. Emotionless.

She did not shy away from his lifeless gaze as she stepped back into the arena. This time, there was no applause for her. The crowd's loyalty had shifted as quickly and predictably as the tide.

A bell, somewhere.

Then a sword, slicing the air before her to pieces. She managed to get her own up in time, just barely, but the strength of the king's first blow echoed through her bones. She felt the force of it in her teeth.

A groan escaped her lips as she deepened her stance, digging in, absorbing the impact, shielding against his advance.

He kept pushing, and her back foot slid, compromising her posture. He was forcing her to make a move, to make herself vulnerable.

Did he think she was a fool?

She added a second hand along the hilt of her blade, then shoved back as hard as she could.

He did what she expected, pressing back in equal measure—

And she spun at the last moment, leaving him stumbling forward.

Isla was quicker on her feet, she knew that. It was her advantage.

But Oro was stronger. Even while wounded.

The king's sword found hers before she could truly recover, and Isla fought to keep up, mostly on the defense, blocking blow after blow after deafening blow. He knew his strength. His strategy was to tire her, to use up her energy on taking his hits instead of making her own. Until her arms gave out.

She almost smiled.

He didn't know that when Isla was twelve, Terra had left her hanging onto the branch of a tree, fifty feet above the ground, for five hours.

Fall, and you'll break your legs, she'd said. *They'll heal, but you won't be allowed to go on the tour of the newland if you're injured.*

She had been looking forward to her first tour of her lands for years.

The first hour wasn't so bad. She had been training for a while at that point. Her arms were strong.

By the third hour, she was screaming.

By the fourth, her voice gave out.

By the fifth, one of her shoulders had popped out of its socket.

She never let go.

But she wasn't allowed to go on the tour. A punishment for the screaming.

You take the pain like medicine, Terra had said in response to her tears. *You swallow it down with a smile.*

Then she popped Isla's shoulder back into place without medication. Another lesson.

The king would not be the one to wear her down.

Still—it was to her benefit for him to think he would. She slowed her movements slightly, bent her wrist just a degree. Angled her sword the way someone trying to shift its weight might.

He advanced faster in response, sensing her weakening.

She took a step back. Another, this time with a slight stumble.

He made his final, bold move.

And Isla unleashed the strength she had stored.

The king was caught off guard by the force of her blow. His blade shook with the impact. She advanced, seizing her chance, aiming everywhere. He was now forced to retreat, deflecting her hits, his brows coming together in focus.

She was going to win.

Her blade became a serpent, the one on her crown come to life, striking for the kill, fangs and all. Again, again, again, she pounced, nearly reaching his heart. Almost grazing his neck.

She leaped forward, ready for the final blow—

And hesitated.

Celeste was a silver reminder in the wings, right behind the king. She wasn't supposed to win the trial. This wasn't part of the plan.

Don't you want to be free? a voice in her head said. That was more important than her pride. Than winning. Than anything.

At the last moment, Isla aimed lower, to a place Oro would easily be able to deflect. When he did, she loosened her grip on her hilt.

So, when his sword struck, her own went flying across the stadium.

Cheers erupted, not only Sunlings, but every Lightlark realm getting to their feet. Honoring their king.

But he only watched Isla, eyes narrowing.

He *knew.*

Somehow, he knew she had let him win.

The tip of his sword eventually, half-heartedly, slid up her stomach, to her heart. Then away. But the king's gaze was relentless, studying her far too closely.

Isla shrank under it, folding herself over, bowing, recognizing defeat.

She retreated to the wings as Oro was crowned the winner of the demonstration.

Her eyes didn't meet his again. But she could feel his gaze on her, not lifeless any longer—but merciless as flames.

CHAPTER EIGHT
CELESTE

The first time Isla met Celeste, she'd felt relief. She had learned about the other rulers of realm her entire life. Four of them were terrifyingly old and skilled, alive when the curses were spun. The original heirs of the fallen rulers who had sacrificed themselves for the prophecy. Isla was no match against them, no matter how long and hard she trained. They were the stars of her nightmares, each of them killing her in her dreams a thousand times before the Centennial invitation had even arrived.

The Starling was a mystery. Young like Isla. Disadvantaged because she would have no Terra or Poppy, no one ancient and wise to guide her, thanks to their curse.

Still, Starlings were powerful.

She is your enemy, Terra would tell her. An informant had long ago announced to her guardians that the latest in the long string of Starling rulers was a girl. *One of you will lose.*

Terra convinced her that as the youngest two, they would be preyed upon to fulfill part of the prophecy. Only one of the two would live.

It must be you.

So, when Isla accidentally portaled her way directly into the Starling ruler's newland castle with her starstick, and the girl just looked at her and smiled, a weight was taken from her chest.

"I think the starstick knew I needed you," Isla would tell Celeste years later during one of their many secret sleepovers.

"And that *I* needed *you,*" Celeste replied, squeezing her hand tightly.

Not enemies—

Friends.

Sisters. That word did a much better job at encapsulating their bond, a relationship Isla could have never prepared for after a life alone. She loved Celeste more than anyone. Even her guardians.

It was only natural to tell the Starling her secret, three years after they met.

It was because of her love for her friend that she had been honest.

"I understand if you don't want to work together anymore," Isla had said. "Truly, Celeste. I would understand."

Celeste had held her tightly as they both cried. Knowing Isla's powerlessness complicated everything. Knowing there was a big possibility that the other rulers would find out during the Centennial, and Isla would die once the rest of the prophecy was fulfilled.

"No," the Starling whispered into Isla's shoulder after a long while. "We work together. Always." Taking her face into her hands, she looked right into Isla's eyes and made a promise. "I will protect you. We will walk away from the Centennial and into the rest of our very long lives together."

That was why Isla listened—or tried to. Celeste had put herself and her entire realm in danger, forming an alliance with her.

And Isla might have already ruined it.

"I'm sorry," she said, looking at the floor of Celeste's room. It was past midnight, so no one would hear their whispers. They had barely seen each other, knowing being caught visiting each other's rooms would mean the end of their secret plan.

But tonight, Isla had taken the risk.

Celeste shook her head. Sighed. She was braiding her silver hair just to do something with her hands. Her friend often busied herself when she was anxious. Before the Centennial, Celeste had made a blanket with her stress, knitting for hours on end, until Isla had finally hidden the needles. "We can't mend what is done," she said simply.

Silence spread, and it always made Isla uncomfortable. She filled it with excuses. "I mean, was I just supposed to lose against Grim? I couldn't. That's what he *wanted.*" Though his grin at being defeated hinted otherwise . . .

She had no idea what he wanted.

Celeste gave her a look. "You weren't supposed to make yourself a target."

Isla didn't know why she rolled her eyes, but she did, suddenly annoyed.

That was when the Starling stood. Energy crackled in the room, a sure sign that she was angry. "You need to think long term," she said sharply, hands in fists at her sides. "Islanders were watching. All the rulers were watching. You beat *Grimshaw.* You nearly beat the king. Do you mean to make enemies, Isla? Do you mean to become someone the other rulers want to *get rid of?*"

Isla looked away. "Of course not."

"Then you need to *listen.* We have a plan. Complete the demonstrations without notice. Be the young, inexperienced rulers they already see us as, so the winner of the demonstrations hopefully pairs us up. That allows us to search for the bondbreaker, to work together, without having to hide our alliance." Isla was surprised when Celeste's voice broke. She had only seen the Starling cry a handful of times before. "It allows me to spend time with *you* without making anyone suspicious. To protect you." A silver tear shot down her cheek. She took a shaking breath as Isla made her way to her friend, instantly ashamed. "I can't protect you if you won't listen."

Isla threw her arms around Celeste, holding her close.

The truth was, if the Starling ruler only wanted to survive and save her realm, she would have abandoned Isla. She knew her secret, after all. It would be easy to share it with everyone else. To guarantee Wildling would die, over Starling, when the time came to choose a ruler and realm to sacrifice.

But she hadn't. Because they were sisters.

Celeste was a better friend than she deserved.

"I'm sorry," Isla said. "I promise, I'll think of the plan. I promise to listen."

Later, Celeste told Isla that she had searched the Star Isle library.

"It wasn't there," she said. One library off their list.

A pang of disappointment rattled through Isla's stomach. Their plan would have been far easier if the bondbreaker had ended up being a Starling relic.

"I'm going after the gloves next," she said.

Isla's head jerked up. She met Celeste's eyes.

"Don't look at me like that," she said quietly. "Like you didn't know this was next." She dipped her chin. "Like this wasn't *your* idea."

Of course Isla knew this part of their plan was next. If the bondbreaker wasn't in the Star Isle library, they would need a way to get into the protected sections of the other isles' collections.

The gloves were crucial to getting inside them.

This particular type of enchanted accessory was well-known throughout even the newlands—gloves that were able to harness a whisper of a realm's power. Isla had researched them obsessively, believing they could help her during the Centennial. All she would have to do was capture a bit of Poppy's or Terra's ability to wield nature and use them to pretend . . .

Unfortunately, the gloves were dangerous to procure. It was said they were made of skinned human flesh. Only dark markets in the newlands would dare sell such a thing—and Isla had searched nearly all of them.

They were rarer nowadays. Not regularly made. Doing so wasn't typically worth the hassle. The power they held was minimal. Inconsequential.

Unless someone found a very specific use for them.

Isla had suggested the gloves when they needed a way to get into the libraries, as a last resort.

"You look ill, Isla," Celeste said, frowning at her.

She swallowed. "How are you going to get a pair?"

Her friend studied her. Sighed. "Don't ask questions you don't want answers to."

Perhaps she *would* be ill. "If you have to make new ones, go to the prison. Pick a killer, someone terrible—"

Celeste grabbed Isla's shoulders almost painfully, bringing her back into the moment, steadying her. "This is my part of our plan," she said. "Focus on yours."

Right. Hers. Isla had volunteered to search the other three libraries. Once they had the gloves, her role would truly begin. "Speaking of my role . . ." she said. It was her turn to share her bad news about not being able to secure the Sunling clothing.

Celeste's brows folded together. "That's strange . . ." She pursed her lips. "Though, on Star Isle, the nobles *did* tell me suspicious things have been happening since the last Centennial. Sunling has separated itself more than ever from the other realms. They stay mostly on their own isle."

"Do you think the king is behind it?"

Celeste frowned. "I'm not sure. But I don't trust him at all."

Neither did Isla. Even if he had saved her the first day of the Centennial. After their duel, she was willing to bet he didn't trust her either.

"That's not the only thing," Celeste said, and Isla braced herself for an added obstacle. "Moonling has also been acting oddly. My nobles said they have guards on their bridge every day. *All* day."

Isla cursed. How was she supposed to sneak onto Moon Isle and search its library with guards at its entrance?

She was allowed to enter, but her movements would surely be shared with Cleo.

Who would immediately become suspicious.

"Did you check?" Isla asked.

Celeste nodded. Her friend was always thorough. "I went for a stroll along that part of the isle and confirmed it. Two guards, right at the front, checking everyone in."

Two Moonlings would not stand between them and their plan.

"I'll find a way," Isla said, eager to help after her display at the duel.

And hoping it wasn't just one more promise she couldn't keep.

CHAPTER NINE

CROWN

Thankfully for Isla, the rulers did not dine together every meal. Some nights, Celeste, Azul, Cleo, and Oro ate on their isles. Others, they ate separately in their chambers. Group dinners were preceded by an invitation and were awkward affairs, for Isla especially, since she would sit with an empty plate in front of her. Ever since their first dinner, eight days ago now, the king had honored her request to eat in her room. Wildlings only needed a heart or two a month to survive, yet weekly hearts were to be provided—and quickly disposed of in secret.

Cleo's constant insults also made dinners uncomfortable. The Moonling had made her distaste for her well-known, ever since that first meal when Isla had foolishly bitten back. She had regretted it ever since, especially when Celeste's eyes would meet hers, a reminder of why it was important to stay under the radar.

Unnoticed. Unremarkable.

Isla was about to enter the dining room for one of these group dinners when she stopped suddenly.

There were too many voices inside. Dozens.

The doors opened by someone else's hands, revealing a room filled with nobles from every Lightlark realm. Many turned to watch Isla, fear and curiosity in a battle across their features, studying her as carefully and critically as a jeweler searching for flaws in a diamond.

Every one of Poppy's lessons pummeled into her head at once.

Back straight.

Chin up.

Shoulders down.

Look right ahead—pay them no mind.

Fingers relaxed at your sides.

This was clearly a demonstration. Whoever had planned it had decided only to invite Lightlark's nobles.

No invitation had preceded it. There were often surprises during the Centennial. *You must be prepared for anything,* Terra had told her.

Demonstrations were opportunities for the rulers to assess each other. To decide who was weak. To potentially win the power to choose the pairs that would work the remainder of the Centennial to figure out the prophecy.

Isla racked her head for what kind of trial this could be. Her guardians had a list of demonstrations from past Centennials. Some were more elaborate than others. Quests. Challenges to tame a wild beast. Scavenger hunts, even. Tests of physical strength, or strategy, or the mind.

There weren't any clues around her. All she saw were tables set with wineglasses and crystal plates.

It really did look like a dinner. Her nerves curbed a bit. Perhaps it *was* just a meal and the nobles were simply invited as guests.

They had seen her during the first trial, from a distance. And she had clearly caught their attention. Some of them looked too long at the parts of her dress that hugged her body. Others watched her like she might be getting ready to shed her clothes or burst into flames. A few backed away, eyes trained on her mouth and fingers, as if half expecting to see claws.

She was a temptress. A monster who subsisted on the hearts of easily seduced prey.

They thought they knew her.

They knew nothing.

A few people gasped as Grim appeared beside her from thin air, making himself visible. His expression did not change.

The people who weren't watching her before were certainly looking now. The temptress and the ruler of darkness. A winning pair.

"Grim," she said curtly, avoiding meeting his gaze. Remembering she knew nothing about him or what he was after.

"Hearteater," he whispered, so only she could hear it. His eyes dipped, studying every inch of her new crimson dress. The two thin straps. The simple scrap of silk of a bodice. Her waist, where the dress cinched tightly before tumbling into more sheets of fabric that clung to her body. Gloves to her elbows, which she rarely wore but had opted for, if only for a bit more coverage, the same color and material as her dress.

He looked shamelessly, eagerly, like it was important to commit every inch to memory. She had never been studied so thoroughly.

Did he mean to embarrass her?

Or seduce the seductress?

His dark eyes seemed to get even darker as they met hers, and he said, "I'm not sure what I enjoy more. Seeing the way you grip a sword . . . or the way your dress grips you."

If looks could kill, the Nightshade would be dead, and Isla would have broken the first rule of the Centennial. Grim's lips formed a devious smile in response to her glare.

She took a step toward him, emboldened. She still wasn't sure what game Grim was playing, but she *did* know he enjoyed it when she bit back.

"And I don't know what *I* enjoy more. Replaying the image of my sword against your throat . . . or thinking about how your heart might look on my plate."

Grim's dark eyes flashed with amusement. "Careful, Hearteater," he whispered, towering over her, standing far too close. "I might just give it to you."

For the last few moments, it might as well have been just her and Grim in the room.

Applause brought her back into the crowd. Isla turned to see that Azul had positioned himself at the head of a table already filled with the other rulers. "Welcome," he said. "If you could all make your way to your seats, we'll get started."

Isla rushed to the table, grateful for an excuse to put some distance between her and the Nightshade. Though the only two remaining seats were next to each other. Perfect.

It was clear this *was* a demonstration, not an elaborate dinner event, even though food was being brought out by dozens of staff. Her mind began spinning possibilities. She was alert, studying every detail, mentally preparing herself for whatever trial she might face.

The nobles had settled in their seats. Isla studied the suits and dresses, all made from dazzling fabrics. The tailor must have been busy in the prior months. She wondered if he had noticed his two missing pieces yet.

But the shop had hundreds of clothes . . . it would be nearly impossible to take inventory each day.

Then again, the tailor seemed deeply committed to his profession. Perhaps he *had* noticed. Would he report the theft?

Would he suspect the Wildling who had been in his shop that same morning of being the culprit?

"Let us begin," Azul said heartily, smiling widely. The Skyling ruler had the most perfect, shining teeth she had ever seen. Tonight, he wore robes with triangle cuts along the sides, revealing markings painted across his dark skin, symbols she didn't recognize. Some Wildlings inked themselves with needles and paint after their training or honorable feats. Isla was never allowed. Her body did not belong solely to her, Poppy said. It belonged to the realm. She was its representative, its lifeline. Even after having been born so wrong.

"Tonight, I would like to celebrate the tremendous abilities that will allow us to succeed in shattering our curses," Azul said. "Rulers of realm, would you honor us with a demonstration of your power?"

Isla almost dropped the goblet of water in her hand she had absentmindedly reached for.

Grim's eyes were on her cup. Her fingers were shaking against the stem, water rippling inside her glass. If she thought her legs would be steady beneath her, she might have run right out of the room.

She had no powers to demonstrate.

Grim—he could make the lights go out. He could make her disappear, or at least cause a diversion. If she asked, he would. He would love the chance to cause chaos. And, though his intentions were murky, he had helped her before.

But then she would have to explain why. She swallowed, weighing the risks.

Before she could say a word, Azul said, "Grim. We haven't had a Nightshade on our island for centuries." His voice was tight. Untrusting. "Would you go first?"

Grim stayed seated for a few moments, and Isla wondered what would happen if he simply ignored the ruler of Skyling. Finally, he stood.

He opened his palm.

The room changed. Suddenly, there were a hundred Grims, standing between each chair. All smirking. The ceiling cracked open, the floor split, large slabs of stone fell right onto their heads, screams pierced the air—

Everything disappeared. The room was back to normal. There was just one Grim, looking bored, as if the display hadn't used even a whisper of his power.

The room was silent. Someone dropped a glass.

Nightshades had mind abilities, Isla knew. But this was more, a vision on a grand scale.

How dangerous would that skill be in war?

Or *now,* in this game?

She looked over at the king. Oro watched Grim with hard eyes, like his display was a threat. A declaration of exactly what he was capable of.

“Cleo, if you would,” Azul said, a bit less excitedly.

She had to come up with something. Quickly.

Terra and Poppy had prepared her for this very possibility. But *their* complicated plan had hinged on her already having gotten close to the king and stolen one of the enchantments he supposedly had in his personal collection, a Wildling flower able to multiply and live forever. She’d had specific directions to get it as soon as possible.

Something she had completely forgotten about, in favor of her and Celeste’s plan.

She hadn’t even spoken to the king directly since that first dinner, avoiding him as much as possible. Perhaps *too* much, in blatant defiance of the first degrading step of her guardians’ strategy.

Now, what would she do?

Admit her secret not only to all the nobles, but to the rulers as well?

She might as well count herself dead the second the clock chimed midnight on the fiftieth day. Not even Celeste could protect her from all the rulers. She had admitted as much.

Celeste. Isla finally looked at the Starling ruler, who was staring her down, clearly trying to get her attention for a while.

Her expression was strained, eyes wide in worry.

Isla was a burden. Always needing to be looked after. Cared for.

She didn’t know why, but she smiled back, easily, nodding her chin slightly as if to say, *Not to worry, I have a plan.*

Though she never had her own plan, did she? She’d only ever gone along with others’ strategies. Never her own. Not really.

Cleo was in front of their table now. Her arms lifted dramatically.

Wine red as blood shot up from every goblet, into the center of the room. She moved her hands as if petting a wild beast, and from the wine emerged a massive shark with three rows of teeth. It rushed at the crowd, falling from the sky, its monstrous jaw coming apart—but before it could reach Cleo, her hand made a fist, and the shark froze

into ice. Its teeth became mauve icicles that landed in a perfect circle around the Moonling, digging deep into the floor. The rest became a dizzying steam.

Applause rang through the room, the nobles not looking upset in the slightest that their goblets now sat empty. Cleo looked very smug as she walked back to the table.

"Celeste?"

The Starling slowly stood, shoulders tense. Isla knew her friend wasn't nervous, at least not for her *own* demonstration. She walked carefully to the front, hair shimmering below the chandelier flames. Celeste raised a finger to the air.

And the room exploded.

Fireworks burst from every corner, silvery sparks showering down like miniature shooting stars. They screeched and roared, flying through the room, before shattering against the walls into silvery specks.

The crowd cooed, some reaching up to touch the stardust that fell like confetti, draping the tables in glitter. Some of it landed in Isla's hair.

It was beautiful.

Isla's stomach lurched, waiting for her name to be called. She needed a plan . . . a way out—

"My turn, I suppose," Azul said, smiling good-naturedly.

The Skyling stood with grace, his cape curling behind him in a self-created breeze. He spun his wrist toward the ceiling, and the air began to ripple. Three clouds like spun sugar appeared, growing wider and wider, until their corners touched. They darkened, then lit with flashes of light—storm clouds. Thunder echoed through the room, before the clouds calmed and became white as parchment. The audience looked up in wonder as they floated down toward their heads. Their fingers went right through them. When the clouds reached their table, even Isla reached a gloved hand up, trying hard to smile while dread boiled in her stomach.

She needed to think . . . she needed help . . .

Azul took a deep breath and blew with so much force that everyone's hair flew back, their capes cracking behind their chairs. And the clouds were no more.

The Skyling turned toward her and grinned.

Now there was no doubt.

Isla's heart was a drum in her chest as Azul spoke her name.

Powerless, powerless, powerless—the word was a chant, a taunt, so loud in her head, she wondered how no one else could hear it.

Compared to all the other rulers' demonstrations, she felt as useless and unremarkable as a piece of coal among diamonds. But she still had to pretend for a few more weeks—long enough to find the bondbreaker.

Celeste couldn't help her. Her guardians couldn't help her. Grim couldn't help her.

She had to find her strength.

Isla stood, feeling eyes on her like stage lights. Nobles whispered, disgust and fear clear on their well-powdered faces. She pressed her lips together, her plan a roughly made puzzle still forming in her head, then smiled, trying to look confident, though her knees trembled beneath her dress.

"King? Would you assist me in my demonstration?"

Oro blinked at her. Now, in his nearly always lifeless eyes, she read many things. Curiosity. Irritation. Perhaps even worry. All of it gone in an instant. He was expressionless by the time he stood, towering over her, offering his hand.

It was foolish garnering his attention after their duel, after he had looked so suspicious of her actions. But being bold was the only way she was going to get through this demonstration without having everyone question her and her abilities.

She led the king to the front of the table, her grip too tight on his hand, a sign of her nerves. "Stand there," she ordered. Then, trying not to look at the faces that showed their outrage at her audacity at commanding the king, that were as hungry for her to fail as they were

for the red meat on their plates, she walked to the opposite side of the room.

Slowly, willing her fingers not to shake, she shed her many rings, placing them on the nearest table, before a Sunling who gasped at the wealth piled in front of him. She took her gloves off and kept one clenched in her hand. With the other hand, she pulled a pin from her hair.

Not any ordinary pin. A throwing star, disguised to look like an accessory.

The room was silent, so Cleo's voice carried as she said, "I didn't realize you came to dinners *armed,* Wildling."

Isla lifted her chin slightly, taking the cool metal into her palm. "I'm always armed," she said.

She could have sworn she heard someone near her gulp.

Oro did not make a move, standing still before her, yards away. She did not break his gaze as she took the throwing star between her teeth. And tied her remaining glove over her eyes.

The crowd gasped, but she couldn't see their expressions anymore. She couldn't see anything behind the dark-red fabric.

She took the star from between her lips and put it between her fingers, its deadly sharp points digging into her skin.

Isla breathed in, slowly, as Terra's lessons ran through her mind.

Be still, child.

Do not be easily troubled.

You are a warrior.

Let them fear you.

Let them see what it means to be wild.

The star flew.

Isla heard the unmistakable clang of metal against metal as it found its mark.

She lifted the fabric from her eyes—and couldn't help but smirk as she saw Oro, king of Lightlark, still glued in place, his gaze not on her but on the crown she had knocked from his golden head.

It clattered loudly on the ground before settling, echoing through the silent room.

Isla sauntered over to Oro, forgetting her rings. His eyes finally went to hers. She couldn't read him in that moment and didn't try to. Instead, she bent down and picked up his crown.

"You dropped this," she whispered before handing it over and taking her seat once more.

She hadn't used a drop of power in her demonstration. But no one questioned her, shocked at her nerve. Outraged.

And for just a slice of a second, she felt like the most powerful ruler in the room.

Oro was the last ruler to perform.

Isla expected fire. A raging inferno from his hand.

Instead, the king stood, placed a palm on the table—

And the stone turned to gold. It happened in waves. The metal overtook the marble, then dripped down the side and smothered the floor. In seconds, it was all gilded.

An impossible power. Thousands of years ago, it was said Starlings could make diamonds. Wildlings could make emeralds and rubies grow in their palms like flowers.

Sunlings could turn goblets to gold.

It represented a complete mastery of power.

Could he turn a person to gold? Kill them by gilding them?

Rulers decided how their trial would be judged. Azul announced that the nobles would be voting for the winner, with the caveat that they could not vote for their own realm. As if that made it fair.

It was no surprise the king won, again. He *deserved* to, Isla had to admit, with a display that had rendered them all speechless.

Even the Sunling nobles looked shocked. They had clearly never seen Oro use this power before.

Which only made Isla wonder what else the king was keeping secret.

CHAPTER TEN

JUNIPER

The night tasted of salt. Wind blew the scent of the sea up and over the cliffs and trees, to where Isla crouched, on the outskirts of the agora.

Patterns formed for the patient, Isla knew, and she had learned to be a very special brand of persistent while trapped within her glass castle. It had been five days since Azul's demonstration. Celeste was busy sourcing the gloves. No other trials had been announced. So Isla had focused on her part of their plan. She had visited the agora almost every night, watching. Waiting.

She knew the nobles who frequented a storefront that sold art during the day but turned into a secret brothel past midnight. She knew the shops that had back entrances and exactly what time they truly closed. She counted the number of songs the band played before packing up for the night—always fourteen—and noted the members who would go to a bar before setting off for home.

The important information was gleaned when the Sunlings were long gone, lest they burst into flames with the rising sun. When the first rosy hint of day coated the horizon and the only people left in the marketplace were too full of drink to notice her, she would walk the back streets, paying attention. Listening.

That was how she learned about the barkeep.

The man locked his door for the night with a key he kept in the pocket of his immaculately pressed light-blue pants. There was a strange rhythm to the jingle of his lock—it took five turns to get it right.

He turned around and startled.

Isla sat on an unsteady stool, hands clasped in front of her. The place reeked of alcohol. Sharp, pure, concentrated liquor. She had never tried a sip, thanks to Poppy and Terra, but she knew the smell well.

Your head is already in the clouds, they said. *No need to cloud it even more.*

"It seems business is booming," she said, motioning at the dozens of empty glasses left discarded on the tables, the leftovers from a euphoric night.

The barkeep grinned, making his strangely shaped mustache curl upward on either side. "Well, the years haven't been kind. But bad times are good for business."

Isla wasn't wearing her crown, or any of her brighter colors, but the barkeep stared at her eyes. "You know who I am, then," she said.

The Skyling's gaze remained fixed upon her as he made his way to the other side of the bar. He uncorked a bottle, poured it directly into a glass, and took a sip of the honey-colored substance, eyes never leaving hers. "Of course I do, Wildling. The question is . . . do you know who I am?"

Isla had watched countless islanders walk in and out of this bar, too quickly to have had a good time, without any drink in their hands. Some left without smelling of alcohol at all. She had followed some of them, brushed past them, seen there was nothing new in their pockets. Which meant the barkeep was selling something other than liquor. Something invisible, yet priceless. Gossip on the street had all but confirmed it.

"You're the person islanders come to for information."

The Skyling pursed his lips, considering. Finally, he put his drink down and bowed. "Juniper, at your service."

"What is your price?" she asked. She had arrived prepared. Without waiting for him to answer, she dropped a handful of precious gems on the counter, next to a large pile of coin. Ready to pay whatever she needed to for the right information.

Juniper looked at the display and grinned. "I require a different sort of payment . . ." he said.

Her breath hitched. What was he implying?

He must have seen her tense, because he added, "I deal in secrets, dear."

"Secrets?"

Juniper nodded. "Give me one of yours . . . and I would be happy to provide you with any information you require."

The mention of secrets made her blood go cold. Her secrets would mean death. Isla straightened her spine. "I have none," she said steadily.

Juniper only smiled. "We both know *that's* not true."

She swallowed. What exactly *did* he know?

Panic rose in her chest, bile up her throat.

Part of her wanted to flee.

But to get into the Moon Isle library, Isla needed information. She took a steady breath and, before she could stop herself, said, "I let the king win during the first demonstration. I could have bested him—but didn't."

Juniper took a deep breath, as if the secret invigorated him, then said, "That will do. What is it you wish to know, Ruler?"

Isla leaned in so she could whisper and he would hear her. "How do I get past the guards on Moon Isle?"

He put a finger against his lip, considering. "There are no guards during the full moon, when the Moonling curse is at its strongest. All Moonlings retreat to the safety of their castle then."

Good. "And when is the next full moon?"

Juniper answered immediately, as if he'd known that would be her next question. "The twentieth day of the Centennial."

That was in a week.

She nodded. "Thank you." Part of her wanted to ask about all the remaining libraries. Where they were. Tips on getting inside them.

But she couldn't trust the barkeep with any more of their plan. Doing so would be foolish. Dangerous.

Isla turned to go.

"Oh, and, Wildling?" Juniper said, thrumming his fingers against the bar.

She froze. Looked back at him over her shoulder.

"The tailor is missing clothing. *You* wouldn't know anything about that, would you?"

Isla's stomach twisted into a braid. But her face revealed nothing. Poppy's training ensured her emotions were always left off her face.

This was a game. For *all* of them. The islanders' lives were also at risk. She needed to remember that. Needed to remind herself she couldn't trust anyone. Especially not Juniper.

She grinned. "A secret for another time," she said before leaving through the back door.

CHAPTER ELEVEN

FEAR

The tailor knew his clothes were missing. It was more important than ever for them to find the bondbreaker before any of the rulers learned of the robbery and became suspicious.

A problem—she couldn't begin her search of the libraries until after Celeste's demonstration. It would provide them with the final thing Isla needed to locate the bondbreaker.

Luckily, the Starling's crisp gold letter from Oro arrived the very next morning. A ruler had the right to choose the time their trial took place, as long as it was within two days of receiving their paper.

Celeste chose to host hers immediately.

When Ella knocked upon Isla's door, she took her time answering it, as if she wasn't already dressed in the perfect attire for the next trial. As if she hadn't been running scenarios through her head for the last few hours. As if she hadn't coincidentally requested her meal to be delivered early.

The paper she was handed was silver, sparkling. The words were made in Celeste's perfect cursive.

A test of fear, it read.

Location: The Hall of Glass

Time: Now

Isla followed Ella through the Mainland castle. She had never been to this wing before, a part that looked ancient, nearly untouched for hundreds of years.

The walls were covered in paintings. Portraits. Sunling leaders.

She saw what had to be Oro's predecessor, his brother, King Egan. He had ruled for centuries before sacrificing himself on the night of the curses. Isla recognized the same golden hair. A similar set in their brows.

King Egan, however, had lively eyes. A glimmer of joy in them.

Nothing like his brother.

Isla wondered if Oro had always been the way he was now . . . or if five hundred years of curses had taken their toll on the king.

The Hall of Glass was frosted over, sunlight choked and muted, a protection for Sunlings. She wondered if Oro ever even bothered opening the blinds of his windows at night, knowing that forgetting to close them again would mean death in the morning.

Then she remembered when he had saved her. He had been on the balcony as soon as the sun went down, as if desperate to be within inches and minutes of sunshine. Sunshine adjacent.

A cruel curse.

All of them were so very cruel.

Celeste was already there, speaking to a group of Starling nobles. Her friend's cape was magnificent, specially made for her demonstration. Somehow, a tailor in the Starling realm had managed to make silk that was so thin, so translucent, it almost resembled glass. Faintly silver, with stars sewn into its edges, crystalline and glittering.

Isla had to stop herself from smiling at her friend, from acknowledging her at all.

The king was there too, surrounded by his own nobles and advisers and by wealthy islanders who wore gold cuffs and necklaces, who were so decked in gold, they looked like statues gilded by their king.

Cleo entered, joined by her entourage, who trailed her like guards.

Azul laughed with a group, interacting with them more like friends than a leader speaking to his subjects.

Isla was alone. Not surrounded by anyone. Even Ella had left her side, waiting in the wings with the other attendants.

So was Grim. He appeared across the room, making the nobles closest to him scuttle like roaches.

His dark eyes found hers, and she saw an understanding there.

Both were alone.

Was that why he had helped her?

Was it because he knew what it felt like?

No. He was her enemy. She had to remember that.

"Welcome," Celeste said. She was standing by something tall and cloaked. It looked like a statue with a sheet shrouding it.

It was not.

"My demonstration is a trial of fear. Whoever conquers their greatest fear first is the winner." A silver hourglass sat across the room, counting the seconds down.

Demonstrations were planned carefully. Some were chosen to showcase the hosting ruler's superiority. Some were chosen to demonstrate a particular opponent's weakness. Some, like this one, had a more mysterious purpose.

With a silver-gloved hand, Celeste tugged at the glittering sheet, revealing a towering mirror.

It was an ancient Starling relic the ruler had brought from her own realm. Isla had watched it for over a year, standing in the corner of Celeste's room like a specter. It could only be used by a person once, so Isla hadn't been able to practice. But she was almost certain about what her biggest fear would be.

"Who would like to begin?" Celeste asked.

Fear was perhaps a ruler's greatest weakness. What they feared most could doom their realm. It was a good test.

But it was not why Celeste had chosen this challenge.

The king stepped forward. The moment he pressed his palm against the mirror, its glass rippled, water shifting in a goblet.

Suddenly, it stilled. And so did he.

For minutes, the king went on a journey none of them could see. Oro just stared blankly at the mirror, hand still pressed to its face, brows occasionally jerking together.

Everyone had a fear. Isla wondered what the king was so afraid of. According to Celeste, the mirror trapped someone until they succeeded in besting their greatest fear. Someone could be stuck inside it forever. Many had died using the relic.

Oro straightened, the spell broken. The king's hand was released.

He had conquered it.

In just three minutes.

Isla swallowed. The king had been alive for more than five hundred years.

What if she kept the crowd waiting here for hours? What would that say of her and her abilities? Of her worthiness of surviving the Centennial?

What if she *never* bested it, and the mirror kept her?

Isla knew how important the use of this relic was to their plan. But she suddenly wished her friend had chosen a different trial.

Azul was next. He took five minutes. More than the king, but not by much.

When he left the mirror, Isla couldn't help but notice that his smile was a little duller than usual. Something in his expression looked haunted.

What had he seen?

What fear had he been forced to face?

Isla's palms began to sweat. She brushed them against her cape and took a deep breath. *Get it together.*

The moment Cleo placed her pale hand onto the mirror, Isla knew things would be different. The glass didn't ripple nearly as much. Her eyes closed and she froze completely, a ruler turned to ice.

It was not two minutes later that they reopened.

Gasps sounded among the crowd. Cleo had beaten even the king. By over a minute.

Isla's teeth ground against each other. The Moonling must be heartless. Or fearless. Both dangerous qualities in an enemy.

Grim finished his exercise in just under three minutes.

Celeste did hers in five.

Then it was Isla's turn.

The room was silent as she made her way over to the towering object. Her heels echoed through the hall. Her knees trembled beneath her dress, and she was grateful for its length.

Too soon, Isla found herself holding up her hand. Her fingers shook slightly before pressing against the mirror.

It moved—shifted.

Then something yanked her through the glass.

CHAPTER TWELVE

SHATTERED

Isla was pulled through the mirror into a crystal world.

In the many months she had anticipated this demonstration, she had determined her greatest fear: failing her realm.

She had readied herself to see a field of fallen Wildlings. Burned forests. A dead Poppy and Terra at her feet.

Now that she was in the trial, there were no bodies, no flames, no dying wildlife.

Only a room. *Her* room, in Wildling.

It looked exactly like it did when she left it. Clean. Proper. Her wall of swords glimmered at one side, winking their hello.

She expected to feel a rush of relief at being back, at being in a place so familiar after two weeks surrounded by strangers. In a strange land ruled by secrets.

But all she felt was dread.

If she failed, this was where she would return. She would live out the rest of her short, cursed, powerless, mortal life hidden away again. The realm would need a better heir for the next Centennial, so she would be forced to have a child.

She would continue to be sheltered.

One book from the library at a time.

Visits to her people from a distance, if at all.

Choices made for her by Wildlings who knew better, who knew more than just these glass walls.

Secret travels with her starstick.

Not even training, because there would be nothing left to train *for.*

Forests and people that would continue to die, flowers that would become extinct, Wildlings forced to kill for survival, unable to ever fall in love, turning them more and more into the beasts the rest of the realms believed them to be.

No.

She couldn't bear a life like that.

Lightlark was dangerous but full of wonders. Now that she had tasted freedom, she couldn't be locked in her glass box again and be content.

She wanted more than she had ever wanted in her life.

Isla watched herself reflected in the glass windows before her. As if spurred by her thoughts, her reflection began to move of its own free will.

She watched as it paced around the room. Lay in bed. Read a single book. Again. Again. Again. The reflection sped up, her movements a blur, and the days passed by too quickly, like time had tripped over itself, again, again, again. This time, instead of reading the book, her reflection tore its pages out. Banged on the windows instead of staring out of them. Pulled at her hair instead of braiding it. Forced back the floorboards, one by one, searching for something, fingers bleeding. Her starstick? *Had her guardians found and gotten rid of her starstick?* Years seemed to flip by in seconds, and eventually the reflection stood still in the middle of the room as time continued to pass her by, her body weakening, hair falling out, her soul scooped out of her chest. Her eyes had gone lifeless.

She couldn't see herself like this. Empty. All the best parts of herself stripped away. Isla reached a hand out to touch her reflection, to comfort it—

And suddenly, she was looking back at her own self.

Her heart was beating too quickly.

Was that her fate, should she fail? Was that what she was destined to become? A hull of herself?

A prisoner?

Something lurched, screeching—

The room became smaller.

Isla startled, moving closer to its center. Somehow, the walls had moved, the floor had been eaten up.

Smaller.

The glass rattled as it shrank. Perfumes fell from her vanity and smashed against the tile, her leftover makeup soon joining them, blots of color bleeding, bright powders making plumes of dust.

Smaller.

Isla's heartbeat rang through her ears in warning; her fingers shook, and sweat dripped down her forehead. The room was going to swallow her whole, press its glass against her skin, make her and her reflection one and the same.

Smaller.

The ceiling concaved, nearly skewering her in place. The walls folded together, getting smaller, smaller, smaller.

Her bed was gone, her things were mangled in the mess, and the room was getting smaller still, shrinking all around her.

This was her fate. The reflection had told it to her.

Locked forever in a room.

A secret too shameful to share.

A curse too painful to bear.

The room creaked, and Isla's bones vibrated with the movement of everything around her being eaten up, enclosed, matted over.

No.

She refused.

Isla hadn't worked for years for her efforts to be useless, to be a victim of this room and her circumstances.

She hadn't even known how much she was missing. Now that she saw how much the world had to offer, she wanted it all.

She wanted *everything.*

Isla wouldn't return here. She would either break her curse—or die trying.

Before she could make a single move to stop her fate, however, it seemed she was too late. There was nothing she could do as the remaining walls all fell down atop her.

The bites of a million pieces of glass were a constellation across her body as the room shattered. Before she could move out of its path, a massive solid pane crushed her without breaking. Her breath was torn from her chest. The world was black and silent. Her face pressed against the glass, so closely she couldn't breathe.

Was she permanently in the mirror?

Had she joined the girl in the reflection?

She tried to move a foot, a leg, *anything*—and finally managed to feel around with her fingers. Only one hand hadn't been crushed by the wall.

Give me a chance, she told her broken bones. *Give me a chance, and I'll make sure we never become her.*

Her fingers searched blindly, desperately, until a blade cut through her skin like butter. She grinned beneath the rubble. It was one of her swords. She gripped its hilt—

And broke through the glass that had smothered her.

Isla gasped.

She was back in the hall.

The mirror had gone still again. Her rattled reflection stared back at her. This time, it did not move of its own accord.

Isla tore her hand away, her palm cold as ice.

There was no applause. No sound as she backed away, and the demonstration ended. Cleo was crowned the winner.

Isla remained in the hall until it was just her, the mirror, and Celeste.

"How long?" Isla finally asked. She was certain her time had been far longer than everyone else's. *That* was why the crowds had left so

suddenly. *That* was why no one had caught her eye, why Celeste hadn't nodded at her or touched her nose or done any of their subtle tricks to speak to one another in secret.

Celeste frowned. "Six minutes," she said simply. "Why didn't you look at the hourglass?"

Six minutes. That wasn't bad.

Isla didn't bother answering Celeste's question, because she didn't want to admit that she had been afraid to look. That she felt on edge.

She might have faced her fear in the mirror . . . but she had never been more scared.

Now she had seen her worst fear embodied, brought to life.

She would do anything to keep that fear from becoming reality.

And that, perhaps, scared her most of all.

The Starling ruler was circling the mirror, looking at it carefully. Isla watched from a distance as Celeste strung her fingers together and smiled. "It worked."

Isla straightened. "How do you know?"

Celeste snapped her fingers, and sparks illuminated the hall. Handprints glowed silver across the mirror's glass. Every ruler's print and essence had been stored by the relic.

The Starling pulled a pair of gloves from her pocket. They were so thin they looked translucent. Isla nearly retched. She had done it. She had completed her part of their plan.

Isla opened her mouth, ready to ask if Celeste had truly managed to find a pair of the gloves in a dark market somewhere on Lightlark. The alternative—

Celeste shot her a look that made her think better of it.

Frowning in focus, the Starling slowly rolled on the new gloves. They sounded both papery and leathery, crinkling as they slid down her skin. Isla winced. When they were fully on, Celeste carefully pressed them against each handprint, letting the marks soak into the gloves. They would absorb the energy the enchanted Starling mirror had taken from

all the rulers, to be used later. It was an inconsequential amount. Not enough to be used in battle or make any meaningful display.

But every library on Lightlark had a protected section, a home for each realm's most valuable relics. Each was guarded by enchantments that only allowed a ruler and their essence to enter.

Wearing these gloves, Isla would be granted access.

Now, she had everything she needed to begin searching the libraries for the bondbreaker.

CHAPTER THIRTEEN

TOWER

The next night, Celeste stared at the materials between them and frowned. "Is this really everything?"

"Yes." Or, at least, what Isla *thought* she needed to make the elixir.

It was the fifteenth day of the Centennial. Isla was anxious to search the next library for the bondbreaker as soon as possible. It hadn't been on Star Isle, but perhaps they would get lucky and it would be in the Sky Isle collection. If not, she would have to wait until the full moon to go to Moon Isle. And she still hadn't come up with a plan to get onto Sun Isle unnoticed.

She tried to remain positive. She could very well find the bondbreaker that night. Then they could use it, and both of their bloodlines would be rid of all the curses that afflicted them. Isla would get her Wildling powers she had been denied at birth. The Wildling realm wouldn't have to kill their beloveds or live on hearts any longer. Celeste and all Starlings would live to see their twenty-sixth birthday.

The bondbreaker was the key to both of their freedoms. And right now, they were counting on some sparse hair dye instructions to get it.

Isla held the torn piece of parchment between them. She couldn't have asked Poppy for help with this alternate plan, so she had taken a page from one of her guardian's books, swiped some Wildling-specific ingredients, and hoped for the best.

She read the list out one last time.

"Rose water."

Check. She had swiped a vial of it from Poppy's vanity.

"Ash-leaf extract."

She had only been able to find an ash leaf during a last-minute expedition in the forest and hoped that would do.

"Soil from the ever-changing tulip."

Check. She had grabbed a small shovel of it from Poppy's collection. The enchanted flower only grew by the coast in the Wildling newland, where her great-great-grandmother had planted it, straight from the island's soil. Many of Lightlark's flowers had been transplanted there in the aftermath of the curses, attempting to create some sort of ecosystem like their island.

And many of them had died since Isla had been born.

She poured a portion of the small pouch of dirt into the pot of hot water Ella had brought her, supposedly for tea.

Finally, she needed some of the color she wanted her hair transformed to. Though Azul's own hair was dark, many Skylings had hair the color of their realm. Maybe it was fashion, or a way to honor their power source, or perhaps it was natural, like Celeste's own silver hair—she didn't know.

All she knew was that she needed to fit in, and this would be the most inconspicuous color.

The recipe called for a flower petal with the shade, but there weren't any in Wildling. As a substitute, she carefully ripped the bottom of her stolen dress's hem and threw the fabric into the potion.

It bubbled a bit, thickened. Isla and Celeste watched as it became a paste.

The Starling peered into the pot carefully. "Is it supposed to look like this?"

"I don't know," Isla mumbled. Nerves flurried in her stomach. She wasn't just sneaking onto another ruler's isle. She was *impersonating* another realm. None of the Centennial rules stated against it, but it was still dangerous.

No one could recognize her. It would immediately put her and their plan in jeopardy.

The enchanted dye had to work.

"It's cooled," Celeste said. She had dipped a gloved finger into the mixture.

They took the bowl into the bathroom, and Isla sat in the bathtub as her friend coated her long brown hair in the light-blue paste.

Celeste worked in silence, her fingers careful, rubbing into her scalp, then making her way down to the ends.

"How does it look?" Isla finally asked after most of her hair felt like it had been covered.

Celeste said nothing.

She whipped around to look at her friend's expression.

And found a smile tugging on the corners of her lips.

"What?"

She finally laughed. "It— You just look different," she offered. "But it's good. The color is nearly exact."

"Nearly?"

Celeste waved her concern away. "No one will be able to tell in the moonlight," she said. "And no one will be in the library this late . . ."

Isla groaned. So many excuses, so many elements out of her control that had to go right.

The mixture was enchanted, thanks to the ever-changing tulip soil. Without it, the color wouldn't have stuck nearly as quickly or effectively on her dark hair. Still—the blue would only last a few hours.

Her friend took her stained gloves off and gripped her hand tightly. "This will work. You do this all the time."

Isla gave her an incredulous look. "I sneak onto another realm's isle *all the time?*"

"No. But you sneak into other realms' *newlands* all the time. Wearing stolen clothing. Impersonating another ruler's people. With your starstick."

That was true. But this was different.

This was the Centennial.

"You move like a shadow," Celeste continued. "You strategize like a general. You can blend in anywhere—I've *seen* you."

Her friend was right. She had spent years unwittingly gaining the skills she now needed to find the bondbreaker.

Isla washed the paste out of her hair, combed it, and hoped it would dry by the time she reached her destination.

"Right," Isla said, staring at her reflection, feeling strange in a color she had never been allowed to wear. "So far, I've been a thief. A liar." She sighed. "Time to become a fraud."

It took forty-five minutes to reach the Sky Isle bridge. Once, the island was whole. Then, thousands of years ago, it was sliced into pieces, so each realm could have its own. All the isles were connected to the Mainland by rope and wood that didn't look even remotely steady. Wind whistled through large gaps between each plank. The strings holding them together were thin and frayed. The entire thing rocked back and forth like a pendulum. Isla looked down at what had to be two hundred feet, the water churning roughly below, a soup ready to boil her.

"No," she said simply, the word slipping out of her mouth, into an empty night.

She had read about these enchanted bridges. Though everyone was traditionally allowed on any isle they wanted to visit, some realms had been known to restrict access during political turmoil. If Azul or the Lightlark-based Skyling government had decided those outside their realm weren't allowed to pass, the bridge would collapse, sending her hurtling hundreds of feet below.

It was unlikely—but not impossible. If she fell, no one would hear her screams. Worse, if someone did, there would be nothing left of her to save.

Her entire realm would die in an instant, just because she was foolish enough to fall off a bridge.

It was too big a risk.

Isla took a step back.

Right into someone's chest.

She stilled, forcing herself not to scream, then whirled around, hands splayed in apology.

A tall, freckled Skyling man stood there, eyes half-closed, a large cup of drink in his hand. "Crossing?" he said merrily, staring down at her as if nothing was amiss.

He didn't question her hair.

Didn't stare at her clothing or face like he recognized her.

His gaze narrowed then, and Isla froze, wondering if he was about to yell to all Lightlark that Isla Crown, ruler of Wildling, was trying to get onto Sky Isle.

Then she remembered he was staring at her strangely not because he was putting the puzzle pieces of her identity together but because she had been gaping up at him for several seconds without responding.

"Yes, of course," she managed to say, forcing a smile.

He smiled back. His eyes flickered behind her, as if saying, *So, are you going to cross, then?*

Now she had no choice. Isla took a step, feeling at least a glimmer of comfort that should she plummet hundreds of feet, someone would know her fate right away.

Her foot was met by a steady plank.

Relief needled down the backs of her legs.

The rest of the way across was unsteady and filled with at least half a dozen more stomach-sinking feelings, but she made it to the other side in one piece.

Only to stop and stare at the world she had entered.

Sky Isle was a floating city. Giant chunks of rock hovered high above, strung together by bridges like beads on a bracelet. Waterfalls

spilled right off levitating mountain ranges, their triangular bases and roots trailing far beneath them, almost to the ground. On the largest floating piece sat a palace with spires that shot so far up into the clouds they must have scratched the sky itself.

The ground beneath the floating city was far inferior—Isla felt like someone walking on the seafloor, looking up at the surface in wonder. Poppy had taught her that Skylings used to be able to fly, once upon a time. Before their curse bound them forever to the ground.

The only person who could fly now was Oro. As an Origin, he had all the Lightlark realms' powers. But not their curses. Only Sunling's, since his family had claimed the realm as their own long ago.

The second city, built beneath the first, covered every inch of a mountain. At its peak stood a tower tall enough to reach the very bottom of the closest floating rock. Isla wondered if *that* was how one entered the flying city—and who was allowed to. At the mountain's base sat a marketplace that smelled of peppermint and ale.

Mostly ale.

Someone tumbled from the closest pub, right into the street, face bright pink, barely missing a puddle of vomit.

Skylings were well-known for their celebratory nature. Part of her wanted to rush into the closest bar and down her first drink, knowing it gave others courage.

But she couldn't risk the distraction or an adverse effect. Not tonight.

Celeste had found out the location of the library through her attendant, a Skyling boy with pale skin and a voice so soft it was hard to even hear him. It supposedly used to be located high above but now had taken over a tower in the newer Sky Isle castle, at the base of the great mountain.

Isla had wondered about the best way to sneak into the palace—but, it turned out, Skylings weren't as pretentious or paranoid as other realms. The castle doors were open, welcoming any of its people, from nobles to other islanders, inside. No guards were present.

This late at night, there were just a few visitors milling through the halls. A couple, walking hand in hand, sharing a foaming drink between them. A cluster of teenagers, taking turns throwing a ball at each other, only using their power to harness wind.

The people of the realm were not unlike their leader. Content. Happy.

It was a bit unnerving, more than two weeks into the Centennial. Weren't they anxious? Did they know something she didn't? Did Azul have a plan for this Centennial that he had shared with his people?

Isla made a turn to the east side of the palace. She studied it carefully. It was surprisingly well-kept for being the home of a ruler who only returned for a few months every century. It was just a fraction of the size of the Mainland castle and painted light blue, a giant bird's egg. Its ceilings were designed to resemble a massive, endless sky and were remarkably tall. Wind whistled through the corridors, from various windows left open.

Free. Airy. Light.

The tower wasn't difficult to find. It was one of just a few and had unlocked glass doors, which revealed its interior.

Books. Floors of them, in a circular shape, going around and around, in a spiral leading up to a rounded skylight. All empty. Celeste was right. No one seemed interested in reading at this hour.

Now she just needed to find the protected section.

She studied the space and frowned. There were no hidden back rooms. Everything in the library was on full display, shelves built into the walls. Isla started up the spiral walkway, forcing herself not to look too carefully at the books. If she saw any of their titles, she wasn't sure she would be able to resist the temptation to sit down and read.

You will have plenty of time to read once your curses are broken, she told herself. After using the bondbreaker, she would have the freedom to pillage the library in the Wildling realm and devour every book if she wished.

She just needed to find it.

The tower was taller than it looked from the bottom—it took several minutes to reach its top.

When she did, she frowned. No protected section.

No relics. Just books. Thousands of them.

Isla gripped the railing, staring a hundred feet down at the bottom. The library was empty. Hollow. She barely resisted the urge to fill it with her frustrated screams.

But she hadn't colored her hair and stolen her clothes and stepped foot on another realm's Lightlark territory to give up so easily.

Every isle's library had a protected area.

This one must just be hidden.

Isla backed toward the wall and felt it carefully, knocking gently. It was solid, books covering nearly every inch of the tower's interior. Its middle was air.

No room for a secret.

Unless—

She looked up at the skylight. If she stood on her toes, she could reach it.

Her stomach roiled as she carefully grabbed the gloves from her pocket. They felt rough and thin enough to tear if she wasn't careful. She tried not to think of what they were made of, of *who* they were—

No. She had to keep her mind on the mission, lest she retch her dinner.

Hoping Celeste was right, and Azul's essence was indeed imprinted on the fabric, she rolled them on, then pressed her gloved palm against the glass—

It dropped open, along with an elegant pair of metal stairs that unfolded before her eyes.

Isla's grin was a primal thing, pure satisfaction. She had uncovered a ruler's secret. She had figured it out alone. A powerless young ruler.

There is no time to celebrate. Terra's scolding was in her brain. Whenever Isla beamed after mastering a skill or managing to disarm her guardian, she would be chastised.

Time can stand still for just a moment, Isla once said.

Not for you. From the moment you were born, the clock began counting down, Terra had replied. Any time not used to prepare for the Centennial was wasted. Wanting anything more than to defend and protect her realm was selfish. Her life had never been her own.

With the bondbreaker, it could be.

Isla took the first step up the ladder.

The skylight was a door, leading to a small glass room awash with moonlight. There was a bundle of ancient scrolls. A scepter with a gemstone top that was milky, the color of someone blending clouds and sky together with their thumb. A sword with a braided blade, two sheets of metal intertwined, locked together like lovers.

But there was no oversize glass needle.

There was no bondbreaker.

Disappointment made her reckless. Isla entered the Mainland castle without her normal precautions. She did not wait in the shadows to ensure no one was around. She did not cloak her steps, which would require slowing her pace. She did not take the long way, through halls that were always empty because they were ancient and let cracks of moonlight and cold drafts through holes in the stone and didn't have any of the monstrous hearths that filled the rest of the palace.

All she wanted was to get to her room as soon as possible, wash the dye out of her hair, tear the light-blue clothes to pieces, and get any remainder of sleep the night allowed.

By the time she quickly turned a corner into the main hall, it was too late.

Cleo had already spotted her.

Isla was gone in an instant. She kept walking straight instead, not knowing where she was going, heart thundering, wondering how good a look the Moonling ruler had gotten at her face.

It was dark. She had been on the other side of the hall.

No, not close enough to have seen it was her.

But certainly close enough to make her suspicious.

Seconds later, Isla heard the unmistakable sound of steps behind her.

Following her.

Just a few long strides and the Moonling would catch up to her, confirm that the girl with the light-blue hair and Skyling clothing was a fellow ruler.

An impostor.

The discovery would spin so many questions and stab so many of her secrets, Isla began sweating, panting.

Cleo wouldn't give up until she had Isla backed into a corner. Her steps were just a few moments behind hers.

Another turn came up, and Isla took it, using the few seconds that the Moonling ruler couldn't see her to take off at full speed.

She ran, ran, then took another turn—

And crashed into something solid.

Her mind spun behind her eyes. She would have fallen backward if it wasn't for two strong hands catching her by the waist.

Grim.

Footsteps sounded behind her, echoing through the last hall. One turn, and the Moonling ruler would find her there, *both* of them.

The Nightshade ruler stared down at her, confusion drawing his brows together. His eyes caught on her colored hair, her clothes, a question in his expression.

No time to explain.

"*Please,*" she said, gripping his arms, hating the way her voice broke on the word.

He seemed to know what she wanted.

Because before Cleo could turn the corner, Grim gathered Isla to his chest and they both disappeared.

The Moonling ruler froze at the entrance of their corridor, finding it empty. Isla might have found pleasure in the shock on Cleo's face, if she wasn't so afraid.

She was trembling. Cleo was just feet away. If the Moonling discovered her, Celeste's plans and help would be for nothing. Just because Isla was foolish enough not to be cautious. Just because she was upset that she didn't find the bondbreaker on her first try.

The Moonling took a step forward, right toward them. Silent as a shadow, Grim lifted Isla as if she weighed nothing and shifted them both to the side of the room. The rough stone wall dug into her back. Grim was shielding her. She could feel his breath against her forehead.

Isla tried not to focus on what *else* she could feel. His tight grip on her waist, the cold emanating from him searing through the thin fabric of her stolen clothing. The chill that licked her spine like night blossoming in her bones.

Out of fear, she told herself, fear of being discovered. Nothing else.

The Moonling walked the entire length of the room—before finally retreating the way she had come.

Only after her steps were too faint to hear did Grim make them visible again.

And Isla was shocked by his proximity.

She was pressed against the wall, and he towered over her, head bent so low his nose almost grazed hers.

He looked down at her. "Have you decided to change realms, Hearteater?" he said, reaching up and taking a strand of her colored hair between his fingers. "If so, you might consider Nightshade. We can't compete with Skyling when it comes to sweets or inventive drinks, but if debauchery is what you're after . . ." His dark gaze gleamed

in amusement. "We are most famed for our thorough exploration of pleasure."

What was he implying? His hands were still on her waist, his fingers long against her ribs. She took a shaky breath.

Then batted him away, scowling. "Count me uninterested," she said.

But Grim only grinned as he took a step back.

Of course. The demon could feel her emotions, the heat pooling in her stomach as she thought about his surprisingly gentle touch. The way his lips had curled around the word *pleasure* . . .

No. What was wrong with her? She had always judged the Wildlings reckless enough to begin to have feelings for someone. They risked the relationship ending in death.

Isla's actions put her entire *realm* at risk.

She wanted freedom. She wanted to break her and her people's curses. That was all.

That was *everything*.

"Thank you," she said simply.

Then she darted out of the hall as quickly as she could.

CHAPTER FOURTEEN

AZUL

Isla's invitation arrived the next morning. Her demonstration was next.

All night, the Nightshade had haunted her dreams. Their brief encounter in the hallway had affected her more than she cared to admit.

Grim had made her invisible, just because she had asked. He had no reason to help her. If it hadn't been for him, Cleo would have discovered her, and all of Isla's plans would have been ruined in one disastrous night.

She knew she would regret this. If Celeste ever found out, she might seriously reconsider their friendship.

It was foolish, *dangerous,* but Isla set off looking for the Nightshade.

She knew all the rulers' habits by now, thanks to her regular snooping during the last sixteen days. Azul was always with his people and spent a surprising amount of time walking along the coast. Cleo was always surrounded by nobles she seemed to keep at an arm's length and visited her isle far more than the other rulers. Oro left the castle nearly every night, and she still hadn't had the nerve to follow him.

Grim's movements were more of a mystery, since he was often invisible, traveling from place to place unnoticed. A few times, though, she had caught him slipping into a bar in the marketplace in the middle of the afternoon. That was where she headed.

She was nearly at the agora when her name was spoken.

Isla whirled around, only to find another ruler standing there.

Azul.

Her blood went cold. Did he know that she had been on his isle the night before? Had someone seen her?

Had *Grim* told him? They didn't appear to be friends, but alliances were easy to hide during the Centennial. Isla and Celeste were the prime example of that.

If she hadn't been distracted, she would have heard him approach. She wouldn't have leaped in surprise at his voice.

She pasted a practiced smile on her face. "What a pleasant surprise," she said, her tone sounding so genuine, Isla wondered when she had become such a good liar.

"Likewise," he said, matching her expression. "What brings you to this part of the Mainland, Ruler?"

Isla tried her best not to let her voice tremble, the way her hands were. She clasped them behind her back. "The castle was getting a bit dreary. I thought I would do some exploring."

Azul's grin grew, but it did not reach his eyes. They remained as cold as the gems he hoarded. Was it possible she hadn't been as discreet on Sky Isle as she thought?

Or perhaps he was just wary of her. And why wouldn't he be? She was wary of him too.

"If it's the Mainland you'd like to see . . . allow me to take you to one of its greatest wonders."

She didn't want to go anywhere with a ruler who might or might not know that she had been disguised as one of his people the day before. Their chance encounter was too great of a coincidence.

He must know.

Refusing his offer would make him even more suspicious of her, though. "How generous of you."

They started in the direction of the mountain range that framed the Mainland. The rock was brown and red in some places, marbled in others.

"How are you enjoying the island?" he asked lightly, as if the Centennial was a vacation, and not Isla's only chance at living.

Of course, he couldn't know that. A Wildling ruler was supposed to be nearly immortal.

"I can understand its appeal . . . though I have much to explore." She had learned that it was better to let others speak when she had much to hide. Most people liked to talk about themselves, anyway. "And how is your fifth Centennial?"

He laughed without humor. Something about that laugh was strange, Isla thought. Bitter, maybe. "It's . . . interesting." He pursed his lips. "The first Centennial, I'm sure you've heard, was a nightmare. Almost worse than the war . . . With the second came rules, and some order. We had plans. Strategies. But no alliances. None of us trusted each other, you see, after the first time. For good reason too."

His voice trailed off, and Isla saw something flash in his eyes.

Was it pain?

"The third was better. It was the first time we split into teams. We believed we were very close to breaking the curses—to figuring out all parts of the prophecy. We were wrong, of course. By the fourth, it seemed most had lost hope. Cleo did not even attend . . . did you know that?" Isla nodded, though she most certainly hadn't known.

Any ruler who didn't attend wasn't eligible for the grand prize . . . and their curse wouldn't be broken with the rest, should someone find a solution. Why would Cleo stay away?

More importantly—why had she returned this year?

Dread danced in her bones, and Isla had the feeling there was something everyone else knew that she didn't.

"Even without her, we really thought we had it." He shook his head. "The curses have ruined so much. But one of the worst things it has done is tear our realms further apart. Before, we were very close to unity."

Isla knew this from Poppy's history lessons. She was happy to speak about anything that didn't involve her sneaking into the Sky Isle library. "That's why King Egan was getting married to another ruler, wasn't it? To try to bring the realms back together?" Isla used to wonder if the king had decided, atypically, to marry outside his realm for love. That was certainly how Poppy told King Egan and Aurora's story. A Sunling and a Starling finding love, despite their differences. It was the only time her guardian hadn't spoken about love as a cautionary tale.

"Precisely." Azul sighed. "Now, here we are at the fifth." He looked at her briefly over his shoulder, pity in his eyes. "And I'm afraid I don't know if I have it in me to attend a sixth."

Isla swallowed at his dark tone. Was this a warning?

Was he telling her that, despite his typically jovial disposition, he wasn't above killing her if it meant this Centennial was the last?

Isla was desperate to change the subject. "Are you close to your nobles?"

Sky Isle had been surprisingly well-kept. The nobles seemed to be doing a good job of running it in their ruler's absence.

Azul frowned. "There are no Skyling nobles." She must have looked confused, because he continued. "We've had a democracy since I came into rule. The Skylings who are invited to the smaller events are elected officials. All big decisions are made based on voting from my people."

Isla blinked at him. "So, if they decided they didn't want you as ruler . . ."

He shrugged. "I would step down. Though that would certainly complicate things, what with the Centennial and the way our powers are passed down," he said. "I'm lucky they have been happy with my rule."

She had never heard of a realm being run that way.

As she considered Azul's words, she found him watching her.

Studying her.

What was he looking for?

They had stopped at the base of a mountain that looked peculiar, but not special enough to have made the trek. Azul had told her many things, things she wouldn't have expected another ruler of realm to be so up-front about during the Centennial.

Was it because he knew she wouldn't be alive long enough to use what knowledge he had shared?

The fiftieth day was just over a month away. Isla tensed, wondering if the Skyling was counting down the hours before he could kill her without breaking the rules. Perhaps his people had already cast their votes, wanting her to be the one who died when the time came to fulfill the entire prophecy.

Azul only stared upward. Isla followed his gaze warily and saw that there were tunnels dug above them, high into the sky. If she squinted, she could see bright blue on the other side, through the mountain. She counted seven, all lined up next to each other, perfectly carved through the stone.

"I used to come here as a child, with friends," he said, smiling. This time, it did reach his eyes. "We would fly through the tunnels as fast as we could, timing ourselves. We made a game of it."

It had been five hundred years since he had flown. It appeared he missed it as much as Grim missed night and Oro missed day.

He turned to her. "Nowadays, it has a different use." He planted his legs in a wide stance and shot up with his fist.

Isla instinctively backed away, then watched a burst of air travel through one of the tunnels. A moment later, it made a beautiful sound.

"It's an instrument," she said loudly, her excitement real this time.

In response, he sent air through all the tunnels, one after the other, fast as wind.

A song broke through the afternoon.

Isla hummed, matching the pitch, overjoyed. The mountain was an instrument . . . she couldn't believe it. Azul indulged her, playing song after song, his air never weakening. The wariness from his eyes disappeared, little by little.

She found herself happy that Azul had happened upon her, if only for a limited distraction.

By the time Azul escorted Isla back to the Mainland castle, it was nearly dusk. Grim would have already left the agora.

Instead of finding him in the bar, she had to go to his bedroom.

Isla had figured out the location of all the rulers' rooms several days before. She could have asked Ella where the other rulers were staying. It would have saved her hours of snooping. But Isla felt safer spreading her requests around, not allowing anyone to know too much about what she needed, lest they put any pieces of her plans together. The rulers were harder to follow through the castle without notice, so she had trailed their Lightlark-provided attendants.

That was how she knew Grim's chamber was on the other side of the castle, farthest from another ruler than anyone.

Isla had already made up her mind, knowing the potential consequences. Knowing what she was putting at risk. She had traveled here regardless.

Standing in front of his door, though, she hesitated, her knuckle inches from the stone.

Before she lost her nerve, it swung open.

Grim stood there, looking down at her with an eyebrow lifted.

"I'm sorry I ran off," she said. It really was rude, after he had helped her. "I came to thank you, again. And to offer something to you, in thanks for—for what you did."

A grin began to overtake his face at the mention of an offering. "Oh?" he said, voice somehow growing even deeper.

Isla glared at him, as if to say, *Not that kind of offering.* He was shameless. Was he like this with everyone? Was she only the latest person he had decided to flirt with?

It had to be part of his plan. Which only made what she was about to do all the more foolish.

His eyes only glimmered deviously.

"My demonstration is next," Isla said, the words rushing out of her before she could change her mind. "Tomorrow. It requires preparation."

Grim's face went surprisingly serious. "Hearteater, you don't have to—"

No. She did have to. Grim knew one of her secrets now, after finding her in the Skyling clothing. He had *helped* her, by turning her invisible to avoid Cleo. Isla was beholden to him. She didn't like that. She would tell him this information, then be done with it.

"It's demonstrating the worth of your realm by showing something of value it's created, for the future of Lightlark."

The Nightshade did not break her gaze. He did not grin. He did not thank her. He simply nodded.

She nodded back.

It was only late that night, staring up at her ceiling instead of sleeping, that she wondered if she had made a grave mistake.

CHAPTER FIFTEEN

ELIXIR

Isla had given them an hour.

Instead of a trial focusing on the power of their ruler—for obvious reasons—Isla wished to test the ability of their realm. Her people might not be on the island, but it was a chance for her to show Lightlark all they were beyond their bloodthirsty curse.

Her guardians had wanted the demonstration to be something different. An opportunity to further their own strategy.

Isla had convinced them that showing that her people could *heal* just as much as they could *kill* might convince the other rulers of Wildlings' value, especially over Nightshade, who only destroyed.

Her warning Grim of the demonstration negated some of that strategy. Complicated everything.

They were back in the arena. Isla wanted as many islanders as possible present to see what she had brought from her newland.

She had already announced her trial to a wary audience. Her voice had been surprisingly smooth, no hint of her nerves peeking through.

The rules had been stated as well. The audience would vote for which demonstration of a realm's abilities was most useful in securing the future of the island. No one could vote for their own ruler—though Isla was under no illusion that it would give Wildling a fair shot. She wouldn't win. But she didn't need to. All the crowd needed to know was that Wildlings were more than wicked seductresses.

The rulers stood on the sidelines. She wondered if an hour had been enough time to prepare—for the ones who didn't already know about the demonstration, anyway.

Their expressions gave nothing away, waiting for her to call out their names.

"Azul."

The ruler swept into the center of the arena, followed by a trail of other Skylings, who were aiding in the demonstration. "Our realm has been working on a form of communication that uses wind. Easier communication means more efficiency, streamlined processes . . . faster invitations to parties." The crowd laughed. Azul certainly knew how to present himself. Isla thought back to what he had said about Skyling's government the day before. His people did seem to adore him. Was it because he had given them choice? She of all people could understand the importance of freedom . . .

He grabbed a piece of parchment from an interior pocket of his cape and wrote a message on it. Then he folded it carefully into a square and used his power to fly it across the arena, right into Isla's hand.

All eyes were on her. She folded open the page and read the words the ruler had scrawled: *Of course, we also have our music . . .*

Isla couldn't help but smile.

"This can be replicated on a grand scale," Azul added. He motioned to the rest of the Skylings who had joined him. They carried stacks of sheets of parchment. Without warning, they threw all of it into the air. Before her eyes, each page folded neatly, then set off, one after the other, on dozens of paths the Skylings had created in the sky, wind currents for the messages to use as trails to their recipients. A true infrastructure for mass communication.

It was a grand display. An innovation that would surely make an impact on Lightlark.

The crowd certainly seemed to think so as well.

Isla wondered what the pages Azul had distributed even said. Perhaps an invitation to a festivity the Skyling was throwing in the agora after this.

"Cleo."

Isla hoped that the lack of time to prepare had flustered the ruler. She imagined the Moonling struggling to put together a demonstration and nearly smiled.

Cleo only radiated confidence as she strolled toward the center of the arena. She had no helpers. No tools . . . or anything visual to display.

Her words were simple. "We have ships," she said. "For the past two centuries, we have built many, *many* ships."

That was it.

The Moonling walked back to her place, and Isla felt a tinge of anger in her chest. She wondered if the crowd would be silent. Confused. If the other rulers would balk at her lack of display.

But no one did. Moonlings cheered, all but confirming that they had spent decades making the fleet Cleo had so casually described.

She could be lying. But Oro looked like he believed her.

He looked like he hadn't known about the ships at all.

Interesting. Celeste was right. There was tension brewing between some of the Lightlark realms.

Though a navy wasn't logical while the Moonlings were still haunted by the deadly full moon, it *would* be useful in a postcurse world. The ships could be used to bring the thousands of Moonlings, Starlings, Wildlings, and Skylings back to Lightlark, to unify the realms in one place once more. They could explore distant lands beyond the island and the realms' newlands.

They could also be used for war.

"Celeste," Isla said, wondering if the way she spoke her friend's name was different than she had said the others. Wondering if saying a person's name thousands of times made it sound different coming from a mouth.

The Starling was prepared, of course. A dozen of her subjects joined her.

"My realm has been developing a way to manufacture tools and weapons, using solely our power," she said, gesturing to her people, bidding them to begin.

The crowd watched in wonder as they demonstrated the way they pooled their energy, making it so concentrated that, before their eyes, a sword was created in just moments. They had turned energy to metal, almost like Oro had turned the table to gold.

Almost.

This took a dozen Starlings and much effort. For one sword.

The king could likely gild them all in a single breath.

Celeste took the finished sword in her hand and lifted it up, to the endless cheers of all the Starlings in attendance.

Isla wanted to smile, wanted to say something to her friend. But all she did was call out the next name.

"Oro."

The king did not meet her gaze as he took his place. He had always looked at her with disdain. Now, after likely knowing she'd let him win the duel and using him as a prop for Azul's demonstration, it seemed he deemed her below his notice.

"We have found additional ways to spread light and heat throughout the island." He lit a fire in front of him with a curl of his fingers. Then he dipped his entire hand inside it before dragging it out again quickly, fingers splayed. The flames came apart, the fire like spatters of paint, flying across the room. There were screams—some islanders blocked themselves using their power.

But the flames had been contained in dozens of orbs. They landed harmlessly in hands and laps. "They will not go out, as long as the original flame is lit."

Between the endless hearths inside the castle, torches across the Mainland, and this demonstration, the king clearly had an obsession

with making sure flames were everywhere. Was it because they represented his rule? His realm?

He allowed the crowd a few more moments of inspecting the orbs of fire, throwing them in the air, marveling at their warmth, the light like a hundred fireflies lighting up the arena, before curling his hand. Smothering his flames.

The lights shriveled and died, just like he said they would.

Applause seemed to follow everything Oro did, and this demonstration was no different.

"Grimshaw" was the next name Isla spoke.

The Nightshade brushed past her. A stripe of chill danced down her arm at his slightest touch.

She needed to get herself together.

The crowd was silent. But they were clearly curious about what the Nightshade would show them. His realm had been a mystery ever since they had created their own stronghold. They were the enemy during the war. Even with a peace treaty, his kind weren't trusted at all. Many, Isla imagined, still believed Grim's people were responsible for the curses.

And maybe he was.

Grim stopped at the center of the arena. He gazed right back at the curious faces, turning to face them all to allow them to get a clear look at him.

"My realm has nothing productive to offer you," he said.

Then he left.

Silence. Whispers.

Isla felt her face go hot. With rage? With surprise?

She had given him more than enough time to prepare for her demonstration. Against her better judgment. Behind her friend's back. And he had made a mockery of it.

He had arrived empty-handed on purpose.

Why?

The Nightshade had the nerve to walk right toward her on his way back to the wings and say, "You're next, Hearteater," before becoming one with the shadows.

Demon. Monster.

She straightened. She wouldn't let him unnerve her. That was surely what he was after.

Isla didn't bother announcing herself as she readied for her turn. There was one thing she needed.

From the king.

"Would you make me a fire?" she asked him.

For a moment, he just frowned down at her. She wondered if he might ignore her, or refuse her, and she would have to ask some other Sunling for help. As if they would.

Then, with the smallest whip of his wrist, a column of fire appeared in the center of the arena.

"Thank you," she said tightly.

He did not nod, or even acknowledge her, before she walked toward the flames he had created.

All eyes on her. She should have been used to it by now, but their scrutiny was like a thousand knives, all turned in her direction.

Isla pulled a vial from her pocket, glass in the shape of a heart. It held a liquid thick and crimson as blood.

"Wildlings have developed advanced healing remedies," she said, holding the container up for all to see.

Now, she just needed to demonstrate its potency.

Before she could lose her nerve, the same way she had done a half dozen times before in preparation, Isla took a deep breath.

And put her entire arm in the flames.

Yells. Cries of horror. The crowd gasped, horrified, as Isla's skin charred. Melted.

She did not flinch. Even though the pain threatened to swallow her

whole. Her arm shook in the fire. Her other hand was curled so tight, her nails drew blood in her palm.

Just a little longer.

Tears welled up in the corners of her eyes, and she lifted her head, willing them not to fall. She must have looked triumphant to the audience. Pain-free.

She was not.

Not being able to take it any longer, not without falling to her knees and breaking like an egg in front of them all, she removed her arm.

The skin had peeled off in coils, leaving only angry red.

It was sickening to look at, to smell. Her stomach turned—a moment more and she would retch.

She took the vial's top off with her teeth, lip quivering uncontrollably. Then she poured every drop of the liquid across the burns.

Before her eyes, and everyone else's, the skin calmed. Knitted itself back together. Grew back, until her arm looked just as it had a few moments prior.

There was no mark of the fire.

The pain was not gone—not even close—but she kept it off her face as she bowed her head, signaling the end of her demonstration.

No one clapped. But they didn't need to. Isla could see the wonder in their faces.

Moonlings were the only ones on Lightlark who were supposed to be able to heal, using water. If Celeste's intel from her nobles and Ella were to be believed, they had begun making their skills scarce on the island. Charging too much. Healing less and less.

Almost *wanting* the rest of the island to be weaker.

Isla had just proven someone else could do what they did. Perhaps even better. Which, she knew, would only make Cleo hate her more.

In the end, Azul won.

Some would say the decision wasn't fair, but neither was the game.

CHAPTER SIXTEEN

SHADOWS

Isla's skin was still sore that night. She flinched as she slowly inched the thin strap of her gown down her arm, cursing herself for not wearing a different dress.

Then there was the matter of the zipper. From where it was placed, it typically required both hands to maneuver, to reach it—

"If you need help undressing, allow me to offer my services, Hearteater."

She jumped at the deep voice, spinning around.

Grim sat in a chair bathed in shadows, nearly all the way hidden. He leaned forward, elbows on his knees, eyes trailing her now bare shoulder, the strap hanging off it. The top of her dress slightly slipping down . . .

She righted it with her bad arm, then groaned, the flash of pain lightning behind her eyes.

The Wildling elixir might have healed her, but it hadn't been advanced enough to completely dull the ache. It was either take away the pain or heal—one, or the other. Of course, the rulers and islanders didn't need to know that.

It was why it was so important Isla never flinched. Never let anyone else see her pain.

It was why Terra and Poppy had made her practice, again and again, until she got it perfect.

"How did you get in here?" she demanded, voice thinner than she would have liked. He was so crass. So suggestive. She might have claimed she hated it.

But she didn't hate it.

She hated *herself* for not thinking his words were repulsive.

He shrugged. "Through the walls." Of course.

Isla remembered his demonstration. Anger replaced her pain. "Good. I suppose you can *leave* through the walls too, then," she said, pointing at one.

Grim stood. She swallowed. His size was always surprising. The height. The power that emanated off him in invisible tendrils.

"I will admit," he said, wicked smile tugging the side of his mouth. A step toward her. "This is not how I imagined you would want to spend our time in your chambers."

She scowled. Glared at him. Neither had enough bite. Both were offset by the blooming emotions she knew he could sense.

He was trying to distract her.

"You made a mockery of my demonstration, demon," she said, lest she forget why she was mad. "I told you about the trial. I gave you time to prepare."

Her inexplicable hurt must have peeked through her expression, because his eyes softened. "Hearteater," he said, his voice surprisingly gentle. "I thought you would have guessed by now, but let me make this clear. I have no interest in winning the Centennial. Or forming alliances. Or playing this game at all."

There was silence as his words washed over her.

He could have been lying.

But she had always focused on actions above words. They reflected motivations much more accurately. And Grim's words matched his actions. He hadn't attempted to be allies with the other rulers. He hadn't taken any of the demonstrations seriously.

She felt her face twist in confusion. "Then why are you here?" she said, finally voicing the one question she had about him. The one that blared over and over in her head every time he got close to her. Every time she wanted to get close to *him*. The Nightshade did not answer, so

she took a step toward him, filling the gap. Everyone wanted something. Everyone had motives. She had been trying and failing to uncover his the entire first fifth of the Centennial. Her gaze locked on to his, demanding an answer. "What do you want?"

Grim looked down at her, and she could have sworn his expression turned sad. But a moment later, the wicked smile was back. "I believe I've made it clear what I want," he said, running a finger down the arm that had been seared.

Isla braced herself for the pain—but it never came. It was as if, somehow, he was masking her hurt. His skin was cold to the touch. Soothing. Ice against a burn.

Still, she stepped away. "You didn't come to the Centennial for me," she said, refusing to allow him to get away with the nonanswer.

"No," he said simply. "I did not."

"Then why?"

He frowned. "Do you know how Lightlark was created, Heart-eater?" he asked.

Her hands curled into fists. She couldn't help but feel he was evading her question, but she preferred him speaking to simply vanishing, so she played along. Perhaps she would get useful information from him anyway. "It was formed by Oro's ancestor, the first Origin Horus Rey."

"That is a lie. The island was created by *two* people. Not just Horus, but also Cronan Malvere."

Her eyebrows came together.

"My own ancestor."

Isla had only ever heard of Horus Rey forming Lightlark, thousands of years before. Nightshades weren't even welcomed on the island, didn't even have a dedicated *isle* anymore.

"Lightlark became more powerful than either founder could have anticipated. It made both men greedy. Turned friend against friend. It

ended in a duel, and when Cronan lost, all of Nightshade fled to form their own land, one not nearly as strong as Lightlark."

His dark eyes found Isla's. And, though she wanted to, she found she couldn't look away.

"Nightshade power built this place just as much as Sunling's did. My father believed it was time for us to regain control of a land we had claim to."

That was the reason for the war between Nightshade and Lightlark.

No wonder Grim hadn't been invited to any of the previous Centennials. Isla wondered how Oro could host the person who had invaded his home and killed his kin. The king must have truly been desperate to end the curses.

Why? What was he hiding?

"And what do you think?" Isla asked, voice barely above a whisper and still feeling too loud.

Grim ground his back teeth together. "I told my father to sign the treaty. We had lost too many people. We were going to lose everything if we didn't agree to peace. As part of the agreement, I was sent to live on Lightlark. A reminder that if Nightshades slipped up, they could kill my father's only heir. I lived here for twenty years, until—"

Until. He didn't say the words, but Isla knew the next part well.

Until the curses were cast, and all the rulers of realm died in sacrifice on one horrific night. Until power was transferred to heirs for the last time. Until the new rulers and most of their people fled the island and the incoming storm that would engulf it.

Isla dreaded her next question. But she had to ask it. "Grim, did you cast the curses?"

He looked at her, really looked at her. "If I did, would you ever speak to me again?"

She moved back, tensed. Her nostrils flared. Her answer was immediate. "No. The curses killed countless of my people. Turned us into monsters." Her voice thickened. "It's the reason my parents are both dead."

Something like sadness flashed in Grim's eyes. "The curses killed my family too." His head dipped, and he did not break her gaze. "No, Isla, I did not cast those curses."

She knew it was foolish to believe any of the other rulers. But Grim's pain was real. And it mirrored her own.

"So why are you here?" she demanded. "To get revenge? To try to invade Lightlark again?" Another thought formed in her mind, and she paled. "To ensure the curses *don't* get broken?"

Grim raised an eyebrow. "Why are *you* here, Hearteater? What are you after?"

Her body went still. Lies filled her mouth, ready to be spoken, but Grim grinned. He had felt her nerves. Her hesitancy. He would know she wasn't telling the truth.

Isla did not break his gaze. But she also did not say a word.

The Nightshade only shook his head. "You know," he said, making his way toward the wall through which he'd come, "you ask a great deal of questions, Hearteater." He studied her from head to toe before frowning at her arm, as if he could sense the pain it still gave her. "For someone with so many secrets of her own."

CHAPTER SEVENTEEN

FROZEN

Isla spent the next day with her arm wrapped in ice. Ella had fetched a bucket of it from the kitchen and replaced it regularly, without question. The burns still hurt. But not as badly. She alternated the ice with her Wildling elixirs. The faster the skin fully healed, the less it would feel like a layer of herself had been sliced away.

Later, the lingering pain—and perhaps the equally pestering thoughts of the Nightshade—had made her restless. Instead of trying to find sleep that wouldn't come, she roamed the halls, doing her typical snooping.

That was when she noticed the commotion around the wing of the castle that held the arena.

They were setting up for a demonstration. Dozens of islanders milled around, yelling orders. She tried to get as close as possible, to get a hint of what the trial might be. But there were too many people. It wasn't long before her arm flared in pain again, calling for its ice.

Her efforts hadn't been fruitless, however. The vast majority of those wandering the halls wore white. Moonlings.

She shouldn't have been surprised when Ella knocked on her chamber door twenty-four hours later, in the dead of night.

Her skin still burned, but not as sharply. She had tried her best to speed up the healing process after seeing the signs of a trial being set up, doubling her creams and taking other elixirs by mouth. Still, she thought she'd have more time. Only someone as cruel as Cleo would plan their demonstration to happen at midnight.

"A test of desire," the Moonling ruler said, hands pressed together in prayer. She stood in the center of the arena, which had been transformed into a maze of waterways. Each of the rulers stood on points of its perimeter. Once they dove into the lanes, they wouldn't be able to see each other anymore, thanks to walls of ice that made the confines of the labyrinth.

There had been no warning. No time to change. That was how Isla had ended up in the freezing snow globe that the stadium had been turned into, in nothing but a tank top and tiny shorts. Surely, she would freeze in the water. The rest of the rulers weren't in their typical capes and elaborate dress. But they also weren't in sleepwear. Somehow, they had managed to put on clothes that would fare well in the water. Did something in their powers allow them to do so? Or had they insisted upon the time to change, while Isla had blearily followed Ella through the castle?

"A true ruler must deny the selfish wants of their heart, for the good of their realm. You will be guided through the maze by your own heart. It will lead you to what you desire most. The winner will be decided *not* by their desire, but by who can reach it first. For worse than desiring something above the good of one's realm is not being sure of what you want at all."

The king stood just a few feet away, eyeing the water like it had personally offended him. *He* wasn't wearing dainty pajamas. He wore gold trousers and a shirt, with sleeves he now carefully rolled up his wrists.

A patch of skin on his hand was slightly swollen, a rash forming.

"Giselroot, nasty thing," she said quietly, almost to herself.

He stiffened. Looked at her, as if it was the first time he noticed she had been positioned in the lane beside him. "You know what this is?"

She shrugged. "Of course. Plant with five points? Green spots? Yellow buds?"

Oro nodded slowly.

"Giselroot. Poisonous. Causes a rash, and bad dreams."

He blinked at her.

"All right, the bad dreams might have just been a tactic by my guardians to keep me away from them." Giselroot grew in the forest just outside the loose pane of her window. After Poppy and Terra had it sealed, they had warned Isla against the plant, lest she find another way out of her room. "You'll want to treat that with an elixir of milk, tomato paste, honey, willow bark, pasted ash, and crushed mulberries."

Oro's lips pressed together before he said, "Thank you." Like it was a very hard thing to say.

She narrowed her eyes. "Giselroot only grows deep in the woods, where the trees are close enough to touch. What in the realm were you doing in a place like that?" Her tone said, *Don't you know how dangerous it is?*

Oro fixed her with a strange look. Isla stared back.

Without warning, a bell sounded.

And Isla was forced to jump into her lane.

The water was a thousand needles piercing her skin. At first, the cold was almost welcomed against her raw arm. But it quickly sharpened, becoming too much, making it hurt even more. She immediately gasped for air, her chest a block of ice, the tips of her fingers and toes already numb.

Hundreds of islanders greeted her above, yelling, relishing in her weakness, jeering at her, cheering for their rulers.

Keep going, a voice in her head said, though her body screamed to get out of the water. She was surely at a disadvantage, coming from a place like the Wildling realm, which never saw a winter.

But she had been tested in the elements before.

Terra knew some of the trials might involve harsh weather conditions. When Isla was seventeen, she was left blindfolded in the middle of the woods, during a hurricane.

By the time she tore the fabric from her eyes, her guardians were long gone. The trees were bent in grotesque shapes from the wind, dirt

and leaves stuck to her skin, and bugs had already started gnawing at her ankles.

Forests were deadly to those who couldn't control them. It was why the king's choice to venture into them was so shocking.

It took her three days to get home. In that time, she drank spoiled water and sat shaking beneath a hastily made canopy of palm fronds, the fever in her head like a bell, ringing over and over. Knowing she would die if she stayed, she forced herself to walk, remembering her survival lessons. She hunted for food with bows and arrows she made herself, using the dagger she always kept strapped to her thigh.

In the haze, she cut her fingers, and the blood smeared her weapons, acting as a siren call to even more insects, which feasted on her flesh as if she was already dead.

By the time she collapsed outside the Wildling castle, she was so sick, it took their best healers weeks to bring her back to health.

You could have killed me were the first words out of her mouth once she could speak again, directed at Terra.

Her guardian had only smiled. *The only way not to fear death is to meet it.*

Isla knew what dying felt like. This wasn't it. So, she kept going, pushing, though the needles sank deeper, until they clicked against her bones, her entire body overcome with cold.

Ahead, there was a split in the maze. Isla wondered which route to take when she felt a faint pull in one direction.

Then, a pull in the other.

She stopped, angling her head to take a deep breath.

One direction felt like home—Poppy and Terra. Her people.

The other felt like more.

She couldn't quite make out what it meant, but the emotions were powerful. Intoxicating. Startling.

Cleo's words played back in her mind. Her heart was supposed to guide her. Why was it so undecided?

Time froze over as she treaded water.

Had it been a few moments?

Or minutes?

Or longer?

Snap out of it, a voice in her mind sounded.

She wanted freedom, that was for sure.

But was that truly all she wanted?

A whistle sounded somewhere, breaking her out of her thoughts. The first ruler had reached the end of their maze.

Isla was so far behind. It was time to make a choice.

To follow her heart.

She chose a direction and swam, reinvigorated, her chest full of frost, white plumes coming out of her mouth each time she gulped for air.

Her hair had divided into thick, frozen strands; her clothes did nothing to keep her warm. Her skin felt too stiff, her muscles fighting to flex in the unrelenting temperature of the water.

Just a little longer, she pleaded with her body, knowing it had been through worse. She had trained for this.

Her lungs began to shut down first, choking with water that had somehow broken through her mouth.

Another turn.

The maze seemed to be closing in around her; each time she went up for air, the crowd became blurrier. Their cheers farther away.

Was she even moving anymore? She couldn't feel her arms.

Everything became colder. Her lungs lurched.

Her eyes fought to blink open, one more time, and all she saw was light, retreating.

She was sinking.

If the trial killed her, she wondered if part of the prophecy would be fulfilled. Perhaps the Moonling ruler had chosen this trial, knowing it might kill one of the weaker rulers for her, without having to break the rules. At least, in that scenario, Celeste would live.

But her people wouldn't.

Terra and Poppy wouldn't.

This was not death. This death was too quiet. Too much like slipping into sleep.

She wanted all life had to offer. The long life of a ruler with powers, exploring all Lightlark, a lifetime of friendship with Celeste, perhaps even . . . love. Something she had judged others for. Including her own mother. Something she had always seen as reckless. She *wanted,* wanted so strongly, selfish things beyond just saving her realm and breaking the curses—

Slowly, her fingers uncurled from their fists. A groan sounded in the back of her throat, and she fought the urge to keep her eyes closed, willed her limbs back to life.

She clawed through the ice-cold water like it was the only thing standing between her and everything held in her heart.

Her vision went in and out, but she felt the end of the maze. She grabbed the glowing tablet of ice waiting there and hauled herself out of the water with all her remaining strength.

Isla didn't see what was written on the slab, didn't hear the crowd. All she felt was something warm washing over her body. Ella. The Starling draped a towel across her back.

She was shaking, her vision going in and out. "Please, get me to my room," she managed to say.

Isla owed Ella far more than pain cream, she thought as her attendant rushed her out of the stadium, using the cheers of the crowd and the crowning of Cleo as the winner as a cover. The Moonling had clearly chosen her trial to showcase her superiority over the others.

She might have been more concerned that Cleo was now tied with the king, and could potentially be choosing their matches, if she didn't feel so weak.

Ella was small but stronger than she looked, holding Isla up as they slowly made their way through the empty castle. Water dripped an

endless puddle behind her. The rest was frozen. Her lungs ached, two buckets of ice in her chest.

"I'll draw a bath," Ella said when they finally made it to her room. "And get tea." She rushed out of Isla's room.

Isla was going in and out of consciousness. Her body had gone numb.

Her mind was full of her mission.

She needed to find the bondbreaker.

For so long, she had denied her desires. Pushed them down. Her guardians' warnings were always on her mind. Saying her life didn't just belong to her. Teaching that wanting anything but saving her realm was selfish.

Now, she couldn't lie to herself any longer.

She wanted many, many things.

And she was willing to do terrible things to get them.

Not just for her. Her desires made her understand her people more than she ever had before. They deserved to have what they wanted. So did Celeste's people—including Ella.

I promise, she might have said aloud, or maybe her words never reached her mouth. Ella had helped her into the bath, and the hot water scalded her frozen skin, made her scream out, too dazed to hide her pain. *I'll find the bondbreaker. I'll break the curses.*

Even if it means breaking myself.

CHAPTER EIGHTEEN

CASTLE

Isla awoke feeling on the brink of death. There was a relentless cold at the center of her chest. All day, she stayed in bed, drinking broths. Ella fed the fire. Kept bringing tea. Drawing hot baths. By night, Isla only felt a little better.

Celeste risked a visit, bringing a special Starling soup recipe she had procured from Star Isle. "I'll go instead," she said as soon as she saw her.

And Isla knew she must have looked on the brink of death too. A groan escaped her as she pushed herself off the bed. She shook her head.

It was the twentieth day of the Centennial. Tonight was the full moon. Her only chance to go to Moon Isle undiscovered. "No offense, Cel," she said, "but you can't move like I do."

Her friend sighed. "I know. But—"

Isla shook her head again, cutting the Starling off. "If you get caught, it's over. We can't risk it."

Celeste frowned. "Can we risk *you?*" she asked pointedly.

Isla waved her concern off. She stretched her limbs as she formulated the hair dye again. "I'm fine," she lied. Celeste knew it was a lie.

But she also knew as well as Isla did that they didn't have another choice.

Everything she wanted was on her mind as she forced down the pain of her arm, the cold with every breath, her need for rest.

None of it meant anything compared to their need to find the bondbreaker.

***

Juniper might be the most or least trustworthy barkeep on the island, Isla still wasn't sure. But his information had been correct.

There were no guards on the bridge that night.

The Moonling curse meant that every full moon, the sea sought out Moonling blood. Ships were cracked in half by hundred-foot waves; girls were swept off cliffs by monstrous surges. The sea swallowed them, then went still.

Tonight, it was ravenous.

The entire isle was empty. It was so quiet, Isla could hear the sea banging against the cliff of the castle, over and over, knocks on a door, death demanding its due.

Moon Isle was an ornament encased in ice, water, and glass. From the first step off the bridge, Isla felt the frost, cold in her chest like regret. Harsh as the ruler who ruled it.

And, also, just as beautiful.

Fountains and thin rivers snaked across Moon Isle, giving the water-wielding Moonlings constant access to their power. The ice palace sat perched above, watching her as closely as the moon. The paths were carved out of mother-of-pearl, lined with marble statues depicting sea creatures with winding tentacles, fish-tailed women, and ships floating on nothing. No guards anywhere.

Unfortunately, she was going right toward where they all were hiding.

Celeste had learned the Moonling library was deep within the castle walls. That was where Isla was headed.

Her hair had been painted white with Wildling elixir. She wore the right dress. But something told her that being a Moonling was much more than that—and if any of the guards took one look at her, they would immediately know she was an impostor. Being outside during the full moon was the greatest hint to her identity of all. No Moonling

would survive being outside the palace tonight, so Isla needed to move like a ghost, get inside undiscovered. She stuck to the shadows, should anyone be watching from above.

The castle sat high on a hill of white rock. A thin, exposed path led from the gardens up to the castle entrance. Easy to monitor. Impossible for Isla to use without being detected.

She circled the mountain's perimeter, hoping to see another entrance. The rock was impenetrable—except for a window, fifty feet up, right at the bottom level of the palace.

There were no bars on its glass.

That was her way in.

Isla readied herself. Her palms were wet with nerves, so she smoothed them along the chalky rock, coating her hands in the stuff.

The cliff was nearly flat, but there were pockets. She had been trained to see the tiniest of holes, the invisible recesses.

Her hands found its first two placements, barely a few inches to cling to.

Then, with a grunt, she hauled herself up.

The first few moments of climbing were never too bad. The ground wasn't that far away. One wrong move, and she could just start over.

Things became more precarious thirty feet up.

She moved quickly, so as not to lose her momentum and not make time for fear, similar to swallowing down medicine too fast to taste it.

One of Terra's lessons. Her guardian had made her watch the monkeys that swept across the forest effortlessly, climbing trees with ease.

They didn't plan out every movement. They swung, knowing there would always be something for their arms or tail to latch on to.

Climb until your muscles learn the movements; leave your mind out of it, Terra said. And Isla climbed the tree, the cliff, the wall, again. Again. Again.

Her hands were used to this. They moved on their own, looking for grooves in the stone. Finding them. Going up. And up. And up.

Another move. One hand latched on to a slight bump. Her other fingers felt around for purchase.

But for once, the rock was smooth.

Nothing to hold on to.

Higher. She would need to look higher. Arm shaking with the effort, she lifted herself up, to find somewhere else for her other hand to hold. She barely muted a cry as her still-sensitive skin screamed in pain at the movement.

Nothing.

That was the problem with climbing an unfamiliar rock face. There were no guarantees. Still, there was always *something*. Some way to get up.

Her fingers were starting to get sweaty. The grip on the point of rock less secure. She felt both freezing and too warm. Did she have a fever? Was she sick?

No. Just weak. Her arm's skin was still slightly raw. The cold in her chest had intensified.

She needed to find placement for her other hand quickly.

Higher.

Despite her efforts to be silent, Isla grumbled with strain as she forced her arm to lift her even *higher*—

Only then did she find a slight hollow in the rock. She didn't waste a moment before shoving her fingers painfully into the pit, distributing her weight again.

That was close.

The window was just a few feet above. It was large enough for her to fit through, with a ledge, even, for support.

Isla made her next move. And just as her hand was about to lock on to another hold, the knob holding all her weight gave way.

She fell.

This high up, she might break her legs. Or, depending on how she landed, could crack her ribs. Or her spine.

In any case, she would be discovered. Found in a broken heap right outside the castle walls.

No bondbreaker.

No future that she wanted more than anything, a future that was changing every day the more she saw and experienced.

No.

So fast it was muscle memory, Isla unclipped the back of her necklace—a dagger made to look like a choker, sharp point instead of a clasp—and dug its hidden blade into the rock with all her strength.

She stopped falling.

Barely.

A moment later, the blade gave out.

By then, she had new hand placements.

She was twenty feet down from the window now. But she was alive. Whole.

Her stomach felt like it had been turned inside out, her heart drummed against the cliff.

No time to celebrate. Sweat licking the back of her neck despite the cold, Isla traveled the rest of the way up to the window. Roaring still filled her ears, from the sea, or the adrenaline, or her body warning that she wasn't ready to exert so much effort—she wasn't sure.

Minutes later, she hauled herself up the ledge, lifted the mercifully unlocked window, and dragged herself through.

The Moon Isle castle was quiet.

Every inch had been sculpted from white marble, dark-blue veins weaving through it like rivers. It reminded Isla of Cleo.

Spotless. Ageless.

Something about it was unsettling.

It was late. The Moonlings must have retreated to their rooms within the castle. Ever since the curses, Celeste said, most of them had moved

into the palace, the only building on the isle high enough to escape the monthly surges.

Even inside, Isla could hear the snarl of the sea, desperately rising in curls toward its inhabitants.

Most people must be asleep. Or perhaps there were rules. Cleo seemed to take pleasure in wielding her power. There could be a mandatory curfew. Or restricted areas of the castle.

It was a labyrinth.

Isla didn't know where she was going, just that the library was at the very back of the castle, overlooking the sea.

So, she went deeper.

The occasional footstep sounded through the hall, followed by orders. Guards, patrolling certain corridors.

There were so many. Much, much more than she had seen on other parts of the island. Now that she thought about it, there hadn't been *any* guards on Sky Isle. There weren't many on the Mainland either, except for the ones who lit the torches in the agora.

What was Cleo up to?

Isla hoped the library wouldn't be as highly monitored. The restricted section required Cleo's touch to be accessed, after all. But the farther she made it into the palace, the more she heard. Whispers through the walls. The gurgle of water being wielded. The high-pitched crackling of water being turned to ice.

Was she close to the dungeons? Or were the guards simply practicing?

For what?

There was a flash of white at her side, and she darted into the closest room she could find.

Empty. Just four stone walls that chilled her to the bone as she pressed against them, hoping the passerby hadn't seen her.

For a few moments, there was just silence.

Then, she heard voices.

"Were you patrolling this hall?" A man.

"No." A woman.

"Was Lazlo?"

The woman grunted her no. "Why?"

A second. "I saw someone."

"Here?"

Isla froze. He *had* spotted her.

The man and woman were walking down the hall now; she could hear their boots clearly against the marble, clacking like clinking china. Every step brought them closer to her.

"How would they get past the legion?" the woman said.

Legion?

Cleo was building an army.

Why?

What was she planning?

Isla didn't have much time to wonder.

Because a moment later, the door of the room she was hiding in flew open.

CHAPTER NINETEEN

UNDERWATER

Isla didn't give the guards time to reach for their ice blades or wield the sloshing water held in vials across their belts.

Before they could even yell for help, she had hit them in six different places, special points Terra taught her to target.

Their muscles slackened.

One good hit each in the back of the head, and they slumped down to the floor, passed out. Not one drop of blood.

Terra would be proud.

The moment she stopped moving, she was panting. The climbing, the fighting—it had taken too much energy. She really shouldn't be out of bed, let alone deep in another ruler's territory.

Too late now. She was here. And things were already starting to get out of hand.

As quietly as she could, and with all the strength she could muster, she dragged them fully into the room, closed the door behind them, and ran down the hall.

Either they would wake up and call for help, someone would realize they were missing and would call for help, or someone else was about to stop her and call for help.

It was clear that the time for being a shadow had passed.

Now she just needed to get into the library. As fast as her quickly weakening legs could take her.

The next passageway was empty, but the one after that had four guards, pressed against the wall, chins up, ice swords to their chests like

nutcrackers she once saw in a market. At the sound of her steps, they came to life, turning right to her.

Time to go, she thought, taking another turn instead, and hoping she was going in the right direction.

Their boots echoed loudly behind her, the sounds growing as more guards joined the pursuit. Isla ran as fast as she could, white dress curling behind her like a plume of steam. Her chest made concerning sounds with every breath. Her bones and muscles ached.

The halls were endless. Isla couldn't help but feel she must have taken a wrong turn. She wouldn't make it much longer.

Maybe she was getting farther away. Maybe she had become disoriented in her struggle to outrun the guards. Maybe—

Then she heard it.

The sea, louder than before, echoing like thunder. A beast shaking the walls of the castle with its firm grip.

The library had to be close.

She took off toward the sound of the sea, following its force, wincing at the pulsing of pain of her arm and her chest and her head, like the three of them were having a conversation. The farther she made it into the castle, the more the chandeliers on the ceilings shook, pale crystals clinking together. The more works of art teetered on their hooks. The Moonling curse was ruthless.

How many more cycles would it take for the castle to simply be knocked off its cliff, into the ocean's waiting mouth? When would the sea be rewarded for its efforts by getting the entire palace and its inhabitants in one fell swoop?

Not tonight, she hoped, as she ran and ran and ran, faster than the guards, as fast as she could without collapsing.

Until she nearly crashed into a wall.

A dead end.

No more halls. No more turns. No doors.

Just a wall.

She hunched over, hands on her thighs, and began coughing, the cold in her chest crawling up her throat. Her knees wobbled.

The steps behind her had turned into a stampede, and they were closing in. A few more seconds, and they would have her surrounded.

The ocean made another move against the palace, raging. She expected, this close to the exterior, to feel the hit in her bones, the sea colliding directly against the stone in front of her.

But as she braced herself for the impact, the wave hit—and the rock in front of her did not shake nearly as much as it should have.

Which meant there was something else behind this wall.

Just as the guards rounded the corner, Isla slipped on Celeste's gloves as quickly as she could and pressed against the bricks.

The stones began turning, a puzzle undoing itself, unlocking a door.

It opened. And she pushed herself through, then slammed it closed, hoping it would seal behind her.

The guards were a flurry of sounds on the other side, alerting more of their crew. The *legion*, perhaps.

"Intruder!" she heard. "In the library!"

She was trapped inside. Cornered.

But at least now she knew for certain she had found it.

Isla turned to find a frozen library. Perfect. As if she wasn't already cold enough. Every book was trapped in walls of ice. Slab after slab formed rows, an entire room of parchment and frost.

She should have suspected that Cleo would have made the *entire* library restricted, instead of a specific section.

Bangs sounded outside as the guards tried to break the wall down.

No time to waste. She took off, running through the icy rows, nearly slipping on the frosted-over marble floor. Her feet skated as she rounded the corner—

And came face-to-face with a monstrous wave. It hit the set of glass doors with a force that seemed to shake the castle to its foundations. If

it wasn't for her last-minute gripping of an ice-coated shelf, she would have fallen to the floor.

The doors led to a curling white balcony now flooded with sea-foam like a rabid mouth, the aftermath of the sea as it retreated, gathering its strength to strike once more. It was a wonder the glass doors hadn't shattered. They must have been reinforced with enchantment somehow.

Enchantment.

Where were the relics? All she saw were books.

"She's inside!"

"Get the ruler!"

Ruler? Isla swallowed. Cleo was supposed to be sleeping in the Mainland castle. It was tradition to spend the most time there, especially during the first twenty-five days.

She had to hurry. Her eyes strained to take in every inch of the library. It only had one floor.

Nothing. Only books contained in ice, for as far as she could see.

She must have missed something.

Isla whipped around, ready to take a closer look at the front shelves, when another crushing wave sent her tumbling forward.

This time, she hit the floor.

There was a terrible cracking sound as her head smacked against it.

For a moment, there was just blinding white. She blinked, willing her vision to come back, telling her body there was no time to waste, no time to give in to pain.

Her cheek had nearly stuck to the ground. Her mind spun as she lifted it, and the world tripped before righting itself.

Her arms shook as she made to get up.

That was when she saw it.

The floor was frosted over. Her body heat had warmed it enough that the icy coating had cleared, revealing a second library beneath.

Water. Dozens of relics were encased in water, chained down, floating below the floor.

A cape, its fabric moving unnaturally, flipping this way and that.

An arrow with a snowflake point.

Crystal daggers.

Books with locks.

Keys long as her arms.

No bondbreaker.

Nothing that even resembled an oversize glass needle.

Disappointment quickly turned to anger as she stood on shaky legs, stumbling to the side, having to steady herself against a block of ice.

Something hot dripped down her cheek.

Tears?

Was she crying and she didn't even know it?

She lifted a trembling hand that came back crimson.

No. Blood.

Isla stepped forward and nearly collapsed.

Her other foot made to move, but her knee gave way.

First, her sore, burned arm. Then, the effects of the Moonling's demonstration. Now, this head injury.

It was too much.

Isla had sworn she would break her curse, even if it meant breaking herself.

Perhaps she should have worded her promise a little differently.

Bangs echoed through the room—but they weren't coming from the balcony or the sea. No, they were coming from the wall through which she had entered.

"We have the entire legion out here," a voice yelled from the other side. "The ruler is on her way. You are cornered. There is nowhere to run. There is no way out."

Isla smirked.

He was right. There was nowhere left to run.

But *no way out?*

In that, he was wrong.

"Good thing I never planned on getting out the way I came," she said to no one. Every part of her ached as she reached back her good arm and pulled her starstick from its place against her spine.

She didn't know how to use it accurately for small distances or places she had never been before. But her room in the Mainland castle was neither.

The wall came down just as she portaled away.

CHAPTER TWENTY

TEA

For two full days, Isla slept. She only awoke to eat and sip broth, then she drifted away again. She had strange dreams. Grim was in some of them. Flashes of him. Of her. Of *them*.

By the twenty-third day, when Ella came with news of afternoon tea, Isla knew it was time to get up. To shed the pain and weakness like the snake on her crown shrugging off its skin.

The bondbreaker wasn't in the Star Isle, Sky Isle, or Moon Isle libraries. Which only left one place.

Sun Isle.

The king's own land. It made sense that a relic as powerful as the bondbreaker would be kept there.

But Isla had no way of getting gold clothing. Barely any hair dye left.

And more problems than ever.

Cleo knew someone had attacked her guards, gotten into her library, and left without a trace.

She must have suspected Isla immediately. Ever since that first dinner, Cleo had had her sights on her. The physical description the attacked guards would have provided would have simply confirmed her suspicions.

Cleo didn't have proof it was her. But she *knew.*

She had to.

The wound to her head had mostly healed, thanks to her Wildling elixir. The white had washed out of her hair. She had thrown her Moonling clothing into the fire.

Still, Isla felt like the truth of her whereabouts three nights prior was written across her body as she walked inside the tearoom.

It must have been beautiful, once upon a time. Now the windows, giant arches every few feet, were covered with thick fabrics like mirrors in an old house. Like her room back home. The ceiling, domed and made of glass, had been painted over, trapping the sunlight outside. The only light came from hundreds of orbs of fire that floated precariously overhead, the same ones the king had displayed at her demonstration. Marble columns lined the room the way guards might if Oro allowed them inside. The king didn't need guards, however. Not even against rulers of realm. He was more powerful than all of them combined.

Isla felt that power ringing through the room as Oro entered it.

Cleo swept inside next, and her eyes immediately locked onto Isla's. Her expression revealed nothing.

But Isla's palms began to sweat. She forced herself to keep the Moonling's gaze until an attendant guided Isla to her seat.

The Moonling ruler knew. Isla felt it in her bones.

Cleo was a dangerous enemy. One who was building an army. For what? Did any of the other rulers know that between the legion and her supposed ships, the Moonling seemed ready for war?

Once all the rulers were seated, staff came pouring out of a large set of doors, carrying gleaming trays of china. They circled the table once, then stopped suddenly, their movements perfectly choreographed. Behind each chair stood a Skyling, a Moonling, and a Starling.

Oro nodded.

The Starlings lifted their hands, and tiny plates flew in a flurry, landing carefully on the table, followed closely by teacups, which fell atop them with a clink. Three cups total sat in front of Isla. Ornately decorated teapots hovered overhead, high above the table, heavy with liquid. Water-wielding Moonlings lifted their hands, and steaming tea Sunlings had no doubt heated fell from the pots like tiny waterfalls,

through strainers the Starlings held steadily, rich red liquid that spilled into her first mug. The pots straightened and moved in a circle before her second cup was filled with honeyed gold. The third tea was the deep blue of sapphires.

The Starlings lifted their arms again, and cubes of sugar fell into each cup, followed by drops of honey and shots of cream. Each flavor of tea received its own treatment, the blue tea getting a slice of lemon, the red receiving a mint leaf, the gold gifted a candied orange peel.

Finally, the Skylings whipped their wrists, sending a gentle breeze over their drinks, cooling them.

Grim sighed. "I suppose this isn't the moment to mention I detest tea?"

Oro ignored him. "Please enjoy," he said.

Isla loved tea. She would have smiled under happier circumstances. Wildlings were experts at collecting the richest herbs, leaves, and spices that, when steeped, created the most delicious drinks.

She reached for the red one first. The drop of cream had turned it the pink of dahlias. She brought the cup to her lips tentatively, bracing herself for the burning liquid. But the Skylings had cooled the tea perfectly—she took a deep sip and almost groaned. It tasted like berries without the bitterness, honey without the heaviness.

Her eyes had fluttered closed, and she only opened them when the tea was drained from its cup. She lowered it and found Oro watching her.

"Any match to Wildling tea?" he asked.

"It's certainly drinkable," she said flatly. Then she reached for the second cup.

Cleo studied her. Too carefully. "How *do* Wildlings take their tea?" she asked, sharp eyes gleaming. "With a splash of blood?"

Isla sipped the second tea slowly. This one—the gold one—tasted of caramel. "And we drink it from the skulls of our conquests," she said steadily, smiling good-naturedly, like the Moonling's words were a joke from a friend and not a barb from a now certain enemy.

There were a few moments of clattering and quiet as they drank their tea. Isla finished her first cup and peered into it, noticing a strange pattern in the leaves that stuck to the bottom.

Her next one had something similar.

By the time she finished her third, her blood had gone cold.

Oro rose.

"Welcome to my demonstration," he said. Tension filled the room. Power surged.

Demonstration? But there weren't even any islanders present.

Though, she supposed, that wasn't truly a rule. Just a custom. Something most rulers preferred too, to display their excellence at their own trials.

The king's pointer finger circled the lip of one of his teacups. "This is no ordinary tea," he continued, his tone steady. "It is a truth tea."

Isla went still. Dread dripped down her spine.

"Your greatest secret is written in the leaves."

She risked a look down at her cups.

And saw her greatest truth written across the three of them, in careful script.

I have no power.

It took every drop of her training not to let her horror filter through her face. She remained calm, though inside she was a tempest, desperate for escape.

She studied the other rulers as a distraction from the panic that had turned her skin to thorns. Cleo had gone paler than usual. Azul simply frowned. Grim looked ready to coat the entire room in Oro's ash. Celeste darted a rare, risky look in her direction, eyes wide with a message.

It's you, she seemed to be saying. Of course. The Starling's greatest secret was one she was keeping for Isla.

The urgency of her glance said *run*.

Before Isla could debate any move, the king picked up his first cup and said, "Whoever shares their secret wins my trial."

There was a shatter of glass as Celeste dropped her cups to the floor, taking herself out of the challenge. She looked over at Isla meaningfully, for just a moment, and her heart swelled. Celeste was a better friend than she deserved.

Azul's broke next.

Without wasting another moment, Isla pushed hers to the floor and watched them break into a thousand pieces, her secret lost in the shards.

Grim let his own fall one by one, eyes trained on the king. Isla had never seen him look so murderous. He had transformed into the famed Nightshade killer, the ruthless ruler she had heard warnings about. His expression held promises of torture and darkness.

The force of his invisible power lashed out, waves of searing chill coating the room. For a moment, her bones felt hollow, dead.

One thing was for sure. Grim *did* have a secret. And if even the idea of it being revealed produced this much anger, Isla was afraid to know what it was.

Just Oro and Cleo were left.

This was the last trial.

The king had won the duel and the demonstration of power. Cleo had won her own trial and Celeste's.

They were tied.

Whoever won this one would decide the matches the rulers would break into. The decision was important. Because of the first rule, a ruler could not kill the person they were joined with. The choice would force alliances, guide their search for the meaning of the rest of the prophecy, shape the rest of the Centennial. Perhaps even decide who would be targeted to be killed.

Oro's gaze was unrelenting as he stared down the Moonling, daring her to reveal her secret. And for a moment, Isla thought she might.

But, thinking better of it, Cleo sent the glass to the ground.

The king had officially won the trials.

His eyes were lifeless as he stared down at his first cup, and said, "I."

He let it fall to the floor.

The second. "Am."

For the third, he looked up and caught Isla's eyes. He frowned a bit, as if disturbed his gaze had shifted her way. But he did not look away as he spoke the third and final word of his greatest secret: "Dying."

CHAPTER TWENTY-ONE

PAIRED

The king was dying. What did that even mean? Chaos erupted at his confession, but he said nothing more before sweeping out of the room. Claiming his win.

It was a secret that affected them all.

Oro's life-force was directly correlated with the island's. Did that mean Lightlark was at risk?

He was the strongest of them. An Origin, who was Starling, Skyling, Moonling, and Sunling combined. If *he* was dying . . .

What hope did the rest of them have?

Isla heard a soft knock at her door, far past midnight. *Celeste.*

The Starling hurried inside, looking as if she had seen a ghost.

"That was close" was all she said.

Isla's stomach dropped, remembering the words printed in her cup. She imagined Celeste's were nearly the same.

"I know." She frowned. "Thank you. You shouldn't have to protect me like this, but—thank you."

Celeste waved her thanks away, as if it was nothing. But it wasn't nothing. The only way Isla could ever repay her friend for the risk she was enduring on her behalf was to find the bondbreaker.

"What do you think it means?" Isla asked.

The Starling seemed to know immediately she meant the king's confession. She shrugged. "I'm not sure. But it's reason enough for us to hurry up and find the bondbreaker so we can get off this island."

She was right. Once they were free of the curses, they could be free of Lightlark. The king's death wouldn't affect them or their realms.

But there were even more factors that rushed their already limited timeline. And complicated their plan.

She told Celeste about the disastrous display in the Moon Isle castle and Cleo's almost certain knowledge that Isla had broken in.

Celeste walked around Isla's room, hands coated in sparks. Her emotions often triggered them, which was part of the reason she always wore gloves. To keep her energy in check.

"I'll do my best to get information on the Sun Isle library" was all she said after a long while. Isla nodded, though that wouldn't solve their biggest issues. How was she supposed to sneak onto Sunling land without gold clothing? Celeste finally stopped pacing and clasped her palms together, making the sparks fall away like ribbons, vanishing before they hit the floor. "In two days, teams are being decided. Oro will hopefully match us together. Then we won't have to work in secret. We will find a way for you to get onto Sun Isle undetected."

Isla didn't want to question her friend, especially when she had complicated everything by making Cleo suspicious of her, but she couldn't help voicing a doubt. "What if we aren't paired together?"

Celeste frowned. She placed a gentle palm, still buzzing with energy, against Isla's cheek. "*I* know how incredible you are, my brilliant friend," she said. "But they do not. The king is not going to pick you. Or me, for that matter."

Isla had to admit she was right.

"Now," Celeste said. "It's not all bad news, is it? We know for certain that the bondbreaker is in the Sun Isle library now. We will get you inside. You will find the bondbreaker. We will use it. Break our curses. You'll get your power. Our realms will be freed. We could be off the island in a week. Two weeks, at the most."

Said like that, it sounded easy.

But Isla knew now that nothing on Lightlark ever was.

***

On the twenty-fifth day of the Centennial, they returned to the throne room for the pairing ceremony.

"King." Azul's tone was steady, though his eyes flashed with urgency. "Are you going to explain your . . . *truth?*"

This time, the king sat on his throne, as if reminding the rest of them of his position.

Even if he was, supposedly, dying.

Oro's crown glinted beneath the light of the flames above. He frowned.

The rest of the rulers were silent, clearly wondering the same thing Azul had so helpfully verbalized.

Finally, the king spoke. "Since the last Centennial, the island has been steadily weakening. Elders have died. Buildings that have stood for thousands of years are now ruins. Our most ancient creatures have vanished." He gripped the sides of the throne so strongly, his knuckles turned white. "The curses. Centuries of rulers living away from the island. Thousands of our people leaving. It has all taken its toll on Lightlark. On *me*."

Isla thought of her own realm. The same things had happened. All signs that too little power was being injected to the land and not enough ability was being used.

Oro rose from his throne. He looked at each of them, eyes hollow as ever. "I fear this Centennial is not simply *a* chance to break our curses. I fear this is our *last* chance."

The room was silent.

Surging power—from anger or fear or wariness, Isla didn't know—filled the hall.

Azul spoke again. "How do you know you're dying?"

With that, the king lifted his sleeve. Starting from his elbow, his golden skin had started to gray. It looked almost blue. "It's spreading," he said. "Quicker than I anticipated." His jaw locked. "Part of my power

and role has been to keep the island warm and full of light for centuries, even during the endless storm." He frowned. "That power has weakened. The last decade has been our coldest in history. It is causing plants and animals to die. I have been trying to lessen its impact . . . but soon, I won't be able to stop it."

That was why he had commanded that all the hearths remain lit. Why there were so many torches across the Mainland, and fire in nearly every room of the castle. They were all masking the king's weakness.

He stepped down the stairs, putting him at their level. "I hope you see now why it is more important than ever to figure out and fulfill the prophecy."

The king motioned to the wall. Words began to be carved along the stone in large, fire-coated letters. The oracle's riddle, the one Isla had been taught years prior. The key to breaking the curses.

Only joined can the curses be undone
Only after one of six has won,
When the original offense
Has been committed again
And a ruling line has come to an end
Only then can history amend.

"'Only joined can the curses be undone,'" Oro read. "That is why we break into teams, to fulfill the prophecy. And attempt to solve it. A reminder of the first rule. A ruler is forbidden from assassinating their partner."

Isla wasn't really concerned with the prophecy. Her and Celeste's plan didn't require it.

Still, she pretended to read the words on the wall while running ideas through her mind. Perhaps she could tweak her elixir potion to dye clothing . . . she might be able to make one of her own gowns gold.

It would never work. Plus, she barely had enough elixir for one more shot at dyeing her hair, let alone an entire swath of fabric.

She could rob a Sunling in the market and take their clothes?

Isla winced at that idea.

Horrible. Also, the Sunling would immediately report the crime, and Oro would know someone meant to sneak onto his isle.

Isla was so focused on feigning interest in the prophecy and plotting her attempt to sneak into the Sun Isle library that she didn't realize her name had been spoken until it was repeated so loudly she startled.

"*Isla,*" the king was saying.

Her expression must have given away that she had no idea what he had said previously, or if she had been asked a question, because the king gave her a grating look.

"My choice of partner," the king repeated through his teeth, clearly hating every word coming out of his mouth. The room fell away. She forgot to school her expression or control her emotions around Grim. Her mouth might have been hanging open. She might have accidentally shot Celeste a horrified look. "Is Isla."

CHAPTER TWENTY-TWO

DEAL

This was bad. Dangerous.

She was supposed to be matched with Celeste. They had a plan.

This was yet another factor that complicated everything.

Why in the realm would the king want to be matched with her?

The last thing Isla wanted was to be forced to spend time with the Lightlark ruler. Not just because he was insufferable, but also because doing so would surely mean having to use her powers in search of a way to break the curses, using the prophecy.

Powers she didn't have.

Would he be able to sense her powerlessness if they spent more time together? Grim hadn't. But Oro was the king of Lightlark—his abilities were endless.

She had to find a way out of it . . . an excuse. She waited for Celeste to knock on her door, to brainstorm.

Celeste. Her friend had been paired with the worse possible ruler. Cleo. She felt a pang of dread.

Everything had gone so wrong.

Because of the king.

Hours later, there was a knock on her door. She had done everything she could to distract herself, waiting for the Starling to finally arrive. Isla had taken a bath, as if she could wash the day off. She had put on her comfiest clothes, the pieces she had sneaked into her luggage before leaving the Wildling realm—an oversize long-sleeved shirt Poppy had let her wear at night. Tight pants that were just as soft as the shirt.

Celeste, finally, she thought as she threw the door open.

But it wasn't Celeste.

Oro's eyebrows were slightly raised as he took her in. She supposed she looked like a completely different person—makeup off, hair in a bun atop her head, shirt five sizes too large. She might have been worried that the king had seen her like this, without her Wildling temptress mask on, if she wasn't so annoyed.

She crossed her arms across her chest. "Do you normally call upon rulers at midnight?"

He matched her frosty expression before looking over her shoulder, into her room. "May I enter?"

Her chest tightened. There were many things in her room that would give her and her secrets away. Her starstick. Her reliance on elixirs. But she couldn't say no. It would only make him suspicious. "I suppose."

She should have anticipated he would seek her out. He *had* decided to pair up with her—for whatever reason. Isla had excused herself as soon as possible, fleeing to her room, fearing everyone in the hall would be able to hear the unsteady beating of her anxious heart if she stayed too long.

He strode past her and frowned at the state of her room.

It wasn't even that messy. There were a few dresses she hadn't managed to put away strewn across the furniture, and teacups littered her nightstand, but, what, was the king's room perfect?

She closed the door and didn't stray far from it. "Yes?" she said flatly.

Oro carefully picked up one of her dresses, placed it on the bed, and took a seat on the chair that it had previously occupied, leaning back as if it was his own room. And Isla supposed it was.

His fingers trailed the curling sides of the seat as he said, "I would like to make a deal."

For a moment, Isla considered grabbing her starstick from its hidden place in the wardrobe and portaling somewhere far away. It would be so easy . . .

Somehow, she forced herself to stand very tall and say, "Oh? What is it you propose?"

They were already paired. She didn't understand why he wanted to make a deal on top of that but decided it would be best to allow him to speak. Perhaps she would finally get some answers.

He laced his long fingers together. "I have a theory about the curses, one I've been working through the last half century. And I believe you are able to help me." She wanted to laugh and say if it was power he needed, he should ask someone else. She wanted to make any excuse she could. "You see, I require a knowledge of nature. One you clearly possess."

So that was why he had saved her that first day. Why he had paired them together. He *did* need something . . . "What is the deal?"

"You are, of course, aware of the second-to-last line of the oracle's riddle. One of our realms must fall for the curses to be broken." Isla nodded. "As we are a pair, I cannot harm you. And, if you help me find what I seek, I will do my best to protect you from the other rulers as well."

Protect.

She hated that word, though she clearly needed to be protected.

She wished she didn't.

Also—*his best?*

She gave him a withering look. Her unfiltered thoughts came out. Why bother playing the game she did with everyone else, acting a part, telling them only what they wanted to hear? Every time she looked at him, all she heard was the first step of her guardians' plan in her head. To seduce him. To steal his powers.

Did they think so little of her?

Did the *king* think so little of her that he believed she needed his protection?

"*You* want to protect me? I thought you were dying."

Oro's eyes turned hot as fire. She imagined if he didn't need her, or wasn't forced to adhere to the rules, he would have lit her aflame with a single look.

"Is it a deal or not, Wildling?" He spit out the last word like it burned his tongue.

Isla smirked. "I disgust you, don't I?" she said. She took one step toward him. "Is it the heart eating?" she asked, pleasure blooming as his frown deepened. "Or the dresses?" She feigned compassion. "What a shame the only person who can help you with your supposed *theory* repulses you so much."

Oro stood.

He didn't answer her question, but she could see it clear on his face. He *was* disgusted by her and her kind.

"You are wasting my time," he said through his teeth. "Do we have a deal, or not?"

For a moment, she considered.

She had no idea what the king's theory was and didn't care. What she *did* care about was that this proposed alliance offered her something she needed.

The closest chance she might have at getting into the Sun Isle library.

Isla didn't have to go along with his plan. He just needed to believe she would.

Still—

In case Oro's strategy did end up having merit, it could make a good backup plan. So, she needed to assure Celeste's safety as well. But if she asked outright, Oro would suspect their alliance . . .

"It's only a deal if I am able to decide a second realm that will remain safe."

His frown managed to deepen even further. "Is there one you have in mind?" he demanded.

She shrugged noncommittally. "If I'm helping you break the curses, I should at least get to determine one other realm that deserves to be

saved." Her smile was feline. "And, since you *require* me, it seems there might be room for negotiation."

Oro's jaw tensed. It seemed he hadn't expected any opposition. Chimes sounded, almost making Isla jump, marking the hour. Officially midnight. When they were over, Oro said, "Fine. So, it's a deal?"

It felt good, deciding on her own. Forming a backup plan. Her entire life, she had listened to others. Her guardians. Celeste. Even though they only had her best interests in mind, it felt freeing, making this choice.

"It's a deal," she said firmly, wondering what in the realms she was getting herself into.

"Good."

She walked toward her door, eager to have this meeting be over. "When do we start?"

The king did not follow her the way she planned. "Now."

"Now?" Her voice was too panicked. But she needed time to figure out an excuse for her powerlessness . . . to prepare . . .

"Is that a problem?" he asked, gaze narrowing.

She glared at him. "Well, I did have plans to *sleep*." Speaking of sleep . . . this close, she could see the king had purple crescents below his eyes. Was the king sleeping at all? Oro didn't budge, or react to her words, so she said, "Fine. Just let me get dressed." She reached for one of her new dresses. "If you could step outside—"

Oro frowned at the gown she had chosen, as bright and revealing as the rest. "You can't wear that."

Back when she was still preparing for the Centennial, Isla had dreaded meeting the king. She had wondered if she might cower in his presence, or if he would sense her lack of powers and kill her as soon as he could. Now, looking up at Oro and his disapproving frown, Isla realized that her main problem would be controlling her urge to throttle him.

"Are you telling me how to dress now?" she demanded.

Oro blinked slowly, annoyed. "During our excursions together, no one can know you are ruler of Wildling."

She stiffened. "Why?"

"Lightlark doesn't like you."

No kidding. Still, Isla scowled. "Excuse me?"

"Some ancient creatures on the island, the ones that still live in the deepest pockets of Lightlark, believe Wildlings abandoned them five hundred years ago. If they sense you, or hear rumors that you are near their lands, they will attack. Which would only end in spilled blood and too much attention to our efforts."

She knew Wildlings weren't liked but had never heard this reason. *Abandoned?* The bloodthirsty Wildlings had practically fled the island. Or, at least, that was what she had always been taught. "So . . . you want me to dress differently?"

"Not just that." He took a step toward her and lowered his voice. "I can't sense your abilities, Wildling."

Her stomach collapsed. She made to step back—

"I can tell that you're cloaking them," he continued, without missing a beat. "I just ask that you keep doing that when we're on the isles."

Isla blinked. Again. "So . . . you don't want me using my powers." She felt like falling over. This was a *good* thing. A great thing.

Lucky—she had gotten lucky. Isla was both grateful and anxious. Luck was dangerous.

Because just like any rare elixir, it was bound to run out.

He nodded. "If you do, those ancient creatures will be immediately drawn to you."

Isla wondered about these mysterious ancient creatures. And why even the king of Lightlark wanted to avoid them. She pretended to look pained, inconvenienced. Angry, even. "Fine."

"Good." He looked down at her clothes and said, "That will do."

"These are pajamas . . ."

He just blinked at her.

Isla wanted their time together to be over as soon as possible, so she shrugged, quickly braided her hair, and left without her crown.

CHAPTER TWENTY-THREE

STORM

Oro stepped out into the darkness with ease, a king of day who now walked only through night. Isla wondered if it pained him to be outside his castle, remembering how things looked in the sunlight. Or maybe he was used to it.

Five hundred years was a long time.

She didn't ask him any of it as she struggled to match his pace.

Isla assumed they were going to the agora, or to one of the isles beyond it. But, before they could reach the valley, he turned sharply to the left.

"Where are we going?" she asked.

Oro walked several steps without saying a word. They continued down the green hills of the Mainland, far away from islanders enjoying their night. Far from any trail.

"Are you going to ignore me?" Part of her wanted to stay silent. It didn't really matter where he was taking her as long as she got what she wanted from this pairing, right? But his disdain had turned disrespectful.

He kept walking, and she had a good view of his golden cape, floating gently with the nighttime breeze.

She stopped, arms crossed.

The moment she stopped, he did too. His back tensed before he slowly turned around. He opened his mouth, but she beat him to it.

"Just because you *asked* me to wear *this,*" she said, motioning toward her too-big shirt and pants fit to ride a horse, "and asked me not to wear *this*"—she reached up and flicked his crown, the metal singing in

response. Her nail sang too, in pain, but she didn't dare wince—"doesn't mean I'm not *also* a ruler of realm. You will treat me with respect, *King*." She spat the last word out like it was poison.

Poppy would have dropped dead hearing the way she dared speak to the king of Lightlark. Especially with what her guardian had commanded her to do.

But she had tired of filtering herself, of shoving her emotions down, of telling everyone what they wanted to hear. What had it gotten her?

Cleo now almost certainly wanted to kill her. They hadn't yet found the bondbreaker. The matches had turned out to be a disaster.

He glared at her. No, he didn't like her tone or the crown flicking one bit. "We are going to the storm," he said sharply before turning around and continuing on his way.

The storm?

She had no idea what he meant. But she followed him again, content at least to have gotten a response.

They were walking toward the coast. The one she knew Azul often liked to visit. The air began tasting of salt. Her hair blew back, braid whipping wildly.

In Wildling lands, the wind whispered. It sang songs and passed along gossip and whistled melodies high-pitched as clock chimes. Before Terra and Poppy had it sealed shut, Isla had sometimes kept the loose pane in her room open during the day, hoping to catch bits and pieces of what the wind said.

The wind spoke of heartbreak, from Wildlings who had made the mistake of falling in love. Of hearts, eaten and torn apart by nails sharp as knives. It told her stories that seemed old as the trees themselves, born of seeds that were rumored to come straight from Lightlark.

The Wildling newland had been formed just five hundred years prior, but its foundation was ancient. It was said that after they fled the island and its cursed storm, a hundred Wildlings sacrificed themselves to create their new land, relinquishing their power to the dry, infertile dirt.

Flowers bloomed from their blood, forests grew in a matter of weeks, and the newland was born from their bones.

That was what the wind said, anyway. Isla had found it to be quite dramatic.

Sometimes, she would answer it. Confide in it. Trapped in her orb of fogged glass, she spoke her thoughts to the wind.

It never responded. Not once.

But Isla hoped it listened.

They reached yet another steep incline. Her calves began to strain.

She wasn't sure why the king would take her to this part of the Mainland. What was there even to see? The ocean?

Then, she spotted it. Something had swallowed the coast.

A storm gone still.

Dark clouds like blotches of ink stained the sky above the beach. Silver lightning strikes thick as blades shot out of them and down to the sand, glittering in jittering energy. A ringlet of fire hovered close by, its flames stuck in time. Enormous, deadly spouts leaked from gaps in the clouds, long sheets of water like beams of moonlight tinged in purple.

The sea had been pulled back like a blanket and stacked high—a wave tall as a tower crested but never fell. It was frozen, though not in ice. Even from her height, Isla could see the water running within it, bubbling. Waiting. It had left a long stretch of sea floor uncovered. Sparkling gems and long-lost ancient trinkets coated the sand, alongside shells.

It was the curse on the island, temporarily subdued. The enchanted storm.

Was this what Azul was always visiting?

There were whispers, calling her forward. The storm pulsed with power. She wanted to see it up close.

The cliff closest to the storm was broken into shards. Parts of it had fallen away, leaving two-hundred-foot gaps between half a dozen islands

of rock. Some were connected by hastily made bridges, with planks so far apart it seemed easier to fall through than actually reach the next step. They made the bridges to the isles look safe.

The king took a step toward one.

"No," she said simply.

Oro turned to look at her.

"No?" he asked, as if he must have misheard her.

She didn't meet his eyes but could have guessed he was looking down at her with something like disgust.

The king sighed. She saw a flash of movement, like he had pressed his fingers to his temple in frustration. "It is steady. But if for some reason you did fall, I would obviously save you."

Isla turned and pinned him with a glare. "*Save* me? Like you did the first day?"

Oro stiffened. Then he returned her look and said, "*Yes, like I saved you the first day.*"

She barked out a laugh. "I hit the water! And you left me in a puddle on the balcony, like discarded trash, without even bothering to wait and see if I woke up!"

He scoffed. "You might have hit the water before I got to you, but you also had a head injury that you would *not* have woken up from if I hadn't healed you."

Isla remembered the pounding of her head, how there hadn't been any blood. She straightened. "You just admitted you didn't get to me until it was practically too late, so the only way I'm crossing this bridge is if you're tightly by my side. So, if I fall, *you fall.*"

Oro looked at her as if he might just shove her over the side himself. "Fine," he said through his teeth, and roughly took her arm in his.

Before Isla could hesitate, he dragged them both onto the bridge.

Isla didn't breathe. Wind blew up through the cracks, sending chills up her legs. They had suddenly gone as stiff as the thin planks of wood shifting wildly beneath them.

"Quickly," she whispered, closing her eyes. She stepped one foot in front of the other, trying not to think about how it had felt to plunge, plunge, plunge into the sea from the balcony. How her breath had been ripped from her chest. How she had—

"You can open your eyes now," he said, dropping her arm like it had burned him. And Isla had never been so grateful to feel solid ground.

She did as he said and looked around. They had reached a shard of mountain that was narrow at the top but joined the rest of the hill toward the bottom. If she slipped from here, she would only plummet about a hundred feet before ending up in some crack of the cliff. She winced. Not that that sounded much better than simply falling off the side of the island.

The storm seemed close enough to touch, curled toward them in its frozen dance. The whispers she had been able to hear at the cliff were louder now. Insistent, almost.

Oro had stopped at a gaping hole a few feet away, perfectly round like a well. In the near darkness, Isla couldn't see a bottom. It went all the way through the mountain, for all she knew.

"I'll go first," Oro said from her side. "Then you."

He made to take a step forward, into the black hole, and she gripped his elbow. *Go first?* They were jumping *inside?*

"Will something . . . break my fall?"

"Obviously."

She peered into the hole and squinted. It was as dark as the backs of her eyelids. If she couldn't see anything, that meant the fall would be long. The drop could be deadly.

"Are you . . . sure?"

Oro sighed. "Fear of heights. Fear of falling. Fear of bridges. Should we make a list of your fears, Wildling?"

Isla glared at him. Instead of pointing out that those all likely classified as one single fear, not *three*, she nodded toward the hole. "Go ahead, King."

He held her gaze as he stepped forward and fell completely away.

Isla tensed. It was her turn now.

She didn't move an inch.

Oro could *fly*—no drop would be deadly. He had a million ways to survive a fall. Isla had none.

All she had were his words, promising she would be fine. Her life relied on his honesty. Something he seemed to pride himself on, if his demonstration was any indication.

Still. If she died this way, technically he wouldn't be breaking the rules . . .

Was this an easy way to get rid of her?

Were all the other rulers, except for Celeste and Grim, in on it?

Seconds ticked by. The whispers from the storm became louder. More insistent.

She was afraid. Though Terra had trained her not to fear death, she did.

But it wasn't what she feared most.

Her greatest fear was the one she faced in Celeste's trial—not living. Being trapped for eternity in a room without having done everything she dreamed of.

They were so close to finding the bondbreaker. Whether she liked it or not, Oro had become an integral part of their plan. He was the key to getting into the Sun Isle library.

Before losing her nerve, she took a deep breath.

And jumped.

It was like tumbling between worlds, worse, so much worse than falling from the cliff or portaling. The hole was just big enough for a body, and there was barely any air, nothing but the musky walls, and the smell of mold, and her screams, her voice scratching painfully against the back of her throat, her eyes shut so tightly that her head pounded, ached—

Isla was swallowed up.

Before she could process the cold, the freezing water biting into her like a thousand mouths, two strong arms pulled her out, onto cool stone. She pushed him away with as much force as she could manage and gripped the ground, hair a wet fan around her head as she alternated between panting and coughing up water.

When her breathing slowed, she looked up through her curtain of hair and saw Oro standing there, completely dry. He was frowning. "Took you long enough."

She was on her feet at once, in front of him in less than a second. Her hands fisted and pulled back and struck—

But she was soaking wet, and her head was spinning, and he was too fast.

Oro gripped both of her wrists tightly. "This was all a test, wasn't it?" she yelled. Her back teeth clattered together. "You wanted to see if I could trust you."

The untrusting king, the paranoid ruler who always thought everyone was after his power. It was hypocrisy. He wanted her to trust him—when he trusted no one.

Oro stilled. And that was answer enough.

"I knew it." She fought against his grip, but his giant hands might as well have been chains, wrapped more than fully around her wrists. If only she had brought a sword, a dagger, *something* other than her knife-tipped earrings, which wouldn't do nearly as much damage as she wanted—

Isla spat at his feet and hoped that told him what she thought of him.

Oro's frown deepened. "Listen closely, Wildling. I don't care if you like me. But if we're going to work together, you need to trust me."

She bared her teeth at him. "How am I supposed to trust you if you haven't even told me what you're looking for?"

He considered her for a moment. Dropped her hands.

Then he said something that sent her rearing back in surprise.

"Are you going to divulge what I tell you to Grim?"

What? Why would he ask her that? Did he think she and the Night-shade were working together?

The Nightshade *was* constantly seeking her out. It was an easy conclusion to make, she supposed.

Isla wondered if perhaps that was the reason Grim made such a show of wanting to be near her. Was it for others to think they had allied?

"No."

He seemed to believe her, because the next thing he said was "I'm looking for Lightlark's heart."

Isla raised an eyebrow. "Its what?"

"Its source of power. Its life-force."

She tilted her head at him. "Isn't that . . . *you?*"

Oro gave her a strange look. "No. I'm the island's conduit, if anything. My connection to Lightlark, through blood, binds me to it. Through that bond, I can funnel power."

"But if you die, Lightlark dies."

"If its power cannot be funneled or is unbalanced, the island will crumble. Not because I am its heart, but because everything we have built, everything we are, relies on the power I channel."

"Oh. So . . . it has an actual heart?"

"Yes," he said. "But it doesn't look like the type you eat." *Interesting.*

"Then what does it look like?"

The king shook his head. Already annoyed. It seemed to Isla that he only had an allotted amount of patience and number of words for her, and she had already run out of both. "I don't know. Every time it blooms, it looks different."

Blooms? She had so many more questions. Why he was looking for the heart. How it even fit into the prophecy. How he thought she could help him find it.

But before she could say another word, Oro was speaking again. "Yes, Wildling. This was a test of trust. But we did come here for a reason."

For the first time, Isla looked around at where she had landed.

An oasis at the center of the mountain. Impossible. Beyond the stream she had fallen into stood hundreds of plants, growing right out of the cave floor, as if the rock was fertile.

The cave was freezing. She still shook from the cold of the water dripping down her face, her clothes soaked tightly against her skin. It was a wonder *anything* grew down here without sunlight or soil, let alone hundreds of different species. It didn't make any sense. This cave had to be infused with Wildling enchantment.

"What is this place?"

He frowned down at her dripping clothing. It pleased her knowing she likely looked terrible, the long, oversize fabric swallowing her up, her hair in wild strands stuck to her cheeks. He made a move as if to dry her using his powers, then didn't. Good. She didn't need his warmth. "Wildlings built a garden in the center of a mountain, to protect all of the island's flora. This cave harbors plants from every isle on Lightlark."

Something in her chest tightened. So many Wildling plants had died since she was born, thanks to her powerlessness. She had believed them to be lost forever. But perhaps they still lived on, here.

"The heart of Lightlark blooms every hundred years, attached to a living thing. A plant. If you could identify which types of plants something like the heart might be drawn to, they could guide our search. We could go to where they originate on the island." So that was why he needed her.

This, she could do. She had never seen most of these Lightlark species, but growing up raised by Wildlings meant she knew how they worked. What to look for.

She bent down, studying the plants closest to her. "For the heart to blossom regularly, it needs to feed off life on the island. It needs a willing, nurturing host."

Isla made her way through the garden, and, after a while, the king followed her, deeper into the center of the mountain. The floras were fascinating. She saw a tree with leaves every shade of a fire. A small

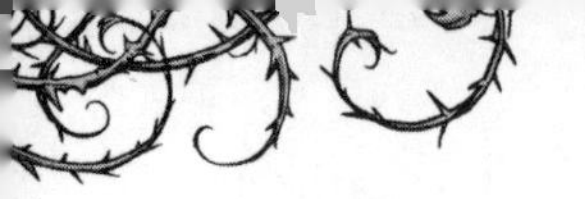

cactus that grew a single, stunning, no doubt poisonous flower. A bush with vines that curled and uncurled like beckoning fingers.

One wall was covered completely in a mess of dark red roses. Isla could have sworn they were humming.

"Are they—"

"They only grow over dead bodies," he said impatiently. "Or where blood is spilled. It is said they capture the last words of the dead who give them life."

Oh. "Like the willow strands," she said quietly. In Wildling, there was a crop of ancient, sacred trees where the memories and voices of the dead were kept. Twirling some of the limp branches around one's wrist could make them speak.

Did that mean there were bodies buried in the mountain? Or had the Wildlings simply replanted them here?

Only when she reached the back wall of the garden, an hour later, did she speak again.

"Those," she said, pointing at the uncurling and curling plants. "Something can be hidden in their middle. I've seen even birds live in plants like them. We call them purses. They . . . carry things. Without killing them." She looked pointedly at a plant on the other side, a carnivorous one that looked almost exactly like the purses except for the row of teeth she knew lined its core. She turned again. "And those," she said, pointing at two trees with thick trunks. "We have something similar called coffiners. They have been known to grow around living things . . . almost like a shield. Or, in some cases, as a prison." Poppy had told her about a girl she knew who had gotten lost in a forest for weeks. A tree had grown around her in seconds, trapping her in its trunk. It had fed her and given her water but had tried to keep her. It had taken three Wildlings to free her. She shrugged. "It would be a perfect place for the heart to hide while also leeching off a living thing."

Finally, she pointed at the pond she had landed in.

"Those water lilies have roots," she said. "It could be stuck to a root like that, at the bottom of the water."

Oro nodded. Made to turn around.

"So, what now?" she asked.

He worked his jaw, irritated, like every piece of knowledge he shared sliced against his very core. "I will decide on a place to start. One that has the plants you've indicated."

That sounded fine. She smothered a yawn, exhausted. Her eyes searched for a way out of the cave. But there was no other exit. Only the hole, a hundred feet up, visible even from this side of the cave. She frowned. "How—"

He turned to look at her. And there was something wicked in his eyes, something that took great pleasure in the horror that overtook her face.

"Absolutely *not*. You must have spent too much time under the moon, you lunatic, if you think that I—"

"It's the only way we get back to the castle before sunrise," he said.

She opened her mouth, ready to refute that claim, but he interrupted her.

"Trust me, if there was another way, if there was a way to do this without *you,* we wouldn't be here."

Isla waited to feel the sting of his words, but none came. He disliked her just as much as she disliked him. And she was fine with that.

Quickly, before she could warn him what she would do if he dropped her, one arm knocked her legs from under her and the other caught her back. He looked down at her, sighed when he saw her blinking back at him, eyes wide in fear and threats—

Then shot up into the air. He must have angled in such a way as to go through the hole that hadn't been directly above them, but he certainly did not stop or slow down—he flew fast as a shooting star, a strike of lightning in the opposite direction.

Isla screamed so loudly in his ear, it was a wonder he didn't simply let her go, especially when her nails dug so deeply into the back of his neck, she was sure they drew blood. Feigning bravery felt impossible. They propelled faster than the wind for just a few moments before everything went weightless.

He was simply . . . walking. Had they reached ground already? She moved to jump out of his grip, but he hissed and his arms gripped tighter, almost painfully so. Only when she opened her eyes did she see that they were still very much in the air, hundreds of feet up. Oro was walking on nothing, an invisible bridge instead of the flimsy one, right toward the cliff. The exposed beach sat far below, rocks poking out of it like shards of glass. She gasped and promptly stuck her face tightly in the space between his neck and shoulder.

Oro laughed meanly, amused by her fear. She whispered words into his ear that made him frown. "It's almost like you *want* me to drop you."

Before she could say something she might regret—and that wouldn't have much bite, anyway, given how tightly she was clinging to him in terror—Oro took a step that felt much more solid.

Finally, they were back on the Mainland.

The second it was safe to do so, she stumbled out of his arms, relieved to be away from the king. She glared at him. "That was horrible," she said, lest he have any doubt about her feelings about flying—about being so close to him.

He returned her cold look. "I'll see you tomorrow," he said, baring his teeth, making it sound like a threat.

Then he shot back into the air, toward the castle, leaving her to walk home alone.

CHAPTER TWENTY-FOUR
SEEKING

Isla might have promised she wouldn't tell Grim about the heart. But she had said nothing about telling Celeste.

The first place she went once she reached the castle was her friend's room.

She knocked, and the door swung open immediately, even though it was nearly dawn. The Starling must have been waiting all night to speak to her.

The pairings had complicated their plan.

She told her friend everything. To which Celeste demanded, "Are you sure he said *heart?*"

Isla nodded. "He must believe it fulfills the prophecy. An original offense committed again, somehow. Maybe finding it was the original offense?"

Celeste shook her head. "I don't know. But I don't like this. Not at all."

"Me neither. The king is clearly desperate to break the curses this time," she said. "But I think this can be good."

Her friend looked at her as if she had sprouted a flower from her forehead.

"*This* is how we get into the Sun Isle library."

Celeste considered that. "You think you can convince him to show it to you?"

Isla winced. The king hated her. Still, she would find a way. She nodded.

"All right," the Starling said. "Get him to show you the library as soon as possible, then. There are just a few weeks until the ball."

A few weeks until rulers are allowed to kill were the words she didn't have to say.

On Isla's way to the door, her friend called to her once more.

"Oh, and, Isla? Be careful." Celeste bit her lip in worry. "The rulers . . . I'm afraid of what they'll do to win, now that we know Lightlark is in trouble. I don't trust any of them." She looked her right in the eyes. "Especially not the king."

Oro arrived at her room the next night, as promised. He barely spared her a look before leading her to their next destination.

This time, Isla didn't ask where they were going. She had been to some of the isles now, knew where nearly all of them were. She could figure it out herself.

Twenty minutes into their walk, she was positive they were going to Sky Isle.

Crossing the bridge confirmed it.

Oro thought this was the first time she was seeing the isle. Isla didn't go so far as to pretend she was in awe of the floating city, but she did keep quiet.

They left the base of the lower village and walked into a set of woods. Isla couldn't help but swallow. She wondered if the forests on Lightlark were like the ones on Wildling. Dangerous. Deadly. Even fools feared the forest. No one went inside without protection. It was why Oro's rash had been so surprising. Plants could be as wild as animals. They could strike, maim, kill. Terra said that was why powerful Wildlings were so important. Only they could tame nature. Protect others from it.

But Isla wasn't a true Wildling ruler. Plants did not obey her. She had many scars that had taken years of elixirs to fade to prove it.

What would the king think if they struck her?

Would he blame the fact that she was supposedly cloaking her powers, at his request?

Would he become suspicious?

Luckily, when she entered the woods, nothing happened. The trees stood tall, like everything else on Sky Isle, like the people themselves. They bore sky-colored berries the size of buttons and wore dandelions up their branches, like they had gotten caught on bits of cloud. The temperature dropped quickly, and Isla wished for a cape, one of the ones big enough to wrap around herself. She thought of the king's secret. It did get noticeably colder away from the endless hearths and fires on the Mainland.

Oro didn't consult a map, but he walked assuredly, the island seeming to have a gravitational pull just for him. "I've identified two places on Lightlark that have an unusual number of the plants you indicated in the garden," he finally said. "One here. One on the Mainland."

The forest ground turned into a steep incline, and they climbed it in silence. The king could have flown, she knew. It would have saved a lot of time. There must be a reason he wasn't. He had alluded to searching for the heart for over half a century. Perhaps he had flown over every inch of the island and had still been unsuccessful.

This time, it seemed he wanted to be thorough.

Finally, the hill crested, and Isla stared down into a valley full of purse plants. Relief was cool down her back. This variety of nature wasn't dangerous. She would be relatively safe here.

But there was a new concern. There were thousands, taking up every inch below, from mountain to mountain. Miles and miles. Searching the entire area as carefully as they needed to, on foot, would take days. "How will we know we've found it?"

"You'll know. The power it radiates is unmistakable. But only detectable from a very close distance." So *that* was why he hadn't abandoned her to fly the length of the valley in minutes.

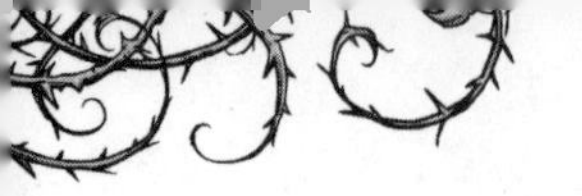

Isla didn't trust her ability to sense the heart solely from its power. Not when she didn't have any of her own.

"Will it . . . look special?" she asked.

The corners of his lips turned down, their favorite placements. "Yes, Wildling," he said. "It will look *special.*" He turned to the left without giving her a second glance. "I'll start over there."

Good. At least they wouldn't be searching side by side.

She looked back into the valley and swallowed. There really was a lot of land to cover. It all looked the same too. It would be easy to mix up where she had and hadn't looked, especially over days. She needed a strategy.

Isla found a pattern in the plants, rows that weren't clear cut but were easy to spot once she knew their shape. Now, she just needed markers to indicate the areas she had already searched. Her eyes took in the land, looking for a color that stood out. A different sort of flower, maybe. A special type of vine.

But there was nothing. The plants all looked the same. Even the ones in the forest behind her were too similar in shade.

She was the only thing that stood out in the entire valley.

Isla sighed and reminded herself this was the best way to gain access to the Sun Isle library before ripping the bottom of her favorite shirt.

There. That would have to do.

She was efficient. After four hours, Isla had covered a good chunk of her area. She had developed a system. Purse plants opened when their tops were stroked. It took a few long moments for their leaves and vines to uncurl, and a couple of more seconds to get a good look inside before they closed again. At her fastest, she was able to get to five a minute. Once she was finished with a row, she marked it by tying a strip of fabric to its last plant.

By the time Oro came to collect her, Isla had looked inside over a thousand purse plants. And her shirt had been reduced to ribbons. Before, it had nearly reached her knees. Now, it ended far above her navel.

The king looked horrified. She grinned, reveling in the fact that she looked as wild as he believed her to be, covered in dirt, her hair curled around her face, clothes cut to pieces.

"What did you do?" he demanded.

She crossed her arms across her chest. "What I *did* was cover this entire area," she said, motioning toward a large grove sectioned off by her fabric.

The king's eyes briefly darted to the spot she had indicated. He didn't look impressed.

He didn't look anything.

Isla narrowed her gaze. "I'm assuming this means you didn't find it?"

He didn't humor her with a response before turning around toward the way they had come.

The next morning, Ella arrived with clothing. More long-sleeved shirts that looked just like the one she had torn to ribbons. Pants that were like her other pair—now coated in a layer of dirt—but thicker, with reinforced fabric on the knees, better for the elements. Boots that were far better suited to the task of searching forests and valleys than her now soiled-beyond-repair slippers.

"The king sent this," the Starling said.

Isla rolled her eyes.

She almost wanted to rebel and wear her same clothes from before, just to spite him. But she thought about her mission. Get him to show her the library. He wouldn't honor her request yet. But perhaps if he saw her trying to help him, to find the heart . . .

Still. She decided she *would* wear her crown that night, as at least the faintest reminder that she was *also* a ruler of realm, not to be trifled with. Even if she had hidden most of it in the folds of her hair, so it wouldn't give her away to the mysterious ancient creatures the king had warned her about.

Before they parted ways to search each half of the grove, Isla asked something she had been wondering since he had shared his plan with her: "How did you find out about the heart in the first place?"

He said nothing.

She casually walked the few feet between them, smiling sweetly. She reached up and flicked his crown, just because she knew he had hated it the first time. "You should tell me. Because if you don't . . . I'm not opening another purse plant."

Oro's eyes flashed with irritation like crackling firewood. Still, he said nothing.

Isla clicked her tongue. "An untrusting king who always keeps all of his cards close to his chest . . ." Her hands circled her waist, fingers pooling in the oversize fabric of her new long-sleeved shirt. She stared pointedly at his arm, where the bluish gray had started spreading. The sign of the king's impending death. "Tell me, how has that worked out for you?"

Oro glared down at her. He took a breath that seemed to shake his shoulders. Power emanated from him in thick waves—a sharp wind she couldn't see, a riptide she couldn't pull free from. Suddenly, the cool air went hot as Wildling.

The force of him made her knees wobble. But she couldn't allow him the satisfaction of seeing that. Instead, she smiled again, blinked her long lashes, and lifted on her toes so she was just inches from his face as she said, "Well?"

Immediately, his power was ripped from between them, swallowed up. He did not flinch away from her proximity. "I'll take my chances, Wildling," he said coolly before flicking her own crown. The movement sent her back on her heels, stumbling a few steps. Her head immediately throbbed. *How hard had he flicked it?* She reached up to trace her finger along the metal and came upon a deep indentation.

Something in Oro's eyes glinted with wicked pleasure as anger twisted her features.

"You dented it!"

He simply turned away and began walking toward his side of the valley.

"Fix it!" she demanded.

All she saw was his back as he got farther and farther away, golden cape billowing softly in the wind.

"Wretch," she whispered angrily under her breath. "If we weren't paired, I really would gut you."

That made him stop. He turned like he had heard every word.

She made a gesture at him that she hoped proved just how much she had meant them.

Oro frowned and turned back around.

And only because he was her best chance at getting into the Sun Isle library and finding the bondbreaker did she fix her hands in angry fists and walk toward her rows of flora.

They spent three more nights searching the purse plants. They worked from after the sun went down to an hour before it went up, enough time for the king to reach the castle before day reached him. Just as her room filled with light, Isla would collapse into bed, sometimes without even a bath, exhausted.

Her fingers were stiff, the muscles in her palms sore. Her arms even hurt after lifting them one after the other, thousands of times. Her neck ached from straining to peer into the centers of the plants. Her lower back was a lost cause.

Every day, Oro and Isla got closer in proximity, starting from the edges of the valley and making their way to the center.

By the thirty-first day of the Centennial, they met in the middle. Both covered in dirt. Both tired. Both frustrated, if the look they gave each other was any indication.

"It's not here," Isla finally said. Her voice was raw. Sleeping for a couple of hours during the day and working at night had begun to take its toll. Especially since she hadn't started their search in good health in the first place. Her arm had fully healed, but the cold hadn't completely left her chest.

The king wasn't standing as straight as he normally did. He ran a hand through his hair, not seeming to care he was coating it in dirt. "No," he said. "It isn't."

She must have groaned, because he looked down at her, eyes ablaze, almost daring her to make a snarky comment.

She might have. If she didn't need him.

It took everything in her to take a deep breath and say, "Where is the second place?"

CHAPTER TWENTY-FIVE

SECOND PLACE

It was night, and the castle's lights were off. The darkness was so deep it seemed to seep everywhere, like spilled ink all around her.

Isla looked around for lights, for curtains she could open. She found a candle and lit it.

Her shadow loomed before her, trapped against the wall.

Another one joined it. Far bigger than her own.

She whipped around, and there he was. Grim. He was dressed in armor. Shining sheets of black metal.

He was the thing of nightmares, the monster in the dark.

For a moment, she was nervous. But not afraid.

Still, she took a step back, until she and her shadow were one and the same.

He stepped closer. Reached up to pull the helmet from his head. Dropped it to the floor with a loud clatter. Lifted her from the ground by the backs of her thighs, just as her hands fisted in his hair, and she said—

Isla gasped. Blinked at the ivy that snaked across her bedroom's ceiling, a thin shard of sunlight peeking through her curtains. She was in the Mainland castle . . . not the dark room.

Not with Grim.

Fool.

She blamed her exhaustion for the dreams. Her sleeping patterns had changed, and her body still hadn't gotten used to it. Yet—

Isla hadn't seen Grim in a week. Not since the matching ceremony.

A week. Before, he had sought her out whenever he could. Had he gotten whatever he had needed from her and moved on to the next step of his plan?

Her chest felt too tight thinking about it, but she sat up and tried her best to ignore the feeling. She would be a fool to spend another moment on him.

Isla should be focused on her *own* plan. That night, she and Oro would travel to the second location. It would be best to try to get more sleep . . . but the idea of dreaming of Grim again—and worse, *liking* it—sent her out of bed, toward her balcony. By the position of the sun, she guessed it was still early morning.

She got dressed, deciding to seek Ella out on one of the bottom floors of the castle. She remembered the recipe of a Wildling sleeping elixir. All it required were a few ingredients.

Yes, she told herself as she swept through the palace, *that* was what she needed. One cup of the tea, and she would sleep soundly through the day, no Nightshade haunting her dreams. No waking up every few hours clutching her blanket, covered in sweat.

She was just about to round the corner when she heard low voices.

Taking the abandoned old halls was second nature by now. It ensured she rarely saw any attendants and never ran into another ruler. It was how she had visited Celeste a handful of times undetected.

It seemed she wasn't the only one who used these empty halls for privacy.

Without making a sound, she pressed herself against the wall, straining to listen.

"Your plan is madness."

Isla froze. The voice echoed even in a whisper, deep and angry.

Oro's voice.

Another voice responded, too quiet for her to make out the words. But she knew who had spoken them.

Azul.

What were they doing, meeting in such a strange, hidden place?

Isla crept closer to the voices, walking silently, just like Terra had taught her. Tips of her toes, then the sides of her feet, her heels never reaching the floor.

"You will be sentencing thousands to death," Oro snarled.

She didn't dare take a breath. There was a pause.

"A realm has to die, Oro," Azul finally responded.

Isla took a step back, shocked—the heel of her shoe made the slightest noise.

The voices quieted.

A moment later, a door slammed shut, blocking out the rest of the conversation.

That night, they remained on the Mainland. Isla and Oro entered the vast woods to one side of the castle, which stretched all the way to the coast. She felt the familiar prick of fear down her neck. This forest was wilder than the one on Sky Isle. Energy coursed through the air. Branches seemed to curl toward her, as if straining for a closer look. Vines across the floor tightened as she passed, as if making to trip her.

The nature here seemed intrigued by her. Sweat pooled down her chest as she watched it. At least it hadn't hurt her. Yet.

Panic began to poison her thoughts, so she turned her attention to the king instead, hoping the less she looked at the forest, the less it would stare back. His eyes were squinted and slightly more creased at the edges. He walked more stiffly than usual.

"You haven't been sleeping at all, have you?"

He said nothing to indicate he had heard her speak.

"You could at least try to sleep during the day if we're going to work at night."

Oro continued through the forest, ducking to avoid branches that Isla could barely touch if she reached her arm up.

"Unless you have another ally you're working with during that time?"

"I don't have other allies," he said curtly.

"Really?" she said. "Not even Azul?"

Oro looked bored. "Eavesdropping is lowly, even for a Wildling."

So, he knew it had been her listening. Good. "What's his plan?" she demanded. Before she could stop herself, she added, "You promised to protect me from the other rulers. Should I be worried?"

Oro sighed, irritated. He turned to her. "Azul is harmless. You, of all people, have the *least* to worry about when it comes to him."

That didn't make sense. Azul had talked about ending an entire realm. If he hadn't been talking about Wildling, which realm *was* he talking about? "But—"

His sharp look silenced her. "I will not be revealing any more of our private conversation, so you can save your breath and be grateful you heard anything at all."

The way he spoke to her . . .

Oro wouldn't tell her any more details about their conversation. But perhaps learning Azul's story would help her understand his motivations. "Did something . . . happen to him?" she said a few moments later. The Skyling was always jovial, but she had caught a haunted look on his face a few times. She was willing to bet there was sadness, or perhaps anger, behind his good-natured mask.

Seconds ticked silently by, and Isla thought he was going to ignore her again. But he finally said, "Azul lost someone. Someone he loved."

Oh. Isla wasn't expecting that. She supposed all rulers had lost someone close to them the night the curses were spun. This seemed different. "A partner?" she guessed.

He nodded. "His husband."

Isla felt a knot in her chest. She didn't know Azul very well, but

the thought that he had lost someone so close to him made her hurt in an inexplicable way.

"Was he also Skyling?" she asked.

He shook his head.

It made her think of Oro's brother, and the wedding the curses had destroyed. Two rulers were set to marry for the first time in centuries, a chance to bring the island together. She didn't want to ask directly about King Egan, but she did say, "Is marrying between realms common on Lightlark?"

"It has become more common" was all he said.

She frowned. "How does that affect power, then? Children . . . are they born with just one realm's ability?" She looked at him. "They don't get both, do they?"

He shook his head.

She waited expectantly, wanting a better explanation.

The king sighed. "They are born with one power, Wildling."

Interesting. Isla opened her mouth, another question ready, when Oro gave her a look that silenced her again.

Fine.

Though he was the one who had ended their conversation, not ten minutes later did he say, "The entrance to Wild Isle is near." He murmured the words, as if not really meaning to speak them.

Isla stood still. She knew Wildlings had their own isle on Lightlark, of course. She had even searched for it during her snooping. But she hadn't found the bridge anywhere.

"How do we know the heart isn't on Wild Isle?" she asked, suddenly desperate to see it. Oro had kept walking, and she raced to catch up. "Surely most of the plants are there."

The king looked over at her. "You said so yourself. The heart needs a willing, nurturing host to survive." He shrugged. "All the nature on Wild Isle is dead."

Dead. The word was a rock to the chest.

She shouldn't have expected anything different. But it still hurt to hear it spoken.

A moment passed. "What did you think of them?" she asked, even though she practically knew the answer, given the way he had sneered at her during their first dinner together. "Wildlings."

He frowned, and Isla readied herself for a string of insults that she might just slap him for. "They were my favorite realm, besides Sunling," he finally said.

She scoffed. "You can't possibly mean that."

He peered at her over a shoulder. "I said *were,* Wildling."

"Why?"

They kept walking. The trees began changing. Thinning. Until they entered a clearing.

"Wildlings were advisers in our court," he told her. "When I was a child, they taught me to wield a sword, how to pick the right berries. They were loyal. They were good."

Isla just stared at him. "And now?"

"And now . . ." They walked into another set of woods then, made up entirely of coffiners. Hundreds of them. "Wildlings are all the things they say."

They spent the entire night peeling back bark, peering into each coffiner tree. Oro did so without having to use a knife, thanks to his Starling abilities. Isla used her hands and a tiny dagger she had sneaked onto the island, disguised as a bracelet. With each cut of her blade, she winced, waiting for the tree to retaliate. But none of them made to hurt her. Isla moved quickly enough that she hoped Oro wouldn't suggest she unmask her powers for the task. Every hour that ticked by, she worried even more, waiting for him to say the words.

At the end, he finally did. "This would be easier with your abilities," he said, frowning.

Isla stilled, wondering if she should prepare to run. And what good it would do her.

"But the creatures it would draw out . . . I'm not sure it's worth the risk." Isla wondered about these creatures, the ones he had mentioned before. Who were they, and why did they hate Wildlings so much?

Why was even Oro afraid of them?

Isla had always assumed that the rulers were the worst things at the Centennial. The most powerful. Most lethal.

The way the king spoke about these ancient creatures made her think that wasn't true. Made her wonder how deadly they could be.

And also made her hope she never found out.

CHAPTER TWENTY-SIX
THORNS

It had been ten days since Grim had sought her out. She should have been relieved. But part of her wilted at the fact that Celeste had likely been right.

What other explanation could he have to suddenly avoid her after seeking her out so consistently? She really had just been a part of his plan—whatever it was.

Fool, she called herself, for believing anything else.

It was their third night in the coffiner forest. They had looked inside hundreds of trees, all heartless. Isla was starting to wonder if she hadn't paid close enough attention in the garden.

Was there something she had missed? She had identified the plants most likely to harbor the type of power Oro had described . . . but she could have been wrong.

On their way across the Mainland, she had asked the king more questions. Every day with him was a test, seeing how much he would tell her.

"Why didn't Cleo attend the last Centennial?" Azul had mentioned it before.

The woods hadn't hurt her yet, but she still felt their energy unspooling around her, as if the nature was simply waiting for the right moment to pounce. Even the king was careful where he walked, not underestimating the power of the forest for a moment.

"You should ask her. The two of you get along so well."

Isla might have thought that was an attempt at a good-natured joke, and might have keeled over at the possibility of the king making one, if his tone hadn't been so hostile.

She gave him a look. "It isn't my fault she's had a target set on me since I made that comment at dinner."

The king shook his head. He seemed in disbelief at her foolishness. "Cleo wouldn't kill you because she dislikes you."

Isla scoffed. He clearly hadn't seen the way the Moonling had studied her, as if she was counting down the hours until the fiftieth day of the Centennial. "You seem to think highly of her."

The king, to her surprise, nodded. "I do. Cleo thinks of the good of her realm above all else."

Isla remembered the Moonling's trial. It had tested one's desires.

Terra and Poppy had preached the same unrelenting commitment to one's people. Only on the island had Isla understood how big of a sacrifice it was to give up all the world had to offer. "Really?" Isla said incredulously. "She has no hobbies? No lovers?"

Oro didn't meet her gaze. "She did have different relationships, with both men and women, before she came into power," he said. "But since she has been ruler, she has focused completely on her realm's future. Her focus is admirable." He worked his jaw. "That does not mean she is not a problem, however."

Problem. Isla wondered if he knew about her legion. Her guards. He must.

"Wouldn't that commitment to her realm mean she would kill any ruler she could to fulfill the prophecy? To make sure she and her people don't die?"

The king came to a stop. "Any ruler?" he repeated.

She shrugged. "The first she had the chance to assassinate."

He had never looked as repulsed by her as he did then. "Don't you understand, Wildling? Killing a ruler isn't the hard part. We all have had several opportunities to fulfill that portion of the prophecy. Do you know why killing isn't allowed until the fiftieth day?"

He looked so upset, she didn't dare form a response.

"It's because choosing the *right* ruler and realm to die is the difficult part. Not just because we would be sentencing thousands to death. But because *all* of our futures depend on making the right decision." His voice became louder. She had never seen him more impassioned. Or angry. "All of our realms are connected. You can't begin to understand the consequences of losing one of them. Even if we did know for certain the offense that needed to be committed again, the decision of who needs to die would be nearly impossible. *That,* more than anything else, is why the curses haven't been broken until now."

Isla didn't know why she spoke her next few words. But she needed clarity. Answers. "Why not just kill Grim, then?" she wondered, even as the thought made her insides twist with a surprising amount of pain. Even if he seemed to have forgotten about her. "He's not part of Lightlark. Isn't he the obvious choice?"

His smile was mocking. Cruel. "I can't," he said. Perhaps it was because he was so angry, so eager to throw in her face how little she understood, he told her more than she expected he would. "Grim is the only thing standing between us and a greater danger you can't even begin to fathom."

Greater danger? What could be more dangerous than the Nightshade? Or the curses? Or the Centennial?

He looked down at her like she was a fool, a naive ruler. And it did seem now like she knew nothing. Terra and Poppy had always framed the Centennial as a survival-of-the-fittest game. One where the weakest link would be murdered, if the others were given the chance. If Oro was to be believed, the hundred days were more about making the *right* choice over the most convenient. Before she could ask anything else, he had stormed off.

The king was on the other side of the woods now. She could hear him every few minutes, slicing into the bark with his powers, just enough

to look inside the trunk. He didn't get distracted, no matter how many hours they did the same task.

Isla couldn't say the same. Not when she now had so many questions on her mind.

She had finished her section for the night. No hearts. Just the occasional animal burrowed inside the trunk that would peek up at her with curious eyes.

Celeste had visited her that morning, looking for an update.

I'm trying, Isla had said. It just never seemed like the right moment to ask the king about the library. Too soon or out of the blue, and he would become suspicious of her request.

Now, she wondered if she had burned all her chances at getting him to take her to the Sun Isle library with their earlier conversation. The king had looked furious.

It was dangerous, stupid, but she walked deeper into the woods, hand trailing along the coffiners until they ended. The nature changed, becoming wilder. Flowers bloomed, red like the dresses she most often wore.

Rosebushes. Bulbous petals guarded by halos of thorns.

The last Wildling Eldress, the one she had found in the forest, had called her that once.

You are a rose with thorns, she said. A pretty thing capable of protecting itself.

If only.

Her blades should have been enough. She was a great warrior. But against power—metal might as well be paper.

The rosebushes became thicker, turning into another plant. One that had spines long and thick as fingers, jutting everywhere. It looked like a weapon. She didn't know why, but she followed it through the forest, watching the bush become larger, taller.

Until she reached an entire wall of spines and thorns.

Her pulse raced.

Thorns formed on plants to guard them. They were defense mechanisms, just like her own throwing stars and blades.

This entire wall of spikes had to be protecting something.

Maybe the heart of Lightlark.

Isla turned to yell for Oro, triumphant.

That was when it struck.

The thicket of spines came to life—wrapped her in its embrace.

And pulled her right into its nest of spikes.

Her scream was a guttural thing. Dozens of barbs stabbed through her back at once, sharp as blades. Thorns needled themselves through her arms.

She was well practiced in pain, but this was not rehearsed. Not expected.

Isla tried to tear herself away from the wall, but she was stuck to it, the spines curved into her skin like hooks. Keeping her. Every push away sent them farther within. Blood ran hot down her back; tears shot down her face. A choking sound escaped her lips.

Then there were warm hands steadying her.

"Stop moving. You're making it worse," a voice yelled.

She wanted to spit at his feet for chastising her at a time like this. She wanted to warn him to get away from the evil plant. But she could barely even see. The pain had eaten all her senses.

The king cursed, and she imagined he was inspecting her back. "I'm going to have to break them to free you," he said.

Isla nodded and, a moment later, screamed at the top of her lungs as Oro tore the first barb in two with his Starling energy. No matter how steady or gentle his power was, she felt the spine in her back, twisting closer to her bones. The plant didn't like Oro's handling of it. It dug its other barbs deeper inside. It did not strike the king, however. As if it only had an appetite for her.

"There are . . . several."

She couldn't take another one. The first—

She cried out again. Saw flashes of hues behind her eyes, the pain so deep she swore it had its own color.

Again.

Again.

Again.

Isla couldn't control herself. The next time he broke one of the spines, and the plant retaliated by digging farther inside, she retched all down the front of her clothes.

If it got on him, he didn't say a word. He just held her steady as he broke the spikes in two.

Again. Again. Again.

Isla insisted on being the one to pull them out.

She was on the ground now, away from the wall, Oro kneeling in front of her. The rest of the forest had gone still. Watching her.

"How did this happen?" he asked.

Right. Of course he was confused. Plants wouldn't dare attack their ruler. Even if she was supposed to be keeping her abilities cloaked.

"I . . . tripped," she said, wincing. He kept studying her, and she narrowed her eyes at him. "Go, look for whatever the wall is guarding," she spat. "I'm fine. I can take them out myself."

Even when she was injured, even soaked in blood, the king had the nerve to glare at her. "You're covered in your own vomit," he said flatly. He reached toward her back to help her, but she reared back, then groaned.

"I said I'll do it myself," she growled.

Oro bared his teeth at her. "Are you truly this stubborn?"

"Are you truly this *overbearing?*" she demanded. "I said no. Now leave."

The king stayed put for a moment.

Then he got up and walked back toward the thicket, cursing beneath his breath.

Good.

When he was far enough away, Isla folded over and gripped the ground with all her strength, arms shaking in a sob. The pain—

It was like nothing else she had experienced. *Evil, wretched plants.*

And it wasn't over.

Wincing, Isla reached back and felt around for the first spike. Gripped it with shaking fingers.

And pulled with all her might.

Her scream echoed through the forest; she could have sworn it rumbled the trees. Their shaking leaves sounded almost like laughter.

She had never hated herself more for being born powerless than she did now. If she was a true Wildling ruler, she could control every inch of the woods. They would never have hurt her. They would have *helped* her.

Her hand shook as it released the bloodied spine. It fell unceremoniously to the ground.

Only ten more to go, if her count had been correct when Oro had broken her free from the bramble.

The king was back now, crouching next to her.

Her entire arm shook as it bent backward, feeling for the next one. "I told you to go look for—"

"I did," he said. "No heart."

Tears rolled down her temples from the angle her head tilted. All this. For nothing.

"You can—you can go," she said, closing her eyes tightly.

A few seconds passed. She didn't hear him move and wondered if he had simply flown away in that soundless way of his.

But when she opened her eyes, there he was, frowning down at her no doubt gruesome-looking back.

Oro reached toward her, and she flinched. He held his hands palm up. A peace offering. "The spines are all yours," he said, eyes clear. Reasonable. He motioned toward the dozens of thorns embedded in her arms, thin crimson streaks raining down from them like tears of blood. "I'll get these." She started to shake her head. "It's faster," he added. "The sooner this is finished, the sooner we can resume our search."

He had a point. She supposed she could let him help her if it meant completing their mission. And getting out of this wicked forest.

"Fine," she whispered.

His hands were hot against her skin but surprisingly gentle as they worked, pulling the thorns out, one by one. Each was followed by a prick of pain.

But nothing compared to the spikes in her back.

She wrapped her hand around another. Pulled. Screamed into her knees.

Another one. This one was curved, just an inch from her spine. She pulled, and a jolt tremored through her entire body, needles through her bones, poison in her veins. In the shock, her teeth bit down hard on her tongue, and an animalistic sound left her throat. Blood pooled immediately, dripping from her mouth.

"Here." Suddenly, Oro was offering her something to bite into instead. "You're going to bite your tongue off," he said. "I've seen it happen before; you have to have something in your mouth for something like—"

Isla pulled another barb out, knowing it was impossible to feel more pain than she was feeling now.

But she was wrong. It doubled, tripled, and she bit down hard on what he offered.

Again.

Again.

Her eyes were closed so tight, her head hurt. She slipped in and out of consciousness. But she pulled every spike out herself.

It wasn't until she was done and slumped against a tree that she realized she had been biting into Oro's hand. It was covered in bite marks. She had pierced the skin in various places.

She was too tired to feel shame. All she could do was count her breaths as Oro used a canteen of water and his Moonling abilities to close her wounds.

By the time she stopped bleeding, it was time to leave. Dawn was approaching.

"What now?" she said, her voice barely making a sound.

Before the wall of spikes had attacked, she had already finished searching her assigned trees. She assumed Oro had too. The heart clearly wasn't in this forest.

His jaw clenched. "There are too many places with the plants you indicated. I thought—because of the quantity, we would . . ." *Get lucky* were the words she filled in.

Isla almost wanted to laugh. Or cry.

If there was any luck in the world, she and the king had never encountered it.

He shook his head. "I have another plan. One I hoped to avoid." He looked her in the eyes. "You know those ancient creatures I told you about?"

She nodded.

"Well," he said, "I think it's time we meet one of them."

CHAPTER TWENTY-SEVEN

THE HARBOR

Oro hadn't knocked on her door in five days. He was supposed to be attempting to seek out the ancient creature, to make a deal that would guarantee their safety.

"Would one of these ancient creatures really try to hurt the king of Lightlark?" she had asked.

"I can't be sure," he said. "Though they would certainly not hesitate to hurt you."

Isla had been grateful for the break. Oro had healed her back with his Moonling powers, but her body had shut down for two days after they had returned to the castle. She was wrecked. Exhausted. Broken.

But her mind had never been clearer.

Her encounter with the barbs and thorns had only made her want to break her curses more. Not just for the freedom . . . but for the power.

Never again would plants harm her. Never again would she be powerless against them.

After the third day, when she was ready for their next mission and still hadn't heard from the king, she began to worry.

Had he decided a Wildling who had been attacked by plants wouldn't be much help to him? Had he decided to continue the rest of his plan on his own?

She refused to sit in her room and wait for him to fetch her. If his plan had changed, so had theirs. She needed to speak to Celeste.

Isla had slipped a note under the Starling's door, asking her to meet

her in the agora. Since they weren't paired, she thought they needed to start forming a superficial friendship seen by the islanders, so if they were somehow caught together, it wouldn't be so suspicious. They were supposed to serendipitously run into each other in the Starling weapons store. Isla *did* need a dagger—one that didn't double as an accessory.

But, more than that, she needed to speak to her friend.

She had been so focused on her work with Oro that she had nearly forgotten the Starling had been forced to spend time with Cleo. What had that been like? Celeste was the type to avoid telling Isla things, so she wouldn't worry. But she wanted to be there for her. Just as much as the Starling had always been there for her.

The agora was busier than even before, vendors filling their storefronts with their best accessories—silk hats, crystal-covered gloves, gowns that were as puffed up as the pastries sunbathing in the nearby bakery windows. All in preparation for the ball.

It was just ten days away.

Ten days until killing was permitted.

Ten days to find a way into the Sun Isle library.

Ten days to find and use the bondbreaker.

Ten days to break their curses and get off the island.

Isla stopped in front of the Starling store. Just as she was about to enter, someone bumped into her.

Strange. Usually the islanders gave her a wide berth, as if her skin was poisonous.

Then she felt the note that had been slipped into her hand.

It was a small piece of paper. The words made her go still.

You are in danger, the paper read.

What? Isla whipped around, looking for who had given her the warning. She spotted a white cape weaving through the market, head down. That had to be them.

A Moonling?

She wasn't going to sit around and solve the riddle of who might want to harm her. There were too many people on that list.

Instead, she followed whoever had slipped her the message.

Music was playing in the streets, a quartet no doubt hired to build excitement for the ball. Stores kept their doors open, and young boys and girls shouted advertisements—*special offer! Two pairs of gloves for the price of one! One-of-a-kind hats for one-of-a-kind islanders!*

Isla rushed through the crowd, pushing past shoppers holding stacks of boxes tied with ribbon. Children holding cones of cream. She whispered apologies that were met with frightened gasps as she nearly collided with a wagon holding ripe fruits and freshly roasted nuts. But there, far ahead, she saw it. A flash of white fabric, disappearing around a corner.

Celeste was suddenly in her path then, on her way to the Starling shop. Her friend's eyes narrowed with confusion as Isla ran past, whispering, "I'll be right back," leaving without waiting for a response.

Her arms tight by her sides to slip through the busy road, she moved like a ribbon in wind, her feet finding free places on the pavement, her body filling gaps in the sea of people. Moments later, she was turning that same corner, onto a street that was almost empty. So empty she could see the Moonling racing away, the trail of their cape billowing in the breeze.

This tendril of the marketplace went down instead of up into the mountains. The air was heavy with salt and fish and brine. The rough cobblestone became wet beneath her shoes, and she nearly slipped in her rush to catch the Moonling.

She turned another corner. And they were gone.

Too slow. She had lost them. The sea was near. She was in the remnants of what must have been a harbor, hundreds of years before, when the island wasn't entrapped in its curse.

Isla forced herself still, refusing to give up. She looked around, squinting, searching for a sound or a ripple of fabric.

She turned in the other direction—and found it. The curl of the white cape, disappearing behind a ship that had somehow made it onto land. It looked like a washed-up whale, flipped on its side.

Isla took a step and gasped.

Chains from nowhere locked around her wrists and ankles.

And the cool edge of a sword pressed firmly against her throat.

"That was a little too easy," a low voice said in her ear. Isla yanked against the chains and found that they weren't chains at all. They were braided water, firm as a rogue wave, strong as the tide.

Five more men peeled away from where they had been hidden, behind ancient boathouses and landlocked ships. They wore crisp white suits, with diamonds in place of the top button of their shirts.

Moonling nobles. She recognized them from the demonstrations.

A growl escaped her throat. She became a little more of the beast they believed her to be.

The person in the white cape appeared then, and Isla bared her teeth at them, her gaze promising violence. The figure didn't even glance her way before it was handed a handful of coin and slipped away.

A trap. She had been tricked.

Fool.

No. *They* were the fools.

She lifted her chin high and said with as much venom as she could manage, "Release me, and I will show mercy. Keep me bound, and you will all see what happens when you try to trap a Wildling."

The men only smiled.

"Wild, even captured," one said. His white hair was slicked back, and he gingerly held a cane with a crystal top, though he clearly didn't need it. He pointed the cane in Isla's direction, and the water chains tightened, forcing her onto her knees. Isla seethed as her bones screamed and her skin broke against the damp stone floor. "But even wild things can be tamed. And caged. Tell me, will you beg for your life, Wildling?"

Now, it was her time to laugh. "So, your ruler sent you to do her dirty work?"

It wasn't the fiftieth day yet. Either Cleo had skated past the rules by not exactly *ordering* Isla's assassination . . . or the Moonling ruler didn't care about breaking the rules. Perhaps she wasn't after the prize of the power promised after all.

So much for Oro's theory that Cleo wouldn't kill her just because she disliked her.

Though, admittedly, Isla sneaking into the Moon Isle library likely had more to do with it.

The Moonling with the cane stiffened, insulted. Others turned to look at each other, and that told Isla enough. Cleo might not have sent them to assassinate her, which would have directly violated the rules. But their efforts were sanctioned.

"I'm sorry," one of the men said, surprising her—and the rest of his group, it seemed. "But the Centennial isn't just a game for rulers. One of the realms must fall. And we have families . . ." He shook his head. "We don't want it to be us."

She *did* understand. The Centennial was a deadly game with many players. And grave consequences.

She spat at the man's feet anyway.

"Enough." Isla was hauled up by the man behind her, sword still against her throat. "Say farewell, Wildling," he rasped into her ear, pulling the blade back for a clean, clear sever.

Isla yanked at the watery chains with all her strength, made to escape—

But her efforts did nothing against their Moonling power.

Back in the Mainland forest, Isla thought she had never wanted her Wildling powers more. She had been wrong. Now she not only wanted them—she *needed* them.

Words pummeled through her mind, the last she would ever hear: *Too late. Failure. Powerless. If only—*

Before she was ended, she heard another word.

"Farewell," a voice said, stopping the blade just an inch from her throat.

And the man was hurtled back through the air.

Celeste made a fist, and the water chains went limp, disappearing in a mess of silver sparks. She must have followed her. One of the nobles sent a wave of sea hurtling toward her, and the Starling spun on her heel to meet it with a stream of energy.

Unshackled, Isla was unleashed. She reached both hands toward their opposite wrists and unchained her bracelets, which snapped into throwing knives. She sent them flying with ease, each finding their marks.

Two Moonling hearts.

The men slumped to the ground, and Isla turned—only to be thrown by a wave of power.

Her hand managed to grip a shard of glass from the floor, then the world went sideways as she was slammed against an old ship.

Isla tasted blood on her tongue; her head pulsed between her eyebrows. The man's hand was around her neck, lifting her up. She heard a roaring that was not the sea and made a terrible sound when she tried to breathe.

Still, she smiled.

She might not have been a match chained up.

But the restraints were gone now.

Isla wrapped her fingers around the long shard of glass in her hand—and stuck it through the man's throat.

He released her immediately, reaching for his own neck, trying to speak. No words left his mouth.

The other Moonling nobles hadn't fared any better. She raced back to Celeste, only to find her standing in the middle of a mess of dead, laid out across the wet harbor stone.

"She tried to have you killed," Celeste said, voice surprisingly steady. "You need to leave a message. One that shows you're strong. One that

makes her think twice before another attempt on your life." They worked together to scrawl a response in blood.

When they were done, Isla looked down and smiled. Once, she might have had the urge to vomit. But she had been on the island forty days. In that time, she had dueled against famed rulers. Survived countless trials. Swallowed down unspeakable pain. Pulled barbs from her back with her bare hands. She stood straight and steady, remembering how the men had threatened her. Remembering how weak she had felt, chained in place. Powerless against power. Never again, she promised herself.

Try harder, the message read.

CHAPTER TWENTY-EIGHT

PLACE OF MIRRORS

Isla had never wanted power more in her life. First, the barbs. Then, the assassination attempt at the harbor that was proof her blades meant little on Lightlark.

They *did* serve well as an outlet for the anger that roiled through her like a storm, though.

She had marched straight into the Starling shop after the assassination attempt and purchased her dagger. One with a curling snake around its hilt, fit for a Wildling. She held it now, cutting the air to pieces. The metal was weightless in her grip. She twirled it around her fingers, threw it up in the air, and caught it without having to look. Mimed stabbing someone right in the gut.

The Moonling nobles flashed in her mind, and she carved her blade through the air, through *them*.

Her lip curled. She stabbed them all, one by one, the men and the memories.

"Did the wind do something to offend you?"

Isla whirled in an instant, and her dagger flew—piercing the stone of the palace, right above Grim's dark hair.

He grinned. With a fluid motion, he dug out her dagger and threw it back at her.

She caught it without her gaze ever leaving his.

Grim. Her stomach stumbled for a moment at the sight of him. Then, anger swelled. She glared at him. "I never thought the ruler of Nightshade would be so indecisive."

"Indecisive?"

Isla took a long step toward him. "*Indecisive*. You can't seem to make up your mind. One day, you act like we're friends, and the next, strangers. You disappear for weeks."

Grim did not shy away from her gaze. "Which would you prefer?" he asked, as though he truly wanted an answer. "Friends, or strangers?"

She swallowed, begging her emotions to stay in check. "Neither," she lied. "I just want you to stay away from me. Consistently."

He stepped toward her. Grinned, just a little. "Is that *truly* what you want, Hearteater?"

Her breath hitched. He felt her everything.

She turned away before he could feel any more.

Grim's grin vanished. He suddenly became deathly serious. "We really should stay away from each other," he said. "That is why you didn't see me."

So, he *had* been avoiding her.

"Why?" she asked, though she could fill in a thousand answers.

He shrugged a shoulder. "I'm the famed Nightshade warrior—thousands of kills on my blade. Everyone hates me. No one trusts me. For good reason. They shouldn't." He peered down at her. "*You* shouldn't."

She wanted to ask what he meant. But before she could, he took a step closer. Her hair was wild around her face, and her shirt seemed too tight against her skin—she had changed into pants and a shirt to train. Even though her gowns were all designed for a fatal temptress, at this moment, these training clothes seemed far more revealing.

"You know what it's like to be hated, don't you, Hearteater? To be seen as a monster? A savage?"

It was true. Still, it hurt to hear the truth spoken.

"You're feeling irritated, Hearteater. Do you deny what you are?"

She was breathing heavily. She didn't even really know why. "No. Do you?"

Grim shook his head. He took a step toward her. "Never. I am the monster."

Isla knew she should probably run away, or leave, or do something other than take a step even closer. He tilted his head. Something about the way he looked at her, the way he stood so close. Closer than anyone had ever dared.

"I'm not your enemy," he said, voice softer than she had ever heard it.

Then why couldn't she trust him? Why was he pushing her away?

Why did she even care?

"Prove it," she dared. "Tell me something."

"Anything."

She remembered the king's words in the forest. The reason he had given for why the rest of the rulers hadn't simply decided to kill Grim to fulfill the prophecy. "Oro said you are the only thing standing between us and a greater danger. What was he talking about?"

Grim didn't look particularly surprised by her question. Though he took his time answering it. "There are worse things in this world than the curses. Or even me."

"Like what?"

He shook his head. "I could tell you. But it would only distract you. Believe me, right now, the curses are the more pressing danger."

Isla scowled. Who was he to decide what would and wouldn't distract her? What was too much to know? Still, she could tell by his tone that he wouldn't budge.

"Fine. Show me something, then."

"Anything," he repeated, though the word meant less now that she knew it had limits.

"Show me where the Wildlings lived when they were on Lightlark."

The request surprised even her. She still hadn't found the entrance to Wild Isle. Oro's comments about it in the woods had only fed her curiosity. There was so much about her realm she didn't know.

And now, she was more curious than ever. She wanted the endless power her Wildling ancestors had once possessed. Perhaps they had left something behind. Something that could help her now.

Grim stared at her, and Isla held her breath, wondering if he knew how much she had thought about him in the last few weeks. Wondering if he knew that however hard her heart was beating, however many times his words had already echoed through her mind, he was right—she couldn't trust him.

And he couldn't trust her.

"Of course, Hearteater."

Isla did not speak a word as he led her into the Mainland forest, in the shade of the castle. Not far from the crop of coffiner trees, but in the opposite direction. The way was wild. The stone path had long been overtaken by weeds, untamed plants that smothered it completely. Isla flinched as she watched the woods, bracing herself for another attack. Her back prickled, as if remembering. But the forest did not dare strike her in Grim's presence. They stepped over vines thick as limbs and under spiderwebs large as umbrellas. Soon, the trees lost their leaves and became sharp, bare branches that resembled clusters of swords. Stones that might have lined a riverbank replaced the grass. She couldn't see the end of it until she was out of it.

Sunlight blinded her momentarily, and she stilled.

There was a bridge. It was broken in many places. The sides were made of braided vines.

The isle on the other side gave no indication of life. But something about it called to her. Isla stepped onto the bridge first, without hesitation, and was on the other side before she knew it.

The king had been right. There was no life left here.

Wild Isle had been reduced to a forest of hulls. The trees were bare and twisted, skeletons swaying in the wind. The vines and roots along the floor were dry and crunchy beneath their feet. The ground was a

mess of broken branches, in the shapes of striking snakes. No animals. No green. No . . . anything.

In the center of death stood a structure.

Grim was by her side. “They call it the Place of Mirrors.”

Every inch of the palace was covered in reflective glass that cast back the bare forest, mirroring its surroundings. Its edges winked in the sunlight.

The Place of Mirrors looked fragile, like a strong wind could shatter it. But it had survived when everything else on Wild Isle hadn’t. It was shaped like the carnival tents she had seen on the outskirts of the Skyling newland with her starstick—bulbous, as if blown up by air, and pointed in three places.

Somehow, though the outside was mirrored, the interior was clear. She stepped inside and saw the razed woods through endless windows, cut in a million shapes. The ceiling was curved.

It was almost empty. Just a few statues remained, along with leaves that had swept inside. Isla walked deeper into the Place of Mirrors to find that the rest of the large palace was not made of glass at all. The walls became stone and opened into what must have once been interior gardens, where the ceiling ended altogether. Dead vines grew up columns. A small fountain now held dark water. She kept walking, into rooms and corridors that had been left abandoned and overtaken by the dead forest, until she reached its very back wall, which was sturdier than the rest, carved into the base of a mountain.

It was covered in markings, the most prominent a large swirl. The rest depicted battle—men and women dressed in armor, holding swords and shields. Some rode giant beasts she didn’t recognize. She traced the drawings with her fingers.

“Is it everything you hoped it would be?” Grim asked.

She turned. “It’s much more.”

“Even if it’s almost empty?”

Isla hadn't gotten to explore the entirety of the palace, but she guessed she would find it cleared out, the same way the other rooms were.

"The fact that it's still here . . ." She pressed her palm against the wall. "Gives me hope. That Wildlings can survive all of this."

Grim was somewhere else—she could see it in his eyes. She wondered what he was thinking about. Every move he made was confusing.

"What are the Nightshade lands like?" she asked, not really knowing why.

Even with her starstick, she hadn't dared travel to their territory. Terra's warnings about them had kept her away.

Grim looked at her for a long time. "One day," he said, "I'll show you."

Isla waited for the cloak of darkness before leaving the castle. Oro still hadn't returned to her door. The night was hers. And she made careful use of it.

She wished for Grim's power to see easily in the dark as she took the path through the Mainland, the moon her only guide. On their way back, she had made sure to study the route to Wild Isle intently, but everything looked different touched by night.

The path continued too long when it should have disappeared under overgrowth. She must have taken a wrong turn or missed it completely. Soon, she was back at the Mainland castle.

Isla cursed and tried again. She strained to remember the curve of the trees, or the number of steps she had counted hours before while trying her best to mask her emotions around Grim. He couldn't know that the entire time he was answering her questions, she was thinking about what she had spotted in the Place of Mirrors—and how soon she could go back. Alone.

She squinted through the darkness, then bent so that her fingers could trail the path, waiting for the wildflowers to begin smothering the stone, marking the place she needed to follow.

If she had Wildling powers, she could simply call to the forest and listen for its reply. Follow its song to the palace.

But she didn't. So, she continued stumbling blindly through the night.

Finally, grass brushed against her fingers, a second path veering from the first. She followed it to the forest and hesitated. The moon was locked out of the woods, blocked almost completely by hunched-over trees. She would have to feel her way through. And hope the forest was satisfied with the amount of blood she had already shed for it.

Isla ducked her head lower, wondering if she should come back in the morning. She wondered even as she continued through the woods, thorns catching on her ankles. Even as she tripped over a vine and landed on her hands and knees.

No—no one could know about her midnight journey to the Wildling palace.

Not even Grim.

By the time she stumbled into Wild Isle, her hair had been tangled out of its braid, and she felt the sharp sting of cuts across her palms. But even the pain stilled as she regarded the building in front of her.

At night, the Place of Mirrors reflected only darkness. Her light-brown clothes cut through it like a blade. She watched herself peel from the shadows of the bare woods like a specter.

Inside, moonlight showered down once more. The floors above groaned, as if awakened from a slumber. Wooden walls somewhere cracked. *Normal ancient palace noises,* Isla told herself. Something thudded against the glass above. *Just a fallen branch.* Still, she quickly made her way through the halls and rooms, only stopping at the back wall.

She had seen it, earlier in the day, with Grim. And knew she had to go back.

Isla recognized the spiral on the wall as a door. It was the same shape as the one hidden within her chambers, beneath a broken panel in her closet. The same place she had found her starstick, tucked within her mother's things.

If the Wildlings had a secret door, whatever was inside must have been important enough to hide. And it must still be intact, unlike the rest of the palace.

She had a feeling whatever was inside could help her now. That it held something she needed.

Isla had to get into the vault.

She pushed against the spiral door with all her might, expecting it to creak open with enough effort, just like the one in her room had.

But this one didn't budge.

Isla studied the wall and spotted a gap. A place for a key. No . . . it was too long for a key to fit. Unless it was massive.

She looked around for something that matched its intricate design, a strange pattern like a miniature mountain range. A short candlestick holder seemed close to the right size. She tried to shove it into the hole, but it didn't fit. Not even close. She tried getting some vines and fashioning something similar. But when she turned it like she would a key, the vines snapped.

Her back teeth slammed together. If there was a way to open the door, it had to be inside somewhere.

Isla walked up a winding staircase, covered in dead leaves that were a symphony of crunches beneath her feet. She roamed through hall after hall, into room after room, shards of moonlight her only guide. Minutes later, she had an armful of objects that might fit into the hole. An old, abandoned comb. A thin champagne flute. A vase just big enough to hold a single flower. A miniature harp.

She shoved object after object inside, trying them like keys, until dawn peeked through the palace, bathing the glass entrance in violet. But none of them worked.

The door remained closed.

CHAPTER TWENTY-NINE

THE ABBEY

Isla was more convinced than ever that the Wildling vault held something she could use to find the bondbreaker. Or help her in some other critical way.

And if anyone on the island would know the secret to opening it, it was Juniper.

She walked into his bar the very next day. It was empty, save for a man sitting at the back corner, hat over his face, as if he was napping in the pub, waiting for the livelier evening crowd.

"My favorite Wildling," Juniper said from behind the bar. He wrung his hands together. "To what do I owe the pleasure?"

Isla needed to make this quick. Hopefully no one had spotted her entering the pub, and she wanted to keep it that way. "Moonling nobles attempted to assassinate me." There. That was her secret.

Juniper's head reared back, as if this news surprised even him. "What information do you seek?"

She leaned in closer. "The ancient Wildling palace on Wild Isle. What do you know about it?"

He pursed his lips. "Admittedly, not much. Is there something specific you're wondering about?"

"Is there something hidden inside? If so, would you know how to find it?"

Juniper frowned. His brow creased. It seemed he wasn't used to not knowing about a subject. Isla had to admit it was a long shot.

Wildlings hadn't lived on Lightlark for hundreds of years. She doubted most islanders knew the palace even still stood, if its abandoned state was any indication. "I apologize, Ruler. I have never heard of something hidden inside the Wildling palace. From my understanding, anything of value was looted long ago."

Isla nodded sharply. She had known the chances were low that anyone knew about the vault. Her secret would have to be used another time, for another sort of information. She made to leave, but Juniper spoke once more.

"I do know *something* about the Place of Mirrors, however."

She sat down again. Juniper had used the castle's name, the same one Grim had told her. "What is it?"

"The Place of Mirrors is the only place on the island where all powers other than Wildling's are repressed. Only Wildling ability works inside."

What?

Only powerful enchantment could do such a thing. She didn't even know ability like that existed. Something in the vault must be responsible.

It wasn't the information she was looking for, but it was enough to make Isla desperate to know what was behind the door.

And more positive that whatever it was could help her now.

Isla walked back out into the agora with more questions than answers. A storm was on the horizon. The sky above was filled with dark clouds like a pack of wolves circling, gray fur and all. They seemed to mimic her troubled mind.

"How do you think that dress would fare in the rain?"

Grim. He was leaning against the outside of the bar, waiting for her.

She blinked. "Are you following me?"

Going from completely avoiding her to trailing her . . . it made no sense. What had changed?

What was he after?

Grim raised an eyebrow. "No. I was here for my own reasons, and I sensed you."

"Sensed me?" *Own reasons?*

He nodded. "Your emotions, they have a tinge . . . a color, almost. I knew you were nearby."

She didn't know how she felt about that. Wanted to know what color she was but didn't ask. Instead, she raised her chin and said, "Creep."

Isla turned to walk out of the marketplace, and Grim easily matched her pace. "You know, if you're asking Juniper for information, I might recommend taking precautions. I can make him forget your conversation, if you would like. Or simply threaten him for his silence . . ." She glared at him while simultaneously considering taking him up on his offer. Juniper had helped her, but it was impossible to trust a barkeep who traded secrets.

She really had hoped Juniper knew how to open the vault in the Place of Mirrors. It clearly required a key—one she had no time to look for.

Finding the bondbreaker had to be her focus.

Though, something told her whatever was in the vault could help her locate it.

She couldn't describe it . . . but the door pulled to her, spoke to her. Told her in its own silent language that she needed to get it open.

If only she had the time and resources to make that happen.

"You're disappointed, Isla." She blinked, and there Grim was, stopped in her path, watching her. The castle loomed far ahead, high on its cliff like a crouching giant.

Her back teeth clashed together. She stopped too. "I told you not to read me."

"And I told you I couldn't help it."

She crossed her arms, mouth already open in reply—

When the sky cracked open like an egg.

Rain soaked her clean through in an instant. It stormed so hard that she could barely see through her lashes. Grim was just a dark figure before her. She heard him, though, his deep laughter like a rumble of thunder.

Wind blew her hair and dress back, hissed in her ears. The trees at their sides arched, their leaves dancing wildly.

Grim reached out a hand. And she took it.

The castle was too far, and Isla wasn't sure any of the Nightshade's powers could shield them from rain. He led them to the closest building, the abbey she had seen many times before, with the stained-glass eye at its front.

Grim opened the front door with a blast of dark power and pulled them through.

She was panting, freezing. Drenched. Her hair stuck to her face in wild strands, and her dress—her dress clung to her, outlining her every inch. She reached up to take her crown off and found it knotted in her hair.

Grim stood a few feet away, watching her.

He was soaked too. Dark hair splayed against his forehead, dripping tiny droplets down the sides of his face. The black fabrics he always wore now seemed too fine, barely even there, the muscles beneath them now perfectly defined. His cape dripped softly against the wooden floor of the convent as he slowly walked over. And when she looked into his eyes, she found no humor there, no amusement.

Grim stopped just inches away, and Isla stopped breathing. He reached toward her, and she went still—but his hands simply went to her crown. His fingers gently, carefully, pulled at the strands of her hair wrapped around the metal, unknotting it from her head.

He pulled a little too hard on one piece, and she made a sound that made Grim immediately meet her gaze. Something wicked danced within his eyes, something that made the bottom of Isla's spine curl.

There were no lights in the abbey, no flame. Only the single, rounded stained-glass window offered muted daylight as the storm raged on, rain pattering violently against the glass. And Isla could have sworn the dusky corners of the room darkened further, ink spilling over, shadows lengthening toward the rows of pews.

She took a tight, shaky breath and convinced herself it was because of the cold. Grim watched her mouth and said, "You're feeling . . . distressed, Hearteater."

He was so close she could feel his breath on her cheek, cold as the rain outside, cold as the fingers that were still partially knotted in her hair.

"And you?" she said, her voice just a rasp. "What are you feeling?"

Grim grinned. "Oh," he said, eyes trained to hers, as if he wanted to make sure she heard every word, "what I'm feeling can't be said in a place like this."

Her breath shouldn't have been catching; her pulse shouldn't have quickened at his proximity or words. She still didn't know why he had come to the Centennial, what he was after. Isla had judged her people for their recklessness with love. Now, she understood them a little better.

And herself a little worse.

What was she doing? She had always thought herself above such desires. Stronger than her mother. More focused. Grim had told her she couldn't trust him. He had proven it time and time again.

Why did that make her want to get even closer to him?

With a final tug, he freed her crown. He frowned down at it, and Isla watched as his thumb ran across the dent Oro had made days before. It smoothed over instantly. He handed it to her, in the limited space between them.

She took it with treacherous, trembling fingers.

Then he turned, leaving her standing there, words caught in her throat. She gripped her crown so hard, its rough edges pierced painfully into her hand. *Get a grip.*

Celeste's warning flashed in her mind then. He was a distraction. He was playing her.

She could play him too.

"Where were *you* that night?" she asked, voice still a little breathless. "The night of the curses."

He looked over his shoulder at her. Shadows danced at his feet, their sharp edges ebbing and flowing. Like night itself was seeping from him. "Do you really want to know?"

"Yes."

"I was in bed."

Isla's eyebrows came together. "You were *sleeping?*"

He stared at her. "No."

Oh.

Suddenly the stained-glass window seemed very interesting. Isla studied its four illustrations intently, hoping the heat she felt on her face wasn't visible in the darkness.

Grim sat at one of the benches in the abbey, elbows on his knees. He watched her—she could feel his gaze on her but couldn't bring herself to look back.

In an instant, he was behind her. She felt his breath on her bare shoulder and tensed.

"When I left my chambers, everything was burning. And all of the rulers were dead." She turned and found his face drawn, more serious than she had ever seen it. "I was a ruler of realm. When all I had ever trained to be was a warrior."

Darkness billowed out of him in waves, snuffing out even the limited light creeping in from the window. A flash of lightning struck outside, but its light did not reach them.

Isla swallowed. Turned to face him fully. "I know what it's like to have responsibility you never wanted . . . and never thought you deserved."

Grim's hands were tightly wound by his sides. She tentatively reached

out and opened one of them. Ran a finger across his palm and felt him tense in front of her.

"Will you show me?" she asked, knowing she shouldn't.

He seemed to know she meant his powers. The extent of them, beyond the simple demonstration he had given weeks before. And she seemed to know that he needed a release.

Grim looked intently into her eyes. "Are you sure you want to see?" he asked.

She almost said yes immediately, then remembered the bite of disappointment she'd felt at his answer the last time he had prefaced his response. He was warning her, she realized.

Warning her that she might see something she wouldn't like.

Still, Isla nodded. She wanted to see it. Raw power. The thing she wanted more than ever.

He was so close his nose almost touched hers. "Not here." He glanced at the window. Isla heard the rain, still raging, but not as violently as before. "Do you mind going outside again?"

She shook her head and followed him back out of the abbey.

Isla felt it all once more, the water in sheets, but she was already wet, already cold. Her eyes stayed glued on Grim as he walked to the cliff, to its very edge. His back was tense, his cape glued to his shoulders, and the muscles there rolled back.

Fast as lightning, he turned, hand shooting in front of him—and darkness erupted in a violent line, a wall of ink that rippled like water, peaked like flames. It whipped right past her, inches from her face. She stumbled back, the force of it almost making her fall over.

As quickly as it had struck, the darkness dissolved. Isla took an unsteady breath. In the places night had touched, life had been ripped away. The grass sat charred and matted; trees were reduced to hulls that decayed into ash right before her eyes.

If that power had been unleashed on a human, she could imagine

their skin would melt right from their bones. And those bones would splinter and crack until they were fragments in the wind.

This was worse than fire.

Grim's darkness left nothing behind.

He had turned back to the cliff, hand fisted at his side. A hand that wielded terrible, terrible power.

Grim went still when she trailed two fingers over the back of that hand, against her better judgment. When she said, "Show me more," he grinned.

And gripped her by the waist.

They shot off the cliff, to the sand below—and this time, Isla didn't scream. Because somehow, they had skipped the entire middle of the jump.

The sea foamed and raged like a crazed animal in the storm, clouds bubbling and frothing above, melding together to form a gray gradient. She couldn't see where the ocean ended and the sky began. They both churned and eddied, desperate to touch.

Isla stood close enough to Grim that she heard him over the rain, over the wind that blew in from the sea, whipping against every inch of exposed skin and leaving it numb. She still had her crown in her hand and, for a moment, considered simply throwing it into the angry ocean, wondering if that would solve her problems.

"Hearteater," he said.

She looked up at him, only to see something peculiar in his expression. He looked *worried*. Devastated.

Worried that she would cower from his terrible display of ability? Hate him for what he was?

She remembered his words.

I am the monster.

Part of her was afraid of it.

But she wasn't afraid of *him*. Even though part of her screamed that she should be.

“Tell me how I’m feeling,” she whispered. She could try her best to control her thoughts, her actions—but if the Nightshade had taught her anything, it was that her emotions were far more difficult to bridle.

Rain fell from his hair and onto her cheeks.

He swallowed, reading her. “You’re feeling . . . intrigued.”

She motioned toward their surroundings and shrugged. She had asked him to show her more. “Well?”

Instead of grinning again, Grim’s expression darkened. The ocean curled with a giant wave that crested before them and collapsed into cliffs just feet away. His mouth was suddenly at her ear. “I could open a black hole that would swallow the beach. I could turn the sea dark as ink and kill everything inside of it. I could demolish the castle, brick by brick, from where we stand. I could take you back to Nightshade lands with me right now.” His voice was deep as dreams, dark as nightmares. “I could do all of those things.” His lips pressed against the top of her ear, for just a moment. “And I might—if I didn’t think you would hate me for it.”

Isla’s shoulders and fingers shook—from the cold, or the rain, or his proximity, or his proclamations, she wasn’t sure. She looked down at their bodies, pressed close. Just flimsy, drenched fabric between them. Red dress against black, a rose dipped in midnight. Like tea in boiling water, darkness still seeped from him, around him, ribbons of it that reached toward her before recoiling. “Why do you care what I think? You barely know me.”

Grim’s shadows flared, though his expression did not change. “I know enough,” he said.

“What about staying away from me?”

His lips were right above hers now, his words practically pressed against the corner of her mouth. “I gave it an honest effort,” he said. “But it turns out . . . I’m not that honest.”

Isla stumbled away from him, afraid of what she might do if she stayed so close, close enough to feel the power that leaked from him,

close enough for it to brush against her as harshly as the wind—it was magnificent.

But she was a fool. He had been hot and cold for a reason. He had his own plan.

If anything, he'll use you. *Us.*

Grim took a step back. Another. The shadows at his sides flinched, hissing over the rain. "You're afraid," he said.

She didn't know what else to do, so she nodded. Because she was terrified. Terrified of the way her heart was beating wildly, of how her head was as fogged and clouded as the sky above.

Her people deserved better than her, an unproven leader who was at that very moment gambling away their salvation.

What was she doing?

What was *he* doing?

He must have felt all her emotions, fear weaving with confusion and desire and shame. Because he said, "Let's get back to the castle." And all the darkness and shadows fell to his feet before being washed away by the rain.

CHAPTER THIRTY
SPECTER

On the forty-third night of the Centennial, the king finally knocked on her door again.

She opened it. Looked him up and down. "It's been eight days," she said.

He was expressionless. "It took five to find her. Two to coax her out of hiding. One to make a deal."

Isla stared at him, wondering if she could trust him. Wondering if she even had a choice. She had spent the last few days trying to find another way to get into the Sun Isle library. Unsuccessfully.

Part of her considered simply walking straight inside herself, without an invitation, without a disguise, and allowing the king to make his own conclusions. She had proposed the plan to Celeste, who had gotten back to her a day later, with bad news.

Sun Isle library is heavily guarded and monitored, she had said after asking around. *It is also always full. It would be impossible to search for the bondbreaker unnoticed.*

She needed the king to allow her an unmonitored invitation. Which meant earning his trust.

So she accepted his explanation. And followed him to their next location.

Star Isle was silver. The ground glimmered with cosmic dust. Trees stood thin and crooked, turning into themselves in spirals, tiny glittering leaves growing from even the trunks. The castle was a monstrosity with endless arches, bright jewels tucked into the stone itself, like stars had been stolen and used to fortify the palace, trapped in stone before they could fly home. Celeste once told her that to Starlings, the stars looked brighter than they did to everyone else, like millions of moons, or shining fruits ripe for the picking. Only they could see how brightly they truly glowed.

Starlings manipulated energy from the stars, concentrated power so bright and shining that it could once make buildings topple over, throw bodies soaring without a touch, and shatter all a palace's windows. Now, with their curse, Starling masters no longer existed.

The isle was glittering, beautiful. But in ruins. Unlike Sky Isle, run by its people and their representatives, or Moon Isle, run by the strict Cleo and her harsh nobles, these lands were unkempt. Overgrown. It was a wonder the castle still stood. All other structures looked either unstable or were already partially fallen apart.

That was what happened when an entire realm died before twenty-five, she supposed. Their government was almost nonexistent, run by nobles who were practically still children when they died.

A pity, Isla thought, as she walked through Star Isle. Something about the realm dazzled her, every living thing coated in a shining gloss, like someone had dipped their hand inside a star and smeared its silvery glow across the land.

A bird that looked crafted out of shining metal sat in a tree nearby, beneath a cluster of silver acorns. A metallic snake crept along a branch, its scales like chain mail. They walked through the strangely hued forest for just minutes before coming upon a stream, water silvery in the moonlight.

Isla's skin prickled, not just because of the cold, but because of nerves. They were about to meet one of the ancient creatures. The ones Oro had warned her about.

"Do as I say," he had said. "They are tricksters. Some more violent than others. Some will eat you for dinner and pick their teeth with your bones. Others are more scheming than murderous. They are as old as the island itself."

The king had promised the one tonight would not try to kill her. He had made sure of it during his final meeting with her the night before. But Isla was still on edge. There had to be a reason this hadn't been Oro's first plan.

The trees stopped suddenly, revealing an ancient building, all arches and columns. The windows had long been blown out; the stairs had partially fallen away. Silver roots and vines swept inside, curling around the pillars, in and out of the entrance, around its base, then back into the woods, like the forest was desperately trying to keep the structure from floating away.

Oro took the stairs two at a time, careful to avoid steps that had long since crumbled into powder. Isla followed and once inside saw just how much the forest had taken over. The ceiling was high and vaulted, split into shards—and covered in leaves. Trees had grown up the sides of the interior columns, and brambles swept across the walls. Smaller plants had budded between the stones of the floor, some sporting flowers, others sprouting silver berries that resembled bells, thick thorns between them. They were much smaller than the ones that had pierced her, but even looking at them made her stomach turn.

Oro took one of those thorns and pricked his palm with it. The drop of blood that formed dripped onto the floor.

And a woman stepped out of the wall. She wore a simple dress that floated around her, just like her hair, both suspended as if she was underwater. Her body was silver and slightly transparent.

A specter.

This was the ancient creature? A ghost?

"My king . . . you have returned for me," she purred, her voice like wind chimes.

The temperature had suddenly dropped. When Isla breathed out through her mouth in shock, a cloud puffed from her lips.

The specter turned sharply to face her. Her smile deepened. "And you brought me a gift."

"Not a gift," Oro said. "But yes, what you asked for."

Isla took a step back. "Asked for?" she said, tripping on a vine. She barely caught herself before falling.

Was this his new plan? Was he going to trade her for the heart?

The specter approached quickly, hair moving like a whip behind her head. "Ah, yes . . . exactly as I requested. How were you able to find her on such short notice? I've never seen a face quite like that." She frowned. "The clothes do not flatter her, but I see the hint of a nice figure there . . ."

Isla pulled her new dagger from her waist and brandished it. "Don't take another . . . float," she said, looking down and not seeing any feet.

The specter's head fell back at a gruesome angle as she laughed. "That metal would just go through me, girl." She squinted milky eyes at Isla and said, "Now knot that shirt. I want to examine the body I will be wearing."

"Wearing?" Isla whipped around to face Oro, who seemed content to watch.

He sighed. "It's just for a few seconds."

The specter pouted. "I had hoped you had changed your mind about that."

Isla was a moment away from plunging the blade into Oro's side. "You have one second to explain before I run from this place screaming and never speak to you again," she said through her teeth. He conveniently hadn't mentioned *this* on the walk over.

His expression was bored. "The specter's price for helping us is being allowed to walk in a body for a few moments."

Her hand tightened on the knife's hilt. "Why not yours?"

"I offered. But she requested . . . something specific."

The specter was suddenly at her side. "The most beautiful girl on the island, that's what I requested." She reached out a silvery finger, making to touch Isla's cheek. "And you're *perfect.*"

"Absolutely not," Isla said, stepping back. "How do I know she won't stay in there? That you're not in love with her and just want a body for her to inhabit for eternity?"

Oro gave her a look, just as the specter turned to regard him in a way that told Isla that was exactly what she was hoping for.

"Well?" Isla demanded.

"Do you trust me?"

"No! You didn't even tell me about this until you summoned her!" But that wasn't completely true. She did trust him, at least a little, after all they had already been through.

Anger burned down through her chest. *This* was the deal he had made with the ancient creature?

Oro sighed. "What will it take?"

Nothing! she wanted to scream into his face. But then her heart began beating faster, doing a little dance in her chest. This was her chance.

This was the moment she had been waiting for.

She was so excited, so nervous, she didn't bother glazing the request. "Take me to the Sun Isle library" was all she said. "Let me look inside. Alone."

Oro frowned. "Why?"

Isla straightened. "I like books. I want to see what your isle has to offer," she said casually. Then, to draw attention away from her admittedly random request, she added, "Sunlings do *read,* don't they? Or do they prefer to spend their time frowning, sulking, and burning things like their ruler?"

That did the trick. He stared down at her like he wanted to throw her off the nearest cliff but finally said, "Fine."

Something cold plunged into her chest.

He had stabbed her—that was her first thought as her mind went dark and she drifted far, far away.

She was suspended, weightless, a whisper in the night. Free and bound, loose and tethered. Dancing. Falling.

"*That's enough.*" Oro. She gasped.

Isla blinked. Oro blinked back—an inch away. Her body was pressed firmly against his, her fingers were laced through his golden hair, and her lips were almost against his lips. He wasn't holding her at all, but she was clinging to him.

She startled and likely would have fallen back and cracked her head open on the stone if he hadn't reached for her.

A true Wildling wouldn't have been so fazed by the king's proximity, but Isla didn't have a long list of conquests like the proud temptresses of her realm.

Isla turned to glare at the specter, who floated nearby, beaming. "You're lucky you're already dead," she spat.

Her cheeks burned and she refused to look at Oro again, who said with just as much venom, "You got what you wanted. Now tell us what you know."

The specter sighed. She sat in an invisible chair. "What you seek is not on Star Isle. Not this time." *This time?* Before Oro could leave, she said, "A warning, King. The underbelly of the island is rising up. Darkness is at work . . . We feel it."

"Feel what?" Isla asked.

"Dread." With a final smile at Oro, the specter disappeared through the wall. Isla wanted to turn to Oro, to scream something at him, but she knew it would make him even more suspicious of her.

Besides, she had finally gotten what she wanted.

Though—it seemed too good to be true. She needed to make Oro fulfill his word tonight, lest he go back on his deal. It was still early. They could go right now. "Great. That was traumatizing," she said. Her shoulders hiked with a chill as she thought of that ancient being wearing her skin. Even if it was just for a moment. Of being close enough to the wretched king that she could feel his breath against her mouth. "Now you know the heart isn't on Star Isle. Thanks to *me*. I'll admit, it's valuable information. Must narrow locations

down significantly." She looked him right in the eyes. "Now, take me to the library."

Oro turned and walked back through the Starling forest in silence.

He was really taking her. She couldn't believe it.

Sun Isle's was the only library they hadn't searched. The bondbreaker had to be inside. She could find it and break their curses that very night.

Celeste would be thrilled. She couldn't wait to tell her—

At the bridge, the king took the wrong turn.

She stopped. "Isn't your isle that way?"

He just kept going as if he hadn't heard her.

"You made a promise, King," she yelled at his back.

"I will take you to the Sun Isle library," he said over his shoulder. "But I don't recall specifying *when*." His gaze narrowed. "Perhaps when you have helped me find the heart, as promised in our original deal."

Her fingers spasmed, itching, pleading to choke him. She shook her head, so angry she felt the prickle of tears at the corners of her eyes. She was so close. He had *promised*. Had she not done enough?

"Come back," she said. He did no such thing. He ignored her, a specialty of his.

Her body was broken and tired—this was all she asked for in return.

This time, Isla's voice shook with rage. "You . . . you are a self-centered, heartless wretch."

That made Oro turn around. He took a few steps back toward her and grinned meanly. "Is this your plan, Wildling? To try to win my heart by tormenting me?" His wide eyes searched hers, waiting. He was serious.

Isla had felt the sting of tears, but now she laughed. Breathless, infuriated, she laughed and laughed. She took a step forward and said slowly, so he could hear every syllable, "I have absolutely no interest in you whatsoever, *King*."

She waited for him to call her a liar. To say she was just like the countless Wildlings before her who had undoubtedly also been instructed to seduce the king as part of their strategy.

Instead, Oro looked taken aback. Shocked. Was it really that surprising that a Wildling wasn't trying to make him fall in love so she could steal his abilities and bring that power back to her realm?

Could he tell by her anger that she was telling the truth?

"Then what *are* you interested in, Wildling?" he demanded. "Why do you want access to my library? What are you looking for?"

She stood very still. And said nothing.

He took a step closer. "I have watched you. You are a chameleon, becoming everything everyone wants you to be, all of the time. Except around *me*—you don't seem to give a damn what I think of you." His gaze was fire. "The lands I have been entrusted with are dying. *I* am dying. I will do anything it takes to break these curses. You, or whatever you are planning, will not keep me from that end." He looked down at her so closely, it was as if he was trying to see right through her. "So, I will ask you again. What do you want, Wildling?"

The king was suspicious. And perceptive. He knew she was looking for something.

She had ruined it.

Hurt and a million other emotions pooled in her stomach. Her voice had never been so cold. "You are taking me to the library. Now."

Oro's expression did not change. "I will take you once we find the heart," he repeated.

His tone was final. Isla knew he would not change his mind, and they were nowhere near finding the heart. She couldn't wait until then. Not with the ball a week away. Not when Moonling nobles had nearly succeeded at assassinating her even before then. The handwritten note in the agora might have been a trick, but it was true. She *was* in danger.

"No," she said, laughing without humor. She felt her sanity unspooling around her. "You know what? I'm *done*. With you, with this plan." Her voice became louder and wilder the more she spoke, but she didn't care. "I have bled. I haven't slept. I have been possessed. I have had the thorough displeasure of being in your presence for far too long. I am *done*. Our deal is off. And guess what? I don't need you to get onto your isle, King," she sneered. "Unless you want to stop me?"

She kept her eyes locked on his. Daring him to deny her access.

He did not.

"Good. Perhaps I'll go during the day, then," she said, hands in fists at her side. She spoke her last words right in his face before passing him by. "That way, I'll have your land all to myself."

CHAPTER THIRTY-ONE

FIRE

Terra had been right. She had always scolded Isla and her emotions. *Your feelings will be your ruin,* she had said countless times. They made her weak. Vulnerable.

And now, they had ruined her plan at gaining access to the Sun Isle library.

She shouldn't have gotten so angry at the king. She shouldn't have expected him to be anything but insufferable.

Of course he would use her own words against her. Of course he would have a specter use her body for his own purposes yet deny her a simple request.

Isla had gone about it all the wrong way. She knew that now. But she refused to tell Celeste she had failed them. Again. Not when her friend had gone to such great lengths to secure the gloves.

She wouldn't give up. Not yet.

Sun Isle was empty during the day, as expected. There was no one to gape at her bright-red dress. She hadn't bothered wearing a more neutral shade. Any hue other than gold would stand out immediately, anyway.

The isle was gilded, just like its king. Gold everywhere. She didn't waste time looking at its wonders, or lingering. She marched right up to the castle with resolve.

She didn't care if all the guards in the palace tried to stop her, she was getting into that library.

As soon as she entered the castle, the sunshine from outside died. The only light came from fiery orbs and chandeliers. They filled every inch of the ceiling, doing what the king couldn't.

"Isla, ruler of Wildling?"

She turned around to the guard who had spoken, ready to tell him he couldn't keep her from the isle. That she was *allowed* to be here. But before she could, he spoke again.

"We've been expecting you. Please, follow me." The guard's gold-plated armor clinked as he turned on his heel and made his way down the hallway.

Expecting you? She took off after him.

"You . . . have?" she said, looking around carefully, expecting to see more guards soon. To possibly be brought to some sort of dungeon.

He nodded. "I've been given orders to take you to the library." Isla was silent. That couldn't be right . . . it had taken her three days to find her nerve to venture into the Sunling land. The guard had been waiting right at the doors. There was no way he, or others, had been waiting for her to arrive.

Before long, he stopped in front of an entrance. "The king has ordered the library to be closed this week. You will be alone and are to have full access to any of the floors."

She blinked. Oro had refused to take her here himself, yet he had given her exclusive privileges?

It had to be a trick.

Though, as long as she was able to search the library . . . she didn't care. Isla bowed her head in thanks, pasting a smile on her face as if this was all normal. Expected. "Thank you," she said.

"I will be out here, should you need anything."

The library doors closed behind her with a thud.

The guard was right. She had the entire space to herself. Ten floors of books. Galleries so long, she couldn't see their end.

If she didn't have a specific task, she would have loved to spend days in here, exploring.

But that wasn't why she had fought so hard to get inside this room.

Isla took off, not knowing if more guards were coming to trap her, or if the king himself would appear any moment, to demand she tell him what she was looking for.

She fetched the Starling gloves from a hidden pocket in her cape and pulled them on with only minimal disgust. With so little time, she needed to touch everything and hope she got lucky.

The books were beautiful. Their covers were gold, gems up their spines. Knowledge seemed to be prized on Sun Isle.

Dozens of tables filled the space, unlike any other library she had visited on the island. Did this mean Sunlings were granted full access inside?

No time to wonder. She looked for anything out of place, anything that looked special at all.

At the very end of the hall sat a hearth, big enough to swallow her whole. The flames inside crackled, almost like a beckoning.

She stopped in front of it.

The Skyling hidden section had been at the very top of the tower, high in the sky. The Moonling one had been engulfed in water.

Perhaps Sunling's secret section was hidden in flames.

Before she could think better of it, Isla reached one glove toward the fire, knowing it could very well wilt to pieces. She braced herself for the pain and smell of double layers of flesh burning.

It did not. The fire vanished immediately, and she stepped into the mouth of the hearth. Pressed another hand against the stone wall behind it. And watched the brick fall away.

Her chest felt too tight. Her throat too dry.

This was it. The last library. The last place to search.

She stepped inside.

Sunlings had more relics than any of the other realms combined. There were shelves of them, sitting in the near darkness.

Isla didn't waste a moment.

She was thorough. She picked up every single enchantment in the room. Held it for a few seconds. Pulled some apart, making sure nothing was hidden inside. There were dozens.

None of them resembled a giant needle.

None, besides a few swords, even had a point.

No. This couldn't be right. They had searched *every* library on Lightlark. The text had said—

It had said the bondbreaker was in a library centuries ago.

More than enough time for it to have gone missing.

Or to have been destroyed.

Or maybe . . . it never even existed in the first place.

Her chest filled with fury, then worry, then sadness. Celeste and Isla had planned for years. *This* was their way to break their curses. *This* was the key to her freedom.

This was the plan that guaranteed she would be off the island before the fiftieth day.

Now, the ball was just three days away.

And there was no bondbreaker.

CHAPTER THIRTY-TWO

NEXT

Celeste took the news surprisingly well.

The Starling paced for a few minutes before saying, "There must be another library, then."

Isla loved her friend. But in that moment, she felt like shaking her by the shoulders.

There was no other library. No bondbreaker.

"We need to consider another plan," Isla said. "This one failed. We searched every library. Every isle. The fiftieth day is almost here."

The Starling shook her head. "Exactly. The Centennial is just halfway over. We have time to find the library. We—"

"I don't have time," Isla yelled, cutting her friend off. She tensed. She had never raised her voice at her. But the words had come flooding out. Isla swallowed, and her tone became gentler. "*I* don't have time," she repeated. "Cleo means to kill me. She will, after the ball."

Celeste frowned. Grabbed her hands. "I know, I know," she said. "But didn't I protect you last time? With the nobles?"

Isla sighed. "Of course. But you said so yourself. You can't protect me from all of them. And I'm not sure Cleo is the only one who wants me dead."

Her friend insisted on continuing their search for the bondbreaker. But Isla had made up her mind.

They needed another plan.

And she knew just where to find it.

***

Isla found him in front of a crescent window in the Mainland castle. He stood watching the moon, as if staring at it hard enough might make it a sun.

The king stiffened as she entered. But he did not move an inch. Not when she crossed the room. Not when she walked to his side. His eyes remained firmly on the window.

Clearly, she would need to be the first one to speak.

"Thank you," she began. "For allowing me access."

He stared straight ahead. "You said so yourself. You did not need my permission."

They both knew that technically wasn't true. If the king hadn't wanted her on his isle or in his library, he could have kept her out.

Silence stretched on, seconds tripping over themselves.

"Did you find what you were looking for?" he finally asked. Only then did he glance over at her.

"No," she said sharply, and he faced the window again.

More moments ticked by, cartwheeling between them.

"Did you?" she whispered.

It had been five days since she had seen him. More than enough time to have sought out another ancient creature for help. If he had somehow found the heart without her, she would have no other plan. Her only hope was that Oro would take her back. Would honor the terms of their deal again. She would get his protection after the ball, and a chance at still saving her and Celeste.

"No," he said. Relief tasted sweet on her tongue.

"Good." She turned to face him. Oro turned too. "What's next?"

CHAPTER THIRTY-THREE

THE BALL

At the midpoint of the Centennial, on the fiftieth day, the Betwixt Ball took place. It was the Lightlark event of the century, a beautiful excuse for a party that was intended to muddle the anxiety and anguish of the Centennial with bubbling drinks, gowns made of gossamer, and a feast that celebrated each of the isles.

It also marked a turning point in the games. At midnight, killing could begin.

Her guardians had designed a specific outfit for the ball. Precariously placed leaves trailed across her chest and along her stomach, leaving strips of skin exposed across her ribs. The green leaves continued down her middle, just past the tops of her thighs—below there was just sheer material, the occasional leaf sewn into the tumbling fabric. Her cape was deep green and offered at least some sort of modesty.

It also hid her weapons. Throwing stars disguised as brooches. Blades tucked into the folds. Chain mail was stitched into the fabric, making the cape into a shield.

She knew how useless it would all be against a ruler set on assassinating her that night. But she refused to die without a fight. As much as it annoyed her, she would have to trust that Oro would hold up his end of their newly re-inked deal. They were set to seek out the next ancient creature—one the king had promised would *definitely* try to kill her—the very next night.

A knock sounded at her door. Ella. "They're ready for you," she said.

Isla knew exactly what to expect. Nevertheless, her fingers shook at her sides as she walked down the halls, trailed by staff who carried baskets of crimson rose petals, crushed leaves, and freshly picked wildflowers.

Too soon, she stood before double doors, and Ella left her side. Her spine straightened. Her chin rose.

The doors opened, and Isla stopped breathing.

The ballroom had six grand staircases—one for each ruler. She locked eyes with Celeste across the room. Her friend looked determined, seeing through this glittering ball's mask into its bloody underbelly. By the next morning, one of them could very well be dead.

It had been twenty-five days since the rulers had been paired together, with the task of figuring out all aspects of the prophecy. Who knew if someone *had* identified the offense that needed to be committed again and now just needed a ruler to die?

She thought of the king's words in the forest. He claimed the reason the curses hadn't been broken wasn't because it was hard to kill another ruler but because *choosing the right ruler and realm to die* was the difficult part.

Cleo's assassination attempt negated all that he had said about her and the games. Isla spotted the Moonling then, at the top of her own staircase. Anger curled in her stomach. It was the first time she had seen Cleo since she had tried to have her killed.

It was quickly replaced by a dark satisfaction. *That didn't go the way you planned, did it?* her smile said as she stared at the Moonling from across the room. The ruler met her gaze, but there was no triumph in it. Or *anything,* really. Her face was a mystery, revealing nothing.

Snow fell in sheets from clouds that crowded the glass ceiling, shadows danced along the walls, trees grew from the marble floor, silver stardust was smeared like paint down the stairs, and dozens of rings of fire hung above their heads.

Isla knew exactly what to expect.

But it was still magnificent.

The rulers began their coordinated descent.

Lightlark nobles and, in Skyling's case, representatives, awaited below. Many stared at her dress. Some whispered and grinned at each other behind ornate fans, as if gossiping about her impending assassination. Coins clattered as they were exchanged between hands. Were there bets on rulers' deaths?

Some Moonlings regarded her with clear malice. Perhaps the nobles she and Celeste had killed were their friends. Or family.

Isla stared them down and hoped they feared her.

As soon as her heel reached the marble floor, a single brave man peeled away from the crowd. A Starling in a silver suit. Other nobles gasped at his foolishness. He bowed his head and offered his hand. "Would you honor me?" he asked.

Normally, Isla might have refused. She already felt on edge and off-kilter, the snow and smeared starlight and flames bright in every corner of her vision.

But it was important she appeared unaffected by the prospect of the first rule expiring at midnight. Fear would only make her an easier target.

Isla took the Starling's hand, and he immediately whisked her into the center of the ballroom. Poppy had taught her all the traditional dances. She moved effortlessly through the steps, as easily as twirling her blades in her hands, and the Starling kept up, spinning her perfectly, keeping a firm hand on her lower back and his feet away from hers.

The song changed, and she had another dance partner. Then another. Another. Celeste was nearby, dancing with just as many people, doing a better job at looking like she was having a good time.

Cleo was sitting in one of the corners of the room, surrounded by Moonling nobles.

Watching her.

Waiting?

Azul stood by a long spread of food, goblet in hand. He wore a cape entirely made up of Skyling jewels, his every knuckle glimmering

with gems. From across the room, he gave a nod of appreciation to the large diamond teardrop earrings she wore that skimmed the sides of her neck.

She smiled back politely.

Some nobles tracked the exchange, perhaps suspecting an alliance.

Good. Let them suspect anything but the truth.

She thought back to the conversation she had heard between him and Oro. Had he really not been speaking of her realm?

If so, which realm had he been speaking about ending?

No one was busier than Oro, who lingered by his throne. He wore gold, as always, with sleeves covering every inch of the bluish gray she now knew was growing down his arm. Dozens of nobles surrounded him, asking questions he answered lazily between sips of drink. But his eyes were alert. A handful of women seemed determined to get a bit closer to him, not afraid to discreetly push each other out of the circle to do so. Isla rolled her eyes. Just when she was about to look away, he met her gaze. And nodded before taking another swig of wine.

She looked around for the last ruler . . . but didn't see him anywhere.

After yet another dance, she excused herself, her head spinning and throat dry from small talk. She stumbled out into the hallway, into the closest room, and closed the doors firmly behind her.

It wasn't a room at all. At least, not one with four walls. Her steps echoed against the stone floor until she reached an interior balcony. There were more of the same levels, above and below it, like layers of a cake crafted out of marble. Her eyes closed and her fingers gripped the railing as tightly as if it was a starstick that could transport her anywhere else.

Isla hated the fake smile she had worn all night. She hated the nobles who had watched her every move. She hated how closely *she* had watched the clock, every bell marking the hours making her stomach sink with dread. She—

"Looking for me, Hearteater?"

Isla whipped around, and Grim was there, towering over her. He wore a much nicer version of his typical clothing, a black suit with a shining cape.

He took in her every inch and grinned. "Now you look satisfyingly terrifying, don't you?"

Sparks twirled around her bones, and his grin widened, sensing it . . . sensing how he made her feel.

She didn't even bother hiding it. Not tonight. Not with everything else going on in her mind. Grim was the least of her worries.

"I didn't see you," she said.

He shrugged. "Sometimes the only way to keep people from bothering you is to not let them see you at all."

Isla wished she'd had that power an hour ago. "Then why bother going visible again?" she asked, her voice barely above a whisper.

Grim took a step toward her. Took her hand into his with such brazen possession that she nearly took it back. "To dance with you, of course."

Before she could say a word, she was whirling around, the sheer bottom of her dress draping across the marble floor, leaves crinkling. His hand, cold as night, was at the base of her spine—the other wrapped completely around hers.

His grin was devilish, and she swallowed, knowing exactly what he was sensing as her hand gripped one of his wide shoulders, as she looked up at eyes that might as well have been two pools of ink, the space between stars.

Did it frighten him? Everyone in the six realms lived in fear of having a Wildling love them. It was a death sentence.

And she didn't love him . . . she barely knew him.

But shouldn't he be afraid of what she was feeling now?

She pressed herself closer, completely against him, reading his

reaction, surprising herself with her boldness. And Grim only laughed darkly. His hand ran a slow trail down her spine—then up once more. "Hearteater," he said into her ear. "You're killing me."

Isla didn't breathe. His breath was against her cheek. He smelled like stone and storms and something spiced, like cinnamon.

She bit her lip, and he watched the movement, swallowing.

Then he was gone.

No, not gone. Invisible.

And so was she.

A crowd of nobles entered a moment later. Their voices were high-pitched with the pleasure of passing along gossip, though Isla didn't pay attention to their words. Grim was shadowed next to her, visible . . . but not truly there. Her own body looked similar.

The sight of the nobles made her sick. Betting on lives. Looking at her as if she deserved to die, simply for being born.

Suddenly, she craved a distraction. The ball would soon turn bloody. She would either stand and fight—or flee to a safer location. She still wasn't sure. What she *was* sure about was that these could be the last few minutes that she didn't have to watch her back, the last hour she might enjoy just for herself.

"Let's go," she whispered. They were both leaned against the balcony, facing the crowd.

Grim raised an eyebrow at her. "Leave the ball?"

"Just for a bit. Right now, I want to be anywhere else."

Grim grinned wickedly. He wrapped his arm fully around her waist. "Then allow me to whisk you away, Hearteater."

He fell back and took her with him. They plummeted right off the interior balcony, backward, to the floor below.

Grim's hand was over her mouth before she could scream—half a moment later, she was in his arms. It was all a blur, the marble and ceiling lights and the sheets of her gown mixing to make their own galaxy, and then she was on the ground.

Isla looked at him like she wanted to gut him, and he just laughed. The nobles were huddled like wolves above, oblivious to them. She ceased being shadow, and Grim went solid before her. He took her hand once more and said, "Night is a wicked time, Hearteater . . . you can get into all sorts of trouble."

Trouble. That was exactly what he was, leading her through room after room before turning into a hall. He knew the way well, and Isla had almost forgotten that it had been his home once. Centuries before.

Grim went down a set of stairs, and Isla matched his pace. Around and around they went. Down, down, down. She was smiling—*why was she smiling?*—even as she could barely see the steps before her. No light shined there, the brightness of the ball far behind them.

"Where are we going?" she asked, and only got a grin in the dark in response. She almost tripped on the folds of her dress, but he held her firmly, all the way until the bottom of the stairs.

They must have been at the base of the castle—underground, maybe. Orbs holding white light crowded the corners of the room, floating like balloons. The walls were arched, held up by columns, and beyond them sat a slice of dark water like a piece of the nighttime sky trapped below.

It shimmered, startling her, and she took a step back.

Right into his chest. She stilled.

Grim placed a hand on her waist. Her shoulders hiked up, his body ice-cold but leaving heat blooming beneath her skin. His fingers trailed down to her hip bone. His thumb circled the delicate skin just beyond it. Closer and closer to even more sensitive places. Isla pinched her lips together.

In her heels, she was tall enough so that when she leaned back, her head rested against his shoulder. From that angle, she imagined he could see down her dress, only a few leaves keeping her from being completely exposed. Still, under his piercing gaze, she felt bare. Breathing became difficult. One hand gripped her hip harder, pinning her to him, while the other traveled across her stomach. His knuckles trailed up her ribs,

only stopping once they reached the heavy underside of her chest. They grazed her there, and she was suddenly aching, her skin prickling, heat pooling. She met his eyes and found them dark with—

She didn't know what that was.

Was it desire?

Was it . . . sadness?

"What are you thinking?" she asked, turning to face him.

Grim looked at her like he knew her, like he saw her for what she truly was and not what she pretended to be. She felt naked before him, not just because he had touched her where no one else ever had but also knowing he sensed her every change in emotion. The pulsing desire for him to touch her *more,* for him to pull her dress down and touch her everywhere without any fabric between them.

"I'm thinking . . ." he said darkly. *Thinking what?* He reached for her.

And blinked. His entire expression changed.

The hand he had reached toward her now reached inside his pocket.

". . . that I have something for you." He pulled out a necklace. It had a dark chain, holding a black diamond as large as a plum.

Isla's eyebrows came together. He was giving her jewelry? She didn't know what to say. Her face was still hot. The diamond was beautiful, but she didn't want a gem—she wanted him, pressed against her. Immediately.

Grim grinned, sensing everything. He looked ready to take her into his arms once more but seemed to think better of it, because he turned his attention to his gift. "May I?"

She nodded, hoping he didn't mistake her disappointment for not liking his present. She lifted her hair, and he clasped the necklace into place, tight around her neck, his fingers lingering for just a moment.

"I know you are more than capable of protecting yourself," he said, head bent low, breath against her nearly bare shoulder. "But should you ever need me, touch this. And I will come for you."

She glanced down at it again with greater appreciation.

I will come for you. He had said it like a promise.

She needed any protection she could get. Something like this would be useful, especially after seeing his display of power. Especially now that they were minutes away from killing being permitted.

Yet—

"Grim. I can't . . . I can't wear this." It would be a statement. Oro had already suspected they might be working together. This would all but confirm it. She couldn't do anything that would compromise her and Oro's alliance, not when it seemed like the only chance to break her and Celeste's curses.

"I know." Two of his fingers pressed against the chain, against her neck, and it went invisible.

She looked up at him. Didn't know what to say, wanted to thank him . . . but the words formed and died in her throat.

Grim reached toward her again, all restraint gone, and trailed his knuckles down her cheek, the necklace, her collarbones. Down the center of her chest. "Hearteater," he said gently. "You don't want to know what I'm thinking," he finally answered. Her body tensed in anticipation, taut like an arrow a moment away from careening through the air. She wanted his hand lower, higher, everywhere . . .

But he dropped it instead.

He did not touch her again on their quiet walk back to the ballroom. She wanted to say something, do something, tell him . . .

When she opened her mouth, he was already speaking.

"I need to go," he said, looking over her shoulder. Was he looking for someone? He almost looked nervous. Wary.

Of who?

"You're leaving?" she asked, eyebrows coming together.

"Don't worry, Hearteater," he said. "I'll be back before midnight." His gaze shifted to the corner of the room where Sunlings had gathered, Oro at their center like a sun they all revolved around. "In the meantime . . . perhaps you should dance with the king," he said.

Oro? Isla frowned. Grim had just run his hands down her body. He had gifted her a necklace. Why would he suggest she dance with someone else? Especially his enemy.

It didn't make any sense. Before she could ask anything, he was gone.

Isla turned around, back to the party, slightly dazed. She trailed a finger across the chain of her necklace, invisible to everyone else. It felt like another secret.

One she actually enjoyed keeping.

"There you are." Celeste casually slipped to her side, pretending to study the table of desserts nearby. "Half an hour until midnight. What will it be? Fight or hide?"

The rules required they attend each Lightlark event. But nowhere was it specified they had to stay the entire time. She and Celeste could leave, barricade themselves somewhere safe. Her friend had suggested portaling to Star Isle and staying there awhile.

But their alliance would be compromised. And though their plan had gone to shambles, secrets were still sacred during the Centennial. Letting their friendship be known could endanger them both.

"Fight," Isla said, surprising herself by the conviction in her voice. At the beginning of the Centennial, she would have said *hide* without any hesitation. But though she didn't have power, Isla refused to be a coward. She would face Cleo's rage head-on. *That* was how she would survive. Not by hiding.

"Are you—"

Before Celeste could say another word, the floor lurched. And Isla was suddenly careening through the air.

She landed on her side, temple banging against the marble.

Air shattered with high-pitched snaps of metal chains as the fiery chandeliers fell, taking most of the ceiling with them. The floor split into fractures, strikes of lightning across the marble. Cracks of collapsing stone and hissing fire filled the world—everything solid turned out to be delicate, crumbling like cake, breaking as easily as glass.

As the castle collapsed, nothing and no one was safe.

Isla only had time to reach an arm up in front of her eyes as a ring of fire fell, right at her face—but before it broke her skull, Celeste was suddenly there. The Starling raised her own arms, and it stopped midair.

Screams echoed against the stone walls, the metallic scent of both power and blood filling the room. There was a roaring, a ringing, as the world stumbled, then straightened, only to fall again.

The woman to her left, a Skyling in a cornflower-blue dress, was swallowed up by the floor. A Moonling man stood still in shock—he took a step, but it was too late. A chunk of the ceiling crushed him, no water around for him to wield in defense.

She turned to where Celeste had been. But her friend was gone. Isla's heart pinched. She raced to her feet. Dust clouds bloomed, and she squinted through them, searching desperately for the glimmer of her silver dress, fearing the worst—

But Celeste was nearby, lifting debris off a group of Starlings.

Isla backed toward the wall, her mouth opening and closing, her lungs frozen in her chest, her hands outstretched, but doing nothing.

It wasn't even midnight yet. What was this?

Azul was at the other side of the room, his arms working in wild strokes, creating a shield of air under which dozens of guests hid. Cleo was healing a group of Moonling nobles who had been badly burned by the fallen flames.

Oro.

She found him on his knees, at the back of the room. His face was twisted with pain, and his fingers had gone through the marble floor.

That was when she realized what was happening.

Lightlark was falling. It was just as the king had described. People dying, structures collapsing. For hundreds of years, the rulers had failed to break the curses. It was finally taking its toll on the island.

But why now? Why at the ball?

She reached toward a group clinging to what was left of the floor, a bloody bridge snaking across the room. One she was able to pull up. Another fell through the cracks.

Her blades could do nothing. Her cape might shield some debris, but it was useless against the thick slabs of marble raining down around them.

If she had power, she could save them. She could wield the vines decorating the room, use them to pull people to safety.

She might not have abilities. But Oro did. He needed to get up—he could stop this.

She shouted his name. But he remained hunched over, forehead now nearly against the floor. The roar muted her voice. Furniture fell through the ceiling. He was across the ballroom. The space between them was half-gone, the rest falling without warning.

Isla cursed as she kicked her shoes off and ran toward the king. She jumped over the largest hole, sharp pieces of rubble embedding themselves in her heels upon landing. The pain was a whisper compared to the spines she had pulled from her back—if she could live through that, she could live through anything. She dodged a chair that nearly crushed her, pushing a young Moonling away from its path too and earning a look of disgust that she had dared touch him.

Next time I'll let it crush you, she thought as she ducked beneath a piece of the ceiling that had concaved and finally made it to the king.

"Oro." She knelt before him, the same way he had when she was on the forest floor, full of barbs and thorns.

He didn't acknowledge her presence.

Nothing new—but this wasn't just about her.

She grabbed him by the shoulders and said, "Get up! People are dying. They need you!"

Oro raised his head enough to meet her gaze. His eyes were hollow. As if every ounce of energy had been drained. Another tremor shook

the floor, and he growled, his fingers going deeper into the marble. The pain must have been unbearable to have brought the king to his knees.

"*Please,*" she begged. A few feet away, rock rained down into a pile that crushed half the group Azul had been trying to block. He rushed to fling the rubble away with his wind, but blood coated the stone. It was too late.

Oro did not move an inch. But she heard him say "*Leave*" through his teeth.

No. When Isla was hurt and had demanded he go, he had stayed. She wasn't leaving. Not until he stopped this.

Isla took his shirt in two fistfuls and shoved him against the wall with all her strength, tearing his fingers from the floor. She screamed right into his face. "You might be dying, but you're not dead yet, you miserable wretch, now get up and do something before you allow your brother's sacrifice and everything we all have lost to be for nothing."

Oro did not meet her gaze or get up.

But, with a groan that shook his shoulders, he leaned forward, pushing past her—and his hands fully pierced the marble. Power erupted from his touch, filling the room.

Forcing it still.

Then he collapsed against the floor.

Screams and calls for help and final breaths became a symphony that overtook the violins and harps that lay in splinters in the corner of the room, along with most of the orchestra.

When Celeste found her, and they rushed out of the room, Isla thought about the king's words—that this Centennial was not simply *another* chance at breaking the curses . . .

But perhaps the last chance.

Dozens were dead. The wing of the castle had been reduced to little more than rubble. And it would get worse, Isla knew, if they didn't break the curses soon.

She had somehow found herself in an alliance with the king. They had a plan to find the heart. Grim, Celeste, and Oro had all promised to protect her.

Even without the bondbreaker, it had all seemed almost possible to survive the Centennial and break their curses before it ended.

But as the broken ballroom doors managed to slam closed and the screams were swallowed up, Isla wondered if the island would even last the rest of the hundred days.

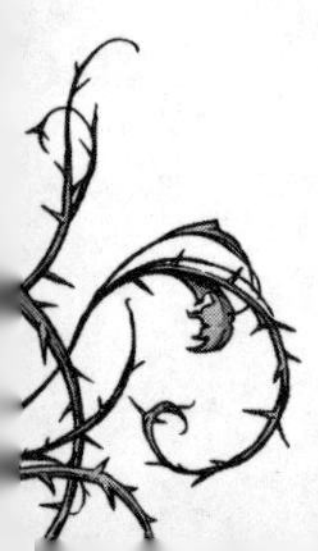

CHAPTER THIRTY-FOUR

ORO

The aftermath of the ball left the island fractured in more ways than one. Part of the castle was in ruins. The streets of the agora were so empty, wind whistled down them. Store windows shuttered, and their walls did not fold open at night. Islanders were afraid to leave their homes, let alone their isles. There were whispers that the tragedy at the ball was Grim's doing, after his demonstration weeks before had shown the same thing happening. Except this hadn't been an illusion.

The Mainland became a place only for specters and rulers.

They did not pretend any longer. Cleo abandoned all pretenses of working with Celeste and moved to her isle, breaking tradition. Oro uncharacteristically pushed their excursion back a few days, needing to deal with the wreckage and keep the nobles from rebelling. Tensions had never been so high.

They had always known that the Centennial had a timeline. A clock of a hundred days.

But it seemed as though that clock had changed.

"Tell me more about the heart," Isla said on the fifty-third day.

A screech echoed through the night, so loudly the wood beneath her hands quivered. Isla took a steadying breath, keeping her grip, refusing the siren call in her head that dared her to look down at the hundred feet below her toes.

Oro paused for a moment, waiting for something. His gaze flicked to the sky. Then his arm reached up for the next branch. They were

climbing up a lattice of wood, thick trunks that had been woven into webbing. Oro couldn't fly wherever they were going, Isla assumed. She hadn't asked why.

Isla had many questions. Which meant she had to be selective.

Another second passed without a response, and she was very close to pulling him off the grid by his foot. But he said, "It was made during the creation of the island and contains pure, concentrated energy from its creator."

"Who created it?"

"Horus Rey."

"And Cronan Malvere?"

Oro paused before his fingers could reach the next branch. She watched the muscles in his back tense. Slowly, very slowly, he looked down at her.

She stared back, eyebrows slightly raised. It seemed he didn't have the energy to glare at her any longer. More than two dozen nobles had died at the ball, and each life lost weighed on him. She saw it in the firm set of his mouth, the tense shape of his shoulders. "Did Grim tell you that?" he finally said.

"He did. He's much more forthcoming than other rulers of realm," she said pointedly. Part of her wanted him to glare at her. Wanted him to do anything but look so hollow.

Oro still hadn't reached for the next ring. She climbed up to his level so they were matched. "Is that all he told you?" he asked.

She nodded.

He frowned. "Not as forthcoming as you think, then," he said. Then he climbed up to the next level.

"What is that supposed to mean?" she asked.

Oro said nothing.

"Hello?"

He turned to look down at her and said, "Ask Grim. He's the most *forthcoming* ruler."

Isla's mouth was already open in response—when a hand reached through the lattice and pulled her through.

She was dragged forward, into an endless maze of wood. She couldn't see her attacker; the moonlight was far behind her back. Isla reached for her dagger, which she had tucked into her waist, but another hand bound hers together. There was the unmistakable burn of rope against her wrists.

A moment later, she was on her knees in total darkness.

She was trapped again—but this time, it was on purpose. Isla had proposed using herself as bait. Oro had agreed, seeming willing to take more risks after the disaster of the ball.

And it had worked.

Light erupted, illuminating everything. The walls were honeycombed. She and Oro must have been climbing the outside of it.

Oro.

She saw the unmistakable curl of his cape as he stepped next to her. He wasn't bound, he was simply standing there, looking down at her.

"Release her," he said sternly.

Isla looked around to see who he was talking to. That was when she saw them, standing in the gaps of the hive. Dozens of them.

They had long, transparent wings that hung limp at their sides. Their skin was light blue, like someone had stuck a paintbrush in the air to get the color. Their eyes were too large, limbs too long.

Not one of them moved.

Oro bared his teeth. "Did you not hear me?"

Steps sounded before her, at the center of the hive. From the shadows stepped a man as tall as Oro. He had the same light-blue skin as the others, but his wings were larger and perched high, the tops peaking above his muscled shoulders. His hair was dark as Grim's. "Oh, no, they heard you, *King,*" he said. "They are hesitant to listen to a ruler who has abandoned them, however." He angled his head at Oro. "You can understand, I am sure."

Oro made to step forward, but a sword appeared from thin air—and pressed firmly against his throat. The winged man had a hand raised, keeping the blade hovering in place.

Oro's finger twitched and the blade drew closer, sending a droplet of blood spilling down his neck.

The winged man clicked his tongue. "A move, *King,* and we'll see just how easily you can die like the rest of us."

She had to think, do something. Stall, until she could come up with a better plan. "You would destroy the island just to kill him?"

Slowly, the man turned to her, as if noticing her for the first time. She expected a sword against her throat next. Oro had said he would try to kill her. That he, like other ancient creatures, hated her kind.

But he only grinned, pleased. "The island is well on its way to destruction," he purred. "And it would be a gift . . . We all have suffered enough, *Wildling.*"

He turned to Oro, amused. "Did you think you could disguise her from me?" He smiled, and Isla saw too many teeth in his mouth, all crowded together. "That might work on others . . . but me?" He laughed. "Or did you think she would be enough to convince me to work with you? Are you truly that cornered, King, to ask me for aid? You fool."

The winged man turned to face the others. Their hair was blue, not dark like his. And they looked too pale. Sickly. The way their wings hung made Isla think they didn't work anymore. Was it because of the Skyling curse? Did it affect them as well?

"What do you say?" he said loudly, a leader rallying his people. "Are we ready to be free of this island? To see how we fare on the other side?" His hand turned to a fist.

And the sword sliced across Oro's throat.

Isla gasped. The blade had not cut deeply. But blood streamed down his neck, staining his shirt. They had to get him to water so he could close the wound before he lost too much.

Even with the gash across his throat, the king's face did not change. He did not wince.

They needed to abandon her plan. He had been right—

It had only taken a few seconds of the winged man speaking to his people for Isla to retrieve her dagger. A few more to cut through the rope. She felt cool metal in her fingers.

And then her arm flung through the air.

The blade flew true, aimed perfectly, right at the winged man's heart. It whizzed fast as an arrow, blade glimmering in the light.

An inch before hitting its mark, the dagger froze.

Isla stilled, preparing for the winged man to send it back through her chest.

But he had not frozen the blade. His eyes were wide; he looked as shocked as anyone to see the tip pointed at his heart.

It wasn't alone. The sword that had been at Oro's throat was now at the man's neck.

Oro had stopped Isla's blade.

Everyone stilled. Not by their will, but by Oro's. His nostrils flared. "Perhaps *you* are the fool for believing you could immobilize a Wildling with a bit of rope." He stepped forward. Blood still flowed steadily from his wound. He did not reach up to wipe it away. Oro grinned meanly. "Yes, she knew she would pique your curiosity enough to get us into your hive. And I knew you would be prideful enough to believe you could capture us so easily." He reached the platform the winged man stood upon. His voice became almost a growl. "Now, tell us where we can find the island's heart."

The winged man was silent for a moment. Then he smiled. "How I love a surprise . . . and *she*"—he looked curiously at Isla—"*she* certainly is a surprise. More than you know . . ." Isla froze. She could hear it in the edge to his voice—he knew. Somehow, he knew she was a Wildling ruler born without powers. She braced herself, waiting for him to say it.

Waiting for what Oro would do with that information. But the winged man simply laughed. "Curious, so *curious, Wildling*. Born so strangely."

He turned to Oro, still smiling joyfully. As if he had not just sliced the throat of the king of Lightlark.

"What will you offer me, *King?*"

Her blade drew closer to his heart. "I'll offer you the chance to keep your hive, and people, intact."

The man's expression didn't falter. "I want the Wildling."

Before Isla could make a move, Oro's hand was at the man's neck. And it was coated in flames.

They danced in the man's eyes as he calmly said, "I want the Wildling *to visit me*. Once this is all over." He glanced at her. "She will come willingly, I assure you."

Isla stepped forward before Oro could make another move. "Done," she said. His skin was too pale. He needed to be healed immediately. She sighed, feigning boredom. "Now tell us where to find the heart. I'd like to get at least a *wink* of sleep tonight."

The winged man's smile widened. "Very well. The heart blooms somewhere new every time. I have seen it. I know not where it is now . . . but it seems to always choose a place where darkness meets light."

Isla had no idea what that meant. But Oro plucked her dagger from the air and held it firmly as he turned his back on the man and the rest of the winged people. He grunted as he walked past her, a sign for her to follow.

They walked through the maze of the hive until they reached its outside layer. He handed her back her weapon. Isla began to climb down, but Oro stumbled through one of the openings and grabbed her before falling. He soared for a while, breathing a little too fast. His blood stained her cheek, her hair.

"A plan," he said, voice hoarse. "We have a plan."

"Oro," she said as they half flew, half fell, the trees just inches below. She tried to keep the panic out of her voice. "*Oro.*"

He glanced at her—and his eyes were bloodshot. Had he been sleeping at all? They closed for a moment.

And they began to fall.

They hit the trees, and Isla screamed. His hands tightened around her, and the air flurried, shattered as something like a shield appeared around them. Branches snapped, wind roared in her ears as they tumbled, dropped—

She hit the ground with a thud. Even with the shield breaking their fall, the breath was knocked from her lungs. She gasped, gripping the dirt, leaves crunching between her fingers. Stars dotted her vision, mixing with the real stars, and darkness threatened to swallow the rest.

Isla forced herself up, her bones screaming in defiance. Oro was a few feet away, sprawled across the ground. Blood pooled at the side of his neck. The cut didn't look deep, but he must have lost too much for him to have been weakened so thoroughly.

Water—he needed water. Then he could heal himself with his Moonling abilities. She forced herself to go still. To listen.

Her breath was too loud, so she held it. Her lungs pulsed in pain, her head spun, but finally, she heard it. The trickling of a stream.

Not nearby, no. She grabbed Oro's hand. "Get up."

He didn't stir. But blood was still flowing. That was a good thing.

"*Get up.*"

Nothing.

She slapped him across the face as hard as she could.

His eyes opened at that. And began to close. "I can't carry you," she said. "You need to help me."

Slowly, with her help, he rose.

"Can you call the water to you?" she asked. But it was like he couldn't hear her. So, she half dragged him toward the sound, his weight on her like a boulder.

He was too heavy. She wanted to stop. Wanted to crumple to the ground.

But if Oro died . . .

All Lightlark would.

She needed the heart now, just as much as he did.

He needed to live.

She walked until her legs burned, until her breath was hot against her lips. Until Oro's skin began to cool, the unmistakable Sunling heat dying down.

Just as her knees threatened to buckle, the dirt softened beneath her boots. And the roaring of the stream was in front of her.

Her legs nearly collapsed with relief. She pushed him into the water with all her remaining strength. He seized for a moment before falling still.

She worried it was too late. But the water seemed to know him. It glowed faintly and got to work. He began to sink, but she kept his head out of the water. She held him firmly by the shoulders, the back of his head in her lap, the rest of him deep below.

His sleeves were rolled back. The grayish blue he had shown them before had spread. A lot. It now covered his entire left arm, down to his hand. Was this why the cut had weakened him so quickly? Why the ballroom had broken in half during the ball?

Isla stayed like that, gripping him, her legs in the cold stream, for a long while. Waiting. Waiting for the island to begin to crumble around her, like it had at the ball. For trees to fall. For Oro to stop breathing.

The water worked intently, all through the night. Slowly, slowly, the slice across his neck knitted together, new skin replacing the broken shreds. The blood on her dried. She could feel it on her cheek, smell it in her hair, but didn't dare wash it off. She just kept holding Oro.

And waiting.

She must have drifted off, because her head knocked against her shoulder. Her spine straightened, and fear gripped her chest. *Had she let him go?*

No. There he was. She hadn't let him slip. His wound was nearly healed.

Still, his eyes remained closed.

A stream of light had begun peeking through the trees. The first dewy, honeyed tinge of day. Isla's first thought was that this was good. Maybe the heat would be good for him, maybe he could draw upon its strength . . .

Dread stabbed her through the stomach.

The curse.

She had to get him inside. If the sword hadn't killed him, the sun would. And the water wouldn't be able to heal him from that.

"Oro," she said, shaking him.

He didn't move.

"Oro," she yelled into his ear. "The sun's coming up. We have to go."

His eyes did not open.

Light had almost found them. It made lazy lines across the forest, peeking through the trees. Day had almost broken open.

He was going to die. She was going to watch him burst into flames, the same way, using her starstick, she had watched a child burn to ash in the Sunling realm, years before, helpless—

No.

Not helpless.

She spotted an opening in a mountain twenty feet away. A cave.

Isla didn't know if they would make it inside before the king became fire. She had no idea how she was going to get him there.

But she gripped beneath both of his shoulders and pulled.

CHAPTER THIRTY-FIVE

THE CAVE

It was midday by the time the king finally opened his eyes. Isla was curled against a corner of the cave, watching him. Still covered in his blood.

"You saved me," he said, frowning.

Hearing him say the words made her realize how absurd it was. Oro was the most powerful person in all the realms . . . and *she,* a powerless ruler, had saved him.

Perhaps she really wasn't as powerless as she thought.

She gave him a look. "I'm not as weak as you think I am."

He didn't return the glare. "I've never thought you were weak."

She blinked. He couldn't mean that. "Well, now we're even, I suppose." That day on the balcony seemed realms away.

"I suppose we are." Oro took in the cave. They were at its mouth, buttery sunlight spilling inside, just a few feet away. Those streaks of gold had nearly seared him through. She had pulled him to safety with a second to spare.

Oro turned his attention to the other side of the cave, the tunnels that led through the underground. Pretty blue lights illuminated the ceiling like a constellation of stars.

"We're beneath a Skyling graveyard," he said gruffly. He nodded toward the bright blue. "Glowworms. They eat the bones."

Isla scowled, the mysticism of the place ripped away. But she remembered the winged man's words. "Is it a place where darkness meets light?"

He nodded and winced. "One of the few on Sky Isle. Once the sun goes down, I'll search it." He seemed to sense her confusion about the winged man's information, because he said, "Nightshades did build the island, along with Sunlings. When they were banished from Lightlark, their lands were built over. But some parts, and some creatures, still dwell in the in-between."

"So, this is our plan," she said, needing confirmation. "We're going to check all the places on the island where Nightshade and Lightlark meet? That's where the heart is?"

He bowed his golden head. His crown was covered in mud. Both of them were caked in dirt and blood. "There aren't many. Especially with Star Isle off the list, thanks to the specter's information." He stretched. "Besides the graveyard, there is only one other place on Sky Isle that qualifies."

"How about Sun Isle?"

"I will search those locations myself."

Isla gave him a look. "Yourself?"

Oro sighed. "Do you truly not trust me yet?"

She frowned. "Do you trust me?"

Oro did not answer her question. Instead, he said, "I never break promises. I do not break deals on a whim." He looked at her pointedly.

Isla rolled her eyes. "And what about Moon Isle?"

"There are a few. But that's the last place we check."

"Why?"

"Because Cleo has her isle heavily monitored, and if she thinks we're looking for something there, she'll try to find it herself."

Oro was being unusually forthcoming. She needed to get every detail out of him that she could. "How many total places are left, then, where darkness meets light?"

"Eight."

Eight. That wasn't a large number at all. Hope bloomed in Isla's chest.

"Don't get too excited," he said, frowning. "There are risks."

Isla didn't care. They had a firm strategy and a manageable number of places left to search. Still, something made her uneasy. "The plan is entirely based on what others have told you. The specter. The winged man." She swallowed. "Did it ever occur to you that they could be lying?"

"They can't lie to me," Oro said simply.

Isla didn't know what that meant. Was it because he was king of Lightlark? Could all his subjects not lie to him? She certainly could. And she had.

She asked another question, since it seemed like he might answer it. "In the oracle's prophecy, it says the original offense must be committed again to break the curses. You believe the original offense was wielding the heart of Lightlark, don't you? Using its power?"

Oro glanced at her. Nodded.

So that was why he needed the heart of Lightlark. To fulfill part of the prophecy.

"You said that when Sunling and Nightshade created Lightlark, they trapped a fraction of their power in the heart." Her eyes widened, realization dawning. "That's why you invited Grim here for the first time," she said, the words toppling from her mouth. "You don't think he or any Nightshade spun the curses. You think someone used the Nightshade power trapped in the heart to cast them."

Oro nodded again. Something in his eyes, a gleam, looked almost impressed.

She lifted her chin. "That means you didn't know about the heart until after the last Centennial. Or else you would have invited him to the previous ones . . ."

Oro's silence confirmed it. But his expression had turned wary. "You should go," he finally said, not meeting her eyes. He was stuck there until dusk . . . but she could leave at any time.

Her dry lips pressed together. Part of her wanted to run out and

up to the surface. Take a bath and wash the hair that was stuck to the blood on her face. The mud that covered her clothes. The film of dirt across her skin.

Another part wanted more information. The king had never been this forthcoming before. And she had one more question she needed answered.

"I'll wait with you," she told him.

Oro blinked, surprised. Then frowned, annoyed. She ground her teeth together—*wretch*. The king tensed as he trailed a finger across his neck, making a line through the dried blood.

She shot a look at the light at the mouth of the cave, a carpet of gold across the floor. "Seems like we'll be here awhile longer," she said. "Let's play a game."

"A game," he said flatly.

Isla nodded, undeterred. "Questions, back and forth. I'll answer one. And then you will. Honestly."

She expected he might say her proposed game was foolish or might even decide to brave the fiery sunlight rather than spend another moment stuck with her. But he leaned the back of his head against the wall and looked at her, chin lifted. "Fine, Wildling. You start."

She sat up. Her important question barreled through her mind, but she couldn't ask it. Not yet. She had to start small. "Be honest—do you ever tire of wearing gold?"

Oro gave her a look that said, *That's what you want to ask me?* He sighed. "Yes, Wildling. Though I can wear blue, white, or silver if I choose."

Right. He was an Origin—he could wear colors from all the realms he had powers from. She wondered if he did wear other shades, outside the Centennial.

"Your turn."

He studied her for a few moments. "What is your life like, back in the Wildling newland?"

It wasn't the question she might have expected, but it was an easy one, so she was grateful. "It's . . ." She opened her mouth. She had an answer queued up, ready to go, about how wonderful and exciting it was.

But she had promised to be honest.

Isla wanted him to trust her, so they could find the heart and break her and Celeste's curses.

Which might mean trusting him in turn.

"It's awful." She studied the ground, running her fingers along its rough patches. "I love my guardians—they're my only family." She took a long breath. "But—" She squinted, not knowing how to say it. She met his gaze and found him watching her intently. "Have you ever felt like a bird in a cage?"

She expected him to sneer at her.

But he nodded, just a slight dip of his raised chin. "Every day for the last five hundred years."

Of course. Her limited existence locked away in her Wildling castle was nothing compared to the centuries Oro had endured.

"Who trapped you?" he asked, though it wasn't his turn.

Isla winced, then cursed herself for even suggesting this game. Why would someone with so many secrets do such a thing? He had no idea how close his question was to the truth . . . to unraveling all the lies she had built up like a fortress around her and her realm.

"Not *trapped* . . . just . . . protected."

Oro didn't push the subject, and she was glad. She hurried to ask a question of her own. "Have you ever been in love?"

His answer was immediate. "No."

"Why not?"

"Kings of Lightlark do not fall in love. It makes us vulnerable. Our power becomes unprotected." He glanced at her. "I suppose we are similar in that regard . . . in our inability to have that."

Because of the Wildling curse. "I suppose so." She thought of Grim. His hands across her dress. Clutching her to his chest. It wasn't her

turn, but she had to know. "Do you think it's possible for a ruler to love another ruler? Truly, without any agenda?"

"No." He shook his head. "Not truly."

A part of her wilted inside. But he had to be wrong. Just because he had never experienced love didn't mean it wasn't possible. "So, your brother really wasn't in love with his bride-to-be?"

Oro shrugged a shoulder. "Egan loved Aurora. But not in that way."

"How would you know?"

Oro met her gaze. "They didn't share abilities." Falling in love meant sharing access to one's power with their beloved. It was what made rulers falling in love so dangerous.

"Your turn," she said quietly. She had asked several questions in a row and was surprised he had answered them.

"Did you know Grim previous to the Centennial?"

Isla stilled at the mention of him, as if Oro had plucked him from her thoughts. She answered honestly. "No."

He looked at her strangely.

She rolled her eyes. "I'm not working with him against you, don't worry." It was true.

Oro's expression settled into something she hadn't expected . . . relief mixed with surprise. Isla immediately shifted the subject away from the Nightshade ruler. "What's your favorite part of Lightlark?"

He scratched the side of his head, just below his crown. "There's this secluded stretch of beach on Sun Isle, along a cliff . . . with giant coals in the water that sizzle when the sea hits them." He lifted his gaze, eyes on the ceiling. "The sea is a strange shade there . . . dark green. The color of your eyes."

Isla glared at the word *strange* to describe her eyes but mumbled, "Sounds beautiful."

His arms stretched over his head. "Your singing," he said simply.

She blinked. Part of her had forgotten that he had heard her, so many weeks before. "What about it?"

He shrugged. "Tell me about it."

Isla looked toward the mouth of the cave. The sunlight still glittered brightly. "It's calming to me. Something I was born being good at, without really trying."

"Like swordplay?"

"No. That was hard. I wasn't naturally good at it, not like the singing. It used to frustrate me to no end . . . Terra, my fighting instructor, would scold my impatience constantly." She sighed. "So, I practiced. A lot. Every day, all day, all the time. Until the sword was weightless in my hand. Until it was a part of me, just as much as my voice was. I *forced* it to be."

Oro studied her but said nothing. It was her turn.

Finally. It was time to ask her question, for the sake of her own sanity. Just to make sure she had made the right decision in calling off her search. It was a risky thing to say aloud. But now, on the fifty-fourth day of the Centennial, every action seemed like a risk. "Is there a relic on the island that can break any bond? That can break the curses of the ones that wield it?"

She studied his face desperately, looking for any sign of recognition, any hint of surprise. The king's eyebrows *did* come together. But, more than anything, Oro looked confused. "No," he said firmly. "If there was, I would have found a way to use it."

She believed him. It was a foolish thing to do, but she did.

Which meant the bondbreaker either never existed . . . or was destroyed before the king had learned about it.

"Is that what you were searching for?" he asked. He knew she had been looking for something in the Sun Isle library. And that she hadn't found it.

No use in hiding it now. She nodded.

It was her turn again. "How long have you been able to gild?"

Oro looked surprised by the question. He blinked. Isla wondered if this was the one he would refuse to answer. A few moments passed

in silence before he said, "Since I was a child." His eyes were trained on the ground. Deep in thought. "I was told to hide it," he said, frowning, as if he hadn't expected to be telling her this. "Egan was the eldest. The heir. He was supposed to be the strongest."

"But he couldn't gild," Isla guessed.

He met her eyes. Nodded.

"So why now? Why show everyone?"

Oro sighed. Shrugged a shoulder. "I figure I'm dying. Might as well share all my secrets." He said it casually, but his eyes were hard. Serious. She thought of the bluish gray she had seen hours before. How much it had spread since he had first shown it to them in the throne room. Moments mounted, and silence stretched between them. She wondered if he wouldn't take his chance to ask a question, right up until he finally met her gaze and said, "What was your secret, Isla?"

Isla. He so rarely called her by her name, instead referring to her as *Wildling* most of the time, as if to remind both of them of what she was. Or, she supposed, what she was supposed to be.

She felt her throat get tight. "What?"

His stare was unrelenting. "Your secret from my demonstration. What was it?"

She swallowed. Shook her head no.

The king laughed without humor. "I didn't think so." He scratched the side of his neck. "How about this—why did you let me win our duel?"

So, he *had* known. The duel seemed so far away. So much had changed. "I didn't want to make myself a target."

"Ah."

Her turn to be bold. To prove that, even though he had proclaimed that he wanted to share all his secrets, there were still some he wasn't willing to divulge.

"What is your flair?" she asked. She had wondered for a while if the king had one of the rare powers that didn't relate to their realms, the ones rulers so often possessed.

The way Oro paused made her positive he did. The Sunling inclined his head at her. Considering. "Share your secret, and I'll tell you."

Wretch. She said nothing.

And the king smiled. It unnerved her. She had never seen him smile, not really. Not genuinely. "How about this?" He sat up straighter. His eyes were not hollow at all—they were full of something she couldn't read. "Tell me your secret, and *you* can be the one who wins."

Silence. Her heart was beating so loudly, it was a wonder it wasn't echoing through the cave. "What?"

Oro did not so much as blink. "When we find the heart, you can brandish it, fulfilling the prophecy. *You* can win the great power promised." He shrugged. "But only if you tell me your secret."

Win?

Isla had never even thought of winning. She had been too focused on surviving. On breaking her and Celeste's curses. Lately, on finally getting her Wildling abilities.

He couldn't be serious.

"Why would you do that?" she demanded. "Don't you want the power for yourself?"

Oro shook his head. "I do not wish to become a god," he said. "Too much power is dangerous. I have never wanted to win. I simply want to save Lightlark."

Isla scoffed. "You would give it to *me?*"

"Who else? Do you suppose Cleo should have it?" Isla bared her teeth, and Oro looked ready to grin at her reaction. "Precisely."

"How about Azul?"

Oro shook his head but did not offer an explanation.

Power. Isla had wanted it more and more. The power promised was prophesied to be endless. The things she could do—

No.

Isla hadn't ever handled even a drop of power. What would she do with a sea of it?

Especially since the price was revealing her secret.

Isla shook her head.

The king looked surprised. Then he frowned. “Either you are the only other ruler not interested in the Centennial’s prize,” he said, “or your secret is worse than I suspected.”

“That’s not a question” was her only response.

For the rest of the time, they barely spoke, their game over.

Isla watched the sunlight streaming from the cave entrance until it withered and disappeared.

CHAPTER THIRTY-SIX

ORACLE

Each day after the ball held ruin. An ancient building fell into the sea. Another elder died. Another crack formed overnight, dividing the Mainland. The cursed storm grew along the coast. Still trapped in place, it began to rage. Thick bolts of lightning would strike at the same time every night, loud enough that Isla heard them wherever she was. Counting down the days.

The heart was not in either location on Sky Isle. Or Sun Isle, which Oro searched himself.

It was the last place Oro had said he wanted to look. But on the fifty-ninth day of the Centennial, the time came to search where darkness met light on Moon Isle.

Isla wondered about the guards. Oro had hinted at not wanting Cleo to know they were looking for something on her isle.

But the king had a solution. One that Isla didn't appreciate.

"I'll go slow," he said, surprising her.

Isla gave him a look.

"Slower," he amended.

She didn't want to ever experience flying again, but she also couldn't think of another way past the guards that didn't require telling him about her starstick. "If you drop me—"

"You will gut me, I am aware."

Then she was in the air. She buried her face in his chest, scrunching her eyes against the wind. His hand was splayed across her back, his grip a bit too loose for her comfort, so she clung to his neck tightly.

"You know," he said into her ear, "I used to wonder how Wildlings carved hearts out with only their nails." One of the hands that was supposed to be holding her securely reached back and smoothed down her own fingers, one by one, until they didn't dig into his skin any longer. "Now, I know they're sharp as daggers."

Isla poked her head up to give him a withering look. "I wouldn't have to cling so much if you held me properly."

"Properly?"

She nodded. "More tightly. More securely."

Oro shifted his hands. Suddenly, instead of being loosely held in front of him, she was cradled against his chest. Her entire body warmed from his heat. It was almost comfortable. "Better?" he asked. She expected his tone to be mocking. But it wasn't.

"Better."

Before she knew it, Oro landed, his arms tightening around her as they made contact.

The second she was away from him, frost filled her chest. Moon Isle had gotten significantly colder since the last time she was here. Her eyes darted to Oro. *He* was the reason. Since Lightlark and his control of it was weakening, he could no longer keep it warm. Or bright. The days were dimmer. The sun set sooner. All parts of the island were noticeably cooler. Dozens more hearths and torches had been added across the Mainland and inside the castle. But they were only a temporary solution.

They had landed on the edge of a forest of trees that looked more like knotted, twisted roots, delicately braided at the top. Streams navigated between them, transporting water lilies and fat white flowers as big as her palms. It was so silent, she could hear the snow falling. She shivered, cold air puffing from her lips. Her fingers already felt frozen; her toes were tiny blocks in her boots. Wind bit against her cheeks and nose, and her eyes watered and stung.

Suddenly, Isla screamed.

In the middle of the silence, a dark-blue bird like ocean made into wings landed on her shoulder and screeched right into her ear.

Oro turned and struck immediately, without waiting to see what the threat was. His fire curled through the night, right to where the bird had been—but it was too fast and went flying away, back through the woods.

His arm dropped as he watched it. When he turned to Isla, his eyebrows were slightly raised. "Aren't you supposed to be good with animals?"

"Not when they blow out my hearing," she said, gingerly cupping her ear. "Aren't *you* supposed to have more care with your fire?"

Oro's jaw tensed—she had struck a chord, it seemed. "Yes," he said tersely.

They walked in silence until the ground turned to ice. She could see the roots of the trees below the crystal-like veins, dark as night. They reached a cliff where snow began to cake the ground like frosting. Her boots quickly got stuck in it, so she trailed behind Oro, whose steps melted a path. Snowflakes got lost in her hair and piled on her nose, and she felt as cold as one of the ice statues that sat in front of the Moon Isle palace.

After an hour, her breathing became panting, and she must have slowed, because Oro finally turned. One look at her, and he offered his hand. "I can warm you."

She wanted to say no. But she was done being proud. She gripped his hand with her own, and he frowned.

"You're freezing." He said it like an accusation.

Isla wanted to glare at him, but her eyes stung too much to make the movement.

In a quick sweep, he removed his golden cape and draped it around her. It was so large, it wrapped Isla like a blanket. She wanted to reject it, but the moment it touched her skin, her body was flooded with heat that seemed to melt through her bones. Her face buried in the fabric,

shoulders shivering as she tied it closer around herself. It smelled like honey and mint leaves, deliciously soft against her skin.

When she finally peeked her head out of the cape and buttoned it around her neck, Oro was watching her warily. "Are you . . . all right?" he asked, as if the idea of hypothermia and dying of cold had never once crossed his mind.

"I'm fine," she said quickly, raising her chin as if doing so did anything to make her look less ridiculous. She walked past him, into snow that drenched her ankles in cold. "Thank you."

Oro followed behind, and she must have been walking in the right direction, because he didn't say a word. She did not stop until she reached a slab of ice so large, it was like a glacier that had gotten trapped on land.

Isla squinted at it. There was something inside. She inched closer and wiped at it with Oro's cape. Some of the frost cleared, and she startled, tripping backward, right into Oro, who steadied her before she could fall into the snow.

Three women were trapped within the ice.

"The oracles," he said, hands falling from her shoulders.

She blinked too many times. "I thought there was *one*."

"Only one has thawed in the last thousand years."

"Why are they here?"

Oro stepped to her side. "A king far before me trapped them in ice, so they would never leave, or die. Three women born with the gift of prophecy. Enraged at being imprisoned, two of them joined forces with Nightshade, calling to the dark part of the island. When Night Isle was destroyed, they froze forever."

"So, this is a place where darkness meets light."

Oro nodded as he placed a hand against the ice. It immediately began to thaw.

The middle woman's eyes flew open. She floated in the water, her white hair a halo around her head. Her gaze went to Isla, then Oro, then back again.

Her voice echoed, sounding like a million voices trapped in one throat.

"It's been a long time since I saw a Sunling and a Wildling side by side." She angled her body toward them, her face just inches from their own. "I've been warned not to help you . . . but this is just too curious . . ."

This was the woman who had spoken the prophecy of the curses. The key to breaking them. Her words were the ones they followed like law. The ones she had learned from the time she could talk.

"Warned by who?" Oro demanded.

The oracle shook her head. "*That* I cannot say. But I will say more than I've promised not to."

Cleo. It had to be Cleo.

"So many secrets, trapped between you," she continued. The oracle scratched along the ice with a long nail, and the sound made Isla wince. "But, just like this wall, they too will one day give way and unravel and fall . . . leaving quite a mess and madness."

Isla avoided meeting Oro's gaze. The oracle met her eyes with a knowing look. Knowing everything. She grinned.

"Enough of your riddles," Oro said. "We seek the heart of Lightlark. Is it here?"

The oracle smiled wider. "It is near. Nearer than you know."

"So, it's on Moon Isle?" Isla said.

The oracle nodded. Relief nearly brought her to her knees. "Where?"

The woman shook her head. "That I cannot divulge. You both must find it on your own. That is the only way to successfully wield the heart."

Isla glared at her.

The oracle stared back. "You . . . have many questions. There are so many things I could tell you . . . though I should not." She looked at her knowingly. "All will be revealed soon enough."

Isla's stomach puddled. Could she truly mean that her secret would be revealed? *No.*

"Know this," the oracle said. "There are lies and liars all around you, Isla Crown."

Lies and liars.

Who?

"And one of the six rulers will indeed be dead before the hundred days are over." Which ruler? Did that mean the curses would be broken?

Isla took a step forward, willing the right words to form in her head, the right question. But before the words could leave her lips, the oracle smiled.

And the water hardened into ice.

Isla banged on it with knuckles that immediately spotted with blood. Still, she kept pounding, over and over, her hand raw and throbbing.

Finally, Oro placed his hand over hers, stopping it. "She's gone," he said. "And she will not awaken again anytime soon."

Her hand stayed splayed across the ice for another long moment before she tore it off. She turned to Oro. He had secrets too. The oracle had confirmed as much.

So much for sharing them all.

Lies and liars . . . Had the oracle meant him?

Or someone else?

And which one of the six rulers would perish?

Though she was disappointed, terrified . . . the oracle's information had been invaluable.

"How many other places on Moon Isle qualify?" she asked, voice barely above a whisper. The oracle had warned her that her secret would be revealed. They needed to find the heart soon, before that happened. Before the island was no more than rocks and ruins.

"Three."

Three. Isla breathed out and leaned against the ice, relief making her limbs go weak. The cape kept her warm, and she cradled her bloody knuckles against the fabric. "Three," she repeated. "Can we go tonight?"

Oro shot a look at the sky. "No," he said quietly. "We . . . *I* don't have time. One place is easier to access than the others. And, for both of our sakes, let's hope that is where the heart is."

Isla nodded, though her teeth locked in disappointment. She wanted to find the heart that night, as soon as possible, so she could break the curses, free her people, and get the power before the oracle's words could come true. Before her secret came to light and made her a target for fulfilling the rest of the prophecy.

"Tomorrow?" she said, cape wrapped tightly around her.

"Tomorrow," Oro agreed.

CHAPTER THIRTY-SEVEN

PUDDLE

Later that night, Isla stood in her room, holding her starstick.

Before the Centennial had even started, she'd promised herself she wouldn't use the relic to look at her home. Part of her feared she would miss the Wildling newland so much, she would make a rash decision and leave the game, portaling away.

Now, so much had changed. She wasn't the same person who had arrived on the island two months prior.

Before, she had never even spoken to a man unsupervised for more than a few minutes. Now, one had touched her up and down her body.

Before, she thought she would cower before the rulers. Now, she had beaten them in trials. Threatened them. She had even saved the king.

Before, she believed it was wrong to want anything other than to break her and her realm's curses.

Now, she wanted everything.

She drew her puddle of stars, almost hoping that her old self would click back into place at the sight of her realm and people.

The edges quivered, alive—spilled ink and diamonds. The stars faded into different colors, the hues sputtering and forming quickly before her eyes. They scattered until she was looking at Wildling.

Blood drained from her face. Her heart became all she could hear, beating unsteadily in her chest.

It was gone.

The forests had been razed. The Wildling palace was nearly destroyed. Villages were empty.

This had to be a trick—an illusion.

Her hand trembled as she touched the starstick, leading it somewhere else. The colors scattered until she was looking at a woman, sprawled across what was left of the forest floor. Her tan skin had hardened, turned to sheets of bark. Strands of her hair had become vines. One hand was already roots in the ground.

It was Terra.

Isla stopped breathing.

Her guardian had started to be taken by nature, just like the Eldress. The first steps of a Wildling death. Isla's stomach went watery, her mouth went dry, her vision blurred—

She was about to jump into the puddle, to go to Terra, but forced herself still.

There was nothing she could do. She was powerless. Reversing a Wildling death that had already begun required endless ability and enchantment.

And her realm had none of that to spare.

Terra. Her fighting instructor, the closest person to her in the world. The one who had taught her nearly everything she knew.

Poppy was kneeling next to her, applying an elixir that would delay the transition. But it wouldn't save her. It wouldn't save their realm.

"I reach my hand into the dirt, to speak to the trees," Terra told Poppy, voice frailer than Isla thought possible. "But the dirt is dead in my hand."

Poppy held Terra's few soft fingers. "We still have time," she said. "Our little bird is still fighting for us."

Terra only closed her eyes. "How many more are like this?" she asked.

"Almost all of them," Poppy answered.

Isla had thought her people would be just the way she had left them. Wildling had weakened during her reign, but it had been gradual.

How was this possible?

The land had been without power for too long. The ground was demanding its due. Taking powerful Wildlings, one by one.

Breaking her curse and theirs wouldn't save them. The Wildling realm was too far gone. Even the powers she was supposed to have been born with wouldn't be enough. Not when they had weakened with every ruler's generation.

To save them all, she needed more—more than even a single ruler could give.

Tears streaming down her cheeks, Isla remembered the prize. The single person who broke the curses was fated to be gifted immeasurable ability—more power than the realms had ever seen. The type that could save the Wildlings. The type that could save Terra. The entire Centennial, Isla had been focused on making sure she didn't lose.

Now, she knew she had to win.

Isla felt like she was going to be sick. She had cried for so long, it didn't seem possible her body had any liquid left.

"What happened?" Oro's voice was surprisingly gentle when she found him, pacing around a room in the Mainland castle. "I just saw you a couple of hours ago," he said in confusion, in anger, muttering almost to himself.

Her eyes must have still been swollen. She didn't answer his question. "Does your offer still stand?"

Oro seemed to know she meant the one he had extended in the cave. To her relief, he nodded.

A tear ran down her cheek. "Can I trust you?" she asked.

Oro stared at her. "Yes. I've never lied to you, Isla. Not once."

She hoped that was true. Her stomach felt like it was flipping inside out. If Celeste knew she had willingly shared her greatest secret with the king, she would be furious. But the Starling would understand.

Isla had no choice now.

Oro was directly in front of her. His hand went to her forehead. He was frowning. Did he think she was sick? He studied her body quickly, clinically, looking for damage. Did he think she was injured?

She wished she was. Physical pain would hurt less than this.

Isla couldn't believe she was going to tell him her secret. She closed her eyes, unable to look at him as she did. Every bone in her body and vein and muscle and swath of skin screamed against it.

Your secret is your greatest weakness. You can never reveal it. The rule was like a favorite blanket. She had learned it before she had learned anything else. All other lessons were birthed from it. She needed to know how to fight because she was powerless. She needed to hide in her room because she was powerless. She couldn't meet anyone alone because she was powerless.

She was a disappointment because she was powerless.

She had to follow the rules because she was powerless.

Terra and Poppy had to rule in her stead because she was powerless.

She had to survive the Centennial and lie, cheat, steal, and kill because she was powerless.

No. She forced her eyes open. Forced herself to look right at the king as she said the words she had built her entire life around—the foundation of everything.

"I was born powerless."

There. The words were out. Birds let free. Their cage propped open. Nothing and no one could take them back.

Oro went still. She could see it in his eyes—he had expected anything but that.

His brow creased, confused. He squinted at her.

A million thoughts were going through his head, and Isla imagined none of them were good.

It was too much to ask for her to stand there in the aftermath. She was strong enough to say the words—but not enough to stay.

Isla turned on her heel, but Oro stopped her with a gentle hand.

He looked strange. Slightly horrified. "Are you saying you have never used power?" he demanded.

She blinked. Was she going to have to repeat it? "Yes," she said, her voice trembling. She swallowed. "You can't use something you don't have."

For once, Oro was speechless. She might have enjoyed seeing him so flustered if she wasn't having the worst day of her life.

And she supposed the oracle had been right. Her secret was revealed.

Just not in the way she would have ever imagined.

She turned to leave again.

And this time the king did not stop her.

CHAPTER THIRTY-EIGHT
TOMORROW

The next morning, Isla entered the throne room with her head held high. She had told Oro her secret and survived.

The king claimed he was a man of his word. Which meant now, the power promised would be hers. All they had to do was find the heart. And now they knew it was on Moon Isle. There were only three locations left. They would search one of them that very night.

They were so very close.

Hope was the only thing keeping her from falling to pieces.

I'm coming for you, she whispered to Terra. *I'm coming to save you, just as you trained me to.*

Killing was permitted. Isla should have been scared, walking into a meeting with the other rulers of realm. But she wasn't. She had Oro. Celeste. Grim.

The king had called the rulers together for an update. Isla was safely by his side. Grim appeared next. She hadn't seen him since the ball, but every night she ran her fingers across her necklace, wondering when she would get the courage to pull the diamond and summon him to her room.

Cleo strolled inside wearing a cape that buttoned down its front, with a slit for her pants-clad legs. She looked at Isla with little interest, but Isla didn't make the mistake of believing it meant the Moonling didn't want to kill her. Cleo likely knew she couldn't get near Isla with Oro as her partner.

Good.

Celeste joined them. Then Azul.

They all stood far away. Their eyes alert. Ready for attack. Ready to wield their powers, should they need to.

Oro finally spoke, his voice filling the room. "It has been sixty days since the start of the Centennial. Would anyone like to share their progress?"

No one said a word. Isla wondered what, or how much, she should say. They hadn't discussed the meeting beforehand.

To her surprise, Oro said, "Isla and I have scoured the island for a relic we believe might have been used five hundred years ago. We think wielding it was the original offense, and that its power created the curses."

The truth. Nearly all of it. She blinked, shocked.

Azul frowned. "What sort of relic could possibly have cast curses?"

"One infused with Nightshade power," Oro said simply.

Again, the truth. Isla stared at him, lips parted. Hadn't he said he didn't trust the others? Why hadn't they discussed this beforehand?

The Skyling ruler whirled to face Grim. "Could such a relic exist?"

Grim had gone still. "It could if it was created long enough ago that a Nightshade ruler could afford to sacrifice a part of their power."

Azul looked incredulous. "Then shouldn't we all search for this relic? Shouldn't the Nightshade look for it? Perhaps it would call to him."

Isla glared daggers at Oro. Why would he give so much away?

"No," the king said, his voice absolute. "We cannot take the risk of focusing our efforts on one avenue, should we be incorrect. Not with the urgency of our situation." He lifted his sleeve, showing them how far the bluish gray had spread. His body was like a map, demonstrating the crumbling of the island. She straightened. At least he had the good sense to keep the others away from their plan. "*However,*" he said, "I believe it's time for a change in matches."

The blood drained from Isla's face.

Oro turned to the Moonling ruler. "Cleo, would it suit you to be matched so we might search Moon Isle for this relic together?"

Isla wasn't breathing. A roaring had overtaken her hearing. She had to have heard him wrong . . . had to have misunderstood. Could he even change the matches?

She knew she should have shielded the outrage in her eyes, burning angry holes in Oro's face. Or the shocked set of her mouth.

But the king did not even turn to look at her.

Cleo's smile was feline. "Are you sure, King?" she said. "It seemed you and the Wildling were getting along so swimmingly."

Oro matched Azul and Celeste next. Then Isla and Grim. But she barely heard his voice over the roaring. Her body hardly resisted barreling over the table and slicing the king's throat with his own crown.

The realization hit her like a boulder to the chest.

Oro had been using her—up until she had become useless. Just as Celeste had warned.

Now that they knew the heart was on Moon Isle, he had changed alliances to suit his plan. He had chosen Cleo.

For the entire time she had known him, every choice Oro had made was for the good of his people. *I will do anything it takes to break these curses,* he had said.

Even if it meant betraying her.

"Are you really sure, King?" Cleo said, staring at Isla with pursed lips. "I have to admit, I'm suspicious . . . This isn't just a strategy between you and the Wildling, is it?"

A sprig of hope grew in Isla's chest. They had worked together for weeks. She had saved his life. He had saved hers. Maybe he wasn't betraying her. Maybe this *was* a strategy . . .

Oro's smile was pure mirth. "I'll let you in on a secret that might explain my decision," he said loudly, for all to hear. He turned to look straight at her. "Isla Crown doesn't have powers."

The world froze.

Then shattered.

She was a fool. A fool for believing the king would let her have the power promised in the prophecy. A fool for believing his promises held any weight. A fool for believing he would keep her secret.

The oracle's words rang through her head, to the tune of dread.

There are lies and liars all around you, Isla Crown. She had been talking about Oro. Trying to warn her.

Betrayal seared through her stomach, iron being formed into a blade. She wanted to stab Oro through the heart with it.

Cleo turned to face her, seeming to put together that Isla was unprotected. Alone. Powerless.

She took a step forward—

But before any of the rulers could make a move on her, Grim took her hand and they were gone.

CHAPTER THIRTY-NINE

PROMISE

They knew. All of them knew.

The secret she had kept for her entire life, the reason she had been trapped inside her room, the one thing that would make her the number one target at the Centennial.

Because Oro had *told* them.

The pain was a hand unraveling her insides.

No. This couldn't be real.

He had said he had never lied to her. He had said she could trust him. He had gotten kinder, more caring—

Fool. Even now, she was defending him. Even after he had ruined her chances at breaking her curse and saving her realm.

Oro had sentenced her to death. He had used her. This *was* real.

One moment she was in the throne room, watching the look of horror on Celeste's face. Watching Cleo take a step toward her. The next, she was on the other side of the Mainland, down the cliff, on a beach.

Grim still clutched her hand.

Grim. He was the reason she wasn't dead. But how did he—

Isla must have looked confused, because he said, "My flair."

His flair. *This* was what it was.

It was a dangerous power. Isla thought Grim could simply turn invisible—she had never imagined he was able to travel across the island within a single breath.

She remembered his proclamation on the beach, then.

I could take you back to Nightshade lands with me right now.

Did the other rulers know? Or did they simply suspect he had made her invisible?

What *was* clear was that he had risked his flair being found out, for her.

"Thank you," she said, tears prickling the corners of her eyes. "I—"

He watched her carefully. His eyes were crowded with worry.

Of course. Grim knew her secret now.

Did he think less of her?

She took a step back.

Did he regret potentially revealing his flair to save her?

She felt ashamed. Weak. Foolish.

"I knew," he said gently.

A second. Another. "Knew what?"

He stepped closer. Until he was right in front of her. He pressed two fingers to her chest. Pushed. She shivered. "I knew that you aren't bound by the curses. And that you've never wielded power."

Isla's entire world blurred, tilted.

He *knew.*

"What?" She imagined her emotions were a tidal wave of feeling, fear and shame and surprise and anguish dueling each other.

"Nightshades . . . our powers include curses. I can sense all the others. I knew from the first time I saw you that you weren't bound to them."

She remembered how he had saved her from eating the rest of the heart, demanding it be taken to her room during the first dinner. He had known then.

He had known the entire time.

"I'm not a danger to you, Isla," he said, voice firm. Eyes clear. "I would never hurt you. Or divulge your secret."

"Why?" she said, breathless. Why wouldn't he tell the others? Why hadn't he given her up the moment he had sensed that she wasn't bound to the curses?

Grim grinned then. It was unnerving the way, even in this moment, it made her insides puddle. "Because we're monsters, Hearteater," he said. "Or, at least, that's what they think." His grin widened. "And monsters stick together."

I am the monster.

The puzzle began to form. Grim's immediate fascination with her. His pursuit of her, without fear of her curse.

The parts of her that had recoiled in fear now settled. Half of her felt bare and broken in front of him. Flawed. Powerless.

But the other half slackened in relief. He knew her secret. And hadn't told anyone.

She had suspected him of using her during the Centennial. But he hadn't. Every interaction with him had been genuine.

Her lips quivered. She willed them to stop, but they didn't.

Grim took a step forward, feeling her everything. Her sadness. Her lingering self-hatred. He squinted at her, confused, then trailed his knuckles down her cheek. A tear had fallen, and she hadn't even noticed.

"Grim . . ." she said, voice unsteady. "What's wrong with me?" A ruler born without power was an oyster without its pearl.

Grim's eyes flashed with anger. "Nothing, absolutely nothing, is wrong with you, heart," he said.

Then he took her into his arms. She stayed there, trembling.

"I think they're going to kill me," she said quietly, then looked up at him.

He surprised her by smiling. He placed his hand carefully against her cheek. "If anyone makes a move to harm you, I will ruin them and their entire realm." His fingers trailed down her face, past her throat, then tugged gently on the pendant at the end of her necklace. "Pull this," he said. "And I'll be there."

Isla believed him.

She believed *only* him.

CHAPTER FORTY

TOGETHER

Oro's betrayal was a glacier in her chest, throbbing and raw. She had *trusted* him. They had been through a flurry of challenges and obstacles. Together.

Didn't that mean something?

The weeks she had spent helping Oro had been wasted.

The only thing that thawed her pain was Grim. He filled her dreams, then her days.

Isla knew they were numbered, not just because the island was crumbling around her. Cleo and Oro would be close to finding the heart . . . had possibly already found it. And when they did, and they wielded it, only one last part of fulfilling the prophecy would be left—killing a ruler, and their entire realm.

Soon, Isla would be dead. She would never have her Wildling power. Terra would be gone.

And there was nothing she could do about it.

For a week, Isla thought only of survival.

With Grim's help, she had moved into the Place of Mirrors on Wild Isle. If Juniper was to be believed, only Wildling power could be wielded there. It was the only place where she and Cleo, or even Oro, would be matched in power, should they attack. Her blades were not meaningless there.

She had taken over one of the abandoned rooms upstairs.

Every morning, she wondered if it was her last. She locked her door and put furniture in front of it, knowing all it would do was give her notice before someone struck. She tried to stay awake at night, every creak of the castle making her jump—but eventually her body shut down, forcing her asleep.

Her hand was never far away from her dagger.

Ella risked grave danger in the deadly forest, venturing to Wild Isle to bring her whatever she needed. Food. Water. One of the last times she had stopped in, Isla had handed her most of the gems she had brought to Lightlark, a sack full of diamonds and precious stones. "Hire a healer," she had said.

She had wondered if the Starling wouldn't return after that, having gotten what she wanted. But she did. Every day, she returned.

So did Celeste.

Right after the betrayal, she had called Isla a fool for trusting the king. Then she had pulled her into her arms, and they had cried.

Isla had wondered if that would be the moment Celeste would leave her behind. Her friend had her own life and realm to worry about. It was foolish continuing to ally herself with Isla.

But Celeste was still convinced the bondbreaker was an option.

"I'm searching for it," she said. "I'm making progress."

Isla spent most of her days drawing her puddles of stars and looking inside until seeing Terra made her stomach twist with guilt. The entire right side of her body was part of the ground now. She could barely speak.

Once, she wondered if she was being selfish by hiding. If Cleo and Oro did indeed find and use the heart of Lightlark and fulfilled most of the prophecy, didn't it make sense for Wildling to be the ones to die?

Her newland and people were nearly gone. She was powerless. Isla and her realm offered nothing to the future of the island.

Perhaps they made the most sense . . .

Isla mentioned it to Celeste, who had looked ready to slap her.

"We need Wildlings," her friend had said. "To rebuild. To grow. You and your realm are more important than you know."

That night, she had wandered the Place of Mirrors, stopping in front of the carvings of her people and the vault she had tried and failed to open.

Celeste was right. Wildlings were once great. Integral to the island.

What a shame they had such a weak leader, she thought, staring at the wild animals that once roamed free here, the glorious floras thousands of Wildlings once grew, the weapons they had wielded before their focus became hearts and blood.

What a tragedy this was how their chapter ended.

CHAPTER FORTY-ONE

LETTER

The next morning, Isla found Celeste at her door in the Place of Mirrors. "You have sulked enough," she said.

Isla blinked. *Sulked?* She had been trying to survive.

"You really are a massive fool. Do you know that?" Celeste said.

Isla nodded weakly.

"Good. But you know what you are not, Isla Crown? A failure. And neither am I. So, you got betrayed? We expected this. We *knew* we could trust no one. Or did you forget?"

Isla's back teeth bit together painfully.

"We didn't plan for years to be stopped by this," she said. "And all hope is not lost, not yet." She surprised Isla by grinning. "I've been speaking to the Starlings who work in the castle, your Ella included. About the hidden library."

Isla resisted the urge to scream. The bondbreaker was a lost cause. She knew that. Her friend's insistence on finding it was getting infuriating. Isla needed a *real* solution—not a legend.

Still. Celeste could have abandoned her the moment the rest of the rulers had learned her secret. But she hadn't. So, Isla said, as gently as she could manage, "Do any of them know where it is?"

"Not yet—but they're looking. I have them each searching a specific section of the castle and asking around to anyone they—"

Isla gave her friend a look.

Celeste lifted her arms over her head. "So, what's your plan? Sit and hide here until the island falls apart around us? Wait until Cleo and the king find the heart—if it even exists—and kill you? Wait until the Wildling realm is officially extinct?" Isla bristled. Even though that was exactly what she had been doing.

She had told her friend about what she had seen in her puddle of stars. She had shown her.

I will help you, her friend promised. But Isla knew nothing short of the power promised in the prophecy would save the Wildlings in their state of deterioration.

Her problems seemed insurmountable.

How was she supposed to find the heart of Lightlark when everyone now not only wished to kill her but knew they easily could? The moment she stepped out of the Place of Mirrors, she would be a target.

How was Isla supposed to win now?

She looked down at her hands. Her shaky words surprised her. There was a lump in her throat, and the corners of her eyes prickled. "I don't want to give up," she said honestly. Every time she closed her eyes, she saw her guardian. Suffering. Slowly becoming part of the forest. Poppy and Terra were counting on her . . . and Isla had purposefully gone against all their plans and preparation. She had truly thought that she could fulfill her duty and get what she wanted most on her own terms. How foolish she had been. "But how can I not? We have no plan. No allies."

Celeste took her hands in her own. There was something bright in her eyes, an intensity like two glimmering stars. "We have exactly what we started the Centennial with. Each other."

If only that were enough.

If she had power, she could face off directly against Cleo and Oro, maybe even get the heart from them, instead of waiting to be slaughtered.

The Starling ruler paced the room quickly, as if invigorated by her own words. "This game is not over. We've been on the island over two months. We must have made some sort of progress, some connection. Someone here must be able to help us."

Connection.

Celeste's word gave her an idea. Her breath caught. Her thoughts scattered. One person had proven useful, time and time again. Someone who dealt in secrets.

And if Isla had learned anything during the Centennial, it was that secrets were everything.

"Parchment," Isla demanded.

The Starling ruler smiled. "I'll be right back."

An hour later, Celeste returned with parchment, ink, and Ella. The Starling now knew of their friendship, but Isla didn't worry. Not when Ella had been loyal and was one of Celeste's people. It was in her and her realm's interest to keep their secrets.

Isla wrote the letter quickly, showing it to Celeste before folding it in half and handing it over to Ella to be delivered.

Finished. Isla had done something . . . She wasn't giving up. Not yet.

As Ella left with the letter, Isla felt a spark of hope. She might be young and powerless and foolish. But if Oro and Cleo *had* found the heart, they would have already used it. One of them would be dead, and the curses would be gone.

Something had gone wrong.

Celeste was right. The game was not over. Not yet.

The letter was for Juniper, whose bar had been closed since the ball. If anyone knew the location of a rumored hidden library, or anything at all that could help her win, it was him.

It read, *Details of my greatest secret in exchange for yours?*

Isla couldn't sleep. And, it seemed, neither could Grim. He stood with his back to her in the long room, staring out a window—a threshold he could not pass. He took a deep breath, and his head fell back as he exhaled, as if just seeing the dark beyond invigorated him.

She took a step, and he whirled around.

He looked surprised. Relieved.

"Heart," he said quickly, forgetting the last part of his name for her again. Was she no longer "Hearteater," now that he didn't have to pretend not to know her secret? Grim took long strides toward her, never once breaking her gaze, and, before she could say a word, he swept her into his arms.

She made a sound she had never made before, and he touched her possessively, like he knew her every inch and wanted more, wanted everything. Soon, his armor was on the floor, next to her puddle of a dress, and—

Isla gasped as she sat up, blinking away the bits of dream like the scraps of dress that Grim had . . .

She swallowed.

Just a dream.

Just another—

Dream.

The next day, Isla could hardly meet Grim's eyes when he visited her in the Place of Mirrors. He came whenever he could, walking into the castle like anyone else, unable to use his flair to get inside. Juniper hadn't replied yet, but she hadn't lost hope that he would. The barkeep wouldn't be able to resist her secrets. Not if he had heard about her powerlessness.

Grim had brought her chocolate from the market. She thought all the shops in the agora had closed after the ball, when the island had started crumbling in earnest. But she supposed Grim could be very convincing when there was something he wanted.

Isla had almost been able to feel his hands on her during her dream. It had been so vivid, the way he had—

"Hearteater?"

She blinked.

He grinned. So wickedly that Isla scoffed. Her eyes narrowed into a glare.

"Did you—did you *send* me that dream?" she asked, voice very tight. Nightshades had that ability. With her own eyes, she had seen him create illusions during the demonstrations. "Have you been sending me all of them?"

Isla thought about Grim more than she should. But the number of times she had dreamed of him was absurd. He filled her head nearly every night.

She should have known. All those dreams she'd been having lately . . .

"What dream?" was all the Nightshade said. But his eyes looked devious.

She got up from her makeshift bed and stormed over to him. Something about him planting the dream in her mind felt invasive—no matter how much she had liked it—and her hands made angry fists at her sides. "You know very well *what dream.*"

Grim had the nerve to still feign confusion, though the corners of his lips twitched, fighting not to grin. "I'm not sure what you mean," he said. "But . . . from what I'm hearing . . . and *sensing* . . . it might be one I would enjoy hearing more about . . ."

She fought the urge to stomp on his foot before sending him away for the day.

Isla tentatively stepped out of the Place of Mirrors the next morning.

She expected to find Cleo's legion waiting, or Cleo and Oro themselves, jumping at the chance to kill her.

But no one was there.

No one was waiting.

Isla didn't want to leave. It was too soon and seemed reckless. But Juniper had sent a reply—and it had hinted at something worthwhile.

I know who cast the curses, he had written.

It wasn't the type of information she had been anticipating, but it seemed crucial. All this time, she had been focused on how to break the curses instead of who had created them.

She didn't know how this would help her win the Centennial. But it was a start. It was the only lead they had.

When she and Celeste entered the agora, Isla's pulse quickened. Again, she anticipated an attack. Just like at the harbor. People jumping out of the shadows.

But it was abandoned. No islanders lingered. The only sound was the creaking of shop signs, coated in dust, moving in the wind.

Celeste scrunched her nose as they walked into the pub. Isla squinted. Though it hadn't seen patrons in weeks, the smell of alcohol had intensified, so strong it burned her eyes.

And there was something else—another scent.

Isla raced to the bar and peered over it, only to gasp. A scream scraped the back of her throat.

There was a message.

Scrawled in blood.

No, not just a message. A response. She remembered the words she and Celeste had painted after the attempt on her life at the harbor: *Try harder.*

Written across the wooden cabinets that housed shelves of bubbling drink were the words *Hard enough?*

And below the words, Juniper was dead.

CHAPTER FORTY-TWO

CLEO

The island was built from hearts and bones and blood. Death was at its very core, from the duel that had killed Cronan Malvere to the lives lost since. For the three days after Juniper was found dead, Isla remained in the Place of Mirrors, knowing she was next.

Cleo hadn't killed her yet—but her influence was everywhere. She had intercepted Isla's note or found out about it somehow. No communication was safe. And her bloody message was clear.

The Moonling hadn't come for her yet . . . but she would.

Sometimes, late at night or early in the morning, Isla slipped out of the Wildling palace and ran. It was the only activity lately that cleared her head of the never-ending images of her realm dying. Every day she went farther, risking venturing deep into the wicked forest. To the cliff. To the outskirts of the castle, even.

At least it made her feel something.

She felt useless, doing nothing to win.

But where would she start? Oro hadn't—purposefully—shared the remaining locations on Moon Isle where darkness met light. She couldn't go search them herself. Even if she did know where they were, Oro and Cleo had likely already looked. Which meant they must have the heart . . . or must be close to getting it.

Guilt piled onto her shoulders and stacked high, weighing down her every step. She had failed her people. She had failed her guardians.

And she had failed Juniper. Cleo had killed the barkeep because of her—because of the knowledge he had been about to share.

Which meant his clue had been important.

Isla wouldn't let Juniper's death be for nothing. And, as she ran through the woods, she felt a tinge of hope.

If Cleo and Oro had already found the heart, the Moonling ruler wouldn't have bothered sabotaging Isla. Something had gone wrong . . . which meant maybe there was still a chance to right everything.

The island was a pastry, crumbling into the sea, day by day. But at dusk, it was pretty. The sun was a running yolk, smearing gold and orange and red across the sky, as if desperate to leave its mark. The clouds were cotton dipped in pink dye.

Isla watched the sunset from a cliff, hands on her knees, panting. She had just run for over an hour. The roots of her hair were wet with sweat, the day's heat reminding her of Wildling. A salty breeze blew her braid back and receded, sticking her hair to the side of her face.

She was wearing the clothes the tailor had made her during her first week on the island. Clothes meant for running and fighting. The fabric was thin but offered protection against the elements. Isla had planned to wear this same outfit to find the heart—

Together.

She sat down as the last of the sun reluctantly dipped below the horizon. Her hands gripped the grass, and she felt it—power, coursing through the soil, though weaker than before. Power she could not access.

"Mom," she said to the incoming darkness. "I don't blame you." She spoke to her sometimes.

Isla had never known her mother. She was killed the day Isla was born, by Isla's father, before he had turned the knife on himself. Both were victims of the Wildling curse. Her mother had refused to kill her love, so the curse had demanded its blood.

And their daughter was born without abilities.

"I couldn't do it either," she said quietly.

Isla thought about it, sometimes. The impossible choice. Killing a beloved . . . or dying. Before, it had seemed obvious. Now she knew she could never kill the person she loved.

Perhaps that made her mortal. Perhaps that made her weak.

No. Not weak. A weak ruler wouldn't have made it this far into the Centennial without powers.

"I understand you. And I don't blame you. And . . ." Her voice shook for just a moment before smoothing again. "And I wish I'd known you."

By the time she walked back into the woods, the moon was a wide eye in the sky, watching her. She sneaked through the shadows, keeping at its perimeter, watching the Mainland castle through the darkness.

She missed her room there. She missed her secret and the safety it had allowed.

Isla was about to turn back into the Mainland forest when she saw her.

Cleo.

Her first reaction was to freeze, draw her dagger. But the Moonling hadn't spotted her. She was too far away.

As Isla watched Cleo slip through the night, her white cape pale as bone, her fear dimmed.

Celeste was right. She had sulked for too long.

Soon, she would be forced out of hiding anyway for Carmel, the twenty-four-hour-long celebration that took place on the seventy-fifth day. Attendance was mandatory, lest she wish to officially take herself out of the game.

She couldn't. Not with the state of her realm being what it was.

Isla would be forced to face Cleo there. Part of her wondered if that was when Oro and the Moonling planned on killing her—if they wanted to make it dramatic, in front of the attending islanders. Her heart hammered at the thought.

She wouldn't live any more days afraid. If her destiny was to die, she would face it head-on.

Sweat sticky on her forehead, Isla began to trail the Moonling ruler through the night.

Perhaps she would lead her right to the heart.

Cleo swept across the Mainland, white clothes shining through the night, illuminated by the spotlight that was the moon. The Moonling ruler basked in it, stopping for a moment to roll her shoulders back and lift her face to it. It was said that Moonling had become the strongest realm since the curses had been spun. Unlike Sunling or Nightshade, they could still access their power source. And, unlike Starling, many of their members were still ancient. Their curse, if anything, affected them the least. Thousands of Moonlings had died at the hands of the sea over the years, that was true, but the survivors hadn't been physically weakened.

Isla's stomach twisted. She didn't know how she hadn't thought of it before.

Cleo must have spun the curses. *That* was what Juniper had tried to tell her. *That* was why the Moonling killed him.

Had she created the curses and given her realm one to erase suspicion? A curse that wouldn't weaken her in the slightest?

She hadn't suffered at all. She was still as strong as ever.

If that was true . . .

Cleo wouldn't want the curses to be broken.

Did Oro know? Was that why they hadn't yet wielded the heart? Was Cleo making sure Oro never did?

Isla was breathing too quickly. Cleo was dangerous. Deadly. But she did not turn around and go back to the castle, to Grim or Celeste.

She followed Cleo to the Moon Isle bridge.

For the first time, there were no guards there. The Moonling ruler must have removed them after she and Oro had been paired. *Why?*

She didn't have time to wonder and took their absence as a positive sign.

Isla waited a few minutes for Cleo to disappear down the bridge.

Then she crossed it.

***

Cleo walked past her palace. Isla trailed her through the same forest she and Oro had visited two weeks before. Where was she going?

The Moonling's white dress floated gently above the foliage, not staining in the dirt or getting wet in the weaving streams. The water shifted its current in her direction as she passed—called to her, it seemed.

Isla's outfit kept away much of the cold. Her cheeks and nose stung, but her chest was warm. Her boots kept out the frost. Cleo walked easily, unbothered by the snow. Perhaps it invigorated her, the same way the moon did.

Without warning, Cleo stopped, and Isla stilled before diving back into the cover of the forest. The Moonling ruler had paused before a mountain, coated in ice like armor. Her arms raised overhead, fingers splaying—and she dropped them with the grace of a snowflake falling from the sky.

Instantly, the ice began to thaw, slipping down in sheets that hit the ground, then hardened again. Isla squinted through the darkness. What was Cleo doing?

She needed a closer view. Isla stepped forward, one foot out of the forest. She squinted as the ice continued to fall, revealing a hole, almost like a portal. Or a hidden passageway. Her eyes narrowed. Was this where she and Oro met? Was it where she was keeping the heart? Or something else entirely?

Isla took another step—and a loud screech pierced the air.

The dark-blue bird from before swooped through the trees, aimed right at her head. She ducked just in time, but it looped back around, snapping its beak wildly. It squawked loudly—an alarm, Isla realized too late. The bird was a spy for Cleo, alerting its master that she was being followed.

Isla dared a look up. The Moonling ruler had turned. They locked eyes.

In a flash of crystal blue, she was hurtled through the air by a thick sheet of water. Her breath was ripped from her chest. Cleo flung her against the side of the frost-coated mountain, and Isla cried out as her spine seemed to shatter. The pain was shocking, blinding, and she screamed again just as the water that had flung her back crackled into ice.

Cleo stepped forward, looking surprised.

"I have to admit," she said, "I'm impressed by your stupidity. A powerless ruler, following me onto my own isle?"

She was going to kill her. Just like she killed Juniper.

Isla tore against the ice—

But it might as well have been iron.

"Oh, as the night grows colder, the ice will only get stronger," Cleo purred. "Now tell me, Wildling, why have you followed me here?"

She had to be smart, keep Cleo talking as long as she could. And pray it would give her enough time to come up with a plan.

"I know," Isla said, her voice coming out deep and fractured. She took a shaking breath, the pain in her back like daggers through the gaps in her spine. "I know why you killed Juniper."

Cleo looked curious. She took a step closer to Isla. Her white hair glimmered in the moonlight as she shook her head. "You are a fool." *Fool.* The word was an old friend, or maybe an enemy, waving hello. Though she had done foolish things, Isla was not a fool. "But a courageous one, showing up to the Centennial without abilities . . ." She raised an eyebrow. "And using the skin gloves to get into protected sections of our castles? Ingenious." She pursed her lips. "Let's see if you are clever enough to get yourself out of this mess."

The Moonling snapped her fingers, and the ice keeping her in place expanded. Thickened.

Anger warmed her core, though not enough to keep the frost from turning her numb. Her lips were two chips of ice when she whispered. "You're afraid," she said. "Because I know . . . I know you spun the curses." Isla raged against the ice, pounding over and over. But

it was no use. "I know, and if a *fool* could figure it out, so can anyone else."

Cleo raised a hand, and the ice traveled from Isla's collarbones all the way up her neck, like a crystal choker. Isla gasped, every breath now frozen. "You don't know what you think you do, Wildling," she said. "But even if you did . . ." She smiled. "Corpses can't talk. And corpses can't break curses, can they?"

With that, Cleo smirked before disappearing into the icy hole.

Time ticked differently when you were dying, Isla realized. The seconds were miles long, and the minutes were endless howls of wind. It might have been hours, or only half a chime, but soon, Isla stopped feeling the pain in her back like a hundred knives. The ice had frozen it over, just like it had muted the limited heat that her outfit had provided.

She remembered the first time she had portaled to the Moonling realm. How she had hated it. The snow and ice and frozen everything had looked beautiful—but had felt like a bite. Mosquitoes, all over her body. She had only stayed minutes, which was long enough to watch the full moon swallow a ship whole.

Never did she think that something as simple and natural as the cold would be the thing that ended her. A curse or a blade to the heart, maybe. But never the cold.

First Isla was sad. Then she was afraid.

And then she was angry again.

Cleo was right . . . she was a fool. She had followed the Moonling ruler without a plan, so desperate to get answers. And the heart.

And revenge.

She took all the words to her mother back, calling them from the sky, roping her prayers down. If she had powers, she could maybe lift a finger and access the rock deep below the ice. Or a tree. Or call to an animal that would help her free.

I do blame you, she said in her head. *If I die, I blame you. What kind of Wildling falls in love, knowing the costs?* She wondered what her mother would look like now. An older version of herself, she supposed. Once a ruler had children, they began to age more properly, looking older and older the more their family line grew. Each family only had access to so much power. After the curses, the island and realms grew weaker. But in a way, some people, by losing their families, became stronger.

Isla had no family. And she was still weak.

Alone.

No . . . not alone.

Her necklace. Grim had told her to touch it any time she needed him. He could save her. Her hands were too far—she had no chance of breaking them free. But her chin—maybe she could touch it to the chain . . .

A sound from deep in her throat echoed against the surrounding mountains as she strained, the nerves at the base of her neck crying out in pain. She angled her head the farthest she could, head pounding.

But with the ice Cleo had trailed up her throat, it was not enough.

She collapsed, her head hitting the back of the mountain. She barely processed the ache. Even if somehow she could touch the necklace, Grim couldn't be out at night, she realized. He couldn't get to her until morning.

And by morning she would be dead.

CHAPTER FORTY-THREE

LIES

Hot breath puffed against her cheek. She heard splitting ice—someone was heaving a blade against it. Cutting through the frost to get her out like carving a statue.

Isla couldn't open her eyes. They had frozen over, like the rest of her. Her eyelashes had glued together. Though she could not see, she knew it was still night, for it had gotten colder.

Her lips tried to part, to thank whoever was setting her free. But they were sealed closed, knitted together by frost. Whoever they were, they banged their weapon hard against the ice, over and over, the vibrations going through her bones. They were going to strike her if they weren't careful.

"It's her, isn't it?" a voice said. It was wickedly deep—and amused.

Another voice. "Look at that face. Of course it is." She felt something sharp against her cheek. A blade? No, a nail. A long one. "We'll make a broth from her bones that will fill us with power. We'll burn her hair and inhale the smoke to make us beautiful again."

Isla stopped breathing.

The first voice said, "She's awake, isn't she? Do you think she can hear us?"

"I don't care. Where is Thrayer? This ice isn't breaking easily."

Something rustled nearby. Then, "I'm here. You found her like this?"

The first one squealed. "Trapped like a rat in honey."

"Good. Very good . . ."

The ice went warm, shifting into water. She slipped down the side of the mountain, landing at its base. Even though her body was freed, she couldn't move a muscle, even to reach her neck.

Someone gripped beneath her shoulders and hauled her up.

Who were they? Cannibals who would roast her on a spit and eat her charred flesh?

It was so cold, the promise of heat was almost welcomed.

Whoever they were, a Moonling was helping them. Someone had unfrozen the ice.

They carried her through the forest. And she could hear that ridiculous bird, the one that had announced her presence. *Cleo's* bird. Was she watching her, somehow? She imagined the Moonling ruler would take great pleasure in seeing her roasted alive.

"Shoot the bird. It's making my ears bleed."

She heard the familiar sound of an arrow hissing through the night. For a moment, there was silence.

Then more screeching.

"If you can't shoot a bloody bird, why should you get her heart?"

"I found her!"

"Perhaps I'll shoot *you* and keep her for myself."

The bird screeched and screeched, almost happily.

The forest went still.

She felt a current through the air, metal in her mouth.

One of her captors screamed, and the heat of flames roared past her face. The smell of stars shattering something nearby, blood splattering against her skin. The one holding her dropped her.

But before she landed on the ground, someone else's arms were around her.

And she was in the air.

She was metal being fashioned into a blade, filled with so much heat she screamed and wondered how she even had strength to make the sound.

"Just a little longer," someone said.

At the sound of that voice, she stilled—and kicked with all her might, moved any limbs that had been thawed.

A hand came over her eyes, warming them, and finally, she could open them.

Oro was standing above her, frowning.

"*You,*" she said through her teeth, her voice venomous. Her hands pleaded to choke him. To gut him, slice a blade right up his center, tear his heart out with her bare hands.

Was he here to kill her? Had he finally found the heart of Lightlark?

"Before you do whatever horrific thing I am sure you are imagining," he said, "let me speak."

She would have lunged at him without hearing another word if her body wasn't still so numb.

Oro sighed. "I did not betray you, Wildling." Isla opened her mouth, but he kept talking. "Though you believing so helped tremendously . . ."

"Helped what?" she growled. He was lying. She didn't trust a word that came out of his wicked mouth.

"One of the places where darkness meets light on Moon Isle was impossible to access without Cleo. It had been encased in a maze centuries before to keep others out. I needed her . . . so I changed the matches."

Isla's nails dug into the flesh of her palm. She could move her fingers now. Maybe, if she was quick enough, she could choke him. She attempted to get her hand up. But it barely got an inch off the bed.

Bed.

She looked around, wildly.

She wasn't in her room. She was in *his*.

The walls were plain, but the ceiling was solid gold. The floors were stone. All the windows were covered in heavy fabrics.

Oro took a step back from the bed, noting her gaze—and possibly her panic. "I brought you here after I found you. I figured you wouldn't want others to know what had happened."

None of it made sense.

Why had Oro saved her?

He claimed he hadn't betrayed her . . . that their plan was still on. That all his actions were in *service* of their quest to find the heart.

Lies. Too many to count.

There are lies and liars all around . . .

Oro continued. "She finally took me there tonight. That's how I found you. I was on Moon Isle, in the maze. The heart wasn't there, which is good, because I suspect Cleo would have tried to take it . . . But now we have just two places left to search."

We. There was no *we* anymore.

She shook her head. Tears fell down her cheeks, his betrayal still raw. "This isn't just about changing matches." Her voice broke. She hated it. "I trusted you. I— *You.* You told them. You—"

Oro closed his eyes for just a moment. "I know. I'm sorry. Truly. Cleo had become suspicious. She knew we had visited Moon Isle the day before, somehow." Isla thought of the bird. Her spy. It had spotted them. "The only way to convince her to help me was to discard you. Publicly. Your reaction and actions in the last few weeks had to be genuine."

That wasn't a good enough reason. She opened her mouth to tell him so, but he continued.

"And," he said, "my sources told me Cleo has become increasingly convinced that Starling must be the one to die."

What? Isla barely resisted the urge to shoot up in alarm.

"That makes no sense. She wants *me* dead."

Oro frowned. "Cleo would have killed you tonight if she wanted you gone."

"She nearly did," she said, exasperated. If Oro hadn't saved her, she would have been someone's meal. "Why would she choose Starling?"

"She believes Starling is the weakest of us. It is the smallest realm. The least developed in the last five hundred years due to their curse."

Isla's voice shook as she said, "You . . . you don't agree, do you?"

He shook his head. "No. Starling is essential. I told your secret not just to get Cleo to trust me but also to cast doubt on her decision. Before, when Cleo and Celeste were paired, she couldn't kill her. When I changed them—"

"She could have gone directly for Celeste," Isla finished.

Oro nodded. "Exactly."

Isla didn't think Cleo even cared about following the rules or winning the power promised. Not if she was the one who had spun the curses.

Though, if Oro was right, and sharing her secret had saved Celeste . . . she was grateful.

Everything he said sounded logical. If he was telling the truth, then everything he had done in the last two weeks was to keep her and their plan safe.

She shook her head. "I don't believe you."

"I have never lied to you, Isla." He took a step closer. "Even though you have lied to me repeatedly." Another step. "You told me your secret. Now let me tell you my flair. No one can lie to me." She remembered his words from the cave. "Because I know when people are lying."

His flair. Isla blinked.

She had lied to him too many times to count, throughout the Centennial. Throughout their time working together. And he had known, every time.

He narrowed his eyes at her. "All you did was lie to me, and I still told you about the heart. I told you everything, except for this. Because Cleo *loved* how betrayed you looked. It was why she was willing to finally take me anywhere on Moon Isle I wanted. She was *thrilled* that I exposed you and chose her as a partner instead. That I revealed such a critical secret." He stopped just a foot away. Her hands were still in fists, and she briefly considered how good it would feel to slap him across the face.

"You put me in danger," she said. "Cleo could have killed me!"

"I was never far from you," he said. "I knew when you moved into the Place of Mirrors. I guarded its entrance. Had guards stationed nearby. How did you think Ella was able to get through unharmed? Wherever you went, I followed. And when I could not, I had guards monitoring Cleo so I could ensure she wasn't anywhere near you."

Isla laughed without humor. "And tonight?"

"Tonight, I went to meet her. You slipped through the cracks by trailing her. But I found you, didn't I?" He shook his head. "Cleo is planning something. She has been forming a secret legion." So, he *did* know about it. "The heart is on her isle. If she gets her hands on it before us, I'm afraid of what she will do."

He was right. Isla was convinced Cleo had spun the curses. If Oro was correct about his theory, that meant she had used the heart before. What was keeping her from doing it again?

Oro's gaze was relentless. "I trust you, Isla, though you have given me countless reasons not to. Are you going to trust me? For the sake of both of our people?"

Our people.

Isla never wanted to speak to the king again. But she didn't have a plan. Celeste was still helplessly pursuing the bondbreaker.

And her people were dying.

"Your offer holds, then," she said, every nerve ending in her body screaming at her not to trust him. To stab her blade through his back and let him see how it felt.

Oro nodded. "When we find the heart, you will wield it. You will receive the power promised."

Isla would be a fool to trust him again after what he had done. But part of her hoped he wasn't lying—that there was truly a chance to save her people, and herself.

She also couldn't ignore the fact that Oro had saved her life. Again. It didn't make any sense. If he was working against her, why wouldn't he want her dead? It would fulfill part of the prophecy.

She released her hands from their fists, and the dagger she had swiped from a hidden pocket in her pants while he had been talking clattered to the ground. Oro eyed it on the floor, unsurprised.

"Fine." She pinned him with the coldest look she could manage. "You know now that I don't eat hearts," she said slowly. "But betray me again—earnestly or otherwise . . ." Isla bared her teeth at him. "And for you, I'll make an exception."

CHAPTER FORTY-FOUR

CARMEL

"Cleo spun the curses," Isla told Celeste the next morning. She told her friend everything: The attack. Her and the Moonling's conversation.

At that, Celeste had frowned. "To what end, though? If she did create them, she hasn't acted on it. It's not like she used the other realms' weaknesses to invade them. She's done nothing."

Isla had been thinking the same thing. "I don't know. Maybe she *has* done something and we just don't know it yet."

She also told her that the Moonling wanted Celeste dead. And her friend only shrugged. "I figure everyone here except for you does. I'll be more careful, of course. But I've never trusted her for a moment."

Finally, Isla told Celeste that Oro had saved her. And what he had claimed.

She had readied herself for Celeste's judgment, for her disappointment. But the Starling almost looked pleased. "This is good," she said.

"Good?"

Celeste nodded. "I told you, I've been looking for the hidden library. I'm positive it's in the Mainland castle. And he must know where it is. You can ask him. He told everyone your greatest secret—he would need to tell you. To earn your trust again."

Celeste's insistence on continuing to search for the bondbreaker made her want to scream, but Isla promised she would ask when the time was right, just to mollify her friend.

Since the ball, islanders had sequestered themselves on their isles. The lack of power being used on the Mainland had quickened its crumbling.

It was no time to celebrate. Isla and Oro needed to search Moon Isle's last few locations as soon as possible, before time ran out. Before Terra was nothing more than wood and vines.

But Oro was bound to the rules of the Centennial with his life. And Isla had to follow them if she wished to win.

On the seventy-fifth day, Carmel went on as planned.

A twenty-four-hour carnival meant to celebrate the last quarter of the Centennial, Carmel was a celebration of the realms for all islanders, not just nobles. Isla didn't think anyone would show up for the event, not with what had happened at the ball, but, sure enough, the day before the carnival, shops opened their doors once more. People started filling the streets.

Isla didn't need to attend the entire event—just some of it. She skipped the picnic in the morning. The festivities on the east side of the Mainland in the afternoon.

She wondered if Cleo would make an appearance, given her suspicion that the Moonling didn't care about the rules. If she *had* spun the curses, she would want to keep them intact . . . not break them.

The Moonling would also want to keep anyone else from breaking them too.

Isla waited in her castle all day, listening at her window for echoes of the festivities. Music played far away. Glasses clinked as the celebrations moved toward the castle, into its gardens.

If tonight hadn't been Carmel, she would be on Moon Isle, searching the final locations. Both of Terra's legs were underground now. Flowers bloomed from the crown of her head.

It wouldn't be long before the forest took her completely. It wouldn't be long before there was no forest left.

One day of rest, she told herself. Then she would find the heart and get everything she wanted.

"You look ridiculous," Celeste said.

It was just after dusk. The Starling had just returned from the festivities to call upon Isla. Isla had moved back into her room at the castle, at Oro's insistence, since they were working together again. He promised he would take precautions to keep her safe.

Guards heavily monitored their hall. The king himself checked on her throughout the day.

Celeste and Isla were both dressed in elaborate, gleaming representations of their realms. The Starling ruler was covered in crystals, from the top of her neck to her long gloves and down to the fabric that puddled at her feet. Her hair was spotted with tiny diamonds that looked like stars that had been coaxed down from the galaxy just for the day.

That night, Isla was a rose in bloom. A crown of flowers had been placed atop her own, bright red against her dark hair. Pink petals had been pressed against her neck and trailed onto a bodice split into three parts. They became more and more elaborate until her waist—cinched tightly by ribbons crisscrossed down her spine—before blossoming from her hips in giant sheets. Rows of petals, all knitted together, trailed all the way to the floor. Her cape was a train of roses that ran five feet behind her.

They couldn't walk into Carmel together. Oro likely knew of their friendship if he and his guards had been tracking her movements. But that wasn't particularly alarming. Of course the youngest rulers would become friends. Still, they didn't want anyone suspecting their alliance had predated the Centennial.

Celeste promised to be close by. And Isla only planned to stay a few minutes. Vendors lined the streets outside the castle, selling pickled porridge, elderberry scones, spun sugar that really did spin, and goblets and goblets of drink. Revelers from all daytime-dwelling realms roamed through the festivities, dressed in elaborate versions of their colors, their wariness fading with every second that passed without a disaster. Starlings

wore glitter, Skylings wore hats that floated precariously above their heads in the breeze, and Moonlings wore white formal suits and dresses.

Everyone was staring at her. She imagined news of her powerlessness had spread. Though most of them had seen her at the duel. They had witnessed what she could do with a blade. She twirled one through her fingers, watching them back. Daring them to make a move.

Isla immediately noticed she was being followed. But not by Cleo.

Oro had arranged a guard of about half a dozen to trail her through the gardens. They were discreet, but Isla could feel their eyes on her.

Their protection made her bold. When a Starling carrying a tray of drink passed her by, she took one of the goblets.

She knew the odds of finding the heart and getting its power. This could very well be her last celebration. Her last chance to try wine.

Isla swallowed the drink.

It tasted like malted honey and burned its entire way down her throat.

The guards continued to trail her throughout the gardens. It only took a few moments before she began to feel weightless.

Wine couldn't be that strong, could it? Had it been some sort of celebratory drink that was more potent than usual?

Celeste would know. Nobles stared at her as she walked past, searching the crowd for her friend. She didn't see her anywhere. Perhaps she had left. Maybe she hadn't been able to find Isla and went searching for her in her room.

Time to go, she thought. She had been at Carmel long enough to satisfy the rules. And the drink's effects were firmly taking hold.

By the time she stepped up the stairs of the castle and into the halls, the world seemed to be stumbling. Or maybe that was her. She was *hot,* too hot, the ridiculous outfit sticking to her like molasses. She took off her flower crown and let it drop on the ground. She peeled off the petals that trailed down her neck, choked by them. The entire outfit was

entirely too much. She undid her cape and let it fall behind her. Already, she felt so much better. *Freer.* Wilder.

Isla imagined the guards trailing her finding the bits of her dress and laughed.

All her worries had fizzled away like bubbles in champagne. She couldn't even think of one of her fears for more than a few seconds if she tried—they were slippery in her mind.

Isla smiled as she began picking the petals off her dress. "I bet a flower has never picked itself . . ." she said to absolutely no one. Then she laughed as she ripped the bottom layer off, stepping out of it with relief.

She turned around and found herself in a hallway she didn't recognize. Had she already passed her room? Had she been too busy ruining her ridiculous dress to notice? She shrugged and kept going, unraveling herself until the flower dress ended high above her knees, leaving behind a trail of petals. She walked until she reached a dead end. Isla frowned at the wall, then whipped around at the sound of a voice.

"Isla?"

She smiled far too wide, excitement flooding through her veins as quickly as the wine had. "Oro," she said, his supposed nonbetrayal feeling worlds away. All she remembered was she was supposed to be nice to him and hope he kept his promise. She walked over to the king, bare feet stepping over petals. She must have taken her shoes off at some point. Isla laughed at herself for what she was about to do, barely keeping it together enough to stand high on her toes and flick his crown.

He blinked at her. Then he frowned. "Are you all right?"

Isla rolled her eyes. "You're always so angry . . . *why?* Do you ever smile?" *Yes.* He had smiled at her, just once.

She was still on her toes, and the ground seemed to slip under her like a rug. Before she could fall back, Oro grabbed her elbow to steady her. He immediately dropped her arm.

Isla scowled at him. "I'm not *poisonous,*" she said, rolling her eyes again for good measure.

She turned and swayed down the hall to music that seemed to be playing through her bones.

"I'll take you to your room . . . if you would like?" he asked.

She shrugged. "Fine. I was going there . . . but the hallways changed." She looked at him for explanation, and he glanced at her like she had said something ridiculous. Isla blinked, not knowing what it could possibly be.

He suddenly looked alarmed. "Did you drink the haze?"

Isla nodded enthusiastically. Was that what the wine was called? She was humming something. No, she was singing. She opened her mouth, and her voice flooded the halls. She liked the way it echoed, and she sang louder.

She had never felt so alive . . . like her throat and arms and face were on fire and glowing, buzzing.

Why hadn't Poppy and Terra ever allowed her such pleasures?

She didn't realize she was partially speaking her thoughts aloud until Oro said, "Your guardians?"

Luckily, Oro was leading the way, because she hadn't processed any of the last hallways or turns. She nodded. "Did you have guardians?"

He was silent for a few moments before he said, "No, I didn't. I was never supposed to be ruler, or king. My brother was the one with guardians."

"So, what did you think you would be?" Words slipped off her tongue so easily, she wondered why it had ever felt hard to ask him anything.

"I led our armies."

Isla stopped in the hallway. She placed her hands on her hips. "*You* commanded the Lightlark armies?"

She expected him to glare at her, but he didn't. He just nodded. It made sense, though. That was why he had been so good at dueling. She

started walking again, slower this time. He matched her pace. "That's why you hate him, isn't it?"

He seemed to know she meant Grim. While she had heard of the Nightshade's previous title, Terra hadn't ever told her about Oro. She wondered why. Did she even know herself? She supposed the Sunling king's reputation and history prior to the curses had been smothered by everything that had come after them. "We both lost many warriors," he said. "And I didn't agree with the way he fought." He didn't explain further, and then they were at her door. "Are you going to be all right?" he asked. Oro looked over his shoulder, verifying the guards had followed. They had and stood in their places against the wall, guarding the entrance to the hall.

Isla nodded. "I'll be fine." When he turned to go, however, she caught his wrist. "Wait. I still have so many questions. Will you come in?" Oro looked like that was the last thing he wanted to do, but Isla wasn't deterred. "I'll make tea," she added.

She entered. At her insistence, he followed. Oro warmed some water, and she found the pouch of Wildling spices and flowers that made her favorite drink, a tea she called yellow bee.

"Why yellow bee?" Oro asked before taking a sip. He seemed to like it.

Isla plopped down next to him on her couch and shrugged. "The plant that grows these flowers was always swarming with bees," she said. "I used to get at least three stings every time I tried to collect them for tea. But it was worth it."

Oro gave her a strange look.

"You haven't been sleeping well, have you?" she asked, leaning toward him, squinting at the purple beneath his eyes.

She expected him to ignore her question, like he had before, but he said, "No. I haven't for a long while."

"Why?" Her voice, surprisingly, was gentle. Not judgmental, the way it always had been with him.

Oro looked at her tree, its fruits ripe and swollen with juice and so heavy the branches dipped. "I have a lot of guilt," he said quietly. "That keeps me awake." *Guilt.* She knew the word intimately.

"How did you find me?" she asked suddenly. She remembered that night in shatters, like a broken, scattered mirror.

"In the hallway? I followed the trail of petals."

She shook her head. "No . . . before." *In the Moon Isle woods.*

The air cooled and stilled, and Isla hummed softly to its current. "I heard the bird," he said. "That's how I found you. I followed the bird."

Stupid bird, she thought. The same one that had almost gotten her killed. At least it had done some good.

She was suddenly tired, her energy unraveling as easily as her dress had. Her eyelids were heavy, and she smiled. She lay down on the couch, her head against his leg. The drink made her mind spin behind her eyes, and she groaned. "I have honey in my head," she said, because that was exactly what it felt like.

Oro laughed, and it was such a surprise that she wished her eyes would open to see if he really had.

Isla woke up warm. Wine still fogged her mind, but it was more of a mist than its previous storm. She remembered the celebration in pieces—Celeste coming for her. Noticing the guards. Drinking wine. Going to the castle. Ripping her costume off. Her eyes flew open.

Her head was in Oro's lap, her cheek against his leg. He was leaned back against the couch, exactly as she remembered him.

Except he was asleep.

She wondered what in the realms went into wine. And knew why Terra and Poppy had kept it from her. Isla remembered her conversation the night before and shuddered—her questions had been so brazen. But Oro had answered them, hadn't he?

How long had they been asleep? She turned to the balcony. The

curtains were closed, but no sunlight peeked through their slight gap. Night, then. Which meant a party was going on at that very moment, in the gardens below.

Oro looked more peaceful than she had ever seen him. It almost pained her to poke him in his chest. But he had to attend at least the last few hours of Carmel. He startled, a hand going up quickly in defense, almost reaching her throat. His eyes were wide for half a second when he saw her across from him in the darkness. Then he straightened and lowered his hand.

"You fell asleep," she said. "Thank—thank you for staying with me. I'm sorry, I think you missed part of the . . . party."

Oro's eyebrows came together a bit, and Isla wondered if he had forgotten about it. He did look better. The purple crescents beneath his eyes were fainter, the set of his jaw stronger.

Isla remembered the sound she had fallen asleep to—Oro, laughing. And not meanly, the way he always had. She had never heard him truly laugh before. As she looked at him, she wondered if she really had imagined it. He was frowning as he studied the room. As if he regretted having agreed to step inside it.

Isla rose. She didn't dare look down at her dress, which she knew was in shambles, ripped high up her thigh. Oro didn't look either as he stood.

"I should go to the celebration," he said gruffly.

Isla nodded. "You should." Without thinking, she reached up and fixed his crown, which had gone wayward while he was sleeping.

Her eyes met his when she was finished. And there was something like anger there. She fell back on her heels, surprised.

"Two more places on Moon Isle," he said flatly, unmoved by her expression. "Tomorrow, we'll go to one. The next day, the other. Then we're done."

"Good," she said curtly before turning to her balcony and slipping through the doors.

The night air was like a caress, rustling the remaining petals on her dress. Far below, she could hear the celebration—the clink of glasses and hiss of conversation and pluck of joyful music.

She was still on the balcony an hour later when pounding sounded against her door. Her eyes rolled, expecting Oro might have returned to check on her, on his way to bed. She opened it with a sigh.

And found Ella standing there, red in the face. That was when she noticed that the party she could hear from her balcony had gone quiet. The music had died.

"What's happened?" Isla asked, retrieving her dagger in a flash.

Ella didn't even wince at the weapon as she said, panting, "A ruler has been attacked."

"Which one?" she asked, roaring filling her ears, filling the world.

Ella's silver-gloved fingers shook at her sides. "Starling."

CHAPTER FORTY-FIVE

VANISHED

Isla moved through the castle like a storm. If she'd had power, it would be everywhere. She ran like she was running from something, wielded her dagger like she might throw it; her teeth chattered like the marble beneath her feet was ice.

Ella, a Starling, was alive. Which meant her ruler had to be too.

Had to be.

As she approached the screams and rushing islanders desperate to get out of the gardens, she remembered her mask.

She wasn't supposed to know Celeste, beyond the last few months.

She wasn't supposed to care so much.

Isla pinched her palm to keep from crying. Smoothing the worried lines across her face was like trying to move metal, but she did.

Still, when she entered the gardens, she was running.

She gasped. Stilled.

Celeste floated in the middle of a miniature maze, looking a lot like she was sleeping. Silver fog and string thin as spiderweb wrapped a thin veil around her.

The only other ruler there was Oro. He turned to her, face drawn. "This is old enchantment. I haven't seen it in a while. It's a poison."

Cleo. She had gone after Celeste. Just as Oro had suspected.

"How do we fix it?" Her voice was breathless.

Oro shook his head. "We can't. Only her body can mend itself. Moonling healing ability strengthens this poison." Isla's lips trembled. She watched Celeste like watching a corpse in a coffin.

During the last seventy-five days, she had begun to feel strong. So unlike the unsure, inexperienced Wildling girl who had stepped foot on the island.

Now she felt completely powerless again.

No. There had to be a way to heal her. She couldn't just not do anything.

"Whoever did this was interrupted," Oro said, studying the webbing around the Starling ruler. "It should have killed her immediately. That's the only good news."

Her hands were in fists. "When will she wake up?" Isla demanded. Her voice was too loud, too raw.

Oro eyed her. "If she does . . . it could be days. Weeks." The island might not last that long.

"It was her," Isla growled. "Cleo."

Oro didn't meet her gaze. "Perhaps."

"Perhaps?" Isla wanted to scream. She wanted to cry. But she did neither of those things and patiently waited for Oro to leave.

When Isla had almost been assassinated, Celeste had saved her. When she had almost been crushed by the ceiling at the ball, Celeste had been there. When Isla was reeling from Oro's supposed betrayal, Celeste had pulled her out of her gloom.

She had always been a good friend. The best friend.

And Isla had failed her. She had been full of drink and moody on her balcony when her friend had needed her most. She had left Celeste *alone* at the celebration, knowing the risks.

She felt the air change as Grim appeared, in the safety of the closest room to the gardens. Finally.

"I need you to do something for me," she said, her voice finally steady.

"Anything."

Isla took a breath that felt like there were leaks in her lungs.

"Whoever attacked her will come back to finish the job. I need you to make her disappear until she wakes up."

She was grateful when he didn't question her request. Grim simply nodded.

And a moment later, Celeste's body vanished.

CHAPTER FORTY-SIX

POISON

Everything changed in an instant. Now, Isla wasn't just fighting for herself, or Terra, or her people.

She was fighting for Celeste.

Tears streamed down her cheeks as she left the castle just past dawn. Isla had failed her friend in so many ways—and she had been blind to it until now. Seeing Terra slowly die should have reminded her that her friend would suffer the same fate if they weren't successful. Instead, she had quickly abandoned the plan they had spent years formulating, partly because it wouldn't benefit *her* realm. She hadn't thought enough about Celeste's.

She couldn't fix the past, but she could try to help Celeste now.

Oro claimed that she couldn't be healed by Moonling ability . . . but perhaps she could be by Wildling remedy.

Soon she was cutting through a path covered by wild grass. Through a forest that seemed determined to mark her skin a thousand times. Crossing a perilous bridge.

Until she saw herself reflected in the barren woods. Against the Place of Mirrors.

She had to open that vault. By any means necessary. There could be ancient Wildling remedies inside, plants that could draw Celeste's poison out. She hadn't seen any in the oasis Oro had taken her to so many weeks before, but perhaps they had been locked away here instead.

Isla knew the door wanted her to open it for a reason. Maybe this was it.

She walked steadily to the wall, not willing to leave without figuring out the lock. It was a strange, long shape. First she tried her fingers. Stuck them in painfully, shoving part of her palm inside to fill the gaps. But when she tried to twist her hand, all she did was scream out as her skin got caught in the metal. It took her nearly an hour to free herself, and by that time, she had cuts across her hand, dripping blood.

She did not give up. She searched every room of the enormous palace that had been her home for weeks. There were strange, curved weapons. Instruments she didn't know how to play. One, a thin wooden box with holes, she shoved into the lock so forcefully it broke. So, she spent a while trying to get the splinters out, cutting her fingers again in the process.

By noon, she was furious.

Vowing to return, she went back to the castle empty-handed.

Isla had wanted to kill Cleo for a long time. Especially after the assassination attempt at the harbor.

But now . . . seeing Celeste lifeless, floating like a specter, wrapped in webbing . . .

Now she wanted to kill Cleo and take a long time doing it.

Isla was thinking about all the ways she would make the Moonling ruler suffer as she stepped foot onto Moon Isle with Oro by her side.

Two more places, she told herself. Celeste couldn't play the game anymore. Isla would have to play for both of them—make sure she won and saved her friend's realm. It was all that mattered now.

Only two more places left to look.

Snow fell with the hurry of rain, soaking into the crown of her head and dripping in streaks down her cheeks. This time she had worn a thick cape over her long-sleeved shirt and pants to shield her from the cold. Still, it didn't do much, and she didn't veer far from Oro, who radiated heat like a sun that had slid down from the sky.

Soon they came upon a tower sticking out of a mountain of snow. Oro climbed through its only entrance, a window, and she followed

him inside, down, then through a hall, until she realized they weren't in a tower at all.

They were in a palace.

It was abandoned but still ornate, built completely out of white marble. They had entered from its highest peak—the rest was buried in ice, trapped in the forever winter that was Moon Isle. She followed Oro down floor by floor until they reached the top of a grand staircase.

The wide steps led down to what must have been the main floor once upon a time.

Now it was completely underwater.

Somehow, the furniture remained tethered; everything in the room below looked perfectly in place. Just . . . submerged.

Oro began taking off his clothing.

Isla whirled to face him. "What are you doing?"

He glanced at her. "There are creatures in that water that won't be easy to face. I don't need to be weighed down or give them something to choke me with." His cape was now discarded on the ground. His shirt soon joined it.

Isla stared, though everything in her mind told her not to. Oro looked remarkably like the marble statues on Moon Isle, his chest and arms muscled like a warrior, toned as sharply as a blade.

More than half of him had now been overcome by the bluish gray. He was part gold, part ice sculpture. She studied him, wondering if it hurt to lose one's powers, to die slowly, inch by inch.

She looked for other reasons too.

Oro stared back at her, surprised. "I'm sure you've seen plenty of bodies before," he said flatly.

Isla bristled. He hadn't said it meanly, more matter-of-factly, and she supposed she couldn't blame his assumption. A *true* Wildling, even a powerless one, would have seen countless naked bodies. They were famed for their romantic conquests.

A fact—nothing more.

Isla swallowed. "Of course I have," she said a bit too quickly.

Oro raised an eyebrow, sensing her lack of curse wasn't the only thing that distinguished her from her people.

He took a step forward, still shirtless. Tilted his golden head at her. "Tell me, Wildling . . . how *many* people have you been with?"

Isla's face flushed. She barely resisted the urge to slap him. "What kind of question is that?" she demanded. In her realm, love was forbidden. But intimacy was not shied away from. It was *celebrated.*

He seemed to know it, and his expression became even more surprised. "A curious one." He shrugged. "I've been with many women. It's not something I deny."

Isla sneered at him. "Well, that must have been a long time ago, judging by how uptight and insufferable you are."

The sides of Oro's mouth twitched. Amused. "That might be so. But you didn't answer my question."

"And I won't," she said, glaring at him. He grinned. Was he laughing at her?

For some reason, she was compelled to prove him wrong. To wipe the smirk off his wretched face. Without breaking Oro's gaze, she unbuttoned her cape and let it fall to the floor. She slipped off her oversize shirt and pants until she was only in the clothes she wore beneath, over her underclothes. A tiny tank top that reached just above her navel and a pair of high-waisted, tight shorts that ended high on her thigh.

She wasn't in her underwear, but only wearing scraps of fabric, she felt bare in front of him.

Oro stood very still.

She shrugged, trying her best to look carefree. "It's just skin," she said, her voice slightly breathless.

"Just skin," he repeated, his mouth barely moving.

She walked past him, down the steps of the stairs. Until her feet splashed. Until the water reached her knees. She heard him slip off his

pants, then socks, then shoes. She shivered, the cold biting every inch of exposed skin.

A moment later he was by her side, just in undershorts. This time, she looked away. A bit reluctantly.

"Water lilies grow here," he said, not looking at her either. "The ones you pointed out in the mountain." Isla remembered that day, which seemed realms away. "You said something like the heart might attach to their roots, correct?"

He glanced at her, and she simply nodded.

"These waters house ancient, vicious creatures," he said. "Be on guard."

The water rippled as he dived into it. Isla took a deep breath and followed him. He swam quickly, out of the main hall and into the corridor. She stayed near the stairs. The ceiling was fifty feet tall, and she was at the top of it, diving down toward a room that looked nearly perfect except for a painting that had slices through it, ribbons of what had been a landscape curling in the water.

Her gaze traced the edges of the floor, beneath the furniture. No sign of any plant. She turned, to try a different room, and almost swallowed a mouthful of water in shock.

A face, lovely and vicious as a nightmare, floated before her.

Half of the girl's face was scaled; half of her hair had the transparent silkiness of a koi fish's tail. Her arms and legs were scaled too, creating the effect of submerged silk around her limbs.

Mesmerizing.

Isla squinted. Her mind had suddenly become just as murky as the water. She was there for something . . . but she couldn't quite remember what that was.

The girl smiled and reached out a scale-covered hand with nails sharp as knives. *To help,* Isla realized.

She didn't know why . . . but she took it.

And the girl led her deep below. Through a bedroom, into a hall. Isla saw the water lilies then, sunken, their roots like braids that went down for yards. Something about them seemed important, but she didn't know what.

Luckily, she had the girl to lead her. Lead her *where,* though? she wondered.

Something drummed in her ears, an echoing or roaring, as her chest contracted. The pain was muted, as far away as the surface. But the beating continued. Beating like . . .

The heart. That was what they were there for, Isla remembered now.

She stopped following, and the girl whipped around. Pulled at her arm.

Isla shook her head, the movement making her dizzy. Her eyes had started to close. She needed something . . . air, maybe.

The girl was insistent. She yanked her arm, yanking Isla along.

Something wasn't right. Isla slipped out of the girl's grip.

The creature didn't like that. She whirled around and sliced across Isla's middle with her razor-sharp nails.

Clouds of crimson stained the water like blotches of ink.

Isla began swimming out of the room again, not knowing anything, but knowing she needed to get away. She made it through the door, back through the bedroom, until she could see the stairs. But the steps were too far, and her legs had gone stiff.

She wasn't here alone though, she realized, the fog in her mind thinning. She could call to him—

Something pulled her foot so sharply she gasped, swallowing water, and sank again.

It was fire in her throat, burning her lungs, the salt water straight from the sea. She jerked, her organs pleading for air, for relief, just as she turned to look at her feet, at the girl who had claimed her once more.

She grabbed the dagger she had hidden in the middle of her chest, tucked in the wiring of her bra—dropped it. Her free foot caught the blade with her toes.

And she stabbed the dark figure right in the eye.

It hissed, disappearing far below in a flash.

She was at the top of the stone stairs in an instant, coughing up the water from her lungs.

In the air, her head cleared completely.

What happened? she wondered. Why had she followed the girl like a fool?

"That was a night creature," Oro said somewhere close by. His voice was tight. "They can invade your mind. Shut it down completely."

He knelt beside her, and she wondered why until she screamed out, her pain rushing at her in full force. There was a long gash along her side where the girl had cut her.

Oro made a gentle, calming sound that seemed totally at odds with his hulking presence. He towered over her even on his knees.

She shivered on the cold stone floor, and he placed a hand against her bare stomach. At once, heat flooded her core, followed by a sting—he was healing her. Oro made the calming sound once more when she flinched, and Isla looked at him, really looked at him, grimacing as her skin knitted itself back together. He stared back.

Something about his proximity, maybe, or his hands on her—or the blood she had lost, more likely—made her feel a little dizzy.

Isla groaned again, the healing like electricity against her skin. He flinched as her hand came over his own, both pressed against her wound. It was hot as a coal beneath her fingers, and enormous, spanning almost fully across her stomach. Before long, it moved.

She watched his knuckles trail down her ribs, healing the very edges of the wound.

"Finished," he said, just as Isla braced herself for another sting.

Isla blinked at him. She had been panting, the salt in her wound like flames against her skin. Now, her breathing settled.

Oro slowly removed his hands from her bare skin. As soon as he did, she shivered, the cold rushing back.

At that, he touched her again, this time against her knee.

She straightened, willing her strange thoughts away, remembering why they were in the wretched palace in the first place. "Did you find it?" she asked, eyes wide. Desperate.

Oro's gaze darkened. "No," he said. "It wasn't there."

She closed her eyes, disappointment hurting almost as much as her wound had. She was Celeste's and her people's only hope. She couldn't fail, not again. When she opened them, she forced herself to look more confident than she felt. "It can only be in one place, then, right?"

"Yes. But that place is one I had hoped to avoid."

"Why?"

"It's right at the center of Vinderland territory," he said.

Her face scrunched in confusion.

"The group that tried to kill you."

Oh.

"Who were they?" she asked. She hadn't seen them, but their voices . . . what they had wanted to do to her . . .

Oro blinked. "I thought you knew."

Knew what?

"They were Wildlings."

What? Her face twisted. "There aren't any left on the island, and they were *men*—"

"There aren't any left. They *were* Wildlings. Their group left your realm long before even the curses. They had already renounced their power, so their kind wasn't affected."

So, they ate hearts and flesh out of desire . . . not because of a curse. She shuddered. There was so much about the Wildlings she didn't know.

Why had the group left their realm in the first place?

"I can go alone," Oro said. Unlike every time he had said similar words before, there was no mean edge to his voice. "If you would prefer not to take the risk."

But she had made it this far. If she was going to win, if she was going to save the people she loved most, she needed to be there when they found the heart. "I'm coming," she said.

That same night, Oro took her to a place she never would have expected to be invited to—the castle's ancient store of weaponry. She grabbed too many things—arrows, bows, knives, throwing stars, swords. Celeste and Terra were on her mind—the strongest people she knew.

She left the vault ready for the next day.

Ready to take on the former Wildlings who had almost picked her apart.

CHAPTER FORTY-SEVEN

BLOOM

As soon as they stepped foot on Moon Isle the next night, the dark-blue bird found them. It harped loudly, and Isla pointed her arrow at it. "Make another sound and you're stew," she said meanly. Wondering if she was speaking directly to the ruler of Moonling herself. She should shoot Cleo's bird right in the chest for what she had done to Celeste.

It squawked once more, then flew away, far from the sharp tip of her arrow.

"On edge?" Oro asked. He didn't have any weapons on him. And Isla supposed that was strategic. The ex-Wildlings couldn't know the king of Lightlark considered them a threat.

Most of all, it was a message to Cleo. Wherever she was on Moon Isle, whether or not she was using the dark-blue bird as her spy, she would know they were on her land again. Oro entering her isle so many times unarmed sent the greatest message of all.

The Centennial was a game. And Oro was still its most powerful player.

Isla tried not to think of the white-haired ruler as they made their way across the snow to the final location. Instead, she thought of the heart.

Would it bloom as beautiful as a primrose?

Would it be as cold as the heart of the king of Lightlark?

So close.

They were so very close.

She turned to Oro and found him watching her. His expression was resolute, hard as the slabs of ice at their sides. He nodded once, as if able to read her thoughts.

One more place. Then it's all over.

Vinderland territory sat far beyond the reaches of Cleo's snow kingdom. At its northeast corner sat a stretch of land so treacherously cold it was almost uninhabitable. Isla relied on the warmth blooming from Oro like a shield. He extended it so that it engulfed her fully, and she barely felt the frost on her nose.

Ice, sharp like teeth, stuck out from the ground at an angle, a cluster of swords. Isla held the hilt of hers tightly, eyes alert. Studying everything. They entered a forest of dead trees, skeletons covered in snow.

They came in a wave.

One moment there was silence. The next, the night split apart in screams as bodies leaped from trees, right into their path. Others had been hidden behind trunks, and they showed themselves now, arrows pointed at their necks.

But Isla was ready.

She smiled, just a little. And unleashed.

Three of her arrows flew at once, each finding their targets. Bodies fell from the high branches. She ducked, barely missing a flying blade, then turned, her sword now in her fist. She gutted the man in front of her who had a dagger to her heart, turned and did the same to a towering woman who had a rusty hatchet aimed at her temple.

Throwing stars from her pocket flew from her other hand, into the neck of a man half a moment away from burying his blade in Oro's back. They landed in a perfect line across his throat like a macabre necklace.

Oro's fire hissed and roared as he took out five people at once, their metal weapons dropping into the snow with barely a sound. He froze one against a tree. Another, he sent hurtling back with a burst of Starling energy.

Isla whipped around, fast as a twirling top, her blade finding flesh and slicing through it as easily as Wildling teeth sinking into a heart's soft tissue. Her metal clinked against other metal before she hit the weapon away and cut down the one who wielded it. She did the same to another. And another.

With a grunt, she was knocked onto her back. The ground was coated in ice, and she gasped but felt no relief, her lungs turned to stone.

A man towered over her. His teeth were sharp as blades—cut into weapons. Tools to eat with, she realized.

He reached a hand toward her neck. To break it. To make a clean kill so that the flesh would be unmarred by injury, suitable to feast upon.

Isla watched, frozen. She lifted a shaking hand from the ground, gasping, willing her body to get over the shock of the impact—

And a blade went right through the man's chest. He made a gurgling sound, then choked on his own blood before falling over onto the snow.

Oro stood there, holding a sword.

But he hadn't been armed . . . or so she had thought. She watched in wonder as the silver sword disappeared in a burst of sparks. He had *created* it from Starling energy. She hadn't known a thing like that could be done.

When her breath returned, she stood, looking around at bodies that never would again.

Dead. They were all dead.

"There are more," Oro said quickly. "Who will come to investigate. Let's go."

Isla took his hand, still gasping at air. He heated her through their touch, and they ran, Oro pulling her so quickly he was nearly flying, only stopping the moment it came into view.

A tree of white feathers, blooming from the ice.

Of course. The perfect host for the heart. A secluded tree, frozen in time. It could be hidden in its feathers or even among its roots.

She stepped forward. Once. Twice. Then she ran.

Finally. After everything . . .

There it was. Their salvation. Her chance at being the ruler and friend the people she loved deserved.

She heard Oro right behind her. His heat grew, relieved that it was all over. The months of searching.

The centuries of suffering.

Isla reached the tree and began searching its branches. The feathers were soft as snow. They danced quietly in the wind, rustling together, tiny bits of feather falling.

When she didn't find anything in its brush, she looked down at the roots. The ice allowed her to see their every inch, thick and twisted into braids.

"Isla."

She studied the tree again. And again.

"It has to be here," she said, hands going through the feathers furiously now. Desperately.

She fell roughly to her knees to get a closer look below, biting down the pangs of pain that nearly blinded her vision. She pressed her hands against the ice and searched closer, studied every knot.

But there was nothing intertwined in its roots.

"It's not here," Oro said. His voice was as hollow as his eyes had looked that first night at dinner.

They had been wrong.

Or they had been right, and Cleo had gotten there first. Perhaps Cleo had sent her bird to mock them when they had first stepped on the isle.

Isla stilled. If Cleo had the heart . . .

She heard Celeste's warnings and doubts—the ones she had ignored—echo through her mind as she pressed her head to the ice and cried.

CHAPTER FORTY-EIGHT

HIDDEN

Twenty days of the Centennial remained. And Isla didn't think the island would make it ten.

Terra wouldn't make it five.

After all Oro and Isla's searching across the island for the heart, they had failed.

Isla had made countless mistakes in the last eighty days. She had trusted the wrong people. She had made the wrong plans. She had followed the wrong leads. She had blindly chased power when she should have done everything to protect the people who loved her.

But she refused to give up. Not this time. Not when Celeste would have demanded she didn't.

Isla banged on Oro's door three days after their last journey to Moon Isle, her knuckles still raw from the cold of the Vinderland expanse, even after she had repeatedly smeared Wildling elixir over the broken skin.

At the feathered tree, Isla had seen the light go out of his eyes—she had watched him fold back into himself, ready to become the same king she had met that first night. More closed off and guarded than his own cursed island. When the heart hadn't been where it was supposed to be, part of him had vanished, the same way Lightlark would if they failed. This time, perhaps forever.

Oro opened the door just as her fist was coming down in its wide swoop. He caught her arm before it could crash into his chest. He held her wrist and looked down at her, confused.

Isla pushed past him into his room, and he let her.

"This isn't over," she said, nostrils flaring and voice cracking in half as if she was still trying to convince herself of the fact.

Oro stared at her. He said nothing.

She took a step toward him. "I refuse," she said, shaking her head. "I refuse to believe this is how it ends." She jabbed a finger in his chest. "You are the king of Lightlark, the most powerful person in all of the realms." He raised an eyebrow, seeming surprised that she was speaking about him in any manner that didn't include the words *wretched* and *insufferable.* "There has to be another way. Another ending."

Her finger was still against his chest, and he looked down at it before looking at her. "What do you suggest?" he asked.

Such a simple question . . . but one he had never asked.

Even in her search for the bondbreaker, she had been following Celeste's plan.

For the first time, Isla made her very own.

"We start from the beginning," she said firmly, turning, taking in his room. "From the most basic truth, the root of all of this." She bit her lip, thinking. Thinking about the first thing he had told her, the basis for their entire search. A question she had asked before, that he hadn't answered. She turned to him. "How *did* you find out about the heart?"

He frowned. "I read about it."

"Where?"

"In a book."

"What book?"

"An old one. One I found in a hidden library."

The world went quiet. All of Isla's senses began to fade.

Hidden library. Just like Celeste had said.

Why hadn't she listened to her friend?

She tried her best to mask her surprise, her knee-wobbling relief, and her crushing guilt as she said, very quietly, "What library?"

Oro did not hesitate as he walked across the room and opened the door of his balcony. He pulled the door all the way back until it pressed

against his room's largest wall and turned the handle again—this time, pushing forward, against the solid stone.

It opened.

Isla followed him into a room tall as a tower, wide as the king's chambers. Filled to the brim with books and enchanted objects.

A library.

Isla barely breathed, barely moved, hoping her treacherous heart, beating far too loudly in her chest, wouldn't give her away. All she saw were books. The bondbreaker must have been well hidden. Not that it mattered now.

Celeste was on the brink of death. Isla couldn't use it with her in that state. And, even if she could, the bondbreaker wouldn't save Terra. Only an excess of power would. Only the power promised to the person who broke all the curses would.

Oro walked to one of the shelves assuredly, as if he had done so countless times before. He plucked a book from the rest and opened it.

Markings had been etched across the page in swirling ink, an ancient language she didn't understand.

"You can read this?" Isla asked.

Oro nodded.

"Read everything," she said. "Everything about the heart. Please."

He agreed. But instead of looking down at the page, he looked at her. "Before I do, there's something you should know, Wildling." He was serious, no amusement or meanness in his expression.

Her stomach sank on instinct. Ready to be disappointed.

"I would have informed you at the beginning. But after what Grim told you . . . I was waiting for him to reveal the information himself." She swallowed. Tell her what? What could be so important? "I'm guessing he never did."

Isla just stared at him. Waiting.

"My ancestor, Horus Rey, and Grim's, Cronan Malvere, created the island."

She nodded. She knew that.

"And so did yours."

She blinked. No. That wasn't true. Isla placed a hand against the table just to feel something steady. Wildlings weren't even really accepted on the island anymore . . . they didn't help *create* it. "That doesn't make any sense."

"Lark Crown. She made the land we stand upon. The island was named after her."

Lark Crown. She didn't know that name.

"You're lying. If that was true, everyone would know it. It wouldn't be a secret."

Oro's eyes darkened. "I've never lied to you," he said. "And it wasn't a secret, not for a long while. Until, like much of our knowledge, it was lost to time. Thousands of years went by. Sunlings ruled for so long, *who* created the island was forgotten. But not by everyone."

He was serious. And Isla knew he had nothing to gain from a lie like this.

If it was true, why hadn't Grim told her when they had discussed the creation of the island? She remembered what Oro had said after she had called Grim the most forthcoming ruler.

Not as forthcoming as you think.

Her lips pressed together. No, it was not a lie. Now she understood why Oro had wanted to make a deal with her. Why he hadn't yet truly betrayed her.

"That's why you needed me," she said, her voice very tight. "To find the heart."

Oro's expression did not change as he nodded. "It can only be found and unlocked by one of us. Sunling, Wildling, or Nightshade. I assumed . . . with both of us . . ."

Only joined can the curses be undone.

He was simply following the prophecy. An inexplicable part of her shriveled inside.

All Oro's words had edges, and they cut into her mind. Oro had confirmed, weeks before, that he believed the *original offense* was someone using the heart of Lightlark to cast the curses. He now claimed only a Sunling, Wildling, or Nightshade could access the heart's powers.

Which meant one of *their* realms had spun them.

Not Cleo. That didn't make any sense . . .

Had Isla's ancestor used the heart to cast the curses? Or Oro's brother, King Egan?

Or Grim's late father?

No. It had to be Cleo.

Isla looked carefully at the book, though she could feel his eyes on her. Studying her reaction to this new information.

"What does the book say?" she asked through her teeth, willing her mind still. Willing herself not to give away a single thing.

Finally, Oro's eyes left her face. And he began to read.

Two chimes later, Isla and Oro sat hunched over in the library, countless books and frustrated silence spread between them.

The book's details had been scarce. It spoke of a heart containing pure, unfiltered Sunling, Wildling, and Nightshade ability. Energy greater than their own, the type of power that had only existed thousands of years before.

The heart is hidden until it blooms and becomes a part of Lightlark when it is needed most. That was the translation Oro had offered her.

By the time Isla stood again, her legs had cramped, and she was surprised to see light shining through the very bottom of Oro's curtains. They had spent hours reading and weren't any closer to the heart than before.

But Isla hadn't lost hope.

In fact, she was more hopeful than she had been in a while.

"This is the key to finding it," she told him, motioning to the books. "I know it is." Oro offered a nod, but his eyes were more tired than ever.

Purple rings and creased edges. When Isla had suggested they rest for a bit before meeting again, he had only refused once. Then, thankfully, he had relented.

Isla walked the halls, quiet as a specter, the castle opening up and dawn's reddish fingers peeking through long, uncovered windows. She was far from Oro's quarters. Far from her own.

Celeste appeared as soon as Isla walked into the room where Grim had hidden her. She looked exactly like she had every night that Isla had visited. Still as a statue. Floating peacefully.

Tears stung the corners of her eyes. From the beginning, Celeste had been intent on finding the bondbreaker—a plan to break their curses without killing another ruler. Without needing anyone else except for each other.

For so many weeks, Isla had hunted for it.

Though Celeste couldn't hear her, Isla's voice shook as she finally said, "You were right, Cel. About the hidden library."

She grabbed her friend's hands, knowing how excited she would be if she was awake. And that was when Isla noticed one of them was curled into a fist. As if she had been fighting, right before the poison had made her go still.

Not fighting, Isla thought, as she carefully pulled her friend's fingers back.

Sending a message. To Isla.

There was something in Celeste's fist, something she had managed to grab, to tell Isla who had done this to her. A clue. She finally fully pulled her friend's pale hand open.

And the diamond ring she had given Azul fell to the floor.

CHAPTER FORTY-NINE

DIAMOND

Azul had poisoned Celeste. He wasn't the jovial, haunted ruler who had charmed Isla with his music. He was a calculating ruler with a plan.

She remembered the conversation she had overheard, so many weeks before. Oro had been fighting with Azul over a strategy to end one of the realms. The king had assured Isla she was safe. She had assumed Azul had meant to destroy the Moonling realm.

Now she realized he must have been talking about Starling. Celeste. Worse—Isla hadn't even told her friend about the overheard conversation. After her best friend had been paired with the Skyling, she should have at least warned her *then,* but she had been too focused on Oro's betrayal. On herself—always herself.

How had she not considered the possibility that Azul might be targeting Starling?

But why?

What was his plan?

So many questions, pieces that didn't make sense. Every time she thought she knew something for certain, the truth shifted and scattered. But not for long.

Isla remembered what the oracle had said.

You . . . have many questions. There are so many things I could tell you . . . though I should not.

All will be revealed soon enough.

Isla stood in the Place of Mirrors, spine straight. Dead leaves blew lazily at her feet, wind peeking in from a fracture in the glass. She faced the grand staircase that led to rooms that once were full and now sat empty, cobwebs and cracked mirrors instead of laughter and music.

She could almost hear them, their voices just as honeyed as her own, as she reached up to her neck to the giant black diamond that sat against her throat and pulled.

A minute ticked by. His power didn't work in the Place of Mirrors. He would have to appear at the edge of its forest on Wild Isle and get to her on foot.

The door slammed open so hard it seemed close to shattering, and she whirled around to see Grim, running, frantic.

His eyes were wide—filled with fear. His breath was wild. There was a sword by his side.

He was in front of her in an instant.

"Heart—are you hurt?" His giant hands cupped both sides of her face, thumbs at the corners of her lips, studying her for any damage. He looked down at her as if she was made not of blood and bone but of ice and mist, a moment from vanishing . . . panting from the run . . .

"I'm fine."

Noting her tone, he dropped his hands.

No need to skirt around the reason she had called him here. "Why didn't you tell me that Wildling created the island with Sunling and Nightshade?"

His expression did not change. Not the way she had thought it might. For a moment, all he did was study her.

Finally, Grim said, "Some things are better uncovered ourselves." His gaze was steady. "There are many things others told me that I would have preferred to have learned on my own. In time. When I could understand it all better . . ." *What things?* she wanted to ask. But she stayed focused.

"Were you ever going to tell me?"

"In time, of course. I brought you here . . . answered your questions . . . but I didn't want to force everything onto you at once." He shook his head. "You had just arrived somewhere new. Not knowing much. Forced to carry the burden of the curses, to represent your entire realm. Powerless. You were terrified. I couldn't make it worse. I didn't want to."

Isla shouldn't have been shocked he had been able to sense her terror throughout the Centennial. Her confusion. Still. That was no excuse.

"Is there anything else you're hiding from me?" she demanded. She couldn't trust anyone. Azul had poisoned Celeste. Cleo had tried to kill her on multiple occasions. Isla remembered the oracle's warning.

There are lies and liars all around you, Isla Crown.

Was Grim one of them?

His eyes flashed with something. She knew him well enough now to recognize it.

She took a step back. "There is, isn't there?"

Grim tensed. Nodded.

"What is it?" Part of her was angry. The other half was scared. And he felt all of it.

Grim took a step closer. She stepped back and almost lost her footing. "There are a *few* things I haven't told you," he said. "Not explicitly." Another step.

Just say it, Isla thought. She couldn't take another moment of wondering.

He frowned. It was an unfamiliar expression on his face. He frowned at other people, a *lot,* but never at her. With her, he always grinned. "I haven't told you what you do to me."

She blinked. "What?"

"I haven't told you that you've ruined me."

"Ruined?"

He nodded. "*Ruined.* Tortured. You haven't stopped tormenting me since the first moment I saw you."

Isla opened her mouth. Closed it. Considered apologizing, even.

Grim continued. "A few conversations with you, and I was ready to make the most disadvantageous trade—all of me in exchange for any part of you you'd be willing to spare." He shook his head. "You have invaded my mind. I have questioned my sanity. I think about you all the time."

The way he said *all the time* had her cheeks burning with its insinuations. "All the time?" she repeated, voice breathless.

"Late at night, I ache for you. I ache for you *all the time,*" he said, face truly looking tortured. As if he had waited a long while to say those words. As if she had been a curse worse than all others.

Then he kissed her.

She gasped, just a little, and he pulled away. *No.* Before he could get far, she pressed herself against him, arms around his neck. She tilted her head back to meet his gaze. All anger was gone, replaced with emotions that made Grim's eyes darken.

Before he could grin, she pressed her lips to his. He was cold as stone, and she became even colder as he pinned her against the glass. Their kiss deepened, mouths opening, heat burning its way down her center. Her head fell back, and he kissed the length of her neck, teeth just slightly grazing her throat, below where her necklace sat.

He moved her cape aside and ran his lips along her bare shoulder. She made a sound, the cold making her skin prickle, and his hands gripped her waist, pressed her harder against the wall. She reached up to unbutton his cape, and it fell soundlessly to the floor.

His eyes snapped to hers. But she was already pulling at his shirt. He let her take it off in one quick movement. Then she paused. And stared at him.

Built for war. Toned completely. A ruthless warrior towering over her. A large scar marred the center of his chest. It sat inches from his heart. She pressed her hand against it, and he watched her movement, his breathing a bit unsteady, as if he was trying very hard to stand still.

"What is this from?" Her pulse was already racing. So was his.

Grim shivered as she traced the scar's jagged mark. "Just someone trying to kill me." He placed his hand over hers. "Hearteater," he said, the ghost of a smile on his lips. *The name was back*. "Right now, *you're* killing me." His voice was deep as the dreams she'd had the last few weeks. The ones he had sent her. The ones she now wanted to make real.

She took his crown between her fingers. Let it drop to the ground with a loud clatter. She did the same to her own.

The ruler of darkness and the ruler of the wild, both breathing a little too quickly. She stepped over her crown, to him, and he took her into his arms. This time, his kiss was desperate, like the sun was setting and they only had a few more minutes left, like the glass room was just a moment from being blown to pieces. He held her tightly, as if afraid she might just float away, a bird uncaged.

Her legs locked around his center, and she could *feel* him—every inch of him against her, even through the fabric of their clothes. *I haven't told you what you do to me.* His words echoed through her mind as she found their meaning. *I ache for you* all the time. He was aching for her now. She moved herself against him slowly, and a low growl escaped his lips. With a burst of unchecked desire, he gripped her by the backs of her thighs, fingers digging sharply into her skin, and ground himself even closer. Her eyes fluttered closed at the friction, her head falling back. He leaned her against the glass as his hands went to the front of her dress, making quick work of the ties and straps. Before she knew it, the fabric was gone, and Grim's mouth was on her chest.

The world could fall to pieces, and she wouldn't notice. Her sole focus was on the path of his tongue and teeth. She was burning for him, for his taste, his touch, the way he made her skin feel like a path lightning had struck.

"More," she said, or moaned, she didn't know, all she knew was that she wanted every single thing he had to offer her. "*Please.*"

He held her close to him, and she gripped his arms, bit down against his shoulder to keep from making more sounds as he lifted her higher and his hand finally reached right where she wanted it. Over fabric. Then, under it. Isla groaned at the first press of his calloused fingers against her, and they quickly began to wander slowly, steadily.

More. He gave it to her, and she gasped against his mouth as he used them to explore her deeper. Deeper. Need overpowered everything else, and Grim cursed as she started to move against his hand. "That's it." His voice was barely above a growl, coaxing and strained, as if he was enjoying this just as much as she was.

Before she could wonder what she might do next, he angled her head back up at him and said, "Look at me, heart. I want to watch you come undone."

She dug her nails into the back of his neck. Their foreheads pressed together, and she had never felt more alive, more bare, than she did in that moment, having him watch as endless sensations overcame her. Grim looked her right in the eyes as every feeling intensified, saturated, more than she had ever thought possible.

And something about it all was so familiar, like falling asleep, or humming to the rain, or breathing. Like she had already done it all a thousand times in her dreams.

CHAPTER FIFTY
SLEEPLESS

Isla did not sleep. She spent her days and nights in the library, and they slipped away as easily as the rain racing down the hundred windows of the Place of Mirrors, during the storm that had locked her and Grim in the glass box for hours.

As she flipped the pages, she felt the memory of his hands against her skin, his lips against her shoulder. They hadn't done everything she had wanted to in the moment, and part of her was relieved that instead of making any move to remove his clothes, he had pulled her into his lap on the floor. That they had watched the rain instead, her head against his chest. His chin resting where her crown should have been. Before they left, she had made him promise to find Azul, wherever he was hiding. And bring him to her.

Oro watched her like he could sense the places Grim had touched. She knew he must have noted her daydream eyes. But he hadn't said a word. Part of her didn't want him to know. To suspect.

Isla dug her nails into her palm, forcing herself to focus. Breaking the curses and winning was now more important than ever. She was her, Terra's, and Celeste's only hope.

Also—the heart was the key to unlocking the life she had always wanted. Not only power, but also, perhaps, a future to look forward to . . . with Grim.

"Anything?"

Oro's voice was a bucket of water over the simmering thoughts in her head. She blinked and noted his expression, knowing she wasn't focused on the text at all.

She closed the book and cleared her throat. She had read the same paragraph ten times, and none of the sentences had anything to do with the heart, or curses.

"No," she said, leaning back in her chair. "You?"

He shook his head and stared at the stack of ancient books in front of him as if he was just seconds away from incinerating the entire pile with a flick of his finger.

Isla rubbed her hands across her face, over her eyes, down her temples. She sighed. "This isn't working."

Oro just watched her.

She was exhausted. Her neck and back ached from being hunched over, reading. Her mind was tired from all the work it had been doing, thinking, scheming—and also daydreaming.

"Talk to me," she said, laying her head in her arms. The wooden table was cool against her skin and smelled of pine. "Tell me everything we know."

Oro didn't balk at the order the way he unquestionably would have months before. Instead, he leaned back in his chair and thrummed his fingers against the table, close to her head. "We know the heart is on Moon Isle. We know it contains immeasurable power from Wildling, Sunling, and Nightshade. We know it was used to spin the curses. We know it blooms regularly when it is needed, in different places. Where darkness meets light."

Where darkness meets light.

Behind her eyelids, there was only darkness. She imagined it, darkness meeting light. What it would look like. What colors it would make. She frowned against her arm. She didn't *have* to imagine it. She had seen it countless times, thousands of instances throughout her life.

Isla's head shot up so quickly, pain pulsed through her forehead.

Oro's eyes widened slightly. "What is it?"

She stood, pacing, her mind working too hurriedly, her words coming out too slowly. "What if it's not a place, but a time?"

"What?"

She stared at him. "Dawn. Dusk . . . when darkness meets light."

Oro considered this, eyes narrowing. "Remlar said it would be *where* darkness meets light." That must be the winged man's name, Isla thought.

"What if it's both? What if it's in a place where darkness meets light, but only appears during dawn or dusk?"

Oro blinked away fatigue like clearing cobwebs. Thinking. He was so focused Isla could almost see his mind working behind his eyes, spinning possibilities. He gazed at the table, hand splayed on its top. He shook his head. "I searched the island for decades and never found it . . . Perhaps this is why."

The cursed Sunling king couldn't be out at dusk or dawn, both times too close to sunlight. They had always searched for the heart at night, long after the sun had disappeared. It would explain why the heart hadn't been in any of the places they had checked. Maybe it *had* but had been hidden. He looked up at her. "Isla, I think you might be right."

She stood. Oro did too. They faced each other, and he smiled. *Smiled.*

She had never seen him this happy.

Something about his smile made her remember another happy memory. The moment she had felt the flames against her arms, prickling painfully along her frozen skin, relief sweeter than a mouthful of honey. The moment she knew, surrounded by the Vinderland, that she had been saved. By Oro.

He had found her, against all odds. *I followed the bird,* he'd said.

She smirked. The same creature that had almost marked her death had saved her life.

Oro raised an eyebrow at her, wondering at her thoughts.

Isla froze. She felt the blood drain from her face, and Oro shot out a hand to steady her just as she braced herself against the table.

The bird had followed her relentlessly every time they had stepped foot on Moon Isle. She had assumed it had been Cleo's eyes and ears, but what if she had been wrong?

What if it had been trying to tell her something?

"I know where the heart is," she said.

CHAPTER FIFTY-ONE

HEART

Isla's steps were silent against the snow. Her breath was steady. Her entire world had narrowed into a tunnel. Her normally endless thoughts were replaced by a predatory calm, the sensation right before making a kill, the moment before releasing a bow, the string taut.

She was right this time. She knew it with every one of her bones.

Oro had been waiting for her in the castle foyer that night. The room had buzzed with invisible energy, emanating from him in ripples. He was excited. Hopeful.

She had smiled, in spite of herself. Because she was excited and hopeful too.

Isla had walked over to him, stood on her toes, and flicked his crown. She had grinned at him, testing him, seeing how their months of working together might have tamed his disdain for her.

Oro had frowned. Then he had surprised her by taking off his crown.

And placing it on her head, around her own.

"If you're right about this, Wildling," he had said, "you might become more powerful than even me."

His words had nearly made her knees buckle. He was truly giving her the win. No—acknowledging that it *was* her win.

Isla had figured it out when even the king couldn't.

She had taken off her own crown and placed it in his golden hair. It was laughably small on his head, and her lips twitched. "Wildling suits you, *King*," she had said before walking out the doors.

His crown was still warm and heavy on her head. It was so large, it sank down to the middle of her forehead. But she found she didn't mind it.

It was just under an hour from dawn. Just enough time to search for shelter for Oro. Once they found it, all they would have to do was wait.

Isla's skin itched; her entire body was covered in sparks. Still, she stayed in her tunnel, focusing all her energy on the other side.

The heart. The ones she loved. Her future.

Power was the last thing on her mind. If she could save Celeste and Terra, she would be content. They meant so much more than abilities ever would. She knew that now.

She just hoped she hadn't realized it too late.

"What will you do?" she asked him as they took their first steps across Moon Isle. "When we break the curses?"

Oro walked steadily, eyes trained on the sky. "I'll rebuild," he said. "These past centuries, the focus has been on the curses. How to break them. How to live with them. How to survive them. With all of that erased, I could be free to bring Lightlark to its previous glory."

Isla raised an eyebrow at him. "With Sunling as the reigning realm?"

Oro shook his head. "No. Before that. When the realms were united."

She let out a long sigh. *United.* That would mean Wildlings returning to Lightlark. The ones that were left, she thought, dread dancing in her stomach. "I'm not sure the people of Lightlark would be thrilled if Wildlings returned."

"They will have to learn to be," Oro said. And his voice was so firm, she glanced at him. He met her gaze. "And perhaps you would want to stay."

Isla blinked. She had never considered staying on Lightlark. During the limited times she had allowed herself to dream about *after,* about what her life might look like if she managed to break the curses, she had imagined bits and pieces. Her and Celeste, back in the Starling newland. Celebrating all her friend's birthdays without sadness or fear.

Leading the Wildling newland with confidence, Terra and Poppy strong beside her. And, more recently . . . visiting Nightshade. Spending time with Grim.

None of her futures included the island.

"Perhaps," she said. But it was a lie. And because of his flair, Oro knew it.

They walked the next half hour through Moon Isle in silence.

The wind whipped her cheeks so violently, she wondered if Azul was responsible. *Azul.* She hadn't told Oro about the proof that he had poisoned Celeste. She told him then.

Oro frowned. "There must be a mistake," he said. "Azul has never wanted to hurt another ruler. He has never even tried to form an alliance."

She had just told him how the Skyling had poisoned Celeste. Wasn't that proof enough that he wasn't innocent?

Why was Oro defending him? She wanted to demand an explanation but reared back as something screeched in her ear.

The dark-blue bird.

Its wings flapped slowly, as if its feathers were too heavy for its small frame. It squawked again. This time, Isla did not threaten it.

She followed it.

Isla and Oro ran quickly through the snow, and she squinted, trying not to lose the bird in the dark. She didn't feel the cold, or the hill dipping below her legs, or anything at all as she trailed after the bird, through the forest with branches like skeletons that caught on her clothes as if pleading with her to slow down.

She kept going. Panting.

The bird wasn't the heart. She knew that.

But it would lead her to it.

Ice mountains came into view. The oracles were not far. *Where darkness meets light.* She remembered what the oracle had said . . . that the heart wasn't in her ice but was *near, nearer than you know.* The trees grew farther apart here, with more room for snow to pile. A river

snaked through them, the sound of the water splitting then refreezing again like the tiny cracks of firewood splintering.

Another screech through the night. She found the bird as it dipped down and flew up, into a tree.

Into a nest.

"Here," Isla said. She knew the heart was there, somewhere.

All they had to do was wait until dawn.

They found a cave carved into one of the ice mountains, within view of the tree. Oro made a fire, though she knew he could heat them both without one. It seemed as though he needed something to do with his hands, to distract him from the time that moved too slowly and the bird just yards away.

Or maybe he couldn't warm them. She had seen how much of his skin the bluish gray now covered. She had felt the island getting colder and darker with every day that passed.

Its flames popped and peaked in beautiful curls. Oro's fire was still orange and red, but also tinged in something different . . . a strange shade of dark blue. A signature of his, it seemed.

Isla traced a finger around his crown, perched precariously on her head. She frowned up at it, squinting so she could see its edge, right above her eyebrows. "It's unreasonably sharp," she said, sucking on her fingertip where the skin had been broken by one of the points.

Oro laughed. It was a glorious sound, making her smile immediately. Genuinely. Perhaps because, as far as she had seen, she was the only one capable of making him laugh.

But then he doubled over.

Moon Isle shook. Icicles fell from the mouth of the cave like daggers, some shattering, some digging into the ground. Isla narrowly avoided one that would have gone clean through her arm.

Oro's hands were in fists, and he arched, grunting, face twisted in pain.

Snow slid off the mountains, threatening to bury the entrance of the cave. The bird screeched angrily, its pitch so high it made her wince. A crack like thunder sounded as a glacier split open.

As quickly as the shocks had started, they ended.

The island is crumbling, and me along with it.

Oro panted, fingers dug into the stone. His back trembled like he still felt the tremors, still ached everywhere.

She took a careful step toward him. Knelt until she was right in front of him.

He leaned back against the wall, eyes shut tightly.

"Are you all right?"

Oro nodded just as his entire body seized again, as if he'd been struck by lightning. He slammed a hand against the ground, and long cracks erupted from the place he had hit, Starling energy making the cave smell of sparks.

She couldn't imagine the pain. His connection to the island meant he felt its power . . . but also its destruction.

Isla placed a careful hand on his shoulder, and he stiffened. She quickly withdrew it.

Oro yelled out again, his fingers digging deeper into the stone, fire forming then dying in his palms, ice freezing then melting, sparks coating them, then vanishing. "What—what can I do?" she asked, panicked. There had to be something she could offer.

His eyes were still shut. He swallowed, and she watched the movement, watched him wince once more. Found herself wondering if she would take his pain for herself if she could.

"Sing for me, Wildling," he finally said.

Isla thought she must have misheard him. But he took a shaky breath in, and out. Quiet. Waiting.

She remembered that night on her balcony. Singing when she hadn't known anyone had been listening.

He had clapped. And she had assumed he had done it to be mean.

Perhaps he had liked it.

She began to sing a Wildling song. Her favorite song. The one she sang when she wanted to hear her own voice echoed back to her. When she was alone in her chambers and hoped someone far away might hear her. When she wondered if there was someone realms away, listening.

She sang that song.

Her voice was thick as honey, high as bells, deep as rumbles of thunder. She could do wild things with it, and she did, sitting back on her heels, her knees grazing his legs. Her voice echoed through the cave, harmonies weaving together.

Oro's eyes opened at some point. He watched her, taking steady breaths. Slowly, his fists began to uncurl. He rested his palms against the cool stone and listened.

She smiled at him when his shoulders settled. His expression did not change. She continued to sing, because he hadn't told her to stop, and the sun hadn't come up. She sang until her voice went hoarse and the sound changed. She liked when it got like this, smoky, different.

Part of her wondered if he had let her go on to be polite. But when she closed her mouth, Oro frowned.

"Why did you stop?" he asked.

Isla motioned toward the mouth of the cave, breathless. "Because of that," she said.

The dark sky was brightening. The moon was fading.

Oro was on his feet in an instant. They both rushed to the entrance, watching. Waiting.

In the rising light, Isla noticed something. She squinted. Right below the nest, something was floating in the air, untethered to gravity.

"Is that an egg?" she asked.

Just as the words left her mouth, the egg fell. Slowly, too slowly, it plunged to the ground—

And cracked open.

From its shell emerged a shining, gold yolk. It rose from the ground in tandem with the sun rising from the horizon, just across the cliff.

"The full egg represented the moon," she said, her voice hoarse from singing. "The yolk . . . is the sun." How many times had she thought the full moon looked like an egg? That the sun looked yolky?

She turned to Oro, eyes wide. "That's it," she said. "That's the heart."

The heart is hidden until it blooms and becomes a part of Lightlark. Oro had presumed it was a plant. But this time, the heart had returned as the very basis of life. An egg.

Oro watched the floating yolk and its discarded shell with such awe, she wondered if he might sink to his knees. He met her gaze and smiled so brightly, it was as if the sun itself was shining right through his skin.

He swept her into his arms and spun her around. She laughed, so close to crying in relief her eyes prickled, her lungs burned. She was immediately flooded with his heat, down through her bones. A moment later, she was back on her feet.

Oro shook his head in disbelief. He reached toward his crown on her head, and she wondered if he was about to take it. Instead, he straightened it, smiling. "Go ahead, Wildling. Get our heart," he said.

She grinned back at him.

Finally.

She was not weak. She had solved the riddle of the prophecy, found the heart, *her way.* She had been right. She was going to save those she loved. She was going to do what even her guardians had thought her incapable of.

She was going to win the Centennial.

Isla set off toward the tree. The bird screeched happily. The yolk was bright as the sun, small enough to fit in the center of her hand. It glimmered like pure gold. The source of all Lightlark power. Its heart.

She reached for it. Gripped it. Felt the force of it shoot through her

skin, along her bones, the power like a bolt of cold water, a tidal wave through the crown of her head, flames licking her every inch—

And felt it all rip away as an arrow plunged through her chest.

She choked, falling to her knees. Her chin dipped, and her eyes settled on the long tip of an arrow, sticking right through her heart.

A perfect hit.

A roar erupted somewhere behind her. She thought it might be Oro, right before fire swallowed the forest, burning people . . . there were *people*.

Vinderland. Here to get revenge. Arrows still drawn. They pulled back their strings to strike her again and died. Oro had killed them all in an instant.

A second felt like a lifetime. Her head lolled over her shoulder, the king's oversize crown falling from her head. Oro was there, reaching for her, just yards away . . . but he could not take a step out of the cave to heal her. Not during the day. His face was strange, etched and lined in a million ways. With a desperate jolt, he reached farther, only to roar again in pain, the sun splitting his skin in two. Blood pooled below her in a crimson puddle. Its warmth was almost a comfort in the cold.

She had survived too long already—stolen seconds the heart's power had no doubt given her.

Isla clutched the heart of Lightlark with one hand, her own sputtering its last beats. With the other, she reached up and pulled on her necklace.

Grim appeared from thin air before her fingers could uncurl from the diamond. His eyes widened at the sight of her covered in blood. She was in his arms in an instant.

"Please," Oro said from the cave, and Isla hardly recognized his voice. Why was he begging? Did he want her to leave the heart? Her hand went limp, and the yolk fell to the ground.

The last thing she saw was Oro's face, fragmented into a handful of emotions, each more surprising than the last.

And then she was gone.

* * *

The heart *had* been keeping her alive. She knew that for certain when she dropped it, and the world had gone dark.

And then she was falling through an endless puddle of stars.

The realms were just spokes on a wheel, turning, turning, turning. She was somewhere in between them, drowning, gasping, fading.

Mom. Would she finally get to meet her? *Dad.* And the man who had been worth death, worth bearing a cursed child?

Death was not quiet, and it was not quick.

CHAPTER FIFTY-TWO

PROPHECY

Hearteater."

The word was a bell, somewhere far away. A rumble of thunder. The quick shut of a door.

"Come back to me."

Come back. Had she ever really left?

A shaking sigh. Words drenched in pain. Agony. Whittled down into a whisper. "What did you do to me?" he said, voice pleading. She felt a finger run down the side of her face. "What did you do to leave me completely at your mercy?" Isla opened her eyes.

She was in her room. Grim was clutching her remaining bottles of Wildling healing elixir in one arm.

Isla was in Grim's arms before she could take another breath. He pulled her to his chest, cradling her head, hand behind her knees. His eyes searched hers desperately.

She pressed her forehead against his mouth. He was cold as stone, and it dulled the ache. She was too warm . . . coated in flames, in energy, in sparks.

The arrow.

A hand went to her chest. Nothing. The sharp tip of it was gone. She looked down and saw her shirt, shredded. Ripped open to address the wound. She pulled her underclothes aside and saw it. An angry mark, right over her heart. Where the arrow had pierced.

She should be dead.

"How . . . how . . ."

"I don't know." He held her again, careful as cradling glass.

But she did. The heart had saved her . . . its energy had been enough to keep her alive for the moments it had taken to heal her.

She remembered Oro's words. Only those in Wildling, Nightshade, or Sunling could claim the heart. Use it.

Isla didn't have powers . . . had it still recognized her?

Had she truly been able to wield it?

She swallowed. If she *had* used the heart, then part of Oro's interpretation of the prophecy had been completed.

Only when the original offense has been committed again.

Isla slipped out of Grim's grip and winced at the pain that pulsed through her chest. The sun still shined, but it was fading. She had been recovering all day . . . too much time had been wasted.

"Thank you," she told Grim, hand going to the invisible chain around her neck. To the diamond large as a small potato. She wrapped her arms around him, hands interlocked behind his neck.

"There's something else," Grim said. He was so serious that Isla's stomach sank. What had happened while she was healing? "There is a Moonling shop in the agora, a hidden one long abandoned. I went there, to try to find more remedy, while you were sleeping. And I found something, hundreds of years old. A rare Wildling elixir that does what Moonling healing cannot."

Isla drew in too much air. She blinked at him, a question in her eyes.

He nodded solemnly. Grim looked at the floor, not at her. "Celeste is awake."

"I need to go," she said quickly, both delighted and panicked. What if Azul came to finish the job now that Celeste wasn't hidden any longer? If Grim had found the Skyling ruler, he would have already told her.

Grim looked at the mark on her chest, then up at her. "You need to rest," he said.

She shook her head. No.

Isla turned to leave but stopped when she heard, "*Hearteater.*" His voice broke on the word. She faced him. "I thought you were dead."

I did too, she thought. But she didn't say that. Instead, she said, "I'm alive. Because of you." She closed the space between them. Moved her head so his nose grazed her neck. Her mouth was at his ear. "And I want to do a thousand things with you," she said, shuddering as her chest burned, the wound still tender. "But first . . . there's something I must do."

Grim nodded.

And she pushed past him, out of her room. She ran to her friend's chambers as fast as she could.

Before she could knock, the door flew open. Celeste stood there, eyes wide.

She threw her arms around her friend, even though it still hurt to move. Pain barreled through all her bones, her organs tightened, and she choked the words, "I thought you— Celeste, you—"

"I know," Celeste said quietly. "It was Azul."

Isla pulled back to meet her eyes. "*I* know. I got your message." She held her hand up, revealing the diamond on her finger once more. "Why?"

"I have no idea. He must be planning something."

Isla wanted to sit and speak with her friend, allow herself to feel relief for more than just a few seconds.

But she had to move again.

"I did it," Isla said, voice breaking. "It's a long, terrible story, but . . . I found the heart. And wielded it."

"What?" Celeste said, like she might not have heard her correctly.

Isla smiled. "I'll tell you everything later, but for now . . . stay hidden and wait to hear from me." She gave her friend another quick embrace. "All of this will be over soon."

She turned to leave, then stopped. There was something she needed to say.

"I'm sorry, Celeste. For everything. I've been a terrible friend. Terrible partner. But I'm going to make everything better. I promise."

With another final squeeze of her hand, Isla raced down the hall. Celeste frantically called after her, but she didn't stop. It was dusk. The sun was setting.

She raced back to her room. Grim was gone.

A moment later, her balcony doors burst open.

Oro flew through, landing in the center of her rug, his skin marred and healing right in front of her. He had flown through the waning light, she realized, when the sun still barely shined. Enough to burn him, but not kill him.

She froze, staring at him.

"You're alive," he said sharply, like an accusation, his chest still heaving. His eyes were wide.

She nodded. There was a pause.

"Good." He straightened. Swallowed. His fingers unfurled, and the heart sat in his palm, glowing like Oro had reached a hand into the sun and taken a fistful of its shine. It looked less like a yolk now and more like an orb. Golden. Fiery.

"We did it," she said, breathless, hand going to her aching heart. She smiled, even though her chest felt like it had been halved.

He handed the heart to her. It gleamed in her palm, winking.

"Bathe, Isla," he said. "Get dressed." Only at that moment did she register the dried blood in her hair, the dirt on her clothes. "Then meet me in the library."

Before she could say a word, he flew back through her balcony, into the night.

She gripped the heart in her hand, wondering how Oro could possibly trust her with it. The king of Lightlark, untrusting of everyone, had handed over the island's most prized possession. The key to ending the curses. The key to her future. The key to the island.

Even *she* thought he was foolish for doing so.

Isla didn't part with it, bringing it into the bath with her as she scrubbed herself down quickly, not lingering too long on the mark on her chest, which had further healed but still looked pink against her skin. A permanent bruise.

She put on a dress. Red, like the blood she had spilled.

Ten days.

They had found the heart with ten days to spare. But there was still a rush. The island could crumble away at any minute. Terra could die that very day. Isla had watched her through the puddle of stars before going to find the heart with Oro. The only part of Terra that hadn't succumbed to the forest floor was the right half of her face, her eye still opened wide. The other was closed.

Isla clutched the heart tightly on her walk to the library, and it pulsed in her hand. Glimmering. Speaking to her in its strange language, a siren call that promised power.

Power it had already started to give her, if her miraculous healing was any indication.

Oro was sitting in the library, lost in thought. Looking at a text, but not reading it.

As soon as she entered, he stood. Nodded. Sat again and motioned for her to do the same.

He was oddly serious. The king of Lightlark sat before her, not her companion on many adventures. Not the person she had come to trust with her life.

Isla sat down and placed the heart between them, carefully.

"I think I used it," she said firmly. "I think it saved me."

Oro only nodded.

She repeated the prophecy from memory.

"Only joined can the curses be undone
Only after one of six has won,

When the original offense
Has been committed again
And a ruling line has come to an end
Only then can history amend."

Isla swallowed. "*We* were joined . . ." she said. "Throughout the Centennial. And all of the rulers were joined on the island. That's the first part. Then, I committed the original offense, by using the heart."

Oro leaned back, his crown's sharp tips pointing toward the back corner of the library. He must have retrieved it, along with the heart, once the sun had gone down.

He hadn't returned her own crown. Her head felt empty without it . . . and also weightless. She found herself not rushing to wear it again.

"You will receive the power that was promised. You will officially be the one who *wins,*" he said, looking unbothered by the fact. "When you complete the final part of the prophecy."

Isla nodded, chin high.

"The last step, then, is the matter of which realm will perish." Oro leaned back in his chair. "As promised . . . the choice of which realm to save is yours."

"Starling," she said immediately. Her shoulders settled a bit. She was safe . . . and so was her best friend. Oro's brow furrowed, surprised. *Why?* she wondered.

Then her blood went cold.

"Who dies?" she asked quickly, not bothering to hide her fear. Not anymore.

Oro's eyes softened. But the rest of his expression remained firm. The face of a king. "Nightshade, Isla," he said gently.

Something had punctured her lungs—another arrow, maybe. Her breathing became panting. She was drowning from the inside out.

"But you said he couldn't die. You said he's the only thing standing

between us and a greater danger." From that point on, she had assumed Grim was safe.

Oro nodded. "That was true . . ." he said. "Until we found the heart."

The realization was a boulder to the chest. The heart held unparalleled Nightshade power. With it, the king didn't need Grim anymore. He could kill him and still protect the island against the mysterious danger.

"What about Cleo?" she demanded, voice angry. Fingers curling. "I don't know how, but she spun the curses. She must have teamed up with someone else who could wield the heart. She's the reason for *all* of this." Her voice shook. Her eyes prickled with tears that did not fall. "She tried to kill me. Twice."

Oro's expression did not change. "That might be. And if she did spin the curses, she will be tried."

"*If* she did?" Isla yelled, standing.

Oro stood too, towering over her. "There are thousands of Moonlings on this island. I will not sentence them all to death because of the actions of their ruler."

Her arms shook. But he was perfectly fine allowing the entire Nightshade realm to die. Her hands clenched and unclenched. Her head throbbed. "What about Azul?" He had nearly killed Celeste. "He obviously has some sort of plan to overtake power on Lightlark. He can't be trusted."

Oro shook his head. "I told you. At the second Centennial, Azul's husband died. Each Centennial since, he does not work to break the curses, or form alliances, or overtake anything. He only tries to speak to his beloved one last time."

"What about his plan?" Isla demanded. "I heard you both."

Your plan is madness, Oro had said. *You will be sentencing thousands to death.*

A realm has to die, Oro, Azul had responded.

"His plan?" Oro said, taking a step toward her. "His plan was to

sacrifice himself. Give himself up as the ruler to die to end the curses. He knew the island's days were numbered after my demonstration. He was willing to sacrifice himself, his people, if it meant saving everyone else. They have a democratic rule. His realm *agreed* with him. They voted for it."

"That's not true. He tried to kill Celeste," she growled.

"I don't know why he would do that. I'm sure there's a reason—"

A *reason.* The king seemed to have endless excuses and empathy, but only when it suited him.

Azul and Cleo both had their own agendas, she knew it. But Isla realized then that they must have had help. Cleo had killed Juniper after somehow finding out that Isla planned on meeting him. Celeste had been found away from the Carmel celebration in the gardens, as if she had been led there . . .

Only one other person knew about Juniper's letter to Isla and Celeste.

One person knew about Celeste's poisoning before anyone else.

One person had complete access to the castle and could move freely, practically unnoticed.

Ella.

Isla's eyes burned; her throat was dry. She didn't know anything anymore. Was she wrong? Or right?

She had worked tirelessly to find the heart.

Little did she know, the entire time, she had only been guaranteeing Grim's death. If Isla refused to kill him, Oro would. She knew that.

You could choose him, a voice in her head whispered . . . choose his realm to save. And see if Oro might choose Moonling or Skyling to die over Starling.

No. Isla knew Oro would choose Starling then. It was the weakest of Lightlark's realms, with the smallest population, because of their curse. Celeste was the youngest ruler, besides Isla.

The choice was clear. Either Celeste, or Grim.

Tears streamed down her face. Angry, hot tears.

"Not him," she demanded. "Please."

Why did she think he would choose Cleo? Just because the Moonling ruler had tried to assassinate her? Because Oro had saved her?

She was a fool to think he cared, to somehow allow herself to believe that Oro was anything but the king of Lightlark. A cruel ruler who would do wicked things to serve his people.

And Nightshade was their enemy.

Oro's face was expressionless. He was the king at the dinner table sneering at her wet hair, putting a heart on her plate and demanding she eat it.

"I saw his flair, Isla. He can travel between Lightlark and Nightshade in a moment. Do you know how dangerous that is? When the curses are broken and Nightshade decides to attack again while we are still vulnerable, still healing, he can transport his entire army here in the blink of an eye. Without warning."

"But you didn't even *know* about his flair until now! Which means he could have done that exact thing in the war. And he didn't, did he?"

Oro shook his head, furious. "You don't know *what* he did," he said, baring his teeth. "And that was a long time ago. *Before* he became ruler and inherited immense power."

Isla's hands trembled at her sides. She looked up at him, eyes gleaming. Pleading. "Please. Reconsider."

He shook his head.

She bared her teeth. "You can't make this decision on your own. You said so yourself. The choice is important. It's harder than the killing itself."

Oro's expression was sad—pitying, even. "I'm not making the decision alone, Isla," he said.

He must have Cleo's and Azul's support, then. A majority of the rulers.

He had gotten their approval of his choice behind her back.

Her blade was in her hand in a moment. She lunged at him before he could make a move, pressed her dagger against his throat.

He let her. He did not strike her down with his fire, the way she knew he could with half a thought, even weakened.

Oro stared at her with his honeycomb eyes. Hollow. Emotionless. "Do it," he dared. His connection to all the people on the island prevented her from killing him. But she could make him bleed, make him hurt.

Isla's hand shook, the dagger trembling against his throat. She stared at him for a long while.

Then she took her blade and left.

CHAPTER FIFTY-THREE

CHOICE

Isla had a plan. It wasn't perfect, and it made her a liar, thief, and hypocrite.

But it was nothing she hadn't already been in the last ninety days.

Celeste opened the door, and Isla started talking. "Tell me that you're my friend. And that you'll forgive me."

The Starling straightened her spine. Her expression became resolute, ready for anything. "I'm your friend. And I'll forgive you," Celeste said firmly. Still, Isla heard the hint of fear there that everything had gone wrong. And it had.

Isla had everything. The heart. The promise of power. The chance to save her realm.

But it all had a cost: Grim's life.

For as long as Isla could remember, the thing she wanted most was freedom. Then, as the Centennial went on, she wanted power.

When Oro had declared that Nightshade would die, when Terra and Celeste were in danger, Isla had realized that there was one thing she wanted a little more than both.

A future—happiness. A life with the people she cared about. Terra and Poppy were the closest things she had to a family. Celeste was her best friend. Grim made her feel things she thought had been denied to her as a Wildling ruler. She had always thought freedom, or even power, would change everything, fix her. But they wouldn't . . . She knew that now that she had begun to fix herself.

So, she made a plan. One that would still save her realm. Still save Celeste. It wouldn't give her the power promised. It wouldn't be a permanent solution for Terra and the Wildlings.

But it would give her Grim.

"I think I know where the bondbreaker is," Isla said. "And I have a plan for us to use it . . . but not only us." She took a steadying breath. "Let Grim in on our original plan. Let us split the blood cost of the bondbreaker three ways."

She would save him. And in exchange, he would have to agree to help save her people. She didn't know what love felt like, but this, this sacrifice . . . rulers in love could share power. If he loved her too, she could bring whatever power they shared back to her lands, to save her realm.

Or, if that was not possible, when her curse was broken, Isla would attempt to trade the Wildling abilities she would gain in exchange for Terra and the rest of the Wildlings that had been taken by the ground. The forest on the newland was known to make deals—and a Wildling ruler's powers were too valuable to refuse. It was a sacrifice she was willing to make to right everything.

She *wanted* to win the Centennial; she wanted that immense power that was promised, longed for it like a lover. She wanted the Wildling power she had been denied at birth.

But she wouldn't choose it over Grim. Or anyone else she cared about.

"I know you don't trust him. But please . . . for me," she said. "I'm begging you, Celeste. We don't have much time."

It took a minute for Celeste to say anything. Isla waited, expecting more reasons this was all wrong, more pushback. But her friend must have heard Isla's desperation, must have known how important it was to her. Because she finally said, "Where is the bondbreaker?"

They had a new plan. A last-ditch effort. Celeste was going to make

part of the castle crumble to lure Oro out of his quarters long enough for her to sneak into his secret library and find the bondbreaker.

"We need a place to use it," Celeste said. "One where Oro won't be able to interfere if he finds out we have it."

"The Place of Mirrors," Isla said. Oro's powers would be nullified there, but enchantments like the bondbreaker would still work.

Celeste nodded. "I'll get the bondbreaker. You bring whatever remaining healing elixir you have to close our wounds after the blood is shed. And that's it. That's all we bring, so no one becomes suspicious." Her friend swallowed. "If anyone finds out . . ."

One of them would end up dead. Isla knew that.

Oro had looked so cold. So *himself,* she realized. She had begun to believe that the insufferable, untrusting king had been a mask Oro wore to protect himself and his island.

Now, she wondered if the person she had glimpsed—the caring, trusting partner she had worked with for months—had been the costume instead.

Isla rushed to her room. She had a feeling she wouldn't be returning to it. After they used the bondbreaker to break their curses and Oro found out . . . she would have to flee, with Grim. And Celeste. At least until the hundred days were over and Oro either chose someone else to kill to break the curses or the island disappeared again. Perhaps forever this time.

Isla stood at the foot of her bed, trying to take it all in. The wall of leaves. The bathroom of white marble.

The chair where Oro had sat and offered her a deal.

The couch where she had laid her head in Oro's lap and first heard him laugh.

The balcony where he had heard her sing and saved her life.

She shook the memories away with a scowl. All he cared about was his people and breaking the curses. He didn't care about her.

Something shattered nearby. Tremors rippled through the palace. *Celeste.* Yells filled the halls, echoing. She braced herself against her wardrobe and knew it wouldn't be long before her friend got the bondbreaker and made it to the Place of Mirrors.

Isla had to be quick. The heart was beautiful in her palm, a slice of sunshine. Part of her had considered stealing it and using its abilities to heal Terra and her realm. But taking it would officially doom Lightlark and the thousands who lived on the island. She wanted power—but she wasn't that selfish.

And, as much as she hated Oro in the moment . . . she wouldn't hurt him.

Her hand shook as she wrote the letter to Oro. Explaining whatever she could.

When she was finished, her chest ached, her wound still pulsing in pain. It brought her to her knees, and there she stayed for a while, until the hurt dulled enough for her to move without groaning.

Satisfied she had given Celeste enough of a head start, she pulled her necklace.

Grim appeared immediately. She nearly sagged over in relief, seeing him still living. The determination in Oro's eyes had been clear.

They didn't have much time. Even weakened, Oro's power was endless. And this was his territory. He wanted the Nightshade ruler dead and likely had a thousand ways to do it.

She strode over to him. Grabbed his hand. "Do you trust me?"

Grim looked at her. Blinked. "Of course, Hearteater."

"Oro's going to kill you to end the curses. Celeste and I know each other—we have an ancient relic that will help the three of us. We're going to break our bonds, tonight. And then . . . we're going to have to run."

She studied Grim's face carefully. Watched his features twist. But he did not look surprised. Had he anticipated Oro would try to assassinate him?

"You would do that for me?" Grim asked, gripping her hand tighter.

It was foolish, caring for other players in a game as cruel as the Centennial. But she couldn't help how she felt. "Yes. And you're going to have to help me too. I might need some of your power to save my realm. I—"

"I'll give you anything," he said immediately. "Anything you need. Anything of mine. It's yours."

She smiled.

"Isla—"

"We don't have time," she said, squeezing his fingers. "We need to go. Now. As close as you can get us to the Place of Mirrors."

Grim's eyes shot to the window, where darkness cloaked everything.

He hadn't been outside at night in centuries.

"Do you trust me?" she asked.

He did not answer. He only pressed his hand against her heart. She shuddered, his fingers cold, a rush going through her. "Your *heart,*" he said, frowning. He shook his head. "It does not only belong to you." Isla didn't know what that meant.

Before she could ask, she fell through the ground, to somewhere else.

They landed, and Grim braced himself. If Isla was wrong, his skin would begin to split open, just like Oro's had under the sun . . . he would die—

But nothing happened.

They were at the edge of the woods on Wild Isle, enchanted by ancient Wildling power, shielding it from all abilities other than Wildings' own. She had a theory that the Wildling forest might be a little like her—that its quelling of powers also meant other realms' curses would be nullified.

And she had been right.

Grim's jaw went slack. He stared up at the sky through the treetops in wonder. He couldn't access the dark power that thrummed through his veins, but it seemed the view of the dark sky above was enough.

She gripped his wrist. "Quickly," she said, hoping Celeste had already made it inside.

Isla ducked into the dead forest, and Grim did not move an inch. He watched her. Eyes filled with something like despair.

"Heart," he said.

She stilled. Something about that word . . . about how he said it . . .

"Will you ever forgive me?" he wondered, reaching out and tucking a piece of her hair behind her ear.

Her heart beat once. Twice. "For what?" she asked, taking a step back. Another.

Grim shook his head. Frowned. "You asked me, just minutes ago, if I trusted you. When you should have asked if *you* could trust *me*."

The forest did not make a sound. The dead leaves did not rustle. As if stunned, just like her.

She stumbled away. Said, "What?" so quietly, she doubted he had heard her.

"Heart," he said. He took a step closer. "Your dreams, the ones you asked me about . . . are not dreams."

"What?"

"They're memories."

Memories.

Him standing before her in full armor. Her legs wrapped around him. His lips on her neck, on her collarbones, on the sides of her knees.

The dreams she'd had for weeks, the ones that had made it hard to look Grim in the eye.

"What are you talking about?"

He shook his head. Reached for her, then recoiled when she flinched. "You appeared in my castle one year ago. And you returned . . . several times. Using your Nightshade relic."

Isla was drowning, she was sure of it. The ground shifted below her feet. She gripped a decayed branch for balance. "I've never been to Nightshade lands," she said, shaking her head. Backing away another step.

Grim swallowed. "You have. You just don't remember. I had to take away your memories. All of the ones with me in them."

She was panting. *Like he had offered to do with Juniper.*

A memory raced to the surface of her mind—the second thing that had come out of her mouth when she had first stepped foot on the island, ninety days prior.

Have we met before?

Grim had touched her shoulder afterward, and she had forgotten all about it. At the sight of him, something must have peeked through the veil he had put on her memories. And he had snuffed it out with that touch.

Isla blinked too quickly. Nothing made sense. Though it was the least important thing he had said, her head was full of cotton, and all she could focus on was, "My starstick is a *Starling* relic."

Grim's eyes were sad. He looked like he was falling apart and trying very hard not to show it. "No, it isn't," he said. "It's Nightshade." He frowned when she shook her head again. "Who do you think its power came from?"

She wasn't breathing. Grim's flair was the power to portal anywhere he wanted to go. The same power as her starstick.

"No," she said. "I've never been to Nightshade lands," she repeated, her mind spinning, voice breaking. She hadn't dared, not after Terra's warnings.

Grim's voice was gentle. "Heart," he said steadily. "Where do you think you were before you portaled back to your room for the Centennial?"

Isla remembered arriving at her room, through her puddle of stars, right before Terra and Poppy had entered it. Right before fixing her crown atop her head and addressing her people.

But she didn't remember where she had been. She searched her mind, digging, begging the memories to appear.

They did not.

If what Grim said was true . . . she had been with him that morning.

He had taken her memories. Then, just minutes later, he had pretended not to know her. She had looked upon him like a familiar stranger.

It couldn't be true. None of it made sense. None of it.

There are lies and liars all around you . . .

She didn't know what to do, what to think, who to trust. But she certainly didn't trust herself.

Or him.

So, she ran into the forest her ancestors had created. Grim waited a few moments before taking off after her. And outside these woods, he might have caught her.

But she was fast as the arrow that had pierced her heart. Quiet as a hummingbird. Before, she had cut her cheek and arms in this same forest. Today, she jumped over all the right vines. Ducked under all the trees.

Until she saw her own self, reflected back at her.

She ran inside the Place of Mirrors, hearing snaps and cracks outside. Through the glass, she watched as the dead trees wove together and formed a wall, encasing her inside.

The forest was enchanted. Did it sense her fear? Was it finally protecting the ruler of Wildling who couldn't protect herself?

Isla didn't have time to question it. Grim couldn't use his powers here, but he was a warrior—it would take just a few good swings of his blade to get through the brush.

She almost slumped over in relief when she saw Celeste inside, eyes wide.

"What's wrong?" she asked, and Isla realized she was still panting. Celeste was holding something in her hand.

It looked like a giant sewing needle, long as a dagger. Sharply pointed at both ends. It was gold and part glass and glowed brightly, just as the heart had.

The bondbreaker.

"Nothing," she said, then shook her head. "Everything."

Celeste nodded, seeming to understand that Grim wouldn't be joining them. "I don't know what you needed from him. But I'll help you with whatever it is. We'll figure it out . . . together."

Together. She had ruined everything. But she believed Celeste when she said that they would find a solution.

"We need to hurry, then," Isla said.

Celeste extended the needle toward her. "It's a quick thing. We just pierce our skin with this."

The bondbreaker's cost was said to be at least a gallon of blood from a ruler. Isla wasn't sure how the needle was supposed to hold that much. But perhaps it didn't have to *hold* it. The needle likely made a puncture that wouldn't close until they'd lost the required amount. Isla had brought her remaining healing elixir to close their wounds once they were done.

A crack sounded through the night. Isla whipped around to see that Grim had made a path through the tree hulls, quicker than expected.

They faced each other through the glass. His eyes widened in sight of the needle.

"Now," Isla whispered, and Celeste stuck the needle into her own hand, wincing.

"Heart, no," Grim yelled before she could do the same, loud enough to make her pause. He ran as fast as he could, hurdling through the door.

But Isla felt a sharp stab through her palm. It was done.

She cried out, something critical rushing through her, burning like smoke in her lungs, salt in her throat, sparks in her stomach. Only it wasn't blood. It wasn't anything she could see.

Isla turned to face Celeste. Her friend's eyes had changed. They were darker, a deep silver instead of gray.

She grinned wickedly.

Isla froze. She didn't recognize that smile. Celeste's silver hair began to float around her head. Her back arched just as Isla doubled over, suddenly light-headed—her skin felt too thin, yet Celeste's skin gleamed

far too brightly. The bondbreaker was *taking* something from her and giving it to Celeste. Something important.

Grim grabbed Isla's other hand, tried to pull her away from the needle.

And was flung back against the glass. By *Celeste*. But her powers didn't work in here—

The Nightshade thrashed violently against chains that looked like vines. His arms strained. Just then, the door crashed open once more. Oro stepped through. How had he found her? His amber eyes went straight to the bondbreaker, and he paled.

"Isla," he said softly, looking more panicked than she had ever seen him.

Then he doubled over, falling to his knees. Was the island deteriorating again? But this was different. Grim slumped over at the same moment. Both weakened in seconds—like her. How?

Suddenly, she was shoved straight down to the stone, away from the needle. It fell to the floor just as her head cracked against the marble.

She blinked, vision blurred, and Celeste took a step toward her. Blood dripped from the puncture on the Starling ruler's palm.

Six droplets.

One sizzled. One floated. One burst. One became dark as ink. One froze. One hit the ground and bloomed into a crimson rose.

Celeste's blood contained abilities from all six realms.

Impossible.

It was as if she had just drained Oro and Grim of all their power. But she hadn't even touched them . . . and it didn't explain *all* six droplets . . .

Celeste's head fell back as she laughed. Her eyes met Isla's, and she sneered. "You're not very good at following rules, are you?"

Isla was frozen on the ground, mouth parted. She had a thousand questions and couldn't form a single one, except for, "What?"

"You were supposed to stay *away* from Grim, remember? I warned you . . . and the king of Lightlark! You weren't supposed to seduce him,

that wasn't *your* plan, it was your guardians' . . ." She grinned. "Good thing I counted on you breaking the rules, little Wildling."

Oro had managed to get on his feet somehow, though the color had completely drained from his face. He took a step forward, hand raised—

And was flung against the glass, next to Grim. By a wild root.

Celeste couldn't use her Starling abilities in the Place of Mirrors.

She was using Wildling power.

"How?" Isla said. She must be dreaming. Or having a nightmare. It didn't make sense . . . her best friend.

Isla was at Celeste's feet, staring up at her. Not searching the room for exits. Not reaching for the dagger at her hip.

This couldn't be real.

Celeste's smile only grew more serpentine. The Centennial was a big game—she and Celeste had repeated those words countless times.

And Isla had been played.

"Why don't you ask them?" Celeste said, motioning to Oro and Grim, who both looked like they were a moment away from going into a hundred-year slumber, their muscles slackened, eyelids drooping. Still, they fought against their restraints in vain. Celeste sighed. "Love on Lightlark is a dangerous thing, isn't it?"

Isla knew that. Falling in love meant handing someone else complete access to your abilities.

"I really thought it would be harder . . . but you played your part well. These two ancient, famed rulers fell at your feet like cut-down stalks of wheat." Celeste walked over to them, sneering. "Grim was easy. He already loved you . . . you two have *quite* a history . . . though I suppose you don't remember any of it, do you?"

Celeste turned to Isla for confirmation, and she didn't move an inch. She didn't recognize her friend. It couldn't be her . . . Isla refused to accept it. Celeste shrugged at the lack of response and stopped in front of Oro. His nostrils flared. If he'd had his powers, his gaze alone could set fire to them all.

But in the Place of Mirrors, only Wildling power was permitted.

"The untrusting, cruel king . . . fell in love with a Wildling?" Celeste shook her head, grinning. "It was torture, wasn't it, King? Trying to fight it. Believing yourself under her spell . . . not knowing that she had no Wildling powers to begin with, until she told you her secret."

Oro's gaze shot to Isla. He looked panicked, an expression she had never seen him wear.

She looked at him, really looked at him. *Fell in love?* Celeste had to be wrong.

The Starling stepped closer to Oro. Ran a silver-painted nail down his cheek. "Of course, you were never under any spell." She shrugged. "That, at least, should make you feel better about losing every drop of power you ever had."

Oro tore against his chains. Grim was very still next to him, looking at Isla. She felt his gaze all over her.

But she didn't know where to look. Nothing made sense.

Oro couldn't love her. She didn't even think he *liked* her.

At least, that was how it had started out. But the more time they had spent together, after everything they had been through . . .

Celeste clicked her tongue. "To think, they handed over all of this power to you." She looked down at Isla, still on the floor, and sighed. "And now you've given it to me."

It still didn't make sense. Even if Oro and Grim *were* in love with her . . . she couldn't simply give that power to Celeste. The bondbreaker—

Celeste must have read the confusion across Isla's face, because she said, "There never *was* a bondbreaker, little bird. *This* is a bond*maker.* The only enchanted device that allows a transfer of ability. Created to help Sunling kings shift their power to their heirs without having to die. Isn't that right, King?"

Oro growled and tore against the vines, so hard he almost broke them with a single motion.

When Isla had been pricked by the bondmaker, it had allowed Celeste to take all the power she had access to, even if she didn't know it—Oro's and Grim's.

"*Celeste*. You're my friend. You wouldn't do this." She would fight for their friendship. Fight for the person she loved.

Celeste frowned. She bent down to where Isla was still on the ground and took her face in her hand, like she had countless times before. Isla let her. The Starling ruler sighed, a hint of pity swimming in her bright eyes. Then her mouth twitched. She smiled, wide mouth sweeping across her face. "Don't you understand, you beautiful, beautiful fool? You did everything I wanted . . . and I didn't even have to make you."

The Starling transformed. Her nose shortened. Her eyes changed color. Her cheeks hollowed. Her lips became redder.

A different face. A different person.

An impossible power—a flair.

Celeste wasn't Celeste at all.

Oro finally looked ready to collapse. His eyes flashed with pain. "*Aurora.*"

Aurora. Isla knew that name. The Starling ruler who had died the day the curses had been cast. The one who had been set to marry King Egan.

"I watched you die," Oro said, his voice rasped.

Aurora turned and faced Oro. "An illusion, I'm afraid," she said.

"Why?" Oro's voice was guttural. Then realization hardened his features. "It was revenge, wasn't it?"

Aurora only smiled.

"What do you mean?" Isla demanded. Her head was swimming. Nothing made sense.

Every word seemed to pain him, but Oro said, "My brother was supposed to marry Aurora." Blood dripped from the corner of his mouth. "But he fell in love with someone else. With her best friend."

What?

"With your ancestor."

Her ancestor. The one who had died the night of the curses. Her name was Violet. She knew almost nothing about her. Certainly not this.

Aurora laughed without humor. It had all happened centuries ago, but the pain was raw on her face. "They meant to marry, with a ring already on my finger. I was so angry . . . I used my shape-shifting flair to change into a beautiful Wildling and convinced *this* fool"—she looked pointedly at Grim—"that he would have me that night if he gave me the most beautiful flower on the island . . . one I knew had bloomed on the remnants of Night Isle, just weeks prior. The heart of Lightlark. Something Egan had told me about as children. I had tracked it, intending for it to be a wedding gift. Instead, Grim unknowingly unlocked the heart for me to use. The job was rushed. Since I had not found it myself, I could not wield it effectively. I cursed all the realms without really meaning to. Even my own. Only *I*, as the curses' creator, was left unmarred.

"Then I panicked. With all the rulers except for me dead, I would be the prime suspect. So, I faked my death with a Nightshade illusion, using the heart. You *saw* me die . . . but the person who truly perished was my heir, my foolish sister. I took on her identity, her face. Then, when I formed the Starling newland, I forbade attendants in the castle. Led from afar. Keeping secrets is easy in a realm where everyone dies at twenty-five. I became a new Starling ruler every Centennial. All the while, biding my time. Planning. Waiting."

"For what?" Isla demanded. Tears streaked down her face. This couldn't be real. She still refused to believe it.

"For the right moment to take everything I had been denied. Only this time, I wished to rule all six realms. Gaining access to all of Lightlark's powers proved difficult." She sneered at Oro. "Even with a new face, a new personality, every Centennial, you always rejected my advances. An untrusting king indeed. Egan had told me about the bondmaker. I began searching for it every Centennial. But, even if I was able to trick you, King, into using it with me, I would receive just *four* of

the six abilities. A ruler can only use the bondmaker to gain ability once and lose ability once. I needed a way to get all six powers in one go."

She turned to Isla. She was still on the floor, watching as everything in her life, everything she thought she knew, shattered.

"And that's where you come in, little bird." Isla swallowed. "It was all luck, really."

Grim's voice bellowed across the room. "*Aurora,*" he said in warning. "Don't."

She only smiled. And continued. "Years ago, one of Grim's powerful, curious generals stole one of his relics and used it to visit the Wildling newland. There, he met a beautiful Wildling. And, though forbidden in every way, would you believe they fell in love? The Nightshade general was powerful . . . so powerful, he thought he could subdue the Wildling's curse . . . keep it at bay. And he did." She smiled at Isla. "Long enough for them to have you."

Isla shook with rage. "No."

"Yes, Isla. You are not only Wildling . . . but also Nightshade."

She shook her head. "I'm powerless."

Aurora laughed. "Quite the contrary, little bird. You're *very* powerful. Your Wildling abilities have simply been cloaked by your Nightshade powers. Made invisible. Unusable, unless a skilled Nightshade should untangle them . . . Manifestations of powers are so strange, aren't they?"

Power.

Isla had always had power.

And she had lost it. To her best friend. Who had never been her friend at all.

"I saw my chance to get all six powers and planned accordingly." Aurora pursed her lips.

"Then something I hadn't anticipated happened. I didn't know you had been visiting other rulers too. You apparently mentioned something suspicious about me to Grim, and the very next day, he appeared in my room."

Aurora turned to face Grim.

"And that was when he became my accomplice."

Isla stilled. Grim's face had gone ashen. He did not meet Isla's gaze.

"A person's emotions have colors, apparently. *Celeste's* had the same shade as mine. He figured out my identity right away and was about to slay me, knowing that my survival meant *I* had spun the curses. But before he could, I told him that the only reason I kept returning to the Centennial with a new face was because I could not rest until Egan's familial line was destroyed for good. I presented him with a plan that would kill the king without dooming everyone on the island, break the curses, and give him control of Lightlark. All he had to do was help me."

"Hearteater," Grim said, trying to get her attention. But she couldn't even look at him. He growled, tearing against his binds. But it was useless. "She told me the original offense was a Sunling ruler falling in love with a Wildling ruler—Egan loving Violet." His breathing was labored. "To break the curses and fulfill the prophecy, the original offense had to be repeated again. You had to make Oro fall in love with you. But we were already in love. You would have refused. So, I had to take the memories of us together away."

Isla could barely breathe. That was why Grim had avoided her for weeks when she and Oro were working together. She thought about his strange comment, encouraging her to dance with Oro at the ball.

His voice took a desperate edge as she still refused to look him in the eye. "It was the most difficult decision I've ever made, Hearteater. Knowing that succeeding meant you beguiling someone else. Making you forget our story. Our love."

She finally met his gaze then. "Difficult for *you?*"

His voice turned resolute. "I was going to give the memories back. Once Oro loved you . . . and you remembered you loved *me* . . . we could take all of Lightlark's powers and rule together."

Aurora pursed her lips. "And, once Oro was drained of his abilities and link to the island, I would be free to kill him."

Grim spoke again. "I did it for my realm. Your realm. For *us,* Heart."

It fit the prophecy perfectly. Rulers being joined. Winning immense power. A ruler and their familial line dying.

Aurora sighed. "You have to admit . . . it *was* a great plan." She grinned. "Too bad it was all a lie."

Grim thrashed against his restraints, bellowing in anger. Immediately, thorns from the vines tying him down dug into his skin, drawing blood. He winced, already weakened. And now Isla knew why. Both he and Oro had been drained of power.

And so had Isla. Though she hadn't been weakened . . . not like them. For she had never relied on power.

She couldn't miss something she never knew she had.

"I need to thank you," Aurora said, looking down at Isla. "You not only found the bondmaker for me . . . but you gave me all six powers at once."

Isla was shaking.

Everything had been orchestrated. A game much bigger than the one she thought she had been playing.

Isla finally rose. Grim had done everything for the same reason she had tried to win the Centennial—to save those he loved and bring power back to his realm. On every level, she understood.

The difference was Isla had been willing to give up everything for him. When, the entire time, he had used her as a pawn. She spat in Grim's direction.

Isla looked at Oro and hoped he read the apology in her eyes. Because of her, because he had been foolish enough to love a Wildling, his worst fear had been confirmed. He had lost his power.

He had been right not to trust her. Not to trust anyone.

She should have done the same.

Isla took out her blade, then faced Aurora. Everything made terrifying sense now.

Aurora had killed Juniper after he wrote them about knowing who had spun the curses. Not Cleo or Ella.

Azul must have somehow figured out Celeste was Aurora and tried to stop her during Carmel.

Isla swallowed, knowing she had to finish the job.

She was quick, faster than lightning striking—her blade was at Aurora's throat in a moment.

But before she could pierce flesh, the blade shattered.

Isla and Aurora met eyes. It didn't make sense. Aurora couldn't wield her abilities here. The Starling ruler laughed. "The dagger you chose at the Starling shop, the one *I* planted there. One I had enchanted so it could never kill me should you discover my plot. Of course you chose the one with a serpent on it . . . so predictable, little bird. So weak . . . so *foolish*."

Aurora lifted her arms, and vines crashed through the glass of the Place of Mirrors, sending shards everywhere. They filled the room, squirming like serpents, reaching toward them all.

Oro and Grim were instantly smothered. Trapped firmly against the remnants of the glass wall. Aurora would end them, even with their powers drained, just to squelch any other claim to authority. Isla knew that.

"Killed by your own abilities . . ." Aurora mused, hands lifted, ready to strike Isla down with all the forest offered. She paused, for just a moment. "I did like you, Wildling. But all the rulers must die today. Again."

Before Aurora could send the vines and roots to end her, Isla reached back down her spine, her favorite hiding place. Her fingers wrapped around something that was buzzing faintly. Glowing.

Aurora's eyes widened. "I told you not to bring anything, fool," she said.

Isla grinned meanly. "I'm not good at following rules, remember?"

Then she plunged through her puddle of stars.

CHAPTER FIFTY-FOUR

CURSED

Her room looked just like she had left it, though the outside was barren. No trees near her windows. No grass.

She had fallen roughly, collapsing onto the stone, her knees screaming in pain.

At the commotion, her door flung open. Just as it had three months prior.

Poppy was wearing sleep clothes. At the sight of her, the woman screamed out in joy. Her guardian rushed to embrace her, arms going around her neck. She smelled of cinnamon and blood. It must have been a feeding day.

"You did it, little bird!" Poppy said. She must have assumed Isla's early arrival meant she had succeeded in the guardians' plan. The first step of which was to seduce the king out of his powers.

And though her true plan had been different from the start . . . Isla supposed she had.

She did not embrace her back. Finally, Poppy let her go, and Isla said, "You knew. Both of you." Poppy had the nerve to look confused. Isla ground her back teeth together. "You both knew I had power . . . didn't you?"

Celeste—*Aurora*—had called her a name only her guardians had ever used. *Little bird.* And that was when Isla had realized that the Starling's plot required help. People from the inside.

"And you killed them, didn't you?" Isla said.

Only Poppy and Terra had access to these chambers. Isla had gotten all her information about Lightlark, her parents, and her curse from them.

Lies.

And liars.

Poppy's hand went to the single blade she carried.

Isla drew hers first, one she kept beneath her vanity.

"Why?" she ground out.

Poppy looked pale. "We did it for *you.* The Starling ruler gave us a choice—kill your mother and her lover so that their power would be transferred to you in time for the next Centennial and raise you to be able to seduce the king one day . . . or she would kill the entire Wildling line and end our realm. She demanded we convince you that you weren't born with ability . . . so that you wouldn't ever try to use it. She said it was dangerous, the mix of power, that it could kill you."

Isla stepped forward, pointing her dagger at Poppy. "You killed my parents," she said, the words barely making a sound. Not the curses. Not the fact that her mother broke the rules. *Them.* The people her mother had trusted most. Her head was full of mist. Her limbs were limp. Her chest still throbbed. "I should kill you," she said before uncurling her other hand, revealing her vial of Wildling healing elixir. "I should leave Terra to rot."

She downed the bottle, hoping it would work over the next few minutes, for wounds she hadn't yet gotten.

She dropped her blade. "But I have something more important to do."

Isla strode past Poppy to her wall of swords. She rushed to put on her full armor—shoulder plates, high metallic boots, chest plate, long metallic gloves, and, finally, her helmet. She grabbed two swords.

Then she drew her puddle of stars once more.

She had escaped Lightlark. She was safe, for now. She could flee. She could run.

Yet.

She couldn't leave them behind.

Grim had betrayed her on every level . . . He deserved Aurora's wrath, a slow death at her hands . . .

But Oro did not. She remembered his words, spoken true: *I've never lied to you, Isla. Not once.* He was the only person she could trust. The only person who hadn't truly betrayed her. She wouldn't abandon him.

Poppy gripped her wrist. "You're going back? You made it out. Don't be a fool."

Isla hissed. She shook out of her guardian's hold. "I might be a fool. But at least I have honor," she spat. "I will return with power for Wildling. I will save this realm, and Terra. But afterward . . . I never want to see either of you again."

She raised her arms to the ceiling, her two long swords pressed together above her head.

And portaled away.

The moment Isla landed in the Place of Mirrors, she was moving. The vines Aurora controlled reacted reflexively, lunging toward her from every direction, thorns and all.

Isla might not have had power.

But, unlike the other rulers, she was used to fighting without it.

Her blades made a slicing sound as she peeled them away from each other and turned them both in wide circles, at her sides, at her front, behind her back—and wherever she cut, plants fell.

Aurora had stolen Isla's power . . . and even dead, the enchanted forest sought to protect the Starling ruler. The decaying nature created guardians in response to Isla's threat, creatures crafted from bark. They hurtled toward her through holes in the glass, wielding weapons made of bone and horns from wild animals. Isla roared and lunged, fighting them just as fiercely as any foe, spinning on her heel, turning her blades, shielding from their thorns and bone daggers with the metal across her arms.

The world went silent. Every step was delicate as a dance, every move of her blade targeted, her arms pulsing not with pain, but power—she had trained every day before the Centennial since she was just a girl. She played not with dolls but with blades. She did not braid her hair but wove vines to make shields.

For a moment, she was back in the Wildling woods during a rare training excursion outside, Terra sitting in a tree above, watching Isla move, her sword cutting through the air. Her arrows shooting targets carved into trees. Her throwing blades hitting their marks every time, from any angle.

And she heard claps, somewhere. Terra used to clap only when Isla had conquered a fighting technique. One that would earn her a new blade to display on her wall.

But the clapping didn't come from Terra.

Aurora's hands rang together, and a thin vine punctured the glass, so small it made it through Isla's raised blades.

And wrapped around her neck.

Isla gasped. It gripped tightly as her breath was choked from her throat, thorn cutting against her neck, right against her larynx.

Aurora stood in front of her, laughing. Clapping once more. Amused. "You came *back?* You were free, little bird." She clicked her tongue, suddenly disappointed. "And you flew right back into your cage."

She closed her fist, and the vine tightened even more, bringing Isla to her knees. Isla sliced at its root, cutting it free. But the piece wrapped around her neck remained.

Oro and Grim watched her, both fighting against their chains, eyes wide in fear. Blood spilled down their temples, down their limbs. Aurora had cut them a thousand times with those thorns. It seemed Isla had interrupted her slow torture of the two rulers.

They hadn't even had a chance to stop it . . . hadn't had access to their pools of power before Aurora had stolen them, because of her, because *she* had suggested they meet at the Place of Mirrors.

Still . . . there was an advantage to being here. Grim and Oro might be trapped, but Aurora was limited to only Wildling power. Beyond this place, her new powers were limitless. She could wield all six realms' abilities. No one in history had been able to do that.

Worse—she wasn't bound to any of the curses, as their creator. Leaving the rest of the realms weak, easy to conquer.

No. Aurora could not leave the Place of Mirrors.

Even if it meant Isla wouldn't leave either.

Isla sliced her blade through the air in a flash, right to her neck. The vine choking her was only an inch thick. A centimeter off, and she would slit her own throat.

But Isla's swords were a part of her—without any powers to wield, she had focused solely on them her entire life.

The vine fell from around her neck.

She barreled toward Aurora, swords raised. The Starling ruler sent tree hulls through the glass, made spikes from bark, threw them in her path.

Isla cut them all down. She was fluid as water. Precise as lightning. Fast as a star hurtling to earth. Her swords moved independently, in tandem, in a rhythm like the blood pulsing through her veins, like the ringing through the glass dome, echoing the slicing and shattering as Aurora sent more of the woods inside.

As she neared, Isla felt the tears, hot on her cheeks. The greatest betrayal was not Grim's. Not Terra and Poppy's.

It was Celeste's. She had pretended to be her friend. Her *sister.*

Isla had been alone. And Celeste had preyed upon her loneliness.

Still, even after everything, a treacherous corner of her heart still loved her friend.

Aurora grinned at the pain etched into the pockets of Isla's face. "You could have done it," she said. "Broken the curses. I hadn't counted on Oro finding out about the heart. You two truly could have broken them, if *you* had just been strong enough to let one of the rulers

die. And, of course, there is the matter of the original offense from the prophecy . . ."

Isla whirled around, bracing against the impact of a trunk. She fell to the ground, air leaving her lungs for just a moment before returning, the healing liquid she had just taken still running through her blood, aiding her. One of Aurora's thorn-covered vines sliced right down her side, sending blood streaming, and she screamed—but a moment later, the skin knitted itself together again.

Panting, Isla kept her pace toward Aurora, swords still drawn. "The original offense wasn't using the heart," Isla said through her teeth, grunting as she cut through a vine wrapped around her leg, thick as her limb. Another tried to take its place, to send her against the glass next to Oro and Grim—who were still fighting against their thorned constraints, bleeding in the process—but she cut that one down before it could get to her. "And it wasn't a Sunling falling in love with a Wildling. Was it?"

No, curses so cruel could only be spun through a truly sinister act. The original offense could not have been love or wielding great power . . . blood had to have been spilled to make something of a malice so great.

And not just any blood.

She had learned at a young age about the six rulers' sacrifice in exchange for the prophecy that would break the curses. Poppy and Terra had told her that her own ancestor had led the sacrifice, giving her life up first.

But Isla now wondered if perhaps her ancestor hadn't sacrificed herself at all.

Maybe she was dead before the other rulers had even learned about the curses.

The Starling's eyes glimmered. As if, for a moment, she felt pain . . . remembered the act that had changed her forever, that had been the basis for curses that had lasted five hundred years.

Her face shifted back to its wickedness a second later, and she raised her hands.

The ceiling shattered as a dozen trees crashed through it at once. Isla was showered in shards of glass. She screamed out, watching her skin break, then close, tear, then heal, the Wildling healing elixir fighting to keep up.

Trees pummeled into her, bringing her to her knees. Before they could crush her completely, Aurora twisted her fingers and wove their branches into a lattice around her.

Glass still rained down as Isla looked up at Aurora.

Through the gaps in her cage.

"Little bird," Aurora said, shaking her head from across the room. "You should have stayed in the wild."

But she wasn't caged. Not really. Even when she had been locked away in her castle, she'd always had a portal to the outside.

She gripped her starstick from where she had again tucked it down her spine, ready to portal out of her cage—

And it flew from her hand, whipped away by a vine. She watched it roll across the room, to Grim's feet. He looked up at her. Blood ran down his temples. He panted and winced, as if it hurt to breathe. But he managed to say, "Heart." He gasped, his words barely coming out. "Your *heart,* Hearteater."

Her heart? She remembered the arrow that had gone through it, a shocking pain like a lightning bolt skewering her. She should have been dead. Even Wildling elixir, even *Cleo,* couldn't fix an arrow to the heart.

Only a heart could.

Isla pressed a hand against her chest, and it burned—not from its injury, she now realized . . .

But because of what it now held.

Power in its purest form. When the heart had healed her . . . it had marked her.

Your heart. *It does not only belong to you.* She hadn't understood Grim's words then. But she did now.

Isla felt its pull from across the island. In her room, where she had left it, with the note for Oro. The heart sang to her, the same song she had heard the moment she had stepped foot on the island. A call like the bird screeching in her ear, a chill like the frost that had numbed her tongue on Moon Isle.

Isla felt it—and called for it.

Her arm outstretched. Her fingers flexed.

And something like an arc of sunlight came crashing through the glass. The heart hurtled into her palm, and she glowed.

Her hand closed, and her cage shattered. Wildling power rushed from the heart in an endless stream. Branches snapped, flying across the room. Something shined at her feet—the bondmaker—and she grabbed it with her other hand, sticking it in her pocket.

A moment later, she was running, jumping, a foot in front of Aurora.

Eyes wide, surprised, Aurora changed in an instant, features twisting, until she became Celeste.

Celeste.

Isla did not hesitate the way Aurora must have been hoping she would. She grabbed the bondmaker from her pocket. Stuck one of its sharp ends into her palm.

And plunged the other end into her best friend's heart.

Isla's scream was a wild, guttural thing that rang through the Place of Mirrors. Her face twisted in agony. Her best friend . . . her sister . . .

She felt power barrel through the needle, into her, as Celeste's eyes went wide, then dimmed.

Dimmed.

Until the original offense was committed again. A ruler of realm killing her best friend, in cold blood. A ruling line came to an end. And one of six won.

The world exploded.

Isla was thrown backward by a force wilder than the wind, stronger than a riptide. Tears burned and blurred her vision, hot on her face,

dripping down her temples. She blinked once at the stars as she flew back, and they looked much brighter than they ever had before.

Before she landed on the ground, it collapsed.

The curses broke, and so did Lightlark. The floor had fissured, and Isla fell through the crack, after Celeste's body, which had already been taken by the island. The Starling ruler had fallen hundreds of feet, down into Lightlark's fiery core. The heart fell from Isla's hand and plummeted after Celeste, returning to the island once more.

Isla followed.

She fell, fell, fell, just like she had that night on the balcony. Behind her back, the ground churned, boiled, ready to receive her bones. She felt power streaming through her, everything she had taken back with the bondmaker. But as she reached to grab it, the energy slipped through her fingers. She didn't know how to wield it . . . had never used her own ability before.

Isla closed her eyes. Recognizing her fate.

She only had time to say goodbye to one person. She chose—

And something caught her around the waist. Her back arched painfully.

She stopped falling.

Someone had saved her. But that was impossible. Grim and Oro might have been released from their restraints after Aurora's death, but they couldn't use their abilities in the Place of Mirrors, even with the curses lifted. Even with Isla returning their powers.

Unless—

Isla opened her eyes to see that the thing wrapped around her was vine. It had caught her and now began to pull her back to the surface.

Wildling power.

But she hadn't been the one to wield it.

Love on Lightlark is a dangerous thing.

Someone she loved was using her abilities.

The thick plant lifted her to the surface, out of the pit that had opened right in the middle of the Place of Mirrors.

When she reached the top, Isla hauled herself over the edge, onto solid stone, panting. Her hair was a wild mess in front of her.

Through it, she saw Oro release his fist.

And the vine around her waist went limp.

Oro was wielding Isla's power. And she could see in Grim's face that he knew what that meant.

The look on his face, agony melting into surprise and finally anger, said that he had also tried to access her abilities. And found that he could not.

Isla opened her mouth. Hours before, her feelings had been different. Hours before, she had been ready to run away with Grim, to build a future together. To sacrifice all she wanted, for *him*.

But he had betrayed her in every way. He had taken away her memories instead of including her in his plan. Instead of trusting her to make her own decision. He had made the choice for her.

And Oro . . . he had been her true partner through the Centennial. He had handed her truths in exchange for her lies. She had cried in front of him. Laughed. Conquered her greatest fears. Faced many dangers. He knew her better than anyone else on the island—except for the friend she had lost.

Before Isla could say a word, Grim backed out of a gaping hole in the glass and disappeared into the night.

Celeste's blood was still hot on her hand. Down her sleeve. She fell to her knees and retched. Sobbed. Screamed.

The curses were broken.

But so was she.

CHAPTER FIFTY-FIVE

BROKEN

They had been joined. One of six had won. A ruler's familial line had come to an end. The original offense had been committed again.

And on the hundredth day of the Centennial, the island did not vanish beneath the storm.

Isla had not emerged from her room. She only returned to the Wildling realm once, to inject power into the ground, saving it and her people from total ruin. She didn't know how to use her power yet, but it had been simple. Digging her hands into the ground. Releasing part of herself into its soil. The change had been immediate. Shocking.

Then she had returned to the Mainland castle, using her starstick. She spent her days curled in her tub, the hot water substituting for tears, because she found she had none left. She was empty.

Hollow.

Celeste. Her best and only friend. Hadn't been a friend at all.

Grim. A year's worth of forgotten memories. And some she remembered. Huddled together in the rain. Her body pressed against the same glass that had then shattered and sliced her in a thousand places.

She knew now that Ella had never been working against her. The Starling kept her updated through the door of her chamber. Through her, she learned that Cleo had cut away the bridge to Moon Isle, separating her territory from the Mainland. Isla didn't know what that would mean, what she was planning . . . but it couldn't be good.

Azul had been seen on the beach, watching as the cursed storm finally cleared. Apparently, the storm had held the souls of those killed by the curses. Those were the whispers she had once heard. The bodies trapped inside had supposedly walked just a few steps as specters before disappearing to their peace before they reached shore.

Isla hoped the Skyling had finally gotten to see his husband one last time.

Azul had never been a danger to her—Oro had been right about that. She knew now he had simply been trying to stop Aurora, becoming suspicious of Celeste.

After two weeks spent in the darkness of her chambers, the curtains drawn, she had finally felt strong enough to brush her hair. Put on a dress. And walk outside. She stood on her balcony, staring down at the sun's reflection on the sea, a golden yolk just like the heart of Lightlark. The enchantment they had spent so long looking for that had saved them all. Had saved *her* more than once.

It held unmatched power.

And so did she.

She still hadn't tried to touch her abilities beyond giving some to the Wildling realm. Didn't even know where she would start. She was worried that if she tried to pull just a thread of them, she would end up ripping a seam and they would all tumble out of her in a destructive flurry.

So, she had let them be. Even though she knew the time would come when they would need to be unleashed.

Grim had returned to Nightshade, scathed. Betrayed.

Isla couldn't deny the sinking feeling in her stomach at his name returning to her thoughts. She hadn't let herself look too closely at the shadows in her room. She kept towels over her mirrors, just in case, knowing Nightshades could use them to communicate. Sometimes she drank coffee late at night instead of falling into dreams that she now knew were memories.

Especially since, five days ago, she had heard a voice echo through her mind, just before she had opened her eyes.

Remember us, Heart. Remember it all.

You will remember.

And when you do—

You will come back to me.

Grim's voice had spoken so clearly, it was as if he was sitting in her room. At the edge of her bed.

But when she had finally blinked her eyes open, gathering the covers to her sweating skin, she had found it empty.

With their curse broken, Nightshades would be stronger than they had been in five hundred years. She remembered with a swallow Grim's demonstration of power in the rain. Remembered the words that had made chills snake down her spine . . . they did so now, again, though for a different reason.

I could open a black hole that would swallow the beach. I could turn the sea dark as ink and kill everything inside of it. I could demolish the castle, brick by brick, from where we stand. I could take you back to Nightshade lands with me right now.

Before, she had thought of his words as boasts. Declarations.

Now, they seemed like threats.

She braced herself against the railing, knocked out of her own mind as heat flooded her. It came from behind her.

Oro.

They hadn't spoken since he had helped her back to the castle. She had been a shivering mess in his arms, sobbing, screaming, Celeste's eyes as she died seared into her mind. He had left food, tea, water, comfortable clothing at her door. But she had only ever opened it after he was far down the hall.

Her shoulders stiffened. She stared down at the sea, thrashing beneath her, all white caps and sapphire swirls.

"You're not thinking of jumping again, are you?"

She whirled around and glared at him. "I did not *jump.* You made me fall."

His eyes were serious. But his tone was all mock concern. "Did I?"

"Yes. You and your snooping."

He raised an eyebrow at her. "I could hear you from my room. I went out to investigate. I'd hardly call that snooping."

She tried to keep her glare in place. But as she studied his face, she blinked. She hadn't ever seen him in the sun.

Oro's amber eyes shined just as brightly as the heart had. His hair was sun spun into silk. The sharp edges of his face were highlighted in the light. His skin shined.

The dark circles below his eyes had disappeared. His cheeks looked far less sallow. The grayish blue had all vanished.

He was radiant.

Isla swallowed. "You were insufferable that night," she said, her words coming out without any bite.

Oro took a step toward her. "So were you. Walking into dinner soaking wet, hair dripping. And all I could hear was your voice, ringing through my mind like a curse. I thought it was on purpose, that you were using your abilities to lure me. Then, you were so surly it seemed implausible that was your plan." He frowned. "When you told me your secret, I was . . . taken aback." He laughed without humor. "For centuries, I had shunned any meaningful connection. And when, for the first time, I began to feel something . . . it was for a Wildling that wasn't even trying to beguile me."

Oro was so close, she had to tilt her head up to meet his gaze.

For a moment, they looked at each other. He opened his mouth, then closed it. She did the same.

Didn't know what to say.

"*Isla,*" he said, her name so soft on his lips. She saw her own emotions reflected in his eyes.

Confusion. Not knowing how it happened.

Just that it did.

Love was a strange thing. She wanted him in so many ways. Had for a while, though she had tried her best to deny it. More than anything, she trusted him.

Was *that* the basis of love?

She still wasn't sure.

Of anything.

Isla reached a hand to his chest. Somewhere, she could feel his power, pulsing. An endless stream, gold and gleaming. Sunling, Skyling, Moonling, and Starling. When Isla had used the bondmaker, she had returned each ruler's power, through the same bridge that had allowed her to take their abilities in the first place. Though she still had access.

There was no armor between her and Oro's endless pool, since it went both ways. She could dip her hand in and take it all, if she wanted to. And he could do the same to her.

Oro closed his eyes briefly, as if he could feel her fingers running along the rivers of energy contained within him.

He mirrored her movement. And she wondered what he felt . . . for, when Isla had killed Aurora with the bondmaker, she had known exactly what she was doing. Not just getting her own power—and Oro's and Grim's—back, but also *taking* something from her. All her Starling ruler abilities. A loophole, to kill a ruler and their line, fulfill the prophecy and end the curses, while sparing the Starling realm.

Now, Isla had a Starling ruler's power. And she didn't want to begin to think of what that meant.

Oro pressed two fingers against her heart. Ran them lower, to the center of her chest.

A vine snaked its way across the balcony and bloomed a red rose.

Oro plucked it. Offered it to her.

She stared down at the flower. A rose with thorns, just like her. It was beautiful. Vicious.

Isla took it, then threw it over her shoulder, clean off the balcony. And stood on her toes so her forehead touched his.

Oro stilled. His eyes were amber and burning, nothing like the emptiness she had glimpsed the first day of the Centennial. He looked at her like she was the thing they had torn apart the island for, the heart he had been desperately trying to find all these years, the needle that had finally threaded him together.

Isla took a shaky breath.

Then she turned to face the sea.

Grim. He had wrecked her. And she had been reckless. Rushed in without thinking, without waiting.

She wouldn't make that mistake again. Even though she trusted Oro—no one else but him.

Isla climbed onto the railing, the same way she had that first day of the Centennial, when she had sung the song that had drawn Oro out onto his own balcony. He was behind her, an endless source of heat, so close that when she leaned her head back, it rested against his chest.

Her feet kicked air, high above the churning sea. She looked up at him. "Don't let me fall in."

His eyes met hers. "Never," he said.

Isla glared at him.

"Never again," he amended.

CHAPTER FIFTY-SIX

KEY

The Place of Mirrors had lost its glass. It was a skeleton of a structure, its floors covered in shards sharp as knives. They crunched beneath Isla's shoes as she walked inside.

Oro had worked to close the crack in the ground, using borrowed power, but a scar still ran down the length of the room. A reminder of what had happened here.

A reminder of the ruler who had been buried below.

He was at her side, watching her every move. Without him, she didn't know if she would have had the nerve to return.

No . . . she would. Because she was stronger now. And it had nothing to do with her newfound power.

She continued forward smoothly, head held high. Oro had returned her crown. He had told her about how he had clutched it in his hands after they had found the heart, during the agonizing hours in the cave while the sun still shined and he was unable to go to her . . . or even know if she had survived.

That was the moment I knew I loved you, he had said. *When that arrow went through your heart, and it might as well have gone through mine.*

Isla had felt her crown's absence in the days following the breaking of the curses. She had drawn its patterns on paper, had imagined it in her mind's eye, wondering how it had looked on her mother. And the generations of Wildling rulers before her. Including Violet.

That was when she had realized what it was. The only thing that connected her to her ancestors. The only important object that had survived the centuries.

She stood before the vault, at the back of the Place of Mirrors. Oro was next to her, eyes fixed on its peculiarly shaped lock.

Isla took a steadying breath before slipping her crown into the hole. Its every ridge clicked into place. She turned it, just the way she would a key.

And pulled the door open.

ACKNOWLEDGMENTS

Once, I was a twelve-year-old, writing books in my room and reading acknowledgments just like these, in the hopes of figuring out how to get published. It was my only dream. One I pursued relentlessly. After hundreds of rejections, I finally wrote *Lightlark* for me. It was the place I wanted to visit, the story I wanted to read.

It would have stayed only mine, if it wasn't for those who saw its potential and changed my life.

Thank you to my team, who has made every win possible. To my literary agent, Katelyn Detweiler, for falling in love with this book first and finding a home for it. Your support is like a suit of armor. To my entertainment lawyer, Eric Greenspan, for taking me on and seeing the possibilities of everything to come. To my film/TV agents at CAA, Berni Barta and Michelle Weiner. To Sophia Seidner, Sam Farkas, and Jill Grinberg at Jill Grinberg Literary Management. To Aimee Lim, whose feedback helped shape this book into what it is.

To my unrivaled editor, Anne Heltzel, for believing in *Lightlark* before it went viral and for championing me to the Abrams team. You saw in me what others didn't and pushed me to make this book even stronger—for that, I am forever grateful. To Andrew Smith for believing in me and all that the future holds. To Kim Lauber, Hallie Patterson, Brooke Shearouse, Elisa Gonzalez, Melanie Chang, and Megan Carlson at Abrams, a supreme group I'm lucky to have in my corner. Thank you so much for everything you have done to get *Lightlark* into as many hands as possible.

To my family, who has had the pleasure of being in close proximity to a writer (wink). To my parents, Claudy and Keith, for making it possible for me to follow my dreams. Dad, you always told me the harder you work, the luckier you get, and I've found that to be true. Mom, you are the strongest person I know, and I now see so much of you in me. Thank you to my twin sister, Daniella, who is the reason I kept writing. Your requests for more chapters pushed me to create new worlds. You were my first reader and will always be my best friend. To Sean, who was one of the first fans of my work—I am so grateful for your enthusiasm and help. To Leo and Bear, for bringing so much joy into my life. To JonCarlos and Luna, for being my star and moon. I can't wait to watch you follow your dreams too. To Angely, for always being there for me. To Rose, Alfonso, Carlos, and Maureen, for your unlimited love and support. To my heart, Rron—this book is dedicated to you. You make the real world just as good as a fictional one.

To my friends, who have all helped me navigate this new world. Your support, advice, and friendship mean more than you will ever know. To Chloe Gong, my other twin in so many ways. Our brunches have become a thing, haven't they? To Adam Silvera, for always hyping me up and making me smile. To Marie Lu, Sabaa Tahir, Zibby Owens, and Brigid Kemmerer. How did I get so lucky to know you?

To anyone who follows me on social media. Your messages and excitement for this book got me through every deadline and made me determined to make it worth the wait.

Most of all, thank you to BookTok. *Lightlark* is here because of you. Every video, every comment, every share, every friend I've made there—*thank you.* You are more powerful than you know. I can't remember what I was thinking posting that video about the concept of an island that only appears once every hundred years, but I'll never forget the shock that millions of people wanted to go on this journey with me. We did it!